Relativ

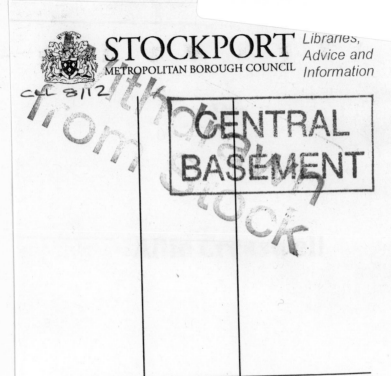

Acknowledgements

I began writing this book in 2006 and finished it in 2008. Those years carried me through a turbulent time in my life during which I learnt a great deal about the importance of family and friends. I take this opportunity to pay tribute to my family for their unconditional love and loyalty; my children over and above all, also my Mum and Dad, sister Sharon and nieces Marianne and Alice. I found out who my friends are – they're the ones who stuck with me. You know who you are. We might not be kin – but I think we are kindred.

For the latter part of the book's creation I was something of a wanderer, working on it in a variety of locales including hotels both dreary and delightful, lounges of the impersonal airport kind and also of the homely, comfortable variety. Thank you for those who gave me shelter and encouragement; my parents and Tim's; friends who put me up; Faye, the breakfast hostess at the Hampton, Stevensville MI whose genuine kindness each morning gave me courage to face the day when I was at my lowest ebb and Lois in Doylestown PA, who allowed me the use of her cosy sitting room and the company of Chico the cat for the re-write in 2011.

Thank you to Tim, who believed in me, and my writing, right from the start and without whose unfailing love, support and encouragement *Relative Strangers* would never have arrived on the page, let alone in print.

This book is dedicated

to my children

Thomas and Abigail

with all my love

October 2004

Friday

As usual, Belinda McKay-Donne waved her husband and children off in the car. Elliot, her husband, in the driving seat, did not even acknowledge her raised arm. He was fiddling testily with his mobile telephone with one hand and jamming the tiny earphone into place with the other. Rob, their son, had his hand on the steering wheel from his position in the passenger seat and miraculously manoeuvred the car, in reverse gear, between the gateposts and out into the Close. Now that he was seventeen, and having lessons, he ought to be driving to school with his L plates on his father's car; practice making perfect. But Elliot was always in too much of a hurry and, in any case, hadn't the patience. Even Belinda's patience had been rather stretched on the couple of occasions she had taken Rob out; he tended to drive too quickly and with reckless disregard for other road users. He had managed, just on the relatively quiet side streets, to have a couple of near misses, and she had had to warn him that, if he wasn't careful, he would end up causing an accident.

Ellie, in the back seat, was the only one to manage a half-hearted wave as the car roared off up the tree-lined road towards the by-pass.

Half an hour later, Belinda too drove away from the house. She'd packed their smart luggage into the boot, ramming Wellington boots and waterproofs anachronistically into the spaces, repeatedly checking her list. The full width of the back seat was taken up by cardboard boxes full of food and cleaning materials and two cold-bags, packed at the last minute, were wedged behind the front seats. On the passenger seat rested her handbag, a Tupperware of neatly cut and tightly cling-filmed sandwiches and a sheaf of papers with directions to Hunting Manor.

Before leaving she'd checked again that the doors were firmly locked, the thermostat was turned down low, the cooker was switched off and the taps tightly closed. Everything was neat and tidy: the beds made, the kitchen floor polished to a high shine, the dishcloth folded and draped over the tap. The linen basket was empty, the ironing done and put away. Even Rob's room, usually a no-go area, was reasonably straight.

A confident driver, she negotiated the back end of the school run traffic with ease, took a nifty short cut through an industrial estate to avoid the road works near the airport turn-off and was on the motorway, cruising at a steady seventy-five in the middle lane.

She had had the idea almost twelve months before: to rent a large house for the autumn half term holiday, coinciding with her parent's Golden wedding anniversary, to get, at last, the whole family together, for something special that everyone, but particularly her mother, Mary, would really enjoy. Left to itself the family would disintegrate. It was always Belinda that got them together, only seemed to be Belinda that cared enough to keep the connections. To her it was a matter of maintaining a firm anchor, reinforcing it with layers of developing association. To the others it seemed to be something that chafed, a kind of restraint, and she was quite aware that when her 'phone calls came, or her emails, suggesting a weekend visit or even only lunch, there would be a palpable shrinking, and their acceptances came with weary resignation.

Geography made it difficult for Simon now that he lived so far from his hometown, and so far, too, from McKay ways. Ruth hadn't the excuse of geography, she had remained local, but she seemed to have drifted away from them all one way or another, especially since poor April had died, and it was all Belinda could do to get Ruth and James and the children to visit once or twice a year. And Heather? She moved in fashionable, glamorous circles and in any case had always been somewhat otherworldly. It was so long since they had all been together for more than just a few hours - and a tortured few hours at that; April's funeral, the chill of the churchyard and the stilted conversation afterwards in the function room of the hotel; Dad's stroke, and the whispering corridors of the hospital. But Belinda would persevere with it for Mary's sake; she, now the harassed carer of their debilitated father, needed to feel, for once, their strength and support.

At one time Belinda had turned to Mary as a first resort in any kind of crisis but recently their roles had been uncannily reversed. Now it was Mary who needed help and Belinda who provided it. Indeed it was to Belinda that they *all* turned, these days, in times of crisis, and their sudden calls for help, like some ancestral clarion cry, would send her scurrying across the country to administer condolence, or nursing care, or casserole. She, now, was the lynchpin of the family, and she was quietly determined to hold it together.

So, she had hatched her plan, quietly, as she did everything, careful to reflect the glory of it onto others, and yet with a dogged determination to overcome every obstacle. The holiday was to be a long overdue reminder, to everyone, that Mary mattered; that *family* mattered. 'Family,' Belinda had read on a picture frame in some gift shop or another, 'is the link to our past and the bridge to our future.' Belinda only wanted to provide the occasion, the venue, to deal with the practicalities which would enable the others to make the links and set foot on the bridges. That, she felt, if any, was her gift. Ruth had once called her, in the new-fangled 'business-speak' she so often affected, these days, a 'facilitator'. Unsure of her meaning, Belinda had finally asked Elliot what it meant. 'It means you let other people get on with the important things,' he'd explained. Well, she'd settle for that.

The whole project had taken some considerable organization, not least among them overcoming her brother and sisters' reluctance, and getting them to commit themselves to that few days. They had such different ideas! 'Oh no! Not *there!* Too far to travel. It isn't like you to be so impractical,' from Ruth; '*That* place? Almost on our doorstep! Have you thought about getting somewhere abroad?' from Simon; 'Oh I don't care! You decide. Only do let there be hills and open spaces, Belinda, and trees, and a positive aura, and room to dance.' This from Heather, her youngest sister. In the end she had found Hunting Manor advertised in The Lady. It was perfect.

A stately home of character and quality peacefully placed in its own grounds, a mile from the village of Hunting Wriggly, easily accessible by road. Luxuriously appointed with every modern convenience, lovingly restored and tastefully furnished with fixtures and fittings from a bygone age of elegance and refinement. Ten principle bedrooms plus servants' quarters.

The image conjured up by this description awakened both longing and anxiety in Belinda. It sounded perfect... But would she arrive to find a dilapidated pile running with damp and infested with vermin? Surely not. Her conversations with the agents regarding the booking had inspired her with confidence. 'Spick and span,' they had promised, 'cosy and warm.' Unlimited firewood, an enormous Aga, a huge boiler, copious hot water, plenty of space for the kiddies, commodious rooms for the grown-ups: convenience, comfort, practicality and beauty. What else could any of them require?

As Belinda covered the miles between the city and the country, the sky, which had frowned rain earlier, cleared to show increasing glimpses of blue sky above driven white clouds. Ploughed fields the colour of bitter chocolate gave way to velvet cropped moorland dotted with sheep, and in the distance purple mountains suddenly made sense to Belinda of a long forgotten Harvest time hymn sung at school. The trees shimmered with green and gold and copper and bronze. The Lorries and vans which had accompanied her like seagulls above a fishing boat began to drop away, and soon she was almost alone on the ever unwinding grey ribbon of roadway. She pressed the accelerator a little more, and edged up to eighty. The car responded without demur.

As she drove, Belinda cast anxious glances at herself in the rear-view mirror. She had, the previous week, for the first time in her life, attended a beauty salon to have her eye-brows shaped and lashes dyed. She was still wondering whether she should also have had something done to her hair; a colour, perhaps. But this would surely have been going too far. She had been discreetly dieting for the past few months, and her face had lost its fleshy roundness, her cheek bones had emerged. Some of her clothes had grown too big for her and she had recently bought some new ones in a smaller size. Nobody at all had passed any comment on these changes in her appearance; certainly not Elliot and not even Mary, usually so quick to spot any physical alterations in her children; a rash which might be the harbinger of illness, a bruise hinting at maltreatment at school, 'that white look' which was the family euphemism for menstruation. Belinda, while feeling rather proud of herself, dared make no conscious acknowledgement of the motivation behind these changes, and now she banished those fluttering wings which troubled her from time to time by concentrating on the road.

Suddenly the traffic slowed. Red brake lights and winking hazard lights indicated a stoppage up ahead. The cars in front of her slowed to a snail's pace and Belinda sighed impatiently; she had so much to do when she got to Hunting Manor; she wanted everything to be ready for when the first arrivals showed up. She crawled along for perhaps a mile or so, keeping pace with a silver Mercedes on her off side and a Walkers Crisps van to her left. Then bollards and the overhead information display indicated that the outside lane was closing, and the Mercedes nosed in front of Belinda with an apologetic wave. A police car and then an ambulance screamed down the hard shoulder, and Belinda knew with a sinking sickness that there must have been an accident. When she came to it, she was surprised to see that the accident had occurred on the opposite carriageway. The outside lane of their carriageway was being closed off for emergency vehicles; this, and the ghoulish propensity of people to slow down and stare had caused the tail-back.

The accident looked very nasty; six or seven cars, mangled almost beyond recognition, littered the carriageway. One of them was covered in soapy foam; plainly it had been on fire. A lorry – not a McKays' vehicle, she noted - had slewed off the road and was on its side down the embankment. A caravan had jack-knifed and rammed the central reservation barrier. Luggage was scattered all over the place, camping gear and, sickeningly, children's clothing. A fire crew was working with cutting equipment on one of the cars. On its windscreen, shattered into a mosaic, Belinda could see blood. Ambulance crews were helping the injured; a woman sat on the hard shoulder weeping over the body of an infant, a day-glo jacketed paramedic in attendance; a man in a business suit stood in the midst of it all and shouted into his mobile 'phone. Then she was past the incident, and three lanes of stationery traffic tailed back behind the impassable scene for several miles, and, amongst it, she spotted the blue and silver of a McKay's Haulage vehicle emblazoned with the nationally recognised by-line 'Going the McKay Way'. The coned off area finished, and the cars on her side of the motorway sped up, and off, and there was clear road ahead. Belinda tweaked the indicator. Her exit was coming up. She reached down to the passenger seat and picked up the list of directions. She was nearly there.

Elliot drove down the slipway onto the ring road which went out towards the industrial estate where the McKays Haulage yard was now situated. His first action as the new Chairman had been to sell their seedy backstreet premises and take a lease out on a splendid new compound and office. He had computerised their systems as well and appointed new staff, whose loyalties would be to him and not to Old Robert, Elliot's father-in-law and the founder of McKays. Most of the drivers he had kept on, however. They knew their vehicles and their routes. And so far it had proved impossible to shift Aunty June from her swivel chair in the accounts department.

Robert's sister, she had been brought in to do the figures in the sixties; Robert believed in family, he wouldn't trust anyone who wasn't family to play any important role in the firm. Les, June's husband, had been taken on as the first additional driver back in those early days of the company. The biggest disappointment of Robert's life had been his failure to persuade his son Simon into the family business. Elliot, taken on straight out of college with an HND in accounting, had soon recognised that his only means of occupying the chair in the boardroom would be via the bed of one of the McKay daughters; he would have to *become* family. The bed, once he had put his mind to it, hadn't taken him too long but he had to wait what had seemed an interminable time before taking possession of the chair. Robert had finally retired the previous year, following his first stroke. Les had retired at the same time as Robert but June had stubbornly refused to let go, still appearing in the office three times a week, interfering with the accounts clerks, double checking their figures, crashing the accounts program and generally getting in the way. She made no secret of the fact that she was 'keeping an eye on family interests', a ridiculous notion since she wasn't even a Director of the firm, but she was, by birth anyway, a McKay, and Elliot had not, yet, liked to oust her, for fear of wounding what he thought of the minefield of McKay family relations.

11

He knew her type, anyway, and it was easily managed: she was a leech. In spite of all appearances to the contrary she didn't have money beyond what she earned at McKays and Les' pension, and her expensive lifestyle - a big thirsty car, golf and bridge with well-heeled women, expensive boutiques and regular appointments at the beauty salon - meant that she was at the mercy of whoever held the purse strings. She had sucked off Robert and Mary for years but now Elliot was in control and when the time came he would make her dance to his tune.

As he drove up the by-pass at something over the speed limit, Elliot consoled himself with the fact that, for a family business, apart from June, McKays Haulage was mercifully unburdened with family involvement. How much worse it would be to have a whole litter of McKay cousins and nephews throwing their weight around, lording it in the compound and lounging in the office cubicles, thinking that the business owed them a living and running up astronomical expense accounts! The McKay siblings had all taken nominal directorships when Robert had had his stroke but they didn't trouble Elliot with awkward questions or requests to examine the accounts, and as Chair Elliot found it thankfully a very rare necessity to call a board meeting. He had them all more or less where he wanted them.

Had Elliot chosen to examine the other side of that coin he might have had to admit that in fact the McKays had him in a similar grip. He nurtured the McKay nest-egg unaided and largely unappreciated. He got results but he got little recognition for them from the family. He got little of anything from them, in fact. They tolerated him, and that only for Belinda's sake. But Elliot didn't care; life wasn't a personality contest, after all. He didn't care that, at conferences, he was avoided, labelled as a piranha, or that members of the club, drawing Elliot's name for golf, would find their hearts sinking. They couldn't argue with his success and his ability to get, in the end, exactly what he wanted.

He swung off the by-pass and began to indicate left, turning into the forecourt of the impressive modern office suite. 'McKays' was emblazoned in blue and silver across the porch; he had settled for just the name. The full strap-line 'Going the McKay Way' had proved to be prohibitively expensive. To his left, the high-walled compound was full of tidily parked wagons, their paint freshly washed and gleaming. A uniformed gate keeper touched his cap at Elliot as he got out of the car and made for the smoothly gliding glass entrance doors. He glanced at his watch. It was ten past three. He had half an hour to sign off the wages, clear his desk and get back onto the by-pass to collect the children from school. The traffic was bound to be appalling at four on the Friday before half term, and Rob had wheedled him into agreeing to go home to collect the computer en route; that would put them back even more.

He was not looking forward to the holiday at all; a week incarcerated with the McKay clan miles from anywhere was nothing like his idea of fun. But Belinda had had this idea and worried at it like a terrier until he had been railroaded into agreeing. Having to keep the kids in hand, play the adoring Uncle to the brats, make jolly conversation with the brothers-in-law and cope with Belinda working herself up into a frenzy over the catering arrangements; none of this struck him as being very appealing, even if it was in somebody else's stately home. On the other hand there were some members of the McKay family who were good value: Simon liked to throw his cash about as proof that he had made it big without McKays, and that foxy new woman of his had a certain appeal. Being seen about with Bob, the famous brother-in-law, had its attraction, of course too, and since Belinda had organised – and paid for, he'd be bound – the whole deal, that would put Elliot in the driving seat as host; certainly that would be very satisfactory; it was exactly where he liked to be.

The whole family deal with the McKays was something that had been as hard – or harder, in some ways – for Elliot to pick up as the business. His own parents had died and his only sibling lived as a semi-recluse on a barge with a posse of whippets, mercifully undesirous of any involvement with Elliot or his new relations. It had taken him a long time to appreciate the tight-lipped restraint which seemed to characterise family relationships. They trod around each other as though on egg-shells, and tolerated each other's failure, feebleness and foolishness with stiff-necked forbearance. Tolerated it rather than confronted it. McKay fools, it seemed to Elliot anyway, were suffered, if not gladly, then stoically. The family tree might be riddled with damp and rot, but as long as the thing looked sound from the outside that was all that mattered. But surely, Elliot thought, glancing over the documents on his desk, the whole thing was a complete charade! The four children had travelled in wildly diverse directions from their humble beginnings. Were they to meet as strangers they wouldn't give each other the time of day, and yet Belinda relentlessly pursued this family connection long after there was any life or purpose left in it. It was a dead horse and he wished she would stop flogging it.

He was late getting to school. The lay-by was empty of buses and grey-blazered pupils; even the staff car park was virtually empty. Rob and Ellie were leaning against the railings. He looked furious, she looked miserable. Elliot forestalled their tirade of complaints by snapping in his most authoritative voice: 'Don't start. I've had a hell of a day and if you say one word you can forget the computer. And don't even start to argue about who's going in the front. You can both go in the back, and that's that.' The children slithered into the rear of the car, looking daggers at each other and at the back of their father's head. Elliot roared away from the school gates, raced down the avenue and took a short cut through half a dozen residential streets and a supermarket car park. He drove too quickly, accelerating and braking sharply, throwing the car round the corners and swerving manically to avoid cyclists, pedestrians and parked cars. Rob got his palm pilot out of his blazer pocket and began to play a game on it. Ellie sent plaintive text messages to her friends berating her father, her brother, school, the holidays, life and God. It was not going to be a pleasant drive.

Hunting Wriggly was a gingerbread village of blue and pink and jasmine cottages with low roofs thickly slated and tiny windows. The main – the only – street curled in the shape of a horseshoe round a village green glassily dimpled with a pond complete with ducks, then snaked down a hill and round to the right to encompass an ancient stone church and minute schoolhouse. The road was washed at its lowest point by a bright stream (a narrow stone footbridge saved the villagers' shoes) then climbed again to the top of a rise, where a cluster of newer houses, a small shop, craft barn and a pub marked the outer perimeter of the village. Further along the lane, terraces of stone cottages punctuated the hedgerows. Low stone walls in front of them served to restrain pocket handkerchief sized gardens burgeoning with bright purple asters and giant-headed dahlias, blooming still, even so late in October. Larger houses and farms were strung out towards the outskirts of the parish, then there was nothing at all until, on the right, a pair of diminutive cottages and on the left, stone gate-posts announced Belinda's arrival at Hunting Manor.

The driveway took her through a tunnel of trees brazen with the colours of autumn. The drive itself was a golden carpet which sloped quite steeply down between thick banks of mixed shrubs and trees. After a while the trees seemed to retreat, held back by a stalwart hedge of glossy rhododendrons. These too were held severely in check by what looked like an intensive coppicing programme; some of the bushes had been cut hard back to allow easier passage along the driveway, skeletal limbs and denuded branches protruded at awkward angles, like broken bones. Amputated boughs had been left to compost down. Then the vegetation petered out as the driveway curved round to the left and opened out into a gravelled sweep. To each side of the sweep, wide, manicured lawns and the occasional stand of grey-trunked beech trees made a green and golden moat around the house so that the gravel made a drawbridge to the massive doors.

The house itself was reassuringly large, three storied, made of pink sandstone, flat-fronted but with a roof line that bristled with chimneys and gables. There were a number of tall windows on the ground and first floor levels and smaller, dormer windows on the upper storey. To the right, a single story wing of newer, but not recent, construction in brick jutted forwards, making an L shape with a pleasant, sheltered paved area in its elbow. Through the tall windows, Belinda could see a snooker table and a grand piano set at opposite ends of an enormous low-ceilinged room. Ridiculously, quite alone on the grand sweeping drive, Belinda clapped her hands in excitement. She walked towards the huge double doors which were set centrally to the main house up two wide and smooth stone steps and under a portico supported on sandstone pillars. The door, as promised, was unlocked. She pushed it open and went in.

The hall was enormous, bathed in light as golden as honey which streamed through the two windows on either side of the door. The wood panelled walls and wide-boarded floor exuded the sweetness of beeswax. To her left, a fireplace so wide and high that five men could have stood abreast within it, was ready laid with wood, its hearth scattered with pine cones and crisp autumn leaves. To the left of the fireplace, a door into the dining room stood ajar. Belinda made a quick note of the number of chairs round the long polished table, (twenty: ideal) before taking in other details; silver candelabra, another huge fireplace, windows draped with heavy folds of beautifully embroidered curtains. Back in the hall, to the right of the fireplace, an alcove stored fishing rods and tackle boxes, a selection of Wellington boots and green waterproof coats, riding hats and crops and even a beekeeper's hat. Their presence gave a somewhat eerie feeling that the proprietors were still in residence; that Belinda was not entitled at all to be intruding upon them. She paused, listening hard, uncomfortably aware of the flop of her own heart within her ribs; but only silence met her, and, tentatively, she took off her coat and hung it gingerly onto one of the pegs, before continuing her exploration.

17

Adjacent to the cloakroom, a door gave access to a small, windowless bathroom, with an old fashioned but immaculately clean white suite and black and white tiled floor. Opposite the front door, a wide and heavily carved staircase rose up ten or a dozen steps before dividing and sweeping further upwards in two broad arcs. To the right of the staircase, leading onwards, a corridor gave access to the nether reaches of the house; Belinda peeped into each room, saving detailed examination until her chores were done; a library, a snug little drawing room and a huge lounge with French windows opening onto a terrace. To the left of the staircase, an anonymous panelled door led the way into the domestic area. The back of it was covered in green material (so *that's* what a baize door is, she thought to herself). To the right of the front door, opposite the dining room, a room that exuded masculinity; (leather armchairs before yet another fireplace, a roll-topped desk, newspaper racks and a collection of cigar boxes). Next on the right, a gallery lined with frowning portraits. Through the gallery, presumably, access to the games and music room glimpsed from the drive, but Belinda, her brief exploration complete for the moment, stood back in the hall and breathed in. Yes, she thought, satisfied: this was a place for family: it would do.

In contrast to Belinda's neat and scrupulously clean house, Ruth's was a bombsite. The narrow, tight hallway was cluttered with boxes of food and wellington boots, a bruised old suitcase, a crate of toys and a hamster cage. A basket of ironing perched precariously on the stairs on its way up, along with a stack of books, a pair of swimming goggles and an odd sock. The children's school bags, their empty lunch boxes and Rachel's PE kit were on the kitchen table. On the bread-board peanut butter sandwiches had been abandoned in the process of construction. A swathe of newspapers carpeted the area around James's armchair and CD cases were in disarray around the stereo.

James, Rachel and Ben were all in a state of high agitation; Ruth would be home from school soon, frazzled after a difficult half-term and wound up about the family holiday to come. They were supposed to be changed and ready to pack the car and set off the *moment* she arrived back from school. James was supposed to have spent his day off getting the house to rights. The hamster was supposed to be round at the neighbour's, Rachel and Ben were supposed to have put their school bags away and washed out their lunch boxes, the peanut butter sandwiches were supposed to be cut and ready for the journey in a Tupperware box. The imminent arrival of Ruth to discover that none of these things had occurred put them all into a state of paralysed anxiety; the three human beings stood forlornly in the lounge and surveyed the chaos, knowing that whatever they decided to tackle as a priority would turn out to be wrong. Even the hamster cowered in his nest of shredded paper. They shouldn't have dallied by the pond for so long on the way home from school watching the fledgling moorhens but hindsight was going to be no comfort to them once Ruth got home. They all knew it but none of them said it. James wrapped his massive arms around the two children and cast a rueful eye at the newspapers and the CDs.

They stood for a while in this embrace; the children leaning against his massive form, feeling the heat emanate from him, pressing into the softness of his flesh. Rachel slipped her thumb into her mouth. Ben played an arpeggio on his father's thigh. Then James gently disentangled himself and strode over to the stereo, inserting a CD and hovering his finger over 'play'.

'Alright, my lovelies,' he said, his voice twinkling with excitement and adventure, 'let us with haste from hence forthwith. Ben, you carry Skippy round to Mrs MacDougal's. Don't forget his food. Rachel, you sort the kitchen, if you can. Finish the sandwiches and wash the lunch boxes. I'll hide the school bags and the PE kit and tackle this mess in here. Stand by to repel all boarders.' He stabbed his finger onto the button and the William Tell Overture at an unsociable volume galvanised them all into action. James flew round the lounge at double speed, like a film in comedy fast-forward, scooping up newspapers and marshalling the CDs back into the shelves. Ben leapt into the hall with a whoop like a comic book hero. Rachel scurried into the kitchen and seized the knife. Their laughter made the house ring like a pure bell.

Ruth's day in the special needs department of the local secondary school had been made more difficult than usual by the over excitement occasioned by it being the last day of the half term. Holiday fever had had the students in its grip and there had been no doing anything with them. She had had an acrimonious staff meeting over lunch and an encounter with a belligerent parent on the school steps. She had a stack of books to mark and tests to grade. The traffic was already beginning to thicken on the main roads and, if they weren't sharp, would be at a standstill by the time they got on the by-pass. Ruth sat and fumed behind the wheel. The petrol gauge caught her eye and her stress level climbed a notch higher. They would have to stop at the petrol station; that would delay them even more. She only hoped that James had spent his day off getting the house tidy and that the children would be ready to set off as soon as she got home. But it was a forlorn hope. James was utterly lackadaisical when left to his own devices; he had no sense of the urgency of anything. He tended to get the children over-excited and giddy so that she had to shout at them to get them into line. No doubt it would all be left to her, again.

Ruth crept three places forward in the queue for the lights, a tricky right-hand filter notorious for letting the minimum of cars through at a time. Distractedly she watched a woman trying to manoeuvre into a parking space outside a parade of shops; she was making a terrible hash of it. On the pavement beyond the parking car three pupils from Ruth's school emerged from a sweet shop and lit up cigarettes, and she gasped and gesticulated at them, but they didn't see her. She sighed and cursed the traffic.

As if the prospect of the journey was not bad enough the holiday itself was feeling like a dreadful mistake in the offing. Ruth wondered what on earth was to be gained by it. She'd never got on especially well with Belinda and although she had been closer to Simon he had drifted away from her since the death of his wife. Her younger sister, Heather, lived life in vastly different circles and in fact had always seemed to inhabit a different plane from ordinary mortals. The family had become brittle and dry, like leather or wood deprived of polish, and the holiday would only reveal the fissures across its surface. Recent family gatherings had been fraught with angst; she had been so distressed at April's funeral that she had scarcely any recollection of it.

The traffic moved forward again. A car emerging from a road on the left nosed itself in front of Ruth's. The driver waved thanks at her as she let him in.

'You didn't give me much choice,' she muttered, sourly.

Even the concept of a holiday was one scarred by unhappy childhood memories. Her father had played a minor role; the driver

21

and provider of ice cream money. Other fathers had built sand castles with turrets and fortifications, or organised games on the hard sand revealed by the evening retreat of the tide, or dammed the steam that flowed onto the beach from some unspecified (and probably unspeakably dirty) source originating in the town. They had been the beach heroes, jolly and tanned, wearing silly hats and sensible sandals. Her father, in long trousers and a short-sleeved shirt, had taken himself off for long walks, leaving Mary with the children and a picnic. Sitting, now, in the sluggish queue, Ruth recalled one memorable occasion when his walk had lasted over three hours. The sky had clouded over and a chilly breeze had sprung up, blowing stinging sand onto tender, sun-reddened skin. Rain, inevitably, had begun to fall and the beach had rapidly emptied, as families struck their camps of deck chairs and windbreaks and rush mats and sun umbrellas, and hurried back to their caravans or apartments or into cafés for cups of milky coffee and plates of sticky buns. Their cardigans and anoraks had been locked in the car and Robert had taken the key away with him. Mary had gathered them together like a mother duckling and they had cowered miserably behind her and their windbreak on the deserted beach and used damp and sand-impregnated beach towels to try and keep warm.

At last Ruth pulled into the drive. The front door was open and loud music boomed from the interior. In the lounge James and the children were dancing and laughing uproariously; Ruth watched them through the window. Neither of the children was changed for the journey and Rachel's hair looked like a bird's nest. Ben was wearing the swimming goggles which had been on their way upstairs since his lesson the previous Monday. James, in spite of his bulk, was careering round the room making silly exaggerated gestures with his arms and legs which had the children rolling around in uncontrollable laughter. The anger and frustration in her made Ruth want to scream at them but a more detached part of her wondered at their untrammelled joy. Like a sudden rainbow across a cloud-darkened sky, it illuminated her, throwing fingers of iridescence into her glowering mood. And yet, like a rainbow, it was uncatchable. Inside the room all was light and glee, but she was outside and it did not touch her, and she knew that as soon as she stepped across the threshold it would evaporate.

Sure enough, as though her thought had conjured it, James' eye caught hers and he said 'here's Mum,' and although he rushed to begin bringing out the luggage to the car, and Ben switched off the music and Rachel proffered the box of sandwiches, and they all, at her behest, became busy and focussed, it was as though her arrival had caused them to close the pages of some exciting chapter, to bury away a marvellous treasure, because she would despise it. She would not have despised it but neither would she have fully understood it; like a foreigner coming in amongst indigenous tribesmen speaking in their own tongue, she could catch only a sense of the passion. Their language, the language of James and the children, the language of silliness and frivolity and make-believe, was alien to her and politely, in her presence, they reverted to her familiar tongue.

Her familiar tongue lashed at them while she packed the boot of the car; why were the children still in their uniform, why was the house in such a state, what had James being doing all day, would *everything always* be left to her? She drank the half cup of tea which Rachel carried out to her in white lipped silence while the others made a last visit to the toilet, then they climbed into the car.

'We need petrol,' Ruth said, accusingly, after a while. James nodded and pulled into a petrol station. While he filled the tank Ruth swivelled round in her seat.

'How was school?' she asked.

'I didn't feel well at lunch time. I didn't eat my sandwiches,' Rachel said, wanly.

Ruth turned back to the front. 'Silly girl,' she said. 'What a waste.'

23

Making her choice, Belinda took the small and unobtrusive door through to the domestic regions. Doors off to the right gave access to a laundry and boiler room and a steep circular stairway leading down to the cellars and serving as a servants' access to the higher floors. One door, on the left, opened cleverly back into the dining room. Finally, at the end of a rather gloomy passageway Belinda discovered the kitchen. It was everything she could have wished for. As big as a squash court, it was fitted out with shelves and cupboards, a fire-engine red six oven Aga, a huge American style fridge, a double sink, a vast dish washing machine and a scrubbed kitchen table, long and narrow, with refectory-style pews along either side and massive carver chairs at each end making seating for up to thirty. A woman with more imagination than Belinda might have conjured up estate workers, house maids, footmen and stable lads sitting down together here for meals while the family ate in the splendour of the dining room. A bustle of activity, the rich smell of roasting meat and aromatic steam from tureens of fresh vegetables, the clatter of dishes and the chatter of men and women at liberty from work for a while. But Belinda, a woman for practicalities, diligently opened the fridge and placed her chilled foodstuffs inside; wine, milk, cheese, ham, red chunks of sirloin wrapped in bloody butcher's paper, cream, butter, yoghurts, bacon, eggs.

Later, having checked the radiators and placed spare toilet rolls, and distributed towels and made sure the beds were aired, and chopped onions and vegetables and placed an enormous casserole in the oven, and baked scones, and tidied away the cooking and baking things, Belinda allowed herself to move around the house and appreciate its preparedness. It was four-thirty. Soon the gravel would grate with the tyres of her family's cars, and the hall would be cluttered with bags and toys and shoes and coats, and the silence would be forced away by the excited cries of children and the exclamations of the agreeable adults and the complaints of the hard-to-please ones. Soon, she would have to share. She had made tea and carried it up the staircase and along the landing to where she had discovered a tall arched window with a deep cushioned seat. The view over the terrace and the sloping lawns was magnificent. To her left, a walled garden showed rows of Brussels sprouts and winter greens, and glass houses steamy with exotic flavours. In the distance, beyond a belt of coniferous woodland, the land seemed to disappear abruptly into a steely blue skyline, like a knife, that would cut the lowering sun on its blade. Soon she would light lamps and close curtains, and even put a match to the logs in the hall grate, but just now she would drink her tea and savour the readiness that her planning and work had brought about.

'Stop the car, James!'

James responded with a characteristic calmness, despite Ruth's rather sudden request. He made a careful assessment of his options. Certainly, this would be a very bad place to stop. The lane was scarcely wide enough to accommodate two vehicles. On one side, a soft verge and a deepish ditch and on the other a rather wild and prickly-looking hedge meant that anyone exiting the car would end up scratched or muddy. On the other hand, at the bottom of the hill the lane took a sharp dog leg round to the right and James could see the entrance to a rough track opening onto its outer curve. Bearing all these considerations in mind, he was yet conscious of the need to be seen to be responding with suitable alacrity, given the sharpness and well known tone of Ruth's command. Therefore he ejaculated: 'Driveway! Down there!' and pressed his foot onto the accelerator in order to demonstrate appropriate urgency and obedience. Arriving, at some speed, at the entrance to the track, he stepped on the brakes so that the car skidded on the loose shale and ground to a halt with its bonnet facing almost back the way they had come.

'Rachel! Get out!' Ruth barked.

Discerning at last the cause of the panic, James fumbled with his seat belt, but his bulk made it difficult for him to move quickly. Ruth was out of her car door and round the back and had her hand on the handle of the rear door before he had managed to disengage himself, and before Rachel had managed to push her various soft toy friends off her knee and unfasten her own belt. Poor Rachel, he could see, in the rear-view mirror, had turned a shade of greenish white. Ruth hauled her step-daughter out of the car and bent over her while she vomited into the hedge. James turned round and gave his son a big wink.

'Alright, Ben?'

Ben looked pale, too, but this was his habitual colour. He gave his father a pallid smile and turned his head so that he was gazing out of his window, away from his retching half-sister. It was just the kind of thing he hated; sudden shouting and heightened emotions. His fingers played a Mazurka on his lap. He had been practising it all term and had recently played it for the external examiner at the Cathedral Music School where he had been a day pupil since the beginning of term. He had found it fiendishly difficult at first but with practise and the help of Mrs Adams, he had mastered it. The examiner, visibly impressed, had made copious notes on his examination sheet.

'How old are you, Ben?' he had asked, at last.

'Nine, Sir,' Ben had replied, clutching his sheaf of music and wondering, with a catch of anxiety, whether this young age might, for some reason, disqualify him.

'Extra-ordinary! Grade three, and only nine!' the examiner had commented, before dismissing him from the room.

'I think I might have passed my piano exam,' said Ben, turning back to look at his father, who was whistling, very quietly, through the gap between his front teeth. James nodded, sagely, as though he had been privy to all of Ben's forgoing thoughts and had just arrived at exactly the same conclusion himself. Outside the car, they could both hear Ruth's voice, her tone vacillating between remonstrance and reassurance; 'I told you that you should have eaten more lunch. Really, what a silly thing to do. Good food wasted, apart from anything else. You know you don't travel well on an empty stomach. Alright, never mind. Let it come, just let it come. Good girl. You'll feel better now. That's it.'

Rachel was looking, now, almost translucent, as though, along with the vomit, she had evacuated all her personal pigmentation. The afternoon was still bright with autumn sunshine and in comparison to the vibrant colours of the leaves and the dun brown of the ploughed fields, the poor girl looked like a spectre in school uniform. Her legs were trembling, too, and from shock, possibly, or shame, she was beginning to cry.

27

'James!' shouted Ruth, 'can you pass that bottle of mineral water, please? And I think Rachel's going to need her fleece from the boot.'

'OK!' James replied, genially, and began again to grope round the overspill of his belly for the clasp of his seatbelt.

'Dad?' James stopped and looked round at his son. 'Cool skid, Dad.' said Ben.

Later, when they were back on the road, and Rachel, exhausted, had fallen asleep, her family of furry animals clasped tightly in her arms, Ruth said, 'I anticipate nothing but trouble from Heather, I'm afraid. She's absolutely obsessed with this child. The whole week's going to revolve around her and Bob and the baby. It isn't as though it's really a McKay! Mum won't be allowed a minute for any of the other grandchildren, let alone for *us*.'

'She has waited a long time for a baby,' James commented, conversationally. Heather and Bob's childless state had been top of the family agenda for about three years. But James was careful to mention this only as a statement of fact. It wouldn't do, he knew, to appear to be defending Heather's preoccupation with the new arrival, nor to remind Ruth that strictly speaking his daughter Rachel wasn't really a McKay either.

'Exactly! Just waited and waited and waited. She hasn't done anything about it; not visited the doctor, had tests, or anything. I mean, I know she wanted to keep things natural, but there comes a point, surely, when it's obvious that Mother Nature needs a little help. Personally, I suspect that it's Bob's fault. All those years of debauched living, drugs, drink, any number of women. Not to mention the fact that he's so much older than she is…. It must have affected his fertility, wouldn't you think?' James, sensing that an opinion was not really required here, simply turned his mouth down at the corners and raised his eyebrows slightly.

'And yet I never heard him suggest that it might be his problem as opposed to hers. Even while she was so down, blaming herself, desperate, just *desperate* for a baby, not a word from him, just that mazy, preoccupied look he has. I don't know how I restrained myself from saying something. And now this. Adopting a child that none of us has ever seen, and to do it right at this moment when all our attention should be focussed on Mum and Dad, doesn't it just make you want to scream?'

'What have they called her? Charlotte?'

'Charlotte!' Ruth almost shouted the name. 'If only! No! That's just the icing on the cake, that is. Starlight! I ask you, James, for goodness' sake! What can she have been thinking of?'

'It's traditional to her ethnic background,' said Ben. 'Aunty Heather told me last week.'

Ruth screwed herself round in her seat. 'You saw Heather last week?'

'No, I talked to her when she rang. I did *tell*......' he broke off, and flicked a look at the back of his father's head. James started to whistle, absentmindedly. 'I did tell Veronica to tell you,' Ben concluded. Ruth turned back to face the front.

'Oh! Veronica! She's a waste of space, that girl! Calls herself a child-minder? She couldn't mind her own business! I've told you before, Ben, you should leave a note if you can't actually speak to Daddy or me.'

'Look, Ben! Look at the name of this village!' said James, slowing the car as they passed the sign.

'Hunting Wriggly!' Ben shouted. He began to laugh. 'Who's hunting Wriggly? Why? Who is Wriggly? Is he Wriggly by name or wriggly by nature?' Suddenly, he was off, exploring, scampering over a landscape that had opened up in his imagination, his mind enraptured by the possibilities of comedy and adventure in the new idea. He lined

29

up the teddies which had escaped his sister's embrace. 'Now, men,' he addressed them, gravely, 'the hunt is on. Leave no stone unturned, no nook unexplored. Wriggly is a fiend, a danger to our citizens….'

'Has anybody seen this child, yet?' asked James, holding the directions Belinda had e-mailed through to him in one hand, and steering carefully with the other. It was a very pretty village, he noted, with a nice looking little pub and a small tea shop; refuges, should escape become imperative, he thought.

'I suppose Miriam and Simon have – they're thick as thieves. Birds of a feather and all that. Money sticks to money. I suppose they swan off to places all the time.' In fact Ruth was incorrect in this assumption. Simon and Heather saw as little of each other as their other siblings, but the impecunious status of James and Ruth's finances was a rankling wound with her. All of her siblings were better off than they were and she found it a bitter pill to swallow. Her efforts the previous Christmas to entertain Simon and his new partner had foundered, she was sure, on the scarcity of smoked salmon and the paucity of good port. It must have been Miriam's influence. Simon's late wife, April, would never have turned her nose up at Ruth's basic but honestly offered hospitality. 'I suppose I'll just have to try and get along with Miriam.' Ruth sighed. She was, on the one hand, dreading seeing her again after the disappointment of Christmas. On the other, she would welcome reconciliation on her own terms. But she had to be realistic. 'No-one seems to see my point of view on the matter and I don't suppose *she's* going to be holding out many olive branches. The truth is that I miss April terribly – more than anyone seems to realise. It's been hard seeing her shoes filled so….inadequately and so…..quickly.' James wanted to avoid at all costs a re-run of the circumstances and almost shouted with relief when he saw the gates to Hunting Manor standing open on the left, as promised.

'We're here! We're here! Rachel, darling, time to wake up.'

Rachel roused herself. 'I haven't been asleep,' she said, yawning, 'only dozing.'

'Are you feeling better?' Ruth scrutinized her step-daughter. Thirteen was a delicate age even for someone as robust and stocky as Rachel. She was the image of her father, big-boned and solid; a weak stomach for travelling was about her only Achilles heel but even so, changes would come soon and must be watched for.

'Are you looking forward to seeing Ellie and Tansy?' Ruth asked.

Rachel shrugged. 'I suppose so.'

'Oh my!' exclaimed James, bringing the car to a gentle halt at the beginning of the sweep. 'I think you're going to like this, Ladies.'

Hunting Manor lay before them in the glow of late afternoon light. The sandstone walls, pink and warm, the still woodland all around, the enticing wisp of smoke from one of the many chimneys.

'You've got to hand it to Belinda,' Ruth said, surveying the scene. 'She seems to have come up trumps with this.'

All at once the children were scrambling out of the car and careering down the drive towards the house. In his mind, Ben was still hunting the mysterious Wriggly. Under his breath, he sang a tune from one of the adventure films he liked so much: in simple quadruple time, four beats to the bar, key of A major, he identified, even as he ran and swerved and leapt across the lawns. Even though he took detours round the fountain and one of the beech trees on the lawn, Ben still arrived at the broad steps before Rachel. She was badly out of breath, her hair was awry and, he noticed with distaste, there was a smear of sick on the arm of her green school jumper.

'You ought to get changed pretty quick,' he said to his sister, carefully avoiding the yellowy stain with his eyes. 'I don't suppose Ellie and Tansy will have come in *their* school uniforms.' Rachel nodded, still too breathless to speak. She hated the grey pleated skirt and

31

formal shirt and tie she was forced to wear. Most clothes looked terrible on her anyway, she thought, miserably, and these were worse than any others. Looking down at herself, both socks were round her ankles and one shoe was horribly scuffed at the toe. On the other, the lace had come undone and trailed dangerously. She looked over her shoulder. Mum (Ruth was not her biological mother, but had cared for her, now, longer than her natural mother had done), and Dad were still driving slowly down the drive. Through the windscreen, she could see Ruth's mouth moving in relentless speech. The car was filthy, quite old fashioned, not at all like the ones her Uncles would be arriving in, she was sure. She didn't know what her parents had done wrong; all her aunts and uncles seemed to have pots of money.

'Shall we go in?' asked Ben. His hand was on the huge brass door handle but he waited for her to nod before he turned it. But at that moment it was snatched out of his hand and Aunty Belinda stood before him.

'Ben! Rachel! Hello sweeties!' she gushed. Ben prepared himself for the inevitable bosomy hug and, when it came, was glad that he had been nearer than Rachel. He couldn't bear the thought of being hugged second, after the sicky jumper.

'You're the first to arrive!' Belinda smiled, discounting herself. 'Why don't you go and explore upstairs? Right up, on the top floor, all the children are going to sleep up there together – you can go and choose your beds now, if you like, before the others come.'

Rachel and Ben stepped past her into the house, hesitating, in the vastness of the hall. Their exuberance of only a moment before evaporated and they felt the years and space begin to press upon them. Unconsciously, they moved closer to one another. Belinda noticed their hesitation and understood it with an unusual flash of perspicacity. 'Don't worry,' she said, gently. 'We're the only ones here. The whole house is ours. There's nothing creepy at all – I've checked!'

Emboldened, they began to mount the wide stair. 'It's so old. So big!' Ben murmured. 'Like a church.'

Rachel hovered uncertainly on the half landing. Looking down to the hall, Aunty Belinda was standing in the doorway waiting to greet the grown-ups. Her body was silhouetted by a golden glow, like a halo, from the low afternoon sun. 'Look!' she gasped, clutching at Ben. 'And there's an angel!' They both began to laugh and the weight lifted from them. They scampered together up the remaining stairs and ran hollering through the house.

Out on the driveway the two sisters hugged briefly. They were utterly unlike. Belinda was short and had always been given, like Mary, to plumpness. She wore, at Elliot's insistence, very expensive and well-made clothes, classic in style, but possessed a fewer number of clothes than other women who buy many things cheaply. She kept her hair long, but wore it in an elegant chignon day in and day out. It was now, and had been through her youth, her only vanity. Losing its dark lustre now, it had taken on an attractive pepper-and-salt colour. Her face bore few lines or wrinkles, except for deep score-lines from the edges of her nostrils to the corners of her mouth, and an engaging dimple which appeared in her cheek when she smiled. She had unfathomable eyes, concealing secrets, suggesting depths that her perpetual preoccupation with trivialities – napkins, raffle tickets – belied. She wore makeup discreetly except for lipstick, which she favoured in bright shades, and was an unvarying user of Chanel No 5. Ruth, on the other hand, took after their father. She was wirily thin, and lack of flesh plus, in her youth, a slavish worship of the sun and a heavy nicotine habit, had caused her face to age prematurely. Her mouth in particular, though large and expressive, was markedly loose, and on her eyelids the skin was becoming quite pleated now, an effect accentuated by the owlish spectacles she wore. Though not tall, she held herself with an air of tallness, a habit acquired early in her working life as a teacher of gangling, rebellious teenagers who tended to tower over her. Ruth affected colourful, multi-layered semi-ethnic clothing, for warmth – she was always perished with cold – and as a throwback from her student days when girls who had been sent off to University with sensible Marks and Spencer wardrobes liked coming home in ensembles rummaged from jumble sales and Sue Ryder shops to shock and offend their conservative parents. Today she wore vivid-print cotton trousers, baggy and a little faded, thick socks and rugged walking boots, a cream polo neck sweater, a man's blue twill shirt, worn like a jacket, sleeveless fleece and a fringed black and white cotton shawl of the kind favoured by Yasa Arafat. Unlike Belinda,

Ruth disdained the use of makeup, except for lipstick, sometimes rather haphazardly applied. Her hair, still the McKay sandy blonde, just about, but threatening soon to become that transparent non-shade that blonde goes before becoming white, was worn very short, mannish, almost, in a style that had been fashionable following its introduction by Annie Lennox in the early eighties, Ruth's formative university years.

Not given to demonstrations of affection, the sisters' hug was brief. Together they turned to the house. Even in childhood, the four years that separated them had seemed an unbreachable chasm; their name and only their name had related them. Now they looked like two women from separate ages; Belinda, dressed beyond her years, Ruth clinging rather desperately to the fashions and enthusiasms of her youth.

There was no escaping the fact that Belinda had pulled off something big and the undoubted coup accorded her, in Ruth's eyes, an unwonted respect. From Belinda, they were used to immaculate but unimaginative dinners, dull but beautifully wrapped gifts, and demonstrations of practical thoughtfulness in times of crisis. No-one was used to seeing Belinda, as it were, centre stage. It was Ruth who had been the drama-queen of the family. The only one to have attended University, her ideologies and both her partners (the first married while still at University, disastrously, it had only lasted ten months) were not as they had expected, or would, indeed, have chosen for her. Even James, as solid and reliable as the other had been shiftless and faithless, had not won their approval because he was a nurse (and nursing, even psychiatric nursing, was no job for a man) and because he was a divorcee with an infant daughter.

Ruth swallowed a phlegmy ball of surprise and the slightly bitter pill of pride and turned from the house to her sister.

'What a splendid place, Belinda! Where on earth did you find it? Expensive of course, but you can see why, now, can't you? Is it nice

35

inside? What time did you get here? What shall I do? What about food? Bed making?' Ruth maintained a torrent of questions designed to accord Belinda due praise while at the same time insinuating herself into an organisational and ultimately supervisory role in the proceedings. Ben and Rachel could be heard inside the house whooping and screeching from room to room. Belinda hugged herself inwardly but could not prevent a flush of self-satisfaction from colouring her cheeks. She cast a look over towards James, but could not catch his eye. He was standing at the back of their car, gazing distractedly into the boot.

'How was your journey? Did you see that awful accident? Come on in and look around,' was all she said.

James, left alone at the back of the car, surveyed the contents of the boot. For such a large man – he was easily six foot four or five, and wide of girth – it was amazing how frequently he went completely unnoticed. It didn't perturb him at all. 'Anonymous', he liked to say, in that quirky, humorous way he had, 'is my middle name.' He began to touch the handles of bags and cases and carriers, tentatively lifting coats and shifting boxes. Inevitably, whichever he chose to bring in first would be wrong. There would be a design, a scheme, some obvious way to proceed which, to Ruth, who had packed the car, would be self-evident, but to James, now, remained a riddle. Suddenly Ben was by his side, then in his arms, propelled by excitement, rendered, almost, to tears by intensity of feeling, a flurry of skinny arms and legs, and big, emotional eyes.

'Dad! Dad!' Ben wheezed into his father's ear, 'you must come and see. It's *magic*, Dad! There's a piano, a *grand* piano, and stairs, and scones and secrets and everything!'

James squeezed his son in sympathy. 'Everything!' he echoed, breathlessly, 'will you show me?'

'Yes, Dad, I'll show you. It's quite alright. There's nothing creepy at all.' Ben slithered out of his father's arms and grabbed the meaty hand in his own Doulton-delicate grasp. 'And can you bring Rachel's things up? She wants to get changed *immediately*, in case the others come.' Together they began burrowing into the boot, James shouldering bags and grabbing boots, Ben manfully struggling with the box of board games and toys. Once in the hall, they dumped everything except for the old suitcase which contained their clothes, and taking only a cursory look around, James followed his son up the wide staircase, along a corridor, through a narrow door and up a slender flight of spiral stairs to the upper storey, where they were just in time to see Rachel, dressed only in her underwear, disappear shrieking through one of the bedroom doors. James noted, with some surprise, that his daughter was wearing a bra, and, with less surprise, that the elastic of her knicker-legs had disappeared into the cleft between the cheeks of her bottom.

'Ben! Ben! Is it them? Is it them?' she was shouting urgently through the closed door.

'No, it's only me and Dad,' replied Ben, pushing at the door and indicating to James that they should slide the suitcase into the gap.

'Unpack your things carefully, Rachel. Try not to crumple all the rest. All our clothes are in that case. I'll come back for it in a while, love. Alright?' James spoke through the doorway, waiting patiently for a response from his daughter before turning back to Ben, who was hopping impatiently from one foot to the other. 'Right Ben. Come on. Show me everything. Everything! But especially the piano, right? And the scones.'

Simon guided the people-carrier through the Buckinghamshire lanes. It was a journey he could make on auto-pilot, now. He navigated it every Friday afternoon and Sunday evening. The children seemed happy at the school but Simon felt guilty every time he dropped them off. They ought to be at home, with him, and April, but life had not allowed him such simplicity.

He had their bags stowed in the rear of the car. They had packed them the previous weekend. He had helped them, of course, but the responsibility of it has been theirs. It was a policy he had evolved, even with little Todd, since April's death had left him to cope alone two years before. Her death had impressed him again with the fickleness of people, and that, in the end, you could only rely on yourself. It was a lesson he had learned the hard way but he would teach it to his children gently if he could. So he had casually suggested to twelve year old Toby that perhaps three pairs of underpants might not be sufficient for a whole week, and patiently explained to six year old Todd why he could not take his bicycle, even though he had just learned to ride it without its stabilisers. 'It won't go in the car, Todd, and no one else will have one, so it won't be fair.'

'I'd share,' stammered Todd, his eyes swimming.

'I know you would, son,' said Simon, ruffling Todd's hair. He was so like his mother that it hurt Simon to look at him sometimes.

'These swimming trunks, though,' he said, tucking them into a corner of Todd's hold-all, 'are an excellent idea. We can find a local pool, or perhaps we might even try the sea.'

Tansy had needed no assistance. She was capable and responsible; old for her thirteen years.

They had gone out and bought new walking boots and assorted outdoor gear, and had clandestine burgers and chips for lunch while Miriam was at the gym. The children were surprisingly enthusiastic about the holiday, about seeing their cousins, and their sense of anticipation overcame to a certain extent his own reservations. Family was something he had learned was safest kept at arm's length. Miriam, he knew, was dreading it, coming along under sufferance and likely, even at this late stage, to find a reason why she could not, after all, accompany them. 'The whole family thing is a foreign language to me,' she had said. She had played no practical role in the holiday preparations, dismissing Belinda's emailed list of the provisions she requested that they supply, and sent him with her own to Fortnum's. She had undertaken only to be at High Wycombe station at a certain time so that he could pick her up before they got onto the M40.

The thing had been arranged for months but now it was upon him he quailed at the ordeal to come. The idea of spending a week with his father was not appealing; it brought back too many memories of miserable, queasy journeys in Lorries and heated arguments about his future. His failure to go into the family business had created a rift between him and his father that time had not healed. His father's rage had filled their house for literally years, like a terrible stench; he had been quite out of control. His mother had wept and wrung her hands, and crept between them, begging and pleading with Simon to reconsider in order to placate his father's wrath. Belinda had cowered and kept her distance, Ruth had escaped to University. Only Heather had seemed unaffected by the turmoil; she would sit up in her room, cutting shapes out of empty cereal packets, snipping and sticking and sellotaping intricate models together, humming gaily to herself as she worked. She alone had been immune from his father's anger. How Simon had envied her his father's unconditional love.

He knew that Mary harboured a fiercer love for him than she had for the three girls, a love which had not been quenched by the years, almost ten years, he had spent *incommunicado* wandering in the States, or by his marriage to April to which she had not been invited, or by the birth of two of his three children which had taken place without the benefit of her support. All this she had forgiven him, along with his occasional appeals to her for cash in times of straitened circumstances. Christmas and birthday cards, finding their way to him sometimes months late, had reassured him that he was remembered by his mother, even if his father's signature never appeared on them. Finally, in the early nineties he had been swept up in the wave of new e-commerce ventures, a wave he had managed to ride out and up and over to success. Only then had he returned home, in a smart car, wearing expensive clothes, with a beautiful and devoted wife and two cherubic children in tow. His sense of justification upon entering the old house and finding everything the same, and only himself so much more confident and self-assured, had been saved from becoming an insufferable crowing triumph only by the sight of his mother, so much aged, by the tearful way she embraced April and the children, and not least by the heart-rending joy with which she enfolded himself back into her arms.

Simon had been careful to re-establish his mother back into his family fold; before Robert's retirement she had been regularly invited to stay with them at times when the business prevented Robert from being included in the invitation. He had encouraged April to call on Mary for advice over childhood ailments, and when April's own health had begun to give cause for concern, it had been Mary who had become their mainstay of support. His father, however, he had kept at arm's length and even now, unmanned as he had been by his stroke, and rendered utterly harmless, yet still Simon was unable to trust the man with a single ounce of tenderness. But to his mother, he felt, he owed it. There was an element of duty about it which was dry and distasteful but he would make the best of it.

The children were waiting for him in the lofty hallway. They clamoured around him and he wrapped the three of them in his embrace before ushering them out to the car. Matron was supervising the departure for the holidays of the pupils, and she ticked the three McKays off her list. Some pupils, whose parents were abroad, would stay on; it was hard to imagine what kind of a time they would have of it in the deserted dormitories with only a skeleton staff to entertain them. They sat in gloomy resignation on the wide stairway while their friends were collected and taken away.

'Isn't Miriam coming?' Toby asked as they approached the empty car. Simon tried to ignore the tone of hopefulness in his voice.

'Of course she's coming!' he replied, perhaps more forcefully than he had intended. 'We're going to collect her from the railway station.'

But they had some time to kill before she would be there. She was not due out of court until four, then she would have to go back to chambers before getting onto the tube. They would get snared up in all the weekend traffic and be late arriving at the house. His suggestion that she might, like him, take the afternoon off had been summarily dismissed.

'Who's hungry?' he asked, as they pulled through the gates of the school.

On their madcap helter-skelter from room to room, James and Ben passed Belinda and Ruth emerging from one of the first floor rooms.

'Oh the whole I thought she'd prefer it,' Belinda was saying, of the room she had allocated to Heather, Bob and the new child. It was the largest room in the south wing, plenty big enough to accommodate all the baby paraphernalia, with an en suite bath. Ruth nodded a little absent-mindedly. Belinda tended to witter on so, and Ruth had stopped listening to the mantra of practicalities after the first few minutes, wishing she could walk through the house with a more sympathetic companion, pointing out its architectural fineness, speculating as to its occupants in times gone by. Such input would be wasted on Belinda, though.

Even as the tour continued, and the wonders of the house unfolded, Ruth was conscious in herself of a rising tendency to criticise. It was almost as though the better the place turned out to be, the more imperative that she pick holes and find fault. It was a characteristic in herself that she knew caused offence and yet could not be curbed. And so, inwardly, she allowed it to romp roughshod over Belinda's triumph. The house was so gratuitously large, for a start. There were twice as many bedrooms as necessary, nice as they all were – her own, indeed, was lovely, easily the one she would have picked for herself, down a mysterious corridor and up a neglected stair – and a superfluity of rooms downstairs which might facilitate division and cliquishness. It was extortionately expensive. Ruth, who had blanched at the amount of money named as their contribution to the holiday, was certain that something smaller and cheaper could have been located. It was alright for her more moneyed brother and sisters - *they* could all afford it without blinking, whereas she and James and the children had positively gone without a holiday during the summer in order to afford their share of this one. Much had been pinned on its success, only a week, to cram in all the relaxation and recreation normally enjoyed during three peaceful weeks camping in the Loire. This being the case, and mean as she felt, Ruth was considering how, as her opening gambit, she could get Heather, Bob and a child who, presumably, would still not be sleeping through the night, moved further away from her own room.

'Don't you think Heather would like to be nearer to Mum? In case, you know, the baby is wakeful?' she said.

'I'm sure Heather might prefer it,' said Belinda, leading the way down the stairs, 'but I want Mum to enjoy the rest. I'll be on hand, and so will you, if there's a problem.'

'And Miriam,' Ruth put in. 'I believe they're very close.'

'Oh yes, and Miriam. But I don't think she's had much experience with babies.'

There was a pregnant pause. They surveyed the boxes and baggage dumped on the hall floor by James. The subject of Miriam, Belinda knew, was very dangerous territory with Ruth, and she was aware already that even the surer ground of the house and the arrangements was beginning to shift under her feet.

Ruth clamped her jaws tightly shut. She could not allow herself to be drawn into a discussion on that subject just now, when Miriam might, at any moment, arrive. It was clear that she would have no ally at all and would have to make the best of things, although the feeling that she, a real family member, should defer to such a Johnnie-come-lately, was galling.

The subject of Miriam left in abeyance, the two women began to tidy up. Belinda carried the boxes of provisions brought by Ruth and James through to the kitchen, trying to ignore the name of the inferior discount supermarket on everything. Ruth hung up coats and arranged Wellington boots in the cloakroom alcove. From down the gallery, the strains of a Mazurka played with gusto and confidence could be heard. James, dancing, a snooker cue in his embrace, appeared briefly in the hall in order to communicate that Rachel was changing upstairs, seemed anxious about the arrival of her cousins, ought to be persuaded to eat and drink something quite soon, and - unnecessarily - that Ben had found a piano. Ruth assimilated this information with a nod, and noted with distaste the crumbs adhering to James' pullover. Evidently, just in his way, he had found food. But Ruth forbore to say anything and in any case he was off again, surprisingly light of foot, down the gallery and into the music room.

Half an hour later, in the kitchen, the delicious aroma of a rich stew emanated from the Aga and hung in the air like a promise. Belinda hovered over the pans of peeled and prepared vegetables and dithered about whether it was time to start cooking them.

'Twenty minutes, that'll make it half-past,' she kept saying to herself, looking anxiously first at her watch and then at the huge clock with swinging pendulum over the mantel.

Ruth sat in the carver at the end of the long refectory table and felt useless. Rachel had made a brief visit into the kitchen and despite the tempting prospect of warm, fresh, homemade scones – something rarely, if ever, available at home – and fresh tea, had drunk only a glass of water before announcing her intention of going back upstairs. She seemed unsettled and Ruth supposed that James must be right; she must be anxious for the arrival of her cousins Ellie and Tansy. This was not, in fact, what James had said, but in her own anxiety about the arrival of Miriam, as, indeed, at other times, Ruth was ignorant of the depths of her step-daughter's insecurities and unfortunately her abrasive persona did not invite confidences. She noted only, with extreme annoyance, that Rachel had put on the outfit brought for the evening of the anniversary itself, leather-look trousers and a long cream jerkin with tasselled belt. Worse, although practically new, they looked tight and rather uncomfortable. It was just typical, Ruth fumed inwardly, for Rachel to grow out of the damned things *now*. It was becoming more and more difficult to get clothes to fit Rachel from the children's ranges in any of the department stores, and Ruth absolutely refused to be drawn at this early stage into any of the teenage boutiques. In any case, clothes in those shops were outrageously expensive and made for thin girls; something poor big-boned Rachel would never be.

'Have you put those on to show Aunty Belinda how nice you're going to look for the party?' Ruth ventured, pointedly.

'You do look lovely, Rachel. Very with-it,' Belinda chimed in, helpfully. But Rachel simply shrugged and muttered something about wanting to look nice *now*. Ruth was prevented from making her meaning clearer by the arrival of Ben and James, exhausted from exploring.

James' eyes lit up at the sight of the scones as though he had not already eaten two of them, which everybody knew he had, and he went on, to his wife's disgust, aided and abetted by an oddly gregarious Belinda, to devour a further two, thickly spread with butter as well as, unnecessarily, jam, before going out through the kitchen door into the gathering gloom with Ben for further adventure.

The kitchen fell silent on their exit. Forty years of shared family history stretched back from this moment: childhood toys (Belinda's dolls always immaculately dressed and cared for, Ruth's naked, and abandoned buried head first in the compost heap); beach holidays (Ruth had teased Belinda with long fronds of seaweed); Christmases glowing with expectation and then dampened with actuality (one year Ruth had pried in all Belinda's parcels in secret, and spoiled her surprises by revealing their contents); school, (Ruth always top of the class, Belinda a plodding pupil). And yet as two adults sharing McKay blood, and so much history, there was scarcely anything tangible which really bonded them together. Ruth surveyed her sister as she fussed and flapped in front of the cooker. Belinda's life bored Ruth, peopled as it was by WI members she had never met and charity events she had not attended, and she could not think of a single question to ask which might begin something like an interesting conversation between them.

Suddenly, without asking, Ruth began to clear away the tea things, deciding that tea was over and that even if someone were to arrive right this moment, tea and scones would not be required, but whisky, or gin and tonic, or wine instead. Indeed she was quite desperate for a drink herself, and having stacked the dishwasher in the face of Belinda's palpable disapproval – Belinda was a strict adherent of Fairy Liquid and Rubber Gloves – she began to open cupboards in search of glasses and bottles.

'What time are they arriving?' Ruth asked, slicing lemon. 'Shall I 'phone? They're sure to have their mobiles switched on.'

'Better not,' Belinda said, 'Elliot only gets annoyed if I telephone him in the car. I'm not sure of the children's numbers off the top of my head.'

'Rob and Ellie have mobile phones?' The extravagance of this appalled Ruth although it should not have done; all the children at school carried mobiles.

'Oh yes,' Belinda shrugged. 'They're pay-as-you-go ones. I buy them a top up card every month. To be honest it's more for my own convenience. Rob's out such a lot and I like to know that I can contact him, and that he can call me, if, you know, he needs to. And Ellie......well, all her friends have them.' Despite this rationale, Belinda felt vaguely uncomfortable with her explanation; it wasn't indicative of good family communication, she thought.

'I really shouldn't worry about the food, too much,' Ruth said, plinking ice into two tall tumblers. People will be too excited to eat when they first get here. They'll want to look round and settle in. That casserole smells delicious but it won't spoil for another hour in the oven, will it? Here.' Ruth handed Belinda gin and tonic and took a long pull at her own.

'What about the children? They'll be ravenous, don't you think....?' Belinda could feel her plans slipping away from her like the string of a helium balloon from the fist of a baby. Ruth shook her head and swallowed more gin.

'Oh! They'll be far too excited to eat straight away. Come on, Belinda. Let's take these drinks and go and light one of those fires you've laid for us.' Without waiting for Belinda, Ruth stalked out of the kitchen and up the passageway towards the hall.

'We could set the table!' Belinda called after her. 'Do you think we should eat here, or in the dining room?' But her question was answered only by the insolent swish and thud of the baize door closing behind her sister.

Rachel had chosen the last bed in the row. There were four of them altogether, with pretty coverlets in mauve and yellow. They had proper old fashioned bedsteads with a head and a foot in metal with brass bobbles at the corners. Each bed had a small chest of drawers to one side. Rachel had arranged her family of teddies very carefully along the bottom of her bed, covering their toes tenderly with the bottom of the quilt. Her clothes she had stuffed without any care at all into the drawers. The beds were arranged along the right hand side of the room, under the highest point of the ceiling, which then sloped down steeply so that you could only walk along without banging your head if you kept to within a foot of the bottoms of the beds. But, into the slope, two deep window casements pushed out, and you could stand up inside these and look out over the garden and fields and woods.

It would soon be dark. Only the very tops of the trees were still alight with the sun; the rest of the grounds were grey, their colours sucked away by the night. They were miles from anywhere, here, out in the wilds. It gave her a stir of excitement to look out on the untamed vastness of it, and to imagine living amongst it. She began to wonder, quite seriously, just how cold it would be sleeping under hedges or in a convenient cave, having a vague idea that there would be piles of dry clean leaves to hand, and choosing not to dwell on the insects with too many legs that might have chosen the same dwelling. She considered whether life could be sustained by berries and nuts gleaned from trees. There was a romantic thrill to the idea of living half-wild, with the roar of the wind in her ears and skin tingling with chill and the sharp scents of autumn in her nostrils, and she could breathe in and in, then something might burst and the real Rachel emerge from the restrictions of her chrysalis. But, infuriatingly, the end of this fantasy was always her father striding through the woods with a powerful torch and a thick woollen blanket, and being gathered back up into childhood and taken home to warm milk and a lecture and then bed with a hot water bottle nestling at its foot.

49

She watched her father and brother now, scampering across the lawns. Rachel noted that neither of them wore coats or wellingtons and predicted a fuss when they came in later with muddy feet and icy hands. Ben's would be icy, anyway. Her father was never cold. Half of her wanted to hurry down to join them. The other half preferred to remain up here and look on; somehow it was easier to know how you felt about things when you were outside of them. Presently it became too dark to see James and Ben properly, and she turned away from the window and drew the curtain across it.

She was ravenously hungry, having lost what little lunch she had eaten in the hedge and refused tea in the kitchen. She took the glass she had brought up from the kitchen and walked into the tiny bathroom accessed through a funny shaped door at the end of the room. The proximity of the bathroom to the bed she had chosen was no accident. She *assumed* that she and Tansy would share. (Ellie, she had noted, had been given a single room, across the corridor, reserved by a post-it bearing her name.) If so, she would be able to dash virtually unseen into the bathroom and close the door every morning, to wash and change in privacy, and last thing at night, she could take her pyjamas in there and do the whole thing the other way around. She hated her body, its wobbling whiteness, the alarming sprouting of thick black hair; she couldn't bear the idea of anyone seeing it.

She filled up her glass from the cold tap. The bathroom, whose every surface was painted a Johnson's Baby Lotion shade of pink, held an old fashioned bath, a wash hand basin and a toilet, and had another of the deep windows thrusting out of the roofline, with no curtain across it this time. Now, with the light on, Rachel could see nothing at all of the grey landscape, but only herself reflected pinkly back into the room, drinking water. She looked like a pink baby-blob, grossly fat. She put her hands to her midriff and pinched the flesh until it hurt. How was it possible to feel so hungry and thin on the inside, and yet be so full and fat on the outside? Suddenly she hated the cream jerkin and tacky fake-leather trousers, and knew with a terrible certainty that both the other girls would have nicer clothes with the right labels, and thin bodies with proper haircuts.

She stepped back into the room and surveyed the beds. Perhaps Tansy wouldn't want to share. With self-discipline and a bit of help from Ben Rachel thought she could most likely manage to spend almost the entire week up here alone. She had her teddies and her books, it was quite warm, and there was water and a toilet. Probably no-one would notice much if she was missing most of the time. The idea of being remote and spiritual quite appealed, it had mystery. At the end of a week she would be thin, surely?

Rachel sat carefully on the end of her bed and tried to imagine being incarcerated in this room, the days passing with only the odd shout of laughter and passing footstep to indicate that anyone else was in the house at all. But the cosy image of herself and Tansy in pyjamas sitting cross-legged and eating chocolate biscuits until deep into the night kept intruding itself. Poor Tansy had lost her mother, after all, and there had been the beginning of a friendship between them started at Christmas before she had suddenly had to go away. It had seemed like they had both been reaching across the space that separated them: a space filled to the brim with insurmountable obstacles like, on Tansy's side, private schools, and horse-riding lessons, and ballet and death, and, on Rachel's, illegitimacy, body fat, second hand clothes and a special needs teacher, and all these things wiping quite away any common ground of family association. But they had seemed to begin to connect, for a while. And maybe Ellie wasn't too old now to want to join in. It might be fun, after all, to share with her cousins. A week was a long time to be absolutely alone and the possibility that no-one would miss her was almost more appalling than the probability that somebody would, and come to drag her without dignity into the midst of the tutting Aunties and Uncles and the bosomy reproach of Grandma.

The crunch of gravel on the drive galvanised Rachel into action. She swept the teddies off the bed and kicked them into one of the window alcoves, then she wrestled her clothing from the drawers and threw that too onto the floor, carefully away from any particular bed. She would let them choose, and that might make them kind.

She met Ben on the stairs, breathless and rosy cheeked.

'They're here!' he wheezed. 'And Dad and me found, oh Rachel, you'll *never* guess, we found, through the woods, the *sea!*'

Mary and Robert were dwarfed by the vast hall. They were standing uncertainly by the door, blinking like shy nocturnal creatures suddenly exposed to the sun. Mary had on her good coat and a large, sensible, black handbag hooked over her left arm. Robert was hooked over her right but, even with her support, still leaned heavily on the walking stick in his right hand. James, having encountered them on his exit from the small bathroom (where he had been attempting, with only partial success, to clean the mud from his own and Ben's shoes), had, in the absence of anyone else, bidden them welcome, without having any idea as to what the arrivals procedure might be. He had sent Ben scurrying off in search of his mother and his aunt, and then busied himself with the enormous fire, making asinine comments all the while about the size of the house and the chill in the air and the warmth from the fire. Mary had responded with characteristic grace ('Lovely, yes, very large. Quite chilly, you're right. Very welcoming, how nice.) while Robert nodded vaguely and looked around him in confusion and awe. Then James had moved across to the front door, still standing open behind them, and closed it with a flourish which he instantly regretted in case his gesture might be misinterpreted as an entrapment rather than an inclusion, which is what he had intended, if, indeed, he had intended anything at all other than to keep the warmth in. Almost at once, there was a muffled thud and shout of annoyance from outside, and James reopened the door to find June and Les on the threshold, Les weighted down with a suitcase in each hand and June with a smile which dripped triumph from its well lipsticked corners. In an action which was to be vehemently criticised later, but having, he felt, no alternative at all, James stood to one side and admitted the second couple. So it was, that when Belinda and Ruth entered the hall seconds later from some cosy spot in the rear regions of the house, they were greeted by the sight of Mary and Robert, looking for all the world like interlopers, hovering uncertainly by the fire place, while June and Les, surrounded by luggage denoting a stay of some duration, took possession in the hall under the full brilliance

53

of the impressive chandelier above, and behind them, James, caught absolutely in the act, his hand on the door, having admitted them.

For once, Belinda and Ruth were in unspoken accord. June and Les must not be allowed to insinuate themselves into this special holiday week. No doubt there was plenty of room and food to spare; certainly the house would be busy and bustling and two extra could hardly matter; but the stark fact was that, frankly, they were not wanted. They were not *immediate* family, and *immediate* family was what this whole week was about.

'June!' exclaimed Ruth, whose complexion was flushed with having been sitting too close to the fire, and from a rather strongly mixed drink, and from indignation. 'What *on earth* are you doing here?' Ruth put into her question every ounce of astonishment that she could muster, so as to communicate without actually speaking the words that it was inconceivable that she and Les could have any place at this gathering.

Without waiting for June's response, Belinda hurried forward towards her parents, expressing welcome and pleasure and solicitude, pointing out the toilet and gently helping with coats, taking her father's arm and sending Ben off to find Rachel, to create as numerous a welcome committee as possible to greet what she termed 'our V.I.P.'s.' James, not knowing what to do, stood by the open door.

'You might well ask!' exclaimed June, beginning to unbutton her coat. 'It's been more trouble than I can say to get here, but when we heard that you'd expected your poor mother to drive all this way on her own, we couldn't stand by and watch, could we, Les?' She concluded with a trill of laughter, utterly false, a habitual characteristic of hers which denoted what Ruth called brass-necked front.

'Only too happy to help,' mumbled Les, paying particular and unnecessary attention to his car keys.

'She wouldn't have been on her own! She would have had Dad with her!' Ruth put in quickly. 'I should think that for a haulage man the drive across three counties would have been reasonably manageable, wouldn't you?'

'Really, I wasn't worried about it, June,' Mary said, gently. She had anticipated her daughters' anxieties about this unlooked for development but had been powerless to resist her sister-in-law's insistence.

'It was such a long way, much further than we realised when we set out. And once it got dark, navigating those narrow lanes was a nightmare. You'd never have coped, Mary, you know, would she, Les? Ha ha ha!' June turned to her husband who muttered something about 'awkward concealed junctions.'

'You're very kind,' Mary said, approaching Les and putting her hand on his arm 'It was a lot of trouble for you.'

'Happy to do it, Mary,' said Les, with genuine warmth.

'Come through this way, Mum, Dad.' Belinda indicated the way past the stairs.

'You'll want to use the toilet before you head back?' Ruth suggested to June, gesturing towards the door of the bathroom.

'I think we'll need a drink and something to eat as well, dear. Poor Les is done in. Ha ha ha!' June handed her coat to Les, her second. The four of them stood in the hall like dancers preparing for a complicated quadrille but unsure of the opening steps; James by the still open door, Ruth opposite him at the foot of the stairs, Les and June and the suggestive suitcases between them. Suddenly Rachel and Ben were on the stairs. All four adults looked up at them and in this momentary lapse of concentration, June took a step in the direction taken by Belinda, Mary and Robert. 'Where's the lounge, is it this way? Come on, children, show Aunty June where the gin is!'

Out-manoeuvred, for the moment, Ruth ground her teeth. 'You might as well close the door and show Les where to put those suitcases,' she snapped at James. 'I assume they're Mum and Dad's?'

'Oh yes,' said Les, 'ours are...'

Les was easier prey than June and Ruth pounced on him mercilessly: 'In the car? What a surprise! I'd better go and make some drinks.'

Left alone, James and Les gave each other a sympathetic moue, before each picking up a suitcase and mounting the stairs.

'Nice place,' commented Les.

'Remarkably nice.'

Belinda led her parents into the drawing room. A fire burned brightly in the hearth, and a number of deep and squashy sofas and chairs were arranged in comfortable proximity to it. Small tables displayed a collection of miniature porcelain flower baskets and a glass-fronted cabinet contained books, traditional board games and a set of model Napoleonic cannon replicas. A French window looked out into a small paved courtyard area.

Ben curled against his Granddad in the biggest chair, regaling him with the unfolding story so far; hunting the ubiquitous Wriggly, Aunty Belinda the Angel, the stairways and the piano and the scones and the woods and, finally, the sea. A torrent of talk, partly fact, partly fantasy, a recipe of Ben's own making, speculative forays into imaginative forests, mythical beasts, police chases and space travel cheek by jowl with precise descriptions of lawns, greenhouses, gravel paths and gazebos. Ben didn't get to see his Granddad very often, but found that his capacity for Ben's conversation had been vastly enlarged since what the grown-ups termed his 'stroke.' A stroke seemed to Ben to be a gentle and welcome thing to experience, a soothing hand on a fevered forehead, a calming and reassuring gesture you might administer to an old dog or cat. Certainly it had rendered his Granddad passive and still, smoothing out under its touch the little rages and storms which had frightened Ben in the past, leaving space for Ben's colourful, sometimes disjointed but always deeply sincere conversational meanderings.

'Very good!' Robert kept saying, even at junctures when such a response was inappropriate, 'Very good!'

On the sofa, Mary and Rachel snuggled together, saying nothing, while Belinda held forth from a position to one side of the fireplace about menus and room arrangements and toilet paper, and speculated about whether Elliot and the children would be here soon, or fairly soon, or not for some time. Every so often, June interjected with a conversational gambit designed to demonstrate her perfect happiness

57

with the arrangements, as though she was affected by them equally with everyone else. Presently they were joined by James and Les, who perched on less comfortable chairs towards the back of the room, and remained silent.

Ruth arrived with a tray of drinks and bowls of crisps and nuts.

'It's rather a trek from the kitchen, Belinda,' she said, handing Mary and Robert their glasses. 'Do you think we should set up a sort of bar in here? On that cabinet, maybe?'

Belinda considered the idea. 'We'd still have to carry the glasses to and fro for washing, though.' She lifted a glass from Ruth's tray.

'That could be James' job, couldn't it James?' Ruth passed James and Les their drinks. Her look communicated to James that this was his cue to establish his determination to make himself useful in some capacity or other during the week.

'By all means,' replied James, good-naturedly. Belinda flashed him a smile.

'And ice,' put in June. 'You'd need ice brought in each evening. I suppose in the old days the people who lived here had servants to run around after them.'

'Some things haven't changed, much,' said Ruth, dryly, handing June her drink.

'This is all very nice,' said Mary, quickly. 'Thank you, Belinda, for all your hard work. Your Dad and I are very grateful to you.'

'To Belinda!' said Robert, abruptly, interrupting Ben to raise the glass which he had suddenly discovered in his hand.

'To Belinda!' they all chorused, obediently, and raised their glasses.

But they had hardly managed to touch their drinks before the door was shoved open and Elliot staggered in carrying a computer monitor with the keyboard balanced precariously on the top.

'Here you all are,' he ejaculated, crossly, as though they had been hiding from him. 'Could we have some help here?' He looked accusingly at Belinda. Here they all were cosily ensconced with drinks; the party had quite evidently started without him. He'd had a terrible drive, the kids had driven him demented with their bickering, there had been no-one to greet him, the place had seemed deserted and it looked like he was expected to unload the whole car without any help from anyone while they all sat around enjoying themselves. His look said all this and more and Belinda leapt into action.

'You've brought the computer? I didn't know. Let me think, now, where would be the best place...'

'What about that room with the desk, off the hall?' Ruth suggested.

'The study? Yes! Of course. Come on, let me show you. James, would you mind helping?' Belinda scurried off down the corridor. Elliot, stopping only to say a surprisingly warm, 'Hello, June! How nice to see you!' followed close behind, grunting and gasping to indicate how heavy the computer was and how unhelpful everyone was being. Rob, in the hallway, held the tower unit and a Bolognese of wires. He, like his father, had an air of panic, as though the machine could only survive a certain length of time in this disembowelled form and might soon be past saving.

'In here!' cried Belinda, opening the study door and switching on the light.

'Clear the desk!' shouted Elliot, nodding towards the stationery and inkwell which took up, to be fair, only the smallest space on the huge desk.

'There aren't any plug sockets, Dad!' Rob almost screamed. 'Move it over there!'

James and Belinda heaved the heavy desk over to the window, and Elliot and his son began emergency reconstructive surgery on the computer.

'Where's Ellie?' asked Belinda, 'is she still in the car?'

'She went looking for you. She's probably got lost. We can only live in hope.' said Rob, over his shoulder, busy connecting wires into the back of the tower. 'Pass me the modem, Dad.'

'Can I help at all?' asked James.

'There's more stuff in the car, Jim,' said Elliot, without even looking up.

James hesitated a fraction of a second before saying, 'Right you are!' and heading off towards the car. He hated being called Jim, but what was the point in saying anything?

In the drawing room, Ben had stopped talking and was simply resting his head on his Granddad's shoulder. The heat of the fire, the long drive, the walk, they were all beginning to tell on him. Only the emptiness in his tummy, still gnawingly present even though he had managed to eat far more than his fair share of the crisps, kept him from falling asleep. Robert had experienced no such obstacle and his eyes were shut, this breathing even. Rachel had left the room at the arrival of Elliot and the children; Ruth assumed she had gone to find Ellie. Ruth was desperate to show Mary around the house but knew that to steal this privilege from Belinda would be unforgivable. Alternatively she would have liked to unburden herself quietly to Mary about the situation with Miriam, but this was impossible too, with June and Les still stubbornly glued to their seats. June's complacency in the situation she had managed to bring about was manifest; she kept on throwing looks of triumph over to Les, who remained on the periphery, steadily eating nuts. He, at least, thought Ruth, had the decency to be embarrassed.

Taking pity on him, Ruth said: 'How's Granny McKay, Les? Will you be seeing her this weekend?'

Robert and June's extremely aged mother lived in an expensive Nursing Home (at Robert's sole expense), hale in physical health but of unreliable and eccentric mental competency. Robert and June took it in turns to visit at weekends, taking her out for runs in the car, carefully controlled shopping trips or even afternoon tea in out-of-the way tea shops. Since Robert's stroke, these visits had been more difficult, as both Robert and Granny McKay was too much for Mary to cope with alone, and she had roped in Belinda or, more rarely, Ruth, to assist. Not to be outdone, June and Les had started taking their shiftless daughter and her unsuitable boyfriend along to visit Granny McKay on their weekend visits. Robert and June's sister Muriel tended to visit their mother during the week, ostensibly because she had to take two buses, and she found it too busy at weekends. However, as everyone understood, the real reason for her midweek visits was that she could thus avoid seeing June. The two sisters had not spoken voluntarily to one another for over forty five years. Knowing that Robert and Mary were to be away, and that Muriel would never attempt a weekend visit, it went without saying that June and Les would be in the Granny McKay chair, so to speak, for the forthcoming weekend.

'Well,' Les began, and Ruth thought she could detect a bloom of awkwardness spread across his cheek, 'she's fine, of course. No change. As for the weekend…' he cast a look at June, who said, irrelevantly; 'Les! Stop eating those nuts!' There was a pause.

'I think,' put in Mary, carefully, 'that Les and June anticipated that they might be quite tired after the drive today, and asked Sandra to look in on Granny McKay for them.'

'Kevin will take her; they'll enjoy the run out!' June cried.

'Really?' Ruth sounded a doubtful note. Sandra's young man did not strike her as the sort for whom car rides in the country would hold

61

much appeal. He was the youngest of a handful of brothers almost all of whom had shady occupations which danced on the periphery of the law; strong-arm debt collecting and illegal wheel-clamping. Kevin, on the rare occasions he had been presented to the family, had remained silent, perching awkwardly on chairs and biting his fingernails.

'She's glad to do it!' cried June. 'She's a marvel, that girl, isn't she, Les? Ha ha ha! Nothing's too much trouble for her. They think the world of her at work, you know, too.'

'Granny McKay'll be delighted to see her, I'm sure,' said Mary, 'and Kevin, of course,' she added, doubtfully.

'And it'll mean you have the weekend free,' said Ruth, pointedly, seeing, now, the whole plan.

'Well, now you mention it,' pounced June, 'yes. Is there any more gin, Ruth dear? Perhaps you'd like to show me where it is?'

Belinda found Ellie alone in the kitchen. She had dragged one of the carver chairs over to the Aga and was sitting with her head resting on the chrome handrail, and her body pressed as close as possible to the cast iron, soaking up the heat. She looked exhausted, wan, with dark circles around her eyes.

'Oh, there you are, Mum,' she said, wearily, on sight of her mother. 'I knew that if I sat here long enough you'd turn up.'

'You look tired, Ellie. Have you had a hard day?' Belinda lifted the shiny lid of one of the Aga's hotplates and slid the huge pan of potatoes onto the dull iron ring.

'Not so much a hard day,' said Ellie, moving to one side while Belinda opened the oven door to check the casserole, 'a hard journey. Dad went off on one the moment we got into the car. He wouldn't let me sit in the front even though it was my turn. Rob made snide remarks the whole time. He stole my 'phone and looked up Caro's number and now he's started texting her. She thinks he fancies her but he's only messing. She's supposed to be my *friend* and she'll think I'm in on the joke.'

'Poor Ellie. What do you think of the house? Have you found your bedroom, yet?' Belinda added more wine to the casserole, gave it a stir and put it back into the oven.

Ellie shrugged. 'The house is cool. I haven't found anything, yet, though. Or anybody, until you. Is Grandma here?'

'Yes. Aunty June and Uncle Les brought them up.'

'Are they staying too?'

'I have a horrible suspicion that they want to. They're all in the drawing room. I suppose you wouldn't like to set the table?'

'Not really. There's a room just for drawing?'

'It's old fashioned. It's short for *with*drawing.'

'Oh,' Ellie moved her chair away from the oven and started to open and shut cupboards, looking for food. 'That's funny. We learned about that in sex education. They had a room for *that*? Are there any biscuits?'

Belinda leaned over the saucepan to hide her smile. 'No biscuits, Ellie. Dinner won't be very long.'

'The girls at school call it supper, Mum. What is it?'

'Casserole.'

'Yuck. Can I have something else?'

Belinda placed the lid onto the saucepan and turned to face her daughter. 'Why don't you have a little explore? Rachel's around somewhere. You young ones are all sleeping on the top floor. I put your name on a single room but you don't have to sleep in it if you don't want to. You might like to share with your cousins. I think Rachel would like that. I don't know. It's up to you. There's time to unpack before supper, and you should go and say hello to Grandma and Granddad.'

Ellie stood in the centre of the room; to Belinda, she looked very young and rather lost in the vastness. Belinda wanted to give her a hug but, these days, hugging was generally not allowed. Now that she had time to think about it, Belinda realised that both the children were out of their school clothes and Elliot hadn't been wearing a suit. They must have gone home – of course – to collect the computer, and got changed. Her heart sank at the thought of the tidiness of the house ravaged by the three of them in a tearing hurry; clothes cast asunder, drawers left half open, snacks hastily prepared on the work surface and not cleared away properly, toilets un-flushed, the doors, probably, not closed properly, the alarm, possibly, not reset.

Footsteps in the passageway distracted her from the awful possibilities. Ruth and June entered the kitchen.

'Hello, Ellie, dear,' said Ruth, giving her niece a hug which was not rejected: which was, in fact, reciprocated. 'Rachel's dying for you to arrive. I think she went upstairs.'

'Hello, Aunty Ruth,' Ellie gave a helpless shrug. 'I don't know where upstairs is.'

'Silly billy. Up the stairs from the hall, then just shout her name. She's bound to hear.'

'All right,' Ellie left the kitchen as though bearing the weight of the world on her shoulders.

'June wants more gin,' Ruth said, reaching the bottle down. 'Oh dear, its half gone. I hope Simon brings some more.'

'We'd have brought some, if we'd thought,' June said, sweetly. She began to tour kitchen, exclaiming about its size and appointments.

'Simon had a list of things to bring, like we all did,' Belinda said, from the table where she was arranging knives and forks. 'I can't remember now, what was on his. In any case, he and Miriam have their own ideas about things.'

'You can say that again,' Ruth replied, darkly. Then, 'You've remembered to set for two more?' Belinda nodded, counting under her breath.

Ruth whispered, in awe, almost, at her own generosity; 'I'll keep June in here for a bit. Why don't you go and show Mum around? Dad's having a doze so now's your chance.'

Belinda looked Ruth in the eye for almost the first time that day. 'Would you mind? I'd so like to.'

Ruth just nodded and took the fistful of cutlery from her hand. Belinda turned and left without a word.

'Give me a hand, would you June?' called Ruth, brightly.

'Of course,' June gushed, 'I'd be delighted, only, where's Belinda gone to? I might just go and see....'

65

'…if you can help unpack the car? Well, if you'd rather.'

'Oh. No. Of course I'll help with the table. How many are we?'

'Nineteen, now.'

In the hall, Ellie sighed and searched with her eyes through the collection of baggage left there by Uncle James. She felt completely weary, and wanted nothing more than to curl up in bed with a hot water bottle and a cup of hot chocolate, if only somebody would bring it up to her. Her anticipation of a week's holiday was utterly ruined, now, obliterated by this whole deal with Rob and Caro. Ellie's habitual sense of powerlessness in Rob's sway had intensified as soon as he had started larking around in the car with her 'phone. Her shrill remonstrance had been curtly and swiftly silenced by her Dad and Rob, smirking, had had free reign. Once he'd accessed her 'phone book, it seemed like her destiny was set. And sure enough, Ellie knew now, from a text message she had received later from Caro, that Rob had promised to meet her later in an internet chat room. Caro, predictably, had been thrilled; she had had a crush on Rob since year seven. And, to be honest, sometimes Ellie suspected that Caro had only chosen her as a friend because she was Rob's sister; certainly, for a 'best friend', she showed a suspicious lack of loyalty.

'I'm sure he didn't mean it. You're too soft. Can't you take a joke?' she'd said in Rob's defence on one occasion when he had done something or other to infuriate Ellie.

'You've no idea what he's like,' Ellie had snapped back. Well, now Caro would find out what it was to be one of Rob's victims; to be teased and bullied and manipulated, to be on the receiving end of snide remarks and the butt of nasty jokes. To everyone else in the family he was faultless, Prince McKay, first son, heir to the kingdom. Oh well, Ellie sighed again, the die was cast, now.

She started slowly up the stairs. From a room across the hall she could hear the voices of her father and brother as they put the computer back together. She paused to listen; they were arguing about which port the printer ought to be plugged into. Elliot, who was not as well up on computers as he liked to think, eventually, with bad grace, deferred to his son.

67

At the top of the stairs an enormous mirror in a gilt frame showed Ellie her own reflection; sleek, dark hair cut in a bob with a long fringe to flop over one eye, dark eyes with long lashes, good skin, developing bust, baggy, wide-legged jeans casually worn low on the still narrow hips, oversized hooded sweatshirt with fashionable sports logo. She was, like her father, of slim build, not tall; the roomy sweatshirt and wide trousers made her look even smaller, waif-like. She felt vulnerable. Caro knew things that Rob must not find out, and she didn't trust her friend to keep a secret. With the weight of these cares upon her shoulders, Ellie felt prematurely aged and even more helpless than usual.

Somewhere along the landing a small door opened up in the wooden panelling, and Rachel said,

'There you are, Ellie. Are you coming up?'

Ellie swung round and smiled at her cousin. In years gone by they had played with dolls and prams and toy kitchens, and made dens in the garden out of clothes maidens and camping blankets, and once, dressed up in Grandma's clothes and beads and high-heeled shoes and paraded around the close. Ellie, older by two years, had always taken the lead in these games and Rachel, who had never seemed to catch on very quickly, had been a happy follower. She had hardly changed, thought Ellie. Looking at Rachel now, she seemed impossibly gauche in her naff clothes and girlish hairstyle. On the other hand, Rachel was still safely cocooned in childhood, possibly an enviable situation. And although she was treated as a cousin in every way, she was mercifully free from the actual McKay blood ties which seemed to complicate everything to do with family.

'Oh yes,' Ellie said, with a sigh. 'Will you show me the way? Mum says there's a room for me.'

Rachel tried to hide her disappointment. 'Yes, that's right. It's up here. Come on, I'll hold the door for you.'

The two of them climbed the narrow stairway, coming out into a corridor.

'It's in here.' Rachel opened the door indicated by Ellie's post-it note, and snapped on the light. She stood back to let her cousin in. It was a very pretty room, Rachel thought, painted in lilac, with a view over the drive.

'Here's my bag. It doesn't look as though Mum's unpacked for me,' was all Ellie said, wearily, indicating the green holdall at the foot of the bed. 'I'd better get on with it. Supper's going to be ready soon.' Ellie hoped that Rachel would take the hint and leave her alone. After the journey, and with the worry about Caro, she just couldn't work up any enthusiasm for playing long lost cousins with Rachel. She wanted, if anything, this week, to be part of the scene with the grown-ups. She was, after all, practically grown up herself; indeed, just at the moment, she felt about a hundred years old. 'I'll give you a hand,' said Rachel, moving into the room and laying a tentative finger on the zip of the holdall, 'if you like.'

Ellie pushed back her fringe with an index finger and tucked it expertly behind her ear. It was an unconscious gesture, made all the more elegant, in Rachel's view, by the thoughtless way it was done. Ellie's fingernails, Rachel noted, were long, and painted in navy blue with silver dots. Was that allowed at Ellie's school? She wore several rings, one, unusually, on her thumb, and a number of coloured bangles and bracelets round her wrists, but, because her sweatshirt was too big for her, the sleeves hid them until she put up her hand to tuck back her hair. Ellie stood helplessly in the middle of the virtually empty and totally tidy room as though surrounded by a chaos that she was utterly unable to sort out. It was a trick, Rachel recalled, she had used for years, especially at tidy-up time or when they had been caught out in some mischief or other, an air of bewildered disconnectedness that generally resulted in someone stepping in the make things right. Rachel had, she realised, just fallen into the trap.

69

'Would you mind?' Ellie smiled. 'Only I need to find a loo. Do you know where it is?'

'Just opposite.'

In the toilet, Ellie locked the door before closing the lid and taking a seat. Surely, if she sat here long enough, Rachel would give up on her and go downstairs. Anyway, she needed time to think: about Caro, and Rob, and how she might stop this thing from going any further. Really, she needed to speak to Caro, but she had hardly any credit left on her 'phone and the chance of borrowing Rob's was....remote. Ellie heaved another sigh, and settled down to wait. It was a strategy that usually worked; if you avoided them for long enough, most problems gave up and went away.

Rachel unzipped the holdall and lifted out clothes - all, as she had anticipated, trendy and pricey – and a beautiful sponge bag chock full of expensive skin-care products. Underneath was a book (Bridget Jones' Diary, very well thumbed), a huge towel, pyjamas, dressing gown and slippers, some very grown-up underwear and, at the bottom, *two* pairs of Nike trainers. Rachel folded, hung up and tidied away the clothes with a kind of reverence and when she'd finished she tidied up the CD's in the CD case, putting them into alphabetical order. She wanted to put a disc into the player but thought she had better not. Finally, when everything was done, she sat and simply waited, whiling away the time by imagining that she was Ellie; slim, elegant, a proper teenager, the owner of nice clothes, reader of Bridget Jones, instead of Rachel; overweight, stuck in childhood, wearer of cheap and tatty clothes and reader (for the third time)of Harry Potter.

Suddenly, the mobile 'phone emitted a series of beeps. Rachel leapt off the bed and grabbed at the phone, pressing one of the buttons as she did so.

'Oh. You're still here,' said Ellie from the doorway. 'I thought you'd have gone downstairs by now.'

'Your 'phone went off,' said Rachel, hastily, holding it out.

Ellie almost snatched it from her. 'It's a text,' she said, and read the message quickly, before switching it off. 'The girl's obsessed,' she muttered to herself.

It felt to Ellie as though the room was closing in on her. Was Rachel waiting for her to say or do something? What? There was an initiative, clearly, and Ellie was supposed to take it, but she hadn't an idea what was expected of her. Being in this little room with Rachel was becoming claustrophobic. She had to get rid of her somehow.

'Are you getting changed for supper?' she asked.

'Well,' Rachel's hands went instinctively to her jerkin, fingers spread, 'no, I ......'

'I won't either, then. We might as well go down.'

Without waiting for an answer, Ellie left the room, leaving the light on, and Rachel floundering, behind her.

The child went to sleep as the jeep pulled off the motorway. The other three occupants of the car breathed a sigh of relief. She had wriggled and struggled in her car seat, spat out her dummy and refused to be entertained by innumerable offers of toys and books. She had set her face against food and drink alike. They had made unscheduled stops at service stations so that her nappy could be checked. They had tried putting her into her push-chair and wheeling her round the car park, and showing her the lorries. They had tried music, a CD of nursery rhymes, turning it up loud and singing along at the tops of their voices, but she had only yelled the louder.

'If Geldof could see me now,' Bob had grumbled.

'Don't be so bloody precious. I'm sure he's been here; he has children,' Heather had snapped. Even Heather's calming sea-shore and bird-song meditation CD had proved ineffectual. Mantras and soothing incantations had only enraged the child more. For a while her attention had been caught by a string of healing crystals and Heather had handed them over, pushing anxieties about possible choking hazards to the back of her mind. But the beads had soon been thrown aside. The only thing which seemed to placate her was being allowed to drive the car, seated on Mitch's lap behind the steering wheel, stabbing at the controls which operated the window washers and screen wash, and especially the horn. Being removed from this activity sent her into paroxysms of rage. Finally, after weary hours, Starlight had finally exhausted herself and fallen asleep.

Heather slumped back into her seat and closed her eyes. She felt close to tears. No-one had warned her that motherhood would be so difficult. Her sisters had never seemed to have any of these difficulties and nor had her friends. The child in the seat next to her was so precious, a gift long desired, and there was nothing at all that Heather was not prepared to do, no lengths that she would not go to, to ensure her safety and happiness. Indeed she had already gone to enormous lengths, into the shadowlands of the underworld, to retrieve this child from a dreadful fate, and there would be, she was sure, in the future, more treacherous ground to be covered. But nothing was more important to her now than presenting his baby to her family as a crowning glory, and presenting herself to them at last as having achieved the self-actualisation of motherhood.

But bonding with the baby was proving so difficult and it was becoming more of a relief than she liked to admit to be able to hand the responsibility of the child over to Mitch, or to Mrs Palfrey, the housekeeper, or to Bob, all of whom seemed instinctively to be able to decode Starlight's sub-text, to be able to identify and supply the need; food, drink, toy, song, rest.

She sighed, and settled her head more comfortably on the leather headrest. Starlight's arrival had completely altered Heather's attitude to the week with her family. From being something of a drag it was now a golden opportunity for the child to *engage*. It would *socialise* her. It was an opportunity for Heather, too. She would be acknowledged at last as a grown-up; a woman, a mother; no longer the baby of the family, indulged and allowed for. They would see her at last as an equal. And Oh God how she needed a rest and some time out. There were so few people she could trust around Starlight but surely her family would take some of the load? They were grounded and real, normal and uncomplicated in ways that Bob's celebrity acquaintances didn't always appear to be. How she yearned for the simple joys of family life.

She realised that she had started to cry. It was growing dark outside. They seemed to be travelling through a wilderness of empty countryside. She felt Bob's hand on hers.

'What's the matter, Angel?' he asked, gently.

'I think...' she stuttered, beginning to cry in earnest. 'I think that maybe I'm not a very good mother,' she sobbed.

'Shhhhh,' Bob soothed her, casting an anxious glance at the child. 'Of course you are, Baby.'

Mitch said nothing, but drove them, safely, through the dusk.

The house was stirring and breathing like a mystical beast which had slumbered for its allotted span of enchantment. Warmth and voices and the scents of cooking floated in the air. The orange glow of logs in the fire grates (too many fires – it was becoming a full time job for James to keep them all tended) and the light from the chandeliers and lamps created shimmering reflections in mirrors and windows, and refracted off silver and gilt, and awoke the patina of years of polishing in wooden panels and boards. The McKays were taking tentative possession. The kitchen was full of cooking smells and steam from bubbling pans of vegetables. The table was set with cutlery and cheerful crockery.

Ruth, halfway down her third gin and tonic, held June prisoner with a lecture on the current secondary education system, its successes and failures, thoroughly enjoying the opportunity to quash every half-baked objection or suggestion that was raised, citing her own work in the Special Needs Unit as proof of both the hopelessly inadequate funding and the Herculean strides forward that were being made. June, skating as she was on extremely thin ice, satisfied herself with the odd placatory remark like 'I see what you mean,' and 'Yes, when you explain it like that, of course it's clear,' and wondered crossly when on earth Les would come and rescue her.

On the first floor, Belinda escorted her mother from room to room, enumerating, like a dirge, now, the towel and toilet paper distribution, throwing open bedroom doors, explaining her rationale. 'Oh the whole I thought she'd prefer it,' she said, at the door of the room she had chosen for Heather. Mary's occasional but wholly satisfactory 'How lovely!' and 'Very wise, dear,' and 'just the thing, I'm sure,' punctuated the diatribe. Finally, Belinda showed her mother into the Blue room where, she was pleased to see, somebody had already put their cases and closed the curtains. She had chosen it quite deliberately as the best in the house. It had an enormous bed with deeply carved head and foot, draped with a heavy and richly embroidered bedspread worked with azure and turquoise and sky blue threads on a cloud-white background, a thick pile carpet in deepest navy and old oak furniture. There was a separate dressing area with a practical and tightly made up single bed, a private bathroom with bath and shower, and windows looking out north and east. On their pillows, she had placed small gifts, and in the bathroom, Mary's favourite Blue Fern soap and talc. Mary exclaimed over everything, especially the little pillow gifts, and Belinda hugged herself, and her mother. They sat together, briefly, on the end of the bed.

'Do you like it, really, Mum?' Belinda asked, removing a stray grey hair from Mary's shoulder.

'We can all be together, that's the best thing,' Mary replied.

'I hope you're right,' Belinda said, quietly. 'I'm worried about Ruth and Miriam, and the men,' she went on. She was beginning to feel, especially with the arrival of June and Les, that she may well have started something that could explode in her face.

'Ruth will have a chance to get to know Miriam. We all will,' Mary said. 'And as long as we keep the men busy, I'm sure they'll be fine. That was always the thing, anyway, with your father.' Mary got up and reached for one of the cases. 'I think I'll put my slippers on,' she said.

'Poor April,' Belinda murmured, half to herself, 'and poor Dad.'

'Your Dad's all right,' Mary replied, quite sharply.

'And you, Mum, are you all right?' Belinda got up and faced her mother. It seemed very important, suddenly, to keep a tight grip on the reason she had started this whole thing off.

Mary pondered the responses she might make to this enquiry. In some ways Robert's stroke had made things easier, putting her in the driving seat, but there were times when he was more awkward than ever. She was worried about being here with them all, the things that ordinarily she could hide might emerge and there would be nothing she could do to stop them. But it wasn't a subject she could possibly introduce, even to Belinda, and she skipped over it onto surer ground. 'Very happy, Belinda, and ready for my dinner!' she said at last, with a smile, slipping her feet into her slippers.

Elliot, placated temporarily by a very large whiskey and soda, was playing a war game on the computer, closely watched and intermittently criticised by his son. The roar of machine guns and the scream of injured men, and the barking of orders by GI's making an alarming contradiction amongst the leather-bound volumes on the shelves of the English country gentleman's study. He was only half concentrating on the game. It had been, in the end, such a pain bringing the computer, what with the traffic and the disassembling of it, and then putting the thing back together again, that he wanted to punish Rob for putting him through it. On the screen, platoons of soldiers under his command took enemy fortifications, a disembodied voice barked 'Target located!' and 'Target eliminated!' or 'Casualties sustained,' depending upon how he was getting on. Behind him, Rob prowled the carpet and muttered to himself irritably.

Elliot thought that on the whole the house seemed rather good; he would enjoy playing the role of host. However he would be sure to complain to Belinda when he got her on her own for a moment. No-one had seemed particularly pleased to see him, or made much of an effort to help. He hadn't been shown around and had even had to send Jim off to find him a drink. All in all he felt that he wasn't getting anything like the attention he deserved and was resolved to rattle a few nerves before the night was out.

Suddenly his division came under massive fire from an enemy emplacement. A blood-curdling cacophony of screams emanated from his decimated troops. 'Game Over' the screen declared. His glass was empty and, annoyingly, no one had been through to offer to refill it. Abruptly, Elliot got up from the chair and, snatching up his glass, stalked out of the room. Immediately, Rob took his place in front of screen.

'Loser!' he ejaculated, under his breath, 'blown up on level one!'

James and Ben had opened the glass-fronted cabinet in the drawing room and were examining the model cannons together.

Robert slept in the armchair. Les remained perched on a hard-backed chair and fiddled with his empty beer glass.

'Heard today that the City Chairman's going to resign,' he said, eventually, to no one in particular.

'Really?' said James, who had no interest in football.

Elliot put his head around the door. He took in at a glance that Robert was asleep, ignored Les and addressed himself to James. 'This is a nice room, too small for all of us, though. Won't be able to use it after tonight. Seen Belinda?'

'Upstairs with Mary, I believe, Elliot. Enjoy your drink?'

'I'd love another, thanks.' He placed his glass on the cabinet and left the room without another word. James stared after him. Les coughed.

'What little balls,' said Ben.

'Yes, son,' said James.

Elliot passed Ellie and Rachel on the stairs.

'Your mother up here?' he asked, brusquely, not stopping for a reply. Ellie, who had not forgiven him for his crabbiness in the car, shrugged. Rachel, who thought all fathers were benevolent gods, said; 'Hello, Uncle Elliot. I think I heard her voice at the end of the landing.' Elliot dashed on past them both, grunting something that might, charitably, have been translated as 'thanks.'

He encountered Belinda and Mary on the landing.

'There you are,' he said, quite sharply, 'been looking for you. Where are our things?' Then, as an after-thought, 'Hello, Mary. Alright?' He kissed his mother-in-law on the cheek.

She endured it stiffly, as one would an injection. 'Very well, thank you,' she replied.

'We're just here, on the right, first door from the top of the stairs,' Belinda waved her arm in the general direction and made as though to pass Elliot on her way down stairs.

'Could you show me?' There was something in his voice that made even the prospect of overcooked vegetables pale. Nevertheless, she decided that she must, in front of her mother, put up a token resistance.

'It's just *here*, but I need to get back to the kitchen. The vegetables will be cooked; I don't want them to spoil.'

Elliot glared at her, and said nothing.

Mary said, 'I'll go down and see to the food, Belinda. Ruth will give me a hand, I'm sure. You haven't seen Elliot all day.'

Reluctantly, Belinda followed Elliot into their room. Quickly she lit the bedside lamps and drew the curtains. 'I've unpacked your things,' she said, dully, 'unless you've brought more.' She really didn't see why he needed her to show the room personally. Couldn't he see how busy she was? Didn't he realise that Mary doing *anything* this week was exactly what she *hadn't* wanted? Belinda's anger and resentment began to rise up in her like a spring, fuelled by the two gin and tonics she had, unusually, consumed, but the upwards flow met a controlling dam. Of course he would not approve of the room she had chosen for them, there would be reshufflings and hurried alterations to be made as Elliot branded his organisational stamp on things. He would strut about like a diminutive General, shouting orders and making people uncomfortable until he had whipped them all into line, apparently unaware that everybody thought him ridiculous.

'Why did you choose this room?' Elliot asked, surveying the heavy furniture and restricted proportions.

She had chosen it with care, not at all wanting the best but very conscious that, for Elliot's sake, she must not choose the worst. 'It's the only one with a desk, so that you can work, if you need to,'

Belinda began, defensively, 'and it's close to the stairs, so I can get to the kitchen quickly, and it has the best shower, which I thought you'd particularly like.' Elliot clicked on the bathroom light and poked his head round the door. The double shower unit, gleaming white, with chrome body-jets and wide showerhead, certainly was impressive, but he said nothing about it, striding past his wife back out into the corridor, throwing bedroom doors open as he went, left and right, clicking on the lights and making a cursory inspection of the rest of the available accommodation, sourly noting the post-it notes she had stuck onto the others' rooms. Belinda stood miserably on the landing, absent-mindedly twirling a large-stoned ring around her finger. Half of her, more than half, wanted to scurry behind the long velvet curtain that concealed the alcove where she had sat with such pleasure earlier, and to hide until his rage should be over. When Elliot finally joined her again outside their room, his face gave nothing away. She said nothing. She was waiting. Her hand, winding the ring round and round her finger was the only movement in the stillness. Elliot fixed his eyes on it, savouring his moment.

Certainly he could insist on changing rooms, and if that meant others having to move out to let him have his way, they would be too polite, outwardly, to demur. They would leap into action, and pack their clothes, and do his bidding. But privately, he knew, they would mutter and pass each other knowing looks, and roll their eyes, and give Belinda sympathetic glances and furtive hugs, in spite of which she would still manage to appear at breakfast with red-rimmed eyes. Belinda must never be allowed to get too far ahead, or away from him; like a runaway horse, given her head she could wreak untold damage.

They faced each other on the wide landing, locked now, into a stalemate familiar to each whose consequences were almost inevitable. With a weary sigh of resignation he slowly reached out and took her restless hand in his. His ambiguous intention kept them both guessing. Her hand, in his, was small and vulnerable, the large-stoned ring weighty between them. Her eyes widened and searched his, trying to discern his purpose, and she made a sharp inhalation of breath as a precursor to speech, but before she could say anything he dropped her hand.

'Right. Well, I suppose it will have to do.' he said. 'You'll have to show me the rest of the house later. I suppose I'll get the guided tour with the other late arrivals. You'd better get back to the kitchen.'

'Are you coming down?' Belinda swallowed.

'I think I'll just wash my face and hands,' Elliot said, disappearing into their room and closing the door.

Rob closed the CD drawer in the computer and clicked on 'play'. Immediately the room reverberated with the sound of musical instruments under torture and people so eaten up with anger and pain that they had become inarticulate. Rob edged the volume up just a little more and immersed himself in the sound, like a diseased bather into the healing waters of a spa. His music was a wall, obdurate and impregnable from without, soft and comforting from within, and when Rob was at the centre of it, he was unassailable. He checked his watch and his mobile phone before returning to his game. He was already on level three. He had surrounded the city and bombarded its defences from the air. Now he would make his assault on the enemy Command centre. It was a castellated fortress, with a swathe of land around it, probably mined, then sheer walls. The building was more real to him, at that moment, than the one he actually occupied. Apart from the hall and the toilet he had seen nothing of the rest of the house. From the outside, as they had arrived on the drive, it had seemed huge and old-fashioned and boring. Certainly it was miles from anywhere. There would be nowhere *good* to go, and no other people. By other people, Rob meant people of his own age: his aunts and uncles and grandparents did not qualify, his cousins did not signify; his parents and sister he discounted altogether. He had whined and reasoned and finally begged to be allowed to duck out of what he considered to be a sickly-sweet and sentimental week of happy-families, contrived relational posing and uncool outdoor activities, but to no avail. 'Who do they think we are?' he had asked himself, 'the pissing Waltons?' Finally he had decided to play no part in it; that's why he had insisted that the computer to be brought along with them. He had lied, and told them that he had coursework to finish. In reality he intended to turn his back on them all and inhabit his own safe and satisfactorily violent world. He would shock, he would offend, he would appal and insult; they would not force him to come on anything like this again.

His opening gambit, to snatch Ellie's phone and to send abusive messages to her friends, had yielded a response which had stopped him in his tracks; he had unexpectedly unearthed a rich lode. Caro had either wilfully or actually misinterpreted his message. Ellie's shocked and defensive response had interested him. If he could bring his sister to tears by the end of the day, perhaps his parents would be dropping him off at the nearest railway station by morning.

He could hear voices in the hall. The high-pitched shout of effusive greeting. More arrivals. Abruptly (or mercifully) he terminated the angst-ridden hysterics of *Tripwire* and substituted them with the vicious expletives of *Jugular Vein*. On the screen before him, a khaki-clad body twitched as Rob pumped semi-automatic machine gun rounds into it; a blooming rose of blood spread across its chest, but the falsetto cries of agony were drowned out by the obscenities spilling from the lips of *Jugular Vein's* lead singer. Or perhaps they were the soldier's words. It was all one to Rob.

A hand on his shoulder alerted him to the fact that there was someone else in the room. He turned his head. Behind him was a tall man with long grey hair tied back into a pony tail, an off-white T shirt and a home-made tattoo across his left bicep enquiring 'Why me?' The man's eyes were deeply set and told a tale of too many late nights, his skin was aged by the sun, lined, his chin unshaven. The hand on Rob's shoulder had long, artistic fingers and immaculately manicured but unusually long nails, and the skin between the index and third fingers was rimed with the nicotine of years. He was, in this room, in this house, like Rob, an anachronism. He didn't belong, he didn't want to belong. He lived life in another lane altogether but had come, under sufferance. There was, between the two of them, a zest of communication; unspoken, and yet, to Rob, tangible and surprisingly eloquent. In spite of himself, Rob smiled. Then he nodded a greeting to his Uncle Bob; words were impossible in the din from *Jugular Vein* and, in any case, quite unnecessary.

'Fuck you pissing wank-head!' shrieked *Jugular Vein's* lead singer.

Bob nodded back. 'Cool,' he mouthed.

Out in the hall, there had been delighted greeting; hugs and kisses. The baby of the family, Heather was used to being adored by everyone. Having brought with her, at last, the child she had longed for, she expected, and indeed received, special recognition, and was, now, deeply immersed in the role of parent that she had watched her sisters and brother play in turn. Now she was one of them, an equal; the production of a child, regardless of the method, proved her worth, her womanhood. The fact that she had married a celebrity, rubbed shoulders on a daily basis with personalities from the music business, was regularly featured on the pages of glossy magazines and had, through her husband, more money than the rest of them put together, none of this counted in her own mind as an achievement compared to theirs of having produced children. Now, she glowed, satisfied at last; they could not consider her to be the baby any longer. Busily, like a real grown-up, she was supervising the unloading of baby paraphernalia; of the new child herself there was, as yet, no sign. Toys in every shape and size and description, brightly coloured, with multi-textured surfaces to explore, and bristling with knobs to press and dials to turn, emitting noises to surprise and delight; houses and cars and ironing boards and kitchens and tool boxes and construction toys, dressing up clothes and musical instruments and crayons and easels and ride-on toys and teddy bears; an entire toy shop disgorged itself into the hall, James and Ben and Les running in and out with armfuls of bags and boxes.

Heather loitered in the hall, picking through the stock, muttering, 'There was one teddy bear she seemed to particularly like, a blue one, I think.'

Robert, passing through the hall on Mary's arm, on his way to the kitchen, where everyone had been summoned to eat, caught sight of his favourite. His face expressed recognition for the first time. He beamed, and opened his arms.

'Oh! Daddy,' Heather said, going to him and being enfolded. 'How lovely! Hello, Mummy.' She managed to reach a hand out from the embrace and include Mary. 'I've brought you a new granddaughter. You'll see her soon. She's a gift from the spirits, a changeling child; I had to rescue her from the depths.' Robert nodded, sagely, as though this gibberish made perfect sense to him. The child he loved had been usurped by this ethereal being with weird enthusiasms and quasi-religious tendencies, yet the sweet face and golden hair was the same, the pale, faintly freckled skin, arresting blue eyes, the girlish form in his arms could have been the fifteen, or ten, or five year old he remembered. She was still his little girl. Now, he understood, there was another just like her, a golden child, much desired and sought for. A new McKay.

Elliot cantered down the stairs. He seemed to have washed away every vestige of bad temper. He was smiling and relaxed, the epitome of the genial host.

'This is marvellous!' he exclaimed, putting his left arm around Heather and reaching his right towards Bob for a manly handshake. 'Welcome. Welcome. Where is the little one?' He managed to ask it as though the arrival of the new family member had been uppermost in his mind all day, whereas in fact only the arrival of the toys and baby things had reminded him of it.

'She's sleeping, in the car.' Heather said, disengaging herself from her father and Elliot alike. 'Mitch will watch her until after dinner, then we'll bring her in. To be honest,' Heather passed a hand with self-conscious weariness, over her eyes, 'she hasn't been sleeping that well. Now she's gone off, it seemed best to leave her for a good long sleep.'

Belinda, flushed from the kitchen, pushed open the baize door to announce, 'Dinner is served.'

Ben and, in spite of herself, Rachel, cheered out loud and Ben, ignoring the chaos of arrival in the hall, made a lone dash towards the kitchen.

'Shouldn't we wait for Simon?' Mary asked.

Belinda shrugged. 'They're an hour late already. I just can't hold this back any longer.'

'They'll probably have eaten, anyway,' Heather said. 'Miriam's very strict about routine.'

'The ladies ought to have a gentleman to take them down, that's the tradition!' cried Ruth, but instantly regretted it. Her tongue felt like it had doubled in size and couldn't adequately get itself round her teeth to form the words. Elliot, eager, now that he had made a new start, to enter into the spirit of things, gallantly offered June his arm. 'You'll have to show me where to go,' he said, good naturedly. I haven't had the tour, yet.' June almost crowed in triumph as she took her place at the head of the line. The others followed behind them down the passageway towards the kitchen.

Bob stepped back into the study, where *Jugular Vein* had completed a paroxysm of blood-curdling profanities with what sounded like a mass suicide pact on the part of the band members and their live audience. The silence of the aftermath was deafening. 'Dude!' he said, cocking his head in the directions the others had followed, 'grub!' Rob swivelled round in his chair. He had resolved to refuse all sustenance but he could probably be more of a nuisance by joining the meal than by boycotting it. Plus, the promise of Uncle Bob's companionship for this holiday suddenly let in just a glimmer of light. He got up and followed Bob into the hall, but finding Mitch there, busy making order out of chaos, made his mood plummet once more.

He had forgotten about Mitch.

Mitch was hardly more than a year older than Rob but even the small advantage that so few months might have given him should have been more than compensated for by the vast discrepancy between their social and material situations. Rob had been raised in a stable home and had known the security of money and a solid middle class up-bringing for as long as he could remember. Mitch's home life – what he could remember of it, or, at least, what he chose to reveal – had been chaotic; he had been taken away from an abusive father and a drug-dealing mother to stay in a succession of foster and children's homes. Rob's education had been the best that money could buy and his future – never actually voiced but tacitly understood by everyone – was already secure in McKay's Haulage. Mitch's formal education had been, to say the best of it, somewhat piecemeal, disrupted as it had been by frequent moves between school as well as an early habit of truancy, and his future, therefore, had seemed correspondingly inauspicious. Rob was a McKay, a family which enjoyed a high profile in the town as a large employer, patron of various local charities and the regular funder of key Borough events. The McKay mantle of respectability would always shroud him and under its shade, by dint of his mother's tireless charity work and his father's role as Worshipful Master, not to mention respect for his Grandfather's stainless reputation, he would be forgiven much of the youthful waywardness to which teenage boys are prone. Mitch had no such protection. He was nobody, and had consequently been exposed to the full force of the law for relatively minor infractions; he had spent time in a Youth Detention unit and even, whilst on remand, in prison. But somehow, far from tipping the balance against him, these disparities had served to enhance Mitch's aura and, fight it as he might, Rob found himself unnervingly in awe of him.

While Rob himself was forever caught up in a maelstrom of angry resentments and violent impulses, helplessly buffeted by their storm, Mitch had, as Rob termed it, 'got it together'. He seemed to stand at the still, peaceful eye, rock-solid, immune to the hormonal angst, the raging blood of youth. The struggles of his life had honed him of his boyhood. Rob, on the other hand, was still hugely encumbered by his, floundering between the unreasonable and demeaning restrictions imposed by his father and school, and the expectations of the family, and the unwieldy freedoms of unearned privileges granted by his mother in an attempt to over-compensate. Constantly railing against the one and proving himself unworthy of the other, Rob found himself treated as a spoilt, immature, unreliable and moody brat whilst Mitch was accorded a quiet, polite respect surely out of all proportion to his true status.

Rob recalled the first time they had met. Mitch had been present at some family gathering or another, hovering in the background, operating as a very lowly factotum, expected to undertake any manner of menial task. He had been finding his feet in his new and unbelievably cushy situation. He had had the look of some wild

89

creature in sudden captivity, a watching wariness, an astonished defensiveness. Rob, even though younger, had looked down upon him with withering scorn and in order to demonstrate the distance between them, had deliberately spilled a drink so that he could watch Mitch clean it up.

Mitch had come under Bob's wing by means of the Prince's Trust, a charity case, a bad lad with a last opportunity to turn good, another in a longish line of lame ducks that Bob and Heather were in the habit of taking on. Sooner or later the lame ducks usually debunked, often with a bag of swag. Rob had heard his father scoff at Bob and Heather as 'easy meat' and had not supposed that Mitch would last long. But it had soon become clear that Mitch would be more than just a temporary fixture; he had settled; he had adapted. He was quiet, utterly unassuming without at all falling into subservience. He made himself useful in a hundred small but important ways, but it was impossible to belittle him. It seemed that he had only been waiting for someone to give him an opportunity, and in Bob and Heather's rather chaotic, unregulated life there were opportunities aplenty for timely, discreet, watchful intercession. He had, 'wormed his way in', (as Rob thought of it) both at home and in Bob's music Production Company, earning, from everyone, a respect untainted by patronage. It was amazing, Rob railed to himself, when you thought about it. Who was he anyway? Nobody! A charity-case, a lad off the streets, penniless and unconnected.

The two lads exchanged a wary nod as they faced each other across the hall. The door stood open onto the night. The hall fire was almost out and Bob tossed a log onto the embers, before kneeling down and lighting a cigarette from one of them. He took an enormous, needy lungful and blew the smoke up the chimney before offering the cigarette to Rob. Taken by surprise, Rob shook his head, then regretted it, as Bob turned to Mitch and passed the cigarette to him.

'Mitch, mate, keep an ear open, will you?' he said, cocking his head at the open doorway.

'Course,' Mitch replied.

Bob made for the baize door, and Rob followed him.

'Brought a guitar and amp with me,' said Bob. 'Want to wire them up for me, later? Jam a bit?'

'Cool,' said Rob, sullenly.

Belinda had lit candles and placed them the length of the refectory table. There was wine, and jugs of water, and tureens of vegetables. The light flickered, diffused by the glassware and silver, glinting warmly off the copper pans which hung from one of the low beams. The red enamelled Aga glowed like a furnace in the half-light. The room was filled with the smell of good food and the approaching chatter of happy and excited voices as the family made its way down the corridor. Belinda, in a flowered apron, leaned contentedly against the dresser and waited for them to come. It was a shame about Simon, she thought, though typical of him to make a late entrance. But it couldn't be helped. The meal was cooked and she was ready. Family is food, and here was the beginning of it all. Rich red casserole and bright broccoli, golden roast potatoes, carrots cooked in her own special way. Food at a table, the sustenance of common genes and the reinforcing of the cords which bound them; family was flesh and bone and must be built up in body, it was strength in numbers and strength grew from feeding. The kitchen would be her powerhouse, her own domain. From here she would stoke the family boilers and nobody, not even Elliot, would beard her here. The alarm bell that Elliot had rung upstairs had not been rung in vain. She would not allow herself to leave him behind again, not from any desire to gratify him, or from any sense of guilt; it was a purely defensive strategy.

Elliot was the first to enter the room. He took a cursory look around the room but no word of compliment could be drawn from him.

'Where would you like to sit, darling?' Belinda asked, pushing herself away from the dresser and going towards him.

'Oh, anywhere at all, but next to June,' Elliot put his hand unnecessarily over June's where it was slipped into the crook of his arm. It was pure devilry in him; a deliberately hurtful gesture. Belinda pretended not to have seen.

'What about here, then?' she indicated the carver at the top of the table. Without another word, Elliot seated himself in it, and, placing June on his right, began assiduously filling her wine glass for her. The rest of the family filled up the seats around the table. Last of all, Bob and Rob ambled into the kitchen and took up a space between June and Rachel. June made an involuntary lurch away from her long-haired nephew-in-law. She knew he was reputed to have millions and she couldn't dispute his celebrity status – his rock band *WillyNilly* had been huge in the 70's – but he looked for all the world to her like the kind of man one saw lurking under viaducts or rummaging in the bins behind expensive City restaurants. He was the last dinner companion she would have chosen from the whole clan.

Rachel, on the other hand, was flustered by the proximity of her cousin Rob. He had grown in height since she had last seen him, and developed broad shoulders and the shadow of dark down on his upper lip. He wore wide-legged jeans, frayed and scruffy at the bottoms, and a black T shirt bearing the grinning visage of some grotesque death-head. He had black lace bracelets and one earring. His hair, as dark as Ellie's, was spiked into points so that he bore a permanent air of untamed savagery. He was very, very handsome. She hadn't seen him for two years; Rob had been absent on a school skiing trip when they had last visited Aunty Belinda's two Easters ago, so it must have been at poor Aunty April's funeral the autumn before that. He had been, then, an unremarkable fifteen year old, uncomfortable in his school blazer and tie. Suddenly, Rachel found herself under scrutiny from her neighbour, and she realised that she had been staring.

'Last time I saw you,' Rob said, loudly, 'you'd wet your knickers!' It was true; too much orange squash, the interminable service spent perched on hard pews in a freezing church, and then the long, slow walk through the churchyard in a biting October wind had combined to embarrass her. There was a shocked silence as everyone

93

wondered how this conversational faux pas should be handled. Rob's comment, while true, was, at this stage, inappropriate. It reminded everyone of the last time they had been together, of poor Simon and dead April and the three little motherless children she had left behind her, and of the promises they had all made to themselves (and not kept) to make up for her absence by lavishing love and care upon them. Rob's remark threw them off balance; they weren't ready for its rawness. James frowned, and looked at Elliot, who half rose from his seat, scraping his chair feet on the quarry tiles with an anguished scrawp. Every eye was on Rachel. She felt herself fold up from the inside, deflating like a tyre with a slow puncture. Her anxiety, her feelings of disconnectedness, her dissatisfaction with her clothes, her hesitancy over the bedroom, her desire to be older, thinner, elsewhere: it had all been warning her of this. She wanted to run. She thought she might be sick again. She put her hands down on to the bench on either side of her, ready to get up, thinking, even as she did so, that even her exit could be nothing other than undignified as she struggled to get her legs from where they were imprisoned underneath the table. But before her body could translate the thought into action, she felt Ellie's reassuring hand over hers, and heard Uncle Bob growl, 'Not cool, man.' James levelled a steady eye at his nephew and asked, with seeming irrelevance, 'Found the potting shed yet, Rob?' a veiled but, to the family, well-remembered reference to Rob's childhood habit of disappearing into his grandfather's potting shed to fill the plant pots with excreta.

'Yes!' shouted Granddad from the bottom of the table, his mind suddenly illumined by this memory from the past, 'You were a mucky little bugger, my lad!'

Everybody laughed. The moment passed.

Aunty Belinda was serving rich brown casserole, Elliot was on his feet and moving down the table pouring wine, Ellie squeezed Rachel's hand and then let go, and poured water into their glasses.

Everybody was talking. Rachel was absorbed into the circle of baby talk with Heather, and Ellie, and Mary. Bob drummed gently on the table top with the ends of his fingers, and spoke modestly of the huge charity concert he had lately done in aid of African famine victims, and politely requested that a plate of food be kept to one side for Mitch. Ruth had stopped talking and seemed to be concentrating on keeping herself together; she was drunk. Rob grinned inanely, but his eyes avoided faces, and when his plateful of casserole and vegetables arrived he hadn't the courage to do anything other than eat it.

At last, when everyone was served, and the busy talk had been succeeded by the busy clatter of cutlery on crockery, Belinda sat down. She had returned the casserole and vegetables to the warming oven of the Aga. She still hoped that Simon and Miriam and the children would join them for part of the meal. The arrival of Mitch with Heather and Bob had thrown her, temporarily; as useful as he was to them, she had not expected them to bring him on *holiday*. He would need accommodation and consideration. There was the possibility that June and Les too would need putting up for the night, although Les, she noted, had drunk nothing after his glass of beer in the drawing room. As though sensing her thoughts, Les leaned towards her and said,

'I heard today that the City Chairman's resigning.' Belinda floundered for a moment. What could he mean? Did cities have chairmen? She thought they had mayors. In her confusion she chewed for longer than was necessary on a piece of steak, while she considered a suitable response, but her father, unexpectedly, came to her aid.

'Good thing, too,' he barked, while Mary wiped gravy from his chin, 'the man's a waste of space, always has been.'

'Franny Lee was the man, he was,' said Les, with feeling. Robert nodded.

'Football bores me,' said Ruth, slowly.

95

'You aren't eating, Ruth,' Belinda commented, 'are you feeling alright?'

'I think I've gone a bit past it.' Ruth creased her face up into an apologetic smile. 'I had a hellish day at school today, if anybody's interested.'

Nobody was, and Ruth relapsed into a sulky silence.

'More broccoli, anyone?' asked Belinda.

'I didn't know you planned to join us,' Elliot remarked, pointedly, to June. He was pretty sure that he was not the only one. Further down the table, startled eyes were turned towards him.

June simpered. 'Ruth has kindly invited us.'

'It was more of an observation than an invitation, June!' Ruth shook herself from her doldrums to exclaim.

June ignored her. '....and I think, if you're sure we won't be intruding...' Now June was looking at him and with a delicious sense of having assumed control at last Elliot decided to dispense largesse. He shook his head as though it were an impossible concept.

'....as it's getting a little late, perhaps we will stay just for tonight, at least,' June finished

'At least.' Elliot echoed. He looked down the table and met his wife's appalled astonishment with an oily grin.

Mary knew how her daughter felt. She had been out-manoeuvred by June for twenty odd years, and so had Les. Mary looked across at Les, now; poor man, how uncomfortable he looked! He was so kindly, dependable and gentle. They had, over the years, spent many hours together, discreetly withdrawn to the kitchen or garden, while Robert and June had raged at each other, and argued about money and the business. In the early days, when McKays had boasted only two wagons, Robert and Les had shared the European and domestic routes, so that when Robert was away, Les would be home. Many a time he had arrived at Mary's modest front door and enjoyed the comfort of her unpretentious front room and a mug of tea and generous slice of homemade cake for an hour, before returning to his own coldly modern executive home where June would be hosting a bridge four or a committee meeting, with tea and bought cake served in the best china, and where she had installed a downstairs shower off the back porch so that he would not sully her carpets with his oily boots and travel-grimed skin. Yes, thought Mary, to herself, Robert's business had changed everything. It had started off as a sound idea to support his family; an HGV licence and a lorry. It had meant hard work, long hours, a tight belt and nerves of steel, but no one who knew Robert's tenacity and energy doubted that he could make a go of it. It wasn't a glamorous line of work and it had meant days and nights apart, no joke for a young bride, or when Belinda had been small. But it had been successful, and June had jumped on to the band wagon, and everything had changed. It had been odd, really, that Robert had tolerated it; his firm opinion on women was, generally, that they should be in the home. But there June had been, stubbornly holding her ground, taking liberties. She had quickly learned to keep her hands clean even though she worked in a dirty business; the smell of oil and grime and sweat permeated it. Robert had made the transition far more slowly, coming to terms only gradually with going to work to sit, uneasily, with his knees under a desk, instead of under the steering wheel. Mary, involved by association only, was affected only in that she had more shirts to launder and suits to take to the cleaners, until a course of driving lessons and her own small car brought it home to her that money need no longer be a worry, she need not knit the children's school pullovers if she didn't choose to, nor walk the length of the high street to save a few coppers. By the late seventies, eating out was, though still a treat, not an unusual one, and they had been abroad on an aeroplane.

But she and Robert had never taken on airs. They had roots. That, essentially, she thought, had been the McKay creed. Hold on to your roots. Looking down the table at her children and grandchildren, though, she struggled to see how these roots were manifested in the new generations. They had utterly outgrown her, their jobs, houses, holidays, experiences, everything far beyond her comprehension, now. How heady and remote their lives seemed to her. Elliot had transformed the company into a bright and shining thing, impersonal and impenetrable; she hardly knew anyone there now and at the Christmas party had sat with Robert at the top table feeling like an interloper. Even this holiday, lovely though the thought had been, so much more extravagant than anything she could have imagined or would have picked. She dabbed discreetly at her eyes as she felt tears welling up. To see them all here together would be really something, she had to admit, even in these rather overblown surroundings, as different and drifted as they all were from their roots, and she would be content with their choice and happy to seem to enjoy what they thought she would have liked, if only Simon would come.

Then Simon did come, causing a commotion in the passageway. He strode in first. Tall and well-groomed, carrying just a little too much weight, casually dressed in pristine cream chinos and a well-labelled polo shirt, he carried a case of champagne with two sides of smoked salmon balanced on the top.

'Hello, everybody!' he cried, 'don't let us disturb you.'

Everybody, of course, was disturbed. Mary, James, Les and Belinda all got onto their feet. James took the case of champagne from Simon and placed it on the floor over by the back door, Mary reached up and threw her arms around her son's neck. Belinda bustled about, Les simply got up from the table as a gesture that he hoped would show that he knew himself to be an impostor and deserving of expulsion. Ben dashed from the kitchen in search of Toby and Todd. Rob, too, in the melee, climbed out of his seat and slunk from the room, in the mixed hope that his actions would be interpreted as downright rude or as an intention to offer help. Elliot smiled genially from his place of power at the head of the table. Ruth shrank inside, her heart beating from the excess stimulus of the alcohol and the anxiety over meeting Miriam. Now that the moment had come, she felt less sure of her ground than ever. When James climbed back onto the bench beside her, and placed his arm around her shoulders, she could have wept.

Miriam and Tansy followed closely behind Simon; the two boys had been hijacked by Ben to be shown *'everything'*; they could be heard laughing manically as they careered around the ground floor rooms. Miriam was, in stature, tiny, hardly taller than Tansy. She wore an immaculately tailored business suit and high heeled shoes, which Ruth dismissively labelled as wholly unsuitable for a week in the country. Her dark hair was long and sleek. She was one of those women who have natural beauty, fine bones, good skin, large eyes and a pretty nose; her makeup was perfect. Her colouring was olive, a throwback, she claimed, from her Persian ancestry. She was certainly exotic, a lover of luxury, with a constant eye to her own comfort and well-being, attractive to men, very intelligent and strongly opinionated, successful in her career, wealthy in her own right, but secretive and sly, bearing herself aloof as though considering herself to be rather above everything. Though cohabiting, now, with Simon, in the suburban home he had bought after April's death, she had retained her London flat, which smacked, to onlookers, of a lack of commitment to the family. She ran both households with an almost military precision. Having no children of her own, she related to Simon's in a business-like fashion; she was rigorous about tidiness and cleanliness, manners, healthy food and plenty of outdoor exercise, limited television and, when they were home, very exacting about bedtimes. She had encouraged Simon to place the children as weekly boarders at their school, arguing cogently that she had her own important and successful career at the Bar and could not be expected to step into April's shoes as mother just because she had taken up occupancy of April's side of the bed. Having said that, as long as the children were good mannered, tidy and clean and neither crossed her nor manifested any overly emotional behaviour, she was happy for them to have or do almost anything.

She carried two Fortnum & Mason shopping bags, Tansy a third. Les, for want of any other useful occupation, took them and tried to help Belinda unpack their contents; *foie gras,* croissants, huge wedges of stilton and brie, sun-dried tomato Ciabatta, malt-whisky marmalade, organic, dry-cured Norfolk bacon, continental butter, bottles of freshly squeezed orange juice, Belgian chocolate: it went on and on.

Now almost everybody was on their feet; Heather kissed Miriam, Ellie and Rachel fluttered around Tansy. Simon exchanged general, genial greetings, his eyes avoiding his father; it was possible, in the hubbub, to ignore him without seeing to. Everyone was talking at once as though words alone could knit up the fissures between them;

the journey, the house, the week before them, were all exclaimed over. With the arrival of this final family group it seemed as though everything could now begin, as though everything that had gone before was some kind of false start. Now they were complete and the McKays, on the surface at least, were a seamless whole. They all worked hard at maintaining the illusion and an onlooker would have seen a family reunion, the gathering of a clan. They were, in fact, a family of strangers.

Miriam said nothing but looked on as the family scurried around reorganising things that had been in perfect order before her arrival. Then Simon led her round to the far side of the table, well away from his father, and lifted her bodily over the bench as one might a small child. Miriam smiled at last and smacked him playfully, indulging his gesture, and nestled into the space between James and Simon.

'Where's Starlight?' she asked, looking round the table.

'Asleep in the car. Mitch's watching her.' Heather ran a hand through her hair.

'Bless her,' said Mary.

Ruth bristled, but said nothing. So far, neither Simon nor Miriam had addressed a word to her.

Rachel arrived back into the room with Ben, Toby and Todd. Toby, a twelve year old, with his mother's pleasant sandy colouring and teeth that seemed too big for his mouth, welcomed neither his Grandma's hug nor his Granddad's handshake; both made him feel awkward and shy. He didn't know where to sit. He would have liked to sit with his cousin Rob but he was nowhere to be seen. At last, Simon noticed his elder son standing uncertainly by the door. 'Come on, son, and sit here with me,' he said, and Aunty Belinda placed a portion of food in his place. Toby's heart sank: vegetables.

'Dad! Dad!' chirped Ben, 'there's a huge dog in the hall! It's enormous, Dad. Whose is it? Can we keep it?' Then, with a gasp, 'You don't think,' he whispered, awed, 'that it could've eaten Wriggly!'

'A dog!' exclaimed Belinda, wondering if she would be expected to feed it. 'Where can it have come from?' The whole thing seemed to be mushrooming before her eyes.

'It's Mitch's.' Heather told her. 'D'you know he has *never* had a pet? Not even so much as a hamster? I sent him off to the animal shelter as soon as I found out. Although I must admit I didn't expect him to get anything so *large*.... Don't worry, Ben's wiggly won't have been eaten, whatever that is. He's no trouble at all. Half the time you don't know he's there.'

'Like Mitch!' jested Simon.

'Mitch's alright,' Bob put in, a little defensively.

'Oh yes, Mitch's alright,' agreed Elliot, feeling that he, if anyone, should be the one to decide Mitch's status in proceedings, if any.

'Mitch's welcome, of course,' affirmed Belinda, 'It's just that I didn't know he had a dog.'

'What's his name, Uncle Bob?' Ben wriggled on his seat. It seemed to him that everyone was losing sight of the really important thing, here. There was a dog, a really big one, and who he belonged to didn't really matter. A dog could be incorporated into adventures, it could be set on the trail of Wriggly, and it could be a faithful companion or a pretend adversary. A dog that big could even, Ben considered, speculatively, be ridden.

'Tiny,' said Bob, dryly.

Everybody laughed.

The meal recommenced, those who had already started making the best of their chilled remainders. James got Ruth a fresh plate and helped her to a small portion of casserole and some carrots. Under his supervision, she managed to swallow a few mouthfuls and immediately began to feel a little better. Elliot, *mine host*, refilled wine glasses, opening further bottles. Heather discreetly pushed a glass of wine towards Ellie; it was the second time she had done it. Perhaps it was the wine, or the incident between Rob and Rachel, but Ellie was beginning to warm towards her cousins. Rachel was describing the bedrooms to Tansy, tentatively suggesting that they might share.

'May I share a room with Rachel?' Tansy asked Miriam.

'Fancy having to ask that!' Ellie exclaimed, archly. She was not accustomed to asking for her parents' permission on such mundane matters.

Miriam ignored the comment. 'Certainly, if you don't keep each other awake all night,' she assented.

'It'll be like being back in the dorm at school,' said Tansy to Rachel, with a sigh.

'So what have you all decided? Fill us in on the plan,' Simon said, through casserole. 'This is delicious, Belinda,' he added.

'Decided? What about?' Elliot's ears pricked up.

'Well,' Simon swallowed and took a sip of wine, 'with so many of us, we can't expect Belinda to do all the cooking, for a start, can we?'

'Oh, I don't mind,' Belinda put in, stirring custard on the hob.

'No. We ought to work out teams, or a rota, or something.'

'Good idea!' said June, as though it had anything to do with her.

'I'm afraid your Dad's not up to cooking,' said Mary, 'are you, Robert dear?

Robert's only reply was to ask: 'Where's the television? We usually have the television on at tea time. Mary? Isn't that programme we like on tonight?'

Mary put her hand over his, and soothed him.

103

'Of course not, Mum,' Ruth put in, defensively, referring to the cooking. 'Simon didn't mean that you or Dad should do any cooking.' She cast her eyes along the table, hoping that her remark would be recognised as an olive branch. 'You're to have a nice rest and let us look after you.'

'I might be a bit busy with Starlight,' Heather said, self-importantly. She hated organised things; she was a free spirit, after all, and couldn't be tied down by routines.

'There'll be lots of people to help with her,' Simon said, gently. 'You look done in, actually. Perhaps we ought to let you recuperate for a couple of days.'

Bob muttered a sentence that ended with the word 'Mitch.'

'We don't mind helping, do we Les? Ha ha ha!' June shrilled.

'Glad to chip in,' Les said. He was perched, now, next to Mary; James had taken his place. With no cutlery or glass, he felt more marginalised than ever.

'That's very good of you, considering you'll only be here for such a short time,' Ruth threw in, with more acid than she had intended.

'What do you think, Belinda?' Mary put in, quickly.

'I have a menu planned,' Belinda said, slowly, 'at least for the first few days.....'

'We could go out,' Simon suggested, 'at least for one meal.'

'Certainly,' said James.

'That pub in the village looked rather good, I thought.'

'Remarkably good,' James concurred.

Ruth jabbed James in the ribs with her elbow. 'I expect it's very pricey,' she hissed, pointedly.

'We'll be a very unwieldy number,' Belinda said, doubtfully.

'We could get into groups,' Simon was saying, 'say three groups of four....'

'Good idea,' Ruth supported Simon again.

'We'll be a group, won't we?' Ben indicated his two cousins.

'That'll be fine as long as we all like toast and cereal, Ben. That's your limit in the kitchen.' Rachel ventured. Apart from Ruth and Simon, no-one else was very keen on the team idea. Belinda had really wanted the sole freedom of the kitchen; she had planned the menus and written the shopping lists, after all. Heather wasn't much of a cook and Miriam, though an excellent cook, certainly had no intention of spending much time stoking an Aga or polishing copper pans. Bob would be happy to chop and peel but wasn't an ideas man when it came to culinary innovation. James would loyally support Ruth, of course. None of them relished being put in a catering team with three over excited children.

'Perhaps we ought to just agree to help out with everything. James has done a very good job so far with all the fires, and I think he's carried everyone's luggage up for them.' Mary tried to mollify everyone.

'Whatever everyone wants, of course,' Simon drained his wine glass. 'But you know what they say about too many cooks.'

'I don't suppose it's going to be a question of *too many*,' Ruth laughed, reaching for her wine glass but finding a water tumbler had replaced it.

Mitch's head appeared round the kitchen door.

'Little 'un's awake,' he said. 'Shall I bring her in?'

'I'll go,' said Bob. 'Here mate, get some grub.' He got up from the table, laid a fresh place and brought over the plated meal that had been keeping warm in the oven. Then he left the room to collect his daughter.

'Lovely! Thanks!' Mitch began to eat. The meal was over, anyway. There was no question that the family should remain at the table while Mitch ate. People were talking about going upstairs, finding their rooms to unpack. Belinda had run a sink full of hot water while James was beginning to stack the dishwasher.

Ellie regarded Mitch from her position over by the dresser. He was taller and broader than she recalled, and in some way sleeker. His hair, which had been very short, had grown out. It was blonde. His eyes had lost a certain shrinking caginess they had had. They met hers, now across the table. All in all, from an inauspicious start, things were looking up.

'I don't want you all to go away, just yet,' Heather said, suddenly. 'I have this sense of, oh!' she put her hand to her forehead, 'I feel it's very important that Starlight sees you all for the first time, together. It'll be her first extended-family memory. Imagine it, burned into her brain forever. This family gathering.'

'I thought Simon and Miriam had seen her already,' Ruth put in, with a note of sourness.

'She was asleep. She didn't see them,' Heather retorted.

The family's anticipation rose. For Mary, Starlight meant the end of Heather's long quest for motherhood, for Robert, a new Heather-child, a golden faced replica to delight his old age. Ruth of course had her doubts about the child's provenance but even she could not but be excited at the arrival of any new child, however achieved. The girls, young as they were, experienced a frisson of something at the prospect of a rosy cheeked babe. The boys just hoped that the new child would attract all the adults' attention so that they could get away with murder for the rest of the week.

Bob's footsteps could be heard in the passageway. Some of the family rose to their feet; such was their sense of expectation. Then he was in the room, and the whole family except for Simon and Miriam let out a startled gasp. Nestled in the crook of Bob's arm was a child of something over twelve months old. Her hair was a mass of black curls, her eyes as dark as night. She looked around her at the gathered people, her eyes sleepy and confused by the dwindling candle light. Mary put her hand to her mouth, Robert staggered, and fell back into his seat. Belinda thought her heart would beat itself out of her body. Ruth thought for a wild moment that there had been some mistake. Elliot wanted to laugh.

'Well?' said Heather, beaming round at her family. 'Isn't she beautiful?'

'That child,' croaked Robert, a tremulous arm reaching forward and a shaking finger extending itself towards Starlight, 'is as black as the ace of spades!'

Mary and Ruth put Robert to bed straight after supper, with a couple of his tablets. The excitement of seeing everyone, the journey, it had all been a bit too much for him, Mary said. He would be much better in the morning. Her own assurances sounded hollow in her ears. He would not be better and he might be much worse. He was unpredictable that way since his stroke.

Ruth found the undressing and washing process rather distasteful. Her father's body was white and cold, and entirely unblemished, like marble. It was as though any mark life had made on him had been completely erased. His muscles had shrunk to nothing; he was helpless as a baby. His skin concertinaed over itself, missing the flesh that had once filled it out. He stood like a child while Mary saw to him, doing absolutely nothing to help her, but Ruth thought that even so her mother was a little rough, pulling his clothes off him, her mouth closed in a hard, business-like line, her actions lacking tenderness. Ruth offered to sit with her father until he fell asleep.

'It isn't necessary, Ruth. He isn't a baby, you know.' Mary said, folding Robert's trousers deftly.

'I know, but I haven't had a moment on my own with either of you,' Ruth couldn't keep the whine of self-pity from her voice.

'Just as you like, Ruth,' Mary said, leaving the room.

In the bed, Robert's body made a pathetically small mound. He lay straight, his arms, where Mary had placed them, at his sides outside the counterpane, the skin of his face falling away leaving his cheekbones like smooth, sea-worn rocky promontories, his eyes sunken into their sockets. He looked, Ruth thought, for all the world like the effigy of a long-dead knight, carved into white marble and placed on a tomb in a quiet church cloister. Indeed, compared to the man he had once been, energetic and vital, volatile, a powerhouse of strength and determination, he was as spent and vacant as any corpse. The rhythm of his sleeping breaths scarcely disturbed the sheets.

Ruth knelt down by the bed, in front of the bedside table. He was a stranger to her. Even as a child, he hadn't seemed to see her, half the time; he had remained aloof from all her earliest experiences. Her memories were of dolls' teas on the small square lawn; she and Belinda pouring dandelion and burdock into miniscule cups and serving iced gems on tiny plates to start-eyed dollies, while Mary hung out washing on the line behind them. Or of herself and Simon adventuring together across the refuse-strewn wasteland between the railway line and the big houses by the golf course until Mary came to unearth them from their malodorous den of corrugated metal and damp cardboard and discarded beer crates to bring them home for tea and bed.

Her attempts to attract his notice had gone unrecognised and she had turned, as a teenager, to sullenness and rebellion; insisting on university, espousing left-wing political movements, CND and a woman's right to choose, even marrying, disastrously, in her second year. Her father had refused to attend the registry office ceremony, or to recognise any marriage not conducted according to the rites of the Church. He had been blind to his own hypocrisy; he never even attended church, although the children had all been religiously packed off to Sunday school every week and been confirmed, the girls in white Broderie Anglaise dresses clutching tiny white leather bibles, Simon, sullenly, in his school uniform. It was the 'done' thing and the McKays did the 'done' thing.

Ruth raised her eyes to look at the man who bore the name of father. His hand in her own was limp and cool, and peppered with brownish age-spots. She touched one of them gently, then tweezed the flesh between her forefinger and thumb, lifting it clear of the bone and tendon beneath. His flesh and blood. That was all they had in common; his DNA. Suddenly, Ruth pinched the flesh of her father's hand, quite hard. Robert gave a snort and snatched his hand away, but he didn't wake up, and in any case Ruth was out of the room and down the landing in a few short strides.

Now Mary was supervising Starlight's evening meal; mashing carrots and chopping up meat, assisted by her other three granddaughters. Starlight, enthroned in her high chair, with Bob on one side of her and Mitch on the other, looked solemnly on at all the activity in her honour, far more interested in the big girls than in the array of toys collected for her amusement on the table. The girls, all three, had suddenly affected ridiculously squeaky voices.

'Is she ready for her din-dins, then?'

'Starlight! Starlight!' (this in a sing-song voice from Tansy) 'Ah! She knows her name. Look, she's smiling at me!'

'Smile at me, Starlight! Smile at – who am I? Aunty Ellie?'

'Not really. Cousin Ellie, I think.' This from Rachel.

'Don't be ridiculous. *You* don't call me 'cousin Ellie' do you?'

'No, but, I mean, not Aunty.' Rachel squirmed at the put-down.

'Say 'Ellie,' Starlight.'

Starlight said nothing. Rachel stood against the Aga and watched her cousins flit like brightly coloured birds around the kitchen, tossing their hair, admiring jewellery, comparing hobbies. They both rode, had seen the same films, liked and disliked the same shops. They twittered and giggled in the same key, they used the same language; everything was *so* this and *so not* that. There was, between them, in spite of the age difference, a connection of the type that Rachel had hoped but failed to find, an embryonic friendship which had to do with that intangible essence that made a person who they were, and the way it sparked an answering response in its soul-mates. Rachel wondered how much of it was the call of blood to blood, and whether, on that score, she would therefore be forever excluded.

Mitch, too, watched the girls, especially Ellie. He liked the way her hair fell almost into her eyes, and the way she had to keep sweeping it out of the way with her tiny, bird-like hand. He liked the way she laughed, showing white and orthodontic-even teeth. He had only seen her once before. She had been a child, then, about the age that these other girls must be now, her body, in its bathing suit, without a feminine contour, diving like a fish into Bob and Heather's pool.

Her mother, the one with the bun, called across to her from the sink; 'Ellie, do you know where your brother is?'

She shrugged. 'On the computer?' She looked at her watch and visibly paled. 'Mum, is he going to be allowed to be on it all week? I thought we were supposed to do things together!' Her voice was a little shrill and Mitch discerned sub-text.

'He has his course work to finish. The sooner it's done the better, don't you think?'

'Course work!' Ellie said, derisively.

Then the thin woman with glasses, Ruth, came into the room. 'The last thing I want to discuss is work, if you don't mind,' she said, archly, making for the fridge. 'I fancy cheese and biscuits and a large glass of port, don't you?'

People made noises which indicated they were still full. Bob shook his head and Mitch followed suit. She went on to cut wedges of creamy brie and blue-veined stilton, and opened packets of biscuits and found a very good old ruby port from amongst the vast stock of bottles by the back door. She poured herself an over generous measure, swallowing down a good third of it in the guise of disinterested tasting and assessment of its quality, then she nodded with satisfaction and topped up her glass. She exited the room without a word, leaving open cheese packets and biscuit crumbs all over the table and the fridge door yawning wide open.

James took Ben and Todd upstairs to find a bathroom, and ran a bath for them. While the water filled, they stripped off their clothes and raced, yelling, up and down the thickly carpeted landing. Leaving them to play shrieking submarines beneath the crackling bubbles, James mounted up to the attic with Toby and Todd's bags, located Ben's belongings abandoned on the landing, and chose a large room with four beds under a steeply sloping ceiling. He unpacked swiftly, paying wry note that while Toby and Todd's things were all almost new, good quality and clean, Ben's, in sad comparison, were shabby, faded and pilled. Ruth's obsession with charity shops and car boot sales was getting out of hand. Fanatical about economy, being careful had developed into being mean. Rachel, sitting alongside her well-groomed and sophisticated cousins, had looked very much the poor relation, even in her nearly new outfit. James would have loved nothing more than to take his daughter shopping, to indulge her, but, when it came to money, as well as other things, he was powerless. It was a conscious choice on his part whose consequences nevertheless often stung. In other ways it was a relief, to abdicate responsibility. His first wife had been flaky and feeble, unreliable and wayward, traits which had spiralled into the early onset dementia which had fully claimed her shortly after Rachel's birth.

James sighed and surveyed the room; beds neatly turned down, the light in the tiny bathroom at the end of the room left on, curtains closed. Briefly, he toured the rest of the attic area. Four or five rooms with single beds, each painted a different, cheerful colour, a small bathroom and a toilet, the girls' room, and, at the end of the corridor, a door secured by three bolts which gave access to a tiny roof terrace over-looking the outbuildings at the side of the house. James stood in the night air for a few moments, breathing deeply and enjoying the peace. Then he went back inside and secured the door carefully.

Ruth carried her plate of cheese through to the drawing room where they had been sitting before dinner, sure that she would find the others there enjoying brandies and mellow bonhomie, but the room was empty and the lights had been switched off. Only the glow from the fire illuminated the room. In its light, Ruth noted dirty glasses littering the table and that the sofa cushions retained the imprint of their former occupants. Standing alone in the warmth and the semi darkness, she hesitated before the comfortable armchair nearest to the fire. It looked inviting and certainly it would be easy for her to stay here alone, drink port and slip into a mood of morose self-pity. They were all fussing with the baby, she thought to herself. No-one wanted to sit with her and enjoy cheese and biscuits, they would rather play aeroplanes and 'one for Grandma, one for Starlight' with the child, who probably originated from a sun-scorched mud village where food did not have to be glamorised to be made appealing; it only, actually, had to turn up. Ruth rolled another mouthful of port over her tongue, and breathed in the fumes before swallowing it. She knew quite well that she had already had enough to drink, and that she was upsetting Belinda's careful menu planning by breaking into food probably reserved for another occasion. She was aware that she had taken no interest in the baby and that Heather, already upset by Robert's reaction, would be very sensitive to slights from any other quarter. She realised that the issue with Miriam had not really gone away, only been politely skirted round. But she was feeling extremely sorry for herself; this was her only holiday, she had made considerable sacrifices in order to be here at all, she had set the table and been nice to Belinda by looking after June, and she had helped with Robert, which no-one else had. Suddenly there was a groan and a sigh. The hearthrug reared up a massive grey head and two black eyes blinked up at her. Either sit down and shut up, they seemed to say, or go away.

'Hello, boy,' Ruth said, tentatively. She placed her cheese and port carefully down on the small table next to the armchair, reserving it, as it were, before stepping over to the window to draw the curtains.

With the lights in the room off, she could see through the inky panes quite clearly into a small courtyard. She turned the key and opened the door, stepping briefly out into the darkness to smell the autumn night. There was a heaviness around her heart which she recognised instantly and with despair as the beginnings of a sense of hopelessness and oppression which would spiral down into a depression. It was a condition she was prone to, amongst others, and she wondered that James had not picked up on the signs he claimed always to be able to spot; a certain look in the eye, he said. She gulped the cold air into her lungs; it tasted of wood smoke and rotting leaves and general vegetable dankness. She shivered with cold, and although the idea of remaining here and freezing almost to death before being discovered and taken care of was appealing, the idea that somewhere else there was good conversation and easy company was too strong; she didn't want to be alone. She wanted to be where Simon was, even if that meant (as it inevitably would) sharing him with Miriam.

Swiftly she re-entered the room and pulled the French door closed, before passing back out into the corridor. She could hear voices from behind a door on the other side, the library, she seemed to recall, and opening it slowly, caught a glimpse of Elliot and June, flushed and conspiratorial, their heads together over a large book of maps, wine glasses at their elbows. They looked up at her entrance, but before they could speak, she withdrew and closed the door.

The next door she tried opened onto the huge and elegant room at the rear of the house. Lamps had been lit and the curtains drawn; for such a big room, the effect was surprisingly intimate. Clusters of graceful furniture gathered round the windows and the fireplace. On one stylish little settee, Heather and Simon were sitting close together; he had his arm round her and she was weeping on his shoulder, like a small child. Ruth stepped into the room. This was just what she had wanted. She would be needed, welcomed. Her heart warmed within her. At her entrance, however, Simon and Heather turned to face her, and Heather raised an arm in a gesture which could have been interpreted as a sign that she should stop, or even retreat. Ruth hesitated. Surely she had misunderstood; she belonged here. She took another step forward, and Heather raised her arm again. Then, Miriam's immaculately groomed head appeared from behind the wings of a chair which faced the settee occupied by Simon and Heather, but which had hidden her presence from Ruth entirely.

'Would you mind, Ruth, just giving us a few minutes?' Miriam asked, smiling.

Ruth felt as though the air had been squeezed from her lungs. She was to be turned out, was she, by this woman? Hurt feelings and seething anger battled within her, but hurt predominated over anger and Ruth, white, mumbled something incoherent and turned back to the door. Her eyes were streaming with tears before she had managed to close the door behind her. She groped her way to the safety of the deserted drawing room, closing the door behind her and sinking forlornly into the armchair. She had been crying for a few moments before she noticed that somebody had eaten her cheese and biscuits and knocked her glass of port to the floor. It was the last straw. She ran, wailing, out of the room, along the corridor, up the stairs to her room.

Eventually Toby found Rob in a study off the hall. A bluish glare from a computer screen illuminated the creepy armchairs and the old fashioned furniture, which was scattered in disarray around the room.

'Oh!' Toby said, hesitantly glad, 'there you are.'

Rob nodded his head and moved the mouse to close the window on the screen. 'Alright?'

'Yes, alright, I guess. Funny place this, isn't it? Not much to do, is there? You been here long? Didn't see you at dinner. Cool computer. Dad wouldn't let me bring mine. Got many games on it? Have you got *Fatal Blow*? I have. Cool isn't it?'

Rob seethed. It had taken him ages to get to grips with the dial-up internet and then the girl, Caro, had not shown up in the chat room. He had discovered that his mobile phone had no signal. His efforts to be objectionable at dinner had backfired on him very badly and now it seemed that he was to be tormented by this gnat.

'I've brought the computer to do my course work,' he said, ungraciously.

'Oh. Right.' Toby said, quashed. 'I could help. What is it?'

'Quantum physics,' Rob said. 'I've got to calculate the size of fissures in the space continuum and hypothesise on the probability of them creating a negative energy field before the end of the next millennium.'

'Blimey. Sounds like something out of Star Trek,' gasped Toby.

'More like Red Dwarf, eh Rob?' said a voice from the doorway. Uncle Bob stood on the threshold, a guitar case in one hand and a portable amplifier in the other. 'Coming?' He cocked his head and raised an eyebrow, before striding through the hall and down towards the games room.

117

'Cool! Yeah!' shouted Toby, hurrying after him. Rob, relieved that his boob at the dinner table seemed to have been forgotten, followed on behind.

Mitch had moved all the toys into the games room. It was a huge space, with bare floorboards and colourful rugs, bright modern sofas, an enormous home-cinema sized television screen and of course the grand piano and snooker table. Bob, Rob and Toby began to wire up the amp and tune the guitar. At the other end of the room, Ellie, Tansy and Rachel sat amongst the toys and played with Starlight. The baby was wide awake. The long sleep in the car had refreshed her and her three wonderful new playmates seemed indefatigable in their efforts to amuse her. Nearby, Mary had settled herself into a sofa and proceeded to produce, from the depths of her handbag, some crocheting. She jumped a little at the first tortured twangs from the guitar but Bob considerately turned the volume down and began to show the boys how to play some chords. In only a few minutes Toby had mastered the three chord sequence of 'You've got me singing the Blues'. Bob showed Rob how to play a syncopated rhythm on his knees and Bob sang along in his gravelly, world-famous voice. The girls took Starlight's hands and began to dance with her across the wide open space of the floor. After an urge to react sulkily to the fact that Toby, and not he, had been given the first chance with the guitar, Rob began to quite enjoy what Bob called 'the jam', especially when Bob noticed a little extra fluttering movement he had but in with the tips of his fingers and said, 'yes, Phil Collins does that, too, sometimes. Good.'

Rachel, less mindful of her figure and unkempt hair than she had been all evening, and keeping her eyes away from Rob, pirouetted across the floor and imagined that she lived in this house and that this was her very own dance studio. Tansy and Ellie twirled around Starlight, who laughed and reached out her chubby hands. Mary smiled to herself, crocheting happily.

The song came to a tumultuous, if rather ragged, close. James, by the door, clapped his massive hands. The sound of his applause echoed around the room and mingled with the laughter.

'Good acoustics in here,' Rob said, coolly, embarrassed, now, by his part in the frivolities. He yawned, affectedly.

'Very,' agreed Bob.

'Belinda's giving a guided tour,' James announced, 'leaving from the hallway in two minutes. Anybody interested?'

'Oh I am,' said Tansy. 'Are you coming, Ellie?'

Ellie shrugged. 'Might as well.' She began to stuff her feet back into her trainers. 'I've seen my room, and the kitchen, and here, but nothing else.'

'I haven't seen anything. Not even outside; it was dark as anything when we arrived.' The two girls began to make their way up the passageway. Toby, Bob and Rob followed them. Rachel was left alone with Mary and Starlight.

'Aren't you going, Rachel, dear?' Mary asked.

Rachel, feeling hollow, shook her head. The other girls had left her behind without a thought. She wasn't one of them. They had also, she noted, left the baby, as though she was as inanimate as the dolls and soft toys scattered around the floor.

'No, I'm not, either.' Mary said. 'Pass me that picture book and bring the little one to sit here. Let's see if she'd like a story.'

Starlight had taken up a stance in the corner of the room. She held a toy hammer in one of her chubby fists and was staring at it with immense concentration. Then her face relaxed and she beamed a satisfied smile at Rachel, who had located a small cardboard book featuring an assortment of improbably cute-looking animals. Starlight tottered over to Rachel, bringing with her a pungent aroma.

119

'Oh, dear. Grandma,' Rachel laughed. 'I wonder where the nappies are. Starlight's been very busy!'

The family gathered in the hall like a class of over-excited school children on an excursion. June was rather tipsy; her shrill and characteristic 'ha ha ha' rising with more energy than usual up to the impressive ceiling. Elliot was urbane, but unusually bright-eyed. Belinda carefully allowed him to organise proceedings. Miriam and Heather went arm in arm, Heather red-eyed but gracefully forgiving; she blessed them all with her beatific smiles. Miriam kept up an incessant commentary on the architecture, style and historical provenance of every artefact, annoying in its authoritative insistence; the smallest adult in the company, she managed to talk down to them all. Bob and the boys loitered by the fireplace, James and Les shrank into the shadows of the cloakroom, Tansy and Ellie trilled and chirruped in the midst of the throng. Mitch, surprised in the act of returning from the drawing room with a bucket of soapy water and a cloth, was eagerly invited to join them.

They began with the large lounge, exclaiming over the elegance of the furnishings. They drew back the curtains and presently James located a light switch which beautifully illuminated the terrace and lawns from dozens of subdued lights.

'Oh!' breathed Heather. 'Tomorrow I shall dance barefoot across that grassy sward!'

'Yes!' said Elliot, benignly, as though he were the Director of a Sanatorium and she an inmate requiring his permission for such outlandish proceedings, 'of course you will, if you wish it.'

He turned his attention to the room. 'I image we'll spend most of our time in here,' he said, 'it will accommodate us all in comfort. We can move the furniture, if we want. But I suggest we allocate the children another room to gather in. We'll want some peace and quiet, won't we?'

'Oh yes,' said Miriam, surprised to find herself in agreement, 'but we oughtn't to move the furniture. It's all so well placed already. Is anyone in to *feng shui*?'

This pretentious enquiry was ignored.

'*We're* not children, are we, Tansy? So they can't mean *us*.' Ellie was quick to put in, as an aside.

'We won't exclude them altogether, will we?' Belinda asked, quietly.

'Not altogether, I suppose, but look at some of the ornaments in here! I mean, it's obvious, isn't it? This isn't a family room!' Elliot waved his arm to encompass the whole room, and gave Belinda one of his most offensive glares. 'Anyone who disagrees with me,' it said, pointedly, 'is clearly certifiable.'

'Perhaps there's a more suitable one?' suggested Bob, knowing that there was.

'As big as this? I don't think so,' Elliot, who had not seen the games room, was derisory.

'I expect all these things are well insured.' James pointed out.

'They aren't valuable, anyway,' said Bob, dismissively, lifting up a china figurine and briefly examining the mark on its base. Elliot threw his hands into the air with a choleric gasp.

'Very pretty though, aren't they, Les?' June commented with a significant look which passed from Les to Elliot.

'Oh. Yes.' Les agreed.

The library, next, was examined, but not in detail, none of the McKays being particularly bookish, and the party moved on to the drawing room. They stopped to open the French windows into the enclosed courtyard to enjoy the music of water on the stones. It was quite lovely out there, they agreed, but chilly, and quickly they re-entered the warmth of the room.

Ellie managed to get herself next to Rob. 'Well,' she said, 'Did you meet up with Caro?'

Rob gave her a knowing smile. 'Oh yes,' he lied.

Ellie felt her heart dip. 'You're not serious about going out with her are you?'

'That's for me to know and you to find out. Anyway, why shouldn't I?'

'She's *my* friend.'

'Really?'

'What do you mean? What has she said?' Rob gave his sister a sardonic smile in place of an answer, and moved away from her. Ellie gave an inner sigh. It sounded as though Caro was already saying things she shouldn't. It was becoming more imperative than ever that she get to speak to her somehow.

'What's the matter, Ellie?' Tansy moved next to her.

Ellie rolled her eyes. 'Rob. He's such an idiot. You should've heard what he said to Rachel at supper. And now he's…..I can't tell you, but he's going to make get me into such trouble.'

'Oh. Dear. Where *is* Rachel, by the way?'

'I don't know. I think she stayed in that big room with Grandma. Tansy, can I borrow your mobile?'

'Of course. Only I don't think there's a signal. Who do you need to 'phone?'

'A friend of mine. Oh God. I don't know what I'm going to do.'

'Poor Ellie. Isn't there an ordinary 'phone?'

Ellie brightened. 'I suppose there is. I wonder where it is.'

'I'll help you find it. I'm sorry that Rachel didn't come. I hope she didn't feel left out.'

'D'you think she might? It hadn't occurred to me.'

The study displayed every sign of being out of bounds. The lights were off and the furniture was disordered, presenting obstacles to be negotiated, which, along with the treacherous tendrils of wires

123

stretching from the computer to the plug and telephone sockets, effectively debarred entry. In case anyone should misconstrue their implicit message, the computer screen-saver exclaimed 'Fuck Off!' in dripping, blood-red letters.

'Rob! Really!' hissed Belinda. She turned to Elliot. 'Shall we move on?'

The dining room, even with its splendid table and shining candelabra, seemed to leave everyone cold; only Belinda felt a thrill of excitement at the possibility of covering the gleaming space with porcelain and cut glass and silverware, of producing dish after dish of fish and meat and vegetables and sauces, of filling the air with the delicate chime of knives and forks on plates and the hum of conversation, the squeak-pop of corks being drawn from vintage wines and the comfortable crackle of logs in the grate.

'I'd hoped we'd eat in here in future, in the evenings,' she ventured.

'Really? Isn't it a bit far from the kitchen?' June objected.

'There's a clever little door hidden in the panelling here, look. I suppose that's how the servants got in and out. It brings you out just before the kitchen.'

'But we haven't got servants, Belinda, dear,' Heather reminded her sister. 'It just isn't a concept that belongs in our modern world.' Mitch shifted his bucket from one hand to the other.

'On the contrary,' Miriam interjected, 'it is a concept that is very much alive and well, I'm afraid. Wherever there is wealth you will find….'

'I know, I know,' Heather interrupted, quickly; 'I meant that it *ought not* to belong.'

'I think we might find it impractical to eat in here every night, Belinda.' Elliot turned to his wife, 'nice as the idea might be. The general feeling seems to be that it will mean a lot of extra work.'

'But for the Big Night, of course, this will be wonderful,' Simon tried to soften the blow. 'Imagine the table beautifully set, the fire, candle light, and all of us all dressed in our best, champagne flowing...'

'Oh yes, thank you, Simon, that's just how I see it too.' Belinda couldn't help turning a baleful look towards her husband, who had so entirely failed to capture her vision. Elliot laughed;

'Stone cold food, yelling down the table and a week's worth of washing up, that's how I see it!' he sneered, pouring cold water on the spark of empathy that had leapt between Belinda and Simon.

They filed out of the dining room and re-crossed the hall. Simultaneously, Ellie and Tansy spied the old-fashioned grey telephone sitting on a side-table. They exchanged gleeful smiles. Somehow, without knowing anything about the nature of the crisis, Tansy felt involved in it. Casually, she lifted the receiver, and listened for a dialling tone. It purred at her, and she gave Ellie a nod. They were back where they had begun. Surely, now, the tour would come to an end? It seemed that Bob and Mitch had some similar idea; desperate, by now, for a smoke, they cast longing glances at the front door. But as Elliot skipped and shimmied around the party, now in front, now at the rear, herding them towards the gallery, it was plain that escape was going to be impossible. 'This is great, isn't it, girls? What do you think of it so far, Bob? Alright there, Mitch? That bucket not too heavy?'

The family ambled along, stopping to admire the portraits as they did so; stern-faced, hook nosed men and pear-shaped, round-faced women.

'We should have a family portrait,' June said. Everybody noted, but nobody challenged, her interesting pronoun. 'This is a golden opportunity, while we're together. I'm wondering, Les, about that photographer we know, the one who does the Captains' portraits at the Golf Club. Could we get him, do you think?'

'To come here?' Les was incredulous. 'To come all the way here, at short notice? Is that what you mean?'

'Yes, Les, thank you. That's exactly what I mean.' June looked around, searching for an ally in scorn. 'Anyone would think that I had suggested he visit the moon! Ha Ha Ha!'

'Mitch is good with a camera. He could take a few shots,' Bob volunteered.

'Really?' June looked doubtfully at Mitch. She had not deigned to notice him before now; he was bracketed, in her mind, in that class of person who she made a habit of not noticing; her charwoman, waiters, and the girl at the salon who pared her corns.

'Yes, really, Aunty June,' Heather didn't like June's withering appraisal. 'He's very good; actually, he took some publicity shots for us recently.'

'I see,' said June, giving Mitch a vinegary stare, 'Well, it was just an idea.'

'Come along, everybody,' Elliot chivvied them along the gallery. 'At this rate it'll take us a week to see over the place.'

Tansy and Ellie found themselves at the front of the group as they entered the games room. Rachel and Starlight were seated on the floor underneath the snooker table. Rachel had lifted up two of the rugs from the floor and draped them over the table to make a tent, and now the two of them were in residence, along with numerous dolls, a toy kitchen and two sit-and-ride vehicles. Mary remained on the settee. Her crocheting had fallen into her lap and her chin had fallen forwards onto an area of mottled chest revealed by the vee of her blouse. She was snoring, gently.

Rachel and Starlight simultaneously put their forefingers to their mouths. 'Shhhhhhh!'

'I've taught her to say it,' Rachel announced, proudly, in a loud whisper. 'She did a poo and I helped change her nappy.'

'Clever girl!' said Heather. No one was sure who she meant.

'Shhhhh!' said Starlight.

Tansy dropped to her hands and knees and crawled into the tent.

'Rachel!' she exclaimed. 'Here you are!' Rachel glowed. Perhaps she had been left behind by mistake.

'Shhhhh!' said Starlight, solemnly.

Ellie took Heather's arm. 'Didn't you always hate your brother?' she said, darkly.

'Simon? Oh no. I always loved him! Don't you love Rob?'

'No,' replied Ellie, decidedly, 'I loathe and detest him.'

'Do you? How strange. Why?' But Ellie had no time to reply before Bob sauntered over to suggest to Heather that they ought to think about putting Starlight to bed. The reluctance in his voice and the look which crossed Heather's face suggested that this was an ordeal which neither of them was looking forward to.

Elliot's tour continued relentlessly. The party trailed round the house after him; up the stairs, looking into every room and closet, and on up into the attics. En route, Belinda allocated rooms to those who had arrived late; a beautiful yellow room, with a bright and careless smile, to Simon and Miriam, the large room in the south wing to Bob and Heather and Starlight, ('On the whole, I thought you'd prefer it,' she recited, wearily); a pleasant but smallish double bedded room without en suite facilities to June and Les, and what was surmised to have been the housekeeper's suite to Mitch; a cosy single bedded room with private facilities and an adjacent sitting room located alone at the far end of a corridor next to the linen room. Surreptitiously, people fell away until only Elliot, Belinda, Les and June remained, finding themselves in a small, obscure and utterly uninteresting annex to the boiler room.

'Excellent. This will be the boot room,' pronounced Elliot, dusting his hands together as though he had just completed a job of work. He unbolted a thick wooden door in the corner, and opened it, poking his head outside to get his bearings. 'Yes, just as I thought. Brings you out in that little courtyard at the back, behind the kitchen. Ideal spot to take your muddy boots off, see? In America, they'd call this the Muck Room. Except there'd be a shower. So that's that. It's too late to do outside, now, I suppose.'

'I'll make some tea,' offered Belinda, 'if anyone would like a cup?'

'Yes, please,' said Les.

'I'll have a brandy,' said Elliot.

'So will I,' June gushed, 'and I wonder if I might use the telephone? I ought to call Sandra.'

Belinda found Heather in the kitchen, making up bottles of formula. Heather had had a shower and changed her clothes; the multi-coloured, multi-layered ethnic-type garment she now wore defied positive definition. It could, Belinda considered, be as suitable for bed as for an opera.

'Is the tour over?' Heather asked, a scoop of milk powder hovering over the tin, 'I heard you in the laundry room but managed to creep by without getting sucked in. Elliot's *so* officious. You have the patience of a saint with him.'

Belinda made a face, but changed the subject: 'Is Starlight still taking a bottle? She seems a bit big.'

'The truth is,' said Heather, concentrating on levelling the powder in the scoop, 'and what, amongst other things, seems to have escaped everyone's notice about our remarkable and spirit-filled little daughter, we aren't sure exactly how old she is. Her age, along with her provenance and cultural influences, remains a mystery.'

'But you must know how old she is, from her teeth, or something.'

'She isn't a horse!' Heather retorted, but went on: 'She could be between fourteen and eighteen months, but with her history, her background, there's no knowing how she might have been held back.'

'I'm not sure I know how it all came about, really. I know it all happened quite quickly.' Belinda placed several mugs on a tray. She was making a large pot of tea, sure that she would find other takers when she carried the tray through.

'It was through Bob's trip to Africa prior to the Famine Fund concert. The hopelessness and deprivation out there you would not believe, Belinda. Villages without a clean water supply, school buildings made of mud and corrugated iron, poverty so abject that all young girls are at risk from the traffickers in human flesh.....' Heather trailed off while she gave the bottles a vigorous shake.

129

'You saw it yourself?'

Heather shook her head. A tendril of damp hair released itself from the cluster at the back of her head and adhered attractively to Heather's cheek. 'No. I stayed at the Cape on a wildebeest ranch owned by a friend of ours. But Bob came back quite shaken by it all.'

'And so he came across her in one of the villages?'

'He came to hear about her while he was there, yes. She's our little refugee, our own little wayfarer, a traveller out of the desert. It's like she's been on a spiritual journey, searching for her home, and has washed up on our beach, the very thing of all others we had needed and desired. She has issued from the very womb of mother nature herself.'

Belinda gave a slightly mocking laugh. 'You do wax lyrical, Heather!'

Heather placed the bottles into the door of the fridge. 'Only someone who takes their ability to produce children for granted could possibly say that, Belinda, if you don't mind my saying so.'

'I don't take my children for granted, Heather!' Belinda turned from the teapot, which she had been stirring.

'I didn't say that you did. But, now we're on the subject, you don't seem to take much notice of them.'

Belinda turned back to the tea. She admitted, bleakly: 'they don't respond well to close scrutiny. They don't like it when I try to take an interest in them. I get accused of being nosey.'

'Rob was very rude at dinner.'

'Yes. I know. Poor Rachel.'

'And he's managed to upset Ellie, too.'

'Has he? Again? I'm sure he doesn't mean to. It's a difficult age. How do you know?'

'I'm very intuitive. My spirit is in tune with peoples' energy forces. Rob's and Ellie's are very troubled.'

Belinda placed the tea pot on the tray and picked it up. She had had enough of this nonsense. 'Would you bring that bottle of brandy and those glasses through, please Heather? If Elliot doesn't get his brandy soon there'll be more troubled energy than any of us can cope with!'

'You're right of course. Elliot's chakras are in turmoil,' said Heather, but Belinda was out of earshot.

Bob and Mitch sauntered around the gravel drive. It was unspeakable bliss to be out in the cool air, away from the chatter, and to be able to smoke, which they did, voraciously. The night was densely black. No light emanated from the windows at the front of the house apart from the unnatural glow from the computer screen in the study. A single lantern hung above the front door but its light seemed too feeble to illuminate anything other than the two steps and the portico below it. The red glow from their cigarettes and the blinking security lights from inside the cars seemed like malevolent eyes winking and waiting under the cover of blackness. On the lawn, the rustle of leaves and the occasional bored snuffle and grunt indicated that Tiny was taking his evening constitutional, but his ghostly grey form was lost in the darkness. He barked, once, at a shadow.

'Quiet, lad!' said Mitch.

The house, in the dimness, brooded like a sleeping dragon in the night. Above, a sky peppered with innumerable stars defied human comprehension. No wind disturbed the trees along the drive and the only sound was the measured tread of the two men as they paced in the darkness, the occasional scream of an owl, hunting in the woods behind the house, and the sound of Starlight's gentle snores which emanated from the baby monitor clipped securely to Mitch's waistband. The air, so cold it seared the insides of their nostrils, tasted deliciously of frost and wood smoke and Marlboro County. Their companionable and untroubled silence spread around them like a contented yawn. Minutes passed.

Mitch dropped his cigarette butt into his hand and flicked away the lighted end with his thumb. He immediately reached into his right back jeans pocket for another. 'Nice spot,' he commented. The wagging of the glowing cigarette tip a yard away from him denoted Bob's agreement.

'Room alright?' Bob asked, presently.

'Fine, thanks.'

'I hope so,' Bob said. 'You might need somewhere.....' His uncompleted sentence articulated all the awkwardness inherent in the difficult family gathering, and acknowledged that for Mitch, not even nominally related, a safe haven might be necessary.

It was true that family association was an unexplored territory for Mitch. He hadn't a single blood relative that he knew of. Family had always been the kind of thing that other people had, like cancer. Everyone he had trusted - foster-parents, social-workers - had come and gone, and he had developed a species of fierce self-sufficiency as a defence against disappointment. Even in the face of Bob and Heather's child-like ingenuousness, he *still* kept a part of himself aloof, at a safe distance, a characteristic that Bob, perhaps subconsciously, recognised now. 'No reason why *you* should put up with all this crap,' he said, glumly.

They had been, from the start, touchingly open with Mitch, hiding nothing of their weird, whimsical lives while asking nothing about his buffeted, dysfunctional past. He, like a one-way valve, had assimilated them, a watchful, impassive sentinel, an alien come to earth. Heather, he had thought, at first, was an odd-ball, full of daydreams and peculiar enthusiasms, girlish and a bit spoilt, and indeed she could be selfish at times but it was the selfishness of a child; an unconscious, almost natural self-absorption. It had gradually awoken in Mitch a protective, avuncular instinct; she must be *indulged*. Bob had awed him at first, of course; the great man, spangled and wild-haired star of the seventies pop group, now a successful Producer and songwriter with his own company; famous for his altruistic embrace of charitable causes. People thought it a stunt – Mitch, indeed, had cynically anticipated it to be no more than a veneer - but now he knew better. He had seen for himself, earlier in the year, Bob cross-legged on the concrete floor of a bush clinic, cradling a tiny baby while its life ebbed away. There had been no cameras, no journalists; his anguish had been real. They had hidden nothing from him but

133

Mitch, in an instinct of self-preservation, had retained a degree of distance, an emotional obduracy, which they, in their turn, respected.

'Well, I might be glad of it,' Mitch concurred now, thinking of the room, but in fact he didn't think so. He was already picking up on the tension amongst the family; the moody boy, the inebriated, snappish sister, the bumptious, weasel-faced brother-in-law, the interloping aunt. To his own surprise he was finding it all quite entertaining, like watching a play on a stage, and from the silent, watchful space he had created for himself he rather looked forward to seeing the drama play itself out. It couldn't touch him, of course, and he wouldn't let it touch Bob or Heather either, or the child, but it interested him. And anyway, it wasn't all bad. There was the pleasant, motherly woman who had cooked the dinner, and the amiable outsized man, and the girl, Ellie.

Yes, there was the girl.

The front door opened and closed, and James strode across the gravel towards them, his features and even huge form being quickly absorbed by the black night.

'Evening, Gents.' James distributed brandy balloons amongst them.

'Ah!' they all sighed, appreciatively, the vapour from the spirit mingling with the chill air to bring water to the eyes. Mitch wiped his eyes with his sleeves, James with his handkerchief which glowed faintly like disembodied miasma. Bob allowed the tears to gather on his lower lashes and then to meander down his life-worn cheek. When the brandy was gone James reached into his capacious pocket and produced the bottle, topping them all up again.

For the first time since they had arrived James felt as though he wasn't in the way, and nothing was expected of him or was being left to him. It was such a relief to be out in the dark, in the quiet, where conversation was superfluous. He liked Bob; he was easy and comfortable, with an utter absence of ego. The sky above them was a riot of stars, yawning away like a dome, and the enormous trees reaching up to them, and the wide landscape of the park which he had briefly explored with Ben earlier all seemed to be the right fit for him. There were not many places where a man like him could stretch his arms wide and not knock into something or someone.

'Nice out here' he said, eventually, summing up eloquently the absence of the chattering women, and the pompous, effusive Elliot, and June's hyena-like laugh, and even the high-pitched noise of the children, much as he loved them.

'Yeah,' Bob and Mitch agreed. Tiny threw himself down on the gravel at their feet with a contented sigh.

Silence reigned between them. They sipped their brandies, and smoked, and gazed at the stars, and took deep draughts of the air. Then, above them, a bedroom light snapped on, sending a shaft of yellow light out into the darkness and bathing them uncomfortably in its glow, like a spot light. By common but unspoken consent, they moved out of its pool, so that when a figure came to the window and looked out, and then opened the window, nothing could be seen except the empty drive and the row of motorcars parked neatly on the sweep. But, in the stillness of the night, the three men couldn't help over hearing the conversation which ensued.

Inside the room, June was busy unpacking her suitcase.

'Really, I'm not tired at all, Les. I don't know why you should be so insistent about us going to bed so early.'

Les, by the window, drew his pullover over his head. When he emerged, his thin, iron-grey hair was mussed and untidy. 'We needed to leave the family alone for a bit, June. We're intruders.'

'We are *not* intruders, Les, and I won't have you say so. They're *my* flesh and blood, remember. And we've been invited.' June opened the wardrobe and began to hang up a number of skirts and several

135

blouses and jackets. 'I don't know where you're going to put your things,' she lamented. 'There's hardly room in here for mine. I don't know why Belinda gave us this inconvenient room. There were better ones, after all.'

'She doesn't want us to stay! That's why. *She* didn't invite us, poor girl. She didn't know where to put herself.' Les bent down to remove his shoes. 'Anyway,' he said, tucking them neatly under a chair, 'I didn't bring many clothes, so it won't matter.'

'I should think she *was* embarrassed! What a social gaffe! She *ought* to have invited us from the beginning, and she knows it.' June was unpacking her toilet bag; jars of cream and tubes of make-up, eye-shadows and lipsticks and pencils, brushes and heated rollers; the dressing table was soon covered.

'Nonsense.' Les placed his razor, comb and toothbrush on the bedside table. 'This was always going to be a family do.'

'I keep telling you, Les, I *am* family.' June insisted. 'This house is quite big enough for all of us; it was sheer selfishness to exclude us. When I think of our Sandra, and Mother.........'

'June! What do you mean?' Les, half in and half out of his trousers, smelled a rat, 'what has it got to do with them?'

'Never you mind, Les. I know what's due to family even if she doesn't, that's all. That girl needs teaching how to carry on and there's no point expecting Mary to do it. She never had an idea of what was right when it came to entertaining. Mary's idea of a buffet is a plate of sausage rolls and corned beef sandwiches, and if she'd ever had a dinner party, which I don't think she ever had, she'd have served up meat and potato pie, like as not.'

'There was nothing wrong with that dinner tonight, and anyway, I like meat and potato pie,' said Les.

'Exactly!' crowed June, making him feel, uncomfortably, that he had unwittingly proved her point.

The three men on the gravel sweep avoided each other's eyes. When Bob swallowed a mouthful of brandy, the noisy closing of his throat made them all gulp to hold back their laughter.

Up in their bedroom, Les sat on the bed and unbuttoned his shirt slowly.

'We'll be going home tomorrow. I don't know why you're bothering to unpack.'

'We certainly will *not* be going home, Leslie.' June set her mouth in a hard line.

Les stood up and mustered what authority he could; in his socks and underpants, however, it didn't amount to much. 'We *can't* stay, June, you must see. They haven't catered for us. They all brought boxes of groceries; we didn't bring anything. They've had this place booked for months and we haven't been incorporated into any of their plans. We haven't paid. We can't stay if we haven't paid our way. We're not wanted, June.'

'*You* might not be wanted, and who can blame them? You never have anything to say for yourself, you're a social liability, Les. Go home if you like, I don't care, but I won't be coming with you. Now for God's sake, put your pyjamas on. You look like an oven-ready chicken standing there like that.'

Les put his pyjamas on and got into bed. The sheets were good quality and crisply laundered, but cold. 'You *can't* mean to stay all week?'

'Certainly I do.'

Les sighed his defeat. The hard-shelled insensitivity of his wife staggered him. June, sitting at the dressing table, had applied fresh lipstick and was tweaking her hair.

'Aren't you coming to bed?' he asked, quietly.

'No. I told you, I'm not tired. I'm going back downstairs to join in the fun.'

The three eaves-droppers heard the bedroom door close and soon afterwards the window was slid shut and the curtains closed. Then the light was extinguished and they were swamped once more in impenetrable darkness. Unconsciously, they had been holding their breath, but now they breathed out and gave each other mischievous looks, discernible only by the enlarged glow from the whites of their eyes. Mitch lit another cigarette, James replenished the brandy glasses. The rattle of the bottle on the rims of the glasses was the only audible sign of his laughter. Then they all began to shake. Suddenly the tension created by the journey and arrival, and the meal, and the baby, and the overbearing behaviour of Elliot, and the over-wrought anxiety of the women, and the over-excitement of the children evaporated into the night air, fuelled by the embarrassment of their shared conspiracy and the heady ambience of the wide, wide night, and the brandy. Doubled up, they shuffled quickly away from the building and onto the lawn. Tiny hauled himself to his feet and ambled after them. Arriving blindly at the fountain, they perched on the cold stone of its parapet and hooted to the skies.

In a remote corner of his conscience, James felt sorry for Les; he knew how it felt to be out-manoeuvred by a McKay. But it seemed to him that the family was like a jig-saw which had been pulled apart and stored in a box in a damp place for too long. The pieces had warped and buckled, and on reassembly had failed to key into each other in a comfortable fit. The genetic chain which linked them together had become all but obliterated by life's experiences and by their choices. And yet just here and now, the three of them had made what seemed like a connection which went far beyond the fleshly. These three, linked however remotely to the main family puzzle, had achieved something more intimate than chromosomes alone could create.

Tansy, Rachel and Ellie had changed into their nightwear. Ellie and Tansy had picked beds adjacent to each other and Rachel gratefully accepted the third, furthest away from the bathroom, it was true, but she put that thought out of her head in her pleasure that they had chosen to share. She hastily re-stuffed her clothes away in the small chest of drawers but left the soft toys in obscurity behind the curtains.

Tansy, used to dormitory living, had stripped off her clothes without hesitation, only turning her back to the others to remove her bra and shrug into her pyjama top. Her pyjamas were thick brushed cotton, yellow, warm and attractively cute, bearing pictures of puppies and kittens gambolling together in assorted poses. They came with a matching dressing gown which she laid carefully over the wrought iron foot of the bed. Ellie's pyjamas were expensive, sophisticated; velour, baggy-legged and strappy-topped, in lilac and pink. Passing on her way to the bathroom, Rachel despaired at the over-washed and shapeless cotton-jersey pyjamas she clutched under her arm, knowing full well that the legs were too short, the sleeves frayed and that her stomach would prevent the top and bottoms from meeting properly. She hoisted herself up onto the toilet seat in order to see in the small mirror the enormity of her grossness, taking the roll of her midriff in her hands and trying to fold it inwards, and wondering whether it would hurt beyond her ability to endure if she was to cut it off with a sharp knife. Rebelliously, at the thought, her stomach gave an inward lurch of hunger, and Rachel sat heavily on the toilet seat to delay the awful moment of her emergence. In the bedroom, she could hear the other girls as they nattered brightly. Once again, in spite of the shared room, she felt hopelessly alien.

Tansy had chosen one of Ellie's CD's and a velvety voice crooned softly in the room. 'How late can you phone your friend?' Tansy asked, folding her clothes up carefully and shaking open a white scented laundry bag for her discarded underwear.

'Oh, anytime. She has her mobile on all the time.'

'So if we go down soon, and check out the hall, you could do it?'

'Yes.'

Tansy sat on the bed next to Ellie. 'I wish you could tell me what the problem is. Is it very bad?' Despite the three year age gap between them, Tansy felt herself slipping into the role of older and wiser cousin; it was something about Ellie's air of vulnerability which made it natural, along with Tansy's adoption of a motherly role towards her brothers after April's death.

'Rob's the problem. He's pretending to fancy Caro, that's my friend. She knows things about me, that is, she *thinks* she knows things that I just don't want him to find out.'

'Surely, if she's your friend....?'

'You'd think so, wouldn't you? But I just can't be sure of her.' Ellie found herself relieved to confide in Tansy, who couldn't possibly understand the complexity of the situation or the potential gravity of it, but seemed, at least, to care.

'We could get some things together for a sort of midnight feast. Make hot chocolate, maybe? It'd be fun and...a good excuse for going downstairs.'

'Yes, alright. Shall we go now?'

'We ought to wait for Rachel.'

'Oh. Yes. I suppose so. She's taking a long time, though.'

Tansy dropped her voice to a whisper. 'Poor thing. Such horrible clothes. Did you notice?' Ellie nodded. 'I'll give her a knock. Rachel? Rachel, are you alright?'

'Oh, yes,' Rachel replied, jumping up and pulling the toilet chain. 'Just coming.' She splashed water noisily in the basin to denote the washing of hands and then, with a deep breath, unlocked the bathroom door. 'You'll never guess what Mum has done!' she cried, as though the whole thing was a hilarious joke. 'She's only packed my old pyjamas! I don't think I've worn these for years!' Tansy threw Ellie a look. Neither of them was fooled for a moment.

'What is she like?' Tansy said, quickly. 'I expect it's because she works full time. Things are bound to be a bit disorganised.' Tansy knew that her remark sounded hollow; Miriam worked full time but their lives were organised to the nth degree.

'It's nice and warm in this room. I don't think you'll be chilly,' Ellie offered.

'No, I don't suppose so.' Rachel made towards her bed. The sooner she could hide under the sheets, the happier she would be.

'We thought we'd go and make some hot chocolate,' Tansy said. 'Are you coming?'

'Oh.' Rachel hovered, half in and half out of bed. 'Isn't that very…' she stopped herself from saying 'fattening' and instead said, 'I mean, do you think we ought to check that there's enough milk?' At home, milky drinks or bowls of cereal were never allowed at night. Ruth insisted that what Daddy called 'the sacrosanct pint' be kept intact for the morning.

'Oh, I suppose so. I hadn't thought. I've been longing for some hot chocolate since the moment I arrived,' Ellie said.

'It'll be fine. I'm going to put my hoody on over my pyjamas. Rachel, do you want to wear my dressing gown?'

'Oh, yes, thank you.' Rachel beamed her gratitude as she put it on. The material wrapped all the way round her and fell down to her feet, hiding her half-mast pyjamas and her exposed belly. 'You *are* kind, Tansy.'

The three of them made their way along the attic corridor. The door with Rob's name on it stood open. The light from the landing showed his bag, unpacked, upon his bed, but no further sign of occupation. Ellie toyed with the idea of slipping back upstairs and

141

having a rummage through his things; maybe if she could find something to hold over *him*..... but she hated herself for the thought, and in any case, illicit telephone calls were enough to be dealing with, for now. Further along the corridor, noises from behind a closed door indicated that Ben and Todd were heavily involved in some game. Ben was shouting at the top of his voice, a narrative of blood-curdling deeds involving a variety of sharp weapons and an unfortunate victim.

'And then he stuck the sword in him, like *this*, and he twisted it round in his guts, like *that*, and he took his axe out and he chopped off his arms, chop chop, like that.'

'Like *that*,' echoed Todd.

'Ahhh!' sighed Tansy, 'Bless!'

The cacophony of a highly mechanised war emanated from the study. Rob's forces were massed in a wood and were hurling mortars and ballistic missiles across an improbably green sward of grass onto the enemy troops, who cried out in authentic agony. Toby looked on, aching for a turn, but unwilling to ask again since his previous request had been less than graciously received. In fact, Rob's 'Oh, fuck off, will you?' suggested forcefully that the chances of using the computer were seriously small.

Tansy put her head round the door.

'Hello you two,' she said, brightly, 'Midnight feast?'

'Yeah!' Toby yelled, cheering up. Rob snorted derisively. Toby jumped up from his chair and made for the door. Unfortunately he caught his foot in one of the trailing wires and the screen went ominously black.

'For fuck's sake,' Rob snarled.

'I'm sorry, Rob.' Toby blanched. 'I didn't see the cable.'

'Level twenty-three!' Rob was incandescent with fury.

'Oh dear, really, I'm so....'

'Sorry. Yeah.'

Toby felt the uncomfortable prickle of tears behind his eyes. Tansy gave him a sympathetic smile. 'Perhaps it's a bad idea to have the lights off,' she suggested. 'Never mind. Come to the kitchen. We've found cake and biscuits and everything.' Rob sighed. He had tried being objectionable, to the point of downright rudeness. It seemed that everyone was determined to ignore his attempts to offend them. Their politeness was a whitewash designed to obliterate every disagreeable thing. Family feeling must, he thought, with a passing queasiness, be stronger than ordinary good manners if it could overcome such offensiveness. In truth, he hadn't wanted to make Toby cry, and in the face of this and Tansy's sweet reasonableness it was hard to maintain his anger and even his eagerness to cause trouble. She was so like his Aunty April, whom he had liked so much. To be truthful, for the past half hour he had been playing the game without enjoying it, but had been unable to think of any way of finishing the game without offering Toby a go, and he had wished to avoid at all costs any gesture which might be misinterpreted as an attempt to establish friendly relations. Obviously he was going to have to find a way to penetrate this veneer of kindred unity before he could blow the whole thing sky high.

'Oh come on' he said, at last. 'Let's go and see what they've found.'

Out in the hall, Ellie was fussing with her hair in front of a mirror.

'Hello, Rob,' she said over her shoulder as he and the others passed by.

Rob grunted and turned to Tansy. 'Did you say cake?'

'Cake!' Ben and Todd, at the top of the stairs, tousled from play, took up the cry. They rushed pell-mell down the stairs in a blur of eager appetite.

'Oooh yes,' Tansy gushed, 'chocolate. I think Aunty Belinda brought it.'

'It'll be homemade, then,' Ben enthused. 'Mum never bakes and I don't suppose Miriam will have done.'

'Very unlikely. Aren't you supposed to be in bed boys?' Tansy held the door open while they all trooped through.

'Nah!' Todd was dismissive.

'It might be Grandma's cake,' said Toby. 'Listen, Rob, I am sorry about the game.'

'Yeah yeah.'

Their voices faded as the baize door closed behind them. Ellie lifted the receiver of the telephone and dialled the familiar number.

Elliot was holding forth expansively on the subject of McKay's Haulage. Simon continued to nod and smile but in fact his attention had long since drifted away from the subject. Elliot was rather drunk; his words were slurred and he kept repeating himself, and asking convoluted rhetorical questions. His eyes had lost their focus and Simon knew that he could safely pursue his own train of thought. In any case, he had heard enough about haulage to last a whole lifetime. He looked down at Miriam, snuggled into his side. She had gone to sleep. She was immaculate, her elfin face without line or blemish. She was as utterly unlike April as it was possible to imagine; worldly, sophisticated, tough-skinned, ambitious, resilient. It was this last quality which Simon loved most about her. April had been so delicate; it had seemed miraculous that she could bear even one, let alone three children. And she'd been good; nobody would choose such an adjective to describe Miriam, who was ruthlessly bad in a determined childish way, completely selfish and as sharp as glass, she would defend herself to the death. Consequently, he could trust her not to be taken from him, not to be diminished in front of his eyes, not to shrink and withdraw and to finally vanish. Miriam would not leave him on his own.

Across the room, Heather and Belinda were maintaining a desultory conversation, but Belinda looked exhausted and must soon make her excuses and take herself off to bed. Elliot continued to ramble on and on; schedules and fuel tariffs and weighting and palletage. June, who had reappeared freshly made up after being escorted to bed by her husband, gushed and laughed and agreed with every imperfectly articulated remark.

In her absence, they had discussed briefly her unexpected presence here on their holiday. Belinda had been both irritated and offended by June's insistent self-inclusion. Miriam had suggested with that wicked and provocative humour which both amused and nettled Simon, that they simply throw June and Les out, bag and baggage, first

145

thing in the morning. Heather, typically, had advocated a graceful if reluctant acceptance of the immutable forces of 'what must be'. Elliot had scowled at them all and retorted haughtily that he believed, as host, it was his privilege to extend invitations to whomsoever he pleased, and since it had pleased him to invite June and Les he would appreciate it if they could be courteously included in all arrangements. Then he had noticed that James had taken away the brandy bottle and sent Belinda off in search of a replacement.

'I expect James took the brandy outside to Bob and Mitch,' Simon had said, regretting that he had not had the idea himself; it would have made an ideal excuse to escape.

'Bloody cheek!' Elliot had blustered. 'If you want to talk about interlopers, what about *him*?'

'You don't mean James, surely?'

'No, not Jim. Mitch. Who the hell is he?'

'He goes everywhere with us,' Heather had said, witheringly, 'you should know that.'

Elliot took a deep breath. He didn't like being put down, especially by Heather, who was as pathetic and nonsensical as it was possible for a person to be without being weak in the head, but the appearance of Belinda at that moment with a bottle of VSOP and the return just afterwards of June, had cheered him.

'….and so we'll be finding a Montessori trained Nanny for her as soon as we get back.' Heather finished.

'Montessori? Really?' Belinda struggled to maintain her attention.

'Yes. It's all very much about self-awareness, learning through discovery, a multi-sensory approach to everything.'

'How interesting. D' you know, Heather, I think I might go to bed. It feels very late.' Belinda unfolded her legs from where they were tucked up underneath her. One knee cracked and she winced. 'Oooh. That joint's stiff.'

'You should see an osteopath. Or take up Pilates.'

'I expect you're right, but it's so difficult to find time for things like that. I'll take these cups through to the kitchen and then go up, I think.' Belinda looked across the room at her husband and gave a little sigh. His head had drooped to one side and he was almost asleep. Only the narrowest line of whiteness between his upper and lower eyelids suggested that a fragment of consciousness remained, and she knew him too well to believe him beyond awareness. By marching everyone around the house, and monopolising the conversation, and drinking too much brandy, he had soured the evening for her. His behaviour had been outrageous and it was not surprising that the other men and all the children had escaped somewhere. She disliked it intensely when he drank too much; alcohol unmanned him and although there were times, many times, when a gentler, more sensitive side to him would have been welcome, drunkenness did not summon it up. Also, she thought it a very bad example to Rob who had arrived home on more than one occasion recently the worse for drink. She noticed that June, who had been speaking brightly to Elliot for a few moments, had realised that she had lost his attention. Her speech faltered as she came to the realisation that nobody at all was listening to her and she brought her sentence to a close with her customary laugh. 'Ha ha ha! Oh dear! I've bored Elliot to sleep!' she said, good naturedly, in the circumstances. 'Did you say you were going through to the kitchen, Belinda? I'll give you a hand, if you like.'

The two women began to gather up the cups and glasses. Miriam stirred in her sleep and then stretched, like a cat. Simon took the opportunity afforded by her movement to slip his arm underneath her knees. He lifted her easily up into his arms. Heather opened the door for him. Passing through, he kissed her lightly on the forehead.

'Night night, Heather. Night night, Belinda,' he said, in their old-fashioned family way, before disappearing down the passageway towards the hall. June and Belinda followed, bearing trays.

'What shall we do with Elliot?' Heather called after them, her hand on the light switch.

'Just leave him,' Belinda said, over her shoulder.

'I'm not asleep,' said Elliot.

'Of course not,' Heather replied, closing the door softly.

The kitchen was in chaos. Belinda could have wept at the state of it. There were two pans in the sink, showing grim evidence of badly burned milk. No-one had thought even to fill them with warm water. The breakfast table, which she had carefully set earlier, was devastated. Spoons and knives and plates had been pushed around. Some of the plates had been used for cake and not washed or even put in the sink. The cake tin containing the chocolate cake she thought she had hidden was open on the table. Almost half the cake had been eaten and the remainder was looking dry and crusty instead of moist and fresh. Two packets of biscuits had also been opened. Crumbs were everywhere. The worktop was awash with milk and dusted with hot chocolate. A fresh 2 litre bottle of milk had been left out of the fridge without its top on. Toast had been made; the bread packet was also open to the air as well as jar of peanut butter and another of marmite. Buttery knives had been abandoned by the toaster.

'Oh dear,' laughed June. 'What a mess.'

'It wasn't a mess an hour ago,' Belinda snapped, defensively. 'I'd never leave a kitchen in this state.'

'No? Well, I suppose it must have been the children, then.'

'I suppose so. Little monkeys.'

'This cake looks quite nice. When did you cut it? I wasn't offered any.'

'Actually it was for Ellie's birthday on Sunday. I was saving it. But never mind. Do have a piece now, if you'd like one.'

'Thank you, I will. But I'll take it up with me. I'm dead on my feet.'

'Yes,' Belinda said, through gritted teeth. 'You must have had a very tiring day. You go on up, June. Goodnight.'

Alone, Belinda filled the sink with hot soapy water and began to scrub at the pans. Her legs ached and there was a heaviness which had descended on her heart. She was tired beyond everything and longed for bed, but strict conditioning and a sense of personal responsibility forbade her from leaving the kitchen anything but spotlessly clean. Somewhere beyond the fog of fatigue, she heard the men coming in from outside; they were comically inebriated, shushing each other like actors in a farce, bumping into each other and falling over things. The stumbling sounds of their progress up the stairs faded. Very distantly she heard the rush of water as toilets were flushed, then silence. Their good humour lifted her spirits momentarily, but the thought of Elliot dead drunk in the drawing room and the mess here in her particular domain dampened them almost at once. Here at last she had the family under one roof, after months of planning, everything had fallen into place. And yet in a way she just could not comprehend, something was out of step. The presence of Miriam instead of April was a little unsettling. Simon had been a closed book to them since April's death and must be accusing himself of inconstancy even while defying any of them to reproach him with it. Ruth wasn't herself; she hadn't forgiven Miriam for last Christmas and the weight of her resentment was making itself felt. The absence of the Dad they all remembered also required adjusting to. Of course all the children were older; they hadn't met up for a while and would need time to become comfortable with one another again. Starlight was very new and Heather and Bob as parents would inevitably be different too. Perhaps she was just expecting too much too soon. James was the only one she felt she could rely on. In his inimitable way he had already smoothed over a hundred little things; keeping the fires going, carrying luggage.

She turned from the sink and began to wipe the worktops. Her head was throbbing with a pain which bored into her skull through a point just above her right eyebrow and, seeking relief, she switched off the main lights, leaving only the glow from the light under the extractor hood to illuminate her work. Her whole body felt leaden, but she reset the table, put away the milk and bread, and replaced the jars in the cupboards. Then she emptied the bin. Last of all she would have to go through the downstairs rooms, checking that all the lights had been switched off, that the fires were safe and the front door locked. No one else would have thought to do it, she knew. But before she could summon up the last ounce of energy for this task, she lowered herself for a moment's respite into a comfortable armchair near the Aga. Its warmth was very soothing. In a moment, she was asleep. And in a moment more, she was dreaming. She was walking through the house to do the last few chores, but somebody had got there just before her. In the lounge, the cushions were plumped and straightened, the hearth swept. The curtains had been opened ready to admit the morning sun. The toys in the games room had been tidied away and the rug removed from the snooker table and replaced on the floor. Belinda walked slowly, in wonderment. She became aware of a presence which preceded her from room to room, anticipating her actions, performing them, just as she would have done them herself, with care and thoroughness. It was as though this was an 'other' self, inherently related to her, intimately connected. She could hear him, the soft fall of his feet across the rugs in the corridor, the gentle clink of glasses or cups which he had collected from tables, as they were clasped together in his hand, the rattle of the poker in the grate, spreading out the embers, the iron rasp of the bolts shot home across the front door. The faster she tried to move, the slower her limbs responded. Her own languor began to frustrate, and then to distress her. It seemed that he would always be unreachable, this soul-mate. Suddenly she realised that close, human connection was what she had craved from this week away all along; she was desperate for intimate relationship, hungry for it. Through the rooms, along the corridors, she pursued him, she could hear him just ahead of her; he was whistling. Belinda woke up with a start. The kitchen was in quasi darkness. Across the room, at last, she could see him. He had his back

151

to her, standing at the sink rinsing glasses with a studied quietness, so as not to wake her, whistling absent mindedly through his teeth. Before she could rationalise her actions, or differentiate between dream and reality, Belinda was out of her chair and across the room.

'At last!'

She put her hand on his arm and turned him towards her. He didn't speak but took in her distress and exhaustion in a glance. Suddenly she was crying. Carefully, he wiped his sudsy hands on the tea towel before taking her gently in his arms.

After all of the others had gone to bed, Rob smoked one of the cigarettes he had stolen from the packet he had found in the pocket of Bob's denim jacket. He didn't often smoke tobacco; he didn't like it much. The effect wasn't anywhere near as good as weed; it was hardly worth the bother. But the anger and resentment which lodged in his guts had to be released somehow. He had to do something bad, as a sign, even if token, of his resistance. Tomorrow, he thought, he would start on his campaign proper. He would sabotage the house, upset the family, infuriate his parents, distress his sister. The veiled hints from Caro that there was something shocking to be known about Ellie, plus the reaction of Ellie herself when he had implied that he had spoken to Caro, intrigued him. But the stupid bitch hadn't turned up in the chat room, and he had no signal on his mobile. A flash of inspiration caused him to switch user on the computer and enter Ellie's password. The quickest of searches in My Contacts revealed Caro's email address and Rob had soon sent her a message which he hoped would flatter her into telling all.

Rob was running a lucrative little business selling illegally copied music CDs which he downloaded from the internet and copied onto disks. He produced authentic-looking CD covers. He was busy persuading his father to buy a rewritable DVD drive on the pretext that he would need it to complete his media coursework, but it was really so that he could move into the movie market. Rob had a few orders to fill over half term and so he set the printer going on a number of CD covers. With Uncle Bob in the house, this had to be done clandestinely; as proud as he was of his enterprise, he was not such a fool as to think that he should broadcast it. As a genuine music producer, Bob was one of the unwitting victims of Rob's little scam. While the covers were printing, Rob toured the downstairs rooms of the house. He spent some time observing his father, lying on the settee in a foetal position with his hand thrust down his underpants. Rob despised him. He despised his mother for being with him; the idea of them in bed together was revolting. And yet he had happy

153

memories of his childhood when his mother had been the very centre of his universe, and the contradiction confused him.

When the covers were printed, he hid them in the back of his coursework folder, and made his way up to bed. He could hear the boys in their bedroom and the girls in theirs, and wondered briefly about joining them, but decided against it and went into the room with his name on it, slamming the door behind him.

Muriel McKay lived in a small terraced house in an inner suburb of the same town where she had been born and grown up. When she had bought it the area had been enjoying a renaissance of popularity; the houses were mostly in the throes of modernisation of some kind or another; skips and builders' vans furnished the pavements at regular intervals. Muriel's house remained immune from such intrusions, but was neat and clean and bright and warm. The street itself was situated adjacent to a rear entrance of the hospital, where Muriel had spent her entire working life tending to the medical records of the patients, a job she had started as a girl of fifteen.

She had worked for forty-five years doing the same job in the same office. For thirty three of those years she had lived alone with and latterly cared for her mother, an arrangement which had pleased neither of them especially. She had enjoyed a close relationship with her sister-in-law, Mary, at first, and had tried hard to be a favourite Aunty to the four children, relishing the invitations, when they came, for the occasional meal or christening or birthday celebration, and even, once, (because Robert was away and one of the children was recovering from a tonsillectomy) a weekend stay. But as the business had flourished, Mary and Robert had spent more of their leisure time with June, which meant that Muriel could not be included. In any case, Robert's rage, witnessed once, had frightened her. Invitations had become few and far between and she had lost any standing, real or imagined, in the hearts of the children. Her hopes of meeting a kind solid man and marrying him had faded. She had never known a grand passion or the painful bliss of childbirth; she had not travelled beyond Britain's shores. She was naive in the ways of the world, inexperienced, gauche and a little under-confident. Her life had been entirely divided between the hospital and the dark little house of her birth. Spring, summer, autumn and winter, the bus carried her backwards and forwards, only the clothes she wore changed, dictated by the changing weather outside and, just a little, by the altering fashions of the times. Externally she grew stout, her hair turned grey, her skin lost its tautness and rested in wrinkles around her eyes, internally her lively spirit shrivelled a little, but never aged, her girlish heart remained intact.

Life really began for Muriel when she was aged sixty. Robert and June had decided that Granny McKay, then eighty years of age, should enjoy her twilight years in The Oaks nursing home. Muriel had used her savings to buy a house close to the hospital. Ironically, two years after moving, the hospital trust had decided to computerise the records department and had taken the opportunity to offer Muriel early retirement.

The first time that Muriel opened her new front door to find Les on her doorstep, neither of them had been able to speak for a full minute. He had hovered, hesitating, on the step, his thinning hair blown around by a stiff breeze. It was late afternoon; Muriel had been preparing her evening meal, which she always ate rather early; a throwback from her days looking after her mother, who had kept early hours. She was wearing a flowery apron and had floury hands from the potato cake she was mixing. She held them up and out rather awkwardly, so that they didn't touch anything. The sight of him on her threshold was a shock; she felt cold and warm at the same time, and her mind half formed questions and offered unsatisfactory answers to account for it. He was as thin and wiry as she recalled him, not a tall man, but with disproportionately large hands, which he toyed with restlessly in a manner which had always been habitual with him. He was smartly dressed, in a shirt and tie and a Harris Tweed jacket. Later she was to discover that he had dressed carefully for his visit, had planned it and purposed it as soon as he had discovered her address. This was no impulse thing; he had waited, he said, thirty five years to undo the wrong he had done. Later, Muriel was to berate him gently for not giving her an opportunity to prepare herself too.

'I could have had my hair done,' she said.

But for those moments there were no words between them. She took him in with her eyes, noted how time had greyed his eyebrows and beetled them, veined his cheek and dulled the intensity of his eyes. His teeth had yellowed and his ear lobes had lengthened. He was no longer a vital young man, but a seasoned one, mellower; the scent of Old Spice had been superseded by Old Holborn. But the set of his jaw and his expression was identical, in spite of the years, to the way he had looked thirty-five years before, standing on another doorstep, just after he had told her that she must release him from their engagement and cancel their wedding plans, because he had discovered that he must marry her sister instead. As she had stood there, struggling to understand the news, she had sensed, rather than seen or heard, the triumphant presence of her betrayer in the hall behind her. June, her seventeen year old sister, had given him what, in three years of courting, she had not. She had tried to hold his eyes but they had slipped away from her. But now, he did not look away. His eye was steady. His look held no expectation at all. She might shout, she might cry, she might hit out at him, she might embrace him; whatever it was, he would take it. His eyes did not flinch but his hands fluttered; it was the only sign which betrayed his quailing nerve.

His visits became regular. She heard all the family news from him. Simon's return from the wilderness, Robert's stroke and subsequent retirement, Elliot's assumption of the chairmanship of the company, April's illness and death, Heather and Bob's failure to have a baby, and, latterly, the plans for the family holiday and June's fury at being excluded. He told her it all week by week as though it was the unfolding story of a soap opera available to him on some obscure cable or satellite network, but not to her. Elliot he portrayed as a nasty, avaricious man who had virtually wrested the company from Robert against his will. Ruth was described as a leftie radical feminist with poor parenting skills and no domestic ones, who nevertheless contended single-handedly at school against uneducable drug-taking thugs. Simon, he led Muriel to believe, was a heroic figure, fighting

157

valiantly against bereavement, bringing up single-handedly his three orphaned children and carving out for himself a career in some fiendishly complicated world of high-tech new-fangled whatsits. Belinda she longed to know; from what Les said, she seemed a homely and kind-hearted sort, although efficient and smart. Only of Heather and Bob did she gain direct information, from the pages of Hello magazine, where they could regularly be seen attending galas and award ceremonies. Muriel hungered to hear of their doings, even though, through Les' eyes, they did all seem very strange.

Les taught her to drive; they went out in a little car he helped her to buy, long drives in the countryside and to the coast. On one of these outings he took her to an animal refuge, where she chose Roger, a malodorous, mangy mongrel. He had nothing at all to recommend him; was under-socialized, which resulted in him being rather snappish and nervous with strangers, given to giddiness. He was unremarkable to look at and suffered from appalling halitosis. But he had been at the refuge for three years without attracting an owner, and would, the Refuge Manager thought, make a loyal and loving pet for the right owner. Muriel chose him because he reminded her so much of herself. ('You haven't got bad breath,' Les said, chivalrously.) Les especially wanted her to have a dog. 'I don't like to think of you being alone,' he said. It was just one more indication of his care and concern for her, and summed up his loving nature. Roger settled in to her little home immediately, choosing the second best chair for his day bed and the sheepskin bedroom rug as his night one. He needed only a short walk each day, as he was rather arthritic, and was happy to sit in the sunshine of the garden or by the fire, wherever Muriel herself was to be found.

On Wednesdays Muriel would leave Roger behind and take the two buses to The Oaks to sit beside her mother, hearing her imperfect repetition of the news she had already heard from Les, sifting out the vague approximation to the facts from the ridiculous assertions which equally made up her mother's world: ('Our June says she'll take me to Turkey one day. I wish you'd bring me some new bras. I saw some lovely ones the other day, in the butchers,') restraining herself from correcting the details; (Torquay, Les had said, not Turkey), wondering if she was sitting in the very chair he had occupied the previous Saturday.

On Fridays he would come and take her shopping, while June helped with the wages at the depot. They would saunter round the supermarket like a married couple, putting items into their trolley as though they would spend the weekend cooking and eating them together. On Monday evenings he would take her out to the pictures of for a meal while June played bridge at the golf club. Muriel never asked Les how he explained his absences, how he accounted to June for the times spent with her. But Les never sneaked or dissembled. He walked close beside her, took her arm openly, never looked over his shoulder. They both behaved as though June did not exist. Thus there was need neither for guilt, nor for choice.

In the bedroom he was as tender and ardent as a boy, delighted by her. To Muriel's astonishment, decades of unexpended sexual pleasures gushed forth from her at his touch, and drowned them both. She loved him with the intensity and abandonment of a girl in first love, indeed in many ways she had never grown up, but had waited in a kind of stasis, like a fairy-tale heroine, slumbering on the doorstep until her prince should come and awaken her.

On one occasion only did she meet Les while June was present. Granny McKay had celebrated a birthday and The Oaks had thrown a small party in her honour. Muriel had gone of course, as had June and Les, Robert and Mary, and Sandra, with her boyfriend Kevin. Muriel had immediately been able to understand Les' concern about his daughter's choice of young man: he had loitered on the fringes of the family gathering offering nothing in the way of conversation or assistance, but spent the entire afternoon staring into space. From

159

what she could tell, Kevin was entirely unsuitable; uncommunicative, insolvent, from a disreputable family which had had more than its fair share of brushes with the police. June had laughed unnecessarily all afternoon, petting her mother and talking loudly about Sandra, who was, for all June could see, an unremarkable girl, rather gauche and not especially pretty. Sandra was not the child who had caused the hasty marriage of June and Les; that baby had been lost only weeks after the quiet ceremony, if indeed, Muriel speculated, it had ever existed at all. Muriel felt nothing for Sandra, even though she was Les' flesh and blood, other than a vague sadness. June was portly, splendidly dressed and heavily made up. Muriel thought that her sister was impossibly brassy and loud. Les, she was surprised to see, kept himself aloof from the proceedings, passing tea cups when commanded to do so, agreeing with June when called upon, as he frequently was, but offering no conversation otherwise, apart from the briefest comment about football passed to Robert. But when it was time to go home, and they had stood together in the overpowering heat of the entrance vestibule buttoning coats and fastening scarves, Les had shaken Muriel's hand very warmly, and kissed her boldly on the cheek before moving on to do likewise to Mary, and June's torrent of inconsequential conversation had stumbled as she observed it.

Muriel's telephone rung very late on Friday evening. For the telephone to ring at all was a shock; it rarely did, and Muriel tended to think of it as a herald of bad news. She would answer it with a mixture of extreme caution and excessive wonderment, as though she could not conceive that the call could be anything to do with her and that, if it was, it was bound to be unwelcome. But for it to ring at such a late hour could only be, she thought, a harbinger of doom and she immediately thought of her mother at The Oaks.

'Hello?'

It was Les, speaking in a low voice, calling to tell her, sadly, that he probably would not be able to see her on Monday. She had been excessively lonely that day, without him. Now she would not see him on Monday either. Muriel's heart sank.

'Before I knew what was happening, I was driving Robert and Mary up here. June's got it into her head that we're staying all week,' he said, gloomily.

Muriel toyed with the belt of her dressing gown. 'Oh,' she said, 'so you're all up there together, then.'

'Looks like it,' Les nodded, 'and, what's worse, I think she's got something up her sleeve for tomorrow.'

'What?'

'I don't know,' Les sounded glum. 'Some carry-on. There's more, but I can't tell you now.'

'I understand,' Muriel sighed. 'Never mind.'

'I'd phone The Oaks tomorrow, and weigh things up, if I were you,' Les said, before hanging up.

Muriel hesitated at the bottom of her stairs in the moonlit hall. Roger regarded her with concern from the top. She considered making a cup of Ovaltine to take upstairs with her. She could drink it while she finished the last three or four chapters of the book she was reading, a Mills and Boon romance. She couldn't help feeling sorry for herself, alone of all the family excluded from the wonderful McKay holiday. She knew it was a bad habit but she indulged the complaint once more, that in spite of having done so very well for themselves, no-one in the whole family ever thought to throw a crumb to their poor maiden aunt. She didn't know why she wasn't frequently called upon for baby-sitting, or included in family trips and treats. Even with Les' companionship, she was so often alone, and in the watches of the night she would frequently worry about dying suddenly without a hand to grasp *in extremis*, and being found decomposing days later by strangers. June, of course, was the cause of all her pain and hardship. From her very arrival she had disturbed Muriel's happiness. Aged only

161

six she had been expected to mind her baby sister, begin helping with the washing and cleaning, and was banished from the embraces of her parents. From her point of view, June had stolen Muriel's place as cherished baby of the family, and later she had taken also, in the cruellest way, her fiancé, her unborn family, her whole future. And now she would keep Les to herself for the whole week and deny Muriel even a few hours of companionship and love. It seemed like the last straw, and as Muriel lay sleepless in her lonely bed, she burned with unhappy self-pity.

When Les got back to their room, June was snoring loudly, and taking up the whole of the double bed. Where ever he lay in the bed now he would not be able to avoid touching her, and he couldn't bear that. He left the room with a heavy sigh in search of an unoccupied bed.

Ruth – A memoir from 1972

On the morning of Ruth's eighth birthday she woke up early. In the room she shared with Belinda, spring morning light was already filtering through the pink curtains made by her mother. Ruth hadn't wanted pink. She hated pink. But pink was for girls and this was the girls' room. They had to share it, now that the new baby was in the little room, the room that had been Ruth's, before she came. This shared room was not the biggest room. Mummy and Daddy had that, and Simon had the next biggest, the exciting room, built into the loft, even though he was the smallest – next to smallest – but he was the boy, so he had to have a big room. It wasn't fair.

In the bed across the room, Belinda wasn't stirring, but Ruth knew that she mustn't get up, yet. On a birthday, the birthday person had to get up last, and go down to breakfast where everyone would be waiting and there would be parcels. But somebody was awake, she could hear movement in the bathroom next door; swishing water and the funny chunnering noise her father made when he washed his face, before he soaped it with the little brush, and shaved his chin. Ruth itched to get up, to see if he had changed his mind. Today, as well as being her birthday, was Saturday. On Saturdays Daddy went to the yard, and tinkered with the lorries, and sorted out the pink delivery notes, and, with painstaking slowness, his tongue protruding from the corner of his mouth, wrote out the invoices. On the rare occasions when she had been taken (under protest, he didn't want to, really, but he had done it two or three times when the baby in her tummy had made Mummy tired) she had thrilled at the size of the enormous vehicles, parked like sleeping dragons in an orderly row, sniffed in their hot, oily smell, loved scrambling up into the cabs to wriggle on the slippery vinyl seats and reach her hands out to the solid wheel. The cabs were a treasure trove of half packets of sweeties and dog-eared maps and they smelled of sweat and chips and cigarettes and grease and Daddy. Her Daddy had a swivelling chair in his office, and there were washed out beans tins with paper clips and rubber bands and pens in them, and mugs with cold, scummy tea, and shelves thick with dust. It was all a marvellous, grubby, exciting, grown-up shambles and she had begged to be taken there today, as her birthday treat. But Daddy had said no.

Instead there was to be a party. Ten little girls from her class at school; games, a birthday tea. Ten little girls plus Ruth, and Belinda, and Simon, the only boy.

On the back of the bedroom door, their party dresses hung waiting. Both pink (inevitably). Belinda's was made of netting, with a full skirt which stood out stiff over a petticoat. It had little pearls sewn onto the bodice and puffed sleeves and its neck was edged in pink satin ribbon. It was completely wrong for a twelve year old, but Belinda liked it and had helped her mother sew on the pearls. It made Belinda, who was chubby anyway, look like blob of pink bubble gum. Not that the McKay girls were allowed to chew gum; it was common. Ruth's dress was made of clingy, slippery sateen, a slightly paler shade of pink. It had a straight skirt to the knee and a round neck, with a large fussy Peter Pan collar which had given Mummy no end of trouble on the machine, and three-quarter length sleeves and a wide satin ribbon at the waist which tied in an enormous bow at the back. It made Ruth, who was skinny, look like a stick of rock. Their white knee-length socks and shiny patent leather shoes lay ready. The only item of clothing which would be left to their own choice would be which hair-band they might wear. The baby would be trussed up in layers of pink knitted woollies and look like a little pink dolly-mixture. Simon would wear shorts and a shirt, and perhaps, if he could be persuaded to keep it on, his gingham bow tie. He would be the only one of them spared the indignity of being made to look like an item of confectionery.

The pink of the dresses melded into the pink of the room. Anaglypta wallpaper painted pink, pink carpet, pink light shade with a pink bulb, pink candlewick bed-spreads and flannelette sheets, pink curtains; it was like being trapped inside a bottle of Johnson's Baby Lotion.

In the bathroom, Ruth heard the click of the toilet lid being raised and a sort of sigh. Then Daddy blew his nose, like a trumpet. Then there was quiet. Presently the toilet roll holder rattled before the chain was pulled. Water swished again, then the door opened and Daddy went back into the bedroom. Ruth heard low voices exchange a sentence or two and she began to wriggle with impatience between the sheets. Even now, it was possible that Daddy might change his mind, put his head round the door and say to her; 'alright, then. Get up quick and you can come.' She began, in her mind, to plot out how quickly she could get up and dressed, where her playing-out trousers and cotton shirt would be; located, in her mind's eye, her old shoes (they would be on the rack in the back porch); planned to grab an apple and a banana from the fruit bowl so that she would not get hungry and make a nuisance of herself by needing food. She didn't care about the ten little girls or the games or the tea; it could all take place without her. She would rather go to the yard. But then she heard her Daddy's footsteps as they hurried down the stairs, the fumble as he put his boots on and the front door open and close. He had gone. Gone without her. Gone before the birthday breakfast and the presents, gone without even saying Happy Birthday.

The party was an agony of embarrassment. At three the ten little girls arrived clutching parcels; pencil cases and jig-saws, a kit of beads and pre-cut felt to make a beaded hand-bag, sweets, colouring books, a board game that looked just like the one she had taken to the same little girl's birthday the preceding month. They were all trussed up in velvet and lace and satin; ruched and smocked and be-ribboned; brushed and scrubbed and curled and preened. Their mothers deposited them on the doorstep with strict instructions to 'be good' and 'say please and thank you' and 'mind their manners.' Belinda was insufferable, behaving like a Mummy, taking coats and echoing Mummy's every 'how lovely! What a lucky girl! Say 'thank you' Ruth.' Simon was giddy as a goat. He ran around making rude noises and pulling silly faces, snatched the parcels out of her hands and even managed to open one or two of them before Mary could be prised from the kitchen where she was putting the finishing touches to the potted meat sandwiches and spearing cocktail sausages with little sticks, to bring him into line. Even so, the hand-bag kit was open and the floor treacherous with plastic beads before he could be stopped. (Belinda made the bag in the end, but she never did get it finished; too many of the beads were missing.)

They played 'pass the parcel' and 'musical statues', Belinda standing at the radiogram in charge of the music. They played 'pin the tail on the donkey' and Simon stuck the pin into one of the little girls and made her cry. She didn't even bleed, but it put a dampener on things for a while. Then, as the girls took their places at the tea table, solemn with good manners, Simon squirmed into the chair at the top of the table, reserved for Ruth, and would not be moved, and Mummy just said, 'Oh Ruth, let him. He's only five and you're such a big girl now. You sit next to Clare instead.' But she didn't want to sit next to Clare. She hadn't even really wanted to invite Clare, who nobody liked because she was a bully, but had been made to because Clare had invited Ruth to her party. Dominating the table, Simon had stood on his chair, and shouted silly remarks, and dropped his sausage in his orange squash on purpose, and shown off the real fly in his shorts by getting his willy out and waving it around, while the girls gravely ate egg-and-cress sandwiches and sausages-on-sticks and crisps and potted meat sandwiches and cheese-and-pineapple on sticks, and fairy buns and chocolate finger biscuits and iced gems and jelly, and remembered to say please and thank you. The girl who had been pricked with the pin snivelled and Clare reached under the table and squeezed Ruth's hand so hard that her knuckles cracked and her fingers went white. Then the cake came; a round sandwich cake (not a

167

lorry, which is what she had hoped for) with pink icing and Smarties, and eight candles. Belinda had switched out the light (it wasn't dark, but it was tradition) and Mummy had carried it in. The ten little girls had sung 'Happy Birthday to you' and Simon had sung the rude version he had learned at a party the previous week, with squashed tomatoes and stew, and, at the last moment, had slid down from his chair, dashed round the table and blown out the candles.

After tea the ten little girls had gone home, with a slice of cake wrapped up in a napkin, and a balloon on a string, and her Daddy did not come home until after she was in bed.

Saturday

Belinda woke feeling refreshed. Elliot's side of the bed remained empty. She showered and dressed, made the bed and opened the curtains. Her window looked out onto the gravel sweep, the lawns, the beech trees and the stone fountain. The day promised to be fine; a lingering mist hovered in the hollows but the sky was a pale washed blue. She determined to have no agenda for the day, to see how things developed. It was alien, not to her own character, which was flexible and compliant, but to the nature she had adopted since marriage, which demanded order and accountability, and she knew that if Elliot required an itinerary, as he inevitably would, she would have to let it go. But, for herself, she was happy to supply the wants of others, while they dictated the pace of things. The only absolute for the day was that she positively must find three more lamb steaks from somewhere.

Downstairs, the house was as she had left it. The kitchen was tidy, the breakfast table ready. No one else was up and Belinda was glad to be the first to take possession of the day. She placed the kettle on the hob and opened the back door and let a gust of fresh air, sunlight and birdsong enter. Tiny loped in from the hall and passed through the kitchen, giving her a blearily exhausted look, before disappearing outside. Passing the sink, Belinda cast a wondering eye over it, then allowed the dream to dissipate in the sharp air. The arrival pell-mell of Ben, Todd and Toby, ravenous for breakfast made practical matters take precedence.

Mitch, carrying Starlight, entered the kitchen.

'Good morning,' he said, sliding the child into her high chair and fastening the straps.

'Goodness!' Belinda cried, 'I never expect to see Rob until after lunch on a Saturday. You're an early riser.' Such a nice young man, she thought, clean-shaven, his hair freshly washed, his clothes clean and

169

respectable, not like the dreadful, grunge style that Rob preferred. Amazing to think that only a couple of years before he had been down-and-out, in trouble with the police, probably, she speculated, involved with drugs.

'Well,' Mitch indicated Starlight, 'let's just say that *one* of us is!' The child had evidently adapted to her new surroundings; she babbled incoherently, and smashed her plastic cup on the tray of her highchair while Mitch mushed Weetabix into milk.

'So did Starlight sleep in your room?' Belinda was shocked, but not surprised that Heather should have passed responsibility for the child onto this young man. They seemed to rely on him for everything, had taken him absolutely under their wing and into their midst just in that all-or-nothing way they had with everything. But he didn't seem to take any liberties; he behaved, in fact, with perfect decorum; he knew his place and knew, presumably, that as fortunate as he was in his situation now, there was no guarantee that it would go on forever. It didn't reflect on Mitch, it was the way that Bob and Heather were, espousing with passionate enthusiasm one thing after another, but nothing much for any length of time. The baby herself, Belinda had to admit, might turn out to be just such another passing infatuation.

'*Sleep?*' Mitch replied, with irony, spooning the cereal with difficulty into Starlight's mouth. She kept reaching out for the spoon and gobs of Weetabix were being distributed far and wide.

'Oh dear. And I never heard a thing.' She placed coffee near his elbow, well away from the flailing arms of the child. 'Why don't you let her hold a spoon herself?' she suggested, passing one over. Starlight beamed as the spoon was placed into her chubby fist, and began with immense concentration, but indifferent skill, to apply it to her breakfast.

The boys were wild with their plans for the day. A walk to the sea, an exploration of the woods, the selection of a suitable camp site, the construction of a bivouac and the snaring of fresh meat for food were all discussed with enthusiasm. Belinda suggested gently that perhaps she would be able to supply food for a picnic, which might be less trouble and more enjoyable than raw rabbit.

'It won't be *raw!*' shouted Todd. 'We'll cook it, on the fire.'

The other two boys gave him a sharp look, but the word was out.

'You won't be lighting a fire in the woods, Todd, dear. That would be very dangerous.'

'But Rob said....'

'Shut up, Todd,' Toby hissed. Then, 'is there any toast, Aunty Belinda?'

Belinda put toast on the table, but needed to extinguish the fire plan once and for all.

'Rob has his coursework to finish. I'm sure he didn't promise to light a fire for you. He's too sensible for that. And so are you, I'm sure. And you wouldn't really want to kill anything would you, boys?'

Ben secretly agreed with her that killing and then skinning and then finally eating an animal would be awful. He had thought so the previous evening when his cousin Rob had described in lurid detail how this could be done but in the interest of self-preservation he had said nothing, and now rolled his eyes in an imitation of the other boys' silent derision.

'Can we go out now?' Toby leapt up from the table. He had been sitting the closest to Starlight and had narrowly missed being larded with Weetabix. Staying longer, he felt, would be tempting fate.

'No, Toby, not until more adults are up and about.'

All three boys expressed voluble outrage at this prohibition.

Presently they all left the table to go to the games room to watch TV. At Belinda's request, they agreed to take Starlight with them on the understanding that the remnants of her breakfast be first wiped

171

from her hair and face, and that they wouldn't be responsible for anything in the nappy department. She toddled happily along between them, looking from one to the other, adding her voice to their incessant chatter.

Belinda cleared the table around Mitch, refreshed his coffee and placed two slices of toast in front of him.

'Did you have plans for today?' she asked him. She hoped her question would give him permission, if he needed it, to slip away from what must feel like a slightly awkward, anomalous position. Plus, to be frank, she thought Heather ought to take responsibility for her own child.

'Oh, no,' he replied, biting into his toast. 'I'll hang around in case I'm needed. Think I'll take this outside, though,' he said, making for the door.

Belinda just had time to refill the kettle, when Mary and James entered the kitchen.

'Good morning, dear,' Mary said, brightly. 'Sleep well?'

'Very well, thanks, Mum. You?'

'Oh yes, very comfortable.' She did look rested, and was nicely dressed in a navy woollen dress and hand-knitted cardigan. James settled her at the table and then stepped out through the back door to take the air for a few moments. As he passed her, Belinda made much of pouring tea for Mary.

'Is Dad still asleep?'

'Oh yes, he sleeps quite late, you know. It's the medication.'

James re-entered the kitchen. 'A will and stindless day,' he pronounced. Belinda liked the funny ways he said things; making the ordinary seem exotic, or the frightening benign. He had a sonorous, low voice, never wasted words, but made them all, even trivial ones, count. His report of Ruth was not good; a disturbed night, bad stomach pains and a blinding headache. He set about making up a tray for her. Belinda tried to imagine Elliot being so considerate.

'Oh dear. Is there anything we can do?' she asked. James shook his head.

'I do worry about Ruth,' Mary confided, after he had left the kitchen. Mother and daughter sat together at the end of the table. Each held her tea mug cupped in her hands.

'About her health?'

'Yes, but more than that. She always seems so.......'

'Tired?'

'Strung out, I was going to say. She's sort of...' Mary groped for the word, 'sour and disappointed. She seems so alone. They never speak of friends; they don't seem to go out, much.'

'I think money's very tight.'

'Oh yes, obviously. The children's clothes...'

'Yes. Well all of them, really. It's almost like a badge; she doesn't seem to do anything to disguise it.'

'She's so busy. I don't think she notices. She doesn't have time for the niceties.'

'If she bought better quality things in the first place.....'

The two women sipped their tea.

'I think she misses April terribly.' Belinda said, presently.

'Oh yes. She was the only one who seemed to be able to get close to Ruth. They were as close as sisters.'

'Closer.'

'Mmmm.'

They avoided one another's eyes.

'Will you have a slice of toast, Mum? I've got some lovely wholemeal bread. Or there are croissants, somewhere.'

'Toast, please.'

Belinda sliced the bread. Mary opened a jar of marmalade.

'D'you think that was the real trouble last Christmas? Between Ruth and Miriam?'

'That she wasn't April, you mean?'

'Yes.'

'Well, she *is* very different from April.'

'Totally. But the children seem to quite like her and Simon's obviously devoted. I just hope it's a two way street.'

'You don't think so?'

'He couldn't bear to lose someone else.'

'Oh no. How's that marmalade?'

'A bit odd.'

'It's from Fortnum and Mason. Miriam brought it.'

'There you are, then.'

Mary ate the rest of her toast in silence. Mitch brought his plate and cup back. James reappeared and reported that Ruth was 'somewhat improved' and was getting up. He seated himself at the table and reached for the tea pot, but Belinda took it from him.

'I'll make fresh,' she said. 'If I grilled some bacon, could you eat a rasher or two?'

James nodded. At the mention of bacon, Mitch placed himself hopefully back at the table. The two gave each other a rueful grin.

'Sleep well, James?'

'Remarkably well.'

Bob and Heather joined them. Bob was wearing his jeans and a clean white t shirt but Heather remained in her ethereal ethnic robes. Her hair was loose and tousled. They both looked rested and rosy and smugly satiated.

'Gosh!' Heather yawned, reaching for the Muesli, 'you're all up so early!'

'Early!' exclaimed Mary. 'It's almost ten!'

Belinda grilled bacon and scrambled eggs, boiled and re-boiled the kettle for tea and coffee. June and Les joined them at the table, Les with diffidence and June with her habitual laughter and front. She was coiffed and powdered and corseted for battle, declared herself very happy with her accommodation and agreeable to any plan that anyone might suggest.

'And Les will be happy to run any errands, fetch shopping, chop wood. Won't you, Les?'

Les nodded, and sipped his tea.

'I think Robert would like to have a bath, later,' Mary said. 'Would you mind very much giving me a hand, Les?'

'Not at all. Glad to help,' he said, gratefully.

The smell of bacon brought the three boys back to the kitchen; they were at the table and reaching for cutlery.

'What news of the twirly-whirly-girlies, Ben?' James turned to his son.

'Oooh!' he rolled his eyes. It was to be his expression of the day. 'They're up there *washing* and *brushing* and fiddling with their *hair.*' He managed to convey his impression that this was the most pointless of activity. Certainly it was something that neither he nor his cousins had troubled themselves with.

Ruth arrived, carrying her tray. Belinda took it from her and kissed her. The unexpected show of affection brought tears to Ruth's eyes. She had spent the past half hour reliving her behaviour of the previous evening, and had had to admit to herself that she ought to feel very ashamed of her maudlin humour, inebriation and hysterical outburst. Her almost uncontrollable urge to find fault with others and feel sorry for herself had meant that she had set off on the wrong foot. Also her failure to deal with Miriam, even if only by showing that the past was forgotten, had resulted in the issue still hanging like a cloud over them. She had no idea what had been decided about anything, and had lost touch with the general atmosphere. This in itself was a serious result of her behaviour and she knew that she had considerable ground to make up. She had decided that an apology was in order, but had dreaded arriving for breakfast after Miriam, who would have smiled with cloying sweetness while she made it. But now she could speak quite genuinely of her regret at having left them all so early, of her ill health, and of her determination to make good the deficit by cooking, washing up, helping with the children or any other chore which might be apportioned to her.

'I've no doubt you all planned everything out last night, but if someone could just fill me in on the details I'll happily fall into line,' she said, slipping into her seat next to Ben. His narrow shoulders and anxious face made her want to cry again. She noticed that his sweatshirt had a hole in the shoulder seam and the sleeves were too short; his puny arms and wrists protruded from the frayed cuffs. It occurred to her with another rush of emotion that Ben hadn't had any new clothes for a while because April had not been there to pass along Toby's cast-offs. It was an arrangement that she and April had had between them and she couldn't expect Miriam to know of it or to perpetuate it. At the same time it was just another reminder of her loss. April had been Ben's God-mother, too. He would never know her, now.

She looked into his face; a broad forehead narrowing to a pointed chin and defined jaw, a good, strong, straight nose; a McKay profile if ever there was one. Grey eyes, sandy blonde hair; the McKay colouring. A wiry frame, but small. He was, in fact, she decided, his grandfather in miniature. The McKay genes were more pronounced in Ben than in any of the other grandchildren. Ellie, perhaps, had something of the delicacy of bone structure, Toby something of the colouring. Rob had the eyes and the stubbornness of character but was wily, like his father. He promised to be reasonably tall; something of a miracle, for a McKay. Todd was like April and Tansy like Simon, who had, like Belinda, inherited a fullness of figure from Mary.

Ben snuggled into her side. The scrambled eggs which had been placed in front of him were too runny and made his stomach feel as though it was too high up. The frenetic activity of the previous day, the lack of sleep, the excitement of the proposed expedition and the disappointment of delay were all beginning to add up to more than he could take. He looked mutely at his mother, who read everything in a moment.

'Why don't you go and play the piano for a while? Dad says it's a lovely instrument and you're lucky to have the chance to play it. Also, the peace and quiet will do you good.'

Ben nodded gratefully, but cast an anxious eye down the table towards his cousins.

'I won't let them go without you.' Ruth assured him, in a whisper.

Ben slipped away from the table and out of the room.

He passed Simon and Miriam in the passageway. 'Good morning, good morning everybody,' they called out as they entered the room.

Ruth leapt from her seat. 'Come and take my place here, Miriam,' she said quickly, determined not to perpetuate the mistakes of the previous evening. 'I've finished eating and I'm going to make a start on the dishes. I'm afraid I was terribly lazy last night didn't do a hand's turn. I'm going to make up for it today. Let me pour you some tea.'

'Thank you, Ruth,' Miriam was taken aback by Ruth's effusiveness. 'May I have a fruit tea? I think I brought some with us.'

'*Fruit* tea?' The pretentiousness of this request almost undid Ruth's good intentions but she tried hard not to let her voice or her expression give anything away. 'Certainly. I'll have a look.'

'Anything to eat, you two?'

'Do I smell bacon?' Simon sat down in Belinda's place, next to Mary.

'Just toast for me, please,' said Miriam. 'I think I brought some organic bread. I'd rather have that if I may.'

The girls came clattering into the kitchen. Tansy and Ellie wore almost identical baggy jeans and sloppy jumpers. They'd done each other's hair into braids. They'd tried hard with Rachel's hair, but it was neither long nor short, too coarse for braids and unbecoming left loose and nothing had looked quite right. In the end they had settled on one of Tansy's hair bands. She wore the same imitation leather trousers and jerkin. Seeing the three of them standing together on the threshold of the room like that, in unavoidable comparison, the heart of every woman except Ruth gave a small clutch.

'Rachel!' Ruth exclaimed from her place at the sink, 'you surely aren't going to wear that outfit again today! It won't be fit to be seen by Thursday!' She turned to the family in explanation, unseeing Rachel's stricken expression. 'We brought it especially for the party, you know!'

'And very nice it is too! Isn't it Les? Ha Ha Ha.' said June.

Poor James remained silent, but his eyes spoke volumes. Tansy suddenly felt terribly ashamed of her good quality, fashionable clothes. She pulled at the sleeve of her own jumper as though spoiling it in some way would make Rachel feel more comfortable. Ellie thought her Aunty Ruth might have gone slightly mad; surely she didn't actually consider that hideous outfit to be presentable on a special occasion? Then she saw Mitch and all thought of Rachel's clothes flew out of her head. She flashed him a brilliant smile.

'I found it very difficult to know what to pack,' shrilled Belinda, like a woman on a tightrope, she didn't know which way to jump. 'I had no idea what the weather would be like or what we might be doing.'

'Me, too,' agreed June, and then realised that to admit as much was probably a mistake.

It was, to everyone's amazement, Miriam who saved the occasion. 'I think I'll probably pop off shopping today,' she said. 'I seem to have packed quite inappropriately.'

'I'll come with you,' said Heather. 'I haven't bought Ellie a birthday present yet. It's so long since I saw her I wasn't sure of the size. I know!' she exclaimed, astounded by her own brilliance, 'why don't you girls all come along? We'll have a lovely girly shopping spree!'

Tansy and Ellie were full of enthusiasm. Rachel looked at her father in panic. She had never been shopping without her mother before, and she knew they didn't have money for the kinds of shops her aunts and cousins were likely to frequent. The idea of taking her clothes off and being inspected in the changing room was appalling. James shrugged helplessly at his daughter, and almost didn't catch Miriam's words as she leaned closer to him and said, under her breath, 'She'll be fine. Don't worry about anything. I'll look after her. It'll be my treat, to make up for Christmas.' James turned to smile at her in gratitude but she had turned the other way and was listening to Todd, so he just smiled at Rachel instead and gave her an encouraging nod and a wink.

'What a lovely idea,' gushed Belinda. She was drying the dishes as Ruth washed them. '*You* don't want to go shopping, do you Ruth? We can have a walk with Mum and Dad round the grounds instead or you could just sit and have a read in the library. I'm sure the men will take the boys out adventuring in the woods, so that'll mean some peace for us all round.'

'I certainly don't want to go; and I'm sure Rachel won't either. She has homework she could be doing.' Ruth scrubbed at the grill pan.

'Not on holiday! What a waste!'

'Not as wasteful as shopping!' Ruth retorted.

'I'm sure she won't want to be left behind,' Belinda said, more gently, lowering her voice, 'The girls are all getting along so nicely, don't you think? And it is very kind of Miriam and Heather to offer to take them. We wouldn't want to cause offence,' she finished, dangerously.

'No.' Ruth pulled the plug out of the sink, resigned to the sacrifice of her step-daughter on the altar of good family relations, 'you're right. I suppose she can go, if she wants to.'

The family chatted around the breakfast table, finishing their final cups of coffee and tea. The plates and cutlery had all been cleared, the surfaces wiped and the cereals and condiments put away. James, Mitch and Les had carried all the bottles and the spare boxes of groceries into one of the store rooms down the corridor. The back door stood open and Tiny was sprawled in the patch of sunshine across the threshold. The boys were anxious to be outside.

'When will Rob be up?' Toby asked.

'I'm afraid he never surfaces much before lunchtime at weekends,' Belinda laughed. 'It's because he's a teenager. They grow in their sleep, you know.'

In the absence of Rob, James, Bob and Simon were quickly conscripted onto the expedition. Miriam and Heather were discussing which car they had better use, and the distance to the outlet village they had both noted just off the motorway junction. The noise of the assorted voices planning and proposing almost drowned out Elliot's cheery 'Good morning, one and all,' as he entered the kitchen, and only a few of them paused their conversations to give him a nod of greeting.

Elliot's person, freshly showered and sleekly groomed, betrayed nothing of his excesses of the night before or of his night spent sprawled comatose on the sofa. Only Belinda detected a certain dullness of the eye which betrayed his true hung-over state. Underwhelmed by their welcome, and riled by the fact that breakfast had evidently been enjoyed without him, that no one had come to find him, or to bring him tea, or missed him in any respect whatsoever, he strode across the quarry tiles towards Belinda in order to wreak his revenge. 'Good morning, my darling!' he beamed, kissing her on the cheek. 'Full English, if you please; tea, juice, and wholemeal toast.' Belinda smelled the lingering acrid odour of brandy on his breath; she shrunk from his embrace. Without waiting for a response he turned to the table and set his laptop computer onto its surface. 'Plug this in, Toby my boy, and lets fire the old girl up. I sense the need for organisation, for leadership, for the mighty hand of authority; in short, I propose we make a plan.'

Belinda turned hastily to the fridge and began extracting bacon and eggs, and reached for the skillets which lay newly washed and dried. The rest of the family gaped at Elliot's rudeness.

Miriam got up hastily from her seat. 'We have a plan of sorts, Elliot, at least for today,' she said, archly. 'Heather and I are taking the girls shopping. Simon and the other men are taking the boys out to climb trees. You see, we've managed quite well without the "mighty hand of authority!"' She flicked her hair over her shoulder imperiously and walked from the room. Mary followed close behind her, to see if Robert was awake, and ready for his bath.

'Give me a shout, Mary, whenever you're ready,' Les called after her.

Elliot continued undeterred to boot up his computer and to make an excel spread sheet with everybody's name across the top and sections of time down the side.

'So all this activity will continue until....lunch time? Later?' he asked, urbanely, keying in the word 'woods' under the names of the boys and his three brothers-in-law, and 'shops' for the girls and his two sisters-in-law.

'I should think we can dispense with lunch. It's eleven o'clock now,' suggested June. She was the only one encouraging him in his efforts to take control, behaving as though making a detailed itinerary for everyone's movements was an entirely reasonable practice for those on holiday.

'Let's say three then, shall we?'

'I think that sounds fine,' agreed June, hiding a private smile, 'You never know what might have happened by then.'

Belinda was busy scrambling eggs. Her face was flushed from the heat of the Aga, and from embarrassment. She knew exactly where this was going. She had left him behind again but it wasn't her fault that he'd got so drunk that he couldn't make it into bed, and surely a lie-in under those circumstances had been a kindness?

But two things occurred to avert the disaster.

Ben sauntered back into the kitchen. He felt calmed by his playing; music worked like a soothing balm to his nerves. Now he was ready for the adventures of the day.

'Oh, Ben. Have you been in the games room? Is Starlight alright?' Mitch rose to his feet. Even a nappy change was preferable to the showdown he felt coming on in here.

'She isn't there anymore,' Ben slithered onto the pew besides Elliot, fascinated with the computer. 'She was there when I went in, posting farm animals into Uncle Bob's guitar. And she liked it when I played Fur Elise, but then when I'd finished a Bach piece I looked up and she'd gone.'

Heather made an involuntary squeak and got to her feet. She'd forgotten all about Starlight. Bob too leapt up. 'You didn't watch her to see where she went?'

'Ben's only nine years old! He can't be expected to be responsible for a baby!' Ruth cried, sharply defensive.

'She can't be far away,' Simon said, calmly. 'She'll be in one of the other rooms. Come on, we'll soon find her.'

The family exited the kitchen en masse, except for Elliot, who remained alone at the table, and Belinda, busy with his breakfast. Some went down the passageway and others out of the back door to check the immediate grounds. Those indoors soon met with an obstruction; Mary, in a blind panic, to report that Robert's bed was quite empty and that Robert himself was nowhere to be found.

Robert found the morning air very refreshing. A lively breeze was blowing the cobwebs out of his head, playing gently with the grey wisps of hair which Mary usually combed so carefully for him. The wind filled his pyjama top so that it ballooned out around his upper body, but the chill on his skin tended to comfort rather than distress him; it was such a clear indication that he was alive. He was alive, that much was certain, but everything else was a fog of uncertainty. He had woken up in a strange bed, in an unfamiliar room, entirely alone. He had called but received no reply. Mary's things were in evidence; her nightdress neatly folded on the pillow, her curlers and hair brush tidily arranged on the dressing table, but of Mary herself there was no sign. This circumstance struck him as being very cruel – she had deliberately abandoned him in this unknown place – or very frightening – she had been forcibly taken from him. Either way she must be found to re-establish order. He had got out of bed and discovered his slippers in their habitual place by the bed; discovered them not as a result of any intention or quest on his part, but simply by the fact that they had been there beneath his feet. In the alien morass he had woken into, they gave him a sense of comforting normality. The corridor had stretched endlessly, nicely carpeted, warm, but a considerable journey to be undergone before he discovered the stairs. In the absence of his stick, or of a supporting arm, he had leaned against the wall. His voice, calling out Mary's name, had seemed muffled and ineffectual. He was unable to increase its volume and the little sound he did make was absorbed into the walls. His steps had felt as though they were dogged by weights, and the entire dream-like experience had caused him to pinch himself hard on the hand; but he discovered that the place was already quite sore and he concluded that this dream, if dream it was, was inescapable by that means.

At the bottom of the stairs there had been music, heavenly music, the notes dancing from the air like melodious motes. The sound of it both comforted Robert and further alarmed him, present as it was in absence of any human hand. He had hesitated in the hall, several doors offering too many equal possibilities of improvement or deterioration of his plight. Then an awareness of a draught on his back turned him down a corridor and into a room which seemed, not familiar, but briefly known. The chair, the empty fireplace, an arrangement of miniature cannons in a display cabinet; they all struck a chord in his imperfect memory. He toyed with the idea of sitting here and simply waiting; surely Mary would come along soon? But the breeze through the open French doors promised a quicker resolution to his sense of disorientation. The ghostly music, the deserted rooms, the absence of Mary, the ethereal quality of it all, everything was suggesting to him a possibility too enormous to consider. He stepped out into the little courtyard. The stone slabs under his feet were reassuringly solid. The water played over the stones of the fountain with a cheerful gurgle, and the water on the green fronds of the plants glinted in the pale sunshine. Robert reached out and put his hand into the water; it was icy cold, but quite normal, and the wind on his skin inside his pyjama shirt made it pucker into goose-flesh. Yes, he was definitely alive.

On the other side of the fountain, a small dark statue, which had been regarding him solemnly from its position kneeling in the fountain's basin, struggled to its feet. The long, loose clothing was the colour of stone, and folded in saturated ridges around her body. Her skin was dark and shone with wetness. The small pearly teeth chattered together with cold, and her hair, an aureole of curls encrusted with water droplets like gems, seemed to crackle with ebony fire. The wondrousness of this sprite-like being distracted Robert from every other consideration, and when she climbed awkwardly from the fountain and ran to the narrow wrought iron gate which sealed the courtyard off from some wider landscape, and reached up in an ineffectual effort to reach the handle, and looked at him beseechingly over her shoulder, he walked over and opened the gate for her without a second thought. Together they walked out onto the terrace, down the steps and onto the wide expanse of lawn. The statue-girl capered around the lawn emitting burbles of aqua-laughter, glad to be free of her watery prison, and Robert stumbled after her, laughing too, his eyes running water in sympathy with the nymph's stony clothing; the house, Mary and his confusion of only moments before entirely forgotten in this experience of release.

The child led him down the slightly sloping lawns, past flower beds straggled with the very last gasp of the summer's show. Their progress was erratic; the child ran in circles, doubled back on herself, tottered on her feet and then rolled on her back. Robert followed her as best as he was able but his legs kept carrying him away from the line he thought he was taking; once he stumbled into one of the herbaceous borders and scratched his leg. He caught sight of a small arbour, with a seat, and a roof twined around with the tendrils of clematis and honeysuckle, but his most determined efforts to direct his steps towards it were in vain. His desire to keep up with the child weighed equally in his head with his duty to do so; he had found her, released her, she was his responsibility and also his prize. This mixed feeling was suddenly very familiar to Robert. He remembered with clarity the sense that Mary and his family had felt to him like an unbearable and ungrateful burden, and also like a precious cargo to be borne with pride and pleasure, the joy and gratification of the one never allowing him to give in to the weariness and heaviness of the other. On the other hand, the great trial of responsibility had led him, often, he knew, to treat his family with coldness and anger, he had resented them, never enough to make him abandon them altogether, but enough to cause them discomfort on their voyage.

The child had disappeared down a steep grassy slope and was running along a small wooden fence towards a gate which led into a wooded area. Robert slipped down after her. Golden leaves had collected in the hollows against the fence, and the child ran through them screeching her pleasure. Robert found them damp and less appealing. His slippers were becoming wet and uncomfortable and he wondered about taking them off and going barefoot, like the child. They were, in some way, too big for him, and he considered, briefly, the possibility that, in this enchantment, he was shrinking, his body following the pattern of diminution recently experienced of his mental grip on life's actualities; his ability to get what he wanted, his control over things, like his business and his family, his memory, his very understanding, shrivelling, becoming unreliable and pathetic, a creature requiring care and medication. Perhaps indeed, though not dead yet he was dying, but gradually, fading and diminishing over time, and today's ordeal was just another step on the way. Perhaps in time he would become like this other-worldly being, a child again, occupied only with enjoyment, impervious, needing nothing, aware of nothing except the potential for pleasure in everything. The idea of becoming a child again appealed. His childhood had ended abruptly with the death of his father. Aged only fourteen he had been the man of the household expected to provide for his eccentric mother and two sisters. But before that, there had been pleasure and adventure, freedom. Yes, to regress to such an existence would make a tidy end to his life.

He staggered along the fence in the wake of the weird, watery cherub, and through the gate. It was shadowy under the trees; the leaves lay thickly on the ground, some crisp, others slimy with damp. There was a discernible pathway but the child slipped off it, between the tree trunks and through the bushes, penetrating deeper into the copse. The branches became denser, prickly and inhospitable, and while the child could to some extent duck and scramble to avoid their most tenacious tendrils, Robert was repeatedly snagged and scratched on their thorny ends. As he followed, more slowly still, an uncomfortable sense overcame him and he kept on casting glances over his shoulder to the gateway back to the lawn, but it was soon hidden from view, and the route back to it also became lost. Suddenly, up ahead of him, a wail pierced the air. Very human pain and fear yelled for attention. His concept of the child as a faerie nymph,

187

insubstantial and eerie came crashing down abruptly as she roared. He came across her quite soon. Her eyes were enormous and swam with distress, her mouth a wide, dark cavern of misery. Her nightdress was filthy with damp green smears, black, peaty soil and covered with skeletal leaves and twigs. The child held her foot in both hands; it was bleeding quite badly. The sole of her foot was pink, beneath the grime, not brown, and, to Robert, the sight of the blood oozing quite freely from it was more shocking. He looked over his shoulder and called 'Mary! Mary!' once or twice. Very distantly indeed he could hear voices calling and he knew that he must return to his own world, powerless and inconsequential though he now was in it, with no hope of even a regressive regeneration. He considered the child, wondering, if he took her back, whether she would have to return to the freezing water of the fountain, whether, in fact, she should have been there in the first place. Statues didn't bleed, did they? But then surely a live child should not live in a freezing fountain? Equally, what could a brown pick-a-ninny baby have to do with him? What was she doing here? What was he? Her cries were getting louder and louder, the longer he failed to meet her need. It didn't occur to him to pick the child up, to soothe her or to offer any word of comfort. He dithered on the cusp of indecision. In the meantime, the voices came nearer, the wood began to reverberate with the noise of people approaching, many people, with high pitched voices and angry tones, like huntsmen, it sounded as though they had weapons to beat their way through the undergrowth; the branches around him thrashed wildly in protest. He realised that he had left it too late, and, as Todd and Ben and Simon pushed their way into the tiny clearing, Robert, too began to cry.

Because of what Miriam called 'All the hoo-ha', the shopping party was very late in setting off. Heather remained undecided up until the very last minute as to whether she would accompany them, whether Starlight's car-seat and buggy and change-bag and cup and toys should be packed into Simon's people carrier, whether Mitch, too, should be brought along to help to care for her, or whether in fact she, Heather, ought to remain behind with her daughter. Her hysteria at the disappearance of the little girl and the deluge of guilt which descended at her discovery, dirty, wet and injured in an impenetrable thicket in the woods, resulted in a period of alternating wordless sobbing, bitter self-chastisement and unpleasant accusation which, for a time, threatened not only the plans for the day but the whole vacation. Why, Heather asked, with angry eyes, had not one of all these relations been able to keep an eye on their new family member for five minutes? Surely everyone could understand why her dear father was not to be considered an appropriate supervisor for a child, in his current incapacity? *Who* had allowed such a thing? Which idiot had opened the French windows? How, she asked herself, could she have failed to check up on Starlight's whereabouts *herself*? What kind of a mother was she, to allow such a thing to happen?

'Oh, oh, my precious daughter,' she moaned over and over into Starlight's sodden and begrimed body, 'Mummy will *never* leave you alone again.'

But after a warm bath and a change of clothes, and a bottle of milk while Bob tenderly administered first aid to the cut on the sole of her foot, Starlight was fast asleep in her travel cot in Mitch's room, Mitch was sitting in vigil in the chair at her side, and Heather, red eyed and limp from expended emotion, was persuaded that no harm at all could result in the child being left at the house in his care, under the watchful supervisory eye of her Grandmother and two aunts, and that some considerable good might accrue to Heather herself from a change of scene and air.

189

'We have learned a lesson, Heather, that's all,' Mary said, soothingly. 'Starlight is nimble and adventurous and this house is unfamiliar to us all; we must all take extra care about leaving doors open, and such like. We'll also have to be quite specific about who is supervising Starlight at all times. We have been spared a catastrophe, this time. We must be grateful that neither Starlight nor your Father came to worse harm.'

'Oh yes,' Heather breathed. 'The wood nymphs and dryads have protected her from harm, this time. I will thank them, when I go outside, later.'

'Personally,' said Elliot, dryly, from his place at the kitchen table where he had remained throughout the furore, 'I'd be giving the child a good spanking to teach her not to go wandering off on her own, instead of cavorting around in the woods thanking non-existent tree spirits.'

'Your opinion doesn't surprise me in the least!' flashed Heather, her eyes narrowed. 'It would be just your idea to bully and beat someone small and helpless, and then to tell them it was all for their own good!'

'Just a minute!' shouted Elliot, rising from his seat. 'Strong discipline is essential to bringing up children. "Spare the rod and spoil the child."'

'Perhaps you ought to take a close look at your own family, Elliot, before you start handing out advice to other people,' Heather said, coldly, before turning her back on him. Poor Belinda, who had been unable to join the search with the others while she served Elliot's breakfast, couldn't help remarking, 'My own feeling is that the grown-up who left the French windows open in the sitting room should carry a greater burden of responsibility than a toddler in unfamiliar surroundings.' Elliot bristled, but said nothing. He sank back down into his seat. His breakfast things remained on the table beside him. Having insisted on a cooked breakfast, he had left half of it on his plate. The food was congealing now at his side and the smell of it nauseated him. 'Take this away,' he said, dully, to Belinda.

'And besides, you know,' put in Simon, quickly, 'we can't wrap our kids up in cotton wool. To a certain extent they need to be able to make their own choices about things and learn from the consequences. There are always going to be accidents and near-misses. We, and they, just have to learn from them.' He wondered whether his words would strike home with anyone, but the morning's events had made everyone myopic; they were too busy being careful where they were treading to take any kind of long view.

The atmosphere in the car on the way to the shopping centre was subdued. Miriam drove briskly, handling the car aggressively through the country lanes. She resisted Heather's attempts to draw her into conversation, and uttered only the occasional expletive at tractor drivers and ramblers who took up more than their fair share of the road. Rachel, in the back, soon began to feel sick and regretted not having eaten breakfast (her cousins had refused even toast and cereal) or taken a travel sickness tablet. She concentrated fiercely on the road ahead, breathed deeply of the fresh air coming through the window, and tried not to feel nervous about the ordeal to come. Ellie felt that the fun of being out with her two trendy aunts, and of shopping principally for her birthday gifts, had all but been stamped out by the uproar over the baby and Granddad. She whiled away the journey time by using up the last of her phone credit to send plaintive text messages to Caro warning her against further conferences with Rob. Her 'phone call the night before had yielded no results; Caro hadn't answered. Tansy alone listened to Heather as she went over and over the events of the morning, interjecting occasionally with 'Poor Starlight' and 'Poor you,' as appropriate.

After about forty minutes, they stopped for petrol. While Miriam filled the tank, Rachel climbed out of the car saying she needed the toilet. In the station shop, hating her weakness, she grabbed a floppy, grey, cellophane wrapped sandwich, paying quickly with the £2 coin which was all her mother had given her to spend, looking all the while over her shoulder through the window into the forecourt. Then she hurried through to the toilet cubicle where she tore and wolfed at the limp bread and indeterminate beige filling, chewing and swallowing with difficulty; her mouth was too dry, but the yawning chasm in her stomach demanded to be filled, and the rising nausea had to be quelled before she could get back into the car. Five minutes later, she climbed back into her seat, muttering about a queue, knowing that this was ridiculous since theirs was the only car at the pumps.

'That's alright, Rachel.' Ellie said, kindly, 'Miriam's bought us some drinks and a sandwich, freshly made from that little kiosk across the road. I'm starving, aren't you?'

'Do you like Ciabatta?' Heather asked, holding up two thick, well-filled rolls, 'prosciutto and garlic roule or brie and cranberry?'

Rachel looked at them blankly. She had no idea what they were talking about.

'Or plain ham?' Tansy offered, holding up the sandwich she had unwrapped, but not eaten.

'I'm not sure,' Rachel said, feeling sicker than ever, but her sickness caused, now, by their kindness and forethought, and by utter self-disgust.

'Let's share, then, and see which you prefer.' Tansy tore her sandwich in half and passed one piece over to Rachel.

'My parents never buy food while we're out,' Rachel confided to Tansy, as the journey got back under way. Heather had fallen asleep and Miriam was intent on a phone-in radio programme about the European Union.

'Really? How do you manage for meals, then?'

Rachel shrugged. 'We take food with us from home.'

'What about when you're on holiday? Don't you ever eat out?'

'Sometimes. But usually we buy things in markets and cook them in the tent, or Dad barbeques.'

'I'd forgotten you have camping holidays. Is it fun?' Ellie sounded doubtful.

Rachel shrugged again. 'It's alright. We go walking and swimming and have trips round museums and castles and things. Usually there are other kids there and we have games of volleyball and cricket. Sometimes we make particular friends with a family and we share meals and have joint excursions to places. We always say we'll keep in touch when we get home but we never seem to. What do you do for holidays?'

'Last year we went to the Caribbean,' Ellie said. 'It was great. We went All-Inclusive and I made friends with two of the waiters. They slipped me alcoholic cocktails even though I wasn't really supposed to have them. One night they took me back to their village for a street party. The village was like a shanty town; they all lived in wooden huts and the pavements were all muddy and churned up. The people were poor and I couldn't understand what they were saying half the time, but very friendly. The two lads gave me some local drink – it blew my head off! They tried to make me smoke some weed but I wouldn't. Mum and Dad never found out about that, by the way, so don't tell them. Anyway, one of the waiters turned out to be a creep and I had to make the other one walk me home. Then I had to explain why I was drunk, why I'd lost one of my pink sandals and why I had a bruise the size of a tennis ball on my arm. It was the creep, of course. Rob offered to beat him up for me but Dad just reported him to the manager and we never saw him again. I was pretty much grounded after that.'

'That was brave of Rob,' Rachel said, 'and nice of him to be so protective.'

Ellie looked arch; 'Don't be fooled. He's not the chivalrous type. You ought to know that, Rachel!'

Rachel turned away to the window to hide her blush.

'We don't have family holidays,' Tansy said. 'We go away on camp, just the three of us.'

'We don't have family *summer* holidays,' Miriam interrupted, sharply, from the front. '*This* is a family holiday, isn't it?'

'Oh yes. That's what I meant,' Tansy replied, quickly.

'Just the three of you?' Rachel was incredulous.

'Well, when we get there of course there are lots of other children. Some of them go year after year, like us, so we get to know each other really well.'

'Is this abroad?' Ellie asked.

'No, it's at a place in the Cotswolds.'

'Oh.' Ellie lost interest.

'We stay in a huge old school and there are activities and outings and themed days,' Tansy went on. 'One time we spent the whole day dressed in togas!'

'I think I'd enjoy that,' Rachel sighed, wistfully. 'I suppose it's very expensive?'

Tansy shrugged. 'I wouldn't know.'

The road widened and soon they entered a small market town. Heather woke up and stretched herself.

'We'll probably be able to get the things Belinda wants from here, afterwards,' she remarked. 'What was it? Lamb, and something else?'

Miriam nodded. 'I've got a list,' she said. The main street narrowed suddenly, the shops became houses and then the houses petered out and they were back on a country road.

'Not much of a place,' commented Heather.

They came to a large roundabout. Miriam turned off the radio and began to indicate. 'Nearly there,' she cried. The girls brushed the crumbs off their clothes. Ellie got a small mirror out of her bag and checked her make-up. Tansy brushed her hair. Rachel fiddled with the tassel on the end of her belt.

The Outlet Village was a modern, purpose built complex of stores and cafés. A pedestrianised precinct with glass-covered walkways and raised flower beds was surrounded by shops boasting the names of internationally recognised designers and retailers. Their

195

windows displayed willow-thin, long-legged, headless mannequins dressed in expertly co-ordinated outfits. Chrome and wrought iron furniture stood outside continental-style eateries, music floated from every wide open inviting storefront. Other-worldly post-modern sculptures in stone and acrylic loomed out of burbling fountains.

They walked across the vast car park; it was almost empty.

'It looks like we have the place virtually to ourselves,' said Miriam, with relish.

'Like a private viewing. We'll have all the assistants running to and fro,' agreed Ellie.

'I don't really want anything. And I haven't brought any money.' Rachel blurted, her voice betraying panic. 'I'll just watch the rest of you.'

'Don't be silly,' said Heather, taking her arm. 'We're going to get you some lovely things to wear, things that fit, and suit you, and you mustn't worry about the money, it's all sorted out. Miriam and I are going to treat you.'

Ellie and Tansy beamed.

'But really, I couldn't. It wouldn't be fair....' Rachel had the sudden impression that this whole outing had been a ruse to get her away from her parents, and her mother in particular. At the thought of Ruth's disapproval, any premonition of enjoyment dissipated into a sense of impending trouble. Loyalty and pride forced her to make one last remonstrance.

'Please, I don't think Mum will like it.' But her voice went unheard.

'Of course she will. It's what families are for. Come on, girls, let's shop!'

In the end, Rachel enjoyed herself. Ensconced in the tiny cubicle, she simply waited while her relations handed in clothes for her to try. No-one insisted on coming in to see, or in her stepping out to show. Sizes were discreetly referred to as 'smaller' or 'looser'; the numeric values were ignored. Once she had found something she liked, she was invited to emerge just into the vestibule where Ellie and Heather would nod encouragement, or suggest a helpful alternative. The threatened assistants were banished at a word from Miriam, once Rachel's white and hunted expression was understood. This process repeated itself in three or four shops. Eventually, a long denim skirt, two pairs of jeans, four t shirts and a couple of hooded zip up tops, two pairs of pyjamas, some decent and modest underwear and a pair of trainers had all found themselves into Rachel's carrier bags. Coating the joyous pill was a bitter shell of shame and fear, and Rachel choked on it while she sat in the cubicle in her bra and pants, mashing her midriff with restless hands. It seemed that the kinder and more generous her aunts and cousins were, the more unworthy Rachel felt. Thoughts of Ruth, poor, thin and shabbily dressed, picking her way through tables full of clothes at jumble sales and along the rails of charity shops kept intruding, and of her frayed-cuffed, shiny-suited, sad-eyed father too. What a lack in their provision would this spree expose? How could this undoubted expense *on her* be justified at all? Wouldn't Uncles Bob and Simon go ballistic when they knew? It wasn't even as though she was proper family!

Later, they went for tea at a smart coffee shop. Rachel asked for a cup of ordinary English tea while the others chose lattes and cappuccinos and frothy hot chocolates. Watching Ellie scooping whipped cream from her drink, and dipping in the chocolate flake, and eating a doughnut dripping with warm toffee sauce, Rachel wondered bitterly how on earth she remained so slim, while she, Rachel, who ate sensible meals, mainly, remained grossly over-weight. At the same time, she was uncomfortably aware that what her mother defined as sensible meals, Aunty Belinda would describe as 'convenience' food, where 'convenience' stood for cheap, or even junk. This awareness nourished a germ of resentment against her mother, which served to alleviate, at least in part, the guilt of the new clothes.

Presently, the three girls went off to browse round a store of accessories next door to the café. Heather and Miriam smiled at one another.

'Mission accomplished, I believe,' Miriam said.

'Oh yes. Poor thing. Shame we can't do the same for Ben.'

'We will, when he's older. I don't think he cares much, at the moment.'

Heather viewed the large, cloudy stone of a mood-ring she had bought. It looked, at the moment, as dull and ordinary as any beach-pebble. 'I don't know how we're going to get it all past Ruth,' she said. 'It wouldn't surprise me if she made us take them all back.'

'I can manage her,' Miriam sipped at her skinny latte, 'We'll just tell her that there was a sale on and everything was 'buy one, get one free."

'Well, that might do it!' Heather laughed, but went on, more seriously, 'I don't think she especially likes getting cheap things, you know. Money is just a preoccupation with her; did it annoy you at Christmas?'

Miriam shook her head. 'Not really. It was just so – oh – so *cramped* for a start. What with the Christmas tree, and all the presents, and the nine of us, and children being children, of course, it was just chaos. But even that would have been bearable just for a few days if Ruth hadn't been so insufferably.... cloying. I hardly knew her, after all, but she was so *intense*. It was as though she expected me – instantly – to be as close to her as April had been. And I gather they were *very* close.'

'Ruth was devastated when April died, as devastated as Simon, really. At the funeral she behaved very oddly – as if she was the chief mourner.'

'I *know* April was an amazing person and I probably ought to be flattered but I'm *not* April and I like to choose my own friends and, to be honest, some of the stuff Ruth wanted to talk about was so *intimate*. I just wasn't ready for that level of relationship.'

Heather nodded, sympathetically. 'Mmmm, I see. In Ruth's defence, I think she'd invested a lot in Christmas; I don't mean money, I mean that she'd planned and prepared and she really wanted it to be a good visit. And when you all upped and left, I think it left things very flat for them.'

'I can understand that, and I tried to explain at the time,' Miriam picked at a mark on her trousers with a flawlessly manicured nail. She sighed. 'I suppose I'm going to have to have it all out with her.'

Heather shook her head. 'I shouldn't think so. It isn't the way we do things.'

'But at the end of the day, what I can't understand is that she should expect me to put her and her family, above my own mother.'

'She fell ill, didn't she?'

'Yes, and when we got the news, of course, I had to go to her.'

'Perhaps Ruth thinks it was just an excuse.'

Miriam considered. 'I'll admit that in a nasty, selfish way that I'm not proud of, I *was* glad to have an excuse to get away. Even without it, perhaps I couldn't have lasted the distance. But the illness was quite genuine and while I'm not close to my Mother, of course I know where my duty lies. What would you have done, in my shoes? What would Ruth?'

'You didn't take the presents they'd bought for you.'

Miriam flicked this away as an irrelevance. 'That was an oversight.'

'Ruth feels it keenly, I think. She inferred from the fact that you left them behind that you expected them to be worthless.'

'Oh dear. Yes, I see.' Miriam sighed.

Heather looked at her watch. 'Nice as this is, I think we ought to make a move. If we go home without Belinda's groceries, there'll be trouble, and the shops may close early in the country.'

Miriam began to gather her bags and parcels together.

'Yes. I mustn't alienate another McKay sister, must I?' she laughed, ruefully.

Calm descended at Hunting Manor. Starlight and Mitch slept, the effects of their disturbed night and the morning's exertions catching up on them. Robert, too, after a shower and a change of pyjamas, and a light meal, and two of his tablets, had gone back to bed. He had complained querulously all the while to Mary, that he had been left cruelly alone, had got lost in a strange house, heard angelic music and finally freed a statue from a fountain. Mary supervised his toilet in silence, while Les and James between them washed, dried and dressed the frail, trembling body of her husband in some clean pyjamas. Belinda fetched his breakfast and Les sat patiently by Robert's side while he ate the meal with a shaking hand. Then the curtains had been drawn on the bright midday and Robert had composed himself to sleep, Les remaining in faithful attendance in the blue armchair; both men as still and as silent as corpses.

Downstairs, in the hall, there was tumult as the boys and the men prepared for their expeditionary journey to the sea. They gathered in an assortment of inappropriate clothes, before being sent away by Simon for long trousers, stout shoes or boots, waterproofs and water containers.

'Oh Uncle Simon! Must we? Waterproofs? It isn't even raining!' complained Ben, stumping back up the stairs. Once reassembled, appropriately attired, they were dispersed again for 'provisions', arriving together pell-mell in the kitchen to beg for fruit, biscuits, packets of crisps and slices of cake to sustain them on their excursion. Elliot, from his place at the table, frowned up at them all as they gathered around Belinda.

'Going to join us, Elliot?' asked James, good-naturedly, slipping two chocolate biscuits and an apple into his good pocket, 'Big expedition; derring-do and the like?'

'I don't seem to be required,' Elliot replied, huffily.

'Oh, come on!' James laughed, but Elliot returned to his computer. James and Belinda exchanged a look.

201

Finally, in a frenzy of excitement, they set off. Simon in an ankle length green waxed cattleman's coat and a matching sou'wester set as a rakish angle, James in his ordinary trousers and an old blue anorak whose zip was broken and which had one pocket hanging off, Bob in a denim jacket and baseball cap, Toby and Todd smartly dressed in matching thick twill breeches, ski jackets and expensive new walking boots, Ben in pilled blue tracksuit bottoms, a yellow cagoule and Kermit Wellingtons bearing the name *Chelsea Witherspoon* in permanent ink on the sides. Tiny lumbered behind them, without enthusiasm; he viewed any kind of exercise as a tiresome bore.

'What a sight we are!' laughed Simon as he herded his troops across the sweep and round the back of the house towards the woods. The day was clear and bright, but a brisk wind whipped in from the sea. The tops of the trees clashed and shivered as it passed, making a noise like a distant round of applause, and showers of golden leaves cascaded down onto the lawns, glinting as they caught the sun. The party stopped briefly to argue over the map. Ben knew the way, having explored the previous evening with his father, but Toby wanted to plot their course, and was laboriously working out the scale in order to calculate their *ETA*. Ben hopped and jumped around him impatiently, pointing to the path and squeaking with excitement and frustration. Todd practised his fighting moves in case they were set upon by bandits. The men stood around them and tried to suggest a compromise, James and Simon, from absurd politeness, trying to make their own boy give way to the others. Finally Toby was allowed to hold the map, as he was the oldest, but Ben was entrusted with the compass, and Uncle Simon even promised to show him how to use it, later. Todd went puce and opened his mouth to roar his objection, but Bob quickly gave him a long stick and told him its use would be imperative in order to ward off attack from bears.

Now men,' Simon said as they set off down the lawn, 'I want you to keep your eyes peeled, in case we find something momentous and important.'

'What?' Todd practiced peeling his eyes by lifting the lids with his fingers.

'The family tree, of course!' James said. 'It'll be somewhere round here, mark my words.'

Back in the house, silence reigned. The house seemed to settle and relax on its ancient foundations, the peace and stillness ebbing out into every corner, to take back possession. Tension exhaled from every room; furniture rested, draperies drowsed, even the boiler slumbered. Mary fussed and tutted as she mended Robert's torn pyjamas in the warm kitchen. Belinda prepared vegetables for the evening meal and worried that Miriam might fail to return with the extra lamb steaks she needed.

'They won't be as nice, anyway,' she moaned. 'They'll hardly get any time at all in the marinade.'

'You haven't stopped all morning,' Mary chided, gently. 'I don't know how many sittings of breakfast you cooked, and now you're straight on to dinner.'

'The family has to be fed, Mum,' Belinda said, 'you know that.'

Ruth, supposing she ought to do something useful, toured the children's rooms and collected together two wash-loads of travel-stained clothes, grubby socks and underwear. There was chaos in the boys' room; clothes were flung about anyhow, pyjamas discarded on the floor, books and toys strewn everywhere, and the debris of a midnight feast crumbily evident. One of the beds was wet – a drink had been spilled. She stripped off the sheet and threw back the duvet to air. The whole room smelled musty and stale; of sweaty, excited boy. The windows were painted shut so she walked along the corridor and opened the door onto the roof terrace to let in the breeze.

She stood for a while looking out over the countryside, breathing the sharp damp autumn scents. She knew that she could easily stand here for hours, lost in her own thoughts, allowing them to spiral her down into a morbid depression; the weight in her chest pressing down on her, through strata of hopelessness and waste, of poverty, of loneliness and wretchedness. And deep in her core there fermented a scalding cauldron of angry disappointment. All she had wanted, as a child, was to be allowed to be part of the business. Her father's world - of trucks and motorways and greasy rags and long hours in the cab - had seemed so inviting to her; a big, important, wide world. She had clamoured to be allowed to accompany him on trips in his lorry during the holidays. She would be good, she had promised, not get in the way, not ask for anything, pass him his sandwiches. She had asked to be allowed to go to the yard on Saturdays, longing to potter in the tiny cubicle of the office, to swivel in her father's chair, to touch the greasy log-books and put the pink, puckered delivery notes into numerical order for him, to scramble into the cabs and put her hands on the smooth, solid steering wheel, and see if her feet could reach the pedals. But he had brushed her aside, had never even known her dream; to be his son in all but gender; not the reluctant son that Simon became, but an eager son, a capable, competent son, who could learn from him and take her place at the helm of McKay's Haulage. But he had dismissed her. The yard was no place for a girl, she would be better off at home with her mother. Simon, on the other hand, was hauled off to the yard when he could barely walk, was taken on day jobs up and down the M1, had slept in the cab and been shown how to load and secure a cargo before he started secondary school.

How she had envied him; then, and since. Wanted - fiercely coveted - everything he had.

It wasn't fair, she considered, when you looked at Simon and her sisters. Out of them all she was easily the most intelligent, the most dynamic, and yet they had left her utterly behind. All her efforts and struggles had achieved absolutely nothing.

Still clutching at the armful of laundry, she perched on the wide stone parapet and looked miserably down at the gravel path which circled the house, and the roofs of the single story outbuildings below, and felt completely alone.

June crept amongst the bedrooms, assessing their relative sizes and facilities, nosing and prying. She pondered the collection of tablets and treatments, supplements and suppositories which cluttered the dressing table top in Ruth's room. She noted that one of the twin beds was immaculately made, almost as though it had not been slept in. The other was tumbled and askew, and a grey, shapeless t shirt evidently relegated to sleeping duties, was scrumpled on the pillow. She wondered, briefly, which bed belonged to whom, or if they had both squashed into the one. It would explain why Ruth had slept so badly. In Heather and Bob's room, she remarked with disapproval the disorder of clothes cast everywhere, baby paraphernalia, and the extremely tangled bed. The idea of the two of them locked together in a knot of limbs and long hanks of hair made June shudder slightly. Then, proceeding quietly in the direction of Mitch's apartments, she found what she was looking for; two single rooms, former nurseries, one with barred windows, not en-suite but close to the master bathroom, and prettily furnished. One of those would be fine, she thought. Finally, returning to the main landing, she opened another bedroom door to discover a nicely proportioned double room with shower and toilet. It was unoccupied, and while she couldn't help fizzing with indignation that this superior accommodation had not been offered to her, yet she was glad to think that her own flesh and blood would benefit from it.

She ascended to the attics. There were two large unoccupied rooms and at least three spare single ones on the top floor. It was clear as day there was plenty of space left in the house and Belinda was only to be condemned for her small-minded selfishness. The girls and boys were all impossibly untidy; their mothers ought to be ashamed of them. Rob was still in bed, at well past lunch time! He groaned and turned over when she opened his door and switched on the light. He wore no pyjamas and directed an expletive at her which had to be heard to be believed.

'You're a very rude boy,' she said, vehemently, as she closed his door.

Her voice in the corridor roused Ruth from her reverie.

She stepped into the doorway. 'What are you doing up here?' There was more challenge in her voice than she had intended. June looked momentarily discomfited before spying the laundry in Ruth's arms.

'The same as you: looking for washing. I thought I'd help out.'

'Hmm.' Ruth breathed, doubtfully, turning back to the view. June stepped out to join her. 'Looks like we're needed here after all,' she crowed. 'Les is sitting with *your father* while the rest of you are all out enjoying yourselves.'

'There are plenty of people willing and able to sit with him,' Ruth rejoined, acidly. 'Les doesn't have to sit with Dad if he doesn't want to, I'm sure. God knows we're not *short* of people here, are we?'

'Well there weren't enough people on hand to stop him wandering off, were there, dear? Ha ha ha!' June laughed. 'It seems to me that it should be a case of 'the more the merrier'.'

'It seems to *me* that that isn't for *you* to decide.' Ruth kept her eyes on the vista.

June sniffed. 'Far be it from me to criticise, but common politeness would suggest that we should have been included from the beginning. Thankfully Elliot has made good the deficit of some people's bad manners.'

'Elliot isn't the head of this family,' Ruth said, 'although he may act as though he were.'

'He's the head of the family firm, which is much the same thing,' June said, mildly, smoothing her hair against the breeze. 'Apart from him I'm the only genuine McKay still working there, protecting the family interests. I think I'm owed something for that, don't you?

207

He does, anyway, and where I feel that I can be of use to the family I'm prepared to suffer any kind of rudeness and insult. I know my duty, even if no one else does.'

'Family isn't about duty,' Ruth retorted, but June had marched off down the corridor, bristling with self-righteousness.

Ruth fumed as she filled the machine with the first load, throwing in Starlight's sodden clothes and the wet sheet. As though *she* needed a lecture from *June* about the meaning of family, she seethed.

As a history graduate Ruth was familiar with the sociological origins of family. At one time, in ages past, it had been about security and mutual protection, clans living and touring the hunting grounds together, or, later, working the land. Vigorous men and child-bearing women connected by a reciprocal tissue of need; their children the healthy seed-stock of future generations of survival. Later still men and women continued to make judicious choices for the furtherance of titles, trades and traditions; a blacksmith's son would become a blacksmith in his turn. A blacksmith's daughter might marry a carter or a woodsman, someone who would shore up the blacksmith's business. The family formed the hub of economic security. But industrialisation, and the Romantic Movement, had interrupted the trend. People worked outside of the family at repetitive and unskilled labour. The mill, factory and shipyard became the economic centres and people became dependent on them, and on their employers and workmates rather than on their families for security and for society. At the same time young people began to marry for love, through choice rather than through expediency, sometimes alienating their families. The welfare state came to mean that no child need carry the financial burden of their parents. They were, as she had said to June, entirely free from duty of that sort. Family, now, was about choice, not necessity, and needed so much more than just tradition to hold it together. But the question presented itself to Ruth as she sorted the remaining laundry into heaps according to colour: what else was it than tradition that had brought this family together now? The McKays traditionally made much of anniversaries and birthdays, the celebration of feasts both religious and pagan; Christmas, Easter, Halloween, Bonfire Night. It was expected, like so many other ways they did things, stained into them, like indelible dye in wool. The McKays did the 'done' thing; wore poppies for remembrance and hats in church, and clean knickers in case they got knocked over. They ate Parkin on November 5th, pancakes on Shrove Tuesday, and fish on Good Friday. They closed their curtains on the day of a neighbour's funeral. She'd despised it all and tried not to comply with all their silly customs, had tried, recently, to distance herself from them all. But doing things differently made her feel too uncomfortable, as if she was wearing somebody else's underwear. She felt awkward, out-on-a-limb and friendless, and her body would respond with a bout of illness as though it had been infected in her attempt to cut part of it away. It was as though myriad familial threads connected her and pulled her inexorably back. Then she would cravenly buy Parkin, or make pancakes, and despise herself.

Poor Ruth was like a living specimen of butterfly, pinned helplessly onto a tray with her kindred types, related and attached in ways it was entirely beyond her power to counter. The pin which held her was cruel and insistent and she often fluttered and fought against its restraint and resented the boundaries she was conscious of it imposing upon her. And yet frequently it was the only thing, in the maelstrom of her world, which connected her safely. She would cling to it as if unconsciously aware that its removal would cause her to bleed to death.

Caught as she was on the pin-point of family identity, she could barely contain herself as she entered the kitchen; 'that woman!' she ejaculated. 'Do you know she had the front to suggest to me that we weren't capable of looking after Dad without them?'

209

Elliot tapped busily at his laptop. The table was strewn with papers and files. Mary sighed and tucked her needle for safety through a fold of the material. 'Your father's like a wayward child,' she said. 'He doesn't know where he is, most of the time. It *is* wearing, a constant responsibility. Frankly, I *am* grateful for help, from any quarter.'

'Exactly my thinking,' Elliot said, an edge of triumph to his voice.

'Pity we're not mind-readers, then,' Ruth muttered.

'What are you making, Belinda?' Mary tried to change the subject.

'Meringues. I've heard that there is no better way to cook them than in an Aga, so I thought I'd give it a go. We can have them for dessert with raspberries and cream.'

'Delicious. Raspberries are James' favourite soft fruit.' Ruth said, with a brightness she didn't feel.

'I know,' said Belinda.

'I don't like raspberries,' said Elliot, 'or meringues.'

'Good. All the more for us.' Ruth said, sharply.

'Meringues were a McKay Sunday treat.' Mary smiled. 'And baked egg custard, rice pudding...'

Ruth sighed.

'Very cosy,' Elliot said, under his breath.

Belinda changed the subject again. 'How were things upstairs, Ruth? Any sign of my son?'

'No, still sleeping. One of the boys' beds was wet. We ought to ban drinks upstairs.' She suddenly felt wretched and hollow.

'Do you know where the linen room is?' asked Belinda, practical as always. 'It's the door just before Mitch's.'

'Yes, but I didn't want to go down there just now, while they're sleeping.'

'Very considerate, dear,' said Mary.

June joined them.

'You've been a long time. What have you been doing? Did you find any more laundry?' remarked Ruth, tartly.

'Tidying my room. Making my bed. *I* like to treat other people's belongings with respect,' June looked accusingly at Ruth.

Belinda looked at her watch. 'Does anyone want lunch? It's well past one.'

'And your son's still in bed!' June quipped acidly.

'Quite normal, for a teenager. He's on holiday, after all.' said Ruth. She didn't approve of it really but she was damned if she was going to let June criticise her family.

'I'd like a cup of tea,' said Elliot, tapping testily at the keys of his laptop. A wire connected his laptop to the mains, so anyone walking from the Aga to the fridge had to walk all the way around the long refectory table. He had spread papers all over the table and was busy transferring figures from a file onto a spread sheet. His briefcase was open on the table, his spectacles case and a calculator too. He didn't seem to care how much space he took up or how he might be inconveniencing other people.

'I'll put the kettle on, darling,' Belinda stood up from the sliding the meringues into the Aga and reached for the kettle.

'I don't suppose it would occur to you to make Belinda a cup of tea?' Ruth said cuttingly, to Elliot. 'She hasn't stopped all day.' She wished he would take his self-importance and his laptop and his fussy files and figures away somewhere else. 'Showing us all how important he is,' she thought to herself, bitterly. She had brought her book down

211

to read but there was nowhere she could sit which would not impinge on Elliot's arrangements.

'I don't mind,' Belinda said, quietly.

'I don't know, Ruth. Would it occur to *you*?' Elliot gave her a straight look across the room.

'It might have done, after I'd finished washing your underpants and socks.'

'Belinda's only trying to look after everyone,' remarked Mary, biting at her thread.

'Not everyone,' Elliot muttered, waspishly.

Belinda steered a narrow course between the sparring forces in the room. 'Well there's certainly plenty to be done. I can't do it all, of course. All the fires will need sweeping out and relaying for tonight. Not that we'll need them all, I don't suppose, but it was lovely, wasn't it, to have them all burning away so brightly last night?'

'James did that,' Mary put in. 'Do we have to chop our own wood? We should have asked the men to bring some back for us.'

'There's plenty on the ground along the drive, I noticed. It will only need collecting.'

'I don't think my back's up to chopping firewood,' Ruth put in, sullenly.

'It's a man's job, really,' June said, inspecting her nail varnish.

'Well *I* can't do it. I'm busy with this.' Elliot looked at them all in turn, daring them to suggest that he ought to leave his figures for another time in the interest of the family's warmth and comfort. 'These are crucially important calculations for some really big quotes. I need Carole to get them into the post without fail on Monday.' He looked round at them all; everyone avoided his eye. 'There's a year's business here!' he exclaimed, 'the business doesn't run itself, you know!' No one replied. Presently the kettle began to whistle and as no one got up to do it, Belinda began to make the tea.

'How's your health, these days, Ruth?' June asked, settling herself into the armchair by the Aga.

'Very indifferent, I'm afraid. I have a basket of ailments. If it isn't one thing, it's another. But I try not to complain.'

Belinda set cups and saucers out on the table.

'I'd have done that, if you'd asked,' June said. 'Except I was too afraid of disturbing Elliot.'

'Don't mind *me*,' Elliot said, 'no-one else does.'

'You work too hard, Ruth,' commented Mary. 'Couldn't you reduce your hours?'

'Not if I want to continue to feed my family, no.'

'Surely James' job pays something...?'

'Next to nothing, as you well know. Vocational work is a labour of love and brings its own rewards – not monetary ones, unfortunately.'

'He is an extra-ordinary man to do what he does,' Belinda said, over her shoulder, as she rinsed her hands.

'Humph!' ejaculated Elliot, to no-one in particular.

Ruth couldn't contain herself any longer; 'wouldn't you be able to concentrate better upstairs, Elliot?' she burst out. 'I thought Belinda mentioned there was a desk in your room.'

Elliot threw his biro so vehemently across the table that it knocked one of the cups off its saucer. Only its handle saved it from rolling off the edge and smashing on the floor. 'Jesus Christ! What is it with you McKay women?'

The violence of his response shocked Ruth. She wasn't used to being shouted at. She was certainly equal to a blazing row with Elliot

213

and for many reasons would have relished the opportunity of one, but from the corner of her eye she had seen Belinda jump at Elliot's expletive and the crash of the cup, and splash boiling water onto her hand. Something sounded a note of caution and instead of meeting fire with fire she said with surprising mildness; 'don't be silly. You could have gone with the men if you didn't want to stay with us. James asked you.'

'I don't seem to be welcome anywhere. And plainly my likes and dislikes have been utterly disregarded when it comes to planning the menu.' Even in his own ears Elliot sounded like a sulky child. 'Perhaps if I went home, that would be best,' he concluded, petulantly.

'Oh Elliot!' frowned Belinda as she ran cold water over her hand.

'You're just very touchy today, that's all. I'm often the same, on the first day of a holiday. It takes us a while to wind down. Look at me last night! I was all over the place,' Ruth soothed, with unwonted self-deprecation. She risked a glance at Belinda, who determinedly avoided her eye. She dried her hands and brought the teapot to the table.

'I don't want you to go home, Elliot,' she said, pacifically, 'but I wish you'd had a better night's sleep.' Mollified, Elliot retrieved his pen.

'I *am* very tired,' he admitted. 'And I have worries which, like you, Ruth, I try to keep to myself. I used to be able to talk things over with Robert but, now, I don't like to trouble him. There's all this to be done,' he indicated the files strewn across the table. 'I probably shouldn't have come at all, but I didn't want to spoil things for the rest of you.' There was silence while everyone considered the possibility that Elliot's absence could have spoilt things.

'I'm always happy to help, if I can, aren't I, Elliot?' June cooed, complacently. 'I've been in the business almost as long as Robert and there isn't much I don't know about it. There's many a knotty little problem that we've unravelled together, isn't there, Elliot? Shall I get the milk, Belinda?'

'Well,' Elliot demurred.

'Please.' Belinda poured the tea. 'Two years ago, I'd have agreed with you, June,' she said, 'but Elliot has modernised the company so radically that I wonder, these days, whether you're quite as up to speed as you used to be. I know I'm not.'

June bristled. 'My dear,' she said, pouring the milk into one of the cups, 'I might not know the new accounting program quite inside out, yet, but I know that some things, like family loyalty and common courtesy, not to mention human compassion, are still essential both inside the company, and out. Perhaps if I can teach others *that*, this week, I shall have achieved something. Now I think I'll take poor Leslie a cup of tea.' June swept a cup of tea off the table and stalked from the room.

'That's telling us,' said Ruth.

'Oh dear,' said Mary.

Belinda passed the tea and they all drank in silence.

'How about that walk round the gardens, after this?' Ruth asked, eventually. 'I wonder if there'll be anywhere to hang the washing out. That first load will be almost done.'

The three women ambled around the paved pathways which dissected the well-dug vegetable beds. Brussels sprouts and several varieties of brassicas showed promise for being ready after the first frosts. Tall bean plants and raspberry canes still clung to wigwams of poles and the south wall was covered with espaliered apple, pear and plum trees some of which still bore fruit. In the greenhouse, the leggy remains of tomato plants remained, yellowed, and ready for the fire. Belinda and Mary sauntered with animation, bending down to exclaim at leaves and squinting at plant labels every few steps. Ruth, who had no interest in gardening, felt restless, and wondered whether to make her excuses and simply go off for a good long tramp through the countryside. If only April was here, she thought to herself. We could walk around for hours arm and in arm and discuss the whole Miriam situation. Except, of course, if April was here, there wouldn't *be* a Miriam situation.

Presently the subject came round to Heather. They all agreed that she wasn't going to find it easy to adapt to motherhood. 'Look at that situation this morning,' Ruth cited. 'Basically, she had no idea where her child was. It looked to me like she hadn't even remembered she had one, until Mitch mentioned her name.'

'Mitch had been up with Starlight all night,' Belinda agreed. 'Whereas Bob and Heather had slept like logs.'

'They're very fortunate,' Mary said, 'to have that young man.'

'I think he's very fortunate to have *them!*' Ruth cried. 'Landed on his feet there, didn't he?'

'I don't think he takes it for granted,' Belinda put in. 'I was thinking this morning how *tenuous* he must feel. It's an odd arrangement, isn't it?'

'They have everything the way they want it,' Ruth said, a hint of bitterness in her tone.

'You make it sound as though they lead an indolent existence,' said Belinda, bending down to examine a plant label, 'I think Bob works very hard.'

'He gets well paid for it,' mumbled Ruth, 'and he enjoys it.'

Mary rummaged in her pocket for a tissue and wiped her nose. 'I don't think she'll find it any more difficult than we all did,' she stated, going back to the topic of Heather. 'It's just that she's started at a different stage. New-borns are hard, aren't they? Look at your Rob – he didn't sleep for months, did he? And poor Ben suffered with colic, I seem to recall. But by the time they were toddlers you'd both got on top of things. On one level, Ruth, you should be more sympathetic than any of us. Heather's starting a whole new relationship with Starlight, just like you had to do with Rachel. On top of that, there are so many things we don't know about her past.'

'You can say that again,' said Ruth, tartly. She was walking behind the other two; the path would not allow for more than two abreast.

'I was lucky,' Mary went on. 'All mine were relatively easy as babies. I was on my own such a lot, your Dad worked such long hours.'

'I hardly remember him,' Ruth sniffed.

'Nonsense,' Mary said, over her shoulder, 'you idolised him.'

They came out through a small door set into the wall, into the courtyard behind the kitchen. Les, his iron-grey hair dishevelled, was in one corner near an enormous wood pile, wielding an axe, splitting logs neatly. He nodded, deferentially.

'Afternoon, Ladies,' he said.

'Has Robert woken up?' asked Mary.

217

'Yes.' Les rested on the handle of his axe. 'I've dressed him and June is sitting with him in the little lounge. I think that young man has taken the baby out in the pram.'

'He'll find it heavy-going up the drive.'

'Thank you for doing the logs, Les,' Belinda said.

'Glad to help.'

They passed on into the formal gardens. The paths were wider and here and Ruth came alongside.

'Speaking of Starlight's past. What I'd like to know,' she said, 'is where on earth this child has come from. Is she permanent, or just on approval? I haven't been told that the adoption has all gone through, or heard mention of a social worker or anything. Forgive me, I know I'm a cynic, but there are processes to be followed, assessments, laws and so on. You can't just spirit a baby out of thin air!'

'I think Heather might disagree with you,' Belinda laughed. 'The way she talks, that's exactly what she did with Starlight.'

'I understood that she'd come from abroad,' Mary put in.

'Africa, yes. But how? Surely they had to have papers, permissions, a passport? If you ask me, the whole thing's a bit fishy,' Ruth said.

'Oh dear, Ruth. I do hope not,' said Mary. 'Poor Heather would never recover if Starlight was to be taken away.'

'Of course I wouldn't like that to happen either,' Ruth softened her tone. 'But I'm a realist and you have to face facts.'

'They are being very vague,' Belinda admitted.

They'd reached the far end of the lawn and stood of the top of the small hill which ran down to the woodland where Starlight and Robert had been found earlier. From here, the house looked splendid, many-gabled, a hexagonal tower at the corner romantic, the walls ancient and resilient. The back of the house was in shadow, facing east, and the shortening day was already turning the sky behind them a deep indigo. The sun hung above the house, glinting off the chimneys, and seemed to slip, even as they watched, into some hidden slot on the roof. The curious light exaggerated the contrast between the golden illuminated roofs and the shadowed walls. In the woods behind them, the wind thrashed the branches and birds hurled themselves across the skies, calling to each other. Apart from that, and the occasional thump of Les' axe, there was silence. From one chimney, a curl of smoke rose into the chill sky.

'Good,' said Belinda, practical as always, 'Les has lit the fire in the sitting room.'

Ruth sighed. 'I wonder who has wandered here before us and turned to look back on this view.'

'Every holiday maker who comes, I expect!' laughed Belinda.

'But before them,' snapped Ruth, testily, 'generations of men and women, children, nurses, estate workers, year after year, generation after generation....' She pictured them in her head, a procession through time, the costumes differing as the centuries marched on, but each connected to the other by some mysterious family vein; strings of genetic material which bound them, irrevocably, one to the other. But whether the cords were lifelines or fetters she could not say.

Belinda looked at her watch. 'It's getting on for four o'clock. Everyone will be back, soon. I expect they'll want tea. I ought to go back.'

'I'm getting a bit chilly, too. We've been out well over an hour.'

Mary and Belinda began to stroll back to the house, but Ruth remained where she was, scanning the blank windows of the house, looking with especial relish at her own room, ensconced in the hexagonal tower, trying to conjure up ancient inhabitants, soaking up the atmosphere of heritage and age-old tradition, and trying to see her

219

own family somehow in the pattern of fathers and sons, heirs and ancestors. The others disappeared, as she watched, through the gate into the courtyard, and it was almost as though they disappeared into another era, so desolate and timeless did the house and garden seem now that they had gone; no light shone from within, no people appeared to establish the century with a mode of dress or idiom of speech. Suddenly Ruth felt cold, and shivered as though someone had walked over her grave, and she thought of April, and sighed once more and began to walk back to the house.

The sun was so low now that only a sliver of it could still be seen over the roofline of the house, and fingers of light stretched over the roof and pointed into her eyes. It outlined with bright gold the rim of the house, the edge of the day, while the grey tide of dusk came on to swamp it over. She walked to the edge of the shadow, her toes submerged in its colourless substance, like a hesitant bather on the border, as it were, between day and night and, with April very much in her thoughts, on a lip that divided the living and the dead, the present with the past. It was a fitting image, too, in her mind, of the frail hold she maintained on life's positives, while perpetual discontent lapped with its insistent tide at her feet. It was too easy, sometimes, just to give up the fight and drown. She lingered as the shadow crept up her body, basking in the last vestige of brightness while conscious of the cold gloom which was submerging her, the sharp dank scent of rotting leaves and the shiver of the chill wind through the trees at her back. The sun at last slipped out of sight and her eyes struggled to accommodate themselves to the empty air. Death, she thought, might be as easy as this, a slow sink into dusky dust, the simple extinguishing of a light. But for April it had not seemed easy; despite the drugs, she had clung and resisted to the last. She had had more, perhaps, worth holding on to.

Then, behind her, she heard the thrash and crash of people in the undergrowth. She turned, and out of the woods tumbled Ben and his cousins, spilling with makeshift camouflage and impromptu weaponry onto the bright apron of lawn where the sunlight still remained.

They all arrived back at more or less the same time. The men and the boys were full of all their escapades; the woods, the paths, the cliffs, the sea. They were ravenous and voluble and as they tore off their outer clothes and boots, all talking at once, and only gradually realised that there were strangers in the kitchen, and that Belinda and June were facing each other across the table with venomous eyes, and that Mary was dabbing hers with a sodden tissue, and that Granddad looked more lost and confused than ever. And just as their talking and movement ground to a halt, the girls bustled in from the passageway, bearing carrier bags and chattering and laughing, and it took them some few moments too to notice that there was an awkward atmosphere in the room, and new people.

Of Elliot there was no sign at all. A yellow post-it note on his laptop declared simply 'Gone out.'

'Well, children,' said Belinda, into the eventual hush, her voice like steel. 'You'll remember your cousin Sandra, I suppose, and Kevin, her young man.' Belinda indicated the drably dressed, greasy-haired woman standing slightly behind June, and her vacuous, buck-toothed companion. 'And look, here's your great Granny McKay.' Belinda turned to the armchair by the Aga and drew their attention to the shrunken, white-haired, be-whiskered figure who sat in it, clutching a large handbag to her flat bosom. 'And let me introduce great Granny's friend, Mr Burgess,' said Belinda, finally, pointing to the shabbily suited old man who stood behind the armchair blinking and opening and closing his mouth over toothless gums. 'It seems that Aunty June felt that Grandma and Granddad's family holiday could not be complete without them, and they have all been invited to join us here.'

'Pleathed to meet you all,' Mr Burgess said, smiling gummily. He clutched to himself a medium sized, very aged portmanteau. 'Thethe are my thingth,' he said.

'Hello,' the family chorused, uncertainly.

At that moment, Rob entered the kitchen. His clothes were creased and his hair was a matted mess. It was plain he had not washed in the past twenty four hours. He had only just got up.

'Is there anything to eat?' he asked his mother, ignoring everyone. Granny McKay shot out of her chair with the energy of a woman half her age, and marched over to her great grandson. The top of her head came level with his chest, and she stared up at him with blazing eyes.

'Robert!' she snapped. 'How dare you come home in this state? I'll teach you, you long drink of piss!' She began to flail at him violently with her handbag. The protests of Belinda and Mary and of Rob himself did nothing to deter her, and eventually only the restraint of Kevin and Les together succeeded in halting the attack.

'She thinks you're your Grandfather,' Belinda tried to explain to Rob as Granny McKay was restored to the armchair. 'This whole idea is just madness. I'm sorry, Rob, darling. You poor thing, are you alright?'

Rob was flushed with embarrassment. 'She's crazy!' he shouted, his voice betraying the nearness of tears. 'You're crazy!'

'Who? Me? I don't think so dear,' said Granny, smiling happily. 'Who is this young man? I don't believe I've had the pleasure.'

'It was just a case of mistaken identity,' laughed June. 'Mother, this is *Rob*, ha ha ha.'

'He doesn't look anything like Dad,' Ruth said, tartly. 'I was only thinking so at breakfast time.'

'He didn't grace us with his company at breakfast time! He was lounging in bed,' June retaliated.

'She hit my son!' Belinda shouted at June. 'And you think she can stay *here* for a *week?*'

The rest of the family looked on in embarrassment.

'It does seem rather…er…..' James began

'Don't be ridiculous. Everything's fine,' June interrupted. She turned to Mr Burgess. 'Leslie will take your bag for you, Mr Burgess,' she said. But when Les stepped forward, Mr Burgess' face crumpled and he held the bag even more tightly to his chest.

'Alright, mate. You keep hold of it, if you like,' said Les.

In the corner of the kitchen, Ben and Todd were overcome by the humour of the situation. 'You long drink of piss! You long drink of piss!' they mouthed at each other.

Belinda took a deep breath. It was typical of Elliot to disappear just when he was needed. 'Tea is served in the sitting room,' she announced, formally. 'And dinner will be at seven. In the meantime, perhaps someone might organise accommodation for our guests, and carry up their bags? I'm afraid I haven't a single idea where they might sleep but no doubt June will direct you. You must excuse me, now, I have dinner to prepare.'

'Her Majesty will be joining us,' announced Granny McKay, solemnly, 'and the Crown Prince of Luxembourg, who is a vegetarian. I shall need my pearls. One always wears pearls in the country.'

'Yeth. Yeth, I should thay tho,' agreed Mr Burgess, nodding.

Belinda remained in the kitchen while the rest of them took tea in the sitting room, politely passing cups and plates, and making unnatural, bright conversation. June presided over the teapot like the family matriarch, a smug smile on her lips and her shrill 'ha ha ha' rising continually to the ceiling. Granny McKay drank her tea with noisy slurps and Mr Burgess mouthed his cake inefficiently so that crumbs cascaded down his shirt and came to lodge between the buttons. His portmanteau remained resolutely on his lap. Ruth was hard-pressed to keep the boys in line. They were relegated to the floor in the absence of sufficient seats for the grown-ups, and sat in an untidy circle behind the settee stifling giggles and guffaws. Toby started to speak in an affected lisp and Rob kept asking loudly what time her Majesty was expected, and how many Corgis they might have to accommodate. In the middle of tea, Elliot returned and expressed, significantly, no surprise at the presence of the new arrivals.

Eventually, Ruth sent the boys off to play snooker, James and Bob went to supervise and everybody else found some reason or other to absent themselves. Simon and Miriam volunteered to go upstairs and take the first baths. The girls went to try on their new clothes. Heather took Starlight out into the grounds.

'We will dance for the tree-spirits, darling, and say goodnight to the birdies, and feel the fresh wind on our faces.'

'Waa Waa Waa' burbled Starlight.

'See what a super place this is?' June turned to her daughter. 'Didn't I tell you?'

'Thith *ith* a nith plath,' Mr Burgess agreed.

'Where is it, again?' Granny frowned.

'I forget,' Mr Burgess shook his head.

'You're at Hunting Manor, Mother,' cried June. 'Robert, isn't it wonderful to have Mother here?'

'I thought she was at The Oaks,' Robert said, vaguely. 'We usually have the telly on. I like Supermarket Sweep.'

'Yes, but she's here on holiday, like us,' laughed June. 'It's something we never did do as children, is it, holiday together? You're here on holiday, Mother! Isn't that nice? Ha ha ha!'

'I don't remember ever having any holidays as a child,' Robert said. 'Mary and I took ours to the seaside once a year.'

'That's what I mean, dear. Don't you think it's time we did?'

'June,' Mary began, hesitantly, 'I'm just a little concerned about the children. They booked this place for a certain number of people and...'

'Oh Mary! Don't pour cold water on Robert's surprise!' snapped June. 'Now, Leslie, you can carry their bags up. I've found nice rooms for them all. There's plenty of space, no matter what Belinda says. They can have a rest before dinner.' She turned to Kevin, 'you must be tired, after all that driving.' Kevin shrugged, and grinned, inanely.

'We had to stop quite a few times,' Sandra said. 'Granny kept thinking she needed the toilet, but then when I got her into the cubicle, she wouldn't go. She said she needed Muriel.'

'Oh. Did she? How odd. I expect that's her Carer at the home.' June said.

'Mum,' Sandra frowned. 'I know who...'

But June had turned to her mother, speaking loudly. 'Muriel's your Carer, at the home.'

'Don't be ridiculous!' snapped Granny. 'You know very well who Muriel is. You must be going soft in the head. And don't shout. I'm not deaf. I've got my hearing aid in!'

'Sorry, Mother. I was just explaining to Sandra about Muriel.'

'Pardon? Who? I don't remember. This isn't The Oaks. Your father will be home soon. He'll sort it all out.'

'No, Mother, this is Hunting Manor.' June's irritation was beginning to show. Les left the room with Mr Burgess on his arm.

'There aren't many staff. I ought to speak to the Matron,' commented Granny as she shuffled down the hallway, assisted by Sandra.

'Thith ith a nith plath,' Mr Burgess remarked, over his shoulder.

'It *is* nice,' replied Granny. 'Where is it, again?'

'I forget,' said Mr Burgess.

Ruth piled the tea things onto a tray and carried them into the kitchen, where she recounted all the proceedings to a dishevelled and overwrought Belinda.

'What on earth is going on?' Ruth asked, rhetorically, running water into the sink. 'I mean, it seems like a bizarre sort of *farce.*'

Belinda's usual composure had deserted her. Her hair was coming down from its chignon and she had a splash of marinade on her cashmere sweater. 'Oh don't,' she wailed. 'There was no reasoning with the woman.'

'June?'

'Who else? I told her that this place just isn't suitable. Granny needs nursing care; a stair lift, a bath hoist, but she just laughed it all off and said that we'd manage perfectly well because - she specifically mentioned this - James is a nurse...'

'Cheek!'

'I know. I tried everything I could think of, Ruth: the agreement with the owners about numbers, the catering difficulties...but she said I – I - was being selfish. She said that this was family, and wasn't that just what I'd wanted all along, and that I was being contrary to start drawing lines where none existed!' Belinda flung herself down onto a chair and rested her head in her hands.

'What did Mum say?' Ruth asked, 'and Elliot? Surely he backed you up?'

Belinda shook her head, miserably. 'Mum agreed with me, about the nursing, but June ignored her. And James tried to back me up of course. Elliot was conspicuous by his absence.'

'He's left this damn computer in the way though, hasn't he?' said Ruth, irritably, taking the long way round to the fridge to put the milk away. 'If I didn't know better, I'd say he'd been expecting them. He and June were very thick in the library last night, after dinner.' She put the last of the tea things away and came to sit next to her sister. She wondered about pouring a glass of wine; there had been an open bottle, she had seen, in the fridge.

'Mmmm. And he's kept his head down today in spite of what he would see as intolerable provocation, from Heather, and from you, and from me.' They regarded each other, then Belinda said, with sudden flash of vehemence; 'I could put up with it *all*, for Mum's sake. All of this was for her, really, and if I thought it was what she wanted, I really could manage to cater for…..' she totted up on her fingers 'twenty five people. I'd do anything for her, you know that, Ruth. I'm sure you would too.'

'I doubt I could do *that*,' laughed Ruth, wryly.

Belinda's voice rose. Her face was flushed. 'I just wish we hadn't been conditioned to be so bloody *polite* all the time,' she burst out. 'Sometimes I want to scream but then I can just hear Mum saying 'little girls should be seen and not……..' she dissolved into tears. Ruth put her hand awkwardly on Belinda's shoulder, and wished she was the kind of woman to have a clean tissue up her sleeve.

'We'll just have to send them back!' Ruth said, rashly, as though it were that simple.

Belinda shook her head. 'We can't!' she moaned, through tears, 'not for a few days, anyway. Granny's room's being decorated while she's away.'

'And what about Mr Burgess?' Ruth got up and made for the fridge to fetch the wine.

'Exactly! Don't ask me where he fits into this family picture!' Belinda blew her nose. 'But then again,' she said, more calmly, 'I suppose you could say the same of Mitch.'

'Mitch goes everywhere with Bob and Heather; it's understood,' Ruth countered, pushing a glass towards her sister.

'I know. I know.'

They looked at each other in blank despair.

Then Ruth decided that they had spent enough time bewailing the situation. It was time they came up with a plan. 'So, what shall we do?' she asked. 'The thing that gets me, frankly, is the money. I can't stand free-loaders. I think we should insist that, if they're going to stay, they pay a hefty chunk of the cost.'

But monetary issues seemed unimportant to Belinda. 'It would seem so rude, sending them away. I don't think I'm capable of it. It isn't really *them* that I'm cross with.' She twisted a ring round and round her finger. Ruth had noticed it before with an envious eye; a large diamond cluster, quite flashy.

'No, it's June, I know that. But they're just as bad, pushing themselves in. Parasites. Not Granny and Mr Burgess. I don't think they have a clue where they are or what day it is. But simpering Sandra and her Neanderthal boyfriend. Talk about front! We can't let them walk all over us!'

'I have a feeling we'll have to, Ruth. The last thing I want is a scene.'

'Heaven forbid!' ejaculated Ruth, with sarcasm. 'This was never a family for confrontation. Everything gets swept under the carpet and left to fester. God knows how much damage has been done in the past in the name of 'not causing a scene'. We probably all need months of counselling!' Both sisters thought about their brother, absent for so long, battling his demons.

Presently Ruth remarked, 'Dad never minded causing a scene. *He* was allowed to. The rest of us kept quiet, as though our opinions didn't count.'

'That was just the way we did things,' Belinda sighed.

'The McKay way,' Ruth cried, ironically, 'so much more than lorries!'

The McKay way. The inviolable routine of the Monday wash, laundry on the line by eight - but never knickers; the neighbours mustn't see the McKay underwear – dried and ironed and put away by four. The sanctity of family affairs; dirty laundry must never be aired.

'Everything in my upbringing and conditioning says that I should be polite and stay quiet,' moaned Belinda, sipping gingerly at her wine – it was drier than she liked, really - 'and let her walk all over us. But it isn't just up to *me*, is it? I don't know what other people will think. People might take sides. Frankly, I'm not sure which way people will jump.'

'It's a downright intrusion. Surely everyone will feel the same?'

'I do,' said Simon, joining them suddenly as though his image in their minds a moment before had conjured him up. He was damp from his bath. He poured himself some wine. The three siblings regarded each other hopelessly across the table.

'What does Miriam think,' asked Ruth, carefully, topping up her glass.

Simon leaned back in his chair. 'Oh, she thinks it's hilarious,' he said. 'And when you look at us, you can see her point; you couldn't make up such a motley crew as we already have here and adding in two geriatric, senile, incontinent....' he ran out of suitable adjectives, 'can only make the picture more colourful.'

Belinda managed a weak smile. 'They've got us cornered,' she said. 'No matter what we do now, it will be us who comes out of this looking rude and inhospitable. All my talk of family values will look like so much hot air. You don't suppose they *are* incontinent, do you?'

Heather joined them. 'I've had some lovely quality time with Starlight!' she said, smiling happily. 'We danced across the grassy sward and curtsied to the wood faeries, and sang along with the wind. Now she's watching *Blind Date* with the three big girlies while I get her tea ready.'

'From the sublime to the ridiculous,' muttered Ruth.

'Just sit down a moment and talk to us,' Simon pulled a chair out for her. Ruth fetched a glass from the cupboard. Belinda up ended the wine bottle and the last of the wine flowed into Heather's glass.

'This is the first time we've been together, just the four of us, for I don't know how long,' remarked Belinda, looking round the table at them.

'Years, when you come to think of it,' Simon mused.

But the realisation of their strangeness was unhelpful and they moved past it quickly.

'What do you think about this situation with June, and our new guests,' Simon asked Heather, carefully.

'Well,' Heather considered briefly, 'it all seems a bit odd. They weren't invited and yet here they are. To be fair, I think Uncle Les feels very uncomfortable about it. Bob mentioned having over-heard something last night...'

'Yes. Poor man. He really does feel awkward. I feel for him.'

'But there's no need for him to, is there? I mean, there's plenty of room and enough food and everything? And he's pleasant enough.' Heather never bothered herself with practicalities. Things generally arranged themselves without any in-put from her.

Belinda demurred. 'Well, these meals don't just throw themselves together,' she said.

'Or pay for themselves,' Ruth put in.

'It's the principle of the thing,' Simon insisted.

'Isn't it just two rather sad old people and two, well, rather sad young people being given the opportunity of a holiday and a nice family party? I don't see any harm in it, even if their arrival was something of a surprise.' Heather toyed with her necklace. It was made of curious beads engraved with runes, and a number of significant crystals.

'You're right, Heather,' Belinda sighed. 'You make me feel unkind. It's just June who's annoyed us all.'

'She hasn't annoyed Elliot,' Heather said, narrowly, twirling wine around her glass. 'I find his aura quite difficult to read; it's sort of murky and obscure. But if he *had* objected, I think we all know that he would have told us by now.'

The clear-sightedness of this remark struck them all with especial force, coming, as it did, from Heather, who could not normally be relied upon to see the wood for the dryads.

'Oh yes,' Belinda agreed.

'And so although *we* would all back you up, Lindy, darling, you need to consider that you might find yourself in opposition to him.'

Everyone around the table agreed, silently, that this was not a situation which they could allow Belinda to get herself into. She avoided their eyes. For that moment there was perfect accord and sympathy between them. It didn't solve their problem, but it felt like they were in it together.

'I think you're going to have to fight fire with fire.' Miriam, whom no-one had noticed standing by the door, made them all jump. She was pink and scrubbed from her bath, her hair shining like wet jet. She lifted an apologetic hand, 'I'm sorry, I know it's none of my business. I shouldn't interfere, but I just thought I'd say that much.'

Simon pulled a chair out for her but Miriam shook her head in refusal.

'I'm not staying,' she announced. 'I only came down to see if there was anything I could do to help.'

'No, but you think we ought to confront her, then?' Belinda probed.

'Heavens, no!' Miriam laughed. 'She'd love that! The reek of burning martyr as she packed her cases would be intolerable. No, I think you're going to have to be far subtler, and use her own tactics against her.'

'What do you mean?' asked Ruth, in spite of herself.

'Well,' Miriam put her head to one side. 'Two things: old people can't participate in the same way as younger ones; some-one will have to miss out on quite a bit in order to care for them. Now I know we've resisted Elliot's efforts so far to make a holiday itinerary, but it mightn't be a bad idea to see how many sea-fishing, pony-trekking and canoeing adventures we're going to be able to fit in. Do you see where I'm going? And also, isn't there another sister? I can't imagine this *"family holiday"*' she lifted two fingers of each had to make the quote marks, 'could be complete without her.'

'Aunty Muriel!' Simon ejaculated, slapping the table with the palm of his hand 'How June would *hate* to have her here!'

'There you are, then,' smiled Miriam, turning to go. 'Simon, if there's any of that white burgundy we brought with us, I'd love a glass, presently.'

Miriam left them looking at each other across the table.

'So we're going to let her get away with it!' Ruth glowered, thinking of the money.

'Not at all!' Heather got up. 'I don't think Miriam implied that. The universe,' she declared, knowingly, 'has a way of righting wrongs. It's part of the natural equilibrium of things.'

'Alright. So here's our angle,' Simon summarised. 'Having arranged their coming here, we'll obviously assume that June is happy to take responsibility for today's arrivals. That's going to mean being left behind here with them for much of the time.' He opened the fridge to find Miriam's wine.

'You can't be expected to do it, Belinda, you're far too busy,' Ruth pointed out, catching on.

'And Heather has Starlight to look after,' Belinda agreed.

'And poor Ruth just isn't well enough; she needs a good rest,' Simon joined in, with a twinkle, coming back with the white burgundy.

'And poor Simon's only a man, so he doesn't count!' Heather laughed.

'I suppose that this way, we can avoid a scene, and make sure that Mum and Dad enjoy themselves....' Belinda began, resolving herself to the situation.

'Oh yes, of course. But at the same time,' Simon put in, 'if we invite Muriel,'

'June will hate it!' Ruth finished, triumphantly.

They all assimilated the plan, the unforeseen benefit of June's manoeuvrings which had united them, so unexpectedly, at last. The atmosphere in the room was perceptibly leavened. Even Belinda felt shored up by it, her despair of earlier quite gone.

Heather walked to the fridge and began to search inside. 'Why *did* June and Muriel fall out?' she asked, 'does anybody know?'

Belinda too got up from the table and began to unpack the shopping which had lain forgotten on the dresser. 'I'm not sure. It isn't talked about. I think it was over a man,' she recalled. 'Oh, good,' she said, 'you bought more bacon.'

'Yes, we thought we'd better. And they really haven't spoken since?'

'Isn't that sad?' Ruth drained her glass. 'I can't imagine *us* falling out over a man. You could have mine, either of you, any time!' she held her glass out to Simon, who filled it up.

'For your own good, Ruth, that's your last until dinner,' he warned, kindly.

'Poor James! You don't really mean that, do you? Oh no!' Belinda pulled a box from the carrier bag. 'You got lamb *grill* steaks! These aren't what I wanted at all! They're only burgers!'

'It's all they had,' Heather said, calmly. 'At least they're organic.'

'I shouldn't worry, 'Ruth soothed. 'The kids will probably prefer them.'

Simon carried Miriam's wine out of the room. Belinda followed him, carrying shopping to the storeroom. Heather rummaged in a drawer for a knife. Ruth remained alone at the table and watched the pendulum of the clock, over the Aga, swinging relentlessly to and fro until she felt strangely glassy and mesmerised. It was warm, in the kitchen, and homely, and curiously peaceful, and the dark shadow of depression she had been conscious of somewhere in the region of her diaphragm felt diminished; the warm glow of the wine on an empty stomach had effervesced it away to a degree but the concord of her brother and sisters had done far more to winnow it. She remained,

235

fixed to her seat, nurturing the pale kernel of hopefulness, immovable, as though the slightest motion would dislodge or dissipate it.

Simon's laugh, when he came back through the door, almost made her jump. 'Well *that* was a bad move,' he chortled, reaching up for more glasses from the cupboard. 'I seem to have got the job of cocktail waiter, now.'

His words dropped a boulder on Ruth's nascent contentment. It curdled and warped and turned bitter in an instant. 'James was supposed to be doing that job,' Ruth griped. 'He really is absolutely *useless*.' Suddenly her wine tasted sour.

Belinda returned, with an assortment of vegetables. 'I've been trying to think,' she said, 'but I can't remember a single time when I've seen June and Muriel together. Although Muriel did come to our wedding, I *think*...'

'But not to speak to your own sister, for years. That's sad.' Heather interrupted, hesitating half way across the kitchen with a packet of ham and some butter.

'I didn't speak to mine for years,' Simon commented, mixing drinks.

'That was different,' Ruth said, with an effort.

'Of course it was!' Heather agreed. 'You went off adventuring, Simon, we didn't fall out.'

Simon and Ruth exchanged a look; its sub-text strengthened Ruth, a little. 'Some families have feuds which go on for years,' she offered, 'they go on down the generations until nobody knows what the original disagreement was all about.'

'It would have to be something terrible,' Belinda pondered, beginning to assemble the ingredients for the evening meal, 'something absolutely unforgivable.'

Heather sucked butter off her fingers. 'I don't think it happens so much in Eastern cultures. Families are so often bound by business interests as well as emotional ones, there.'

'*We* have business interests in common....' Belinda was busy peeling carrots.

'Well......... We're not *hands-on*, are we? McKays Haulage is a closed book to me, even though I am a director. I haven't a clue what goes on. We could be trafficking illegal immigrants for all I know.' Heather looked, for a moment, as though she could bite out her own tongue. 'I'm sure Elliot wouldn't, though, Lindy,' she added, blushing.

Simon set glasses on a tray. 'I wouldn't put it past him, if there was a profit in it,' he said, darkly.

'But what act could one family member possibly do to another which could split a family?' Heather went back to her original question. 'That's what I'm really wondering. I can't imagine anything dividing ours.'

'I hope we'll never have to find out, Heather,' Belinda said.

Ruth laughed, cynically. 'I think the rot's already setting in, isn't it?' she asked. 'Look at us, really. What do we really have in common other than the same mother and father?' She shook her head, and laughed, hollowly. 'I have no idea what you do for a living, Simon. I couldn't tell you where Heather likes to go shopping or what music Belinda likes. I couldn't name your best friends or your favourite restaurants. I could make a guess at your political leanings, I suppose. But I don't know what your dreams are, what you hope for, what you're afraid of...' she trailed off. Her siblings were looking at her, their faces betraying, variously, shock, sadness, reluctant agreement.

Suddenly Heather threw down the knife she was using. 'We must make a pact of unity,' she declared, kicking off her shoes and tearing the rubber bands from her ponytail. Her golden hair cascaded down over her shoulders, and she caught up the flimsy gathers of her ethereal garment in her hands, and began to hop and skip around her siblings, humming and singing in an aimless, tuneless monotone, letting her clothing lift and fall as she twirled and leapt.

'I shall enjoin the good spirits, and summon the forces of harmony,' she cooed, a little breathlessly, 'and they shall appoint unto us guardian angels for our concord!' Tears of sadness which had threatened turned to tears of laughter, as her brother and sisters howled helplessly onto each other's shoulders.

Because of the late telephone call and the consequent disturbed night, Muriel slept much later than usual. It was after eleven when she telephoned The Oaks and asked to speak to Matron. The receptionist, a youngster, seemed upset. The normal sense of orderly decorum and well-heeled calm had evidently suffered a severe jolt. While Matron was found, Muriel could hear definite signs of a flap in progress. The visitors' entrance hall, which was floored in highly polished parquet, reverberated from the hurry of many panicked footsteps, doors slammed and the usually chocolate-smooth voices of the care assistants were raised to shrill and unpleasant decibels. Eventually, an out-of-breath Matron picked up the receiver.

'Hello? Oh, hello Miss McKay. Excuse me, yes, rather a to-do here. Your mother is quite well, no need for concern there, and has departed on her little holiday as arranged. But another resident, Mr Burgess, seems, momentarily to have gone AWOL. Would you mind very much if I were to phone you back?'

'Excuse me,' said Muriel, slowly, in her best National Health Trust Records Department voice, 'You say my mother has gone on holiday? By whose arrangement?'

'Your niece, Miss Sandra, is escorting her to the country. I was instructed yesterday evening by your sister to prepare her things. I hope there hasn't been a change of plan?'

'Sandra has taken Mother to the country?' Muriel repeated, incredulously.

'Yes indeed. And in her absence we're redecorating her room, *also* on your sister's instruction. We think that's what's upset Mr Burgess. Strangers and so on. I'm sorry, you'll have to excuse me, a police officer has just arrived.'

Muriel replaced the receiver slowly. Feelings of abandonment swept over her and she wept a few tears. So the *whole family* except for her would be up there in that big house, talking about old times,

239

laughing and joking, making arrangements for Christmas and she, alone, was excluded through no fault of her own. The cruelty of it was too much to bear. She desperately wanted to speak to Les, to have him come to her, but she knew there was no possibility of that and that she must not ask it.

She looked around her little house. The Saturday jobs waited to be done; the bed was due for stripping and she ought to walk up to the corner shop to pay the paper bill. Saturday was library day, too. Inviolable routine supported her life – she was, after all, a McKay - like rungs of an overhead ladder, she swung from one to the next, having always to have a firm grip, or she would fall. On Monday she washed and ironed, and in the evening Les came. On Tuesdays she shopped and in the afternoons tended her little garden. Wednesday was the day for visiting Mother. On Thursdays she cleaned her house from top to bottom, and on Friday she went out with Les, and they made love in her narrow bed in the afternoon. Saturday was the day for changing the sheets, for paying bills, for the library and, sometimes, a car boot sale. On Sunday she attended the hospital chapel service along with the patients and some of the staff. She would help with wheeling chairs down from the wards and afterwards would hand round luke warm tea in hospital green china. Usually she would sing as she went about her chores but today there wasn't a tune in her body, and she had no energy for anything. She climbed the stairs slowly and began to run a bath.

Later, in the afternoon, just as she had got back from the shops, Muriel's telephone rang again. It was Matron.

'Good afternoon, Miss McKay. I'm so sorry to bother you. We think we may have traced our wanderer.'

'Really?'

'Yes. It seems that as one of the cleaning staff was leaving this morning she left the door unlocked so that the decorators could carry their gear in. At the same time, your niece and her young man were helping Mrs McKay outside to the car. We believe that Mr Burgess must have taken the opportunity to follow them outside.'

'I see.'

'The police have interviewed all the staff, you see, quite routine, I believe, in the circumstances. Naturally, we're very concerned. Mr Burgess requires regular medication, quite apart from anything else.'

'Of course. I see.' Muriel put her bag of library books down carefully. Roger sniffed them, hopefully. 'How upsetting for you all.'

'Oh yes, it is, Miss McKay. We've never lost anyone at The Oaks before.'

Muriel sensed the Matron's hesitation. 'Is there anything I can do to help?' she asked, tentatively.

'There might be. The thing is: one of the gardeners recalls seeing Mr Burgess on the drive. He always has his little suitcase with him and that distinguishes him, d' you see? And we believe, that is we think, or at least, it seems possible, that he must have climbed into the car with Mrs McKay. It's the only explanation we can come up with. The police have searched the neighbourhood and no-one's seen him. He *must* have gone with them. And you see while it might all have been just a mistake, well, I don't mind telling you that the police are pursuing other avenues, far more sinister ones. In fact, they wanted to know,' Matron lowered her voice conspiratorially, 'they were asking me, in fact, Miss McKay, if there is anything *dodgy* about your niece or her young man.'

'He's *very* dodgy, I believe,' Muriel gossiped, gaily. 'He has a number of ne'er do well brothers who are in to all kinds of dicey dealing. I think at least one of them has been in prison for something. Les - that is, my niece's father - doesn't approve of him at all. I believe the family's quite notorious.'

Matron digested this information. 'I see,' she sniffed. 'That puts rather a different complexion on things. I'm afraid I'll have to mention

241

that to the police. It would explain a great deal. We really couldn't understand at all why your niece allowed it, or failed to alert a member of staff, still less why she actually drove off with him. But if there is criminal intent. ...'

'Oh!' Muriel had the feeling that she'd said too much, 'I'm sure Sandra wouldn't have co-operated in anything illegal. Not willingly, anyway....Although I suppose none of us knows what we might do if there was a gun to our heads.'

'Does he have a gun? Good God, Miss McKay!'

'I.... I couldn't say.'

'But it's a possibility. You think he might have coerced her.'

'Well,' Muriel stammered. 'I don't know. It was just a figure of speech. But it does seem an odd relationship in many ways....'

'Is *she* quite reliable, your niece? There isn't anything the police should know about her, is there? Does she have any particularly strong political opinions, for example? Mr Burgess...' Matron lowered her voice again, 'Mr Burgess is related to somebody *very high up*, you know what I'm saying? That's quite apart from being wealthy in his own right.'

'Oh dear. Not that I know of, Matron, but you must understand that I'm not very close to my sister or her daughter. Really, I wouldn't like you to think that I'm suggesting anything dubious.... '

'But it all looks so suspicious, doesn't it? Until we can clear it all up. I don't suppose you have a contact number for the place where Mrs McKay is staying? We need to confirm quite urgently if Mr Burgess is there, and whether he's there *voluntarily*, shall we say? And to arrange for him to be collected, and also to try and organise some medication for him.'

Muriel gave Matron the name of the house and the village, which was all she knew.

'I think the police will manage with that,' said Matron, writing down the details. 'Frankly, there'll be questions to be answered. Even if it was an innocent mistake, it really was most irresponsible of your niece to take Mr Burgess away without a by-your-leave, if that's what's happened. You can imagine the distress it has caused to our residents. The staff are upset, too, naturally. The disruption has been immense.'

'I can't think what they thought they were doing.' Muriel mused. 'But I hope you'll keep me informed.'

Matron telephoned an hour or so later to tell Muriel that the police had traced the number but that it was engaged.

'They think someone's on the internet,' she said, testily. 'We're pretty sure now that he's there: under what circumstances, has yet to be established. But if we don't get through in the next hour we'll be alerting the local constabulary.'

'I quite understand,' said Muriel.

'In the meantime, it's quite likely that the police will want to ask you what more you know about this young man.'

'Goodness me,' Muriel gasped, wondering if she had enough biscuits.

The rare moment of family accord between the four McKay siblings soon dissipated into the flurry of activity which ensued, but it was not forgotten. It lingered like sweetness on the tongue and lent its flavour to the succeeding events of the day.

Belinda began the final preparations for their meal, grilling the lamb-burgers with disapproval. Heather went to give Starlight her sandwiches. Ruth remembered the laundry she had left in the machines earlier on in the day, and went to put it into the tumble drier, and to find clean sheets for the bed in the boys' bedroom. She encountered Mr Burgess on the stairs, trouserless and ranting, and took pleasure in disturbing June from her tête a tête with Sandra in the library so that she could attend to him;

'I'm sorry, I can't do it. I have all this laundry to sort out, and in any case I don't know which room you've put him in,' she explained, in mock apology. June pursed her lips and said nothing.

'Whose bed is this?' Ruth asked, as she stretched the clean sheet over the mattress.

Todd reddened. 'Mine,' he said, quietly.

'I see,' said Ruth. She knew she ought to give him a ticking off, but now she came to think of it, she hadn't really done anything to re-establish relations with her nephews. In fact, she couldn't remember having addressed a single word to either of them since they had arrived yesterday evening. If she waded in like a gorgon now it could well put paid to any future cousinly visitations and Ben did seem to be getting on so well with them both. So she smiled kindly at Todd as she twitched his duvet back into place and said, as lightly and generally as possible, 'do be *very* careful with drinks up here, won't you boys?'

The boys had all had showers. Their muddy clothes and damp towels were strewn around the room. Toby and Todd were pulling on clean tracksuit bottoms and t shirts, but Ben remained in his underpants crouched in a corner, absorbed in a game on Toby's

Gameboy. His hair, Ruth noted, was all on end, and his skin clung to his bones with hardly a shred of flesh for padding. She had a sudden desire to embrace him; she had hardly seen him since this morning, she hadn't heard about his adventures in the woods and at the sea. The tide of information which generally flowed from him, both plebeian and fantastical, had entirely dried up, or, at least, had been washing up on the shore of someone else's ears, and she missed it. Rachel too, she realised, had been stolen away from her. She hadn't been invited to approve the new clothes, or to hear about the shops. 'The family is joined by elastic,' she mused. 'The closer we get to some, the more we must stretch away from others.' She moved over to her son and crouched by his side.

'Do make sure you sit by me at teatime, Ben,' she said, quietly, smoothing his hair to his head with her hand, 'I want to hear all about your adventures.'

'Alright, Mum,' said Ben, not looking up from his game.

'Take your wet things downstairs,' she told them all, standing up. 'There's a boiler room downstairs where you can leave them to dry. After tea we can all play a board game together. You boys can choose from the box we brought with us, OK?' She chose not to notice the qualified enthusiasm which this suggestion provoked.

She proceeded down the corridor to the girls' room. A pile of neatly folded clothing was reverently placed on Rachel's pillow; even the bags had been folded carefully. As Ruth lifted and examined each garment in turn, she couldn't help but be impressed by its good quality and sensible nature, especially when she got down to the underwear and pyjamas. Something had been mentioned about an incredible sale but even so she couldn't imagine but that some considerable money had been spent, money she knew that she could not repay without sacrifice. Her instinct was to make vehement protest, to get on her highest hobby horse and rant about sweat-shop labour and the exploitation of women by the fashion industry, not to mention the

245

money..... But coming as it did from Miriam, this generous gesture must not be snubbed, and, more importantly still, she could not bring herself to spoil Rachel's own obvious appreciation and delight with her new things. Rachel, she believed, would never take good things for granted, receiving them all too rarely, while her cousins evidently had the opposite attitude; *their* new clothes were tossed around the room, crumpled on the floor and flung anyhow.

And underneath these layers of self-justification was a kernel of confession that indeed her children were shabbily turned out in cheaply bought and poor quality clothes, and that in some ways their shabbiness was as much a deliberate statement as any designer label. Their poverty made a fervent declaration. 'Yes, we're poor,' it said, 'and whose fault is that?'

Ruth sighed. Night had fallen outside and she drew the curtains over the blacked out windows. Somewhere downstairs she could hear Starlight wailing; Heather must be trying to get her to bed.

Simon had been delegated to telephone Aunty Muriel and put their master-plan into action. Belinda had written the number down for him from a diary in her handbag. As he approached the telephone, Granny McKay's voice could be heard shrieking; 'Will someone answer that bloody telephone!?' and it instantly began to ring. As he answered it, Simon wondered with a weird shudder if Granny was some kind of psychic. A few moments later, he replaced the receiver on the hook and rubbed his hands together. His task, of inviting Aunty Muriel, had been made blissfully easy. The caller had been the extremely irate Matron of The Oaks, who had enquired initially whether Mr Burgess was at this address, and then, when this was confirmed, demanded to know why an old and infirm man had been abducted, without permission, and taken to some remote and god-forsaken corner of the country by total strangers. On further enquiry, it seemed that Mr Burgess had been taken away from The Oaks without the sanction of his family, or, indeed, the knowledge of the management. The possibility of kidnap had been very much at the forefront of everyone's mind. Only a chance telephone enquiry from Miss McKay had solved the mystery for them. Now, with the confirmation that Mr Burgess was indeed safely (if illegally) ensconced, a local GP would be contacted so that he could deliver and administer some vital medication. Also, she must warn him, a police team had been mobilised and would soon be on the scene. Finally, a police car was being despatched from The Oaks with a member of the nursing staff to recover the errant resident.

It had taken Simon no time at all to suggest that Aunty Muriel also be one of the passengers, in order to calm Granny McKay's distress at the loss of her male companion. A quick call to Aunty Muriel, therefore, to confirm this arrangement, had completed his task. Her satisfaction had been quite evident. Inclusion in the party, even if only at the last moment and under these unusual circumstances, was better than nothing, and the chance to humiliate Sandra in person, and, by association, June, for such foolishness, could

247

not be passed up. And to achieve this at no personal cost or inconvenience in the way of travel was an added bonus. She would throw a few things into a case and be ready for the officer when he called, she said, straight after she had bobbed next door to Mrs Powell to explain the whole ridiculous story and to leave her key.

Simon explained the situation briefly to Heather as she passed through the hall with Starlight, who was to be put to bed. Starlight's co-operation in this process was evidently not to be relied upon; she thrashed and wailed in her mother's arms; Bob had been recruited as reinforcement and his face was grim. They mounted the stairs as the condemned might mount the gallows.

He met James coming from the kitchen bearing a drinks tray complete with ice bucket and a selection of bottles, and gave him a conspiratorial wink.

'Cocktails are served in the lounge, sir,' James intoned.

'More drinks?' Simon laughed, 'Oh well, we'll probably need them. I think there are going to be fireworks. Stand by.'

'Right you are,' James winked. '"Anything can happen in the next half hour."'

'That's about the size of it!'

Simon proceeded to the kitchen where Tansy and Rachel were setting the table under instruction from Belinda. He took his sister to one side and prepared her for a surprise arrival from the police imminently.

'Of course,' Belinda laughed, grimly. 'Apart from the arrival of an escaped convict, it was the only thing left that could possibly happen! I suppose they'll all want dinner?'

Ellie had topped her mobile phone credit up at the shopping centre and had discovered that a weak, intermittent signal was to be found near the empty fountain on the front lawn. She stood and shivered in the chilly air; Caro's phone rang out but she didn't answer. Ellie was reduced to recording a plaintive voice message.

'Caro, it's me. I don't know if you got my texts. You haven't texted back. Please don't say anything to Rob, Caro. If you tell him...... it would just be so awful, for me. There are things you don't know, things that I haven't explained very well. I think I might have given you an impression..... But I can't go into it all now. Caro, please, if you're my friend, don't tell Rob. Please, Caro, *please*, whatever you do, if you care about me at all, *please*, don't tell Rob. You don't know..... you don't know what he's *like*...' The connection broke off abruptly. She had no idea whether any of her message had been transmitted. She sat forlornly on the cold stone of the fountain's parapet. It was quite dark; the grass and the trees just shades of grey in the deeper dimness, and out of the gloom a ghostly figure loomed, two figures; Mitch and his dog.

He was hovering at a little distance, unwilling to intrude, but she acknowledged him with a smile and a flick of her hair.

'Hello,' he said.

He had his hands thrust deeply into his pockets. His shirt, surely too thin for the penetrating chill of the evening, filled and billowed like a sail in the breeze. His hair, just a shade too long, perhaps, winnowed attractively in the wind. She had, even with all her troubles, been conscious of him during the day, a hesitant, self-effacing figure in the crowd of vociferous relatives, physically present and yet somehow psychologically at a distance, not quite at ease, forever poised to leap up and go off at the least indication that something was needed. She wondered how much he had heard of her message.

He jerked his chin up towards the sky. 'Seen that star?' he asked. 'Venus. Always the first one to come out.'

Her eyes followed his up into the blue-black tent of the sky. Venus glowed, an icy white shard, above them. 'Do you know them

249

all?' she asked. She was, in fact, quite impressed. It was not the kind of knowledge that boys her own age would have, or, at least, admit to.

He came over and sat next to her. 'Some,' he acknowledged. 'In Africa, there were more of them, too many to make out with the naked eye.'

The word *naked* hovered between them momentarily.

From the house, the screams of Rob's computer game, mingled with Starlight's angry remonstrances at being put to bed, came to them across the lawns. Silent, but just as agonised, Ellie knew, was the straining of family forbearance within; just June had been bad enough, but now? How many doddering McKays *were* there, she thought, just more distractions that would let her brother get away with torturing her.

'What must you think about us all,' she murmured, rhetorically.

'What do you mean?'

She nodded towards the house and gave a self-conscious laugh. 'You must think we're all *mad*.'

'I don't think anything at all about it,' he said, peremptorily. 'It's none of my business.'

'I should be so lucky!' Ellie grimaced. How wonderful it must be to be unconnected! If only she could sever the ties which bound her to her brother!

'Your brother?' he suggested. Ah. So he *had* heard her message. 'What's his problem?'

She gave another laugh, harsh and hopeless this time, then shook her head. 'He really *is* mad, I sometimes think. He's screwed up, anyway,' she said. 'He didn't want to come on holiday – well, the way things are going, *that's* understandable – and whenever he's miserable he takes it out on me.'

'I see.'

'Really, what he wants,' Ellie said, surprised at how easily, with him, the words came, 'is to be sent home. He's behaved – well – just *so* badly. Having that game on all the time, so *loud*, all that *horrible* screaming, he was *so* rude to Rachel,.....'

'And he's upset you.'

'Oh yes, but that's backfired on him. I can't *tell* anyone....'

'Can't you?'

She shook her head, miserably.

'Would you like it if he was sent away?'

'Oh! Yes! But that's not going to happen, is it. What would the great McKay gathering be without Prince McKay?'

'Sounds like, for you, it would be much more enjoyable.'

Suddenly a bedroom window was thrown open and a piercing whistle shattered the night.

'Oh,' said Mitch, getting up. 'I'm needed. They mustn't be able to get the baby to settle.' He snapped his fingers a couple of times and Tiny emerged from the shadows under the trees. Mitch took a few steps towards the house, and then turned. 'Are you coming in?' he asked. 'It's cold. Don't stay out here by yourself.'

They closed the door on the night and Mitch dashed up the stairs, passing June as she descended with Granny McKay perched frailly on her arm. Granny was wearing full royalty regalia, including several strings of paste pearls and earrings which flashed alternately red, white and blue. Mr Burgess followed, assisted by Sandra and Les. Mr Burgess wore no trousers. His portmanteau, still clasped to his body, had turned out to be entirely empty. He had soiled his trousers and refused to borrow anyone else's. He wore a pair of Les' underpants in the mistaken belief that they were his own. Their progress down stairs was extremely slow; Granny complained querulously at every step that there was no lift. Todd and Toby bowled down the stairs around them and darted down the corridor towards the boiler room, where they dumped their gear in soggy heaps. Simon met them erupting back toward the study where Rob had promised them a turn on *Fatal Blow*. Todd stopped only to look up earnestly into his father's face and pant out;

'Aunty Ruth says we've got to play a bored game after tea, we don't have to do we? I don't want to be bored!' He chortled at his own hilarity, before darting after his brother.

Simon, his sons, Ellie, Granny, June, Les, Mr Burgess and Sandra converged in the hall. Ruth was descending the stairs with an armful of laundry. On the landing above, Heather. Mitch and Bob paced with a wailing Starlight. Elliot emerged from the lounge, pink with pre-dinner cocktails, en route to his room to get dressed for dinner. Mary and Robert were already in the lounge with James and Miriam. Rob was in the study, from where the sound of deafening explosions and blood curdling death throes emanated. Kevin, it later transpired, was with him, having made himself useful there by revealing various cheats and shortcuts on the game.

Then the police arrived.

They spilled out of the two black vans which had arrived at speed on the gravelled sweep, perhaps a dozen or fifteen in number. The men split into teams; one group spread out over the lawns and lay commando style on the grassy sward which, only an hour before had been the stage for faerie frolicking. Another team filtered like shadows into the darkness, circling the house, hugging the stonework round to the rear. A third stood in readiness on each side of the front door. Their spectacular entrance owed as much to many hours of rehearsal as it did to back-episodes of Taggart and The Sweeny. Their knock, and shouted warning caused Tiny, recumbent on the hall hearth, to leap to his feet with unexpected alacrity and begin to bay and snarl in ferocious tones that his Baskerville cousin would have been proud of. The shock as the squad burst in through the door, brandishing truncheons and in full battle cry, caused Mr Burgess to urinate involuntarily. The splash of liquid on the polished floor was surprisingly loud even in the furore of shouting and screaming. Simultaneously, at the back of the house, the kitchen door flew open and three constables stumbled in, causing Tansy and Rachel to scream like banshees and Belinda to drop a tray of meringues onto the floor with a clatter.

'Now look what you've made me do,' she said, crossly.

In the lounge, finding the doors locked, the policemen shone torches into the room and shouted instructions at the people inside to stand against the far wall with their hands above their heads.

'Oh, for God's sake!' complained Miriam, 'where do they think we are, Baghdad?'

In the hall, Sandra knocked into the hall table; a vase of flowers crashed to the floor. Todd and Toby, white faced, threw themselves behind their father. Ruth threw the laundry down and ran back up the stairs, screaming Ben's name. Bob, on the landing, positioned himself in front of his wife and child. Les put his hands up above his head, June prostrated herself on the floor. Granny sank regally into a deep curtsey and said;

'Welcome, your Majesty.'

The policeman in charge established an interview room in the study. His comrades took off their combat gear and slouched around the hall. Presently, they were offered tea, which they accepted in good humour. Belinda served the children with their dinner in the kitchen. The boys' eyes were agog with the excitement of it all. They all talked about the arrival of the policemen at the same time, their mouths full of mechanically extracted, reconstituted lamb. Toby even ate his vegetables without noticing it. Their fear had been utterly forgotten.

Ellie complained that she was not allowed to eat with the grown-ups. 'I'm not a child,' she said, bitterly.

'Hah!' Rob shouted.

Ruth, who had not been forewarned by Simon of the impending invasion, had nevertheless recovered quickly from the ordeal. She poured drinks of squash for the children, and passed tomato ketchup round. 'Goodness knows how long it will be before we can eat anything,' she said. 'It could be hours. Luckily, the lamb steaks won't spoil, whereas your burgers would have been like cardboard if we'd kept them hot any longer.'

'They taste like cardboard now,' said Ellie, sulkily.

'At least we don't have to sit and watch Granddad eat,' Tansy whispered. The old man's table manners had revolted her; he was always spilling and dribbling and he made loud chewing and swallowing noises which were disgusting and made her feel sick.

In the lounge, the other grown-ups gathered round the drinks tray. Elliot was busy topping up glasses. He had assumed the guise of suave and charming host once more. Surprisingly, he had not waged a one-man war of attrition against the police, barring them from his house and promising legal action for the intrusion of his privacy. In fact at first he had been rather afraid, and had sought more to placate than to provoke. Then, as the police officer and Simon between them had explained the situation, he had regained his composure, and suggested that the police weaponry could be dispensed with, and tea provided. Mary, naturally, was shocked and upset. James had taken her under his wing and was seated in the far corner of the room with her, on the raised hexagonal rostrum area, chatting quietly and calmly over the events which had lead up to the raid. Old Robert had been rather traumatised by the whole thing. He had been too young to fight in the Second World War, of course, but he had not escaped National Service and, after that, driving his wagon, had experienced one or two nasty moments in Eastern Germany. Heather sat next to him, and stroked his hand. She had been badly shaken too, completely misconstruing, for a while, the reason for the police raid, and clutching Starlight to her with grim determination. Granny seemed to have forgotten all about the arrival of the police. She stood by the drinks tray and guzzled gin and tonic, and regaled anyone who would listen with an entirely fictional account of her evacuation as a child to Balmoral, where, it seems, she had befriended Princess Margaret and where they had both been seduced by an under-footman. All attempts to put Starlight to bed had been abandoned. Alone, she seemed entirely unperturbed by the arrival of militia. She was busy entertaining the troops in the hallway, trying on their helmets and untying their bootlaces.

Sandra and Kevin had been seized as the main quarry of the police search, once Mr Burgess had been identified and briefly checked over, and his trouserless state explained. An attempt to interview Mr Burgess had proved quite hopeless. He had no idea where he was, or how he had got there, but had been well treated and was especially looking forward to meeting Her Majesty.

Sandra and Kevin had been taken into the study, where the policeman had interrogated them, pressing Kevin quite forcefully to admit that he had attempted to kidnap Mr Burgess with a view to extorting money, and that the whole thing had been undertaken in league with and possibly at the instigation of his notorious, criminally-

255

connected brothers. Kevin, in stammered half sentences, protested his innocence of anything more than 'fetching the old codgers on holiday,' and it did increasingly seem, to the investigating officer, quite unlikely that his suspect would have the wit, let alone the nerve, to conceive and execute such a plan. Sandra had been weeping and snivelling quite openly, protesting their innocence. She wrung her hands while she spoke, and bit her nails while she listened, and occasionally wiped her nose on her sleeve, having no handkerchief to hand. Mr Burgess had had a suitcase, she said. He had been waiting on the drive. He had climbed into the car with Granny voluntarily. She had assumed that this had been arranged the night before and that her mother had simply failed to let her know. It had happened before, she said, *lots* of times; her mother would send her to collect something from a shop and by the time she got there June would have been on the telephone to order extra, or other items. This had been just the same. It had happened in a very natural way which made her think that everyone except her knew about the arrangement. Kevin nodded eagerly, but looked deathly white, and, if possible, more gormless than usual.

June had been in hysterics. Rob and Les had had to carry her up to her room. Ruth had offered a tranquiliser tablet to calm her, but she had called insistently for brandy instead. Now she was lying in a darkened room moaning softly. Les had left her to it. 'This is what happens when you interfere,' he had said, at the door. 'You owe all those good people an apology. Your mother doesn't belong here; she needs full time care. Sandra and Kevin weren't invited and neither were we. I told you we should have gone home on Friday.'

'You're very cruel. Very cruel,' moaned June, from beneath a blanket of cognac-sodden distress, but Les had closed the door and was on his way downstairs.

Presently a local GP arrived. Dr Gardner was a kindly, elderly family doctor. He had thinning grey hair with twigs and leaves stuck in it. He wore a blue pullover with frayed elbows and stained trousers. He apologised for his garb, explaining that he had been helping to build the village bonfire for Guy Fawkes Night when the call had reached him. Dr Gardner took Mr Burgess into the library and gave him as detailed an examination as possible given the patient's inexorable grip on the portmanteau. They looked as mad as each other. Mr Burgess was declared physically fit but extremely confused and the doctor administered a dose of medication. In conference with Ruth, he expressed extreme surprise that a patient in such a far gone state should be anywhere but in a secure nursing unit.

'If you think he's in a bad way, you should meet my Grandmother,' laughed Ruth. 'On the whole, I'd say she was the worst of the two. But we're stuck with her until Thursday. At least this one's going home tonight.'

Dr Gardner shook hands and left. The Police officer in charge approached to explain that he had concluded his investigations and felt that he could now leave. It seemed to have been a case, he had concluded, of an honest if odd mistake. He found no evidence of ulterior motive, political insurgence or international terrorism. However he had cautioned the young lady in the severest tones that her mistake had caused acute upset and consternation at The Oaks and for Mr Burgess' family, had tied up several police officers for the whole day, and cost a good deal of money. He could not guarantee that some liability for costs might not be laid at her door, or even that an official charge of wasting police time might not have to be answered. That would be up to his superiors. His colleagues from the relevant metropolitan constabulary were on their way with a care home nurse to take Mr Burgess back to The Oaks. Having made his case clear, the team thanked their hosts for the tea, said goodbye to Starlight, retied their shoelaces, reclaimed their helmets and shambled back into their transportation.

Fed and watered, the children took Starlight into the games room while the adults at last sat down to dinner. Belinda dished up the lamb with lips pursed like a scar. With the substitution of the burgers there was just enough to go round but she served them with ill-grace. It seemed to her that her dreams had been trampled upon utterly. She felt the presence of June in the house, even from the distance of her room, like a malevolent odour, and the embodiment of June's machinations seated at the table, Granny McKay, Mr Burgess, Sandra, Kevin and even poor Les, oppressed her. Only the kindly and supportive glances and gestures of her siblings gave her any comfort; they acted as one; settling Mary and Robert, passing vegetables, discussing with careful selectivity the positive occurrences of the day, and glossing over the recent unpleasantness which had marred it. Belinda carefully plated up a meal for Muriel, and, very magnanimously, she thought, one also for June, and put them in the warming oven of the Aga.

Sandra and Kevin were utterly ignored. The two of them had been steered to the far end of the table, landed with the two elderly people and served with dinner without a word, then virtually left to get on with it; the rest of them had drifted in unspoken concert to the other end of the table. They had disgraced the family; this was the unspoken verdict upon them. The McKay's had never been in any trouble with the police; hysteria, smashed ornaments, trouserless old men and puddles of urine were unknown in their annals. Les hovered in an agony of indecision, before seating himself half way between the two parties. Mitch, diplomatically, sat opposite him.

Elliot, uncomfortably aware that his ill-advised licensing of June to invite 'whomsoever she pleased' the evening before had seriously backfired, distanced himself from the new arrivals. Perhaps, he mused, in a rare moment of self-doubt, he ought to have consulted Belinda first. There was a kind of accord between Belinda and her brother and sisters, and the in-laws, too, were standing in line. It wouldn't do at all for him to be caught on the wrong side in the event of a schism; he had far too much to lose.

Sandra ate her food miserably, with one hand, while the other kept Granny McKay from falling off the end of the bench. Granny was quite sozzled; she chatted incomprehensibly to Mr Burgess. Mr Burgess, however, was beyond conversation of any kind. He dozed in the carver chair, his medication having taken effect. Granny McKay was unperturbed by his lack of response, in fact he was the kind of listener she most preferred, and she meandered through a confused and half-remembered memoir of a day trip to the Lakes she had taken whilst Secretary to the local branch of the Mothers' Union. Kevin picked at his food in silence, and wondered what he had done to deserve this muck instead of the burgers. He was keen to get back to the computer game or, failing that, to the double bedroom he had surprisingly been allocated to share with Sandra.

Miriam, at the family end of the table, was quite magnificent. She described, with careful deference to Ruth, the shopping trip, the happy camaraderie of the girls, the attractive little market town where they had been too late for the butchers but found the most amusing little grocery store at which one was served by a gentleman in a traditional brown grocer's coat from behind an old fashioned counter. The image evoked for Mary a picture of shops as they had been in the olden days, and Miriam had encouraged Mary in reminiscences of her girlhood, when rationing had been in place, and women had had to be very ingenious indeed to make the food stretch.

'My mother used to queue, with our ration-books, for meat, and fruit,' Mary recalled. 'But quite a lot of things were delivered; not just milk, I mean. Even in poor areas, like ours. Condensed milk was my favourite. I used to climb up to the top pantry shelf and eat it when my mother wasn't looking. I don't know if you can still get it nowadays, condensed milk,' she finished, wistfully.

'You can't get dried egg or sarsaparilla or sherbet or sago either,' Les put in. Suddenly they were all remembering things from their childhoods.

'I was once sick into a bowl of sago pudding,' Simon announced. 'It was at school. I can't say I especially lament the passing of sago pudding.'

'Filthy bugger!' exclaimed Granny, suddenly, waving her fork. 'Matron will have you out if she finds out!'

'You were going down with chicken pox, poor lamb,' said Mary, quickly. 'It wasn't the sago that made you sick.'

'No,' admitted Simon, 'but the association isn't a happy one.'

'My father was a bread-boy!' announced Robert, his mind still on the subject of food deliveries.

'Really?' a few of them chorused.

'Yes! He had a bicycle with a basket on the front, and he cycled all over the town.'

Belinda brought out the meringues.

'My favourite!' exclaimed James, with perhaps a little too much gush. He helped himself to two. Belinda smiled at him. James had the most beautiful eyes she had ever seen in a man, Belinda thought to herself. So sympathetic and honest, thickly fringed with dark lashes, and melting, like milk chocolate.

'Not for me, thanks.' Elliot said, a little abruptly, interrupting the frisson, 'I think I'd prefer cheese.'

'I'll get it out for you,' said Ruth, with what she hoped was a self-deprecating laugh, 'but let me warn you not to take your eyes off it for a second. Mine disappeared last night during a moment of inattention!'

Mitch coughed.

'I think we'll take Granny to bed,' Sandra said, quietly. 'She's had a long day.'

'Haven't we all?' said Belinda, acidly.

'What a good idea. Goodnight.' Ruth dismissed them, literally, with an imperious wave of her hand. Mr Burgess remained at the far end of the table, snoring gently. Sandra and Kevin shuffled out, with Granny, rubber-legged, between them. When they had gone, significant looks were exchanged across the table but, in deference to Les, nothing was said.

After the meringues, nearly everyone had cheese. Elliot poured port. James led Robert into talk of his childhood days. The distant past was so much fresher in his mind than more recent events, and he could describe incidents which had occurred decades before with a clarity which would have failed him if he had been asked to describe his breakfast that day. The sisters and Mary talked about babies. Miriam, excluded from this conversation, encouraged Bob and Simon to describe the afternoon's expedition to the sea, which they did with many an amusing anecdote concerning the discovery of a bear's den (up a tree – but not the *family* tree, which had eluded them -) which they had sent Todd to investigate equipped, as he was, with their only bear-fighting weapon, tracking for hidden treasure using arrows made out of sticks and the compass (the treasure had turned out to be some chocolate hidden under a log by James) and the continuing pursuit of the mysterious Wriggly, directed entirely by Ben, which had involved a good deal of hallooing and thrashing about the undergrowth with sticks. The sea, when reached, had been a revelation; a long, pebbled beach, with some sheltering dunes running up into a fir plantation. The boys and by contagion the men, were sure that a whole day could delightfully be spent there, with a bonfire, beach combing, some bird-spotting and, when the tide went out, maybe even fishing for crabs in the rock pools.

'If only the weather holds,' said Elliot, sourly, 'it is *October*, after all. And don't the clocks go back tonight? That'll mean an hour less of daylight.'

'No, that's next week. And the forecast is good for tomorrow,' said Simon, shortly, 'and if we got an early start...'

'Tomorrow is Ellie's birthday,' put in Belinda. I'm planning a birthday brunch. And I suppose I'll have to bake another cake before I go to bed.'

'Why don't you let Rachel and Tansy do it tomorrow? Tansy loves baking and I'm sure they'd like to do it for Ellie,' Miriam suggested.

'We were planning on going to church tomorrow,' James announced. There was a shocked silence. The McKays had never been church-goers. Ruth looked rather uncomfortable, and then felt angry at herself.

'We've been attending a local church for the last few months,' she said, defensively. 'It started off as a bit of a ruse, to get Ben into the Cathedral School; it helped your application if you were regular church attendees. But recently, we've started going for its own sake. We quite enjoy it, actually.' She looked round the table, daring anyone to challenge her.

'You do surprise me, Ruth,' said Heather, rather archly. 'You've always been so cynical about *my* spirituality.'

'Christianity has a lot to say about social justice,' Ruth said, quickly, 'you know I've always been active politically. I went on the Woman's Right to Choose march.'

'Politics certainly does require faith,' Miriam mused.

'Don't ask me,' said Belinda 'I've never understood any of it, really.'

'No,' said Elliot, rather cuttingly, 'not your strong suit at all, dear. When you talk about politics you just make yourself look ridiculous.'

'Oh now, really,' James began, but Simon cut in quickly, keen to preserve the unity. 'Well. I guess Monday will do just as well for a day at the beach.'

'Yes, we really ought to make some plans,' agreed Miriam, with a significant glance at Les, 'or the week will be gone and we won't have done anything. I think we passed an outdoor activity centre today. Canoes and so forth. I'm sure the young people will enjoy that.'

'And there's the famous mountain; the third highest in Britain? We ought to climb it, while we're here, if the weather's suitable.' said Simon. 'Elliot, could we use your computer to check the forecast?'

Suddenly, with a part to play in proceedings, Elliot was fussing self-importantly with his laptop, which had been removed from the table, eventually, with great care and trepidation, by Ruth. Belinda got up to begin stacking the dishwasher, concealing a welling of tears at James' chivalry. James got up to help her, and, for a moment, placed his hand on her shoulder and gave it a gentle squeeze. The significance of this gesture lay in its very needlessness, and she stored it up like a treasure. Mitch and Les offered to refuel the fires. Bob slipped off for a smoke. Robert's head drooped onto his chest, and he dozed. He and Mr Burgess, at opposite ends of the table, looked like a pair of curious bookends.

'We shall have to be careful,' said Simon, quietly, with a mischievous wink at Heather, 'when the nurse and the policeman come, that they don't take away the wrong old man!'

'Poor Daddy!' sighed Heather. 'He's lost his spark, hasn't he?'

'His spark used to burn, sometimes,' said Simon, coldly. 'So I wouldn't come over all nostalgic, if I were you.'

Ruth and Miriam found themselves sitting a little apart at one end of the table. It was an opportunity at last to re-establish relations.

'It's a funny thing, family,' Ruth offered, by way of an opening.

'It *is*,' Miriam concurred, with a wry smile. 'You don't choose them, sometimes you don't even like them, and yet there seems to be something, I don't know, a bond, a tie, that can never be undone. Even though you might want to, you can't; it goes too deep.' She had uncannily hit on Ruth's own conclusions and it made her feel uncomfortable to have been so accurately read.

'I wonder what it is,' she asked, a little shakily.

'The bond? Goodness. I'm the last person to answer that question, Ruth. I have no brothers or sisters, only Mother. There's only ever been her and me, for as long as I can remember. I don't actually like her that much. She's over-bearing and dictatorial, quite selfish. But even so I couldn't choose to cut the tie between us. But what *is* the tie? Is it duty? I think it might be. She did her duty by me – she was widowed, you know, before I was born, and the pressure on her to have me adopted was very strong – and now, I, as you know, sometimes to my considerable inconvenience, do my duty by her.'

There was silence between them, before Ruth mused; 'Mmmm. No, it isn't duty, for me. It's something far deeper and more......ingrained........ to do with what we have shared.'

'History? Is it a bond of history?'

'I'm theorising.' Ruth glanced over at her mother, 'Even *unhappy* history is still shared and would still count, wouldn't it?'

'I would think unhappy history especially would unite people. Adversity forges very strong bonds.'

'Perhaps that's all it is, then,' Ruth said, quietly, thinking of angry words unspoken, disappointment unvoiced, the crushing years of disillusionment packing themselves down on the McKays making a mortar of misery.

Miriam sighed and stood up. Elliot, Bob and Simon were leaning together over the computer screen. Belinda and James were washing and wiping in companionable silence. Mary had gone into the games room. The two old men slumbered at opposite ends of the table. 'Shall I make some tea?' Miriam asked. Ruth nodded.

'I'll make decaffeinated, if there is any. It's really quite late.'

As though reading Ruth's mind, Simon detached himself from the group at the computer and hunkered down at her side. 'Happy history makes for stronger bonds,' he said, covering her small hand with his. 'We mustn't dwell on the negative. We did have happy times, Ruthie.' Ruth smiled at him, a little wanly, and he went on, 'and we can make sure of it, can't we, for the children?'

'I don't know,' she mumbled, 'if we can take responsibility for *that*.' He squeezed her hand again and then ambled out of the room. Ruth tried to project herself twenty years into the future, and envisage the children on as disparate paths as it was possible to imagine, subject to lucky stars and tragic losses; Ben, say, a famous concert pianist, Toby a recluse, Todd perhaps an explorer and Rob some Buddhist Guru, Tansy in a Kibbutz and Ellie with five children by different fathers on state benefits in a high-rise. What could they do *now* to make sure that in that future time the young ones, no matter how far-flung, would be bonded indelibly with this happy family adhesive? Or would it just be a case of being larded with the same family soup of genes; a network of accidental biological associations? Or would they be strangers, with nothing in common, no loyalty or link of any kind? And how would they feel about it? Perhaps it would be a blessed relief.

Miriam interrupted her thoughts from where she stood with her back to the Aga. 'I'm not sure we'll ever be able to answer this one, Ruth. I agree with you that shared experience – up-bringing - comes into it. I still feel it has a lot to do with duty....' she shook her head. 'Perhaps it's something we'll never be able to pin down'

'I think what I think you're trying to describe is love,' Belinda said, suddenly, from across the room, a dish cloth poised in her hand, 'or am I just being stupid?'

'I can't define that either.' The word, the concept, made Ruth feel suddenly panicked. She hauled herself abruptly to her feet and began to arrange cups on a tray.

Belinda shrugged. 'Isn't it just knowing that you'd do *anything* for someone?'

'Perhaps.' Ruth cast a sideways glance at her father, still sleeping in his chair. 'It sounds like a very one way street to me. I'm not saying that you're wrong, just that it isn't fair. It leaves a vacuum.'

'I don't know about that, Belinda,' Miriam frowned. 'Take these two sisters; June and Muriel. They don't love each other, but there's something between them, still. There's anger and resentment and jealousy.' Miriam poured water into the teapot.

'How do you know?'

'She's coming, isn't she?' Miriam smiled.

'Ah! Yes! But why?' Ruth almost cried. It was just the nature of that connection which she had been trying to define. God knew she didn't dispute its existence! But Miriam left Ruth's question unanswered, and carried the tea tray out of the room.

The children were playing a complicated board game. It involved dozens of playing pieces in different shapes and colours spread over a board which was designed to look like a map of the world. Each player had a small pad of paper and a pencil, and, before each round, had to predict their move, or the move of others, and the outcome. The game was only designed for six players and there had been some initial acrimony over who should be left out. Todd had yelled when it had been suggested that he was too little. Finally Ellie had suggested that they each roll the dice and the two lowest scorers should form a team of two. To her confusion, Rachel had found herself teamed up with her cousin Rob. She had blushed furiously when they had both rolled low, and had hardly dared look him in the eye since. It was clear from his body language that he, too, was unhappy with the arrangement. She had placated him by attempting to make no suggestions at all as to their playing strategy and had contented herself with keeping their playing pieces in neat and tidy order on the floor besides him.

Starlight, initially, had spoiled things by collecting up the pieces, putting the dice in her mouth and scribbling on the notepads, but now she had been distracted by Mary with a storybook. She sat on her Grandma's knee with her thumb in her mouth. She was tired, and would soon fall asleep. Mary thought it was high time her youngest grand-daughter was put to bed, and wondered about advising Heather about establishing routines. She knew also that she ought to think about getting Robert upstairs, and going to bed herself, but couldn't face it. His disappearance in the morning, the unexpected and unwelcome arrival of his mother and June's daughter, and the shocking appearance of the police, had all taken its toll on her. She might seem to cope well, but she wasn't a young woman anymore. The idea of having someone to look after Robert for a change, was appealing. Les, and possibly James, she thought, might do it, if she asked. Here, amongst her grandchildren, she felt content, and with this little one on her knee, there was a sense of completion which made the traumas of the day seem bearable. The storybook had pictures of babies – all colours, Mary noted – enjoying a bath and then being put to bed. Starlight pulled her thumb out of her mouth and pointed to one of the pictures;

'Ba. Ba.' She said, conversationally.

'Clever girl,' said Mary.

Presently, Miriam brought Mary a cup of tea. While she was drinking that, Les wandered in and sank down on the settee next to her. He looked grey with weariness, his skin the colour of newspaper. The children's game was getting quite exciting and their shouts of triumph or indignation meant that he could speak frankly to Mary without being overheard.

'What a mess June's made of things Mary, eh? I can't tell you how sorry I am.'

Mary put her hand on his arm. Here was a man, she thought to herself, who was kindness itself, a gentleman, quiet and capable, a man who would know how to treat a lady. June did not deserve him. 'We all understand that it isn't your doing, Les.'

'I wanted to go home last night. I told her we ought to go first thing this morning.' He shook his head sadly and looked away from Mary. 'Of course, she wouldn't hear of it. Now we know why.'

'You had no idea, then?'

'No. Of course not. She wouldn't tell me, anyway. She always has been a law unto herself.'

Mary nodded her understanding. 'Haven't they both? Haven't they both.'

Les got out his pipe and began to fiddle with it. He addressed his next few comments to it. 'I've told our Sandra that she's to leave first thing in the morning, and I've told her she was wrong to come and wrong to bring Mother.'

'Poor girl. She only did what June said.'

'Maybe. But she's old enough now to make up her own mind about what's right, and this never was.' He put his pipe away with a sigh and turned to face Mary. 'That brings me to June and me. By rights we ought to leave too. We would do, if I had to drag her away by her hair, we would. But things aren't that simple now. There's Mother here and it seems she can't be sent back until Thursday.'

Mary slid her empty teacup onto a nearby table. 'It doesn't seem fair on poor Belinda. She has enough to cope with, with the rest of us.'

Starlight heaved a huge sigh and laid her head against Mary's breast.

'That's right, sweetness. You have a little nap on Grandma,' said Mary, pulling her fingers through the wiry silkiness of Starlight's hair.

'No, so June and me will stay and we'll look after Mother. It's the best I can do.' He looked her, earnestly, in the eye. His eyes were brown, flecked with green. A cataract on one of them gave it an opaque, gelatinous film. 'Then, first thing Thursday, we'll take her back. That'll mean that you'll have your anniversary celebration just with your family, as you always planned. But, look Mary,' he put his hand, briefly, on her knee, 'we can look after Robert as well, I'll see to that, so you can get out and about a bit with the others. You'll like that, eh?' He sat back a little and observed her with greater perspective. 'You look done in. You deserve a rest, and a proper break. You've always had it hard, Mary. Robert was a hard man to live with before he was took funny, and now it's no easier, is it?'

'No, you're right, it's no easier.' Mary felt tears gathering behind her eyes. She buried her face in Starlight's hair. She'd had such a difficult day and was over-tired. At the same time, being here amongst her family, and watching the children together had made her feel over-emotional. Now, the kindness of this lovely man seemed to make all her feelings enlarge, like milk boiling in a pan. He'd always been such a

269

comfort to her. It was so like him to put her first. Les seemed to discern her feelings and he gently took her hand in his.

'The fact is,' he said, quietly, 'June was never the right woman for me, just like Robert was never right for you. It's hard, isn't it, to look back on your life and know that the most important decision you ever made was wrong.' All kinds of shutters began slamming closed in Mary's head. She almost snatched her hand away. The question was a completely no-go area, like a boarded up house, a blocked off street, it was a route that she could never, ever allow herself to travel.

He sensed her reluctance. 'I know, I *know* it isn't anything *you* will ever have considered, but I have, and...' he seemed to struggle to complete his sentence. Mary's hand remained in his. She realised that she was almost holding her breath. Starlight's head, resting on her breast, was like a weight of anticipation. 'And,' Les went on, finally, 'well,' he breathed out, a long breath, 'there it is.'

'I'm not sure what you're saying, Les.'

Over by the board game, a scuffle broke out between Toby and Todd over a disputed game-piece. Rob separated the two boys easily and tried to restore order but neither brother would agree to the other's actually having won the piece and the game began to break up.

'What a shame, and we were winning, too,' said Rob. Rachel looked shiny eyed at his use of the plural pronoun. She had liked sitting next to him. He had smelled nice, of shower gel, and his hair was shiny and smooth instead of spiky and black. Once or twice, in reaching across to collect a playing-piece, her arm had brushed him, and once, in passing him the dice, their hands had touched. It had made her mouth dry and caused an odd lurch in the pit of her tummy.

'Can't we carry on?' she pleaded, for his sake.

'I was getting a bit bored, anyway,' said Ellie. 'I think I'll go and put my pyjamas on.'

'I'd quite like a bath,' said Tansy. The two girls left the room.

'Sod you, then. I'm going back to *Fatal Blow*,' said Rob, mulishly, and stalked after them. Toby scampered after him. Todd and Ben began a playful scuffle under the snooker table. Rachel, left alone, began wearily to tidy away the game.

Les wished he could light his pipe, but he knew he mustn't inside the house. He took a deep breath, and turned to face Mary again. He lowered his voice so that she had to lean towards him to catch his words.

'What I'm saying, Mary, is that sometimes we get the chance to put right things we have done wrong. I'm going to try and take that chance. Life isn't quite over for us yet, and we have to make the most of what we have left.'

Mary allowed the tears to roll unchecked down her cheeks. Her hand was trembling but Les held it firmly between his. She couldn't think of any words to express her feelings, but then words had, so often, been unnecessary between them. She thought about Robert; his child-like dependency, his weakly incapacity, his mental frailty, his rages which still, occasionally, flared through the obfuscated mind, and stood him in her mind against this man. At the same time her sense of loyalty, of propriety and an habitual tendency to self-sacrifice loomed large in her instinct. Before she could say anything, they were interrupted by Toby, who put his head round the door to say;

'There's another policeman and two ladies in the hall. One of the ladies is asking for you, Uncle Les.'

On the whole Muriel's journey by police car had been very agreeable. The nurse who had been dispatched to bring back the old man had been friendly, and had listened attentively to Muriel's stream of conversation. Muriel knew that she spent too many hours alone, and that, even when she had worked at the hospital, her circle of experience had been sadly narrow. And so she had always tended to relate to the patients and other hospital staff with a light-hearted, inconsequential banter which had passed for social interaction, and indeed, for the patients, when she came into contact with them, she liked to feel that her cheerful, trivial repartee had been a helpful and pleasant change from the routines of hospital life and the anxieties of their individual ailments. At the same time it had masked her intellectual inadequacies and limited understanding. She knew that Les found her merry chatter charming and funny and undemanding. The nurse seemed to feel the same. She nodded and smiled as Muriel talked, and interjected with an occasional laugh or sigh or exclamation which was entirely satisfactory. The policeman, on the other hand, had been sour and uncommunicative. He had been very reluctant to allow Roger to sit next to Muriel on the seat of his panda car, which was very silly of him as Roger really hadn't bitten him very hard at all. He had refused to use his sirens and flashing lights and had been very unwilling to pull in at a service station for a comfort stop. He had paid with very bad grace indeed for the afternoon tea and scones Muriel had insisted that they should all have to sustain them when the hour for their evening meal had been and gone, making an unnecessary fuss about a VAT Receipt.

And now, arriving at this splendid house in the countryside, Muriel felt that far more than just a day's journey had been completed. This was an arrival indeed, through space and time, back into the bosom of her family. No one had heard their knock, so they had entered into the lofty hall. The heavy furniture, high, decorated ceiling, polished wood and extravagant flower arrangements were like a film set. The sound of voices at a distance and, nearer at hand, young people and modern music, the faint smell of homemade food, the dying embers of a fire, it had all fulfilled her every expectation. She had accosted a nice young man – he must be one of her great-nephews, and had not been too disconcerted at all by Roger's snarl – and asked for Les, although, with hindsight, she probably should have asked for Simon or Belinda. But the youth went off happily enough to get Les and Muriel waited with her heart in her throat, her battered old suitcase in one hand and Roger's lead in the other.

Les emerged from a long gallery which led off from the right of the hall. His face betrayed that he had not expected her.

'Muriel!' he exclaimed with surprise. Mary, behind him, also spoke her name with a shrillness which suggested that the surprise was not an entirely welcome one. But Les' amazement gave way instantaneously to a cry of genuine pleasure, whereas Mary's face remained a mask of pure astonishment and her bafflement did not diminish when she witnessed Les' approach and kiss. But the germ of discouragement which had festered for a moment in Muriel's mind was soon smothered by the effusive welcome of all her nieces and her nephew, and of most of their respective partners. Only Elliot seemed confused and less than delighted by her arrival. He, like Mary, hung back, their expressions shouting questions. But the others; they seemed to emerge from every region of the house, though doors and down stairways, crying her name and opening their arms in genuine welcome. In a flurry of introductions, her hand was shaken and her cheek kissed, while she was led through a hidden door and down a passageway into a warm and inviting kitchen. There her brother was gently awakened and, when he had orientated himself, he bid her welcome with a tear in his eye. The nurse and the policeman, who had followed the throng, took charge of another old gentleman, half dressed, who reclined at the far end of the table. Before she had chance to say goodbye, they had escorted him from the house and were gone. But she remained, her coat taken, her suitcase carried

273

upstairs, a cool drink put in her hand and a steaming plate of meat and vegetables placed before her. Roger snapped and snarled at everyone, and Muriel laughed at him and told him how silly he was being, and reassured everyone that he was a perfect pet and wouldn't hurt a fly. But Roger unfortunately, seemed to be coping very poorly with the stress of so many people. He appeared unable to show off his more amiable characteristics and finally had been taken in hand by Les, who took him into the garden to 'stretch his legs'.

Muriel ate and drank, and listened and delighted. She declared herself thrilled to have been invited, and more than happy to help with Mother, and willing to baby-sit if the others should wish to go out for an evening; to stay or go, to join in or to sit out, to peel and chop and wash and wipe: in short, whatever would be required of her. After she had eaten, Les took her and Roger up to a lovely single room, situated just off the main landing and close to a beautiful bathroom. Ruth and Simon and James and Heather and Bob and Robert accompanied them. Progressing up the staircase, Muriel felt like the queen on a state visit. Bob carried a sleeping Starlight carefully in his arms and they all whispered so that she should not wake up. James walked next to Robert, who leaned heavily upon his son-in-law. Her Mother, she was told, was sleeping in the room next door. In the morning, it was suggested, she might turn awkward when she discovered that Mr Burgess had been taken away.

'Don't worry about Mother,' said Muriel, with a grim smile, 'I can cope with her. I did, you know, for thirty-odd years.'

Belinda began to tidy up the kitchen, but was stopped almost immediately by Mary.

'Belinda,' she said, a tone of urgency in her voice. 'Today has been the most peculiar day I can ever remember, and the most extraordinary things have happened, but this, *this* beats everything!'

'What do you mean, Mum?'

'What on *earth* is Muriel doing here?'

'That's just what I'd like to know,' blustered Elliot, who had, like Mary, hung back in order to get to the bottom of what was going on.

'I just don't understand it. Surely, *surely* this isn't June's doing?' asked Mary.

'Oh no. Muriel's been invited by *us*. Simon 'phoned her earlier and she took the opportunity to come with the nurse and the policeman.'

'*Us? Us?* No one consulted *me* on the matter, I can assure you!' Elliot raged.

'But then you didn't consult us about Granny McKay, did you?' Belinda rejoined, acid on her tongue.

'She's been invited by you? Why? What on earth possessed you?' Mary was so incredulous that she cut across Elliot's angry retort.

'To be truthful, Mum, it was a bit of a smack in the eye for June. We know they don't get on.'

'Don't get on? *Don't get on?* They've hardly spoken to each other for over forty years! She'll have a fit, she'll go ballistic when she knows Muriel's here.'

'I'm ballistic now!' shouted Elliot.

'Don't mess yourself, Dad,' said Rob, coolly, drifting into the kitchen and opening the fridge.

Belinda faced them across the kitchen. 'Good. I hope June goes home. I'm sorry. I know that sounds very inhospitable but she's forced her way in here, uninvited, and put us in an impossible position with Granny, so we're landed with *her* now as well, not to mention the rest of her revolting family.'

'*I* invited June! How many times do I have to say it?' Elliot was almost shaking with fury. But Belinda, for once, refused to be cowed.

'You didn't invite her, Elliot,' she said, under her breath, her voice like ice. 'For some obscure reason of your own you made use of the fact that she turned up. You don't have a good word to say for her, most of the time. I suppose you must have some devious reason......'

'*Have* you, Dad?' Rob turned from the bread board where he was smearing chocolate spread onto slices of white bread. 'What is it?'

'Shut up, Rob,' Elliot snapped.

Mary sat down heavily on a chair. 'Les isn't revolting,' she said, in a low voice, and then, gathering herself together, 'Belinda, dear. Do you know why June and Muriel don't get on?'

Rob pricked up his ears. Belinda polished the draining board energetically. 'Some argument about a boyfriend, wasn't it? Didn't June steal Muriel's boyfriend? That's funny, isn't it? And she's been preaching to *me* about family values! And *you!*' she went on, pointing at Elliot with the dishcloth, 'have listened to her lecture me all day and never said a word in my defence.'

'Oh dear.' Mary put her head in her hands. 'I don't know where this is going to end. It just shows you that it doesn't always do to keep family history locked in the closet.'

'What do you mean?'

'Yeah. What *do* you mean, Grandma?' Rob licked the knife.

Belinda knelt beside her Mum, and stroked her shoulder. Mary looked up and her face was quite gaunt.

'June did steal Muriel's boyfriend. In fact he was Muriel's fiancé. June seduced him, and fell pregnant, and so he had to marry her, and not Muriel. Do you see?'

Belinda gasped. 'He had to marry…? You mean?'

'Yes.' Mary nodded. 'It was your Uncle Les.'

Elliot began to laugh. 'June! The minx!' Rob joined in. For the first time since their arrival, there was accord between father and son.

The welcome delegation on the landing had been joined by the three girls and two of the boys. The children were all in their night things but had been brought down especially to say hello to Aunty Muriel, who had been such a favourite with them, when they had been small. The gathering on the landing was quite large, therefore, but voices were kept hushed in deference to the sleeping baby, and Granny McKay.

Gradually, above the muted hum of conversation, cries of an urgent and abandoned nature began to make themselves heard from behind one of the bedroom doors. At first they were dismissed, confused with the blood-curdling shouts from the war game which had been played almost constantly in the study. But these sounds were different; they were human, ecstatic; moaning, sighing, panting, shrieking; they spoke of fierce and ravenous desire, the expenditure of super-human physical exertion, mounting plateaux of pleasure, the ever-nearing conquest of a high peak. Conversation on the landing faltered and died. The grown-ups looked at each other and then, with dawning realisation, at their feet. The girls paled, then reddened. The boys, taking their cue more from the reaction of those around them than from any real understanding of the situation, sniggered.

If Les had known which room his daughter and her boyfriend had been allocated, he might have caught on more quickly and acted more swiftly to interrupt the coitus taking place. James, with Robert depending on him so heavily, could only make urgent gestures to Simon that the children should be distracted and removed immediately. Ruth, putting two and two together, was on the point of outrage that such a thing should have been facilitated, much more, so volubly *indulged* under the same roof as her children. But a sight, emerging from a room further down the landing, immediately arrested everyone's attention so entirely that the climax, when it vociferously and abundantly arrived within the chamber of Sandra and Kevin, was almost eclipsed.

June staggered from her bedroom onto the landing. As overcome by hysteria as she had been at the arrival of the police, she had not disrobed, and her suit, badly creased, was sadly in disarray. As she had tossed and turned in her distress, it had ridden up to her thighs and now remained there, caught up, unfortunately, in the fastenings of her capacious girdle. Her unhappiness at the consequences of Sandra's mistake, and the sense, much fought against, that she, June, might perhaps have put into motion a chain of events which could have undesirable consequences, had caused her to take refuge in a large quantity of cognac. On an empty stomach, this had proved unwise, and June had been copiously sick. The evidence of this was also a sad detriment to her appearance.

Her hair, normally so strictly controlled, firmly permed and heavily sprayed, was also markedly awry. Indeed, a good portion of her curls seemed to be slipping down over one eye in such a peculiar way that the possibility of their not being, in fact, attached to her head, couldn't help but suggest itself to the onlookers. June's make-up, generously applied, had travelled unchecked across her visage and the combination of smeared eye shadow and smudged mascara made her look like a victim of a terrible attack. Her lipstick formed a vivid gash across her mouth.

The sum of these parts was not happy, and June herself was plainly anything but pleased. As the ardent squeaks and chirrups of her orgasmic daughter emanated down the landing, June's roar of fury rose to meet them. She pointed savagely at Muriel, blissfully enfolded in the bosom of the McKay family, but her anger was inarticulate; it stuck in her throat and choked her, until it was expelled with astonishing velocity before a shining stream of vomit, which propelled it decoratively onto the opposite landing wall.

From the window of her room, Mary looked into the impenetrable blackness of the garden. She had tried to sleep, but lying next to Robert in the bed had been like lying next to a corpse. No vestige of heat had emanated from his body to warm the chill sheets and any heat she managed to generate herself seemed to be sucked away from her into his still, sleeping form. In a far corner of her mind, she wondered if she was suffering from some kind of shock. It hadn't just been the cold which had kept her awake; her mind had been frantic with the incidents and impressions of the day. Robert's disappearance in the morning had been yet another confirmation in Mary's mind that he just wasn't safe; he couldn't be relied upon to think logically or to act rationally, and it was a burden of responsibility she felt increasingly unable to bear. He was plagued by perfectly ridiculous fantasies, insisting that impossible things had happened to him; that a stone statue had come to life in the garden. No amount of reasoning could dissuade him and Mary found herself finally acceding to his theories in a way which made her feel complicit to his madness. Physically, he was more and more of a handful; he couldn't – or wouldn't – wash or dress himself, or take himself to the toilet. His table manners were unreliable. All in all Mary was coming to the conclusion that the time was fast approaching when she would be unable to care for him herself. As bizarre as it sounded, she was seriously considering whether The Oaks might not be a possibility for the son, as well as for the mother. Before his stroke, Robert would have ridiculed any suggestion that he might someday be unable to make rational decisions, rule his family and control his company, let alone be his own master. Mary, now, was fully mistress of their financial situation, for the first time in all of their married life. It was quite surprisingly comfortable, and she knew that money was available for The Oaks, or somewhere similar, if necessary. Of course Robert would resist all suggestions that he should go into a nursing home, but Mary would enlist the help of her children; now they were so confident and well-launched in the world, he would not be able to resist them all.

Mary had given up on sleep and got up out of the icy bed. She'd pulled off the heavy blue counterpane and wrapped it around her, before sitting in the blue velvet armchair. She wished that she could get away from the skeletal shell of her husband; go down and make a cup of tea, and find a hot water bottle and fill it from the kettle. But she knew that the lights would be off, and she worried about tripping or falling in the dark, or disturbing others, and so she remained huddled in her blanket and allowed her thoughts to roam. She wondered if Belinda was sleeping. Even given June's humiliating display on the landing, and Les' righteous anger at the appalling behaviour of his daughter, and his masterly over-ruling of June's strident if laughable attempts to impose her will on the situation, still Belinda's resentment was not entirely assuaged. As a child Belinda had been mild and forgiving, patient and easily pleased. Mary would have expected Belinda's anger to have melted at the sight of June's misery, but the exchange between June and Les seemed to have left her, if not unmoved, still dissatisfied. And indeed June had made a complete spectacle of herself, struggling to stand, waving an indicting finger in Muriel's direction, insisting incoherently that Muriel be removed instantly, that she had no *right* to be there, and who did she think she *was*, to impose herself. Muriel had blanched, and then become tearful, and had finally been escorted downstairs to the small sitting room to be comforted by Miriam. The children, mercifully, had also been removed. Les had paraded up and down the landing, shouting about pots calling kettles black, and telling June in no uncertain terms that now she had made her bed she would certainly be made to lie in it, until Thursday at least. Mary had thought him magnificent in his controlled, righteous anger. June had begged, *begged* to be taken home, had threatened to drive herself there, if Les wouldn't take her. She had stumbled back into their bedroom and come out again triumphantly clutching their car keys, but Les had taken them off her easily, like

281

taking candy off a baby. In the meantime, he had turned his attention to Sandra, who had emerged sheepishly onto the landing. He had asked her how she dared to show her face amongst decent folks and with children present too, and called her a wanton and a hussy. Sandra had dissolved into tears for the second time that evening. Kevin, sensibly, had remained inside the bedroom. Then, with both his women folk in tears, he had stalked down the stairs, leaving them behind him on the landing. They had clutched one another.

'Please,' June had sobbed, '*please* make Daddy give me the keys.'

By this time, James had walked Robert through to the bedroom. Heather and Bob had gone to put Starlight, who had not, amazingly, given all the furore, woken up, to bed. Elliot, after quickly assimilating the reason for the hullabaloo, had retreated downstairs. Ruth, Belinda and herself had remained on the landing, unwilling witnesses to the scene, and yet, in some way, feeling that it was their right to see June get her comeuppance.

Then Mitch had arrived with a bucket of hot water and begun the grisly job of cleaning up. Sandra had taken her mother back into her room. Ruth had gone to find some clean sheets. Mary and Belinda had hugged each other briefly before retiring to their own rooms. Now, Mary considered it quite likely that in view of the day's events, Belinda might suggest the abandonment of the entire holiday, if she didn't receive some encouragement from the rest of the family that all was not lost. On balance, Mary felt, that on her own account at least, there was more to be gained by staying. She wanted her children to observe the deterioration in their father first-hand, before she broached the question of The Oaks. Also, it was pleasant to have help with him, and distraction, even if today's distractions had been of an unprecedented kind. The next day was to be Ellie's birthday; surely they could all make an effort for that?

There were other issues. Young Robert was sullen and solitary and spent far too much time on his computer. For a boy, Mary considered, the positive influence and guidance of a benign father figure was very important; it was no accident that of all her children, her son had strayed furthest from his family and his home. The ugly and never confessed truth was that Robert had failed Simon in every important respect and Mary wished that there was some way that she could ask Simon to talk over the consequences of this with Elliot. But how could she unearth yet another deeply buried family skeleton? And what further putrid bones might such a discussion itself reveal? It didn't bear thinking about; perhaps some things were better left buried. Simon himself was an excellent father, to his sons and his daughter; they clearly idolised him. Rob was now at such an age – he was seventeen – when a son's love for and trust in his father should naturally begin to evolve into respect and liking between one man and another. From what Mary could see, there was nothing between Rob and Elliot other than mutual irritation. History, she could see, was threatening to repeat itself, and there was nothing she could do about it.

Mary sighed. Down in the hallway, the clock struck four. She wondered if Muriel was sleeping. June's acrimony had been quite terrible. Anybody would have thought that it was June who occupied the moral high-ground, not poor Muriel who had, Mary thought, with admirable, almost noble graciousness, allowed herself to be excluded from the family circle for its greater good. She, Mary, felt bad about it, really. Of the two sisters she had always preferred Muriel, but the business, and June's habit of tagging along on Robert's coat-tails, had made staying in contact with Muriel awkward.

The thought of Muriel brought back to Mary's mind the confusion of the conversation she had been having with Les just before her arrival, and his intention, as she had understood it, to salvage something for himself in his final years. He had likened their situations, very significantly, and hadn't there been a suggestion, or a question, or even an invitation, for her, too, to consider such a course of action? The fact that he had read exactly her own most private musings had disarmed her. There had been, for that moment, between the two of them, a relation of the most harmonious kind, a connection, deeper, that is, from the companionable relationship they had always enjoyed. But the next moment, the understanding she thought that she had discerned had been muddled by a number of inexplicable impressions. Of all the people in the house, Muriel had asked for Les on her arrival, rather than Simon, who had spoken to her on the telephone, or Belinda, who was understood to be the hostess, or even Mary herself, who had known her longest. Then, Les' greeting had been so warm. Mary was sure that he had not expected her and yet his pleasure upon seeing her had been unmistakable. Finally there was the suspicious matter of the dog, which had snarled at them all, been impervious to all friendly approaches, and yet trotted off perfectly happily with Les, for all the world as though they were very well acquainted.

Mary remained seated in her blue velvet chair, enveloped in the blue and white crewel bedspread, and pondered the possible explanation for all these matters, and her frank and detailed examination of them seemed to make them less worrying.

Presently, she began to feel much warmer, and with the warmth, came a feeling that sleep, now, would come to her. She gathered the bedspread around her and took a last glance out into the night. On the far horizon, the blackness was lightening a little. Ah well, she sighed as she made her way towards the little dressing room and its single bed, another day.

The baby had been wakeful and once he had managed to settle her Mitch found that he was past sleep himself. Soon it would be morning, anyway. He decided to go down to the kitchen and make himself a cup of tea.

Waiting for the kettle to boil on the Aga hob, he surveyed the kitchen. Evidence of the family was everywhere; a cardigan draped over the back of a chair, a book left open on the dresser, somebody's reading spectacles abandoned on the worktop. He was beginning to know them now; the cast of relative strangers was taking on flesh. The cardigan, he guessed, belonged to the Grandma, the book to Ruth, the glasses.... he couldn't place the glasses, yet. But his initial impression, that observing the family would be like watching a play, had been right on the money. Today's events, in fact, had borne the hallmarks of outright farce and it would have been all too easy to laugh up his sleeve at it all; the comedic arrival of more and more relations, (and those relations! Drippy, gormless and potty by turns); the family posturing, jockeying for position, furtive discussions in hushed voices; and then, in a climax of comedy, the police, for all the world like the key-stone cops!

But somehow, in spite of the comical potential, Mitch couldn't bring himself to laugh at them. At one time he had found Bob and Heather very funny; their shambolic life-style: they were often overrun by guests who came for dinner and stayed a fortnight; they were at the mercy of sudden unappeasable impulses: they *must* eat *crêpes*, simply *had* to have a hot air balloon. Heather's weird enthusiasms – for liturgical dance, and eastern mysticism – and Bob's vague, artistic preoccupation which made him forget meetings or even mealtimes, or set off in the wrong direction on the M40 to find himself in Birmingham instead of London. Yes, at first – Mitch would admit it – he had been inclined to laugh at them. And his job – he had been told to 'make himself useful around the place' – was, by anybody's standards, so easy, it would have been a cinch to take advantage (many

285

already had), both of their good nature and of the situation. But they were really nice people – sincere and genuinely good – underneath their absurdity, and also (because of their goodness) rather vulnerable, and it was this vulnerability which quashed any urge in Mitch to lampoon them. At the same time it threatened his determination – his need – to retain an appropriate distance, an emotional distance; it made it hard not to care. He had to remind himself, sternly, that, nice as they were, they didn't owe him anything; he was, when all was said and done, only an employee and they could decide they didn't need him at any time. The travel – he had skied in St Moritz, been scuba diving off St Lucia and caddied at St Andrews; the opportunities – to develop his aptitude for all things gadget: cameras and computers and the mixing desk in the recording studio; his little flat above their four-car garage - all of it – could disappear at a stroke. If he started to *care*, where would that leave him?

But it was a constant battle he had with himself, and the baby was the biggest test of it, sweet, funny, wilful little thing that she was. She was beginning to tug on strings in his heart that he hadn't known were there.

It was happening here, too, he acknowledged, as he poured boiling water into his cup and put the last meringue on a plate. He couldn't laugh at the family's farcical predicament because he saw in them, too, genuine goodness. He saw through the thin veneer of their clannishness to a species of susceptibility. He was beginning to care.

He cared about the girl. He fancied her, of course, that went without saying; she was gorgeous, with flirty eyes and a delicious little dimple in her cheek when she smiled. He wasn't very experienced with girls – his job precluded many opportunities for socialising, he was on-call pretty much 24/7. There had been the odd brief liaison with a dancer or a stage-hand, so he knew the general lie of the land, but *this* could not be like *that* had been, and he didn't want it to be. She was helpless and sort of lost in a way which cried out to his protective instincts, to his emotional susceptibilities, not his predatory ones. His conversation with her that evening had struck a chord. He was already no fan of Rob McKay – their few encounters in the past had left a sour taste – and the girl was right, he was neither use nor ornament here on this holiday. Mitch wondered now, as he padded down the passageway, across the hall and into the study, whether he might not be able to bring things to a satisfactory conclusion to all parties.

The study was in a terrible state. There were empty glasses, cereal bowls and small plates littered over the surfaces. Sweet and crisp papers were strewn across the floor. The computer had been left on; its offensive screensaver bouncing around the perimeters of the monitor. Mitch took a bite of his meringue and opened Outlook Express. To his horror, in spite of Ellie's plaintive appeals to her better nature and their friendship, the in-box contained a number of emails from Caro, who was evidently eager to win Rob's approval. She commiserated with him on having to stay at this 'derelict pile' along with his 'insane relatives'. In Sent Mail, Mitch read Rob's account of the day; the arrival of the 'geriatrics', the assault by the police squad, the noisy sexual adventures of his cousin which had sent all of the grown-ups into hyperspace, the drunken sickness of his aunt. Rob made it all sound like an episode in a television program. Mitch could tell from Caro's responses that she hadn't believed half of it. Then his eye caught the word 'secret'. The 'phone message he had overheard had implied a secret and here was Rob asking Caro to tell him what it was.

His opinion of Rob, already low, plummeted further. Brothers shouldn't betray their sisters. People shouldn't slag off their relatives, even if they were a bit bizarre. Rob's derogatory comments about his family and his holiday made Mitch seethe. Some people were so lucky and they just didn't know it. This boy needed to be taught a lesson and perhaps he would be the one to do it. He connected to the internet and visited a few websites. He printed off some material. Finally he

287

used Rob's email account to send Caro an email telling her that she was a cow, an ugly cow, and that Rob didn't want to hear from her again.

Belinda – A Memoir from 1985

Belinda was always tired on Tuesdays; it was her day at the Enquiries window, dealing with queues of people requesting improvements to their houses, or demanding repairs, or objecting to their rent, or lodging complaints about their neighbours. Today she had been held back long after five by a particularly vociferous tenant and as a result she had missed her bus home. She had had to stand in the rain for twenty minutes waiting for the next one. When she stepped off the bus it pulled away behind her through a puddle which had gathered over a blocked drain, and splashed the back of her raincoat with filthy water. Tuesdays was always a quiet evening at home, because Heather went straight from school to the house of a friend for a quick tea before both girls attended Miss Morton's Academy of Music, Singing and Dance. Normally, after tea on Tuesdays, Belinda and her Mum would do some baking, or she would climb the stairs up to the loft room, the one which had been Simon's, where she now had her sewing machine and a large work table for her quilting and appliqué night-school projects. But tonight Belinda thought she would rather have a hot bath and an early night. She felt cold and wretched. She couldn't face Simon's room tonight.

It would always be Simon's room, no matter how vehemently her parents now referred to it as 'the work room'. It had always been his room, from the moment it had been constructed amongst the eaves of the house. He had had his train set up there, and his Lego models, and, when he got bigger, his boxes of mysterious circuitry and wires and sockets and widgets that he liked to tinker with. Then he was gone, just gone into the night, a few days after his eighteenth birthday, with his passport and his birth certificate and his savings book and a backpack of clothes. At first they thought he would turn up again a few days later, muddy and hung-over from a rock festival, or that there would be call from Ruth, staying on at University over the vacation to write her thesis, to say that he'd turned up on her doorstep ravenously hungry but quite unharmed. But there had been nothing. His friends hadn't seen him or heard from him. There was no sighting of him in any of his old haunts. It was as though he had disappeared off the face of the earth. After a couple of weeks Dad had stamped up the stairs to the attic room, packed away all Simon's things into cardboard boxes, and taken them off to the tip; his clothes and books and records, his files from college, the posters off the walls, even the bed and the furniture had been dismantled and hauled away until there was nothing left at all to show that Simon have ever been there. Mum had wept and wrung her hands, and jumped up at every ring on the bell, every passer-by on the pavement, every shrill of the telephone. Belinda found her on several occasions up in the stripped attic room, her head pressed against the roof-light, inconsolable, sobbing; 'I miss you. I miss you, my little man.'

She kept setting one too many places at the table and cooking too much food.

'It would have been better if he'd just died,' Dad said one meal-time as Mum broke down again over one pork chop too many.

Belinda just couldn't understand why Simon, and Ruth, too, come to that, had found it necessary to make such pointless waves in the family. Why had they complained and objected to everything? Why did they want everything to be different? What, exactly, she wanted to know, was wrong with things the way they were, the way they had always been? There was nothing wrong with being a McKay! Increasingly, McKays were looked up to in the town; they employed thirty-odd people one way or another. Dad and Uncle Les had joined the Masons and the four of them went off regularly to dinner dances where they rubbed shoulders with Police Inspectors and Stock Brokers and people who had been members of the Golf Club for as long as they could remember. (Belinda had been with them to a 'Ladies' Night', with her hair pinned up and wearing a sequined cocktail dress, and 'drunk wine' with the Worshipful Master and received a pretty little china dressing table ornament as a gift. She had danced with a pleasant young man with an unfortunate stammer, and another with a shock of auburn hair, and a third, rather older, tall and thick-set, with beautiful deep brown eyes, a low, sonorous voice and a heavy gold signet ring on his little finger. It had been glorious; she was twenty four after all and it was time she was married. The last of her partners had asked her for her number, but he had never called.) But affluence hadn't changed them. Mum still did all her own cleaning and baked every week, and her washing was the whitest and brightest you would see on any line in the area, only, with Simon and Ruth gone, there was so much less of it, now, and it made her sad.

The two of them spoke of him, sometimes, in hushed tones, speculating as to where he might be and what he might be doing, and whether he was safe. Dad never mentioned his name at all, but the frown-line between his eyebrows was more deeply etched, his mouth set in a harder line, his McKay eyes a more steely grey. He carried the burden of the yard alone. Without the support of a son, without the hope of a McKay to pass it all on to, it must all seem, suddenly, very pointless.

Belinda put her key in the door and stepped into the hall. It struck her immediately that something was different. There was, first of all, the smell of something rich and beefy coming from the kitchen. Tuesdays was usually a day for sausages or bacon. Then, as she slipped off her wet raincoat and hung it in the cloakroom, she could see that the table in the dining room was set with the best white cloth and wine glasses, for four. The lamp on the sideboard was lit and the fire was on. Nowadays they rarely used the dining room on Tuesdays, preferring to eat round the little gate-leg table in the kitchen instead. She walked across the hall, tucking her wet and disarranged hair back into its bun as best as she was able. She stood for a moment at the bottom of the stairs, outside the lounge door. There was something else. Something was lighter, released, like fresh wind after a storm, like the relief when a headache has passed. The band of tension she so often experienced as she stepped into the house was slack and negligible. The house itself felt relaxed. She opened the lounge door. In a vase on the low table in the bay window a there was a huge bouquet of flowers. The television was switched off. Mum and Dad were perched awkwardly on the edges of their chairs, sipping sherry. On the settee lounged a young man Belinda had not seen before. He stood up as she entered. He was young, perhaps a year or two younger than her, and only an inch or two taller. He was slightly built, with fine dark hair swept back away from his face. He had a good complexion, rather small, dark eyes, a pointed nose and a thin-lipped, narrow mouth. He was not handsome, but he had an engaging smile. He held out his hand to her.

Dad leapt to his feet with more energy and enthusiasm that she had seen in him for months. Belinda looked across at him. His face was alight, alive. His eyes were shining and his whole demeanour seemed inflated somehow, buoyed up, infused by some impetus Belinda couldn't quite identify. She looked at her Mum. Still seated, Mary looked back at Belinda with an eager, hopeful smile, her crystal sherry glass clutched so tightly between her clasped hands that Belinda wondered why its stem didn't snap. She hesitated to speak, as though waiting, almost breathlessly, for some much hoped-for sign. And immediately Belinda recognised and named the new quality in her father's manner which had eluded her a few seconds before. It was hope.

Dad stepped forward across the hearth rug, and smiled at her. He held out both his hands, taking the young man by his elbow and reaching out the other hand to Belinda's shoulder. He exuded hope, it poured off him in palpable waves, it shone out of him. The room and everyone in it was bathed with it; golden and beneficent.

'Here you are at last!' he cried. 'Let me introduce....'

But the young man interrupted him. 'I'm Elliot Donne,' he said. 'Delighted to meet you at last.' His voice had a thin, nasal quality to it, almost adenoidal. They shook hands. His hand was damp, but then, probably, after the rain, so was hers.

'Now then,' Dad said, rubbing his hands together, 'let's eat. Come on, son, this way.'

He led the way into the dining room and motioned Elliot towards Simon's chair.

Sunday

After the surreal and distressing developments of Saturday, Belinda's determination when she woke on Sunday morning was to sound a note of calm normality. Not least in her desire was the fact that it was Ellie's sixteenth birthday, and she wished above all things to make the day as enjoyable for her as she could. It was hard to imagine what could possibly occur to blight the holiday further. She felt as though almost every ounce of joy had been wrung from it by the interloping relatives; her plans and expectations were in tatters. But nothing, no matter how bizarre, violent or fantastical, could surprise her now. Only one joyful if unlooked for possibility gave her any encouragement, a hope which she dared not even name and yet which shone over every ugly and embarrassing circumstance of the holiday so far with a kind and healing light. It gave her strength, and compensated slightly her sense of deflation, and she determined that nothing should be allowed to jaundice Ellie's special day.

Ellie's birthday always fell in half term and over the years they had made various attempts to overcome the difficulties that this posed; friends were often away and so parties tended to be disappointingly attended. On the other hand, cinemas, bowling alleys and the like were always maddeningly crowded. No matter what they arranged always seemed to be burdened beforehand with the expectation of disappointment. In arranging the holiday, Belinda had specifically mentioned to everyone that it would be Ellie's birthday and she sincerely hoped that the family would have made an effort. While April had been alive she had been reliable about sending cards and presents, but Miriam left these matters to Simon who generally forgot until days or sometimes weeks after the event. Ruth normally managed a cheap card and a sadly crumpled ten pound note; its dilapidation somehow speaking of the reluctance with which it was parted. Heather's solution was to make vague promises about future treats which rarely materialised into anything concrete or which, at best, involved Belinda in time consuming and expensive trips into town to see obscure exhibitions or slightly unsuitable shows to which Heather had sent tickets. Mary usually consulted Belinda before buying anything and therefore in the past had ended up presenting her grandchildren with practical, useful, if unimaginative gifts, but recently she had taken to enclosing (quite generous) sums of money in the card. Both Rob and Ellie had monthly allowances and as a result rarely needed anything. In addition their patience with useful, practical gifts was wearing embarrassingly thin. They preferred to be taken to boutiques – or, in Rob's case, computer shops – and waited for outside while they selected purchases unimpeded by parental suggestions. Belinda had been delighted by Heather and Miriam's gesture the day before although she still had not been shown what Ellie had chosen, but she hoped that there would be some surprise parcels for Ellie today.

Elliot had come to bed soon after her the night before. She was pleased to see at least that he had brought up with him the cursed laptop computer which had been in the way all day. She had been seated in front of the dressing table brushing her hair; it reached, still, well down her back, and although its lustre was gone, it was thick, with a natural wave. Only Elliot ever saw her with her hair down - even the children rarely did - but it was not a sight which seemed to move him unduly. She had always considered her hair her only beauty. The feel of it in her hands and on her naked shoulders awakened in her imagination confused fantasies which drew from sources as diverse as Rapunzel in her tower, lonely and yearning, and Mary at the feet of Christ, intoxicated by the scent of expensive perfumes as she wiped his feet with her hair. Having her hair unpinned made her feel young and girlish, rather vulnerable, undone and undignified. It was at this moment in the day when Elliot would often choose to unburden himself of the day's frustrations. He would rant and pace, often decrying the idiocy of an employee or the senseless bureaucracy imposed by government which impeded his business, but sometimes

295

he would pick an argument with her which she would feel, in her state of undress, ill-equipped to handle. She often wondered if he did it on purpose, waited until she was undressed and her hair down before launching an attack, as an animal will catch its prey unawares and then target its softer, undefended parts. It grieved her that at those times when she needed from him extreme consideration and tenderness, she must instead tap into her own deeper reserves of extra caution and defensiveness.

Elliot had pottered around the room as she brushed, folding his clothes and taking a long time about putting his trousers in the press. She had braced herself for an onslaught but there had been none. Indeed, he had seemed to Belinda, on the whole, rather quiet. She put it down, at first, to his lack of proper sleep the night before, and the last vestiges of his hang-over. While he had cleaned his teeth she had climbed into the bed and switched out her light, leaving his burning dully on his bedside table. She had felt him slide into the sheets beside her and switch off his light. If Elliot had had a day even half as bad as hers had been, she would normally have spent some time soothing his ego and commiserating with him. But of the two of them she felt that she had suffered far more, and if any sympathy were to be offered, she ought certainly to be on the receiving end of it. Her exhaustion and disappointment threatened, in the darkness, to spill into tears. A kindly hand or soft word would have meant the world to her, but she expected none, and, she caught herself imagining with a bitterness which surprised her, the kind of reassurances and encouragements and fondness Ruth would have got from James in similar circumstances. She pushed this thought with difficulty aside, and lay and thought her way instead around the situation from Elliot's point of view, coming to the conclusion eventually that he had been, unusually, out-manoeuvred on all sides. June had used him, and the united actions of the McKays in bringing Muriel had been accomplished in spite of him. His own consciousness of this state of affairs would explain his aloofness.

In a desperate and craven attempt to elicit some kind of communication from her husband, Belinda had turned over and said, 'What time shall we waken Ellie tomorrow?' She'd heard him sigh, and almost sensed his brain computing the requisite actions and words for a McKay birthday. It was a ritual, one of many, carried forward from Belinda's own childhood days and as far as she knew was the norm for all the McKays. Elliot seemed to have no family traditions or routines at all. He never spoke of his childhood or his parents. He mentioned his eccentric sister only in terms of relief that she required no contact with him. One of the most shocking discoveries Belinda had made during the first few months of their marriage was that Elliot had no idea at all about family life; his calendar was empty of the landmarks which measured out the McKay year; Shrove Tuesday, Easter egg hunts, summer holidays, Halloween, bonfire night, stir-up Sunday.

She had thought for a moment, as she lay in the darkness, that he would ignore her question. She had almost given up on him, when he spoke. 'I suppose ten will be early enough. I'll wake her up and do my bit. But after that you can count me out. Personally I plan a quiet day with the Sunday newspapers tomorrow, if I can finish my figures off. Thankfully I'm not required to play a part in this family melodrama you have insisted on acting out. I'll be glad when you all stop being so bloody clannish. In the meantime I may well drive back on Monday. I must let Carol have these figures for the quotes. They simply have to be in the post on Monday afternoon or the tenders will be closed. And there are other things at the office I need to see to.'

If his words intended to wring from Belinda a plea for him to stay, to relent, they failed. She had turned from him, edging as far away from him as it was possible for her to get. At that moment she could not have cared if he had been as good as his word, but she believed that he was bluffing, and she refused to pander to him. They spent the night thus, separated by hard bolsters of disappointment, hurt and resentment. But in the morning, Belinda packed away her

297

feelings as one might pack up photographs and memorabilia of a deceased love - one which would cause distress to look upon. She showered, and dressed, and put up her hair, and descended to the kitchen with Ellie, and only Ellie, focussed in her mind.

Unfortunately Simon's forecast of good weather turned out to be wide of the mark; in the night the wind had herded laden grey galleons of cloud across the sea and as dawn came they unloaded their cargo relentlessly along the coast, over the fields and onto the village. Hunting Wriggly sloshed, ankle-deep in the deluge; the roofs of the cottages seemed to be pulled low over their walls like hats, the merry brook which crossed the road by the school had turned into a turgid brown torrent, the ducks plattered around in the puddled grass of the green. Outside the little shop, a stream of water spilled out of a broken gutter and baptised the early-bird customers as they entered and departed. Les dodged it as best he could. Inside the shop, a musty smell of old stock mingled with the humid hum of damp overcoats and the shop-keeper's bacon breakfast. Les bought a birthday card for Ellie (embossed with a be-ribboned and be-frilled little girl which he hoped would be appropriate), and a selection of Sunday newspapers. As an afterthought, he also purchased a bar of Muriel's favourite chocolate and a packet of Resolve hangover remedy. In the car, he wrote his own and June's names inside the card and added a twenty pound note before sealing it. His coat, even from the short dash between the car and the shop, was soaked. The envelope, pressed against his knee as he wrote, became damp and looked limp and disappointing in spite of his best efforts.

The road back to Hunting Manor was awash with water; it ran in rivulets along the gutters and in translucent sheets across the road surface, carrying dirt washed from the fields. Les drove with great care; the drive of Hunting Manor was rutted and uneven and threatened to grate on the bottom of his low-slung Jaguar. But as well as the desire to protect his aged but well-cared for motor car, he needed to consider his anomalous position in the McKay family milieu. Uninvited, unwelcome, he was yet constrained, now, to stay; Granny McKay and Muriel constrained him, with duty on the one hand, and desire on the other. His wife also, he was absolutely determined, would stay until Thursday and atone for the disruption

299

she had caused. Under no circumstances would he allow her to shirk her responsibilities to Mary and Robert and the family. Neither would he allow her to take out her frustrations on poor Muriel, the inevitable and, frankly, easy prey for June's caustic sarcasm. A position of strength was not one Les was used to taking in relation to his wife and he girded up his loins, metaphorically, for the onslaught.

Lying next to Muriel the whole night long, a luxury their situation had never before afforded, he had gone over and over in his mind the legalities, the moralities, not to mention the practicalities of his situation, and on every count it seemed to him that the rights of it were all on Muriel's side and the wrongs all on June's. Forty five years ago, given June's purported condition, the family had agreed that the right thing for him to do was to abandon Muriel. Her claims, they had implied, were less. How would they respond now when he declared his intention of unravelling time and going back, as it were, to plan A? There was no doubt that the years of employment security that had been afforded him by McKay's Haulage weighed heavily. Les considered whether there was any sense in which he had been 'paid off' for doing what had seemed to be the right thing by June. Perhaps the family would consider that he had been amply compensated and that to change horses now was rather a smack in the eye.

He drew the car to a halt at the bottom of the drive and looked back down the lane of McKay memories; the births, the christenings, the marriages, the deaths, the birthdays, the Christmases, the anniversaries. It seemed to him like an endless auto route, like the ones he had driven interminable hour after hour on McKay business. And each family get together had been like another identical service station; the same predictable packaged fayre, the same layout, the same décor, and him fumbling with the unfamiliar currencies, stumbling over the foreign place names; there had seemed like no escape, he had felt alien, but he had dutifully toed the line. Now, ever the reliable hanger-on, he was faced with the prospect of making waves. His actions were bound to cause a rift; certainly, June would see to that. Did he care? He had made himself useful, and been made use of, in pursuit of McKay glory, but had bathed in only the weakest glimmer of its reflection. No, he concluded, one way or another, whatever he had received from McKays had been bought and paid for. He owed them nothing, for June's sake, but would doubtless be made to pay dearly for Muriel's. So be it. She was worth it.

The house in its rainy hollow looked damp and desolate; the sandstone had turned dark in the wet, the windows were dulled with water, many still curtained. It was still early, and no cheering wisp of smoke rose from the chimneys. But Les was pleased to see that the hatchback of Sandra's little car was open and in the time it took him to navigate the drive and park on the sweep, she and Kevin had stowed their luggage, climbed into the car and had made their shamefaced departure. She gave him a wan wave as she passed, but Kevin avoided his eye. Les' satisfaction at their quiet exodus was double-edged; he had been heard and obeyed, which was grimly pleasing, but as they drove away they abandoned him to a tug of war between June and Muriel from which, for him, there could be no escape.

Muriel and Granny McKay were breakfasting. Granny had shown no surprise at all at being greeted by her elder daughter on waking, and had made no reference to Mr Burgess. She seemed, for now, to have forgotten everything which had occurred in her life for the past thirty odd years, and treated Muriel as though they were still living together in their gloomy little terraced house. As Muriel had washed and dressed her mother's sinewy, resilient body, she had given a tirade of instructions regarding the washing of the best china, poshing of the laundry and the stoning of the step. Muriel had agreed vaguely with all her suggestions and helped her down the stairs.

They had gamely attempted to empty the dishwasher. Granny had gone through the motions of helping; picking up crockery and moving it from one place to another, putting glassware into the refrigerator and the cruet in the sink. They were in the middle of this exercise when Les came in and Muriel gave him a reassuring smile while he found a glass and filled it with water, dropping two effervescent tablets into it. She offered to make tea, eyeing the kettle on the Aga doubtfully. Les placed Ellie's card on the table, then he shook his head and exited the room with a look of grim resignation on his face. By the time Belinda arrived, plates and pans and cups and cutlery were strewn everywhere and the two older women were sitting amongst it all blinking and smiling like two magpies discovered in their hoard of stolen trinkets.

'We weren't sure where anything went, were we Mother? But we like to help, if we can,' said Muriel.

'Although we pay enough, in all conscience,' Granny demurred, making a sudden mental time-leap, 'It doesn't seem right to me that we should be put to work. Matron must be short-staffed.'

'Yes,' Belinda said, placing the kettle on the Aga. 'Well. Now I'm here I'll put the kettle on, shall I? Just a light breakfast this morning; I'm going to cook brunch at twelve. Did you sleep well?'

'Oh yes, very well, thank you Belinda. Did you?'

'Not especially. I don't suppose you'd know, Muriel, but it's Ellie's birthday today. Now you're not to worry about a gift or a card. You came and helped us out at such short notice that no one will have expected you to have thought of it.'

Muriel's heart sank. 'No. No, I'm sorry. I hadn't any idea.' Having been so determined to fit in, and be family, she felt as though she had failed at the first fence.

'Never mind. Milk?'

'Thank you.'

'Who's Ellie?' Granny's spoon hovered over her Weetabix. 'Bloody ridiculous name.'

'She's Belinda's daughter, Mother.'

'Oh. Well that explains it, then. Who's Belinda?'

Belinda laughed. 'I am. I'm Robert's oldest.'

'Don't be ridiculous! Robert's only fourteen. He isn't even married! Wait till I tell Mrs George!'

Muriel and Belinda exchanged looks. 'Mrs George?' Belinda queried, raising her eyebrows.

'Used to live next door,' Muriel mouthed, 'years ago.'

'Oh, I see.'

'Eat your breakfast, Mother,' said Muriel.

'The milk tastes funny.'

'It's because they give you HRT milk at The Oaks. You've forgotten what real milk tastes like.'

'I think you might mean UHT,' Belinda suggested, with a smile.

James joined them. He surveyed the scene from the small window in the back door. 'A met and wiserable day,' he intoned. Belinda passed him a cup of tea.

303

'I'm going up to the village, to the church service,' he announced, sipping. 'Ruth is unwell, and I don't think either of the children will want to come. So, unless anyone else.....?'

'Well,' began Muriel.

'*I'd* like to, actually,' Belinda interrupted, surprising herself. She was not a regular attendee. She and her siblings had been sent to Sunday school with faithful regularity, and all had stopped attending once they had been confirmed. Her parents had only attended services as spectators; when Heather had been singing in the children's choir, the year that Simon had been Joseph in the nativity and, once, when Ruth had been picked to do a harvest reading. Now she, like them, tended only to put in an appearance at the children's Harvest and Christmas services, or at funerals as the official WI representative, but the chance to spend a whole hour with James was not to be missed. 'I expect I'll be cooking for the rest of the day so I'll take the chance to get out now.'

James nodded. 'I think the service starts at 9.30, so we should leave in about ten minutes.'

Les parted the bedroom curtains six inches and June moaned and screwed up her eyes.

'For God's sake, Leslie!'

He ignored her complaints. 'Drink this. It will ease your head. Then you can get up and come down for brunch. There's a birthday. You know the routine.' He turned his back on her as she struggled up from the bedclothes, emptying his trouser pockets before peeling off his damp trousers and crumpled shirt and dropping them in a corner of the room.

'I certainly won't be coming down. I'm far too ill.'

'Rubbish. You're hung-over, and ashamed to show your face. But you *will* show it. You can't stay up here for five days. Here, you can put these on,' Les plucked clothes from their hangers and flung them on the bed.

'You've changed your tune. I thought you wanted to go home,' June snapped. Les ignored her. He wrapped a towel around himself. 'I'm going to find a shower,' he said. 'It's pouring outside and I got soaked.'

June sipped the fizzing drink. 'Is she still here?'

'Yes, she is. And she's staying.' Les hesitated by the half open door.

June sniffed. 'You can take me home, then. I'm not staying here with her.'

Les closed the door, sat down on the bed and looked at his wife. Without all her artificial additives she looked quite like Muriel, except for a hardness of mouth and a steeliness of eye.

'I can't think what she thinks she's doing here!' June blustered. 'She can't possibly fit in!'

305

Les sighed. 'They invited her, when they found out about Mr Burgess, in case your mother got upset. Your mother has to stay until Thursday, and so will we.'

'And Sandra?'

'No. Sandra has gone.'

'Gone? Why? Why has she gone?'

'Because I told her to.'

They looked at each other. For the first time in their entire relationship, Les was in control. It was an unnerving state of affairs for both of them and it nonplussed them, temporarily. Suddenly June's face crumpled and she began to cry.

'Take me, home, Leslie,' she sobbed. 'Please take me home.'

Les got up and passed her a box of tissues from the dressing table.

'I can't,' he said, quietly. 'I can't leave them to cope with your mother, not when it was you who brought her here. And even if I could, I wouldn't.'

'Muriel can cope with mother!' June exclaimed, with tragic eyes.

'But it wouldn't be fair to ask her to. Not on her own. Not when it was *you* who brought her here. And I've promised Mary that we'll look after Robert as well. It's the least we can do.'

June wiped her eyes and blew her nose. She examined her finger nails, then sniffed. She avoided his eyes. It was a well-known sign, to Les, that she was formulating a plan. 'Of course I only wanted to make things special for them,' she said. 'I realise now that I made a mistake.'

'That's all you'll have to tell them. They're kind people. They'll be polite to you, as a guest. And of course, they'll expect you to be polite to .... their other guests.'

'You mean *her.*' June's eyes flicked towards the dressing table. Les followed her glance.

June drained the glass. 'That stuff's horrible. Where did you sleep last night?'

Les got up. He picked up his razor, toothbrush and comb from the bedside table. 'In one of the other rooms, same as the night before.' He walked over to the dressing table and surveyed the cluttered array of belongings strewn across its surface. He lifted his eyes to the mirror and caught June's reflection, watching him. Her eyes stalked his hand like a snake hunting a rodent as it roved amongst the clutter. Then, slowly, he picked up his car keys. Her eyes met his in the mirror, and there was an instant of naked comprehension between them, before the shutters slammed down.

'Go and have your shower. You stink. I suppose you slept in those clothes. I bet you're sorry now that you didn't bring more things. I shall find a bath. There'd better be plenty of hot water.'

307

When Rachel woke up and opened her eyes, the first thing she saw was her pile of neatly folded new clothes. The remembrance of them caused her to stroke the material of her beautiful new pyjamas with furtive pleasure. She put a peculiar sensation in her abdomen down to hunger and excitement. She heard the rain drumming on the roof above her head, and splattering like plastic beads onto the window, but bad weather couldn't dampen her delight in the burgeoning feelings of friendship which were developing between the cousins. Turning her head, she could see that Tansy and Ellie were still asleep; Ellie, in the bed nearest to her, lay on her back, her arms flung above her head, her dark hair tumbled over the pillow like shiny rivulets of lava.

Rachel had been promised that today she might try to put Ellie's hair into a French plait. Last night her two cousins had brushed her hair, and tied it up this way and that, and discussed cuts, and ceramic straighteners, and colours, and indeed any possibility other than the characterless style it currently occupied. The shopping trip, the mutual grooming, and high jinks late last night – although it had taken Rachel a while to cotton on – were all serving to break down the barriers which Rachel had so feared would alienate her from her more worldly, moneyed, mature cousins. Two nights and one very hectic day had given them ample opportunity to discuss every topic of interest. Boys, of course, first and foremost. (Ellie had had boyfriends 'of course', several. Tansy had liked a boy for a while, and been kissed by him once, unexpectedly, on a coach as they returned from a study trip. Rachel shook her head.) School next. (Ellie muddled along at her private co-ed Grammar school, surviving on charm in the absence of completed homework or satisfactory examination results. Tansy, a weekly boarder, did well at most things because there wasn't much in the way of extra-curricular distraction. Rachel liked practical subjects like technology, hated PE and had the help of an assistant in Math's and English.) Bra sizes and puberty were discussed late in the night. (Ellie, 32B, yes, since she was twelve; Tansy 32A, yes, last year; Rachel

36A, no, not yet.) They had been kind to her, overlooking her non-McKay blood, her physical grossness, her naivety, and treating her as one of themselves. Tansy had painted her toenails and Ellie had even offered to pluck her eyebrows although she had declined this offer, on the grounds that her mother would surely disapprove.

'Oh! Mothers!' Ellie had said, dismissively. 'They don't even notice, half the time. And what they don't know about won't hurt them, believe me.' She had yanked down the waistband of her pyjamas to reveal a small tattoo at the base of her spine, just above the cleft of her bottom. 'I've had this three weeks and no-one's noticed, yet.'

Rachel and even Tansy had gasped and exclaimed, but amid the thrill of the revelation, it was understood implicitly by Rachel that Ellie had trusted her with a secret which she must not tell, even to her father.

Rachel rolled over onto her side and groped around on the floor beside her bed for *Bridget Jones' Diary*, which Ellie had lent to her the night before. She knew that it would be disapproved of. The sensation weighed her down, and she found, surprisingly, that anger, and not despair, rose up to meet it. Her bowels lurched and tautened with indignation as she found her page and began, defiantly, to read.

Presently, Elliot entered the room with a mug of tea for Ellie.

'Good morning girls. Happy birthday Ellie,' he said, placing the mug on the bedside table nearest to his daughter. Ellie rolled over and yawned.

'Mmmm?'

'Happy Birthday, Ellie,' Tansy and Rachel chorused.

'The usual birthday rigmarole awaits downstairs. But don't rush. Your mother, for some obscure reason known only to herself, has gone to church,' said Elliot.

James and Belinda sat at the end of one of the ancient wooden pews in the chill interior of the village church. They had been welcomed by a kindly but surprised sideswoman, who had handed them a dog-eared service booklet and a musty copy of 'Hymns Ancient and Modern'. Three elderly worshippers huddled together in a pew further back, which leaned against one of the two old fashioned bulbous radiators; the other was in the porch, and the little heat which emanated from it was instantly lost through the open door into the damp autumn air. The sideswoman and the priest whispered conspiratorially by the shelves of bibles. The organist played a quiet and inconsequential series of chords and arpeggios. Outside, on the spire, crows called to one another. Belinda sat as close to James as was decent and kept her hands clasped on her lap. James, who never felt the cold, unzipped his anorak and then closed his eyes. He didn't kneel, or make any gesture, but Belinda could tell that he was praying, and she wondered at this newly discovered facet to his character. She sat still, fighting the urge to wriggle, or chafe her frozen fingers, respecting his detachment, feeling, at the same time, a breathless excitement at the opportunity which had been presented to her, to be alone with him. Then, from nowhere, she remembered the poor families whose holiday had been ruined by that dreadful accident on the motorway, the families missing a member, now, and wondered who, in the end, would take the blame for it all; which inattentive driver or defective vehicle would be cited as the cause and whether it really helped, at all, to have someone to blame when a chair at the dinner table, a child's bed, was empty forever, and if a family could ever recover from such sudden and wanton loss.

Presently, James exhaled heavily, his breath making a cloud in the icy air. Then he turned to her.

'Now at last I've got you to myself,' he smiled, 'and we can talk. How are you?' Belinda felt like weeping; not, she was ashamed to say, because of the thought of the accident victims, but just for herself. He really wanted to know, indeed, he already knew, largely, how things were for her. He was so intuitive, a reader of people; he had seen things and discerned the truth from the things he had seen. It had become his habit periodically to take her to one side and gently probe with careful questions. It made her feel so blessed to be singled out by him, and made much of, and it added to her sense of connectedness with him which was so markedly absent from her relationship with Elliot or indeed any other human creature. There was no requirement that she should gush or gloss over things, there was no point; he seemed able to divine the truth. It was this genuine care about her, perhaps even care *for* her, and his intuitive understanding which somehow unloosed her inside. She shook her head. 'No change,' she said, sadly. 'I always seem to get caught on the wrong foot. It's only a matter of keeping one step ahead but I don't often manage it.'

Two more people shuffled down the aisle and took the pew in front of them. They flicked the pages of their service books and consulted the list of hymns on the board.

'No.' James lowered his voice further and bent his head down so that he could speak more confidentially. 'No, Belinda. This is *his* problem, not yours. What this all stems from is his lack of self-confidence. He feels intimidated by you.'

Belinda searched his face. 'Me? But I'm hopeless at everything!'

'No, you're not. You're the key to his success. Everything he has and does is down to who you are. He feels it and it irks him.'

'Because I'm Dad's daughter?'

'Yes, you're the genuine article. He's just an interloper, really, so he has to fight all the time to establish his authority. You're the real McCoy. Or, should I say, the real McKay?'

'I see. Yes. I hadn't thought about it like that.'

Above them, in the spire, a mournful bell began to toll, bidding worshippers to come. Belinda considered James' words. He waited for her to digest what he had said. She could feel his breath on her face as it was turned to him.

'Don't let him crush you, Belinda. You have a gentleness and a softness and a kindness which is too precious. Don't let him crush it out of you.' Belinda bit her lip; his own kindness was almost too much to bear. He awoke feelings in her which confused and excited. His huge body seemed to offer comfort and protection, his calmness was a welcome balm after Elliot's volatile temper. She saw herself, through his eyes, as a new person, and the vision was exhilarating. As they sat together in companionable silence, and he watched her assimilate his vision of her, he placed his hand over hers to reinforce the connectedness between them, stilling, at the same time, the restless twisting and twisting of her ring. His hand was large, clean, warm and soft, with neatly trimmed nails. It folded around her icy fingers and squeezed them gently. She squeezed back, instinctively, and as she did so, equally involuntarily, from nowhere, the question came into her mind; what would it feel like to have that hand un-pin her hair, placed on her breast? To have his fingers inside her? She almost cried out at the shock of it, the thought itself, so inappropriate, so wrong, and yet the picture, the idea, shockingly arousing. At that moment, the organist's rambling notes collected themselves into the opening chord of their first hymn, the priest walked down the aisle, the few worshippers stood and James removed his hand to reach for their hymn book. Belinda stood up, clutching at the back of the pew in front to steady herself; her legs were trembling.

Ruth awoke and knew immediately that today was going to be one of her bad days. A familiar pain was making itself felt in her lower gut; like a rough river pebble scraping and forcing its way along her tender fleshy by-ways, it would grow, and be joined by a companion, and together they would grind and grate the inner surface of her digestive tract until it swelled and went into spasm. Of course there were no pebbles, but the sensation so exactly fitted that description, and was so localised, that it was a miracle to her that an examination of her abdomen did not reveal a raw rose of bruise and the physical manifestation of stones travelling under the skin. She knew that at the height of the attack she would crave a knife to stab and slash at the place, to release the pressure and the virtual foreign body in a gush of watery, blood-streaked fluid.

Ruth cast a doleful glance across at her dressing table, where what James called her 'medicaments', an array of potions and pills both preventative and palliative offered her a number of possibilities. No doubt a richer than usual diet, more alcohol than she was used to, especially red wine and port and the disruption of her usual constitutional routine were all factors in this morning's attack. But above all the stresses and outrages of the previous day had acted as a trigger on her vulnerable and sensitive physiology. In this, her oasis in the maelstrom of the autumn term, she had needed rest and calm, and a chance to repress that slough of despair and depression which threatened to engulf her. She sighed, and shifted her position in the bed, knowing as she did so that relief could not be gained that way.

James entered the room. He was fully dressed, flushed with fresh air and his thick, wavy hair shone with wetness, although Ruth had no recollection of him rising from the bed adjacent to hers. He carried a steaming mug, the transparent delicacy of the china looking vulnerable in his large hand.

'Peppermint tea,' he announced, placing the cup on the small table which separated the beds.

313

'How did you know?' Ruth struggled up into a sitting position.

'Ah.' James smiled a knowing smile, not smug, but kind and perceptive. He crossed to the dressing table and surveyed her medication.

'Now then.' He wriggled his fingers over the array like a pianist about to strike the opening chord of a concerto. 'Which of the *pilules* shall we indulge in today? Two of these, to begin with, I think, and one of those, to get things moving, yes?' He began to pluck pills from their packets. 'I'll go and run you a warm bath while you drink your tea. Then lots and *lots* of fluids for you today, not much food, and, later, a nice walk. Then, this afternoon, two more of these and sleep. Yes?'

Ruth nodded and swallowed the two round white tablets he had put into her upturned palm. The other thing, the thing to get things moving, she would take with her into the bathroom. During the day James would bring her drinks, a variety, some warm and some cool, fruit juice, herbal teas, water, nothing caffeinated, and the occasional snack; an apple carefully cored and sliced and arranged on a plate, brown bread lightly buttered and cut into small squares, pro-biotic yoghurt sweetened with honey. His care would be casual, he wouldn't fuss – that would irritate her – but constant. He would monitor her progress and increase the pain relief if necessary. In extremity, he would give her the small, mind-altering pain killers, and put her to bed, and sit by her side, his hand cool on her feverish palm, nodding sagely as she raved and muttered the hours away. Afterwards, she would be parched with thirst, and disorientated. He would fetch iced water, and soothe her with reassuring words. At times like these she knew that she did not deserve him, and regretted the critical attitude and carping derision with which she tended to treat almost everything about his person, character and calling.

'Ellie's birthday brunch is imminent downstairs. I've made your excuses,' James said, collecting her towel and toiletry bag to take through to the bathroom for her.

'Oh, yes. There's a parcel, in the case.'

'Yes, yes. Already delivered. Don't worry. I know the routine.'

Roger had taken up a proprietorial position in front of the Aga, causing Belinda considerable inconvenience as she tried to serve brunch. Earlier, he had cowed Tiny with an alarming display of yellow teeth and black gums, and made Todd cry by rebuffing a friendly advance with snarls and curled-back lips.

'Oh dear, oh dear, what a silly you are,' Muriel had admonished.

'Are you sure that dog's safe?' Simon had asked, cradling Todd on his knee, 'there's the baby to consider, you know.'

'Safe as houses. But he isn't used to children. It would be better if we all just ignored him.' Muriel fussed with Roger's ears from her position in the armchair besides the Aga.

Todd sniffled and rubbed his head into his father's shoulder. This was the second time today that he'd been made to cry. The disrupted routine, yesterday's big walk and two late nights were beginning to take their toll on the six year old.

'Are you sure I can't help, Belinda?' Muriel offered. 'Isn't there anything at all I can do?'

'Well,' Belinda thought for a moment, 'if you're sure you don't mind, I think Ruth started off some laundry yesterday. June's things need washing from last night and I expect you'll be able to collect enough from other people to make up a load.'

'Say no more,' Muriel gushed. 'Just leave it to me.'

Ellie sat in state at the head of the table, unwrapping parcels, most of which were from her parents, but by the expressions of interest and gradual disapproval on Elliot's face, it was plain that he had played no part in their purchase or presentation. Electrical items, clothes, accessories, sensible toiletries (from Ruth), cheques, money and cards were strewn across the table. Ben and Rachel were agog at the sheer number and expense of the gifts, Tansy gushed with good natured enthusiasm ('An MP3 player! You lucky thing! Toni and Guy straighteners? Wow! Oh, talcum powder – always so useful!')

'Thank you, Uncle James,' Ellie said, sweetly.

'*Thank you, Uncle James.*' Her brother, forced to get up and take part in the birthday ritual, glowered from his place at the table.

Mitch, from his position leaning against the dresser, out of the family circle, gave a sharp cough.

'Fix your face, lad, for God's sake,' Elliot hissed at Rob. He needed to take his disapproval out on somebody and his son's sullenness gave him just the excuse he needed. But Rob stood up and said into his father's ear, 'for fuck's sake, Dad, let me go home. This is just *crap.*' Elliot reddened, and gathered himself for an onslaught, but Rob had already crossed the room and was pouring juice from the fridge with moody concentration. Toby, from the table, observed his cousin with wide-eyed shock and ill-concealed admiration.

Belinda served up bacon and tomatoes, fried bread and mushrooms, sausages and eggs. Apart from Ruth she had the entire family to cater for – it was quite a task. She looked flushed and bright-eyed. Mary observed her with surprise, having expected gloomy repercussions from the previous evening. But the whole family seemed to have come to terms and moved on and as Mary looked around she felt hopeful that things might at last settle down. Sandra and Kevin had departed, Mr Burgess was gone. Granny was behaving herself reasonably well under the careful supervision of Muriel, who was herself beaming and agreeable, and made it hard for Mary to square her suspicions into any kind of concrete form. In honour of the birthday even young Rob was up and dressed. The girls were in high spirits, laughing and joking with Heather and Starlight. Rachel looked lovely in her new jeans, white trainers and a good quality t shirt, although she had what Mary called, knowingly, 'that white look.' Starlight, in her high chair, waved a spoon and sang happily at the top of her voice. There was a pleasant hubbub of conversation and laughter, the sizzle and spit of eggs on a skillet and the smell of bacon and coffee pervaded the air. Only Elliot cast a morose shadow as he sat at one end of the table and occupied himself with a newspaper.

Then Les and June entered the kitchen. The happy noisiness petrified like an insect in amber. It was as though a film had been stopped in the middle of a scene: Belinda stood at the Aga, the kettle poised over the coffee pot, Miriam's fork hovered in the air in front of her mouth, Rob held his juice glass to his lips but did not drink. Following June's display the previous night, no-one knew what kind of denouement might ensue. The possibility of strident and righteous accusation, bitter remonstration and emotional out-pourings was very real. On the other hand, the McKay family way dictated restraint and dignity regardless of the provocation even when such restraint might mean an unhealthy curbing of feelings which would have been better expressed. In addition to this, everyone, now, was aware of the schism which existed between June and Muriel, and also of its cause. The presence of June and Muriel in the same room as each other, not to mention Les, the unlikely object of their rivalry, was a potentially explosive recipe. Family skeletons both ancient and modern rattled themselves in their respective cupboards as Les and June stood on the threshold of the kitchen. Les took June's arm in his, and taking a visibly deep breath he guided her firmly to a seat next to Granny McKay. June was coiffed and made up even more copiously than usual, the layers of make-up forming a mask of fixed hauteur which belied the hunted expression in her eyes. Les placed himself next to her. He had showered and shaved and changed his clothes, and girded himself mentally for the ordeals of the day, but his intention to keep a firm hold of the situation had been shaken just by running the gauntlet of the McKay breakfast table, and while he placed a controlling hand on June's rigid back, his eyes searched for an ally who would break this spell.

To everyone's surprise, it was Muriel who came to his rescue.

'Good morning, June,' she said, brightly. 'I hope you're feeling better. I'm sorry to say poor Ruth isn't at all well.' Her comment gave everyone an opening. People who hadn't noticed Ruth's absence turned to James with concern, sympathy was expressed, Ben began to explain to a wide-eyed Todd about Ruth's sundry health issues, with a small degree of accuracy seasoned with large helpings of rather grisly imagined symptoms. Belinda continued to serve breakfast. Elliot remained hidden behind his newspaper.

Rachel said little. Her stomach was still feeling distinctly odd even though she had eaten some breakfast, and she wondered if she ought to mention it to her father. Across the table from her Rob and Bob were discussing music. She admired Rob's hair which was clean and shiny, and free of its bristling spikes, and his face, which had lost its accustomed moody glower. Seeing him like this, Rachel questioned Ellie's insistence on his malevolence. She didn't believe that Rob would do anything to hurt his sister, and the notion occurred to her that she might in some way bring them together, if only she might be brave or clever enough. The idea that she might effect a reconciliation, and be forever regarded by both of them as some kind of confidante and saviour was appealing, and romantic, and Rachel pursued it down hallways of fantasy which led her to an altar and a ceremony which would make her a real McKay, while her tea went cold in the cup in front of her.

The rain cleared after brunch and as though by common accord most of the adults prepared to go out for a walk. Mary was persuaded to join them when Les and June insisted that they would take care of Robert; she especially wished to see the sea. The men pretended to have forgotten the way so Ben and Todd were press-ganged to join them as guides, and they scurried around to get their outdoor clothes with whoops of excitement.

Toby hung back. He would've liked to be allowed to play on the computer with Rob, but he had disappeared into the study mumbling about coursework and closed the door with a sullen flourish. When Tansy and Rachel offered to bake Ellie a new birthday cake, even Belinda agreed that there was no reason, in that case, for her to stay behind. Granny and Starlight were put to their respective beds with Muriel and Mitch in watchful attendance. Ruth had made a pale appearance for half an hour before retiring to the library where James had lit a cheerful fire. Elliot, with bad grace, conceded that *in that case*, he would work on his figures in the bedroom, since the study, the library *and* the kitchen would *all* be occupied by others. The family made a good natured attempt to persuade him to join them, but he demurred, pleading important work which had to be emailed off without fail in the morning.

'I don't know why we bother,' Simon complained to Miriam in an undertone as he helped her into her coat. 'It isn't as though any of us even like the man. It beggars belief that we're spending a whole week with him. If I met him socially I wouldn't give him five minutes' attention, would you?'

With all the adults out of the way, incapacitated or otherwise occupied, the girls took gleeful possession of the kitchen. Ellie brought down her CD player and soon music was blaring into the kitchen and filtering up the passageway. They opened cupboards and got out bowls and utensils and ingredients, and set about deciding what kind of cake they should bake. It turned out that Rachel had never baked a cake without supervision before, but Tansy knew what to do and soon had her sifting flour and weighing out margarine. The busyness took Rachel's mind for a while off the heaviness in her abdomen, a dull ache between her legs and a vague, distracting buzzing noise in her head. Under ordinary circumstances illness would have sent her to a cosy corner with a book, but she didn't want to admit that she was ill, or pass up this opportunity with the other girls. She considered putting Aunty Belinda's flowery and capacious apron on, to make sure that she didn't get her new clothes dirty, but decided in the end just to be very, very careful.

Ellie perched on the kitchen table and began to paint her nails with the varnish which had been in one of her parcels.

'You have nice nails,' said Rachel, looking ruefully at her own, which were badly bitten. 'You keep them very long.'

'Yes. It isn't allowed, really, at school, to have them painted, and I have to invent all sorts of aches and pains to get out of netball but, you know....'

'You'd be made to take the varnish off, at our school,' put in Tansy. 'Matron keeps a bottle of remover in the sick room. Rachel, would you grease these tins? Rub those butter papers round them. That's a nice colour, though, what is it?'

Ellie read the label. 'Plum Beautiful. Caro bought it for me. She sent the parcel with Mum. It has an eye shadow and lipstick to match.'

'That's nice. So she must be your friend, then, after all,' Rachel soothed, smearing butter around two cake tins, thinking how nice it must be to have a friend who bought you birthday gifts.

'Not if I can't trust her. That's what friendship is, after all, isn't it?' Ellie replied, a little snappily.

'Oh, yes, I suppose...' Rachel trailed off. She had recently made a friend at school, a girl who had just moved to the area and joined her class. Rachel had been picked to look after her and had enjoyed

321

showing her where the science labs were and the short cut to the dining room. It had been fun walking round the quad together at break time and having a companion at lunch, but there hadn't been the kind of private sharing between them which would result in secrets or the need for trusting. And anyway the girl had just been picked for the school hockey team and moved into the top set for math's and English, and Rachel knew that their friendship would inevitably cool as a result of these obstacles. After the holidays she would be back to solitary sandwiches in the dining room and lonely periods in the library.

'There are two twins at my school, boarders,' Tansy was saying, above the whiz of the electric mixer. 'Their parents are abroad. They work for the government or something. Anyway, these twins, they don't have any friends but each other. One of them – she's called Holly - told me it's because they move around so much, and go to so many different schools, no friends they ever made really lasted. In the end they only have each other, she says. She says your family has to love you no matter what, whereas friends only choose to and they can change their minds. Do you think that's true?'

'I don't know.' Ellie considered her nails. 'I don't love Rob no matter what.'

'I know you say so, but if he was to run in here now on fire, you'd try and put him out, wouldn't you?'

'Well yes. But I'd do that for anyone, almost. Can it be a chocolate cake?'

'If you like. Or there's strawberry jam and some cream we can whip up.'

'Yes, that sounds nice. Can I scrape out the bowl?'

'In a minute.'

'We're family, aren't we?' ventured Rachel, tentatively, folding the butter papers smaller and smaller. 'Does that mean that we have to love each other no matter what?' The potential of the idea was almost too much to grasp, particularly with the naggingly insistent pain down below and this hissing noise in her head. That someone *had* to love you, by compunction, didn't sound very appealing. Yet there was a certain comfortable security in the notion that she could be loved in spite of her failings. She knew with an absolute certainty that her father loved her completely, and Ben, too, and even Ruth loved her in practical ways which, though they lacked tenderness, were reliable. But on the other hand the idea that someone would choose to love her was more thrilling, and in her ambivalent position in this family, with these girls, it seemed to her like an important thing, at last, to establish. 'Or.....or....are we friends because we really like each other?' At last she lifted her eyes and looked from one to the other of her cousins. She had made a colossal assumption there and it left her on thin ice. 'I just ask because, well, you know, I'm not *really* family, am I?'

'Oh!' Tansy exclaimed, giving Rachel a floury hug. 'Of course you are!'

'You don't have McKay genes,' Ellie conceded, applying herself to the cake bowl, 'but I wouldn't worry about that. You might be the lucky one. Look at Granny McKay. Look at that Sandra girl last night and Aunty June. They all have McKay genes. Oh God! It doesn't bode very well, does it? There's no hope for any of us! It's a wonder those policemen didn't lock us all up!'

Tansy began to smooth the cake mixture into the tins. Rachel dusted flour off the shoulder of her t shirt.

'That would have been funny, wouldn't it, if they had?'

'It depends,' mused Ellie. 'What would have been funnier is the collection of people left behind. What on earth would they have done with themselves, without any McKay glue to bond them together?'

323

'I could have looked after Starlight,' said Rachel. 'And I would have had my Dad here, after all.'

'Bob and Mitch would have been alright, but I think Uncle Elliot and Miriam might have killed each other before the day was over!' laughed Tansy. 'Uncle Les could have taken Grandma home.' She placed the cakes in the oven of the Aga and shut the door carefully.

'Anyway,' Ellie concluded. 'I don't know about us being friends, yet, really. We're only just getting to know each other and I'm not sure I can trust either of you two, yet.'

'Perhaps you only know if someone's a friend if you can put it to the test,' suggested Tansy, running hot water into the sink. 'Maybe that's what the family thing is all about; years and years of putting it to the test. Leave the butter out of the fridge, Rachel, we'll need it for the butter icing.'

'We could each tell a secret and then see if we keep them. Then we'd really know, wouldn't we?' said Ellie, brightly, jumping down from the table and carrying the bowl over to the sink.

'Well.....,' said Rachel. She liked the idea of being trusted with a secret. It would give her an opportunity, she thought, in her anomalous position, or proving herself both as friend and as family. On the other hand, her own only recently discovered secret, or secret feeling at least, about her cousin Rob, could never *never* be told, and what good was any kind of friendship, she wondered, if it didn't work both ways?

In the flagged passageway, en route to the laundry room with Starlight's soiled linen, Mitch was arrested by the conversation he could overhear from the kitchen. Their tone, at first, had caught his attention; their light, bright flutings, and the hubbub of their cheerful activity; it seemed as though the absence of the adults had in some way released them. It was true that the day's good humour had been characterised by a certain heavy, determined, self-conscious quality; the family had almost visibly *girded* itself, in the face of June's continued residency. Their quiet but concerted effort to hoist her on the petard of her own manoeuvrings had allowed her neither the dignity of retreat nor the solace of forgiveness. It had been almost noble, he thought, the way the family had handled it. But the effort of it had lent a certain shrill note which the girls, now, as they chattered and laughed, had expiated.

He liked the fact that they associated him with Bob; their fates, in the event of mass McKay internment, were indelibly linked. He'd like to think so, too, although his experience of such things argued against it. There was a limit to how far these associations, without what the girls called the 'glue' of family, could stretch. Like Rachel's, his position with Bob and Heather was irregular.

But the most interesting aspect of the conversation he had overheard concerned Ellie's continued distrust of her brother; it coloured her view of the whole family gene-pool. It was a shame, Mitch thought, as he traversed the hall. Clearly she did not assume that their unconditional support just *because* they were family could be relied upon; friendship, she implied, even amongst cousins, and, he inferred, *especially* concerning brothers, was something that had to be put to the test.

The study door was closed but from within the soundscape of continued carnage raged, and Mitch glowered. His plan, hatched in the small hours, still hadn't been put fully in train. But it *could* be. It would be dicey, to proactively involve himself, contrary to his habitually

325

reactive, peripheral policy, not just because of the possible ramifications if discovered but because it shortened that safe-guarding space he maintained around himself. It would make it harder – even harder than it already was – to be detached. But, he reasoned, perhaps the very existence of that slight – and decreasing – objectivity made him the only one who could take it.

The walkers trod through the silent wood. Its arching branches seemed to cocoon them from the elements outside its parameters. Only the very uppermost branches shivered with the brisk breeze which drove white clouds like yachts across the blue-washed sky. A thick carpet of pine needles muffled their footfalls as they marched in single-file along the narrow, winding path. On either side of them the trees crowded into the distance, impenetrable and dark.

'Ben said it was like being in Narnia,' James said, over his shoulder. He spoke quietly. The wood, somehow, was cloistral, demanding reverence. 'He said we ought to look out for the lamp post and Mr Tumnus.'

Belinda laughed. 'What a fanciful child he is!'

'He lives in his imagination,' Heather said, from behind her. 'There's much to be said for it. One's possibilities are enlarged.'

'Do you think so?' Belinda asked. 'I'd have thought that in the end it will only lead to disappointment. Searching for things which aren't there.'

'They *are* there if he believes so,' Heather replied, 'but sometimes it's only the search that matters. The finding can be anti-climactic.'

James chuckled. 'Well he certainly enjoyed the search yesterday, for Wriggly, and the family tree.'

'The family tree?'

'Oh yes! Well, look around you. It must be here somewhere, mustn't it?'

Belinda surveyed the trees, hundreds, perhaps thousands of them in this wood. Trees stood cheek-by-jowl; thin, reedy pines stretching up to the sun, dark-leaved hollies, rowan, dripping with blood-red berries, alder (or elder, she always got them mixed up). Unlike the woods on either side of the driveway, these seemed

327

unmanaged. There was no evidence of coppicing or thinning, no denuded branches, no blunt, sawn-off trunks, no sharpened, hacked limbs. These trees had been allowed to self-seed, they pushed and jostled amongst one another, leaning trunks rested heavily on the shoulders of their neighbours, dead boughs decomposed and provided sustenance for their fledgling off-spring. Ivy and bramble scrambled unchecked amongst them. What, she wondered, would it look like, the McKay family tree. Smooth, straight lines, an unblemished bark, a solid, indigenous, ancient English species? The source of wholesome fruits, giving shelter, providing the kind of timber which built houses and strengthened ships? Or twisted and gnarled, its bark pitted and rough, blighted, perhaps, by some disease, increasingly unable to cope in the modern climate, squeezed out by more virulent, insistent breeds? She pictured her family on the tree; living amongst its branches, sustained and supported by it, or, conversely, hanging from it, caught up on its bony branches, impaled and bleeding on its thorns. An echo from the morning's service came back to her. 'They nailed Christ to a tree,' she said, aloud.

'Yes,' James said.

They had come to the end of the path. The wood ended on a coarse-grassed plateau which sloped into sand and then into the pebbles of the beach. Heather gasped as she caught sight of the sparkling waves, and pushed past Belinda to hurry to the shore. Bob was already there, skimming flat stones across the water. Simon picked Miriam up and threatened to throw her into the shallows. Her screams were taken up by the seagulls which wheeled and dived on the wind above their heads. The boys migrated to the other end of the beach and began foraging in rock pools revealed by the retreating tide. Mary found a flat-topped boulder and rested, her face turned up to the watery sun.

'Yes,' James said again, turning to Belinda. It was no surprise to him that, with the family tree as their launching point, her thoughts had come to rest on the ultimate image of punitive self-sacrifice.

The library fire was burning low and would soon require more fuel. Ruth gazed into the embers gloomily. The carafe of cranberry juice which James had left with her was also empty. She felt neglected and lonely. The pain in her stomach had subsided somewhat; it would appear that she was to be spared one of her more excruciating attacks. She had eaten some fruit and had two more cups of peppermint tea, and strolled with James up and down the terrace for a little while. Then she had taken two more tablets before James had settled her in this pleasantly sequestered room with a hot water bottle for her tummy. He had selected three or four books from the shelves for her to browse through and pointed out to her also the old-fashioned radiogram in the corner of the room in case she wished to listen to a play or some music. Then he had departed for a walk, leaving her alone and miserable. No one had come near her for the past hour although she knew from the noises around the house that there were people in the rooms enjoying themselves. She had heard the drawing room door open and June's strident voice shouting, 'No, Robert, for God's sake, you can only have one for his knob if it's a jack. How many times do I have to tell you?' before the door had been closed once more. In the far distance, she could hear the violent explosions of Rob's war game, and somebody somewhere was listening to some music. She wondered about going out in search of company but the tablets made her feel light-headed and she did feel almost comfortable; it would be silly to risk going anywhere. Perhaps she slept for a few minutes. Then Mitch and Starlight hurtled past the library door, Starlight shouting nonsense at the top of her voice and Mitch, presumably in pursuit, hardly more comprehensible. Presently she heard Muriel and Granny McKay pass down the corridor and enter the drawing room.

'Oh here they are, Mother!' Muriel said, brightly. 'Playing cards. I'm sure they'll deal you in. You like a game of cards, don't you, Mother?'

'Only if they're playing for money,' Granny responded, sharply. 'See if there are any shillings in the teapot.'

'I've been abandoned with the weaklings and the idiots,' Ruth moaned to herself, pushing away her hot water bottle. It had gone cold. 'I might just as well not have come on this wretched holiday. No one cares whether I'm here or not. I could die in here of starvation or cold and no one would give a damn. James is cruel and selfish to have left me here alone. He should have stayed. He could have read to me. Even the children don't miss me. April wouldn't have left me alone. I miss her. Oh! I miss her so!' A tear slid down Ruth's face, then another, and she abandoned herself to a paroxysm of self-pity and grief.

The self-obsessed, depressive meanderings of *Suicide Pact* comforted Rob; their black mood suited his exactly, since he had logged on to the internet and downloaded his messages. Caro, the bitch, had emailed him with a tirade of abuse, asking him who the hell he thought he was anyway and telling him to fuck off, and Rob couldn't really blame her when he read the email he was supposed to have sent to her. The fact was that someone had hacked into his system and was sending stuff in his name, and had also, according to his website browsing history, visited a number of really filthy sites. Basically, he was being set up, and when he found out who was doing it he'd kill them. He could only assume that whoever it was knew about his music scam and it was only a matter of time before he'd be for the high jump, something he really now wanted to avoid as he was just beginning to get things going with Bob. Only that lunchtime they'd been discussing music and opportunities in the music business, and Bob had responded quite favourably to the idea that Rob might come down to London in the Easter holidays and shadow him for a few days at *Ad hoc*.

Things had just been beginning to look as though they might be bearable and now this. *Suicide Pact* sank into an oblivion of despair and *Five Mile Pile Up* crashed with metallic screeching onto the speakers. Rob sat and chewed his fingernails, and wished he had a joint, or dared to steal his mother's car and just drive away, and burned with anger as he turned over in his mind who could be responsible. It boiled down really to just one person; Ellie. She was the only one who might dare to do it and have the know-how to carry it off. She had the incentive, too. She would have wanted to nose around to see what Caro was saying and might well have decided to get him into trouble. With all the down-loaded music and the CD covers on his computer there was enough trouble to bury him a dozen times over. Well, if it was trouble she wanted she had come to the right place. Angrily, he pushed his chair back and stalked out of the study, leaving *Five Mile Pile Up* wreaking audio-carnage in the empty room.

Tansy lifted the cakes out of the Aga; they were golden and beautifully risen. She put them to cool on a wire rack on the kitchen table. But the heat from the oven had made Rachel feel funny; the hiss and crackle in her ears had taken on a visible form; she felt as though she was looking at an artist's interpretation of pins and needles tattooed onto her eyeballs. She sat down heavily in the comfortable chair by the Aga.

'You don't look very well, Rachel,' Tansy observed. 'Are you feeling alright? You've gone all white.'

'Are you due on?' Ellie asked, looking up from the table where she was adding a second coat to her nails.

Ellie's question made everything crystallise in Rachel's head. 'Oh no,' she thought to herself miserably, 'not here, not now.'

Just then Rob strode into the room. His face was as dark as thunder. His hair was gelled into indignant bristles.

'I suppose you think that's clever?' he snarled at Ellie, grabbing her arm and jerking her to her feet.

'Ow! Stop it! What?' Ellie protested. 'Be careful, you idiot. You'll make me spill the varnish!'

'You're too late!' Rob crowed. 'She's already told me your filthy little secret, so your pathetic attempts to screw things up haven't achieved anything!'

'Caro's told you?' Ellie herself looked as white as a sheet now.

'Yep. Sang like a bird.'

'Come on now, you two,' said Tansy, like a Mummy.

'But Rob you don't understand,' Ellie began, her voice trembling. 'What Caro thinks she knows isn't....'

'Don't make me laugh!' Rob interrupted, smiling cruelly. 'Now whatever you had planned, you'd better forget it, because I can do you far more harm that you can do me!'

333

'I haven't got anything planned!' Ellie shrieked, struggling to wrest her arm from Rob's grip. 'Stop it, will you, you're hurting me!' Rob grabbed her other arm and began to shake Ellie like a doll.

'You've been nosing in my computer and sending emails and stuff. Trying to get me into trouble, you little bitch, you'll be sorry...'

'No, I haven't!' Ellie managed to gasp out.

Rachel jumped to her feet, seeing everything in black and white, and barely able to hear what was going on for the incessant crackling noise in her head. She saw Tansy cross the kitchen and take Rob's arm. He flailed out at her and knocked her into the table. The cake, on its cooling rack, span off and bounced on the floor. The three of them were shouting but Rachel couldn't hear anything, their mouths were moving in ugly shapes, then vision too began to sink and blur into a crowding blackness; all her insides were draining away from her; she knew she would fall, and nothing could stop it. She keeled forwards and the rush of white noise in her head exploded when her head hit the corner of the table.

Rob and Ellie were arrested mid-sentence. Rob went waxen. He looked down at Rachel. 'I never touched her! I never touched her!' he kept repeating. 'This is nothing to do with me.'

There was blood everywhere, pouring out of the cut on Rachel's cheek bone, smeared on the floor, spattered on the remains of the cake, and seeping, too, into the material of her jeans from between her legs.

'Oh God! Oh God! What should we do? What should we do?' gasped Ellie, backing away from the table. Rob moved with her, his grip on her arm which only seconds before had been possessive, punishing, now seeking and providing support. They cowered together, all enmity, for the moment, forgotten.

'I think she's fainted,' said Tansy. 'Rob, go and get Ruth. She's in the library.' Roused, Rob sped off up the corridor. Tansy pressed a clean cloth to the cut on Rachel's face. Ellie stood back and wrung her hands. 'She's bleeding, she's bleeding,' she kept repeating.

'Yes, yes,' Tansy said, quietly.

Ruth, befuddled by pain killers, coped with a detached efficiency with the situation which presented itself to her in the kitchen. She sent Tansy to telephone Dr Gardner who had kindly left them his number in case of emergency, and Ellie to find an old towel or sheet 'or anything to cover her up.' She didn't know whether to put Rachel into the recovery position, which would be appropriate for someone who was unconscious, or to lift her feet above her head, which would be right for a faint. While she dithered, Rachel moaned and lifted her head up. Then she began to cry.

'Don't be such a baby,' Ruth admonished, gently, 'you're perfectly alright.'

Ellie came back into the room with Mitch and Elliot. Rob shot a look at her, still ashen-faced and shaking. They lifted Rachel back into the chair, which had been spread with towels. When Rachel saw the state of her clothes, she began to cry even louder.

'Poor thing, poor thing,' soothed Tansy. 'The doctor's coming.'

'I want my.......Dad,' Rachel managed to sob out, hiding her head in her hands. One side of her face was wet and slimy-warm. When she looked at her hand it was slick and red with blood. 'Oh God! Oh God!' she choked out. All these people staring at her, and all the blood, especially the blood on her trousers, was just too much. They would all know, they would all be laughing. She didn't dare lift her eyes.

'Who typically, isn't here, just when we need him,' Ruth commented. 'Keep your head up, Rachel! Don't touch that cut. You might get germs in it.'

Mitch ran hot water into a bucket. June arrived, having abandoned her mother and brother in order to enjoy what was plainly a crisis, and one which, for once, didn't have her at its centre. Muriel followed closely behind in case she could help. Roger, in her wake, set to work on the cake.

'We ought to bathe that cut. Is there any iodine?' Muriel said.

'Dear me! No one's used iodine in years!' June exclaimed, derisively.

'We'll just wait for the doctor,' said Ruth, quietly.

'Perhaps someone would like to explain how this happened,' Elliot blustered.

There was a beat. Then Rachel said, 'I just fainted, that's all. I've been feeling funny all day.' With an extreme effort, she raised her eyes to Ellie, and then, with more difficulty, to Rob. One of her eyes was swollen, her hair on that side was matted with blood, which still oozed from the cut on her cheek and was soaking the cloth which Ruth held against her face. She had proved, she hoped, to each of them, that she could keep a secret, even though she had only the vaguest idea about the cause of their vitriolic exchange.

'I heard a lot of shouting,' Elliot said, narrowing his eyes.

'We all panicked when she fell over,' Tansy said, quietly.

Suddenly the room was crowded with people. James, full of alarm and concern. Toby, ravenous for cake, turned grey at the sight of the blood, Todd, looking confused, was flapping a sheet of paper he had found in the downstairs toilet at his father. Belinda took in the situation at a glance and got busy with the kettle. Ben, silent and queasy, squeezed Rachel's arm, the only bloodless bit of her he could gain access to in the flurry of attention and activity which surrounded her, before slipping off to the piano. At last, abnegated of responsibility, Ruth sank down on the floor next to Rachel's chair. 'Look what happens,' she said cuttingly to James, 'when you leave me on my own. You know I'm not well enough to cope with this kind of thing. How could you? How *could* you?'

'I know. I'm sorry,' said James.

Dr Gardner, bearing his medical bag, soon established order. He had James help Rachel up to her room, where he bathed and dressed her wound with sterastrips.

'Will she have a scar?' asked James. The doctor smiled and shook his head. 'She will be a flawless beauty,' he said, 'and this bleeding down here,' he went on, addressing Rachel kindly, 'normal. Quite normal. Your mother, or one of your aunts, will help you.' He left her some strong pain-killers to be taken with food before a very early night.

Ruth was taken back to her own bed by Heather, and also given two strong pain-killers; judged too unwell to assist her step-daughter in any practical way. Mary was deputed to help Rachel remove her soiled clothes, and run her a warm bath in the pink bathroom. Everyone else was sent to the sitting room where Belinda served tea while Mitch mopped the kitchen floor. Rachel sat in the bath, unresisting her grandma's brisk attentions with soap and flannel, feeling like a baby even though she was now a woman, and seeming not to hear her assurances that she was not to worry, that a little bit of blood did go a very long way, and that the nice new clothes would wash perfectly well. Then, dressed in her pyjamas and 'sorted out' down below, she was left alone while Mary bustled off to fetch a cup of tea and a sandwich.

Alone at long last, Rachel dared to breathe, to think. She slipped out of bed, the wadding between her legs feeling foreign, and waddled to the window. Night was falling. Where had the day gone to? The lawn was grey, the trees beyond dense and black. She still had not seen the sea, been in the woods, explored the garden; the adventures inside the house had been taxing enough. The constant talk, activity, posturing and keeping pace, trying to fit in; she had felt like a fish on a quay most of the time; flapping in an ugly panic, out of her depths. The peace, now, was delicious, like a warm woollen blanket. She prodded her cheek carefully; it felt monstrous and distorted; she caressed it, tenderly. In the distance, she could hear the noises of the house; the boys in their room next door, far-off echoes of piano music, the gurgle and splash of early baths being run, Starlight whooping and hollering in some private, exciting game. For someone who was so used to being an observer, passive, preternaturally inclined to shrink away from the lime-light, the last few days and especially the last few hours had been emotionally exhausting. She hated the attention, the fuss, even the fuss of kindness and of friendship, was somehow hard to bear, had brought expectations and pressures which she felt ill-equipped to meet.

Her reverie was interrupted by Tansy and Ellie, who brought the sandwich and the tea. 'We wanted to see how you were,' they whispered, as though there was a baby asleep in the room.

'My face feels sore, and I feel stupid,' Rachel made a moue. She climbed back into bed.

'You mustn't feel stupid,' Tansy soothed, perching on the edge of the bed. 'It happens to everyone. It happened to me in geography.'

'But everyone saw, and everyone knew,' Rachel moaned, miserably.

'I don't think the boys have cottoned on,' Ellie reasoned. They just think you banged your head.'

'Rob knows,' Rachel replied, then wished she hadn't.

'So what?' Ellie retorted, 'he knows about the birds and the bees, you know.' Then, gloomily, she added, 'he knows everything, now.'

Rachel sipped her tea. Someone had forgotten to put sugar in it.

'We covered for you and Rob, downstairs, just now,' Tansy remarked, to Ellie. 'Uncle Elliot knew something had been going on.'

'Yes.' Ellie regarded her nails. She had cleaned off all the polish; the second coat had been smudged in the fracas.

'What a waste,' Rachel thought.

'He has a habit of getting to the bottom of things,' Ellie sighed, 'it doesn't really matter, now. My life will be a nightmare from now on. Rob won't let this drop. He'll hold it over me until I die.'

Tansy got up and closed the curtains, then she switched on the bedside light.

'Eat your sandwich, Rachel. Grandma said you must before you can take those tablets.'

'Aren't they huge?' Ellie said. I can't take tablets. I have to have them mashed up on a spoon with jam.'

'What a baby,' Rachel thought. '*What* will he hold over you?' she asked, suddenly, surprising even herself that the question had been spoken aloud.

'Ah.' Ellie hesitated. 'Well, it's bad whichever way you look at it. I told Caro that I'd been having a fling with a student teacher. Mr Murray – Philip – he's just gorgeous, only 22.'

Tansy gasped. 'You've been having an affair? With a teacher?'

'Teachers are only human,' Ellie raised a cynical eyebrow, 'just flesh and blood. They're not gods.'

Rachel thought about Ruth. 'That's true,' she said, 'but it isn't allowed'

'I know that!' Ellie retorted. 'But you're not listening. I only *told* Caro that I was having an affair. I haven't been, really.'

Tansy and Rachel took this in.

'Why did you tell her, if it wasn't true?'

Ellie shrugged. 'It so easily could have been true. He flirted with me, and all the girls were jealous. He helped me with a project, and we

339

started emailing each other over that. Then there were texts. It was all very inappropriate, of course. But just words, just looks. Nothing actually happened. I never even kissed him. But that seemed a bit tame, so I suggested......I implied......that there was more.'

'Well, surely, then...' Tansy began, 'I mean, if nothing really happened, that's all you have to say, isn't it?'

Rachel's head was beginning to throb. She took a tentative mouthful of the sandwich, which looked exactly like the ones Heather made for Starlight; the crusts had been cut off and the ham had been cut up small. Even so, her cheek hurt when she chewed.

'There are two things wrong with that suggestion,' Ellie was saying, and her voice took on, Rachel thought, a rather whining and self-pitying tone, 'firstly, I'd have to admit that I lied to Caro. Remember what we were saying before? If you can't trust your friend, what kind of friend is she? What kind of friend would that make me? See?'

'But you *did* lie,' Tansy said, quietly.

'Yes. But don't you see? Even if it had been true, the first thing anyone would do when confronted with it, would be to deny it, wouldn't they? Naturally? So when I deny it, no one will believe me. I'm stuck. I'm absolutely stuck.'

There was the sound of furious footsteps on the stairs. Elliot appeared at the bedroom door.

'Ellie!' he shouted. 'Get yourself downstairs right now. Your mother and I wish to speak to you immediately in the library.'

The fire in the library had almost gone out; only a couple of embers still glowed dully in the grate. The curtains remained open and the black night outside reflected the five people in the room like a silvered mirror. The tension in the room was quite palpable, malodorous and ugly. Behind the desk, Elliot had taken up a proprietorial stance, feet apart, hands clasped behind his back. His face was flushed; he had drunk, rather quickly, a very large scotch. Belinda's, on the other hand, was blanched. She perched in the leather chair which Ruth had occupied for the afternoon, her hands in her lap, fluttering and wringing, toying restlessly with her ring. During her walk, tendrils of hair had worked themselves loose from her chignon and she had not had time to recapture them. Rob leant belligerently against the bookshelves, his hands in his pockets, chewing the inside of his cheek. Ellie had taken up a position behind the chair, uncomfortably close to her father, but as far away as possible from Rob. The fifth person in the room was Simon. His face was positively puce, suffused with anger and indignation; his habitual geniality had completely departed.

'Ellie,' Elliot said, in a voice which was taut. 'Little Todd has found something….quite disgusting, in the downstairs cloakroom. Let me ask you to answer this question very carefully. Do you know anything about it?'

'No,' said Ellie, genuinely surprised, and momentarily relieved – this was not the line of questioning she had been expecting. 'What do you mean? What has he found?'

'Let me ask you again,' Elliot repeated. 'Did you put something in the cloakroom?'

'I put my ski-jacket in there, I think, Daddy, when we arrived on Friday. I haven't been in there since. I wore my fleece when we went shopping and I haven't been out at all today.'

Rob snorted derisively in the corner.

341

'Once more, Ellie....'

'Elliot, I don't think this is going anywhere,' put in Belinda, softly. 'I don't think she knows what you mean.'

Simon agreed with Belinda. Elliot's methods of interrogation were like water torture. He decided to get to the crux of the matter. 'This is what he means,' he snapped, striding forward and taking a piece of paper out of his pocket. 'My son found this....filth...in the cloakroom and your brother says you put it there.' Simon unfolded the paper and slapped it onto the desk. It lay before them like the most lurid affront it was possible to imagine. It was a collage of explicit photographs; spread-eagled flesh, brazenly exposed intimacies and pinkly glistening tissue, all wantonly displayed. Ellie gasped, and clasped her hand to her mouth. She thought she might be sick. She had never seen, never imagined anything so terrible. Belinda looked away.

'Rob says that you've been interfering with his computer,' Elliot said, angrily. 'Is that true? Is that what you were arguing about earlier?'

'No. Yes. I mean, it *isn't* true that I've been on his computer but that *is* what we were arguing about. He came in the kitchen and accused me, he attacked me, actually, and he hit Tansy, although I think that was by accident. I didn't know what it was all about, really, until now. I haven't, truly, I haven't. And even if I did, I'd never, I'd *never* print off anything like that.' Ellie looked from her father to the picture and back again. All eyes turned toward Rob, who began to bluster. 'Well someone's been interfering. That,' he pointed an accusing finger 'is nothing to do with me.'

'Why would you accuse your sister, Rob? That seems to me to be the worst thing of all.' Belinda wiped her eyes. 'Couldn't we put the picture away now, please?'

Simon screwed the picture up and threw it in the fire. Mercifully, a glowing ember caught it and it blazed merrily for a few seconds before curling and turning black. With it, Simon's anger seemed to dissipate somewhat. He perched on the edge of the desk and his shoulders dropped a fraction.

But Elliot hadn't sensed that Simon's fury had abated; he waded on with the inquisition 'Rob,' he stormed, 'you have to admit that you're the prime candidate for something like this. For God's sake, lad! And your mother's right, it was a low-down trick to accuse Ellie.'

'And you spoiled my cake,' Ellie put in, plaintively, beginning to cry.

'I told you before. She wants to get me in to trouble. And it looks like she's managed it.' Rob shouted. 'Look at her turning on the water works, now! This is a set up!'

'But not by me, Rob,' Ellie flung back, sniffing.

Rob was beginning to feel cornered and desperate. His father was acting like judge and jury. It was typical that they would believe Ellie and not him. As they squared up across the table, he and Elliot, although physically quite unlike, bore a startling resemblance to each other; angry, accusing fingers pointing anywhere but at themselves.

Belinda looked from one to the other. 'Perhaps you're angry at yourself, Robert, for being so silly, and for being caught out, and that's why you blamed Ellie?'

'What baloney!' fumed Elliot. His powerlessness to get to the bottom of the situation was making him feel weak and ineffectual. Normally he would not scruple to apply aggressive tactics but he knew that a more antagonistic approach here would be labelled 'inappropriate'. His hands were tied, a position which was anathema to him. He decided to employ a more lateral solution. 'They've done nothing but squabble since I collected them from school,' he complained, turning to Simon. 'You know how these things escalate, get out of hand. Isn't it possible that the picture was here when we arrived?'

'If that was so it would have been found before now. I know Dad has used that toilet on several occasions, with helpers.' Simon shook his head.

'I checked all the bathrooms on Friday,' Belinda put in, knowing, as she did so, that she was not helping Rob's case.

'Look, Rob,' Simon cut in. 'Pornography is everywhere and you won't be the only lad of your age to be dabbling in it....'

'I'm NOT dabbling in it!' Rob roared, but Simon went on, 'I suppose that at one time or another every man has looked at pictures like those. It's the carelessness which has made me so angry. In some ways you've been lucky. Todd didn't really understand the pictures and he showed them to me straight away rather than anyone else. It could have been so much worse if Mum, say, or, God forbid, June, had come across them.'

Everyone considered this appalling prospect.

Then Rob made a sound; a grunt, a groan, it expressed frustration and fear. He clenched his fists and grimaced. The unfairness of the situation, his anger, his powerlessness; he knew that it would all erupt into violence or tears at any moment and he didn't know which was to be the less desired. Of course he didn't *know* that Ellie had planted that disgusting picture, he had assumed it, but he *did* know that *he* hadn't done it, and yet every eye and every finger was pointing at him. If only, if *only* he knew, really *knew*, this secret of hers, now would be the time to reveal it. It was his only defensive ammunition, and, unfortunately, just pretending he knew it just wasn't good enough. The family watched him struggle for a moment, wondering whether confession, or further denial, or something else would be the end result of his obvious inner turmoil. But before it had resolved itself, Ellie spoke.

'Last night,' she suggested, carefully, 'the house was full of strangers. All those policemen, that funny old man that Granny brought with her.' There was an exhalation of tension in the room; fury evaporated, seeping in wisps through the walls and into the pages of the leather-bound volumes, curling up the chimney. They all, to one extent or another, grasped hold of the life-line which Ellie had thrown them.

'By God, she's right,' Simon laughed. 'I think she might have it, you know.'

'I certainly didn't check the toilet after they left,' Belinda admitted.

'I told you it wasn't me,' Rob sulked.

'Well, well, yes, perhaps you might have something, or,' Elliot fixed Rob with a look, 'maybe your sister's just got you off a very nasty hook.'

He eyed the others in the room. Faced with this crisis he had dealt with it swiftly and thoroughly. No one could accuse him of not taking charge. But resolution was necessary now, and a final stamp of authority, 'but there are lessons to be learned here, and one of them is that we should never have brought that damn computer. So tomorrow, you can spend the day finishing your bloody coursework and then it's going away. And that's final. Now then,' he turned to Simon and rubbed his hands together, 'it must be time for a drink, and we have a birthday to celebrate.' Enjoying the last word, Elliot pranced from the room, followed by Simon.

'He must be joking, Mum,' Ellie wailed. 'He can't think I want anyone to mention the word birthday after this! This has been the most awful day of my life!'

'Oh, come on now, darling. Cheer up. It's lasagne, your favourite,' Belinda crooned, applying food, her universal panacea, to the situation, before hurrying to the kitchen.

Rob and Ellie faced each other across the chair. Refrains of childhood rhymes, long unheard, echoed in strands down corridors of

345

time. Shared periods of viral infection and busy projects in snow and sand; streams of genetic material; an intangible connectivity looped like veins across the space between them.

'Why didn't you tell?' Ellie asked, at last.

'Why didn't you?' Rob replied.

Granny McKay and Starlight sat at opposite ends of the kitchen table and ate boiled eggs with toast soldiers. Granny had found, in Starlight, a perfect audience for her half-remembered anecdotes and imperfectly understood remembrances from years gone by, and was happily occupied in recounting the tale of a mysterious illness which had assailed her whilst on holiday as a girl, following the ill-advised consumption of a quantity of salad tomatoes.

'Red-heads can't eat tomatoes, you know,' she said, waving a soldier at Starlight. Starlight waved one back. 'Extremely dangerous, although the doctor wouldn't have it, at the time. I know I haven't got red hair now. Not on my head, anyway. But I haven't eaten a tomato since.'

'You've eaten hundreds of tomatoes. Robert used to grow them, out in the yard,' Muriel admonished, spooning egg.

'He had budgerigars in the yard,' Granny corrected her.

'At one time, yes, and hens. But he grew tomatoes against the privy wall.'

'That privy is a death-trap. I saw a rat in there today. I must get your father to look at it.'

'I'd never keep caged birds,' Heather said, wiping Starlight's chin. 'Birds should be free, shouldn't they, darling?'

'I think he got the budgerigars free, from young Arnold George next door. He used to breed them. He was killed, in the war. He had a dreadful stammer. It was a shame. Mrs George and I had decided that he would marry Matron.'

'A shame that he got killed? Or about the stammer?' Heather smiled.

'You didn't know Matron, then, Mother. Come on, finish your tea, then I'll help you upstairs.'

'Don't be ridiculous. Poor thing; Muriel was always so ugly. But Arnold was a nice boy and he wouldn't have minded.'

'Oh Granny, now that's not very kind,' Heather reproached her, looking sympathetically at Muriel.

Muriel fed Roger crusts, and patted his head. 'I'll take you out for a walk later, Roger,' she said, quietly.

The men had escaped to the pub. It smelled of Sunday-lunchtime cabbage and wood-smoke and stale beer. The walls were crammed with photographs of hardy country folk clutching bedraggled sheep and dangerous-looking, unwieldy farm implements, cheek by jowl with brightly polished horse brasses and items of saddlery. The low, beamed ceiling was strung with hunting paraphernalia; bugles and whips, and pewter tankards for slaking the rural thirst. Fires burned in two cast-iron stoves. They were the only customers and from the landlord's rather tousled appearance it seemed as though early-door business was not normally expected on a Sunday. However he quickly adjusted his demeanour and welcomed them with enthusiasm, pulling pints and fetching ice. Mitch and Bob played darts in the games room, smoking voraciously and quaffing frothy pints. James and Simon played pool; James was rather an accomplished player since it was a popular activity in the day-room of the clinic, but he was careful to give Simon the best of the game. Les, Elliot and Robert stood at the bar; Les and Robert drank halves of mild, Elliot a large scotch and soda, his second of the day. He tried to interest Robert in some business matters but Robert wasn't able to take in the details and conversation between them soon faltered. Presently Simon and James came back to the bar. Simon bought another round of drinks and they took them to a table next to the fire.

'We should have brought Rob with us,' Simon said. 'He oughtn't to be left with the women and children all the time. It isn't good for a lad his age.'

'You never wanted to go anywhere with me,' Robert said, with a flash of his old maliciousness.

There was a moment's silence. In all the general chat, the planning and discussions, and even during the bizarre events of the previous evening, it was the first time that Robert had directly addressed his son, the first time that a reply had been specifically required.

Simon took a deep breath. 'I was desperate to spend time with you, Dad, just not in the cab of a lorry, but now isn't the time to go into that.'

Les fiddled with his pipe. Elliot considered Simon's suggestion and on the whole he found that he rather resented Simon's advice, especially in the light of the afternoon's occurrences. 'When he can behave like an adult, I'll treat him as one,' he said, eventually.

'I think you might find it works the other way around,' James said, quietly.

Elliot fumed at the correction, but held his peace. They drank in silence for a time. Then Simon said:

'I think, tomorrow, it would be a good idea to make a new start. What with one thing and another, it's been a disrupted weekend.'

'I told everyone that we needed a plan, but no one would have it,' Elliot crowed.

James nodded. 'I'm worried about Belinda. She looks done in.'

'Oh, don't take any notice of that,' Elliot snorted, swigging whisky. 'It's a ploy of hers. To make you feel bad.'

'I hardly think so,' James retorted.

'I think we should aim to eat out, tomorrow. At the very least we should suggest that we scale down the catering; we don't need gourmet meals every night, nice as they are.' Simon sipped his expensive continental beer.

Elliot laughed, coldly. 'I expect we'll do as we're told, as usual. I may have to drive home, anyway.'

There was a short silence. 'I do hope not,' James said, politely, after a moment.

'I don't think anything's going quite to plan,' Simon said, 'although the children seem to be getting on nicely, on the whole.'

'There are a lot more of you, for one thing,' Les agreed, graciously. 'I know you never banked on me and June. Or Mother. Or Muriel.'

'Ah ha! Now then. And thereby hangs a tale, eh, Leslie?' Elliot had finished his drink already. He pounced on the opening Les had inadvertently created.

'Mmmm, well.' Les stared into the fire.

'June and Muriel have hardly spoken for years,' Robert said, frowning. 'They fell out. It isn't anything to be proud of. We never speak about it. I am surprised Mary invited her. But it is nice to have her here.'

'Nothing's surprised me more than to discover old Les here is a philandering old dog!' Elliot cried with an unpleasant lasciviousness. Everyone looked uncomfortable. Les kneaded his hands together as though in order to restrain them from Elliot's throat. Elliot looked around the table. 'What's the problem? It's true, isn't it? This is family! No need to be coy!' No-one met his eye.

Bob and Mitch came back into the bar. Bob pulled a stool up to their table. Mitch remained standing, his back to them, scrutinizing the framed sepia prints of prize-winning tups and bulls from years gone by. Bob motioned to the landlord that he should bring another round of drinks.

'Not for me, thanks,' Mitch amended, over his shoulder. He was driving.

'What *is* it with this family?' Elliot wouldn't let the subject drop. 'Are all families the same? So many holy cows and no-go areas! I like to say a thing as I see it. I'm only saying what you're all thinking! Come on! Were you having them one at a time, Les? Or both together? It's every man's fantasy, isn't it, that? Two sisters in the same bed?' He grinned round the table again trying to entice them, but no-one met his eye.

351

'Those are my sisters you're talking about, Elliot,' Robert flashed, sharply, with sudden perspicacity.

James stood up abruptly. He wondered which McKay sisters Elliot fantasised about; frankly he found the idea of any of them in bed with Elliot revolting, even Belinda. 'We oughtn't to be late. Belinda wanted to serve dinner at seven.'

'She can hold it back,' Elliot waved James' concerns away. 'And Bob's just got another round in.'

James sat down again. The landlord brought their drinks. Bob rummaged in his jeans pockets for a time before discovering that he had no cash. Mitch produced his wallet and handed over a note. 'The kids asked me to sort out the TV in the big room,' he said. It was a safely neutral topic, he hoped. 'They want to watch a film. I think it just needs connecting up. I'll have a look at it when we get back.'

'Thank you, Mitch. Simon was just saying,' James said, pouncing on the opening Mitch had provided in a determined effort to leave no opportunity for Elliot, 'that he thinks tomorrow we should try and take control of things a bit.'

'Yes,' Simon clarified. 'I think it would be good if we all went out. Some people haven't stirred from the house since they got here.'

'The atmosphere in that place is becoming insufferable,' Elliot muttered, darkly. 'The Happy Family is a farce.'

'Heather wants to take the girls to a pottery, or something,' Bob said, soldiering on alongside James, 'throw plates. Cheers, Mitch, mate.'

'Ideal. Yes, cheers. And there's a place with a climbing wall, canoeing; the boys will enjoy that.'

'June and I will take care of Granny and ….' Les glanced at Robert, 'anyone else who'd rather stay home.'

Elliot, who had not been consulted on any of these plans, and whose nose was feeling distinctly out of joint since Robert's rebuff, and the other men's determined efforts to ignore his conversational gambits, put in, sulkily, 'as I say, my own efforts to organise things were rather frowned upon. But never mind. Have it the McKay way if you must. It seems more and more likely that I shall go back to the office. I have some important quotes to get off tomorrow. I don't want to climb a wall or throw a plate.'

'Belinda would like to visit a stately home,' James said. 'She mentioned it after church. I forget the name, something in-the-forest. A few hours out, just the two of you, would be very agreeable, I should have thought, and she could certainly do with your support.' James sipped his drink. 'I would urge you to get her away from the house, Elliot. Look how much better she looked after the walk today!'

'I didn't notice. I only noticed that I was left to deal with a crisis and that I didn't get my figures finished. As for a stately home - sounds like hell. You take her, if you like. You clearly know far better than me what my wife needs!'

'I'd be delighted to take her,' James said, mildly, ignoring Elliot's spleen.

'Mary likes a stately home,' Robert commented. 'Simon, I think I need the toilet.' Simon gave a slight, involuntary recoil. His eye, indeed all the muscles of his face, became frozen. He stared intently at his drink. It was as though his father had not spoken, or was not even present. There was a beat, awkward, loaded, then Les got to his feet and helped Robert towards the gents. In their wake, the difficult silence stretched itself across their corner of the room.

Suddenly, Simon turned towards Elliot. 'What *would* you like to do, Elliot?' he asked, sharply.

Elliot contemplated the last mouthful of his drink, leaving Simon in limbo. He would not have wanted to take Robert to the

353

toilet, either, but then Robert was not his father. Presently he swallowed the last of his whiskey. 'I enjoy a round of golf,' he said, unctuously.

'Not really a family activity,' Simon retorted, but Bob cut in: 'Grand. Mitch's a good player, plays off a handicap of seven. He'll give you a game, won't you, mate?'

'Be delighted,' Mitch agreed, thinking, ruefully, now, of the long hours spent on Floridian courses.

'Super,' Elliot nodded, looking a little white.

'Now,' James looked at his watch, 'time we weren't here, I think, gents.' They finished their drinks.

On their way out to the car, Bob nudged Mitch playfully; 'Sorry about landing you with the golf. But it'll make a nice change from mopping up blood and vomit, eh?'

'If you say so.'

Rob had cloistered himself in the study once more. *Five Mile Pile Up* yelled furiously from the speakers, their angst bouncing off the walls and finding an answering note in his head. He was on the edge, positively poised, clinging on and yet yearning to leap, in that space between idea and decision where pros and cons clash. His mind was in a maelstrom. He badly wanted a drink, to get very drunk, to rage and lash out. His anger was like a wild animal, caged, pent up, desperate to be released, and it seemed to scrabble with its frantic claws inside him until he thought he might explode. The pointlessness of it all, the unfairness of it, the suffocating falseness was driving him mad. It was almost unendurable, but on the other hand the thought of unleashing the beast was a terrifying prospect too. He had no idea, once he succumbed to it, where it might lead; smashed up furniture, vandalised works of art, bruised bodies, a raging inferno. There was no saying where it might end. Suddenly he was marching out of the room and down the corridor to the small sitting room. It was empty. Some muddled plan over where the drinks should be kept had meant that one or two bottles and glasses had been left on a glass-fronted cabinet. He helped himself to a large whisky and drank it down, with a shudder. Then he poured another and carried it boldly back into the study and slammed the door. The activity, and the whisky, seemed to exorcise some of his torment. He swallowed down some more. It scalded his stomach but the heat of it seemed to put out his rage. He could feel it melting, flowing into his limbs, slowing the frenzied beating of his heart. It felt good. He was conscious of a sharpening of his mind as he considered things; a dark cloud of anger and – he identified it now – fear which swirled around the danger of someone hacking into his computer, the malicious intent which had been behind the printing out and planting stuff where it would be found, the injustice of the accusations levelled against him, and in the hurtfulness of his father's failure to believe him or even to listen to him.

355

But enmeshed in all that, shooting through it with a clear arrow of light there was yet something, just the smallest suggestion of something worth grasping. His conversation with Bob over brunch had been a shining possibility. Much as he might minimise it, the tiny rapprochement between the cousins on Friday night over hot chocolate and cake had felt good; he was quite aware of Toby's developing puppy-like adoration for him: it was both annoying and flattering. Plus, even though it still eluded his grasp, the existence of this supposed secret of Ellie's intrigued and worried him. He needed to be master of it, whether to use it against her or to protect her from its consequences, he could not say. It was all so insubstantial, so fragile and nebulous; the kind of thing he would normally take pleasure in stamping on, and yet it all called to him in a way he did not understand. He was angry with her, angry at himself, afraid of her, afraid for her. It gripped him, or he gripped it, either way, it wouldn't be let go. Its power over him irked him.

In frustration he paced from one end of the room to another, his music at full volume, looking for but failing to find the security and calm it usually supplied; it seemed to bounce around him, elusive. He lit one of Bob's cigarettes and inhaled it rapaciously. He didn't care who came in. He stood in front of the fireplace, his forehead against the wood of the mantelpiece, his arms braced on either side. Gradually his body chemistry reached some kind of equilibrium, so that when a tentative tap on his shoulder alerted him to Toby's presence in the room, to invite him to join them at monopoly, he was able to decline with only an icy sneer, as opposed to a furious tirade of invective, which is what, only moments before, would have been his inevitable response. To his extreme irritation, Toby persisted; 'Only, you know, we thought you might like to, and, well, we'll let you choose who you want to be, you know, the battleship, or the car, or whatever..' Toby trailed off.

Rob took a deep breath. 'Oh *great!*' he said, with withering sarcasm, 'well why didn't you say so?' Toby continued to look at him, his eyes pathetic with pleading. Rob looked back, his eyes hard and cold.

'So? You don't want to play, then?'

'No!' Rob shouted, making Toby jump, and then regretted it. He gathered himself and repeated, more reasonably, 'no. I don't want to play.'

'Ok.' Toby left the room, closing the door behind him but not before Rob's muttered 'for fuck's sake!' made itself heard.

The returning men met Heather and Muriel in the hall. Heather had got changed into her floaty outfit. She put her arms around Bob's neck and they kissed, extravagantly.

'Oh for God's sake,' Elliot growled, shrugging his coat off.

'I put Starlight to bed all on my own,' she said, proudly, like a small child boasting of a great achievement.

James made immediately for the stairs. 'I ought to check on my womenfolk,' he said, cheerily.

'No,' Heather halted him, 'they're both fast asleep. I just looked in on them. So is Granny, isn't she Muriel?'

Muriel was buttoning herself into her coat. Roger was circling her feet, eagerly. 'Yes, out like a light. And June has also retired for the night. Belinda says I have twenty minutes before we eat, so I'm just going to take Roger out for his constitutional. Poor lamb. He hasn't been out all day.'

'I'll come with you,' Les said, hanging Robert's coat up for him, 'it's very dark out there and you don't know the ground.'

'Thank you Les, that's very kind of you.' They stepped out together into the night. Without Les, Robert was suddenly unaided, his incapacity was uncatered for. His eye, fierce but also a little frightened, travelled over the men in the hall. His stick trembled in his grasp.

'I'm going to find my boys,' said Simon, making swiftly for the games room.

Mitch moved off in the same direction. 'Just go and sort that telly out,' he mumbled.

'Come on Robert,' James, at last, took Robert's arm. 'Let's find Mary,' he said. 'Coming, Elliot?'

'No. I think I might throw up,' Elliot glowered. 'I need a drink. And I *still* haven't finished my figures.' He thrust his hands into his pockets and stalked away.

Todd, Toby and Ben were lying on the floor playing a game of Monopoly. They were wearing their pyjamas.

'Oh Dad!' Toby scrambled to his feet at the sight of his father. 'Dad! Aunty Belinda says we have to go to bed early tonight. She made us put our pyjamas on. We don't have to, do we?' He was sick of being treated like one of the little children, the indignity of being sent upstairs with them to get undressed had been galling, that, and Rob's rebuff, had brought him uncomfortably close to tears.

'I think that's a very sensible idea,' Simon said, putting his arm around his son. Toby's shoulders were narrow and bony underneath his pyjamas. He had grown three inches in as many months and his skeleton seemed stretched and thin. 'We've all had some late nights recently and tomorrow ..... well tomorrow, there're going to be untold wonders and excitement!'

'Why? What's happening tomorrow?' Toby sat down next to his father, on the squashy settee, comforted by his solid nearness.

'Well. It seems there's an activity centre, with a climbing wall, and canoeing and high ropes and archery...'

Todd left the game of Monopoly and came to stand by his father. 'Wow! And are we going, Daddy?' He was wide eyed. He scrambled onto Simon's knee. Simon settled him there and put his other arm round Toby.

'We certainly are!'

Ben returned to the board game. He had just thrown a five and a four. He was playing with the motor car and he drove it carefully from Bow Street around to Fenchurch Street station, where he parked it. Places like activity centres cost money, so there was no chance that he would be going. Fenchurch Street station cost £200 but he didn't have any other stations so he decided not to buy it. Toby was telling his Dad about Archery club at school, he had joined last term and was already quite good. It didn't look as though he would want to resume

359

their game. Todd had been losing interest in it anyway. It would soon be tea time. Ben sailed Toby's ship around the borders of The Angel Islington where it was currently harboured.

'So what do you think, Ben?' Uncle Simon broke into his reverie. Ben shrugged. 'Aren't you the outdoor type? I think some of the others might be going to a pottery place. Would you enjoy that more?'

Ben shrugged again. 'Our family doesn't normally do that kind of thing,' he said, quietly. 'It costs money.'

Simon's heart melted in his chest, a drooping, dripping sadness dribbled over his diaphragm. He pushed Todd off his knee and slid onto the floor, crawling across the space towards the game board and lay down next to Ben. 'Well, d' you know what? I can't see your Mum wanting to go canoeing tomorrow, can you? And your Dad's taking Aunty Belinda to a stately home to look at furniture and paintings and stuff. So how about you join our family for the day? *Our* family does that kind of thing all the time and we don't *care* if it costs money, do we, boys?' He rolled over and beckoned to Todd and Toby. They launched themselves upon him; he scooped Ben into the morass of flailing arms and legs and squirming, ticklish flesh, his voice drowned out by their whoops of excitement.

Rob, sent to tell them that dinner was almost ready, stood at the door with his mouth open. The small boys were wriggling over Simon like puppies, he was mock fighting and tickling them; they were helpless with laughter and pleasure. Rob had never seen anything like it in his life, certainly he had never played with his father in such a way, indeed, in any way that he could recall. The realisation added another layer to the festering laminate he was trying to accommodate; embarrassment and another emotion which he struggled to identify; a yearning for something lost; but not lost in any way which would imply that it had ever been enjoyed. It was absent entirely, a black hole of longing.

'Dinner in five,' he said, loudly, into the noise.

Les and Muriel paced slowly around the gravelled sweep, in the darkness. They held hands. Although it hadn't rained since lunchtime, the grass was still soaking wet, overlaid now by golden leaves torn free by the wind in the night. Roger snuffled and rummaged busily, lifting his leg here and there, excited by the foreign scents and country textures under his paws. Les puffed at his pipe, and enjoyed the feel of Muriel's soft, warm hand in his, and the rub of her shoulder against his arm, and listened to her recount the day's events.

'....of course,' she was saying, 'Mother's far worse now than when I had her with me. But she's biddable enough, mainly. And the tablets make her sleepy. This is a lovely house, so clean, and everyone's so kind. Do you think it would be alright if I had a bath, tonight?'

'I'm sure it would be fine. How has June been?'

'Cold. She's hardly spoken. Very proud. Don't worry,' Muriel squeezed Les' hand, 'I can forgive her, now.'

Les squeezed back and they sauntered in silence for a few paces before he asked; 'How do you find Robert? I think he's too much for Mary. I tried to tell her as much.'

'He's had the stuffing knocked out of him. Not altogether a bad thing. He could be very nasty. He's like Mother.'

'So is June. June hasn't a caring bone in her body. Robert could be vicious. They're all selfish and cruel, except for you. Are you sure you're a real McKay?'

Muriel laughed. 'As far as I know! They're not so bad. Robert's children are all lovely, especially Belinda.'

'That's Mary's influence. Perhaps the McKay blood will improve as it becomes thinner and more diluted down the generations. Watch out for Elliot, though. He was horrible in the pub just now. I wanted to hit him.'

'That's not like you,' Muriel shivered. 'It's time we went in. This is turning out to be a real treat, though. I'm seeing more of you than I would do at home. And Roger likes his holiday, don't you, pet?' Roger appeared at their feet, wagging his rear end and wheezing happily. 'It's nice.' She turned to him, and he kissed her, lightly.

'Don't you mind if someone sees?' she asked, scanning the windows of the house.

'No,' he said, 'I don't.'

Mitch slumped in the gloom of his room. He had brought his portion of lasagne upstairs with him, the prospect of the family birthday meal had been too much, a step beyond the limits he imposed upon himself; it would have been, he told himself, an intrusion. They all would have felt it, with the baby safely in bed, Bob and Heather languorous with the day's fresh air and exercise, and no reason to expect a further sanguineous or bilious outbreak there was nothing they could possibly need from him and no reason, therefore, for him to remain. As much as he might have enjoyed the legitimate opportunity to look at Ellie as she presided, the centre of attention, over the celebratory meal, he would have felt like an aberration, his lack of belonging all the more pointed. He wasn't sure, either, if he could have trusted himself in the all-too-likely event of some cutting, malicious remark from her brother. It wasn't *his* place, after all, to defend her, he thought, bitterly.

His scheme to land Rob up to his neck in it had obviously failed. It made Mitch feel both frustrated and relieved. It would have been enough to secure the lad's ignominious ejection, he would have thought, but for some reason the plan had gone astray; maybe someone had found and discreetly disposed of the page he had planted in the bathroom, or removed it, perhaps, for their own furtive enjoyment. If it had come to light it had certainly been dealt with swiftly and discreetly. Apart from the girl's accident in the kitchen, he had been conscious of no significant additional ripple in the family demeanour. It was a pity; he would have liked to have secured for Ellie this one, vicarious victory. On the other hand, his intervention had sailed him dangerously close to the wind, trampling those deliberately self-erected boundaries of passivity. Being pro-active had felt like breaking his own rules. He must, he really must, resist the temptation to become involved.

The golf on the following day would help, he thought. Spending the day with, surely, the least appealing member of the family would cure him of his burgeoning sentimentality.

Heather – A Memoir from 1978

Heather was awoken by a strange and furry tickling sensation on the pillow by her ear. By the time she had struggled to sit up, the mouse was on her bed-spread, looking at her, its whiskers twitching. It had two heads, one at each end, with round blunt noses like a pig, and black beady eyes, and a red belt round its middle. Then she blinked and it had gone.

The room was gloomy; she could barely see Ruth's bed across the room. In the day time, even with the curtains closed, there was enough light to see by, and it was pink and sugary, like a fairy-tale. At night time, when the light was off, you couldn't see anything at all, and Heather didn't like it and Ruth said she was a sissy. Their room was at the back of the house, and behind the house there were fields with no lights at all. In the little room, which she had given up to Belinda, the light from the street lamp came through the curtains all night long, because that room was at the front, but this room was dark, at night.

So it wasn't night time and it wasn't daytime. She was alone; apart from Boy George and Adam Ant, who stared from their posters on the wall by Ruth's bed. Ruth's bed was neatly made, with her nightie folded up on the pillow; Mummy had done that, not Ruth. Heather had a pyjama case for her nightie, in the shape of a white fluffy doggie, with a zip in his tummy where her nightie lived. He was called Fluffy, and during the day he had pride of place on her pillow, while the other toys had to sit at the bottom of the bed, but at night time they all came into bed with her; Fluffy and big Ted and little Ted and Doggie and Duckie and Lamby and Floppy (although the wire in Floppy's ear was poking out through his fur and Mummy said he would have to have an operation to have it sewn up or he would poke her eye out.) Belinda said that it was a wonder there was enough room for Heather in the bed with all those toys, but there was; it was cosy and snuggly and she liked it.

Her eyes hurt when she swivelled them in her head, and her body was hot and wet, and her fringe was sticking to her forehead. Now that she was sitting up, the hot wetness was beginning to feel cold and clammy. Her ear was crackling and popping, especially when she swallowed, and it hurt when she swallowed, and she remembered that she was poorly.

She got out of bed. It was cold, and she was shivery. Out on the landing she could hear shouting from downstairs. This was nothing new. There had been shouting almost every day for weeks now; shouting about money, about how there wasn't any. Ruth had shouted the most; she wanted to go on a school holiday to somewhere on an aeroplane and there wasn't any money to pay for it. Simon had shouted a bit, but not as much as Ruth. He had been picked to play in the school football team and he needed new boots and there wasn't any money to pay for those. Even Mummy, who didn't shout much and then only about things like muddy footprints on the kitchen floor or food left on plates, had shouted a little bit. Belinda hadn't shouted at all; she never did. She was a big girl at college learning to do typing. Daddy had shouted; not as much as Ruth, but more than Simon and Mummy. He had shouted that there would be no seaside holiday next year, no new carpet for the dining room, no new toys for Christmas, no new coat for Mummy. The shouting had reached its loudest when Aunty June had arrived. That had been on Sunday last. Aunty June and Uncle Les always came on Sundays, for Sunday dinner, and after dinner Belinda had taken Ruth and Simon to the pictures but Heather was too little for the pictures at night time and anyway she had a streaming cold, and she had sat at the dining room table doing her colouring while Mummy and Uncle Les had washed and dried the pots and Daddy and Aunty June went into the lounge and shouted.

'Needs must when the devil drives,' Aunty June had shouted, and 'everyone does it,' and 'c-o-d' and 'cash-in-hand' and 'what the eye doesn't see.'

'Smuggling,' Daddy had shouted, and 'illegal,' and 'tax dodge.'

'Needs must when the devil drives,' Aunty June had shouted, again.

On Monday Daddy had gone away for a long trip. He hadn't done that for quite a long time; they had other drivers, now, who did them, usually. Perhaps he had gone to keep an eye on the devil. On Tuesday Heather had complained of ear-ache but Mummy had said she must go to school anyway. On Wednesday she had cried at playtime and Mrs McKendrick had let her sit in the book corner all afternoon. On Thursday she had had a temperature and Mummy had kept her off school. Today, after a night of hot sweats and nasty dreams about Daddy and the devil driving one of the lorries, Dr Wilson had come and put a cold tube in her ear and a lolly-stick on her tongue and given her some yellow medicine. That was the last thing she remembered; she must have been asleep all day.

Heather walked down the narrow stairs, her legs all quivery, holding on at both sides. The shouty voices were Daddy and Aunty June again. Perhaps it was still Sunday after all and the week she thought had happened, hadn't. But there was no lingering smell of Sunday dinner, so that couldn't be right. Mummy's old coat and shopping bag were missing from the hall table, so she must be out shopping. It was Friday, shopping day, a school day. The clock in the hall said something but Heather hadn't learned to tell the time yet. She had been given a wristwatch for her sixth birthday by Granny McKay, who had said, dangling it in front of her, that next time she saw Heather, she wanted her to be able to tell the time. Heather hoped she didn't see Granny McKay for a long while. The television wasn't on in the lounge so Simon and Ruth must not be home from school yet.

'I did what you wanted,' Daddy roared. 'It was dreadful; lurking round the backs of the warehouses, parking up in lay-bys at night time, whispering and looking over my shoulder all the time. Tampering with delivery notes, dealing with a load of shifty bastards who can't be

367

trusted. Stealing and cheating and smuggling! My reputation will be in tatters! This isn't the McKay way, June. But here it is. So now what? Now what?'

'I'll see to it, don't worry,' Aunty June said. 'Nothing simpler. Leave it to me.'

Heather pushed open the dining room door. There was no light on in the room. The day outside was almost gone, faded to grey. The curtains were open and the orange light from the street lamp, just switched on, flickered over the room. Orange was coming from inside the room too, from the electric fire. Simon had shown Heather once that the coals lifted off like a lid and underneath there was an orange light bulb with a silver hat that went round and round and made the flickering. It wasn't real, only pretend, but the two things together, the lamp and the fire, made everything look hot and red. Perhaps the devil had driven Daddy home and brought hell with him, and it was waiting outside, with its burning fire and gnashing teeth, like they said in Sunday school. But the room was cold and Heather was shivering with it.

Daddy was standing by the table wearing his driving clothes. His hair was all stuck up on end and he had a shadow on his chin, because when he went on the road he slept in the cab and didn't shave. Heather wondered if the devil had slept in the cab too and if it wasn't rather a squash, like her and her toys in the bed, and if the devil's pointy horns might poke out Daddy's eye. The light on Daddy's face made it look like he was blushing. Aunty June sat in the armchair by the fireplace. She was wearing her smart work clothes. She was red too but then she always was. On the table was a heap of paper, all crinkly and thrown around as though it was just rubbish; but it wasn't rubbish, it was money. Lots and lots of money. It covered the table completely and the heap was so big that some of it had slipped off the table and onto the carpet, the carpet which Mummy had said needed replacing, but there was no money for it. But now there was money *on* it. So much money that you could have made a money-carpet for the whole room. Aunty June kept looking at it.

Then they both saw Heather, standing in the doorway, trembling and sweating with cold. Aunty June leapt to her feet and began to scoop the money off the table into carrier bags.

'I'll see to it, I'll see to it,' she kept saying, as though she was talking about laundry; as though she was taking their dirty washing home to put into her posh new machine.

Daddy strode across the room and picked her up. He couldn't look at it, the dirty laundry-money, and he snatched her out of the room quickly. But when they were out in the hall he said; 'back to bed, my lady,' not unkindly, and Heather began to cry, because she was poorly, and only six years old.

Up in the bedroom Daddy put her back into bed and covered her up. He sat on the edge of the bed and reached into his pocket for his handkerchief. As he pulled it out, a tightly rolled sausage of money with a rubber band round it plopped onto the bedspread, just exactly in the place where the mouse had been earlier. They both looked at it, the two-headed money-mouse. Its appearance seemed to shock and unnerve them both equally; they both recoiled slightly. Then Daddy wiped her eyes and put his handkerchief on her nose and said 'blow,' and she did, but it made her ear pop and it hurt, and she cried a bit more. Next time she looked, the money-mouse had gone, and Daddy got up and said, 'back to sleep now, there's a good girl,' and he didn't look at her when he left the room.

Often, after that, Heather would reach into her Daddy's pocket to see if there was another money-mouse in there, but there were only ever sweeties. And they would look at each other and they would both know about the money-mouse but they never said. And, after that, there was no more shouting about money.

Monday

The morning was dull and overcast. But there was a spirit of determined optimism amongst the family which overruled any damp squib the weather might try to inflict. Simon restrained Belinda from producing cooked breakfasts.

'Cereal and toast only,' he said, imperiously, shutting the fridge door firmly on the bacon. 'Look, those croissants we brought haven't been touched yet and that organic bread will need finishing too. It doesn't have the preservatives of ordinary bread you know, so it doesn't stay fresh.'

'Oh well,' Belinda said, 'if you put it like that...'

'I do.' He rubbed his hands together vigorously.

She made a last, half-hearted attempt to object. 'We'll need bread for lunch, though, I was going to make soup..........'

'Lunch will be out, today,' James said, pouring flakes into a bowl for Ben with a flourish. 'You and I are going to that stately home you wanted to see.'

Belinda was conscious of a delicious, reckless, inner thrill at the prospect, its potency unquashed by the rest of James' sentence. 'I hope we can persuade Mary to come with us, Muriel too, if she'd like to.'

Ben rolled his eyes at Todd; 'Boring!' he mouthed, through flakes.

'I would so like to,' Belinda gushed, but she caught herself up short. She could not afford to allow Elliot to feel left out of things. 'But what about......everyone else?' she finished.

'Really, Lindy, you mustn't worry about it,' Heather said, misreading the direction of her sister's thoughts. 'You're like a mother hen, trying to keep all her chicks together! We're not helpless, you know. We all manage to feed ourselves quite well as a rule, one way or another.' Across the room, Mitch was mashing a banana into milk for Starlight.

Miriam looked up from one of the Sunday supplements she was reading. 'The men formulated quite a workable plan, last night at the pub,' she said, 'amazingly enough, considering they were absolutely without female guidance. Simon and Bob are taking the boys to an activity centre. Heather and I are going to take the girls to a pottery. She found a leaflet in the hall cupboard. You can throw a pot, apparently, and paint it, and then they fire it and you collect it in a day or so. You and James will go and soak up some culture. Les and June will stay here to take care of Granny and Robert. I'm absolutely certain that June is equal to a pan of soup. You see? Everyone is happily catered for in every way.'

Belinda took a sip of her coffee. 'What about Elliot?' she asked, heavily.

'Elliot was fully consulted,' Simon said, stiffly. 'He didn't seem to want to do anything. But I believe that Mitch has agreed to a round of golf, so perhaps he'll do that. I'll put these croissants in the Aga to warm, shall I?'

Belinda felt only slightly reassured. She didn't think that Mitch would be Elliot's partner of choice. 'Oh, yes, fine, Simon,' she said, distractedly, reaching preserves down from a cupboard. 'Thank you, that top oven on the left. Well, he does enjoy golf. But he was up very late working on some figures. And then Granny gave him rather a shock.' Everyone smothered laughter. Granny's nocturnal meanderings had caused quite a furore in the night. 'So as far as I know he's still in bed.'

'Well, there's no rush, I don't suppose; it's early.'

Belinda placed small plates and knives on the table. Heather was right; she did feel like a mother hen. Her inclusive instinct was not to be suppressed. 'What about Ruth? And what about poor Rachel?' she asked James.

He reached for the toast-rack. 'Rachel's still feeling a bit fragile. A day at home on the settee with her quilt and a good book will be just the ticket for her,' He spread his toast thickly with butter. 'Ruth is much improved, I believe. Slept well. She's rather fancying a trip to the pottery, I think, if there's room in the car.' He left the question hanging. Belinda tried to imagine herself abandoning Ellie at such a time, but said nothing.

James, however, read her thoughts and after chewing thoughtfully for a while, said in a low voice, 'Sometimes, between Rachel and Ruth, less is more.'

The question of Ruth's inclusion remained in the air. 'Well,' Miriam sighed, closed the supplement, and picked it up like a metaphorical hot potato. 'It would be *just lovely* if Ruth came with us, wouldn't it, Heather? Are those croissants warm yet, Simon darling?'

He opened the Aga door and placed his hand on the pastries. 'Not quite. Will Rob enjoy some outdoor activity? I don't think he's stepped out of doors since he arrived on Friday. I do worry about him.....'

'So do I,' Belinda sighed, 'but Elliot did say that he had to get his course work finished today.'

'Oh yes. Well. That's a shame. But I suppose it will be a good thing all round to get that computer off the scene. Maybe tomorrow.....'

Heather cut toast into postage stamp sized squares for Starlight. 'Rob's chi is in melt-down. He's screaming, that young man, just screaming for attention,' she mused, almost to herself, and then, to the room at large; 'the baby slept through!' Her pride could not have been greater if Starlight had been awarded a Nobel prize.

'I've lost my baby,' lamented Granny, from the doorway where she stood between Muriel and Les 'but it might have been Arnold's little brother.' She shook her head, sadly.

'June will be down presently,' Les said, quickly. Lost babies was a tricky area on a variety of levels.

Simon brought the croissants to the table. 'Careful, Todd,' he said. 'They're hot. And don't snatch.'

'Ooh lovely,' Muriel cooed. 'Like being abroad.'

Miriam tore open her croissant. 'I hope June didn't mind us waking her in the night,' she said, with a mischievous twinkle. June had seemed to mind very much at the time. It had taken her a long time to open her door and they had waited on the landing for what seemed like an age while she fussed and flapped and shouted 'I'm coming, just a minute, don't come in.'

'Why would she!' Simon cried, with ironical bluster, 'everyone else was awake, in all conscience, and *someone* had to put Granny back to bed,' he looked around the table where people were nodding enthusiastically, even Les.

Simon showed Todd how to eat his croissant, tearing mouth-sized pieces off and loading them with butter and jam. He couldn't help noticing that Muriel was paying close attention. He had not been able to help noticing, either, that last night, in the melee caused by Granny's perambulations amongst the bedrooms, Les had been conspicuous by his absence. He had certainly not emerged from the room he was supposed to be sharing with June and watching him now at the table with Muriel, as comfortable as an old couple, with Granny playing the part of their wayward child, there was an obvious connection between them that the years had not faded. 'Is this the last of the butter, Belinda?' he asked.

'I prefer the unsalted brand that we brought, anyway, Simon. It's in the fridge, I think, if you could pass it,' Miriam said.

'Oh!' Belinda clapped her hand to her forehead. 'I've just remembered something. I'll *have* to stay home today, after all.'

'What? Why?' Simon and James threw each other looks.

'Tesco are delivering some groceries. I'll have to be here to put them all away.'

'That was a clever thing to arrange,' said Miriam, genuinely impressed. 'I had the grim foreboding that a mass shopping expedition might be on the cards.'

'I like shopping, I'll come,' said Granny, brightening.

James and Simon looked at Les, who came in right on cue. 'June and I can see to the shopping. You go out, Belinda, and don't worry about a thing.'

By eleven o'clock, James, Belinda, Mary and Muriel had departed in Belinda's car, James at the wheel.

'Am I insured?' he had asked, doubtfully, when Belinda handed him the keys.

'Oh yes. The company pays for comprehensive cover for any driver appointed by a Director. I'm a Director, and I'm appointing you.' Catching a glimpse of herself on the edge was what was almost a flirtatious giggle, she reigned herself back, with a business-like: 'It's handy, really, you can imagine how much it would have cost us to insure Rob in this car, with only a provisional licence?'

James viewed the sleek lines of the high-powered BMW. 'I shudder to think,' he said.

Muriel had been persuaded to leave Roger behind in Les' care. 'I really don't think they'll allow him inside the house and it's cruel to leave dogs locked in cars, isn't it?' Belinda had said, briskly, wishing to avoid having the dog in her car – Elliot wouldn't have approved – and in any case an hour spent in any enclosed space with Roger was to be circumvented if possible. He was such a smelly dog.

'Oh well, yes, of course. I'd never do that. You see them sometimes, don't you, locked in cars outside shops and things? Heart rendering.'

James and Belinda shared a smile, over her head.

'I can't think of the last time I went out without Robert to worry about.' Mary had on her best coat and good gloves, and sensible shoes. She was really looking forward to the outing.

'Just relax and enjoy yourself Mary. Robert will be fine. With any luck, and if the weather holds, we'll be able to do the grounds as well as the house. The leaflet says that Hunting-in-the-Forest has the national Salvia collection and now's just the time to see that.'

Mary sighed. 'Lovely.'

Heather drove Starlight, Miriam, Ruth, Ellie and Tansy in Bob's jeep.

'Poor Rachel. I'm sorry she isn't well enough to come.' Tansy said, from her place next to Starlight. Starlight's car seat had innumerable rattles and toys attached to it. Tansy placed one into the baby's chubby fist.

'To be honest she isn't very good at art,' Ruth replied, over her shoulder. After some polite manoeuvring, she had secured the front seat. Miriam had climbed good naturedly into the back, onto the bench seat, surrounded by baby paraphernalia. 'It would have been a waste of money. I wish you'd let me make some sandwiches, Heather. The cafés in these places are always extortionately expensive.'

'Are they? I wouldn't know. You've got the map? I don't mind driving but I'm hopeless at navigating.'

'Yes, don't worry. I've marked the pottery here, with a cross, look.'

Ellie put in; 'I'm not very good at art either. Although I am doing it for GCSE. But Mrs Goddard says I'll get a D, if I'm lucky.'

'You ought to be able to get at least a C on coursework alone!' Ruth exclaimed.

'Mmmm. Well. Coursework proved a bit tricky, in the end.'

'I hope to do art,' said Tansy'.

'But you probably won't,' Miriam said. 'You'll do proper, academic subjects; sciences, languages and so on. You can do art anytime.'

'I don't suppose Starlight's going to produce anything very *good*,' mused Heather, but she will enjoy the experience.'

Ruth was incredulous. 'Surely, you're not going to pay for Starlight to throw a pot are you? At her age?'

'Certainly I am. Which way at this junction, Ruth? Left?

It took Simon and Bob a while to get the boys organised.

'A change of clothes, towel, dry footwear, waterproofs. Come on boys we have to be prepared for anything.'

'Ice-picks, parachutes, scuba-gear....' Bob added, wryly, ticking them off on his fingers.

'Has everyone been to the toilet?'

'Oh, no, Uncle Simon, I haven't.'

'Off you go then, Ben, quick as you can.'

'Why can't Rob come?' Toby asked, sulkily.

'His Dad said he has to finish his homework.'

'It's a shame. I could have been his canoe-buddy. Now we'll have an odd man out.'

'Why?' Todd turned to him.

Toby sneered down at his brother. 'Everyone knows that canoes are for two people, silly. There are *five* of us. Duh?'

'Don't talk to your brother like that, Toby,' Simon frowned.

'I can go in a kayak,' said Bob. 'I'm used to being the odd man out.'

'I want to be with you, Daddy,' said Todd, suddenly rather afraid.

'*I want to be with you, Daddy,*' Toby echoed, under his breath.

'Don't worry, little man,' said Simon.

Elliot made his appearance at last, resplendent in golfing regalia. Mitch, in jeans and a sweatshirt, was waiting for him.

'I'm *so* sorry if I have kept you waiting, Mitch,' Elliot gushed, knowing that he had. 'I had some important figures to email through and the dial-up here seems very unreliable. I've been trying to get them done since Saturday but everything and everyone has conspired against me.' Secretly, he had hoped that Mitch might have given up on him and gone out with the others. It would have suited Elliot to have had a genuine source of umbrage, today. He badly needed to re-establish himself in a position of authority. People were making plans without him, posturing in a ridiculously clannish way, exuding family solidarity from every hypocritical pore. It seemed to him that everyone was secretly laughing at him, even the old crone who had scared him almost witless last night, wandering into his room and poking him awake with her gnarled old fingers and leaning over him so closely that he had been able to feel her whiskers on his face.

At the sound of his father's voice in the hall, Rob appeared at the door to the study. He looked flushed and pained.

'Dad,' he said, 'this is just crap. I can't do my coursework here. The internet keeps dropping off and the printer's almost out of ink. It all just stinks. I just can't do it. Please won't you take me home?'

'No.' Elliot squared up to him. 'You'll get back in there and get your nose back on that grindstone. Finished or not that computer's going away tomorrow.' Before Rob had time to remonstrate, Elliot turned away, dismissing him. 'Sorry, Mitch,' he said, without much conviction. He didn't know how to treat this young man. What was he, anyway? An employee? If so, what was he doing here? Or, with a handicap of seven, for that matter?

'It's OK,' Mitch replied, opening the door. 'We don't tee off until one anyway. I put my clubs in your car.'

Elliot cringed and threw an angry retort over his shoulder 'I suppose I'll have to hire. There was no room for mine once we'd packed that bloody computer. Alright then. Let's go.'

Rachel had brought her quilt down to the games room and was snuggled on one of the settees. The tablets left by Dr Gardner had made her sleep deeply, but her face felt sore and monstrous, with a wide blue bruise, her hair was sticky, Grandma had not let her wash it, and, down below, she ached and throbbed. Ruth had been up to see her, brisk and bossy, to show her what to do.

'Just like you, Rachel,' she had said, her mouth a hard line, 'to choose the most inconvenient moment for this. I was practically dead yesterday, your father went out and left me. This was the last thing I needed.'

'I'm sorry,' Rachel had mumbled, ashamed. 'Are you feeling better today?'

'Yes. And I'm going to get out of here for a few hours. I'm beginning to feel institutionalised. Give yourself a good wash, night and morning, warm water, soap, rinse and dry yourself properly, but don't make a mess of the towels.'

'Alright. Yes, Grandma told me.'

'Now look, here's what you do with this. See? And then wash your hands. But they're expensive. Don't go wasting them; you don't need to be changing every verse end.'

'No. OK.'

'Have you got tummy ache?'

'Yes, a bit.'

'Mmmm. Well, you can have a couple of paracetamols but really Rachel the fact is that we all just have to get on with it. You're not ill. It's normal and most women just soldier on. Heaven knows, if I surrendered to every ache and pain I'd be permanently bed-ridden!'

'Is everyone going out?' Rachel pulled her pyjamas back on.

'I have no idea. Nearly everyone, I should think. But you'll be alright, won't you?'

'Oh yes. Dad said I could take my quilt downstairs.'

'Mmmm. Well. I suppose you can. It *is* cold today. But don't get in anyone's way. People haven't got time to be running around after you.'

'No. I know. You have a nice time.'

'Yes, I'll try.' Ruth regarded the pyjamas critically, before saying; 'Those are quite nice, very practical. You needed some new ones. I'm sorry; I should have thought to buy you some.' She gave Rachel a brief hug, and they smiled at each other, feebly.

Rachel had loitered upstairs until only two cars remained on the drive, her Dad's decrepit old estate and Uncle Les' jaguar. Surely everyone had gone out now? She had bundled up her quilt and padded downstairs to the games room, made herself a comfy space with cushions, visited the kitchen briefly for a glass of juice and some biscuits, and settled herself down with Bridget Jones. She was aware of voices in one of the back rooms but avoided them. Whoever remained in the house, Rachel didn't want to be accused of getting in their way. She would be quite happy here, with her quilt, and her book and she rather hoped she would be left entirely alone.

'*You needn't think* I'm staying in all day. You can take us all out to lunch, Leslie. You'd like that, wouldn't you, Mother?' June was furious. By the time she had got down to breakfast everything had been decided. She had been entirely out-manoeuvred, stranded, and left holding the most cumbersome of babies. They were in the drawing room. Les had lit the fire but the wood was damp and it was smoking badly.

'Stuff lunch!' Granny spat. 'You said you'd take me to Turkey and I'm still waiting!' She was knitting something that looked like a string vest.

Les, June and Robert all ignored her. 'We'll see,' Les said, evasively. 'We have to wait in for the shopping.'

'I want to go shopping. Woolworths. Mrs Pellin's green grocers. I need some new suspenders.'

'That lad of theirs can see to it,' cried June. 'I see he's been left behind, and that girl. Wouldn't you just know it? All the weak-minded invalids have been left to our care. But it's only a matter of signing a receipt. Surely they're up that that, between them?'

'It'll all need putting away. She isn't well.'

'Stuff and nonsense. Silly indulgence. It isn't rocket science, Leslie.'

'Where's Mary gone?' Robert asked, timorously. 'We usually have the television on. Can we have the television on? I like *Cash in the Attic.*'

'There isn't one in here, Robert,' June snapped. 'Mary's *out.* She's gone *out.* They *all* have,' June folded her arms crossly. 'But we can go out as well, if we want,' her voice switched from sulk to silk, 'a nice pub lunch. You'd like that, Robert, wouldn't you? A nice steak? A pint of bitter?'

'I don't know. What does Mary think?'

June sighed. 'Quite plainly she thinks she can dump on me from a great height. Well, we'll see about that.'

'Don't you blame Mary! This is your mess, fair and square.' Les turned the page of his newspaper. 'City are playing Spurs on Tuesday. Should be an interesting match,' he commented, to no one in particular.

'I don't think I could manage turkey, after all. I haven't got my teeth in. Fish, maybe. They taste funny. And my bottom stings.' Granny wriggled petulantly in her seat, in a way that was not very lady-like.

'Mother! Please!' June snapped. She got up from her seat and approached the fire. 'Oh really, Leslie. Can't you do something with this fire? This is intolerable.'

Roger, on the hearth rug, curled his lip, revealing yellow teeth and black gums.

Les did not lower his paper. 'Anyway, there's the dog. I told Muriel I'd look after him.'

'It would be just like you to put her and that smelly old cur of hers before your own wife! I'm sure he's dangerous. We ought to lock him away.'

'Don't lock me away!' Robert said, tremulously. He looked like he might cry.

'I need the toilet,' Granny announced. 'I think it might be too late. I told you I'd need one of those pads.'

'Oh for God's sake!'

'*Uncle Bob? I* was going to ask you...' Bob was helping Ben put on his life-jacket. Bob was squatting in front of him, one knee on the ground, a cigarette dangling from his bottom lip.

'Mmmm?'

'What's it like, you know, being famous?'

Bob's arrival at the outdoor pursuits centre had caused something of a stir. The receptionist had done a classic double-take as they had entered the foyer. A pack of scouts had hardly been able to contain their excitement as the news that Bob Dewar, the *actual* Bob Dewar, was here, at the centre. The instructor assigned to their little party had struggled to behave as normal, giving them their safety instructions, talking them through the equipment, demonstrating correct paddle-handling, but he was plainly thrilled to have been given their group. Two women had asked for Bob's autograph. One of them said she had every *WillyNilly* album and had been to see them perform fourteen times in her younger days. 'I'm absolutely your biggest fan,' she had giggled.

'Well,' Bob zipped up Ben's jacket and snapped the clips into place, 'it's hard to say. Famous is only on the outside, you know.' He stood up. 'There, that's you done. Will you help me with mine, now?'

'Yes.' Ben gave serious attention to Bob's jacket zip. 'I was wondering.... can I play you my Mazurka, later? And, will you show me how to write music?'

'Sure. We can write something together, if you like. I've had a few bars in my brain cell for a day or two, now.' He peeled the damp cigarette from his lip. 'It goes like this,' he whistled, quietly.

Ben hummed the phrase back to him, 'Like that? Oh yes, please. Can, I? Really?'

'Sure. How are you with lyrics? It's those that stump me, usually.'

'I don't know. I could try.'

Bob took the last pull from his cigarette and ground the butt under his heel, then wound his hair through an elastic band into a ponytail. 'Now then, make sure those straps are tight. I don't want to get wet when we do one of those arctic rolls.'

'*Arctic* rolls! You mean *Eskimo!*' Ben chuckled.

'Well. I knew it was something cold!'

Rob met June and Granny in the hallway. He was on his way to the kitchen in search of food. His heart drooped when he saw them, emerging from the downstairs cloakroom.

'Here's your father, rolling in from the pub,' sneered Granny, pointing a gnarled finger in his direction.

'Don't start that again,' Rob scowled.

'He once threatened to kill me, you know,' Granny said, with surprising brightness.

'I'm not surprised,' June muttered. 'Oh Rob. If there's a Tesco delivery, you can see to it, can't you?'

'I suppose so. What is it?'

'Food. Only we want to go out.' Rob shrugged. 'Your cousin will help you. She'll know where to put things, the freezer, fridge and so on.'

'Whatever.'

Rob proceeded towards the baize door, but an after-thought made him say;

'June. Which cousin is it?'

June bridled, wanting to correct his appellation to a more formal 'aunty' but decided, since she did need a favour from him, she would let it go. 'Well, frankly, I'm not sure that she counts as a cousin at all. The one who fell over yesterday.'

'Rachel?

'Yes, that one.'

James and Belinda walked slowly around the formal gardens. The display of salvias was quite breath-taking. Spikes of indigo, pinkish blue fronds, clusters of purple and palest lilac made an ultra-violet haze in the weak autumn sun which filtered through the high clouds. Small plant labels explained the plants' provenances and culinary uses. Mary, a pace or two behind them, bent and read them carefully. Muriel, not a gardener, really, contented herself with the occasional exclamation; 'Oh that's a pretty one!' and 'very nice!'

The gardens sloped down to an ornamental lake. Beyond that, rising up a dappled hillside, an avenue of lime trees lead the eye to a massive stone mausoleum, built by a former aristocratic resident to house the remains of his dearly loved and tragically lost wife.

'Imagine someone loving you enough for that,' Belinda mused, gazing at the imposing testament to love and loss.

'Can you?' James followed her gaze, and her train of thought, in that intuitive way he had.

'Imagine anyone loving me enough for it? Oh no. Not me. And anyway, love like that isn't an ordinary thing. I doubt one person in a thousand experiences it.'

'And what do you, I and the other nine hundred and ninety seven people experience?' He pulled her arm through his and they wandered along one of the formal beds. Belinda felt something rising up inside her, like a tide.

'We settle, we compromise, we make excuses.'

'Because we haven't found the right person. It isn't,' he turned to her, to emphasise his point, 'it *isn't* because we can't inspire that kind of love. It isn't because we aren't, intrinsically, lovable.'

Belinda allowed herself to be held by his eyes for a moment, doubtfully.

'Look at that little white flower over there, behind that shrub,' James pointed. 'It's lovely, isn't it?'

'Yes,' Belinda agreed, thinking he had changed the subject. 'What is it? Phlox?'

'I don't know. The point is; if we hadn't seen it, or stopped to appreciate it, would that have made it less beautiful?'

'No, I suppose not.'

'Our failing to appreciate it would have reflected on *us*, not on the flower. See?'

Belinda nodded, understanding. 'But, the thing is, you could wait forever, to be seen, to be recognised, by that special someone. They might never find you, or they might find you and then circumstances might conspire for you to lose them...' she looked over her shoulder, at Muriel, and she thought of Simon, and of herself, 'Or..... perhaps, to make them unattainable. It sounds very splendid and romantic, but in the end, you'd just spend your whole life – like that flower – in the shadows, being lonely.'

James gave a sad smile and they walked on for a few paces. 'We do accept substitutes – and pale imitations they are too, sometimes. But we mustn't beat ourselves up for being human.'

They ambled for a time, without words. Presently James spoke again. 'That feeling, I'm sure you know; it isn't romantic. It's deeper. It transcends romance and passion. It's almost spiritual.'

'Does it have a name?' Belinda asked, after a few moments.

'This relation? Between people? I'm not sure. I've heard of people talking about being 'connected', soul-mates, as though they're part of the same being. That's how Ruth talks about April. Ruth said they were *kindred*.'

'Isn't that like family?'

James laughed; 'and what's *that* like?'

'I hardly know. I thought I did, before this week. I thought it was security and belonging – all good things. But now it feels like obligation…..'

'Because of June?'

'Because of all kinds of things.' She had Elliot's behaviour in her mind, and her obligation to put up with it. But there was nothing *kindred* in that relationship.

'Kin is family, isn't it,' James pursued his line of thought, 'and kindred must be an extension of it, possibly. I think kin is blood and bone and genes, and history and tradition, and habit. But yes, as you say, it has issues like loyalty and duty wrapped up in it. But kindred, or what Ruth means by it, goes further than that. It's a kind of affinity, a closeness based on something other than blood. It's spirit, and intuition, and a sort of subliminal correlation.'

'It sounds very powerful,' Belinda mused. 'I wonder,' she stopped for a moment, 'I wonder which is stronger?'

'Oh goodness. I hope it never gets put to the test.'

Rob had showered and got changed into clean clothes. He carried two mugs of tea into the games room, their handles clutched together in one hand; one of the mugs had slipped and was pressing onto his knuckles. It was hot, and in his hurry to put the mugs down on the table, he slopped some tea onto the wooden floor. In his other hand he had a plate with two slices of chocolate cake.

'Shit,' he said, under his breath, and wiped at the floor with his foot, allowing his sock to soak up the tea. Then he smiled at Rachel. 'Hello,' he said, brightly. 'Here you are! I've been looking all over for you. I brought us tea and cake.' Rachel was stunned. She hardly recognised the person before her. Dressed, washed, smiling, and acknowledging her existence. She folded the corner of her page down to mark her place, and wriggled herself up into a sitting position, before holding her hands out for the cake.

'Gosh, Rob. That's nice of you,' she stammered.

'I *can* be nice,' he laughed, sitting on the opposite end of her settee. 'This sock's wet now.' He peeled it off and laughed at himself, 'Mum used to sing me a song about that,' he said, wiggling his toes. They were, Rachel noted, very elongated, and the nails needed cutting.

Diddle diddle dumpling, my son John
Went to bed with his trousers on.
One sock off and one sock on
Diddle diddle dumpling, my son John.'

Rachel smiled, and took a tentative bite of the cake; a small bite, and wiped her mouth with her fingers to make sure there were no crumbs.

'Did your Mum sing nursery rhymes to you?' Rob took a slurp of his tea.

Rachel swallowed cake and ran her tongue round her teeth to make sure there was no cake stuck to them. 'Well. No. Not my Mum –

my real Mum – she isn't well, you know. My Dad looked after me when I was a baby. *He* sang rhymes, lots of them. He made some up.'

'Do you ever see your Mum?'

'No. There's no point. She has a kind of dementia. She wouldn't know who I am.'

Rob reached for his cake. 'I never think about you as not being one of us – a real McKay, I mean.'

'Don't you?' Rachel left unspoken her sense of being entirely alien.

'This cake is alright. I don't know why there was so much fuss about a new one, yesterday.'

Rachel made a moue. 'Aunty Muriel's dog ate it, in the end.'

Rob grinned. 'Yes. In all the uproar. I must say: I thought you hurling yourself at the kitchen table was a bit over the top, as a diversionary tactic, I mean. I wouldn't have actually murdered Ellie, you know! What's that you're reading?'

Rachel showed him the book. His anger and violence the previous day had shocked her. It had seemed irrevocable and final at the time; something which could never be repaired, a wound which would never heal. 'Ellie lent it to me.'

'I've seen the film. I took a girl – she wanted to go, it wasn't my kind of thing. But the scrap at the end was pretty good.'

'There's a scrap?'

'Oh yes. But don't let me spoil it for you if you haven't seen the film. Sorry. I just assumed you would have done.'

'Oh no. I think it's a 15, isn't it?'

'And aren't you, yet?'

'No, not till December.'

'You should have gone. You would have got in. You look fifteen, at least.'

There was a kind of explosion of pleasure inside Rachel, at his compliment. It rippled like a physical tremor across the strings of her heart. She sipped her tea, thinking, even as she did so, that a trill of pure joy might sound from her throat through her parted lips. The tea was like nectar - he had even remembered the sugar. 'It isn't allowed, though,' she said, quietly, making a desperate clutch at reality.

Rob shrugged. What was 'allowed' or 'not allowed' played absolutely no part in anything he did. 'My feet are cold now. Can I put them under your quilt?' Rachel nodded, and moved her legs across. Rob slid his legs under her quilt and allowed them to lean comfortably against hers. 'You're hogging all the cushions! Pass me a couple.' He thumped them into submission and stuffed them behind him. 'This is cosy,' he said.

Starlight was larded with clay. She had made a gloopy puddle on the wheel and was slapping it with the flat of her hand, sending grey splashes everywhere. She sat on Heather's knee. They were both swathed in capacious aprons but their bare arms, starkly in contrast, one fair and freckled, the other like glossy dark chocolate, were elbow deep in mud; their faces and hair were spattered. They were both in their element.

'Clever girl! Clever girl!' Heather encouraged. 'Splat splat splat! Isn't that a lovely sound?' Starlight chortled and beamed. The potter kept giving them sidelong glances from the kiln, where she was removing fired pots.

Miriam had had no success at the potter's wheel. Her ewer, an ambitious project, had collapsed and she had stamped off in a huff to get cleaned up and find a coffee. Ruth had made a passable plate, a bit wonky but at least recognisable. She had gone outside to collect leaves and sticks. She wanted to make impressions in the clay which she could paint. Ellie and Tansy were at the painting table. They had both made bowls; Ellie's was a bit squashed at one side, and rather thick, heavy and ugly. 'Rustic' the potter had commented, judiciously. Tansy's was quite symmetrical, and she had managed to get the edge fine and smooth. Recognising a deft hand, the potter had shown Tansy how to use the wheel and a tapered stick to make decorative ridges around the outside of her pot. Regarding her own, Ellie remarked, with some perspicacity, that Starlight could have made it. 'I don't think I'll even bother to paint it,' she said.

It was the first time they had been alone since the previous evening. 'You were very upset last night,' Tansy said, her head low over her pot. 'I heard you crying. I didn't know what to do, if you'd rather be left alone. And I didn't want to wake Rachel.'

'Yes.' Ellie threw down her etching tool. 'I don't know what it is about me and birthdays. They're always a disaster. I dread them.'

'Did Rob get you into trouble?'

393

'He tried! Oh God, he suggested....well, I can't say, but it was just awful.'

'Has Caro told him your....secret?'

'Oh yes, I'm sure she has. But he didn't mention that. This was something else. Something he'd done and then tried to blame on me.'

Tansy had whittled a delicate stem into the inside of her pot. Under her hand, now, it grew leaves and sprouted flowers. 'Had he done it on purpose, do you think?'

Ellie considered. 'No, I think he'd done something stupid, been careless and got caught out. He tried to shift the blame onto me. He always did, when we were children. I should be used to it by now. You know,' she put her head on one side, regarding Tansy's work, 'that's really lovely, Tansy.'

'Thanks.' Tansy sat back and looked at it critically. 'I love doing anything like this. Mum and I used to make things together; salt-dough models, origami, things with lentils and pasta. Perhaps Rob didn't really want to get you in to trouble at all. Perhaps, as you say, he'd got himself into a mess and was trying to wriggle out of it. I'm not saying that was right, but...'

'No. I wriggled him out of it in the end. I thought of an alternative explanation for.... the thing... one which let him off the hook.'

Tansy applied herself to her pot again, adding a bunch of berries to her trailing vine. Presently she said; 'either way, sounds like it could have been worse.'

'What do you mean?' Ellie was using the etching tool to pick clay from underneath her fingernails.

'Well. Suppose he knows your 'secret', he didn't tell it, did he? That makes me think that he doesn't want to. Or, that he doesn't know it at all. You know what it's like when you're in trouble. You think of the first thing to defend yourself, there isn't time to think up complicated stories. Telling about you would have been the most normal thing to do, I think, anyway. So either he doesn't want to tell, or he doesn't know anything to tell.'

'Hmmm,' said Ellie.

Les eventually agreed to take them out for a drive. June was like a caged lion, Robert querulous and flustered, Granny as mad as a hatter. He put his head into the games room.

'You're sure you'll manage the Tesco thing?' he asked. Rob and Rachel were watching a film. They had drawn the curtains across the windows and were snuggled under a quilt. 'I feel bad. I promised your mother. But your Granddad's very unsettled. I think a drive might soothe him.'

'Yeah, yeah! Don't worry,' Rob waved his hand, dismissing them.

'I've put Muriel's dog in her room. He'll be fine in there.'

Rob waved again.

'What's the Tesco thing?' Rachel asked when he had gone.

Rob shrugged. 'Some delivery. When they've gone, shall we have a drink?'

'More tea?'

Rob snorted. 'To hell with tea!'

The boys thrashed around in the shallows of the lake. Simon and Todd spent a good deal of time going round in circles. Simon, in the stern, shouted 'left, right, left, right' to try and get them into a rhythm, but it was clear after a while that Todd had no idea which was which. Bob paddled alongside them and tied a piece of string around one of Todd's wrists.

'String, no-string,' he said, pointing to each of Todd's hands in turn.

After that they got on much better, and the instructor soon sent them up a course of buoys which bobbed about twenty metres from the shore. Simon could be heard yelling 'String! No string!' right across the lake.

Toby and Ben made a poor start. The canoe was bigger and more unwieldy than either of them had anticipated. They had struggled to carry it between them the couple of hundred yards from the boathouse to the shore. Toby had slipped climbing into the canoe and his trainers were soaking. He quailed to think what Miriam might say when she found out. The canoe rocked alarmingly when either of them made any sudden movements. Ben, in the bows, gripped the gunwales, white round the gills. Toby felt clumsy and embarrassed, and angry. Ben's whingeing was beginning to annoy him.

'Perhaps you should have gone potting with the girls,' he said, nastily.

Ben made a lunge for his paddle but it slid into the water and the instructor had to retrieve it.

'For fuck's sake,' Toby said, under his breath. The expletive shocked Ben and he felt tenser than ever.

Out on the water, a bunch of scouts about Toby's age were having a whale of a time. They had got their canoes alongside each other and were taking it in turns to walk across the bows. Toby kept throwing them envious glances.

Bob paddled up to them.

'Alright, lads?'

'No,' Ben said, his voice high. 'It's too wobbly. I don't like it.'

'What's the worst that could happen?' Bob said, soothingly. 'You could fall out and get wet.' He dipped his paddle into the water. It was about three feet deep. 'Look, you wouldn't drown, you have your life jacket, and we brought spare clothes.'

Just then one of the scouts fell into the water. There was a whoop of laughter. Two others jumped in deliberately. 'Look,' Bob said, 'they're not bothered. Try and relax.' With his encouragement, they made their way slowly up the course.

It turned out that Bob was extremely competent in a kayak. Their instructor mentioned it specifically.

'Did quite a bit in the Rockies, one year,' Bob said.

The cloud lifted part way through the afternoon and Elliot and Mitch played their round of golf in pleasant, watery sunshine, chilled by a stiff breeze. It was clear from the off that Mitch, in spite of his youth, was an accomplished player. Elliot fussed with his clubs and his gloves, prevaricated over tees and complained about the greens. He lost a ball in the rough on the third and another in the water on the seventh. He fluffed an easy putt on the eighth. The course was wet, still soaked from the heavy rain of Saturday night and Sunday. Caddying was heavy going. By the twelfth hole, Mitch was a good number of shots ahead of him.

'I'm afraid I'm not giving you a very good game. These hired clubs are useless,' Elliot muttered.

'Don't worry about it,' Mitch shrugged.

'Patronising little oik,' Elliot fumed, under his breath.

The Tesco van arrived early in the afternoon. Rob stopped the film and he and Rachel unpacked the twenty or so carrier bags, begrudgingly carried to the kitchen by the delivery man. He was especially vociferous about the driveway; 'a positive hazard,' he said, 'full of pot holes, steep and slippery.' When he had gone, Rob and Rachel restocked the fridge and put dried and tinned goods into the storeroom. Rachel was intensely self-conscious, in her pyjamas, thinking that she probably ought to go and get dressed, but didn't want her disappearance to be misinterpreted. But Rob seemed oblivious. He laughed and joked as they sorted the shopping. His nearness made her abdomen clutch at feathers.

When the shopping was away, Rob brought them orange juice, heavily laced with vodka.

'I'm sure this isn't allowed,' said Rachel, but sensing in herself a shift about what 'wasn't allowed', from fear to fascination. She sipped gingerly. 'Oh,' she cried, 'it doesn't really taste of anything!'

'I hardly put any in yours,' Rob said, untruthfully. 'I've been left in charge and I say it's allowed. It'll settle your tummy.' Rachel's tummy flipped, at the thought of him thinking of it. 'Open the crisps. Don't you drink, at home?'

Rachel shook her head. '*I* don't. Mum and Dad have wine. Mum makes it. It's horrible.'

'But when you're out with your mates, at parties and things, you don't drink?'

Rachel shook her head again. She was never invited to parties. 'Shall we finish the film?'

'Do you want to?' Rob asked. 'I thought that maybe it was getting a bit gory.' Certainly the film had been the most blood-thirsty thing Rachel had ever seen. People had been tortured and maimed, savaged by tigers, pushed off cliffs, drowned, burned, gouged, speared, slashed, stabbed and hacked.

'Well, it *is* a bit gory,' Rachel put her drink down on the table. 'But if you want to see the end...'

'Oh! I've seen it a dozen times. There's a huge battle at the end; total carnage. We can just chat, if you like. Ellie drinks like a fish, given the chance. She got herself in trouble on holiday.'

'She told us.'

'*Did* she? Been getting quite pally, have you, you girls?'

'Well....' Rachel drank some more of her juice, and helped herself to a crisp. Her tummy was beginning to feel warm and delicious. 'Actually what she did tell us was that you offered to sort that creepy waiter out for her. I thought that was very,' she searched for the word, rejecting 'heroic' as being too transparent, 'nice and brotherly of you.'

Rob shrugged. 'I would have done. She *is* my sister, after all.'

'You don't seem to like each other very much.'

'What has that got to do with it? Do you have to like your sister? It doesn't make any difference whether I like her or not. She's still my sister.'

'Do you mean you feel responsible for her?'

'I was always *made* to feel responsible,' Rob mimicked his mother, *"Look after your sister, Rob, you're the big boy."* She can be a pain. She wraps Mum and Dad round her little fingers, it's always 'poor Ellie,' like she's helpless or something. But,' he sighed, 'I'm stuck with her. I don't have any choice in the matter.'

Rachel took a tentative step towards the nub of the matter. 'You'd never do anything to hurt her? Or to get her into trouble?'

'God no,' Rob stretched his arms above his head and yawned, widely. 'Not really. I tease her a lot,' he said, through his yawn. 'She's easy to wind up. We shout and scream at each other. Like yesterday. But it's only noise. It doesn't mean anything.'

401

Les found an out-of-town shopping complex. There was a DIY warehouse, a garden centre, an electrical store and a supermarket with a cafeteria. They wandered around the supermarket for a while on a fruitless search for suspenders, then, between them, Les and June managed to get Granny and Robert shuffled into a corner table of the cafeteria. Les bought sandwiches, cake and tea, precariously balanced on a tray.

'This isn't what I had in mind at all,' June complained, eyeing the cellophane-wrapped goods disdainfully.

Granny wriggled on her seat. 'My bottom stings!' she said, irritably, in a voice which carried to neighbouring tables. A security guard approached their table.

'Excuse me, madam,' he said, addressing Granny. 'I'll have to ask you to accompany me to the manager's office. I have reason to believe you have goods about your person which have not been paid for.'

'Oh for God's sake, mother!'

The pottery was part of an arts-and-crafts co-operative housed in some converted farm buildings comprising a wood-turners, a glass workshop, a quilting studio, a gourmet *chocolatier*, a candle-making studio, a jewellery workshop and a man who made interesting things out of driftwood. Miriam wandered from one to the other, watching groups try their hands at the different disciplines, lone artists absorbed in their work. She felt peripheral and restless. It was beginning to be a habitual feeling for her, recently. She was finding the family milieu quite a burden, the incomprehensible chords of tribal history underscored by dissonant strains of tension and resentment. She was fond of Simon and had taken on his children to a certain practical if not emotional extent; they were part of his packaging. She quite enjoyed time spent with Heather and Bob, especially away from the children. But she was beginning to feel her anomalous status; she wasn't family in any sense, legal or natural; she wasn't a wife or a daughter or a mother, an aunty or a sister or a cousin, she wasn't even an in-law. Like Mitch, like Rachel, and like Starlight, like poor old Mr Burgess, she had no official position at all and didn't really belong.

The girls met up in the gift shop and café, housed in a stone barn. The café was upstairs, in what had presumably been, at one time, the hayloft. It was thronged with half-term holiday-makers. They trooped up the stairs to find a table, but had to hover for a while until one became vacant. Eventually Ruth grabbed one when it was vacated by a group of Japanese tourists. Ellie and Tansy eyed the tourists' debris with disgust.

'Don't be silly, girls,' Ruth said briskly, marshalling dirty plates and wiping the table with a spare napkin.

Miriam and Heather queued for food and drinks. 'Let's just get a selection shall we?' Heather said, stacking a tray. 'It's all going well, isn't it? Everyone's enjoying it, even Ruth. What do you think? Tea? Coffee?'

'Oh I don't know,' Miriam sighed. She would have preferred somewhere quieter, quainter. All the food was pre-packaged and mass-produced, non-organic, and looked very unappetising. The staff was barely coping with the rush of customers. There was squashed food on the floor, too many noisy children and the queue for the Ladies was snaking out of the door and around the tables. The door was open and she could smell the warm, womanish waft from within.

Below them, in the gift shop, there was a crash as a quantity of fragile, expensive glass ornaments were swept from a display shelf by an unsupervised black toddler.

Rachel felt relaxed and languorous. Rob had brought them more drinks.

'I'm sure I oughtn't to,' she had said.

'Oh go on,' he had laughed. 'Let your hair down.' He flung himself onto the opposite end of her settee, sliding his legs under her quilt. She wished he had got in beside her, put his arm around her; suddenly, anything seemed possible. It was like a dream, so easy and inexorable, requiring no effort on her part at all. His legs felt heavy and comfortable against hers. He had put some music on; it wasn't the violent, aggressive music he had been playing in the study; a woman with a voice like caramel sang to a mellow guitar. 'This is one of the albums Bob's produced,' Rob said. 'I like it. But don't tell anyone. It wouldn't do my street cred any good at all if it was to get out.'

Rachel smiled. 'Don't worry,' she said, lethargically, 'I'm good at keeping secrets.

Under the quilt, he reached for her bare foot, and rubbed it, absent-mindedly. He threw his head back against the cushion. 'Wow!' he breathed. 'I'm wasted, are you?'

'Mmmm.' Rachel nodded, dreamily. 'I think I am.'

The canoe instructor guided his party around the shores of the lake and into a narrow inlet, overhung by rocky cliffs and precariously clinging trees. The day had turned quite sunny, and here, in the cove, they were protected from the brisk breeze which was combing the surface of the silvery lake surface into shining peaks. Toby and Ben had become quite competent at paddling and steering their canoe. They had raced Simon and Todd up a course of buoys and beaten them to the finish quite easily. Disillusioned, Todd had given up with his paddle and leaned over the side of the canoe looking for fish and treasure while Simon rowed. Bob had paddled out into the lake and engraved easy lines through the water with deft, strong strokes.

'Look Daddy!' Todd shouted, pointing into the water at some dully glinting pebbles, 'I can see gold.'

'Wow, son. That's great. Just great!'

'*Just great!*' Toby sneered, under his breath.

Now the instructor pointed out a tiny shingled beach and a narrow path leading out to a high rocky promontory at the mouth of the cove.

'The water there is very deep,' he said. 'You can jump off that rock and your feet won't touch the bottom. Anyone want to try?'

In the end, they all did. Simon, first, had hurled himself off the rock, emerging gasping and splashing only moments later. Toby had gone next, making a blood-curdling yell that he hoped all the scouts would hear as they pulled their canoes onto the shore. Bob and Ben followed; they leapt from the rock hand in hand.

Finally, after tears and much encouragement, Simon and Todd jumped together, Todd's sharp cry of fear as his father leapt with him in his arms turning to yells of pleasure as they bobbed quickly to the surface in the cold water.

'That's the kind of thing you'll remember when you're old men, lads,' Bob had said, sagely, as they'd paddled back to the shore. 'The kind of memory money can't buy.'

The instructor let them use the staff showers; it didn't seem right to ask Bob Dewar to shower with a pack of scouts. The boys went in first while Simon and Bob stripped off their wet clothes.

'I've been meaning to talk to you, Bob,' Simon said, a little awkwardly, stuffing the boys' wet things into carrier bags.

'Oh yes?'

'Not just now, but later?'

'Whenever. What's up?'

Simon sighed. 'Nothing specific. Family stuff. Just want your opinion, really.'

'O oh! Dangerous waters for a non-McKay, really.'

'I know. Strictly 'without prejudice', you know.'

'Fair enough. After supper, perhaps?'

'Thanks.'

The rooms of the house were sumptuously decorated and furnished. Each piece and painting carefully labelled and described. Belinda passed from room to room, borne on a diaphanous carpet of happiness. Even as she examined and read and exclaimed, she went over and over the things James had said to her; affirming, encouraging things which had fed her soul like spring water in a parched land. She felt just like that sole white flower at the back of the border, suddenly seen and appreciated, recognised, named at last. Belinda felt as though she had been woken up, like a princess after a hundred years of sleeping; or like a prisoner released into the light, after a lifetime in semi-darkness.

Suddenly Mary was beside her; she seemed to sense Belinda's mood, and to share it. In her face, Belinda saw reflected all her own wondering delight and new found amazement. It was as though a mask of responsibility and anxiety had been lifted away from her.

'Isn't this *lovely,*' Mary smiled, taking her daughter's arm. 'I feel so free!'

James and Muriel joined them from the library, where they had been examining an enormous embroidered family tree which displayed the relationship of the aristocrat whose seat Hunting-in-the-Forest had been, to the royal family.

'I think it might be time for a cup of tea. Don't you?'

They ate scones and jam in the tea shop. James made them all laugh by making them pronounce 'scone'. The McKay women pronounced scone as though it rhymed with 'stone', whereas he said it as though it rhymed with 'gone'. They each insisted, with an inverse snobbishness, that the other pronunciation was 'posh'.

'If only,' James laughed, pouring more tea, 'if only we could hear Her Majesty say it, just once, then we'd all know.'

'We'd better ask Granny,' Belinda quipped, happily. 'She will have heard the queen say 'scone' a hundred times!'

Mary stirred her tea, thoughtfully. 'You know,' she said, dabbing her mouth with a napkin, 'today has been a real tonic for me. And it's made me realise something I've been wondering about for a while now.' She looked around the table.

'What is it, Mum?'

'It'll need talking about, and lots of thought,' Mary preambled, 'and maybe this week we can all have a think about it. But the fact is,' she paused, and rummaged in her handbag for a handkerchief to wipe away the tear which glistened at the corner of her eye.

'Oh Mum!' Belinda cried, 'what's the matter?'

'Well, the fact is, I just don't think I can cope with your father for much longer. I hate to say it, but he's just getting too much for me.'

'Oh Mum,' Belinda took Mary's hand, all concern, 'we don't help you enough.'

Mary shook her head. 'You all have your own lives, your own families. You do what you can; especially you, Belinda, do more than anyone.'

'I'd be happy....happy,' Muriel began, but Mary stopped her.

'Neither of us is getting any younger, Muriel.' They were in fact the same age.

James rested his elbows on the table. 'What do you have in mind, Mary? Anything specific at this stage?'

Mary nodded. 'I have wondered about The Oaks.'

Belinda had been thinking about home-help, meals on wheels, day-centres, not full time residential care. 'The Oaks?'

'Oh goodness,' Muriel gasped. 'Isn't that very expensive?'

'Yes, Muriel, it is,' Mary looked at Belinda and James. 'That's why I need the whole family to agree. I know that some of you are

409

better placed financially than others, and The Oaks will make a big hole in your inheritance.'

The word dropped like a corpse onto the tea table. Belinda felt her bubble of happiness burst. If there was any word calculated to divide families, it was 'inheritance.'

Mitch drove Elliot's car home. They had spent an hour on the nineteenth and Elliot had had two double scotches. He had been beaten hollow at golf and was a poor loser. He had paid their green fees and for the drinks with very bad grace. Frankly he was embarrassed to be seen in the clubhouse with Mitch, who was, Elliot considered, inappropriately dressed for such a venue – in denim, and without a stitch of lambs' wool, let alone cashmere. Plus they had been given some sidelong glances by the members, leaping, no doubt, to unsavoury conclusions on the nature of their unequal relationship.

But the day, bad as it had been, deteriorated further when, emerging from the bar, Elliot switched his phone on and it emitted a series of bleeps; he found he had missed a dozen calls. He just caught Carol leaving the office. She was besides herself with anxiety. She had done the quotations he had asked for, a number of them for existing clients and some for new ones, including a very big pan-European prospect. She had copied and pasted the figures from his spreadsheet. But she feared some error; the bottom lines were too low. But he had been so insistent that the quotations should go out in today's post, she hadn't known what to do for the best. There was no-one else to ask, everyone was away on holiday. In the end, she had sent them off, trusting that she, and not he, was in the wrong.

Elliot had her read the figures back to him. He paled; something was seriously amiss. He needed to get home and check the spreadsheet. But oh God, if she was right, he'd under-quoted some massive jobs by thousands of pounds.

Mitch drove in silence. Elliot, in the front seat, was white, and silent.

'*Rachel?*' *Rachel opened* her eyes. Had she been asleep? Rob was looking at her, from the other end of the settee. The room was in semi darkness. The curtains were still closed from when they had been watching the film and anyway the afternoon was drawing in. She couldn't see his face very clearly, just the outline of his head.

'Yes?'

'I wanted to say, you know, I'm sorry, for what I said that first night.'

She waited, to see if he would say anything else, to convince herself that she was awake, to see if he was teasing her.

'Did you hear me?'

'Yes. I did. I just don't know what to say. It was true, I suppose,' she looked away, into the dark corner of the room, shame shifting inside her again. She felt his hand move against her foot; his palm against her skin. Something else fluttered into life in her belly. The silhouette of his head dropped.

'But I shouldn't have said it. I hoped you might say that it was OK. That we can be friends. It's been nice, hasn't it, today?' She held her breath, his words, inside her like an inhalation of aromatic incense. 'Rachel? Won't you say something?'

'Oh yes! Of course it is, it has. And we can, if you really want to. I'm sorry, it's just that, you see, for someone like me, that is so.....unreal.' Somehow it was easier to talk in the dark. She heard him smile.

'Someone like you?'

Rachel shrugged her mantle of self-deprecation into place. 'No one cares about someone like me,' she said, with forced levity, 'what I think, what I feel. I don't...' she groped for the word, and when it came to her, she found it was accompanied by the threat of tears, '....I don't *fit*.' Perhaps he heard the threat too as it caught in her throat.

Rob moved up the settee towards her. She could feel his warmth, his breath, see the glint of light in his eyes. He smelled like a man; spice overlaying musk. His voice, when he spoke, was low, concerned.

'What do you mean?'

Her voice too dropped to a whisper. 'Well, I mean, for a start, physically,' involuntarily, one hand moved to her abdomen, the roundness of her tummy, the folds of flesh underneath her pyjama and the quilt. The other touched her round face, the side away from the bruises and sterastrips, not wounded, but none the less ugly. 'I'm not what you're meant to be.' Rob made a noise with his mouth, like a tut, but without a hint of exasperation. 'And here, in this family, I don't fit in. I don't belong. Not really.'

'You do.'

'No. We were talking about it yesterday in the kitchen. When you're family, I mean, really related, then you're loved no matter what. It isn't a choice. Like you were saying earlier about Ellie. It hasn't anything to do with whether you *like* Ellie. You *love* her. Full stop. She's your sister and that's that. Blood is thicker than water.'

'*Yours* is. It took Mitch ages to clean it up!'

'Very funny. But you see, I'm not family. So I'm not loved no matter what. I have to earn it, like friendship and trust. It's a gradual thing. We talked about putting it to the test, telling secrets and seeing if we could keep them.'

'Secrets?'

'Yes.'

'So you all told each other secrets?'

'No. Well, Ellie did, later.'

She could see Rob nodding. 'Well, that will be alright. You're good at keeping secrets. You told me so. They'll soon find out what a friend you are.'

'That friend of Ellie's; Caro? She's no friend at all, is she? She told Ellie's secret.'

Rob moved his head; the slightest nod. 'Mmmm.'

'And Ellie's very worried about it. But you see, that's because she hasn't understood about family, that you'd never use it to hurt her, because she's your sister. She cried last night. I heard her.'

Rob reached for her hand, which was lying on the quilt. His breath, like hers, was quick and shallow. For a heady moment Rachel thought that he might kiss her. His lips were so close that she could see the glint of their moistness in the small light which filtered in from the gallery. 'Did she? Maybe you could help?'

Rachel was aware of talking too quickly, of words spilling out of her mouth, half willing them to go on forever to put off the kiss, half wishing she could stop them up, to hasten its beginning. 'I'd like to. I thought that to myself, yesterday. That I'd like to help. It was upsetting, seeing you two fighting like that...' Rob nodded again, as though he felt the shame of it. He was scarcely breathing. The closer he leaned to her the faster the words flowed out, as though he were a magnet drawing them out of her, until she wondered if he would have to stop them with his mouth, or if his mouth on hers would simply make a siphon, extracting them from her brain and implanting them on his, so that speech between them became unnecessary and he would always instinctively know whatever she was thinking and feeling '...I wanted to do something which would make it stop. I imagined me doing it, and you and Ellie being grateful and glad, and loving me for it. And the most ridiculous thing is,' Rachel concluded at last spilling out the very last thing she had to say on the subject, pulling it out by its roots, 'the most ridiculous thing of all is that it isn't even true!'

Rob's head jerked. 'It isn't true?'

'No! Ellie made the whole thing up! She never had an affair with that teacher at all!'

Rob's surprise made his voice catch in his throat. 'An aff.....? Which...... which teacher?'

'I can't remember now.... Philip? I think she called him Philip. A student-teacher. But it doesn't matter, does it?'

'No, no I don't suppose so.' Rob was shaking. At first Rachel thought he was crying, or angry. But then he started to laugh.

The atmosphere in the car was as angry as an ulcer. Ruth and Heather had begun to argue on the way across the car park and the close confinement of the jeep had not inhibited them from continuing. Starlight, the hapless cause of the disagreement, had fallen asleep in her car seat almost straight away, oblivious to everything, gobs of clay still sticking to her skin and a small plaster on her leg where a shard of flying glass had cut her. Against the darkness of her skin the plaster looked anaemically pink. Heather had complained to the first-aider because an 'ethnically appropriate' plaster could not be supplied. Ellie and Tansy gave each other looks but said nothing. Miriam, in the back with the buggy and the nappy bag, also remained silent for the most part, looking disconsolately out of the window.

'It isn't the money,' Heather said for the third or fourth time. She had had to pay over three hundred pounds for the broken glass ornaments, 'and it isn't the embarrassment although I *am* glad that Bob wasn't with us, just because you can bet your bottom dollar the press would have been there before you could say *paparazzi* .' She reversed from her parking space and the jeep jolted over the rutted surface of the car park.

'I know you're not bothered about the money, Heather,' said Ruth, snapping her seatbelt into place. 'It's the fact that you're not bothered about it which shocks me. I could feed my family for a month on three hundred pounds. I think you've lost all sense of the value of money. *That's* what I think you should be embarrassed about.'

Heather eased the car between the narrow gateposts of the site and accelerated along the lane. 'Well I'm not. I don't give a stuff about it. Compared to the fact that Starlight could have been seriously injured, scarred for life, what's three hundred pounds? I bet you couldn't put a price on your children; well, not on Ben, anyway. Or perhaps you *could?*'

'What do you mean by that? Take the second left, here.'

'Yes, I know. I can read the signs.'

'Oh! I'm sorry!' Ruth folded the map away in a huff. 'I thought you couldn't navigate.'

'Don't be ridiculous, Ruth! Going home's always different, isn't it? And besides, the motorway's pretty clearly marked. I expect I will need some help when we get onto the small roads.' They sped down a slip road onto a dual carriageway.

'Slow down, Heather. There's a speed camera up here,' Miriam called, from the back seat.

'Perhaps someone else had better drive,' snapped Heather, braking sharply.

'I don't care. But I thought a speeding ticket would just about put the icing on your cake, that's all.'

Heather threw the jeep into third gear. 'I'll tell you what has annoyed me *again*, and it's that this family has *once more* failed in its responsibility to my daughter! Why wasn't someone watching her? For God's sake, I can't be everywhere! I found out about the place, I drove us there, I paid the potter, I queued for the food, I paid for that...'

'Thank you, Aunty Heather,' Tansy said, quietly.

'That's the thing about being a parent,' Ruth said, archly, 'in the end, you're responsible. You can't ever *assume* that someone else is in charge.'

'I just don't accept that!'

'Then you're just not ready to be a parent.'

Heather stepped on the brakes and swerved into a lay-by. She opened the car door and rummaged in the door pocket before slamming it and stalking off. At the end of the lay-by she lit up a cigarette and smoked it, one hand under the other elbow, shaking her head. She stared out across the landscape. Directly in front of her was a hawthorn hedge, leafless, with only a few brown and wizened berries

417

still clinging, and long, cruel thorns. Over the hedge, a brownish, spent pasture, its surface ragged and kicked about by careless, dissatisfied hooves. Past that a river, running fast and brown, and more fields beyond. In the distance, over the sound of the turgid river and the disgruntled wind across the sky, she could hear the roar of cars on the motorway. At her feet, against the kerb and strewn in the verge of the lay-by, litter clung in greyish shreds, rusty cans, a pile of soggy dog-ends emptied from someone's ashtray, ribbons of plastic. She stared morosely at them.

'I always thought the countryside was a clean, wholesome place,' she said to herself, gloomily.

'I didn't know Aunty Heather smoked,' Ellie said.

'I wish I did,' Miriam muttered, darkly.

Ruth scrambled out of the car and marched up to her sister. 'Don't take it personally, Heather. Of course it's an adjustment. None of us is ready to be a parent at first.'

Heather turned her back.

'Oh for goodness' sake!' Ruth circled Heather so that she was in front of her once more, but Heather stared resolutely over her head at the dun fields. 'Look, all I meant was that, well, you've heard the sayings; *'you need eyes in the back of your head,' 'an extra pair of hands,'* – they're all true. But we don't grow them instantly, none of us do.'

'You take the biscuit, Ruth,'

'What do you mean?'

'Handing out advice to the rest of us, as if you don't need help .....'

Ruth sagged, visibly, the wind taken out of her sails. 'I don't mean to imply that I'm the perfect parent...' she muttered, turning and staring, like Heather, across the bleak landscape.

'Good! You certainly aren't. Have you looked at your children recently?'

Ruth reddened. 'It was very kind of you to take Rachel shopping.'

'Kind?' Heather lowered her gaze to look Ruth in the eye. 'That's just it. It wasn't kind; it was family: sharing the load, looking out for one another. Just what *didn't* happen today and on Saturday. Miriam and I did it without thinking. You might be interested to know that it cost us rather more than three hundred pounds on that occasion but it doesn't matter. We did it for you, because we're family, and because we can.' Heather lit another cigarette from the glowing tip of the first. That Rachel had had three hundred pounds spent on her shocked Ruth. She didn't really look that awful did she? Or did she? And how much more she, Ruth, could have got for that amount of money: she could have re-clothed the entire family! But that was the last thing she could say, now, so she only observed; 'I didn't know you smoked.'

'There's a lot you don't know about me.'

There was a pause. Then Ruth said, sullenly; 'Miriam didn't have to spend money on Rachel.' She was aware of uncomfortable indebtedness; it rankled.

'Why?' Heather leapt onto her remark like a dog on a rabbit. 'Because Miriam isn't really family? Or because Rachel isn't? Perhaps that explains why you didn't feel you needed to keep an eye on Starlight today: because *she* isn't really family.'

Ruth shivered. She had left her cardigan in the car. Her eyes began to water; she didn't know if it was the wind or if she was crying. She took off her glasses and smeared a ragged tissue across her eyes.

'To be honest, Heather, I feel so confused about the whole issue. I'm beginning to think it's me who isn't really family.' She turned away and walked slowly back to the car.

'Don't try and make this all about you! This isn't about *you!*' Heather shouted after her, but her voice was snatched away on the wind.

Elliot was yelling into the telephone in the hall. He had managed to get through to the manager of the sorting office where the company mail was taken. The man was being obstructive.

'I tell you I'm the Chair of McKay's Haulage. That mail belongs to me and I want it back. You have no right, *no right* to withhold it from me, do you hear?' The manager explained for the fourth time that all mail, once posted or collected, ceased to be the property of the sender. Elliot wasn't having it. He raised his voice and spoke over the manager, interrupting, drowning him out, his voice like caustic, designed to sear away any resistance. 'Put me on to your supervisor. I want to speak to the organ-grinder, not his fucking monkey......Give me his home number then. I *insist* on speaking to your superior...'

Heather and Miriam stepped into the hall. Heather carried Starlight sleeping in her arms. She motioned urgently to Elliot, indicating the sleeping child, putting a finger to her lips. Elliot turned away from her, dismissing her with an impatient wave of his arm. 'That's outrageous!' he bellowed down the 'phone, his face turning purple, the force of his voice almost lifting his feet from the floor. Starlight awoke with a start, and began to cry.

Rachel was back in bed when the girls arrived home. She had developed a headache and the place between her legs was sore. But what troubled her more than either of these things was a niggling, gnawing anxiety that she had made a grave error. She hadn't – *she hadn't*, she kept reminding herself, betrayed the secret. Rob had *already known* the secret; he had acknowledged as much – hadn't he? Caro was the false friend. All she, Rachel, had done was to uncover the happy truth that Rob would not reveal it or use it in any way that might harm Ellie. So why, *why*, she asked herself, as she cowered under her quilt listening to the approaching footsteps of her two cousins, did she feel reluctant to share this good news with them? Surely Ellie would be delighted, relieved, and so grateful? Wouldn't it *qualify* her, wouldn't it *prove* beyond question that she belonged?

And yet something held her back, something she just couldn't put her finger on, a combination, perhaps, of oddities. First: Rob's sudden and total transformation of character and demeanour; for days he had skulked and frowned and grunted and shrugged, joined in under sufferance, determined, she would almost have said, to make himself as unpopular and disagreeable as possible. And then, today, with her, he had been open and charming and helpful and relaxed. Why? Second: His complete U turn with regard to Ellie; all callousness one day, angry, violent and frightening; all kindness the next, his concern as genuine and irreproachable as a woollen blanket. Why? Then, thirdly, as much as she didn't want to look on it, for fear that observation would tarnish its lustre, there was the fact of his particular and tender attention towards herself. Bringing her drinks, sorting out the DVD and the music, helping with the shopping, the comfortable familiarity of his legs against hers under the quilt, the touch of his hand on her foot, the way he had spoken her name. As precious and breath-taking as these things were to her, and as carefully as she cradled them to herself, it was almost too much, too incredible to hope that they had been inspired by herself alone. Everything in her experience screamed at her that it could not be; nobody, and especially not boys, and above all not boys like Rob took that kind of notice of Rachel.

And finally, now that she considered it, the oddest thing of all was his question, weird beyond anything; 'which teacher?' Why had he needed to ask? Surely, *surely*, Caro would have told him. That question irritated like a splinter, festered like a foreign body, causing all the circumstances around it to inflame and suppurate, infecting her wonderful afternoon, her sense of bonding with Rob, her hopes of proving herself to Ellie, with sepsis. She put her head under the quilt and as the girls entered the room she closed her eyes and feigned sleep. Immediately they lowered their voices, and crept around the room. Rachel breathed in, and caught the lingering scent of Rob. Surreptitiously, she slid her hand under her pillow, and felt the thick, slightly damp material of his sock. She clutched it, tightly.

Elliot had set his laptop up on the kitchen table again and surrounded himself with the same spread of documents and files he had been using on Saturday afternoon. It was as inconvenient as possible; Belinda, in response to Simon's request for 'a simpler meal' was busy making a buffet spread of salads, cheese, slices of cold meats and hard boiled eggs. She had two flans, some garlic baguettes and the remains of the previous night's lasagne in the Aga. She needed the table for the prepared dishes; the worktops were getting cluttered and she was feeling flustered. James pressed a tall gin and tonic into her hand. She took a sip of it; it was just as she liked it, he had smeared the lemon around the rim of the glass before plopping it in with the ice. She smiled at him, gratefully.

'It's more of a stew than a salad day, really,' she said, more levelly than she might have done a moment earlier. 'I do hope this will be alright for everyone after all their exertions.'

Elliot snarled. 'I need to get to the bottom of this if it's the last thing I do.'

Simon was making real mayonnaise in the food processor; a complicated process requiring raw eggs and other ingredients added in a strict sequence. He shouted over the whir of the mixer, 'for God's sake, Elliot! Chill! You look like you're about to bust a blood vessel.'

'I'll be busting something when I find out who's cocked this up,' Elliot muttered, menacingly.

'Whisky, Elliot?' James asked, smoothly, 'ice?' Elliot nodded, scrolling manically through his spreadsheet. Over his head, James and Belinda exchanged a knowing look.

Todd was making a complicated Lego model. He had reluctantly allowed Starlight and Mary access to some of the bricks.

'Don't dribble on them, though,' he had warned, as though either one of them might be as likely to do so as the other. Mitch and Muriel had taken the dogs out for a walk; Roger had not appreciated spending the afternoon cooped up in Muriel's room; he was snappish and disagreeable. Muriel too was a little out of sorts. She had looked forward to telling Les all about her afternoon and especially the delicious tea, and she was put out that he was not at the house. Also, he had promised to look after Roger and she could not imagine what circumstances might have arisen to make him abandon the poor dog.

Heather, Ruth and Miriam had poked the fire in the drawing room into life and had retreated around it, declaring themselves perished to the bone and weary as hell; they had eschewed tea and called for cocktails. Rob was at his computer, still beavering away diligently on his coursework. Toby, excluded, played sullenly on his Gameboy. Of Les, June, Granddad Robert and Granny, there was absolutely no sign.

Ben sat next to Bob on the piano stool, as solemn as a statue. He hardly dared to breathe. It was as though Uncle Bob was an older, wiser version of himself, a version which had received answers to all the questions music asked, explored and conquered the territory which music occupied and was here to show him the map.

Bob pulled the paper and pencil towards them, 'I'm a bit rusty at writing music long-hand! But we'll have go, shall we?' He drew a stave and a curly treble clef. 'Now, I'm suggesting that we go for F major. So that will mean.....' he hesitated his pencil over the beginning of the stave.

'B flat,' Ben whispered, as though reciting a holy word.

'Good lad.' Bob drew it in. 'Can you think of any other tunes in F major?'

Ben nodded, solemnly. 'Beethoven's 6th. And 8th,' he said.

Bob smiled. 'Good. Can you play either of them?' Ben shook his head, sadly. 'No, neither can I. But Beethoven was in good company. Listen to this.' Bob picked out *Happy Birthday to You*, 'That's in F major. So is *Bat out of Hell*, *Hey Jude* and *Yesterday*.' Bob played a phrase from each. 'So if it's good enough for them, I guess it's good enough for us, yes?'

Ben nodded again.

'OK. Now let's write down what we started with,' Bob picked out the phrase he had whistled earlier. An octave below him, Ben followed suit. Bob wrote the melody onto their stave. Then they played it again and again, and let the tune find its way, extending itself a few notes at a time, sometimes Bob, sometimes Ben finding the way.

'It's almost like the tune's singing itself to us,' Ben said, wonderingly, after a while. 'We play something and we know it isn't right, it feels sort of uncomfortable and....itchy. But then we play something else and it feels.....at home.'

Bob turned in his seat to observe his small companion with aged eyes. 'Yes,' he said, 'it's exactly like that.'

'*Ha!*' *Elliot ejaculated,* suddenly. He looked up. Belinda was by the sink, whittling radishes into rosebuds, Simon was carving meat, James was counting cutlery. Muriel, in the easy chair by the Aga, was studying a puzzle book. They all jumped at Elliot's cry; Simon sliced his left index finger with the carving knife.

'Fuck, Elliot!' Simon hissed, his finger in his mouth.

'Look! Here! Here it is! An error in the macro on line forty-five!' Elliot indicated the computer. 'It's cocked up all the totals. It's no wonder the quotes are wrong.'

'Oh good, darling. I'm so glad you've found it,' Belinda said, with forced serenity. 'I knew you would.'

'So am I,' Muriel agreed. She didn't know what a spreadsheet was, or a macro; she supposed it was like a very tricky Sudoku puzzle. 'I made a mistake on my crossword puzzle yesterday. Six across. It stopped everything else from fitting properly. It is very frustrating.'

'It's easy to make mistakes like that,' James placated. 'Especially when you're distracted. Just one wrong keystroke.....'

'But I'd checked them all....' Elliot blustered, 'they were *right...*'

'Well,' James demurred, regretfully, 'clearly not...'

'Perhaps you emailed an earlier version of your document. I've done that,' offered Simon from the sink where he held his finger under the tap.

Elliot stood up. 'No, no. Not possible. *I* didn't get this wrong....' he spoke slowly, as though addressing a group of mental incompetents, 'therefore, clearly.....'

'You think someone interfered.' James finished the sentence off for him. There was a portentous pause.

Simon approached the table, his finger swathed in kitchen roll. 'Are you accusing anyone in particular, Elliot?'

Facing both brothers-in-law across the table, Elliot hesitated, fractionally. It would be easy for them to make out he was over-reacting; he had a habitual tendency to over-egg even quite ordinary things which meant that at times of real crisis his behaviour could easily be dismissed as hysterical. He knew it of himself and occasionally a window of self-knowledge would open through which he regarded his actions with critical helplessness. But this was really serious and he seemed unable to make them see it. Indeed in some ways he didn't want them to see it; it could only reflect badly on him. The consequences of the incorrect quotes were almost incalculable. He had been tendering for some enormous jobs, huge contracts, and while some of his existing customers might be persuaded to accept a re-quote, have a laugh at Elliot's expense over a pricey dinner or a bottle of VSOP, he would lose all credibility with the new, prospective clients if he admitted to them that his quotes were wrong. In so many ways discretion would have been the better part of valour but Elliot had set his foot upon the road and was incapable of U turn.

'I suppose it was one of the children.' Even to himself, his suggestion was lame.

'You can't make such general accusations, Elliot,' Belinda put in, bravely, drying her hands on the tea towel. Her snake of anxiety was back, coiling itself around her innards, making her breath come in shallow draughts. But the quiet conversations she had had with James, the gentle way Simon had ensured that she got a day out of the kitchen today, somehow gave her the confidence and balance she needed.

Elliot was beginning to feel cornered. In fact to a certain extent he was literally trapped, between the long bench and the table. Already on his feet, he needed to move, to pace, to wave his arms around, but the wires of the laptop and his files of papers and the encroaching buffet dishes all impeded his way. Physically restrained, his only option was to pick on the weakest member of the opposition. 'The computer was in here all day, with the document open, anyone could have interfered with it,' Elliot's voice was getting louder. He looked at his wife. 'I might have hoped that you would keep an eye on it for me. You knew how important that work was.'

'I couldn't help *but* keep an eye on it, Elliot!' she replied, hotly. 'It was in the way, wires trailing everywhere! I had to work round it all day. But I'm so afraid of the damn thing I didn't even dare to put it away. So I certainly didn't touch it and I certainly didn't see anyone else touch it. Of course I wouldn't have allowed it, if I had.'

Belinda's failure to accept responsibility, to back him up, pushed Elliot over the edge. 'You're afraid of your own shadow, you stupid woman! A complete waste of space. I might have known I couldn't rely on you!'

'Elliot!' James and Simon cried out in unison.

Elliot turned and attempted to climb out from behind the bench. As he did so, Roger, unnerved by the shouting, rushed at him with a snarl and snapped at his exposed ankle. Elliot kicked out at the dog and caught him on the shoulder, unbalancing himself in the process so that he half lay along the narrow bench.

'Oh Roger! Poor pet. Come here to Mumsy,' Muriel cried out in alarm.

Elliot's struggle to right himself sent the bench crashing onto its side. When he gained his feet is face was choleric and his fine hair was damp with perspiration.

'We all need to calm down.' Simon gave Elliot a hard look.

'Oh here we go, the closing of the family ranks,' Elliot sneered, white-lipped. He began to gather up his papers. A pulse in his temple throbbed furiously and his hands were shaking.

'What else do you expect, when you speak like that?' Simon's blood was soaking through the kitchen towel. He had his hand cupped underneath it. Elliot's targets were narrowing. He stabbed again at the weakest link. 'It was sitting here all afternoon and evening,' Elliot exclaimed, addressing Belinda once more. He waved a sheath of papers emphatically as he spoke; a fleck of spittle clung to the corner of his mouth. 'You MUST have seen something!'

'*I* wasn't sitting here all afternoon and evening!' Belinda cried. 'I went out into the garden for an hour with Mum and then, when I came back, all hell was let loose, and you were nowhere to be seen.' She kneaded and wrung at the tea towel, her nervous hands fluttering like trapped birds. She felt it; his anger and accusation, looking for a home, somewhere to land. The instinctive impulse she always felt, at times like these, to manifest it, to bring it into being, was strong; almost overwhelming.

'And in any case,' Simon put in. 'You've been working on those figures for days, on and off, in different places. There's nothing to say that the mistake happened on Saturday. It could have been at any time.'

'You know,' observed James, conversationally, gently taking the tea towel from Belinda and folding it deftly, 'the apportionment of blame is often a futile exercise. In fact it can be a serious distraction. The incorrect figures evidently have serious consequences, Elliot. If you need any support or assistance in dealing with *them*, I do hope you'll let us know.' He put his hand under Belinda's elbow and guided her across the room, away from Elliot, to the sink at the back of the room. He spoke in a tone quite loud enough for Elliot to hear, making it plain that the subject of his calculations was firmly closed. 'I think Simon's going to need a plaster, Belinda. Is the first aid box under here? I thought it was. Oh look! Quite comprehensive! A cornucopia of medicaments, eh? Simon, let me see that finger.' Simon joined them by the sink. The three of them huddled over Simon's finger while Belinda fussed with gauze and plaster. They all had their backs to Elliot. He was left alone at the table with his laptop and his nonsensical line forty-five.

Muriel stroked Roger who had retreated underneath her chair and was trembling. She wished Les was there. Her exposure to this family row had shocked and unnerved her but good manners called for her to fill the silence. 'I had no one to blame but myself, over the puzzle,' she said sagely, to no one in particular. 'As the Chaplain said only last Sunday, 'whenever we point a finger of accusation, there are three fingers pointing back at us.'

James had kept the ladies well supplied with drinks and stoked their fire into a merry blaze. Heather had produced scented candles and a dish of small pebbles and crystal beads which she had placed close at hand on the hearth. 'They produce a positive aura,' she said. Whether assisted by the crystals or not, the warmth of the fire and the glow of good gin and tonic thawed them considerably.

'I suppose,' Ruth admitted, presently, 'that I have just got out of the habit of keeping an eye open for little ones.' It was as close as she was going to come to an apology, or to taking any responsibility for Starlight's accident in the gift shop. Apart from the candles and the firelight there was no illumination in the room. She was sitting in one of the armchairs, her legs over the arm, her face at an oblique angle to the others. She had a strong sense of the potential of the occasion for honesty, but it was a struggle with Miriam being there; she just couldn't get over her notion of Miriam as an *intruder.*

Heather sighed. She was sitting cross-legged on the hearth rug. Her hair shone like gold in the light of the fire. 'It was wrong of me to expect the girls to watch her, I suppose. They're only children themselves. Rachel has been good with her, though; I must say that.'

'It was a shame that Rachel didn't come,' Miriam remarked, sipping her drink, 'she needs including as much as possible.' Then, referring to the afternoon's incident, she added: 'As you know, I haven't a maternal bone in my body, so I'm of no use at all in those situations.'

'You do very well with Simon's three,' Ruth forced herself to say; it was like pulling her own teeth.

'No, no,' Miriam shook her head. 'I'm much too selfish, as you well know but, in the maddening McKay way, are too polite to say. I do what needs to be done for them in practical ways, if Simon isn't around, and I'm happy to spend time with them; they *are* nice children. But I neither offer nor encourage emotional attachment. There's no point.'

433

Ruth and Heather both looked up at her. Heather gave a confused little laugh. 'What do you mean?'

'Oh,' Miriam looked, for a moment, rather uncomfortable. She placed her empty glass down on the table carefully, and then took it up again and ran her fingertip around its rim. 'Family ghosts, for one; April's shoes are just too big. I feel her presence here amongst you all, like Banquo's ghost; I know I don't measure up.' She shrugged, and smiled, ruefully. 'And, as I said, I'm too selfish. I'm not ready for the unspoken but very real expectations of sacrifice and deference to the greater good.'

Heather laughed again, more shrilly. 'Surely, Simon and the children wouldn't be such a hard project to consider taking on?'

'From my point of view it would be a very unequal bargain, I'm afraid. Four of them, not to mention all the rest of you, and only one of me. I can't fight you all.'

'You wouldn't need to fight us!' Heather said, 'isn't that the whole point?'

'But I like being one on my own, Heather. I'm not a team player.'

Ruth and Heather digested Miriam's revelation with difficulty. They looked at each other, almost speechless.

'So...... you don't plan to marry Simon, then? Or to stay with him at all?' The sisters were devastated for their poor brother, who was to be abandoned once more.

'Not in the long term, no. But I don't plan on leaving either, for the time being, so don't make this into more than it is. Simon's attention is focused on the here and now and that's the way I want it to stay.'

Ruth stared into the fire, adjusting her resentment of Miriam's intrusion into pique at her reserve. Could she possibly consider herself *too good* for the McKays? Then Miriam stood up and collected her jacket from the back of her chair. 'Let me just say this, though. I was thinking about all of this earlier today. The conclusion I came to is this: I have a choice. I can choose to become a member of this family or not. But I'm not the only outsider here and the others don't have the luxury of choice; Rachel doesn't, and neither does Starlight. Actually, family is a simple question of legal identity; and unless you legitimise Starlight's standing - which, as we both know, Heather, is going to be easier said than done – it'll become an issue, like it is for Rachel, now. They're kindred spirits, those two. They're in the same boat.'

When she had gone, Ruth said, 'do you think it's an issue for Rachel?'

Heather shrugged. 'If it is, it's one *you* could easily solve.'

Her emphasis made Ruth observe, as though on an unrelated topic; 'it seems to me your Social Worker has done a very poor job of preparing you for parenthood. What kind of support *are* you getting?'

'I've been having chakra therapy, Reiki and crystal healing till I'm blue in the face.'

Ruth made an impatient gesture. 'From Social Services, I meant.'

'Oh well,' Heather looked away, 'none, really. We haven't really gone in for all that.'

'Surely Social Services have to be involved? There must be questions of medical history to go into, as well as the legalities…'

'No,' Heather prevaricated, 'not..... not necessarily.'

435

Belinda looked at her watch. It was after six. The kitchen table was spread with food and James had wrapped knives and forks in napkins. Simon had opened wine and set glasses on the worktop. Elliot had taken himself off somewhere in a fit of extreme peevishness, leaving James to lift the laptop, stubbornly left on the table, onto the dresser for her, before taking Simon off for a game of snooker.

'Everything is ready,' Belinda announced, heavily. 'I think we'd better eat.'

Mary had placed Starlight in her highchair and was feeding her with diced tomato and morsels of quiche. Starlight held a slice of garlic bread in her fist and the butter was running down her wrist and soaking up her sleeve. She sucked at it in between mouthfuls, with large, solemn eyes. 'I hope your Dad's alright,' Mary said, placing a shred of ham on Starlight's tray. 'There. That's a good girl. Eat it up, now. It's time for his tablet. He isn't used to being without me for such a long time.'

'Rob says they went out hours ago. I don't suppose you know June's mobile number? Or Les'?'

'No. Do they have mobile telephones?'

Muriel, in the easy chair by the Aga, opened her mouth and then shut it again. She had had two quite large sherries, she told herself, and must be careful.

'I think we'll have to eat,' Belinda said again, hopelessly. She found people being late for food incredibly annoying. 'There comes a point when re-heated lasagne becomes dried-up lasagne. Muriel. I wonder if you would mind just letting people know that dinner is ready?'

'No, not at all.' Muriel removed her spectacles and folded up a shirt she had been mending, placing it with some other clothing which had needed some minor repairs. 'Good thing I brought my sewing case,' she muttered to herself as she tottered from the room, Roger in close pursuit.

Belinda and Mary were alone in the kitchen. It was ironic, really, that having hoped for groups and gatherings to characterise the week, all Belinda wanted now was time alone or exclusive, one on one conversation. The crowd of hungry, clamouring relations, the menu, the agenda, the list of practicalities which had seemed to her, two days ago, to embody family, were an annoying distraction now from what had emerged to be at the heart of it all. She had been caught up in the packaging instead of enjoying the content. She moved across the kitchen towards Mary and said; 'Mum, what you mentioned earlier, about Dad?' Mary nodded, and placed a quarter of hardboiled egg onto Starlight's tray. The baby chased it around with her grasping thumb and index finger; it slithered from her grasp.

'Yes, dear?'

'I want what's best for you, Mum, and Dad, of course. But this is something we need to discuss as a *family*, just *us*; you know what I'm saying?'

'You mean without Elliot? That'll be tricky.'

'I don't know what Elliot's agenda will be but I know that he'll have one and you know what he's like, no one else will get a chance to say what they really think. I don't know what it has to do with the company anyway, really. Can you afford The Oaks?'

'We already pay for Granny. It is a substantial amount. Maybe June and Muriel could begin to make a contribution? I don't know.' Mary placed her finger in front of the egg, arresting its circuit of the tray, and Starlight seized it at last and mashed it into her mouth. 'Maybe The Oaks isn't the right thing. I just know that I'm weary of it twenty-four hours a day. I just want to talk about it.'

Belinda put her arm around Mary's shoulders. Beneath the thick wool of her cardigan, they were surprisingly thin. 'Alright. Alright,' she

437

said, softly. She looked at her mother, suddenly a smaller and less substantial figure than she had ever seemed before. Uncharacteristically, there was a stain on the front of her blouse, tea, perhaps, a suggestive sign that Mary was letting things slip. She was getting old, Belinda realised, with a shock.

Mary looked up at her. 'I just keep asking myself: when will it be *my* turn?' The fierce blaze of vehemence was not what Belinda had expected. Before she could respond, the thunder of eager footsteps in the corridor heralded the arrival of the hungry hoards.

The young people took their plates of food into the games room with strict instructions to take extreme care against spills. The latest Harry Potter was being screened for the half term holidays and they were all keen to see it. Tansy carried her own plate in one hand and Todd's in the other; there had been some debate as to whether he should be allowed to eat away from the table. 'He's only six and he's had a tiring day,' Simon had said. 'I think it might be risky.' In the end, though, the risk of histrionics seemed greater and Tansy promised to keep an eye on him. 'There's my princess,' Simon squeezed her shoulder, 'I'm looking forward to seeing your pot.'

'It really is going to be lovely. Quite the nicest of all of them.' Ruth said across the table, helping herself to salad. 'Rachel likes Harry Potter. Maybe I should wake her,'

'We went up before. She was fast asleep, Aunty Ruth,' Ellie said, taking a glass of wine without asking anyone.

'Oh well. I expect she's seen it. I'll send James up with some food for her, later.'

Speculation about the whereabouts of June, Les, Granny and Robert was rife. 'They didn't say anything about going out. I just can't understand it,' Belinda said, serving lasagne from the Aga hotplate.

'I wish you'd make your mind up,' Elliot scowled, 'you've done nothing but complain about June and Les being here and now they've disappeared you're still not satisfied.'

'I think it's her father that Belinda is worried about, Elliot,' James said mildly, helping himself to ham.

'Of course I'm getting used to the idea that *you* know what my wife means, far better than I do,' Elliot retorted, wrestling with the lid of a jar of piccalilli.

'What on earth do you mean?' Ruth asked, sharply. She looked from James, to Elliot, and across at Belinda.

'Didn't you know?' Elliot struggled and strained with the jar lid, becoming more and more puce in the face, 'they're very pally. Church yesterday, some old pile of rubble today, and a regular Johnny and Fanny Craddock in the kitchen this evening.' He gave up with the jar and placed it with a petulant smack back on to the table.

'I took Belinda and the other ladies to the stately home today because you declined, as you very well know,' said James, mildly, picking up the jar and opening it with an easy twist of his hand, 'although I must say it was an extremely enjoyable day.'

'I didn't know that you went to church with James,' Ruth said, a little sulkily, to Belinda. But Belinda was busy with lasagne, hot and bothered over the Aga, and didn't reply.

Rob cornered Ellie in the gallery. She was carrying a bowl of fresh fruit salad and another glass of wine. He blocked her entrance into the games room. Every time she stepped to one side, he shifted his position so that she couldn't get by.

'Move Rob,' she shouted at him, exasperated, 'or I'll lose my seat on the sofa!'

He smiled down at her. He was a good head taller than her. 'Your little friend came good, with hardly any effort on my part. A pushover, she was,' he said, smugly, 'and so now at last I know it all. The question is: what am I going to do about it?'

Ellie blanched. 'What do you mean?'

'Well,' Rob raised his eyebrows, as though considering his options. 'I ought to do what I did in St Lucia. *Philip,*' he sneered the name, 'ought to lose his job at the very least, even if he doesn't face criminal proceedings for sex with a minor.' The glass in her hand trembled and wine slopped over its rim, dribbling over her hand and soaking into her sleeve.

'I didn't have sex with him,' she said, her voice high and shrill. Her heart was in her throat. She sounded so pathetic that she didn't even believe herself.

'Oh, well, *if* that's true, there's the question of spreading lies and gossip which stain his good name. I expect your time at St Hilary's will be over pretty swiftly. He might sue you for slander.'

'Rob! You wouldn't.....' Ellie's hands was shaking so badly now that her bowl began to slip and fruit salad threatened to spill onto the floor. 'Careful now,' Rob said, taking the bowl from her gently, 'it wouldn't do for anyone to think you'd lost your cherry.'

The lights in the games room were switched off and on the screen Harry Potter zoomed energetically around the quidditch pitch. Rob settled himself down on one of the sofas and took a pull at a bottle of cold beer. Presently he nudged Toby, sitting next to him, and passed him a bottle. Toby's eyebrows expressed surprise and anxiety, but Rob touched the side of his nose with his finger. He deliberately placed his bottle into an ambiguous position between the two of them on the glass-topped table indicated that Toby should do likewise. In the event of discovery, he implied, Rob would claim both beers.

Todd, snuggled next to Ben on a large beanbag and underneath a fleecy throw, was almost asleep; the outdoor exercise, fresh air, lake swim and big dinner had just about finished him off. Ben had only half of his attention on the film. He'd seen it before and read the book too. His eyes kept wandering to the piano, where their half completed song stood on the music stand. Really he would have preferred to continue with it, but Bob said that these things were best left to 'ferment' for a while. Writing the music with Bob had been like touching a star, a new star, formed almost as they explored it, their fingers shaping the craters and mountains. The music had drawn them like a field of gravity.

Mitch held Starlight in the crook of his arm. The baby's eyes were following the action on the screen but her body felt limp and

441

heavy, as though sleep would claim it soon. Mitch's eyes kept straying to Ellie, who, since she had come back into the room, had been edgy and distracted. Her dessert remained untouched on the coffee table. She kneaded and wrung her hands restlessly, a gesture Mitch had observed in Belinda. Rob, Mitch noted, was not even pretending to watch the screen. His eyes were fixed on his sister, and, in the gloom, they glinted malevolently. After a while, discomfited, perhaps, by their scrutiny, Ellie got up from the sofa and left the room.

Clearly, Mitch thought, Rob's spiteful intention was still in play. The lad's malefic glower was sounding one of a number of discords in the family symphony; his father's impotent rage was another, Ruth's peevish hypochondria a third. And, last night at the pub he had become aware of another; a massive, yawning chasm of hostility between Simon and the old man. Their dissonant notes were spoiling the family's attempts at harmony. Everywhere he looked there were embryonic connections; evidences of new beginnings. He saw it in exchanged glances and understanding smiles; in shared burdens; in the pursuit of common passions. But the filaments of intuitive comprehension which were beginning to loop and link between them were under threat. He hated to see it. But what more, after all, could he do?

Rachel sat up in bed. She had not slept; her headache had not eased and she burned with thirst, but uppermost in her discomfort was this relentless, nagging sense of doom. She slipped out of bed and got a drink of water from the bathroom. As she drank it, the waft of food smells drifting up the stairs and into the room made her aware that the biscuits, cake and crisps, which were all that she had eaten that day, had long since ceased to satisfy; she was hungry. With all that had occurred to her that day, and with everything that she had pressing onto her mind, she was disgusted by her own appetite; people with worries like hers became thin and distant; their anxieties made a blockage so that food could not pass by. But her tummy was grumbling and she cast a glance across the room at Tansy's dressing gown, laid tidily over the end of the neatly-made bed. Perhaps she would borrow it and go downstairs. As she considered this idea the sound of footsteps treading wearily up the spiral steps made her hope that food might be on its way to her. She slipped back into bed. It was cold in the bedroom and her quilt retained the heat of her body. But Ellie brought no food with her. Her face, naked, for once, of makeup, looked white and stricken. Her hair, un-brushed, styled or straightened, was dull and devoid of its usual shimmer. Rachel knew, with a terrible certainty, that in some unfathomable way her good intentions had been hijacked and that her disconnected status in the family would make her a legitimate target for blame.

'Oh. You're awake,' Ellie said, unzipping her top and dropping it onto the floor. Her voice was flat.

'Yes,' Rachel replied, her hands mashing her midriff under the quilt. She waited for the accusations to begin, but Ellie simply stood in the middle of the room, looking around her. When Ellie didn't speak, Rachel pounced in desperation on the only other topic of conversation she could think of; 'Have you had tea?'

Ellie nodded. 'Supper, you mean? Yes. Have you?'

'No.'

443

Ellie looked helplessly at the mess on and around her bed. Discarded clothes, make up, CDs, dirty knickers, shoes, cups with the gritty residue of hot chocolate, carrier bags, a plate with toast crusts. She looked at it as though someone else had come and dumped it while she was out; as though it was nothing to do with her at all but was a deliberate attempt by some cruel hand to burden her even more. She wondered vaguely whether Rachel expected her to do anything about the fact that she had not eaten; there was always this sense with Rachel that she was waiting for you to do or say something and Ellie was never able to grasp hold of the hidden agenda. She waited for Rachel to come out with whatever it was, but Rachel just sat in her bed, her hands moving restlessly under the covers, a hunted expression in her eyes. Ellie gave up on it with a sigh. She kicked off her trainers, slipped off her tracksuit bottoms and pushed them all under her bed. She extricated her pyjamas from her unmade bed, put them on and climbed under the covers. She wanted nothing so much as to go to sleep and not wake up for about five years, until all of this mess would have been forgotten. In five years she would be twenty-one, a free, independent grown-up, and able to run away from Rob, and Caro and anything else that she didn't want to face.

'Are you going to sleep?' Rachel asked, quietly. Although Ellie was clearly very troubled, Rachel didn't dare ask what was wrong; she was too afraid of the answer. Ellie ignored her. 'Good night, then,' Rachel said, quietly. She continued to sit in her bed in the gloom of the meagre light which seeped under the bathroom door. The curtains were still open but the night outside was thick with darkness. She could hear Ellie breathing, a series of stepped in-breaths followed by a wheezing out-breath. She was crying. Rachel felt tears prick the back of her eye balls. She felt sorry for Ellie and sorry for herself. A worm of guilt writhed in her chest, even though she told herself over and over again that Ellie's friend had told Rob the secret; he had *known* the secret. What had she done? Confirmed it, possibly; named the teacher. But he had promised her that he wouldn't use it to hurt Ellie. He had *promised.* But she could see it all thundering back towards her like a vehicle out of control on a treacherous roadway. She would be run over even though it wasn't fair. Rachel slipped out of bed again and went to stand by Ellie's bed. Tentatively, she put her hand on Ellie's quivering shoulder.

'Ellie?' she whispered. 'Ellie?'

The duvet made a lurch and rose up, but Ellie only disappeared further down the bed. 'Leave me alone,' she wailed from within its folds. 'Just leave me *alone!*'

In the end all the adults chose to eat in the kitchen, which made Belinda wonder why she had been persuaded to produce a buffet meal, as though it was less trouble. She appreciated the fact that the children had wanted to watch the film but even that could have been accommodated with a later meal. Now she would have all the plates and glasses to collect from the games room. You always had to produce an excess of food for a buffet; you could never predict quantities very accurately when people were allowed to help themselves, or given a selection of dishes to choose from. Now, she could see, there would be left-overs to sort out and try to incorporate into other meals, which was always annoying.

As a matter of fact there were a number of things she was beginning to find annoying about sharing a house with her relations; it seemed that no one was very keen to clear up after themselves; she was constantly collecting cups and glasses from all over the house. Also strewn everywhere were personal belongings; books and clothes and shoes; they made the place look so untidy. Nobody seemed capable of changing the toilet roll properly or of picking a bath mat off the floor so that it could dry. Her stores of food were being wantonly pillaged; she would never have believed the quantities of gin they could consume.

She had plated up food for Les, June, Granny and Robert. She didn't know where on earth they could be. It was quite dark outside now; nowhere they might have decided to visit could possibly still be open. She wondered if the car had broken down. Mary was clearly very anxious. She hadn't eaten much, perched on the end of one of the benches next to Muriel, glancing one moment at the empty carver chair where Robert generally sat, the next at the kitchen door. Muriel was nattering inconsequentially about this and that, but Mary only made distracted replies. Periodically one of the children would come in, help themselves to food or drink, and leave again. Rob came in twice for beer from the fridge. She couldn't remember having told him that this would be alright but he did seem to have been working diligently on his coursework all day and Belinda decided to let it go. Elliot didn't seem to notice. He had set himself apart from everyone, morosely eating his food and frequently recharging his wine glass with a bottle he kept at his elbow. On entering the kitchen he had cast a sour glance at the laptop on the dresser, but made no comment. Bob and James were sitting on the opposite side of the table; Bob was telling James about Ben's day at the outdoor pursuits centre, and, with a great deal of enthusiasm, the song they were writing together. Their efforts, admittedly rather stiff, to include Elliot in their conversation, had been rebuffed. Simon was seated in the carver at the far end of the table. Miriam was perched on his knee and feeding him forkfuls of food from their shared plate. Ruth and Heather had retreated to a far corner of the kitchen and had their heads together. Belinda, who had, for once, managed to sit in the comfortable chair by the Aga, surveyed them all. She wished she could slip off somewhere quiet to think over everything that had happened, to escape from Elliot; his presence, brooding and malevolent, cast a shade over the brightness of everything, like a volcano over an idyllic Mediterranean island. She was appalled, really, at how little love she felt for him, or from him, now that she understood, so much more clearly, the nature of it all.

Ruth could scarcely believe what she was hearing. She had at last asked Heather straight out about Starlight. Miriam's parting shot about 'legitimising' Starlight's status in the family had intrigued her and the questions she had been asking herself about the child's provenance had all bubbled to the surface with fresh vigour. It turned out that her understanding that Starlight had been rescued from a parched African village was something wide of the mark.

'You assumed it,' Heather explained, 'but I never *said* we'd brought her from Africa. I said we'd *heard* about her there. One of the workers on the Famine Fund tour was a social worker from Birmingham. She was just coming to the end of a career break. Bob

447

got talking to her and she offered to help us out. When we got home, we got in touch with her and she got Starlight for us.'

'*Got* her? You can't just *get* a child like that!' Ruth said, indignantly. 'Didn't you have to do a course, get assessed, all that?'

'No.' Heather took a mouthful of quiche and chewed it slowly. 'She waived all that for us, in the circumstances.'

Ruth put her fork down and looked incredulously at her sister. '*Waived* it? In what circumstances?'

Heather sipped her orange juice. She still seemed unable to meet Ruth's eyes. 'In the slightly irregular circumstances.'

'Heather!'

'Oh alright, I'll tell you. But don't think of climbing up on one of your high horses, Ruth. We've already established today that neither of us can claim any moral high ground.'

'No. Alright then.'

'Monica – she's the social worker – she works at a reception centre for failed asylum seekers. They get families in there all the time in transit for the flight back to wherever they came from once their applications have been assessed and turned down. Sometimes the parents are beside themselves; prospects for children – especially girls – are grim beyond anything in their home countries and they'll do anything to save their children from such a future. You know what I mean? D'you know that in some African countries they believe that AIDS can be cured by having sex with a virgin..... I mean, it doesn't bear thinking about, does it?'

'No, I suppose not, when you put it like that.'

'And then, some of them have been living here for years. This is all the children know. Sending them back to Nigeria or wherever would be like sending them to the moon; they'd feel just as alien.'

'Mmmm.'

'So Monica arranges for the families to be able to leave one or two of the babies and younger children behind, with families who'll love them and care for them, and give them a quality of life they'd never be able to achieve at home. Education, health care, opportunities.'

'And this is all......'

'Oh yes, strictly illegal of course. She doctors the paperwork so that they cease to exist.'

'So you don't have any paperwork at all? No birth certificate? Nothing?'

Heather shook her head. 'Not a shred of anything. She was delivered at three o'clock one morning in the clothes she stood up in. Bob and Mitch and I went to an industrial estate near Solihull and Monica met us there with Starlight. We weren't told her name, her age. To be honest we weren't totally sure of her sex until we looked, although we'd been told to expect a girl.'

'Good God!' Ruth was almost speechless. But then a further question occurred to her. 'I don't suppose Monica's enterprise is purely altruistic?'

'Oh no. We paid a great deal of money.'

'I wonder if the poor family got to see a penny of it,' Ruth couldn't help musing.

'I wouldn't know. But, you know,' Heather paused, as though listening to an echo, 'needs must when the devil drives.'

Ruth pushed the food around on her plate. 'You didn't consider adopting in the conventional way, Heather?'

'Actually, yes. But Bob's too old to be considered as an adoptive father. Which is ridiculous when you consider that he could still father children.'

'And surrogacy wasn't an option?'

449

'You know, I *did* think about it. But then I thought, why create a new baby when there are thousands of them already in existence needing love and support?'

Prompted by Miriam's comment, the legal ramifications of what Heather had told her were beginning to muster in Ruth's mind; they were enormous. Enrolling Starlight in school, getting an NHS number, a passport, a bank account, all of it would depend upon establishing an identity for her. 'How are you going to...'

Heather seemed to be following her train of thought. 'Money,' she said, simply. 'I don't care if it takes every penny we have. I'll never give her up.'

The word was calculated to irritate Ruth. 'Why does everything,' she thought to herself, crossly, 'have to boil down to money?'

Out of the corner of her eye she saw Rachel enter the kitchen. She was wearing her pyjamas and a dressing gown which Ruth didn't recognise. With a lurch she realised that she hadn't been up to check on Rachel since she got home, and hadn't organised any food for her. In the light of Heather's fervour she suddenly felt wholly inadequate as a mother. She rushed up to Rachel and tried to hug her, but Rachel remained strangely stiff and un-responsive. She tried to help Rachel get something to eat but the buffet was sadly depleted. This in itself embarrassed Ruth; she should have thought to save some food for the poor girl.

'This garlic bread's cold but I could warm it up for you. Would you like that? What about some of this quiche – mushroom, I think – sorry, it's a bit bashed around. Would you like it?'

'Don't fuss. I'm alright,' Rachel said. She took a ragged slice of ham, a squashed slice of quiche and a spoonful of salad and left the kitchen without a word.

She almost bumped into June, marching down the corridor. Behind June, Les had Robert on one arm and Granny on the other.

June was purple with indignation. She burst into the kitchen. 'For Christ's sake,' she gasped, 'get me a drink this minute or I shall expire!' She flung herself into the nearest seat.

'Where on earth have you been?' Belinda cried.

'You might well ask! God! What a nightmare! Mother got arrested and while we were dealing with that Robert locked himself in the toilet.'

'Where *is* Robert?' Mary was on her feet in an instant. Robert, when he entered, was trembly and close to tears. 'His hands are freezing!' Mary said, taking them in her own and leading him to his seat. Ruth put the kettle on the Aga while James lifted a crocheted throw off the back of the arm chair and tucked it around Robert's shoulders.

'Possibly a dram of brandy?' he said to Simon.

'Oh! Brandy, certainly,' June shrilled, 'and copious quantities of it.'

'I meant for Robert,' James said under his breath.

Les settled Granny down next to Elliot, an unhappy arrangement for both parties, and Belinda placed a plate of food down in front of her.

'An excellent afternoon,' Granny declared, beaming around her. 'We got to see the President. Top security of course, lots of uniforms, they gave us a stiff talking to.'

'That was the manager of the supermarket, Mother, and his security guards, and two police constables.' June shouted down the table. 'You were lucky they didn't take you into custody.'

'*Is* there any custard?' Granny looked hopefully around the table. 'I can't eat this. I haven't got my teeth in. They taste funny.'

'That's all she's gone on about all afternoon,' June wailed, swigging the large brandy Simon placed before her. 'That and her

451

damned bottom. So embarrassing. It's a good job this didn't happen back at home. I would never have lived it down.'

'Mary, I'm cold. Where have you been? I didn't like it. I didn't like it,' Robert mumbled. The mug of tea which Ruth placed into his hands shook and quivered, and Mary had to hold it steady for him.

'Here you are, Robert,' she said, popping two blue tablets into his mouth. 'These will soothe you. Drink your tea and then you can have something to eat.'

'We didn't have lunch, Mary. The man wouldn't let us eat it.'

'Yes!' screeched June, 'outrageous! Bought and paid for, too. But we were frog-marched off to the manager's office without a by-your-leave. Not that it was a very nice lunch. Leslie was too mean to take us anywhere nice. If he'd taken us to a pub like I suggested, none of this would have happened.' June threw a narrow-eyed look across at Les, who was leaning against the dresser, next to Muriel.

Granny ignored the tea which Belinda placed before her and took a drink of Elliot's wine instead. Her mouth made an audible slurping noise against the glass. Some wine dribbled down the outside of the goblet and she licked it up efficiently. 'Nice!' she said, smacking her lips.

'Oh for God's sake!' Elliot fumed.

'None of *what?*' Miriam's voice cut over the hubbub of voices with surprising volume. 'Could one of you give us a reasonably cogent account of what's happened?'

'Not me, clearly,' June retorted, huffily, 'although I have been trying.'

'Les?' All eyes turned towards him. He was uncomfortable with the scrutiny but launched into an explanation.

'Robert was feeling a bit restless here, you see, without..... well, with you all being out, and so I thought a little drive would settle him.

So we set out and I found one of those out-of-town affairs. We went into the supermarket and walked about a bit. I don't know why.'

'You *do* know perfectly well why!' June interrupted. 'We were looking for some suspenders for Mother.'

'Well, anyway, in hindsight, the garden centre might have been safer....'

'The DIY store would have been more interesting,' Robert put in, with a spark of lucidity.

'Yes. It would. But anyway, we walked around the store for a while and then we bought a bite to eat in the café.'

'Horrible place,' June said, acerbically.

'And then, well, we were approached by a security guard, who thought that Granny might have accidentally put a few things into her handbag without paying for them.'

'I had!' Granny chuckled. 'A nice tin of ham and two packets of Johnnies!'

'And so, we had to go and explain to the manager that Granny wasn't.... wasn't quite...'

'Sane?' muttered Elliot. Granny had systematically been transferring all the food from her plate onto his. He had watched this process in horrified disbelief. When her plate was entirely clean she held it up like a child and proclaimed: 'All gone! What a good girl! Can I have my custard now?'

'Wasn't quite *well*,' Les corrected. 'But it seems that it is their invariable policy to call the police in these cases and two constables arrived in due course.'

'It took an age,' June complained. 'It's a good job I wasn't being kidnapped.' Everyone considered the likelihood of this. The chances of such a thing were, they concluded, disappointingly remote.

Granny took another long slurp of Elliot's wine, then she turned towards him and surveyed him narrowly. 'You are a very nasty man,' she commented, 'and not a gentleman. I thought so as soon as I saw you. I don't like your nose; it's too pointy and your chin is weak. I can't abide a weak-chinned man. I'm surprised they let your sort in here. The Oaks is exclusive. You can be sure I'll be taking the matter up with Matron.'

'Belinda! Really! For God's sake!' Elliot made a direct appeal but Belinda was busy at the Aga and everyone else ignored him.

Les laboured on with his tale. 'While we waited, Robert needed the toilet and so I took him to the staff facilities. Unfortunately the lock was a bit awkward and Robert couldn't open the door.'

'I never let him lock the door,' Mary said, quietly.

'No. I'm sorry, I should have thought. I went back to the Manager's office and he said he'd call the maintenance man, but it would take a while because he was busy in the bakery; something had fused. In the meantime...'

'I didn't like it, Mary. It went dark.'

'Yes,' Les went on, 'I was coming to that, Robert. It seems that to discourage the employees from spending too much time in the lavatory the light is on a timer. Once you open the main door you get five minutes of light and then it goes off. Stupid idea, if you ask me, but there it is. So when I got back to the lavatory Robert had been in the dark for about five minutes, poor old lad. And then every subsequent five minutes we were plunged into darkness again. I tried to talk Robert through it, but it really did throw him. He...'

'He decided to wriggle under the door,' June took up the story. She couldn't bear Les to have all the attention.

'I used to be able to do it,' Robert shook his head sadly.

'You did!' Granny piped up. 'Your Dad locked you in the coal shed once and you got out like that. And I seem to remember you ran away from Sunday School by squeezing out of the toilet window. Little bugger!'

'Yes. Yes.'

'But you were only a lad then, Robert,' Mary said quietly. 'You can't do that when you're grown.'

'Of course he couldn't. He got stuck,' June crowed, 'as though we needed one more inconvenience to top off the day. It was all I needed, I can tell you; mother under close arrest and Robert wedged under a toilet door!'

'You talk as though he did it on purpose, June,' Mary snapped. 'The poor man. He must have been terrified.'

'He was when the fire alarm went off, we all were! We thought we were going to be burned alive!'

'The fire alarm? Was there a fire?' Belinda brought a bowl of soup she had been heating up for Granny to the table.

'Bring me a fresh wine glass, Belinda,' Elliot said, witheringly.

'No of course there wasn't!' June cried. 'But Leslie here decided that the thing to do would be to call the fire brigade, as though we hadn't enough uniformed assistance by that time. Ha ha ha!'

'He was stuck fast!' Leslie re-joined, in energetic self-defence. 'The maintenance man was nowhere to be seen and Robert didn't want me to leave him on his own again. In the pitch dark. I mean I ask you? What would you have done? I'd seen the alarm; it had a hammer in it. I thought I could use the hammer to buckle the metal door frame enough to get him through — it was only aluminium. Or to shift the lock. He was so distressed.' Les looked round the room at them all, his large hands held out in appeal. Muriel took one of them gently and stroked it. June, with her back to the dresser, didn't see the gesture, although others did.

'Dear me. What a to-do,' Mary stroked Robert's back. The narration of all his unhappy adventures was upsetting Robert again. He had hardly touched his supper.

'It was hardly an emergency,' June scoffed, her mouth full of quiche, 'but of course no-one else knew that. They began to evacuate the supermarket.'

'That was exciting!'' Granny waved her spoon. A thick gob of soup flicked onto Elliot's shirt.

'For Christ's *sake!*' he yelled.

'There were check-out girls rushing around with tills full of money; all the grills came down in front of the bakery and the hot food counter, the staff trapped behind became hysterical. People were piling stuff into their trolleys and there was a jam at the exit. You couldn't hear yourself think with the all these sirens wailing....' June said, 'sheer mayhem.'

'Anyway, the hammer idea worked,' Les said, bathetically, 'got you out no trouble, didn't it, Robert?'

'I didn't like it, Mary,' Robert said, quietly.

'We made a run for it,' Granny said, slurping soup, 'and......' she reached into her handbag, 'look! I got my ham and my Johnnies in the end!'

Rachel took her plate and carried it towards the sound of the television. Inside the room was dark; she could just make out the silhouettes of various people sprawled on the sofas and on the floor. She hovered on the threshold, trying to see if she could sneak in unobserved, find a place to sit, eat her food unnoticed. As her eyes roamed across the bulky outlines of the furniture, she recognised Rob's stiffly gelled hair with a start, and her courage failed her. She retreated up the corridor and went into the library. The curtains were open and no fire burned in the grate. It was chill and lonely. She began to eat, miserably.

Ruth had trouble getting to sleep. It was cold and in spite of the fact that she had dragged the counterpane off James' bed and laid it on her own, she just couldn't get warm. She had been cold all day, she realised, wondering if she was coming down with 'flu. The house was cold; the warmth and welcome of the first few hopeful hours had dissipated leaving a chilly, disillusioned disappointment. She wished James himself would come up to bed. She had left him downstairs in the kitchen chatting and he had promised that he wouldn't be long; in fact everyone had been yawning while the final dishes were dried and put away and they had all said how tired they felt. But that was ages ago and there was still no sign of him. The thought of having his warmth in her bed was appealing, for once. Thinking about it, she couldn't quite recall the last time they had made love; he was a good lover, considerate and patient, but it wasn't often that she could get past the chain link fence of her irritation to allow him to touch her. He was so slow to act; too apt to think and talk about a thing and too little inclined to actually do anything. By the time he had thought his way around every angle of an issue she could have it done and dealt with and would have moved on to the next thing. His ponderousness, a physical as well as a personal characteristic, infuriated her, at times, like an abrasive grit between their skins which rubbed her raw. Once she had loved this rock-like dependability, and taken shelter in the lea of his immovableness. He stood like a colossus while the tides of life swirled and eddied around him. But lately she had begun to doubt the value of this quality. A rock was all very well until you wanted it to move.

Lying frozen between the comfortless sheets Ruth fired off angry arrows of indignation. James was her inevitable first target; he had not made any enquiry about her day; she was burning to share the things she had discovered about Starlight but he had made no opportunity for her, making her unique knowledge worthless. A slight shift in aim brought Miriam into her sights. Miriam knew about Starlight of course but from Ruth's parochial perspective Miriam didn't count: she was not family. The fact that she was not family and yet was privy to such a family secret was outrageous; she utterly resented Miriam's inclusion in any family matter, yet still was able to criticise her for remaining resolutely peripheral. She thrashed angrily under the covers at the thought of Miriam's determined preferences for the organic bread, fruit tea and white burgundy she had brought, as if everyone else's groceries must be spurned as though tainted with tedium; as though she might otherwise sully her hands with the McKay mundane. At the same time Ruth accused Miriam of using the McKays, insinuating herself into their midst under entirely spurious pretences, masquerading as a family member, enjoying the company and their hospitality and their trust whilst offering absolutely nothing real back in return. There was, Ruth glowered into the darkness, nothing real about Miriam at all; she was an interloper; a cuckoo in the nest who would gobble up all the good things and then fly away to foreign climes and not give them a backwards glance.

Ruth let fly another arrow: Elliot was just such another; a parasite on the McKays. Lording it over them all, behaving as though he owned them all, throwing his weight about; it made her sick. Given the chance she could have run that business every bit as efficiently as he did and she was a real McKay. She gathered that he had made a real cock-up of something recently and she wondered quite seriously for a while whether she could force a vote of no confidence in the Chair. Naturally Belinda would stand up for Elliot but she might be able to persuade the rest of them to oust him, and with the position of Chair vacant she could ask for a chance to try her hand at it. Simon, she knew, wouldn't want to, and, in any case, he would be back to being a single parent before many months were out.

Ruth reached over and turned on the bedside light to look at the clock. It was gone two. Gathering her courage, she slipped out of bed and struggled into James' enormous dressing gown. Where on earth could he be? She pushed the curtain to one side to look out of the window. The garden was flooded with light; a full moon glowed in a navy sky and swamped the garden with ethereal luminosity. In addition the garden lights were all on; below her the terrace was fully illuminated, its old grey slabs marked by an atlas of moss and lichen. Dew, or frost perhaps, sparkled on the grass. She pulled the curtain back around her to block out the light from the lamp. The sky was studded by stars, cloudless. No wonder it was so chilly. She was about to go in search of James when a movement caught her eye. Down on the lawn, a naked woman danced and cavorted. Long hair flying and swirling, arms above her head, the whiteness of her skin glowing in the moonlight, small, well rounded breasts with unusually large and dark aureoles, a slim waist and narrow hips, a shadow of pubic hair in the vee of her thighs, long, shapely legs and feet which skipped and hopped in the cool wet grass. She ran down the lawn and described graceful curves in and out of the flower beds, trailing a hand over the shrubs, stopping by the arbour to allow a tendril of honeysuckle to caress her face. She arrived at the bottom of the lawn and entered the ribbon of shadow cast by the trees, but the miasmic glow of her skin could still be discerned as she bowed and did obeisance to the woods.

'For God's sake, Heather, you'll catch your death,' Ruth muttered to herself, but was conscious, amid the dampness of disapproval, of a fiery zest of envy. How she would love to be so carefree! So wealthy that no problem could not be solved. Heather had turned from the woods now and was running back towards the house. Her face was open and lifted up, her eyes ecstatic, her mouth open, as though catching drops of liquid moonlight on her tongue. Below her people were stepping out onto the terrace. Bob, smoking a cigarette or, more likely, Ruth thought, with a sniff, a joint; Simon, one hand in his pocket the other holding a large brandy balloon; Belinda, holding Heather's ridiculous dress and shoes, and behind her James, out of things as always, hovering on the periphery, his shirt un-tucked from his waistband and, even in this light, she could see, a stain or smear of something on his shirtfront. Ruth glowered down at them, feeling bitterly excluded. Were they all having fun downstairs without her? Belinda shuddered suddenly, and looked uncomfortable, as though feeling someone walk across her grave. Ruth looked on, and what she saw next caused her to clap her hand to her mouth to stifle a cry; James stepped up behind Belinda and placed his hands on her shoulders. He rubbed his large, soft, warm hands slowly up and down Belinda's arms. He pressed her back against his front, to share his warmth, and bent his head down to say something quietly into her ear. Belinda turned her face up to him, and her face, like Heather's, was open and elated; her eyes shone. A tendril of hair had escaped from her bun and rather than tucking it hastily away again, she wrapped it playfully around her finger.

Simon – A Memoir from 1984

Simon trailed home from school. It was a baking hot June day, and he had taken his tie off and dragged his blazer along behind him as he walked through the building site, between the new houses which had been built in the field behind their house. The new houses were a good thing; new people, lots of families with teenagers, and this new short-cut through to their back garden which saved him the walk the long way round through the avenues and crescents of their labyrinthine estate. And also a bad thing; now it was too risky to open up the roof-light in his bedroom and shimmy along the roof and clamber down the wisteria which clung to the back of the house to meet his mates on the wasteland when he should have been in bed; some new nosey do-gooding neighbour was bound to see, and tell his parents about his nocturnal meanderings, eager to get one over on the whiter-than-white, squeaky-clean McKays.

Also, he missed the view of the fields and the line of trees along the river, and the blackness at night, and the quiet.

Simon arrived at the pond which had once nestled virtually unknown in the corner of the field. (As children he and Ruth had often gone there to play, and had once brought home a bucket full of frog-spawn to keep in the back porch. In time it had hatched into a seething mass of slimy, sperm-like tadpoles, and they had taken most of them back to the pond. Then, one morning, the back porch had been alive with little green frogs, and Heather had had hysterics and stepped on dozens of them, squashing them wholesale under the soles of her little pink shoes; the more she squashed the more hysterical she became, and the more she leapt and stamped about, and the more frogs she squashed until the floor was a carnage of flattened frogs.) But the developers had landscaped the pond into the new estate, and fenced it around; the exuberant hedgerow had been ripped away to make room for uncomfortable wooden seats and mean, formal planting. Now, in the heat, and without the shade of the hedges, the pond was almost dry, the black, sucking leaf-mould and mud making an earthy stink so that no one chose to go and sit there. People hurried past with averted eyes. It had become a depository for litter and the kind of refuse which the Council wouldn't take away, an eyesore which they could barely look at much less address. And so it remained, an ugly but irreversible blight on their smart new semis and neatly landscaped lawns and pristine patio furniture.

He had just, that afternoon, taken his last 'O' level exam and the summer stretched before him with no school, no homework, no revision and no more exams to cloud the prospect. Plus, in only a few days, it would be his sixteenth birthday; he was one of the youngest in the year and all of his mates had already celebrated, with barbeques in their gardens or trips to the Speedway or, once, memorably, a party in a garage, with cider and girls and punk so loud that the stuff stacked on the father's shelves – turpentine and weed-killer and emulsion paint and tile adhesive and WD40 – had rattled and jangled and clashed together and the sawdust and muck had danced and leapt like fleas. Simon had drunk more than his fair share of the cider, and smoked some cigarettes, and snogged a girl called Wendy with his tongue down her throat, pogoed with his friends and been copiously sick in a flower bed. Another lad had sniffed some of the tile adhesive and been taken to hospital. It had been the best party ever. But there would be no party for Simon's birthday.

His sixteenth summer. It ought to be wonderful; hot nights, hot girls, days by the river, an endless blissful parade of empty blue-sky days with nothing to do but laze, and then, in the autumn, Technical College, the end of childhood, the beginning of the future. But none of this was what Simon had to look forward to. He was not going to be allowed to go to Technical College, he had to start work at the yard, straight away, with no summer break, washing the wagons and hosing the yard down. It wasn't that he minded the menial work; it was the sense of being locked in, incarcerated; it felt like a life-

463

sentence. Simon picked up a stone and lobbed it into the mud of the pond. It landed with a satisfying splat and sent a circle of thick black mud spraying in every direction.

He had tried to tell them; he really had. Without saying in so many words that he didn't want to go into the business, he had argued the advantages of further qualifications and pointed to Ruth, who had stayed on at school to do 'A' levels and who, in October, would be going off to University. That was another problem; with Ruth gone he would have no ally in the house at all. Belinda was out at work in the Council offices during the day and at night-school two or three evenings a week. Heather was only a little girl, just ten, and lived in a world of her own.

'There's no point in wasting time at college, lad,' his father had said, 'when all you'll ever need for the future is right there in that yard.'

When he got home, his Mum was in the garden taking washing down from the line; there was always washing; billowing blue-white sheets and brightly flapping t-shirts and tea towels and trousers – but never underwear: that was dried on an airer in the bathroom. She greeted him as he came through the gate and asked him how his exam had gone. Then she smiled, with a peg in her mouth, and told him that there was a surprise for him in the kitchen. He walked through the back porch (and thought again about the frogs) and up the step into the kitchen. On the counter there was a new lunch box and thermos, just like the ones his Dad had been taking to the yard for years. On the kitchen table a new blue yard-suit embroidered with the company name and logo lay neatly folded, and, on the floor (because of course it was bad luck to put new shoes on a table) a pair of new black steel toe-capped boots.

'There you are, my little man,' Mum said, coming in behind him. It was a name she'd called him since he was little, and she still used it occasionally, even though he was taller than she was. She put the laundry basket down on the side, 'all ready for your first day at work.' Simon stared at them, aghast.

He waited until after tea to tell them. Belinda had taken Heather to Brownies and then gone on to night-school. Ruth, who had finished her 'A' levels a week before, was upstairs getting ready to go out to a party, trying on and discarding one outfit after another until the room she shared with Heather was ankle deep in clothing, the beds and chairs festooned with it, while Duran Duran played at top volume on her portable record player. Thinking, as he did so, how stupid it was to be speaking to his own mother and father like this, as though they were judges or teachers or royalty, and how wrong it was that he should be feeling like this, so nervous and awkward and afraid, he thanked them for the opportunity, tried to convey his appreciation of it, while being unmistakably clear on the fact that it wasn't at all what he wanted. What he wanted, he said, was to go to Technical College and study electronics, and then to work in computers. He was sorry, he said, if it seemed ungrateful, sorry that it would be a disappointment to them, but hoped they would understand that this was a decision, about his own future, that he must be allowed to make for himself. His parents simply stared at him, as though he had announced that he was contemplating entering holy orders, or a sex change operation; almost as though either of those options would have been preferable to this. They sat side by side on the settee, their faces drained and parched with disbelief.

Then, his Dad's face changed, like a shutter going across it, like a light going off, like a lid being put down. He got up from the settee and said; 'Need to be at the yard at eight tomorrow. Make sure you're ready.'

It was Simon's turn to display disbelief. 'You haven't been listening to me, Dad. I'm not going to the yard tomorrow, or any day.'

Suddenly his Dad's hands were all over him, and he was being man-handled out of the lounge and across the hall. In the room

465

behind him, his Mum cried out. Ruth, descending the stairs at just that moment, ready at last for her party, gave a shout of alarm and hurried the few remaining steps down. Dad's voice roared in his ear as he was pushed and shoved through the kitchen and down the step into the porch. At the time, and afterwards, Simon was unable to say what words his Dad had spoken; they had been incomprehensible, a rant; they had felt, against his face, like an incessant gushing stream, hot and acrid and choking, like the vomit on the flowerbed after the party. He only knew that they were empty of love.

Ruth tried to intercede between them, as they jostled through the house, pitting her voice of remonstrance against Dad's infuriated tirade. The three of them pushed and shoved at each other, banging into furniture and squeezing awkwardly through the bottleneck between the door and the counter in the kitchen. The iron, left to cool on the side, toppled over and broke the clay pot which one of them had made at school and where Mary kept pens and pencils. The back door was still open, into the balmy summer evening. The man next door was mowing his lawn but the noise of their shouting cut through the buzz of his mower and he stopped in his tracks as Simon and Ruth were both bundled out of the house and the porch door slammed and bolted behind them. They looked across the fence at him, and at each other, and almost laughed at the absurdity of it. Then Ruth was reaching into her bag and bringing out her front door key, and they ran round the side of the house and let themselves in through the front door. He met them in the hall again, with a further eruption of fury, so loud that, like the tins and bottles on the shelves of the party-garage, their mother's carefully displayed willow pattern shook and rang on the plate rack round the hall.

Simon was ejected again, pushed out of the door. He fell backwards over a tub of flowers and landed on his back amongst the roses. From inside the house he could hear Ruth screaming on his behalf and his Mum's voice ineffectually added into the fray, and his

Dad's going on and on, an inarticulate torrent of angry words. Simon got up and went back around the house, setting his foot on the trunk of the wisteria, but when he was only a little way up, the window of the back bedroom opened, and a flurry of clothing fell past him. He thought, at first, for a terrible moment, that his Dad had thrown Ruth bodily from the house, but it was only her clothes, armfuls of clothes; trousers and scarves and tops and underwear, dropping past him onto the lawn, and then, with a splintering crash, the portable record player smashed into smithereens below him.

After that, it was as though, to his father, Simon had evaporated away, like the water in the pond, leaving only a nasty but unavoidable smell, a depository for blame and accusation, an eye-sore which he could barely look at much less address, an ugly and shameful blight on the triumphant McKay landscape.

Tuesday

Belinda was dreaming; she was at the scene of the road accident; mangled traffic and scorched bodies littered the carriageway. Victims were moaning, and crying out to her to help them, but she was unable to move. Elliot's hand was firmly on her shoulder and he was shouting into her face. She, too, was shouting, trying to draw his attention to the scene around them, but she could not make her voice heard above his. Suddenly she recognised faces amongst the injured; Mary, Ruth, Ellie, Rachel. It made her need to escape from him all the more urgent. Elliot was haranguing her about something, on and on, but she couldn't make out what she was supposed to have done. He was telling her that she was stupid and useless; over and over again. Her frustration, at not being able to help the injured, at Elliot's insensitivity, and at his injustice, made her thrash and flail about; she wanted to slap him, to shake him, she wanted to scream. The strength of her anger, her desire for violence, scared her. Then his voice broke into her dream.

'I'm going now. Back tonight, probably.'

The scene of their argument melded into their room, at Hunting Manor. The words and the emotions clung like sticky grey cobwebs to the curtains and the upholstery. They seemed to absorb all the air in the room so that it was oppressive. It was still dark, although through a chink in the curtains she could see that it was almost light outside. Lying in the bed she was pent up in the shock and the fury of the dream; breathless and exhausted; the feelings of rage and impotence remained tangibly present. The smell of Elliot's shaving foam and shower gel was sweet and cloying and seemed to press down upon her. She felt as though, saying goodbye, he might try to kiss her and, amid the argument and the carnage, it was insupportable. She struggled up through the clinging tentacles of the dream to see the bedroom door closing.

'Don't come back,' Belinda said. Her voice, her real voice actually in the room, woke her up properly. She sat blinking in the gloom, trying to get a sense of where the boundary had been between the dream and the truth. For a moment she couldn't tell. She didn't know whether the row had been real or not. Elliot had gone but had left a syrupy legacy in the scent of his toiletries in the air, and in the tremors of her own distress. But the bedroom door remained closed. When she thought about it all, it was obvious to her that the dream had been the manifestation of all the previous day's angst over the spread sheet, which had threatened to spill out of Elliot like an enraged, caged animal seeking release. Denied the opportunity of expiation by her coming very late to bed, it remained between them, and she knew that neither hours nor miles would diminish it, that they would actually augment it, like yeast left to leaven dough until it was knocked back with rough hands.

Rachel woke up early. Sunlight was pouring through the window. The curtains had remained undrawn all night and she could see the frost riming the glass. Her watch said it was six thirty. In the adjacent beds, Ellie and Tansy slept on. Ellie looked like a sleeping beauty; her slumber troubled. She could not see Tansy's face. Perhaps they both knew, now, of her betrayal and would never speak to her again.

She could not face them.

She slipped out of bed and gathered clothes from her drawers; the old ones she had brought with her; she did not deserve the new ones, now. Everyone would hate her; she didn't blame them, she hated herself. In the bathroom she got dressed as quietly as possible, avoiding the sight of herself in the mirror; old pilled tracksuit bottoms, a shapeless t shirt, a faded sweatshirt and a man's warm woolly jumper bought by Ruth at a jumble sale, two pairs of socks. She dealt with the sanitary towel as she had been shown and then crept from the room and down the stairs.

Entering the kitchen she encountered Elliot. He was wore a shirt and tie and was drinking coffee, standing at the sink. He didn't seem very pleased to see her.

'Ah' he said, frowning, 'another early riser.'

Rachel hovered uncertainly in the doorway, feeling like an intruder. She had not expected to meet anyone and didn't want to be asked what she was doing or where she was going. In truth she hardly knew the answer to either of those questions. But Elliot lost interest in her and turned to stare out of the window. She felt embarrassed to be eating the food from the house – she had no claim to it - but she was so hungry. While she found a bowl and a spoon, Elliot emptied his coffee cup and put it into the sink.

'See you later, then,' he said, and left the room, his laptop bag gripped grimly in one hand and his car keys swinging from the other.

Rachel was ravenous. She gobbled two bowls of cereal in quick succession and gulped milk straight from the bottle. She placed her bowl and spoon next to Elliot's cup in the sink. In the hall she slipped her feet into her wellington boots before opening the front door and stepping out into the chill autumn air. It smelled cold and stingy in her nostrils, and she could trace the acrid fumes of Elliot's car, which had gone from its place next to the others on the drive. She hadn't been outside since Saturday, when they had gone to the shops, and everyone had been so kind to her, and she had begun to feel like she might belong. Well, that was all over now.

She walked round the house, treading as quietly as possible on the gravel, feeling as though even that, she had no right to disturb. She passed under the brick archway and round to the back of the house, then down the lawn to the place where Ben had said the path through the woods led to the sea. The grass was coated with white frost, thicker where the shadows were but pale and sparkling where the sun was melting it away from the open places and where her feet left a trail across the lawn.

Simon lay in the enormous bed with his hands behind his head. Beside him, the diminutive figure of Miriam nestled like a small child amongst the bedclothes. The delicate curve of her back, the skin almost transparent over her bird-like bones, the innocence of dark hair against her neck, her tiny ear, all belied the ravening appetite of the woman, and Simon smiled, smugly. He had come to bed late, a tad the worse for brandy, but she had been lying in wait for him, voracious, like a spider, in black cobwebby underwear. She was responsive to his touch, eager for his mouth and his fingers, and in the end he had to cover her mouth with his hand for fear of her waking the house. Afterwards she had turned away from him and slept, as satisfied and selfish as a cat. She had not, as April would have done, cradled his head on her breast, and stroked his hair, and encouraged him to his own climax, and Simon had lain awake for most of the night, missing his wife.

Now, in the morning, he gently laid her back to rest and turned his thoughts to the family. In the end his chat with Bob had been unsatisfactory. When it came to it, he didn't really know where to start. Who was he, anyway, to begin to criticise his sisters' parenting skills? What business was it of his if Belinda and Elliot took little or no notice of either of their children? It was plain to him that Rob was going off the rails; Ellie had got him off the pornography hook but for all he knew it might be the thin edge of the wedge: what else might he be doing on the computer he spent so much time on? Apart from that excruciating quarter of an hour in the study he didn't think he'd seen either McKay-Donne say a single word to either of their children all week. It was just expected that they would toe the McKay line. There were assumed if unspoken expectations that Rob would go into the family firm. Had anyone actually asked Rob whether that's what he would like? Had anyone actually asked Rob anything, other than, possibly, if he would like another helping of pie? Ellie would be expected to join the twin-set and pearls brigade, marry well, in white, and devote herself to charitable works, just like Belinda. They were,

Simon thought, as he lay in bed thinking it all over, like free range turkeys, enjoying a life of plenty but being fattened, ultimately, for the table, for family consumption.

Whereas Belinda neglected her children, Ruth browbeat hers. Neither Ben nor Rachel seemed, to him, to be strong personalities who would be able to stand against her. Indeed James, big as he was, seemed scarcely able to. Ruth reminded Simon uncomfortably of their father; she was single- and narrow-minded, and dangerously short-sighted. Simon could see her railroading the children down paths they had no desire to travel, passing on to them the massive chips she carried on her shoulder, depriving them of the ability to think and decide for themselves, and turning them eventually into people who either with good grace or bad, did as they were told.

He was his own man, now, doggedly maintaining a hard-won distance between himself and his family, especially his father. But he couldn't get away from the fact that he cared about his sisters and he cared about their children and he felt, almost in spite of himself, a sense of responsibility for them. It seemed to be a thing he had no choice about; a biological default program. It had been one of the risks of the holiday, he supposed, this sense of reconnection.

None of this had Simon been able, really, to explain to Bob. In the end he had simply mentioned his own scheme to try to break into Rob's dark and forbidding world.

'Chap I know's given me a demo of a new game to try. Well, you know, if Mohammed won't come to the mountain....'

Robert woke up in one of his nasty, belligerent moods. He had slept badly, shaken by his experiences at the supermarket. He had a bad bruise on his shoulder where he had got stuck underneath the toilet door. Mary knocked it accidentally while removing his pyjama shirt and he winced and snatched his arm away from her. Then, when she tried to dab some arnica on to it, she hurt him again and he snarled and grabbed her wrist. For a second his eyes were a window through to the old Robert, still lurking and fuming inside the helpless shell, and Mary felt her throat tighten. Although he wasn't tall he was taller than she, and she found herself looking up into his face, and seeing the coldness of his old fury burning undiminished in his eyes. She tried to smile, reassuringly.

'I need to put just a dab of this on it, Robert. It will bring out the bruising.'

'It hurts.'

'I know. You must have been stuck tight. Come on. There. Let's put your shirt on now.' She gently eased his grip on her wrist and reached for his shirt.

'I don't want to.' Robert stood like a stubborn statue in the middle of their room.

Mary decided to be brisk. 'Don't be silly now. Let's get dressed and then we can have breakfast. What would you like? Porridge?'

'No.'

'Alright then. Well we'll see what there is when we get downstairs, shall we?' He made it almost impossible for her to get him dressed. He refused to lift his feet up to put his trousers on until she moved the blue chair behind him and made him sit down. Then he wouldn't get up again so that she could tuck his shirt in for him and fasten his belt. Finally he shuffled his feet around while she tried to put his shoes on. Mary suspected – she was almost sure – that he did it on purpose, was deliberately obstructive and unhelpful, exercising, still, what control he could over her by this means.

'Do try and keep your foot still, Robert. I can't tie your laces.'

'Well hurry up then. I want my breakfast.'

'Pop your cardigan on then, and we're done.'

Robert made great show of examining himself in the mirror. 'My tie isn't straight.'

'Well *keep still.*' She straightened his tie for him and did up the buttons of his cardigan. 'There,' she said, eventually, 'very smart.' She took his arm and they began to walk towards the bedroom door. 'It's a glorious day; quite sunny,' she said, with forced brightness. Robert stopped in his tracks.

'I need the toilet,' he said.

Mary sighed and walked him through to the bathroom. She stood him in front of the toilet and began to unzip his fly.

'No,' he said. 'The other.'

She turned him around, undid his belt and pulled his trousers and underpants down for him, then sat him down on the toilet.

'Leave me alone. I can't do it while you're watching,' he said.

While he was on the toilet, Mary straightened the bed and moved the blue chair back to the window. She folded some clothes and spent a while looking out over the gardens. Les and Muriel were walking slowly around the perimeter of the lawn. They were deep in conversation. Les had offered Muriel his arm. Muriel's dog was snuffling and rummaging in the leaves, running backwards and forwards, his pushed up nose and round belly making him look silly, like a seal with legs. They were both laughing, perhaps at the dog, and it occurred to Mary that it was the first time she had seen Les smile since Saturday evening.

Some time passed.

Eventually Robert called her name and she opened the bathroom door. The air was thick with white dust; everything was covered in a film of it; the bath, the mirror, the carpet, and Robert himself was white with it; his clothes, his hair and his skin, his eyelashes, and his eyes red where they had been irritated by the fine powder. It danced in the air and caught at her throat. On the floor at his feet lay the tin of Blue Fern talcum powder.

'Oh Robert!' Mary exclaimed. He smiled up at her, coldly, before rising unsteadily to his feet. Behind him, the toilet seat, the flabby skin of his buttocks and his shirt tail were all soiled, smeared with excreta. His hands, beneath their white dusting, were also filthy. As she watched, he wiped them, deliberately, down his cardigan.

James was the first person Mary found, on the landing taking tea to Ruth, and he quickly set about stripping off Robert's clothes and manhandling him into the shower. Mitch, inevitably, was the next, arrested on the stairs on his way down to breakfast. He brought an enormous cylinder vacuum upstairs and tackled the talcum powder.

'I'm so sorry. I'm so sorry,' Mary wailed as the two men busied themselves.

'Don't worry, Mary. Why don't you go downstairs and have a cup of tea? We can sort this, can't we, Mitch?'

'Sure. No problem.' Mitch eyed the grimy toilet with resignation.

But Mary remained on the threshold. 'No, please, Mitch, don't do the toilet. Don't think of it. I'll do it. No, really, you mustn't.' They all shouted over the din of the vacuum and the shower. Robert made no sound. He showed no sign of embarrassment or unease. He looked, if anything, rather satisfied with himself. He stood in silence as James washed him, and kept his eyes fixed on Mary with an inscrutable expression.

Young Robert wasn't asleep when Simon knocked on his door and stepped into the room. He wondered if the second part of the inquisition about the porno pictures was imminent, but Simon smiled brightly and said; 'Ah! Rob. Glad you're awake. Do me a favour, would you? We're one short for footie.'

Rob groaned, stretched, and yawned affectedly. 'I don't know,' he said. 'Who's playing?'

'Well unfortunately Beckham's cried off so it's just me and Bob and the three junior space cadets. Come on, the little lads'll make mincemeat of us old boys. We'll be dead by half time without some young blood on the pitch.'

Rob knew that he ought to tell Simon to fuck off, remain remote and moody; he was far more likely to get sent home if he held to his line and especially now he had the ammunition to really annoy Ellie. With any luck he could reduce her to a jibbering wreck before the day was out. He didn't care if he had to catch a train or even hitch-hike, although he'd much rather drive his mother's car, and in fact had seriously considered just taking off in it. But Simon was still standing in his doorway, patiently waiting, a good natured, encouraging smile on his face, and Rob liked the idea of being called upon to help out the grown-ups. It showed respect. Plus, burned into his mind's eye, was an image of Simon and the boys rolling like puppies over the games room floor, and the idea of playing with Simon and Bob was appealing on all kinds of levels, some of them so subliminal they were almost impossible to fathom.

'Oh, and the other thing,' Simon said, stepping further inside the room and perching on the edge of the bed. 'I know your Dad said the computer had to go away today and everything but a mate of mine gave me a demo disc of a new game he's trying to market. He wants me to see what I think of it. I wondered if we could use your computer?'

'A new game?'

'Mmmm. I think it's a driving game: *Road Rage*?'

'Sounds cool.'

'It's an 18 so the lads won't be able to play it. But we could. If you like.'

'Alright then.' In spite of himself, Rob smiled. Simon had as good as told him that he was considered an adult, although he would not be eighteen for months. He hoisted himself up in the bed and rubbed his eyes. 'When are you playing footie?'

Simon stood up. 'Lads are limbering up as we speak. Front lawn.'

Breakfast that day was a disorganised affair. Belinda seemed to have abdicated, temporarily at least, control in the kitchen. By the time she drifted downstairs there was an accumulation of dishes in the sink, cereal packets stood open on the table and the area around the toaster was littered with crumbs, open jars of jam and an assortment of dirty knives. She ignored it all and made herself some fresh tea. Ruth, seated in splendid isolation at the head of the table with a book propped defensively up against a coffee pot, eyed her, narrowly. Her hair was softer and less vehemently contained in its habitual chignon. She wore a lighter, pearlier shade of lipstick than was usual for her. Her normal silk blouse had been replaced by a much more casual one in soft cotton, a beautiful shade of pale yellow, and it was open at the neck. She wore, uncharacteristically, and to Ruth's extreme surprise, a pair of tight fitting corduroy jeans in bottle green, and an expensive brand of trainers. Now she came to really look, Ruth noticed that her sister had shed quite a few pounds.

'My goodness, Belinda,' Ruth said, dryly, 'a very fine swan indeed.' Belinda smiled, dreamily, and carried her tea mug out of the back door to sit on the bench in the sunshine.

June and Granny made a bristling entrance.

'Sit down there, Mother,' June said, shortly. She looked around the kitchen. 'What a mess. Isn't anyone serving breakfast today? Where's Belinda?'

Ruth nodded in the direction of the back door. 'Off duty, apparently.'

June blew air between her teeth crossly. 'This house,' she declared, 'will be the death of me. I scalded my hand getting mother washed.'

Granny wriggled on her chair, and winced through toothless gums. 'My bottom stings,' she whined. 'I keep putting the cream on it but it makes it worse.'

'Oh shut up, for God's sake,' June snapped. 'Let me find you some Weetabix. Will that do?' Without waiting for a response, June dropped two Weetabix into a bowl and sloshed on some milk. 'Here you are. Now eat this and stop complaining.' She pushed the bowl in front of Granny and stalked out of the room. She met Les and Muriel in the passageway. 'Oh there you are. Where the hell have you been? I've had to cope with Mother all on my own.'

'I've been out with Roger. It's a lovely morning,' Muriel said, brightly.

'I wasn't speaking to *you*. Leslie. I need the car keys.'

'Why?' The three of them re-entered the kitchen. Les sat on the end of the bench and, picking up an old newspaper, turned to the sports pages. He avoided looking at his wife who stood beside him with her hands on her hips, her face as dark and ugly as a bruise.

'Because I just do.' She lowered her voice menacingly. 'Do we have to have this conversation here?'

Muriel began clearing crockery and running some hot water into the sink. 'I'll just wash these, Les, and then I'll make that coffee,' she called over her shoulder. The noise of water pouring into the sink and cascading over the dishes predominated for a time.

'Do we *really* have to have this conversation *here?*' June repeated, her voice more insistent.

Les looked up at her wearily. 'As far as I'm concerned we're not having a conversation. Muriel's making proper coffee,' he said, as thought that explained everything.

'So?'

'Yes.' Muriel turned the taps off and swished the water around. 'I'm going to try, anyway; I've only ever made instant. Would you like some June? I said I'd take some out to the chaps. The boys are out playing football. Even Rob. So nice to see them all in the fresh air.'

Ruth lifted her eyes from her book. 'Is James with them?'

'No. I haven't seen him this morning.'

'No. Neither have I,' Ruth said, sourly, going back to her book.

'James is upstairs,' Heather said, coming into the kitchen just at the tail-end of the exchange. She had Starlight on her hip. They both looked as fresh as daisies. 'He's helping Mum. Dad's had.... well, some kind of mishap. Here you are sweetie, let's pop you into your high chair and Mummy will make you some yummy breakfast.'

Belinda stepped back in through the back door. 'A mishap?' A few minutes in the fresh air and sunshine had heightened her complexion; she was blooming.

'Yes,' Heather nodded. She walked over to Belinda and kissed her cheek, before whispering a few words into her ear. Belinda, in response, grimaced. 'Anyway, it's all in hand, now, Lindy. I expect they'll be down shortly.'

'A mishap?' Ruth echoed Belinda and expected, like her, to be enlightened.

But Heather just nodded, evasively. 'I wonder if Starlight likes Marmite...'

'Suit yourself,' Ruth snapped, and turned the page of her book.

'Leslie!' June snatched the newspaper away from her husband.

'Temper temper!' Granny admonished, waving her spoon at June. 'Carry on like that, my girl, and you'll go to your room.' She laid her spoon down into her bowl and looked wistfully at Starlight. 'Mrs George lost her baby,' she said, sadly. 'But hers wasn't a black one. It was pink, like normal.'

Ellie and Tansy arrived in the kitchen. Ellie looked pale and her eyes were puffy. Her hair lacked its usual lustre. Tansy pressed her into a seat kindly. 'Toast? Peanut butter?' she asked. Ellie nodded, dumbly.

481

'Ellie, darling?' Belinda took a few steps towards her daughter, but halted when Ellie shook her head and said, 'don't make a fuss, Mum.'

'Well,' Granny considered, 'I *assume* it was pink...'

'There's nothing especially normal about pink, actually Granny,' Heather said, offering Starlight toast and Marmite. 'Statistically speaking, black ones are far more normal.'

'Speaking of not being normal: how are *you* feeling this morning, Heather?' Ruth asked, acerbically, over the top of her book. 'You didn't catch a chill or anything, did you, last night?'

'Oh!' Heather laughed, musically. 'No. Of course not. It was wonderful. You saw, then? Oh dear.'

'Oh yes.' Ruth swept her eyes across the room until she was looking at Belinda, who still stood half-way across the kitchen. But Belinda wasn't looking at Ruth. Her eyes were trained on the kitchen door. The next moment James was in the kitchen with Robert. 'Oh yes,' Ruth said again, with heavy inference, 'Last night, you know, I saw everything.' It was impossible to tell whether the jibe had gone home. Belinda hurried across to the door and helped James to get Robert settled in his chair. Behind them, Mary hovered in the doorway. She looked white and traumatized. The sight shook even Ruth, momentarily, from her black mood. 'Mum!' she frowned. 'What on earth's the matter?' But Mary shook her head, and refused to be drawn.

'Just leave it, Ruth,' Heather said, quietly, before putting her hand gently onto Mary's shoulder. 'Tea? Toast?'

'What a lot of secrets today!' Ruth carped. Surely the taunt would sting *someone* into speaking? She looked from one to another of her sisters, and at her mother, and even at Ellie, but no one was prepared to enlighten her.

'Just tea, please,' Mary said, quietly, giving Heather's hand a squeeze before pouring cornflakes into a bowl for Robert.

But Robert pushed the bowl away from him. 'Porridge,' he said, firmly.

Mary, Heather and Belinda exchanged significant looks. 'I'll do it, Mum,' Heather said. 'Starlight doesn't seem to like Marmite after all. She'll have some porridge, too.'

Whatever was going on, clearly they were all determined to exclude Ruth from it. 'Suit yourselves, then. Be secretive if you must. But don't say I didn't ask,' she scowled, going back to her book.

James sat down next to her, and tried to take her hand, but she snatched it from him and steadfastly read on.

Presently, a general hullaballoo announced the arrival of the footballers. They were hot and flushed with exercise, and they brought into the kitchen a manly, spicy musk. They clamoured around the fridge and poured out cold juice, which they guzzled thirstily, whilst reliving the highlights of their match. They all looked ridiculous, wearing one another's football shirts. Simon was squeezed into one which was so small it left his tummy bare. Todd's on the other hand, came down to his knees.

'Oh dear, have you given up on me? I *am* making the coffee,' Muriel cried, indicating the coffee cups she had made ready on the table.

'Lovely Muriel! Thank you. You're a star!' Simon called out. Simon was perhaps a little more flushed than the rest, conscious of the extra few pounds he was carrying around these days. He mopped his face and neck with a large handkerchief.

'Humph,' June ejaculated, folding her arms across her bosom, 'making coffee is hardly rocket science!' Defeated in her attempts to get Les' attention she sat down heavily on the chair by the Aga.

Ben struggled onto Ruth's knee. She unbent sufficiently for him to squirm between her body and the table. 'I scored three penalties!' he said, proudly. 'Uncle Bob tried to save them, but he couldn't. Look! He got all muddy.' Bob smiled ruefully across the kitchen. One side of his jeans was smeared with mud.

'You're *all* very muddy,' June remarked, critically. 'You shouldn't be in the house at all in that state, I don't think.'

'We took our trainers off, June,' Simon pointed out, indicating them in a heap outside the back door. In the miniscule football top, with his bare tummy, his righteous indignation was less than compelling. June sniffed.

'It doesn't matter!' Muriel cried, spooning coffee grounds into a cafétière. 'I've got the measure of that washing machine now. You can all peel off and I'll see to it later.'

'Am I going to get any breakfast?' Robert roared, so suddenly that Starlight jumped and started to cry. Simon's lips blanched a bloodless white, remarkable against the flush of his face. He threw a steely glare across the kitchen at his father.

'It's coming, Daddy,' Heather sang out, from the Aga.

'And this is his football shirt, look,' Ben prattled on, 'he says I can keep it. Mum, it's a real Man U one! Not even a replica! Look! It' a number 7 shirt. That was Beckham's, and before him someone called Cantona.'

'I thought you didn't like football,' Ruth said, smoothing Ben's ruffled hair down.

'Uncle Bob says I'm good at it!'

'*Does* he, now? Oh well, if Uncle Bob says so......'

'Yes, and later, we're going to finish our song.'

Rob and Simon were over by the sink, loud with manly guffaws. Toby hovered nearby. Simon's cheer was determined, false. Rob looked rude with good health, his hair tousled. He kept throwing triumphant looks over at Ellie, and laughing, like Simon, too loudly. 'This will be the shape of things to come,' he seemed to be saying, 'when little-princess-perfect has toppled off her throne!' He had really enjoyed the football. The men had treated him as one of themselves; they had winked at each other while allowing the younger boys to make passes and score goals which they could easily have intercepted. He and Simon had made blatant fouls in the area so that Ben could shoot penalties, and Bob had made comedy dives in the goal-mouth to let them in. At full-time they had made a great show of asking the younger boys for their shirts, like real footballers. Simon had looked so funny squeezing into Todd's top! Toby had been thrilled when Rob asked for his. His new-found ascendency, amongst the grown-ups and especially over Ellie, was quite intoxicating.

'I'm famished,' Simon declared, 'aren't you, Rob? Shall we make lunch?'

'Porridge is ready! Yummy brekkie!' Heather called, brightly. It was unclear whether she was addressing her Dad or her daughter. They looked up with equal eagerness at her voice.

'I think it's still breakfast time,' Rob grinned.

'Oh sack that!' Simon exclaimed, expansively. 'Breakfast can move seamlessly into lunch.' He rummaged in the fridge.

If Belinda had been shocked at the appearance of her daughter, she was appalled to see how the appearance of her son had made Ellie's pallor, if possible, more pronounced. She seemed hardly able look at him and yet unable to look at anything else. Something Heather had said a night or two ago came back to Belinda. Something was very wrong between her children and she had been too preoccupied to get to the bottom of it.

'Do you mind if we finish this ham?' Simon was waving the packet at her across the room.

485

Belinda dragged her eyes from Ellie. 'No,' she said, 'I don't mind at all. I'm having a bit of a day off today. Elliot has gone in to the office and....' she took another step towards Ellie, preparing to suggest that the two of them have a walk, or go shopping.

'What?' Rob interrupted her. He stood by the open back door, a butter knife in one hand and a slice of bread in the other. 'Dad's gone home?' People began to look around them. They hadn't remarked Elliot's absence but it explained the Belinda's slightly unusual demeanour this morning. Miriam, arriving in the kitchen at that moment said, with hollow concern, 'Elliot's gone home? Oh dear, I *am* sorry.'

A few people stifled sniggers. Belinda made a moue. 'Just for the day, I think. To sort out whatever the crisis was yesterday.'

'I could have gone with him!' Rob blurted out. He couldn't believe that his Dad had gone home without him. After all the times he had asked!

'I wish you had,' Ellie said, under her breath. Tansy gave her arm a squeeze.

'But you wouldn't want to, would you?' Simon took up a position next to Rob and began laying ham on the slices of buttered bread. He sent Toby off to find plates. 'Go home, I mean?'

Rob shrugged. 'I did,' he said, 'yesterday, and the day before. I asked him to take me.'

'Why?' Simon avoided eye contact with his nephew. Young people, he knew, found it easier to communicate at an oblique angle.

Robert shrugged again. 'It all seemed so pointless. *Happy Families.* I could have stayed at home for half term. Seen my mates.'

'No one asked you, then, if you *wanted* to come?'

'Oh God, no! We don't get asked, we get *told*.'

'Hmmm. Shall we have mustard on these?'

'No, thanks.'

'Do you still want to go home now? If you want to, and if your Mum agrees, I'll take you.'

Rob looked up from the sandwiches. 'Would you?'

Simon nodded. 'You're a big boy now. I bet you could survive home alone for a few days. Anyway, I believe in letting people make their own choices. Then, if it turns out badly, they have only themselves to blame.'

Rob hesitated. 'I don't know, now.'

Simon stacked their sandwiches onto plates, 'Have a think about it. See how you feel at the end of today. I'm going to sit with Toby and Todd and eat these. Then I'll get showered. Then we'll have a look at that game. If you want to. Coming?'

They walked over to the table and sat down. Ellie gave a faint, pained mewing noise and got to her feet. She and Tansy left the room together, passing Mitch in the passageway. He stared after them, after Ellie, more struck than ever by her altered, care-worn face.

The beach was empty, wide, with multi-coloured shingle sloping gently down to the silver sea. Drifts of crisp seaweed laced its upper reaches and petrified lumps of driftwood punctuated the swathe like weird, tortured sculptures. Here and there an anomalous deposit - an oil can, a supermarket trolley, a rubber glove - made allusion to the modern world, but other than that the scene was without a reference point in time. The sea sparkled like mercury while, above it, seagulls soared and wheeled in the pale sky. They seemed so free, without a care. Rachel, standing at the edge of the pine forest, on the top of the sandy slope which ran down to the shingle, and looking out over it all, wished that she herself could be like one of the seagulls, just run across the pebbles and launch herself into the air and swoop far away across the sea. She did not think that she would be much missed. It was still fairly early. There had not been time for anyone back at the house to miss her, yet. When Ellie and Tansy woke up and found her gone, they would assume that she was just in another part of the house. No doubt they would take advantage of her absence to pick over her betrayal. How could she have done it? After everything they had said, about trust and secrets?

And, indeed; how *could* she have?

She stepped away from the trees and the cold air met her; a chill shroud which lay over the beach and the sea. The raw iciness of it pricked at her eyeballs and placed an iron cap on her head. She gasped, and the frosty air reached like fingers down her throat and into her chest. It hadn't felt as cold as this in the woods. But she marched with determined steps into the teeth of it, over the pebbles and down to the seashore. She didn't care if it was cold. She didn't care if she died of the cold, and no one else would care, either. She waded into the sea until it was almost at the top of her wellington boots. Insistent tears flowed down over her face, into the cut on her cheek, and dripped off her chin. She mopped them away with the sleeve of her jumper, sobbing and snivelling; there was no one, now, to hear her.

She cried for the loss of everything; friendship with the girls, belonging in the family, the dream of Rob; especially, *especially*, the hopeless, fleeting dream of Rob.

The sea, even through her boots and two pairs of socks, was ice-cold and her toes began to ache with it. She retreated to the shore and set off along the tide-line. She still cried, cried for the stupid, romantic feelings she had harboured about Rob, which could never, *ever* have been returned. 'Look at yourself! Just look at yourself!' she shouted. 'How could *he* ever have thought that *you* were pretty? You're fat! And ugly! And *so* stupid!' They were truths she had always considered about herself and yet she had allowed herself to believe for a few delirious, oh such heady, wonderful moments that he could, that he *did* have feelings for her, and the wonder of it had taken her breath away and with it any vestige of common sense she might have had. The sight of her, she told herself, bitterly, must have made him almost retch; her ugly bruise and stupid hair and fat stomach and wobbly thighs. She stopped and looked down at herself, swathed in layers of nasty clothes and yet still the lumpiness of lardy fat was undisguised. She wished she had a knife, to cut it all away. There, on the seashore, to hack away the loathsome flesh and leave it in blubbery lumps to be taken away by the tide or carried off by the birds. Suddenly her hands were clenching and tearing at her flesh, her legs, her stomach and her face, pinching and wrenching, until the cut on her cheek split open again and blood mixed with the salt of her tears and the waxy stream from her nose to coat her sleeve with pinkish silver strings of misery.

She walked to the very end of the beach, where rocks slippery with mustard-coloured seaweed tumbled into the water. The rock was black and deeply grooved, sharp and difficult to negotiate. She followed its line back up the beach until she found the sandy slope once more, and a place where the ledge had collapsed onto the beach,

489

leaving a sheltered notch just big enough for her to sit in, and offering a little shelter. Hiding in its cleft, she drew her knees up to her chin, and gathered her arms around herself, and cried and cried.

James found Ruth in the library, sitting, alone, with her book. She looked up as he entered and then continued reading as though her attention had been caught by no more than a fly hitting a window. He closed the door softly behind him and drew a stool up in front of her chair. It was a small stool, a footstool, and his bulk spilled over its edges. Of all the seats in the room it was the least suitable and he chose it so that he would look ridiculous. He lifted her foot on to his knee, gently peeled off her thick sock and began to rub her toes. She did not resist him, neither did she respond. For quite a while he said nothing. Ruth's eyes continued to scan across the lines of text but he could tell that she wasn't reading. She was chewing the inside of her cheek, a well-known sign of inner distress. He rubbed his soft fingers over the sole of her foot, kneading the pads underneath her toes, pressing occasionally at points underneath the skin. He kept his eyes on her face but she looked resolutely down at her book.

Presently, he said; 'I believe Mary will wish to speak to you today – to all of you. She has something on her mind.'

Ruth turned her page. 'Nobody wants to tell *me* anything at all,' she said, archly. 'I don't suppose I shall be required.'

'What do you mean?'

'Oh! A number of things. Lots of things seem to be happening that are to be kept secret from me.'

'For instance?'

Ruth removed her spectacles and rubbed at them ineffectually with hem of her t shirt. 'This morning, there was something about Dad. Heather and Mum both refused to tell me about it.' She replaced her glasses and focussed once more on the page of her book.

'Oh, well, that was just not a nice thing to talk about at breakfast. Your Dad had had an accident on the toilet, that's all. He was in a mess. I expect they wanted to spare everyone the details.' James replaced Ruth's sock. 'Do you want me to do the other foot?'

491

She shrugged. 'I don't care.'

'What about a fire?'

'No. I suppose *you* know what Mum wants to talk about?'

James stood up from his stool and stretched his back. 'Well, yes, she mentioned something yesterday...'

'There you are then! I told you, I'm always the last to know anything!'

'She feels she needs more help with your Dad,' James said, mildly, 'and she wants to discuss the financial implications.'

He pretended to examine the books on the shelves. Lovely tooled leather, complete sets of Sir Arthur Conan Doyle and P.G. Wodehouse and Dorothy L Sayers. They looked as though they might be quite valuable but it was hard to imagine that anything of great value would be made available to holiday guests. From the games room the sound of the piano floated on the air into the room, a Mazurka. A tiny hand clutched at a place below his diaphragm, making his chest enlarge.

'I was wondering,' Ruth said, suddenly, closing her book and looking up at him for the first time, 'I was wondering if there is anything *you're* not telling me?' She gave him a hard look through her spectacles.

'What do you mean?'

Her gaze remained straight for a while, her eyes steely as flints. Then she sighed, and looked away, and said, with a deceptive casualness; 'I wonder how Les felt when he realized he'd married the wrong sister.'

James frowned, perplexed, wrong-footed by her question. 'I suppose he knew right from the start....'

'Perhaps you all do.'

'*We* all?'

'You men who marry McKay girls. You all seem to get the wrong ones. I bet Elliot *kicked* himself, when he met me. *I* was the one he should have had, if he'd wanted a business partner. I'm sure that's all he really did want.' She sighed theatrically, 'but it was too late by then.'

James stepped away from the book shelves and stood once more in front of Ruth's chair. 'Has Elliot *said* anything to you? Has he been….'

'Trying to get off with me?' Ruth gave a hoot of laughter, shrill and hollow, eerily reminiscent of June's habitual tick. 'Good God, no! But,' she was suddenly coldly serious, 'you wouldn't like it if he did, would you?'

'I wouldn't think *you* would like it much, either.'

She ignored him. 'You can see he's not right for Belinda, though, can't you? Just look at her, today, with him out of the way! She's a different woman! Soft, dreamy – she's wearing *trousers!*

James hesitated. He couldn't tell Ruth what he knew, it would only make things worse, that he should know something, a family something, that she didn't. But before he could think how to extricate himself from the awkward corner, Ruth had plunged herself into a deeper one.

'Really,' she said, frostily, 'Belinda would have been a better wife for *you*. God knows, she'd have more patience with you than I do. In fact I told her, only the other evening, that she was welcome to you.'

James was so hurt that his eyes filled with tears. The place near his heart which only a moment before had swelled with emotion now felt eviscerated, as though he had been stabbed. He remained perfectly motionless. Then Ruth, with a sigh, crumpled back into the chair and began to cry. Blindly, she reached for a handkerchief from her pocket. It was empty, of course, and James, like an automaton, passed her his.

493

She removed her glasses once more and pressed the handkerchief to her eyes.

When the words came, they were punctuated by sobs and hiccoughs. 'Is that,' she said, indistinctly, 'is that what *you* want? Is it, James?'

There was no reply. When Ruth looked up, she was alone in the room.

The roar of vehicles hurling themselves through junctions and over roundabouts and, just as frequently, across grass verges and over pavements reverberated around the study. Rob was at the controls. He had picked a metallic blue Subaru Impreza WRX and was racing it through the streets of some non-specific city centre with reckless disregard for traffic signals, other road users or the Highway Code. The more cars he hit the more points he notched up. Pedestrians didn't earn you any points but there was a certain satisfaction in watching them bounce off the bonnet. Another vehicle, an Audi TT, was in close pursuit, tail-gating, cutting him up and generally being annoying. The idea of the game was to cause the Audi to have a crash or to close down on it until you could force it to stop, then to beat its occupant to a pulp. Suddenly his game came to an end when he drove his car off a pier and it disappeared into a marina.

'Hard luck!' Simon said.

Rob turned to face him; his face was alight. 'This is a cracking game. The graphics are brilliant. Your go.'

Simon selected a red Ford Mustang Shelby GT 500 and took to the streets with a screech of tyres. 'Your Dad would enjoy this. It might get rid of all that pent up anger,' he commented, swerving to avoid a woman crossing the road.

Rob sneered. 'He's crap at anything like this. He tried *Fatal Blow* on Friday and died on level one. That junction's blocked off; you'll have to go right.'

'Thanks. Ooops. That was close. You know, I don't think this game warrants an 18, do you? I don't see why Toby couldn't play it, later.'

'No. It isn't as bad as *RTA*, is it? No gore and no swearing, so far.'

'I haven't played that one. So what *do* you do with your Dad then?'

Rob was silent for a while. 'Nothing. He isn't one of those Dads.'

Simon's car bounced across a roundabout and hurtled down the wrong lane of a dual carriageway. A Ferrari followed close behind.

'That bastard's going to have you if you don't do something soon,' Rob warned.

'You're right. I'm running out of options though. My Dad wasn't one of those Dads either; the kind you can talk things over with. We didn't speak for years. Did you know?'

'I did hear something about it. You went to the States, didn't you?'

'Amongst other places. It wasn't easy, though. It was – just a minute,' Simon concentrated for a few seconds while he did a handbrake turn in a car park and shunted the Ferrari into a space between a wall and a wheelie bin, 'that's got *you*. Yes, I was saying: it was probably the most difficult thing I've ever done but I had no other option. I was sick of being bullied. Anyway, what I wanted to say was, if you ever felt like you were in a similar position, you must come and see me. I'm the one person who would understand. Oh crap! He's coming to get me. What's that he's got in his hand?'

'A baseball bat.'

'Oh dear. How do I quit?'

'Press esc.'

'Anyway,' Simon said, getting up to make room for Rob, 'I was thinking, tonight, we'd give your Mum a break and cook the supper.'

Rob took his eyes off the screen. 'We?'

'Sure. You and me and the lads. Nothing to it. You don't cook?'

'Well,' Rob laughed, 'I suppose I'll try anything once. What's the worst that could happen?'

'The worst? Well the whole family could die of food poisoning but hey! Let's take the risk!'

The sun had climbed over the trees behind her and was warming her little hiding place. She felt spent and empty; Rachel had stopped crying, the tight coils of misery and apprehension had loosened and she was left with a weary feeling of heavy hopelessness. She eased herself from her hideout and stretched her limbs, and wandered in a desultory way over the beach, picking up pebbles and finding smooth, opaque nuggets of sea glass which she dropped into her pocket. For a time she lost herself in this activity, distracted by the number and variety of the beach's treasures, but always a hollow, anxious foreboding broke in on her, a physical sensation like an ache in her heart from an old wound.

After a while she looked at her watch. It was almost twelve o'clock. She had better go back to the house for a while. She didn't want to but then again she thought she had better put in some kind of appearance or people would come looking for her. That would just make things too easy; far easier than she deserved. To be looked for and found, and to be questioned in a way which would make the whole story come out would be no good at all. They would tell her that it wasn't her fault, and that she mustn't worry, and that Ellie must take the consequences for her actions. But that way wouldn't do. She absolutely didn't want that. Because it wouldn't heal the rift between her and Ellie, and it would get Ellie into trouble, the very thing she feared, and it would get Rob into trouble too, no doubt, about the vodka and everything. She would be saved but they would suffer. But they would never forgive her and they would never love her. This way, *she* would suffer and *they* would be saved. Like they said in church, about Jesus. He suffered and they were saved, and so they must love Jesus. So she would go back to the house, make sure she was seen by people, use the toilet perhaps and get something to eat, and then come back outside. No one would know except for the people who mattered; they would realise, they would understand the punishment she was giving herself; and they might forgive her. Perhaps it would bring them together, Ellie and Rob. Yes, perhaps, in some way, she might be the one who brought the family back together after all.

Tentatively she touched her cheek. It had stopped bleeding but it felt crusty and hard. The white strips were wet and had lost their stickiness. She might have to think up some explanation about that. She scrambled up on to the dune and began to walk back to the place where the path came out through the trees. When she found it she entered the wood. The path wound between the fir trees. In the depths of the wood, after casting a quick glance around herself, Rachel threw herself onto the ground, rolling in needles and rubbing the shoulder of her jumper up against the trunk of the nearest tree. Then, on all fours, she deliberately scraped the tender side of her face against a prickly bare branch. It hurt, and she winced, but what did that matter? She deserved to be hurt. The pain was oddly satisfying, as though it spoke the words of her inner soreness. Touching the cut with a finger she could not feel any fresh blood. There. Now she would not be lying if she said she had fallen over in the wood and scraped her face.

Mitch walked Tiny round the garden, his hands thrust deeply into his jeans pockets, giving himself a good talking to. He mustn't, he just mustn't get involved. It wasn't down to him, anyway. It was none of his business.

But his detachment was a delusion. He felt like a pinball machine, his thoughts the silver bullet, careering violently round his head, ricocheting off raw susceptibilities, lighting him up in an intoxicating blaze of neon but setting alarm bells ferociously ringing. He was drowning, the morass of conflicting emotional responses closing, inexorably, over his head.

Suddenly, he kicked, viciously, at a pine cone on the grass. It was a pathetic, ineffectual gesture. Tiny watched the cone's trajectory across the lawn with a baleful stare; he never lowered himself to chase or retrieve. That was a mug's game.

The girl's stricken face as he had passed her in the kitchen corridor was etched on Mitch's memory. Their eyes had caught one another, just for the briefest moment, and she had given him such a tragic, sad little smile. It had inflated him, made him unfurl, like a new bud. He had almost heard the pop of the bursting carapace, felt the gossamer brush of petals expanding in his innards; a deep, timeless, visceral response. He had had an overwhelming urge to take her, right there and then, in his arms. Only his too-recent dealings with the grimy toilet had held him back, that, and the erection – like a totem pole – which had woken him up that morning. Both had made him feel in some way unworthy of her, just then. His warring impulses – potent, ravening desire, and a softer, purer, protective impulse, confused him.

The family dynamic confused him, too. He was seeing so much that was appealing – very appealing, to someone who had never experienced the comfortable co-operation, the relaxed reliance of secure family relations; the flow of food, the pleasant hum of cheerful chat, the concerted recreational activities. It all called out to a scarcely acknowledged place in him; a hidden, hollow, lonely room deep in his psyche; the small, neglected, cowering boy within. The cohesive response of the siblings to their interfering aunt had been quite magnificent; June had been, again and again, left high and dry with the old woman. The previous evening Elliot's choler had been discreetly – but determinedly – staved off; he had been, quite simply, ignored. Everyone had seen the burgeoning creative connection between Bob and Ben but possibly he, Mitch, had been the only one to remark the tentative honesty which was creeping into all their encounters; the taut, defensive demeanours that they had all arrived with were, gradually, slipping.

There remained, though, unpleasantly prickly areas, like stinging nettles, amongst the family verdure. June; bristling and sniping at poor, hapless Muriel. Simon; ignoring his father with fixed, steely loathing. Ruth; staggering under chips like barge-boards on both shoulders. Elliot; a maelstrom of neuroses and carping, self-aggrandising gambits. All these were being politely skirted round, stepped over, like dog-dirt in the path. Everyone knew it was there but nobody acknowledged it.

But the situation with Rob and Ellie was different. No-one seemed aware of it. Which made it more dangerous. Mitch gritted his teeth and snarled. Tiny, in response, raised a curious beetled eyebrow.

But it was no good. What could he do?

In his trouser pockets, he found his hands had clenched themselves into fists. It would not be the first time he had beaten the living daylights out of someone. The wet, gristly smack of his knuckles into that smug, scoffing eye would be very satisfactory.

He wrestled with it all; the frontiers of his defensive barriers all-but disintegrated, as he walked, round and round the deserted garden.

Belinda had wanted the little trip to town to be just for herself and Ellie. Her daughter looked pale and ill, and close to tears, but so far Belinda's gentle questions had all been rebuffed. But Ellie wouldn't go into town without Tansy, so Tansy had had to be invited along too. June, Heather and Miriam had all, it seemed, been desperate to explore the little market town. So they had taken Simon's people carrier and Belinda had ended up being in the front seat and forced to make conversation with Miriam while Ellie and Tansy had climbed into the back row of seats and whispered away the journey.

The road took them through the village.

'Wasn't that James going into that shop?' Heather said, suddenly. Belinda craned her neck but Miriam was driving quickly – too quickly, probably – and they were through the village. They proceeded along a number of winding country lanes and then out onto an A road which passed between fields and small gatherings of cottages, farms and the occasional petrol station or car dealership. On the outskirts of town, feeling that if she did not say something the two girls would disappear off on their own, Belinda turned around and said as pointedly as she could; 'I'll treat you to lunch, girls, if you like. There might be a McDonalds.'

'Doesn't sound like much of a treat to me,' June commented, morosely, to no one in particular.

'No,' Heather agreed. 'I think the food in those places is notoriously unhealthy, isn't it? You won't get one of your five a day at a place like that.'

'Not unless you eat the napkin,' Miriam quipped, turning into a large pay and display car park. They all disembarked.

'How about lunch, then?' Belinda said again, brightly, to the girls, who hovered near the back of the car.

'No, it's OK Mum,' Ellie said, avoiding her eyes. 'Tansy and I will go off and explore. We'll see you back here in....'

'Two hours,' said Miriam, affixing the pay and display ticket to the windscreen.

'Oh but Ellie I thought...' Belinda stammered, but the two girls had already set off across the grey tarmac towards a footbridge which spanned a wide, smoothly flowing river.

'I need to find a supermarket or something,' Miriam said. 'Simon says he's cooking tonight and he's given me a list.'

'Oh?'

'I'll come with you,' Heather said. 'I'm sure that Tuesday is market day here. That might be interesting.' The two of them turned to follow the girls.

'Just you and me for lunch then, Belinda, ha ha ha!' June beamed.

The girls found a well-trodden but muddy path which snaked through a wide, grassy strip beside the river. The occasional seat offered itself but they were green with moss, some were broken and all were scrawled with obscenities. The sun shone quite brightly but there was a keen wind which made sitting still seem unappealing. They wandered disconsolately along, Ellie lost in a fog of depression, going round and round the hopelessness of the situation in her head, with the odd sentence bubbling to the surface in a vain attempt to escape the relentless merry-go-round of her thoughts.

'He said that Philip could sue me for libel...........I might get expelled....... I'll never trust anyone ever again..... Even if he says nothing, the very fact that he knows means I can never relax, ever.'

Tansy squeezed Ellie's arm. 'I know, I know,' she said, faintly. 'It's terrible for you. Poor Ellie. But something will turn up. I'm sure of it.'

A dog and its owner walked towards them. The dog was old, wheezing and panting. Its owner shuffled behind it, also old and struggling for breath. Ellie waited until they had gone by before

503

replying; 'I'm afraid, Tansy. Afraid of my brother, and of my Dad and what he'll do when he finds out, and of my Mum, who'll be terrified that she'll be thrown off the committee of the townswomen's guild and shunned on the golf course for the rest of her life. I don't know why we have to have families at all. Why can't we just be on our own, and then we wouldn't have these dreadful responsibilities to other people. If it was only me, you know, I wouldn't care so much, but it's everyone else.'

'You don't think that the best thing to do would just be to tell them?' In a real emergency like this one, Tansy would have run to her Dad, although there were some things that she didn't feel she could tell him, like the way Miriam changed when he wasn't around, for example.

The grassy sward narrowed suddenly. A small thicket of prickly bushes growing close to the river seemed to signal the end of the river path. A stile over a fence suggested that they might continue across a field and into a new housing estate, but there were cows in the field and neither of the girls felt brave enough to go further. Ellie leaned on the stile and stared blankly across the field.

'Oh God, no,' she said, after a while. 'No. I couldn't just tell them. How would you even begin a conversation like that with your parents? I'd rather die.'

In the little tea shop which they found down a quaint stone passageway, June ordered smoked salmon salad and a large glass of chardonnay. Belinda stared bleakly at the menu for a few moments before ordering a bowl of homemade soup. June chattered about a recent scandal at the bridge club and a forthcoming election for the golf club committee. In the quiet of the café her voice was too loud and the waitress eyed them from behind the refrigerated display where she was busy arranging cream cakes. Belinda belonged to other clubs and the circumstances and the personalities meant nothing to her. She nodded and interjected occasional comments, and felt annoyed that she had been cheated out of her quiet lunch with Ellie. Suddenly June fell silent and Belinda was aware that she had been asked a question.

'I'm sorry. What?'

'This cock-up with the quotes. How is Elliot going to handle it?'

Belinda looked at her blankly. 'I'm sorry; I haven't a clue, June.'

'Ah,' June swelled self-righteously. 'Ha ha ha! If I might offer a word of advice, Belinda dear, it pays a woman to make close enquiry of her husband's affairs....'

Their lunch arrived. Belinda's soup looked grey and unappetizing, like old bath water.

'If only he *was* having an affair,' she thought to herself, stirring the pallid liquid around with a listless spoon, 'that would solve all my problems at a stroke.' Aloud, she said, 'to be honest, June, I'm too worried about Ellie to think about Elliot's problems. I really wanted the opportunity to chat to her today, with Elliot being out of the way.' Belinda laid her spoon down and pushed her lunch away. 'I don't really want this soup. I'll pay the girl and meet you in the market shall I?' She pushed back her chair and walked away from the table, leaving June with her mouth full of salad, unable to say a word.

Granny and Granddad were in the kitchen with Aunty Muriel, Granny McKay and Uncle Les. The kitchen door was open and as she bent to pull off her wellingtons Rachel could hear their disjointed conversation.

'If it's Tuesday then the chiropodist will be coming,' Granny asserted.

'How much?' Robert cupped his ear with his hand. 'What?'

'To see to my corns,' Granny clarified, loudly.

'I think you should eat some lunch, Robert,' Mary interrupted briskly. 'Muriel's made these nice sandwiches for us.'

'And a nice cup of tea. Careful now, it's hot,' Muriel distributed the cups.

'I don't like that cheese,' Robert said, querulously. 'It smells funny.'

'I think it cost a lot of money,' Muriel said. 'The package said Fortnum and Masons.'

'Mrs Mason smelled terrible. We all thought so and no one would sit next to her in the day room,' Granny piped up.

'Mary, I don't like the cheese,' Robert shouted.

'Alright, alright. I'll see what else there is.' Mary got up and opened the fridge.

'I'm sorry, Robert. I had to make something Mother could eat with no teeth,' Muriel said.

'My teeth taste funny,' Granny frowned.

'The *cheese* tastes funny,' Robert corrected her, crossly.

'There doesn't seem to be any ham left. Perhaps the girls will get some from the shops,' Mary said. 'What about an egg?'

'I want the telly on,' Robert said.

'Tonight, there's a match on,' Les said, remembering suddenly. 'We should watch it on that big screen, Robert. City v Spurs.'

Robert looked mildly interested for a moment, before turning once more to Mary. 'When is *Doctors* on?'

'Goodness, I don't know, Robert. I think it's all different for the school holidays you know. Come on, now, I'll get this egg scrambled for you in a jiffy. Then you can have one of your tablets and a lie down.'

'I wish you'd stop treating me like a fucking child!' Robert shouted. 'I won't have it, Mary. Do you hear?' In his temper, Robert had raised himself to his feet. '*Doctors* is *always* on,' he insisted.

'Now, now, Robert. That'll do,' Les said, quietly.

'That cream the doctor gave me for my bottom is useless,' Granny said, wriggling.

'Has anyone actually looked?' Mary asked, stirring scrambled egg in a saucepan. Her face was flushed.

Les and Muriel gave each other appalled glances and shook their heads. 'At her bottom?' Muriel mouthed, voicelessly, wide eyed.

Mary shook her head. 'No! At the cream! To see what kind it is.'

'Mary!' Robert barked, suddenly. It was intolerable that she should ignore him in this way. He shot his arm out swiftly and knocked Mary's cup of tea over. It spilled across the table and began to run off the edge onto his mother's lap. Les leapt to his feet but he wasn't quick enough to stop the scalding tea from soaking into Granny's dress.

'Ow! Ow! It's hot!' Granny cried, flapping her hands in her lap.

Rachel had been standing on the step for the past few moments waiting for someone to notice her. She hurried to the sink and soaked a tea towel in cold water. 'Here,' she said, 'put this on your legs, Granny. It will take the heat away.'

507

'What a clever girl,' Mary beamed. 'Where did you learn to do that?'

Rachel spread the tea towel onto Granny's thighs. They were as white and fleshless as sun-bleached bones. 'Press that on, that's right,' she said. 'We do a thing called Life Skills at school. They showed us first aid. Can I have one of those sandwiches?'

'Of course you can, darling,' Mary cried. 'Silly old Granddad spilled his tea. Where have you been? Playing out?'

'Yes,' Rachel said, fighting back the emotion which rose into her throat at her Grandma's praise and affection. If only she knew the truth. 'I've been playing in the woods.'

'How lovely,' Granny sighed. 'I used to play in Bluebell woods for hours and hours. Then Minnie Walsh said a man had messed with her down there and I wasn't allowed to go any more.

'Down in the woods?' Les raised an eyebrow.

Granny shook her head and pointed to her groin. 'Down *there*. But I did. I think I'd like my ashes scattered in Bluebell woods,' she said, dreamily.

'They built houses on it, Mother, years ago,' Muriel said. 'Now come on, eat that sandwich up. Where do you usually see the chiropodist?'

'Tuesdays.'

'Where are the other children?' Rachel enquired, carefully.

'Oh gosh, all playing in the house, I think, except the other two girls, they went shopping.'

'Oh. I think I'll take these back to the woods and eat them...... in my den,' Rachel extemporised, getting up and taking two more sandwiches from the plate.

'Oh, alright dear.'

'If you see my Dad, or Ruth, would you tell them that I've had lunch?'

'Of course, Rachel. You run along and have fun.'

Rachel carried her wellingtons through the house and used the little toilet off the hall. She could hear her brother and Uncle Bob playing the piano, a song she hadn't heard before; their two voices were singing but she couldn't make out the words. Uncle Bob's voice was gruff and deep, like a grizzly bear in a cave, Ben's as high and clear as a bird in the sky. If it wasn't so wonderful, it would have been silly. Along the corridor, Todd and Starlight were playing a game which involved hurling soft toys to see how far they would slide along the polished wooden floor. Nearer at hand, in the study, Toby and Uncle Simon were playing a game on the computer; not the war game, a different one. They were cheering and laughing in their excitement. Somewhere in this house her Dad would be sitting, reading perhaps, and if she just went to find him he would open up his huge arms and snuggle her onto his lap, and she could rest her head on his chest and listen to the comfortable flop of his heart as she poured out all her troubles, and he would say 'There now, there now,' and stroke her back, and it would all be alright. And the pull of such balm was so strong that for a moment she almost gave in to it. But then, from the study, she heard Rob's voice.

'Is Toby allowed a beer?' The sound of it in her ears made her heart tighten. He was close behind the door. It was so disorientating to be so drawn towards something and at the same time so afraid that it was not trustworthy. Frantically she began to wrestle with her wellingtons, stuffing her feet into them, awkward with her layers of socks. In her haste she dropped the sandwiches and almost trod on them.

Uncle Simon said, 'Yes, why not. Just one. We're on holiday after all.'

'I won't be a minute,' Rob said. Rachel grabbed her sandwiches and yanked open the front door just as the study door opened and Rob appeared.

'Hello Rachel,' Rob was right behind her, standing so close that she could feel his breath on her hair. 'Mmmm. Cheese sandwiches? Can I have one?' he took one from her hand, and bit into it. 'Mmmm. Nice.'

'Have them all,' Rachel stammered, pushing them into his hands. 'I don't want them.' She ran down the steps and round the house.

James sat in the village café and ordered a second pot of coffee. He hoped he had enough money left in his pocket to pay for it. When he had set out he hadn't had a clear idea of where he might go or considered whether he would need any money. He had exited the house, grabbing his disreputable anorak off the peg, and walked up the driveway. It was thickly carpeted with a layer of golden leaves, crisp on the top, where they were still frosted and where they lay in shadow, but slimy and wet and turning to mush in the rarer patches of sunshine. The drive was quite steep; James had soon been breathing heavily as he strode along it. It didn't make easy walking; deeply rutted, made of loose gravel and ancient hard-core. There was only room for one car at a time. Idly, as he walked, James had wondered what would happen if a car leaving met another arriving; he supposed that one would have to reverse, there was certainly no room for them to pass; the stumpy trunks and pointed limbs of the cut-back shrubs crowded the banks on either side, and, now he came properly to look, on one side of the drive the ground actually fell away quite sharply.

At the top of the drive he'd paused between the grand gate posts and considered. To the left the road quickly narrowed and lost itself on a coarse-grassed common. To the right it led eventually into the village, where the church was, and the pub, and, he recalled, a tea shop. That's where he would go. He'd turned right and kept to the right on the road, facing any oncoming traffic, but no cars passed him at all and he began the walk to Hunting Wriggly.

He had liked Belinda the first time he had met her, at a family gathering one Christmas. He and Ruth had been seeing each other for some months but it was before he had moved in with her. He had liked Belinda's softness, her quiet voice, the calm and capable way she had gone about cooking lunch, the way she included Rachel in the arrangements for her own children. Like him, she had preferred to remain peripheral while louder voices – Elliot and Ruth and old Robert – had vied for dominance in the lounge. He had admired, too,

511

her understated smartness, a considerable contrast to Ruth's flamboyant dishevelment.

The craft barn had been doing a slow trade. Two cars were in the car park. James had entered and heard the shop bell toll forlornly above him. After the bright sun, the barn was gloomy. Haphazardly arranged shelves held scented candles and jars of pebbles, strongly smelling soaps, art and craft kits for cross stitch and tapestry, sticks of rock and bottles of homemade preserves, tiny watercolours in frames studded with seashells, picture books with views of mountains and lakes, wooden toys, jigsaws and colouring books. Necklaces and other jewellery dangled from a many-branched chrome stand. There was a rail of hand knitted woollies, socks, scarves and hats, and below, them, a row of psychedelic wellington boots. The other customers, an elderly couple, had been were browsing amongst the postcards. The second car must belong to the lady behind the counter, a middle aged woman who knitted furiously, glancing up from time to time to survey the stock with a jealous glare. James had wandered around, his hands in his pockets, where he was surprised to discover two twenty pound notes he had forgotten about. Ruth had reluctantly parted with them on Sunday, the night the men had gone to the pub, but in the end he had not had to buy a round of drinks. The following day, Belinda had insisted on paying for their entry to the stately home and for their tea with her platinum credit card, so the notes remained intact. He'd returned to the jewellery stand and at length chosen a lovely necklace, sterling silver, with nuggets of amber interposed at regular intervals along its length. The lady behind the counter had put her knitting to one side while she placed the necklace into a box for him and wrapped the box in coloured tissue paper.

Now the box nestled in his fleece pocket, and he patted it occasionally while he drank his coffee. He liked buying presents but it was a pleasure he could rarely indulge. He had read his way through the collection of tourism leaflets on display in the little tea shop, the parish magazine and the election manifestoes for the three candidates who had wished to be elected onto the local council earlier in the year. He considered asking the waitress which one had won, but the effort of engaging in conversation was too much.

Belinda's kind efficiency in times of family trauma had been like a welcome salve on a wound. Once, when Ruth had been in hospital – he couldn't recall which of her myriad health issues had been in the ascendant - Belinda had cleaned the entire house and cooked for them, and bathed the children. During April's illness, while Ruth wailed and wrung her hands, Belinda had calmly provided meals and taken the children on outings. Later, in the quiet corridors of the hospice, hour after hour, they had waited together while Simon and Ruth sat at each side of the bed and measured April's shallowing breaths.

It was after Robert's stroke, when Elliot had triumphantly attained the Chair, that James had first discerned the cause of Belinda's sadness. Elliot, who had, until that time, veiled his ambition and true character in layers of obsequious amiability, seemed to come out in his true colours. He was not a nice man; mean-spirited, selfish, cold. It became plainer to James each time he saw them that Belinda's soft and gentle qualities were wasted on Elliot Donne. Her name and her family connection had been her only attraction to him. And each time he saw Belinda he had been unable to ignore the calm courage with which she bore the truth of it.

Two Easters ago they had been invited to Belinda and Elliot's for the long weekend. It had been their first visit to the McKay-Donne's new house. Belinda had gone to infinite trouble; lovely meals, an egg-hunt in the garden for the children, baskets of cheerful spring flowers in the bedroom. But Ruth had been sour-mouthed right from the beginning, her mood utterly curdled by envy, and while she had complained about everything from the stuffiness of the bedrooms (they had kept the heating on due to the cold weather) to the richness

513

of the food, it had been obvious that what she could not stomach was the size and splendour of the house in its quiet, fashionable cul-de-sac location, the elegance of the furnishings and the sumptuousness of the hospitality. Discerning the cause of her angst, Elliot had made it his business to lay it all on with a trowel, telling her how much everything had cost, and letting the names of high-class stores and fashionable designers drop like cyanide into a bucket of water beside her chair. Elliot and Ruth had proceeded to get rather drunk and after James had helped his incapacitated wife to bed he had come back downstairs to find Belinda and Elliot in the midst of a terrible row. Elliot had been raving in that incoherent way he had when drunk and at first James had intended to go back up the stairs, but the sound of breaking glass had taken him into the dining room where Elliot was hurling heavy lead crystal brandy balloons at his wife. She had dodged them easily and they had landed explosively on the slate hearth, but one thing had been immediately clear to James; this, or something like it, had happened before. Belinda's face betrayed fear but absolutely no surprise.

That night, after James had manhandled Elliot into bed, and after they had cleared away the glass and put the room to rights, he and Belinda had really talked. She had talked and he had listened, and they had established a deeper, more vital bond of understanding and sympathy. She had sworn him to secrecy; he must never, she had insisted, breathe a word to anyone, not even Ruth.

His anger was subsiding, gradually. It was an unusual emotion for him, and not one he enjoyed. Of course he would forgive Ruth; he was used to her occasional cruelty and unpredictable mood swings, but it was hard to excuse them somehow. She would not ask for his forgiveness, but spend the next few days looking lofty and self-righteous, and giving him the cold shoulder as though he, and not she, had been in the wrong. The McKays didn't do rows, they did moody silences as enormous and arctic and proud as glaciers, which gradually thawed and retreated until things went back to normal with nothing confronted or resolved, but leaving erratic boulders of unspoken words where they didn't belong, which would have to be stepped around forever more.

In the psychiatric unit, where James worked, even the most damaged patients were encouraged, with infinite gentleness, to confront their issues, but where he was so successful at work, he routinely failed at home, despite constant care. Ruth could never get over her disappointment at her sex; that she was not a boy, had not been considered as the successor to her father in the business; was only a girl, was not Simon. What Simon had, Ruth wanted. Her envy of her brother had manifested itself most obviously in her relationship with April, and when April had died Ruth's grief had been as abject as any spouse.

James paid for his coffee, left the premises, and ambled slowly through the village, looking at the houses and breathing deeply, steadying himself for the ordeal to come. He tried the round handle of the old church door and was surprised that it yielded. The interior was utterly silent and bathed in gentle, numinous light. He bowed his head and prayed for the strength to carry his cross.

They were all back for tea. Miriam unloaded the shopping and Simon set about marshalling the supplies.

Ben and Bob were full of their new song, and promising a world premier gala performance after supper. Ben was solemn with the excitement of it, his skin as translucent as porcelain, his eyes as round as saucers. Ruth, looking pale and listless, eyed them all sourly from the chair by the Aga.

'You don't look so good, Ruthie,' Simon said. Her mouth was pursed as though she had sucked on one of the lemons he was stacking onto the fruit bowl.

She smiled at him, wanly. 'It's nice of you to notice.' She allowed her eyes to flicker across at James. She had refused tea and was drinking wine defiantly.

James looked flushed and healthy. 'An excellent walk,' he declared, when someone asked him how he'd spent the day. 'Has anyone seen Rachel?' His hand strayed to his pocket where the parcel nestled in its tissue paper.

'At lunchtime, yes,' Mary said. 'She wanted you to know that she'd eaten. She said she'd been having a lovely game in the woods.'

'Oh?'

'Yes. She said she'd built a den. Didn't she?' Mary turned to Muriel.

Muriel nodded. 'Oh yes, a super den. And she took some of my cheese sandwiches to eat in it.'

'I think I'll go and look at it, after tea.'

'I'll come with you,' Belinda said, nonchalantly.

'You'll have to hurry up or it will be dark,' Ruth muttered, gloomily, 'although that might suit you better.'

Rob was in his element. His had so enjoyed his day; playing football and then the game this afternoon, even when Toby had been allowed to join them. Now Simon was unpacking the shopping, and showing him how to chop an onion, and sprinkling herbs into a bowl, while the rest of the family milled around and got themselves cups of tea and wedges of cake. He had had a few beers during the course of the afternoon, and he felt loose and energetic, and without the menacing annoyance of his father, as though, suddenly, anything was possible. Presently, in a hiatus of activity, he stepped out of the back door and joined Bob on the bench. They sat together in the gathering darkness of the autumn afternoon. Rob took huge draughts of the cold air. He felt inflated and potent. Whether it was the fun he'd had, or the power he had over Ellie, or Simon's attention, or the beers, or just the absence of that lowering cloud which his father always seemed to cast, he didn't know, but he felt new and revived. Inside the kitchen they could hear the chatter of the family, and it was as though he'd successfully tuned into a radio station he had only been able to hear through the muzz of static before. Suddenly he felt related. It felt good. Rob grinned and looked at Bob.

'You hear that?' he asked.

'Yes,' Bob said.

After a while he stepped back into the kitchen. Ellie and Tansy were huddled at the end of the bench. Ellie looked atrocious; pale and ill. Every so often she lifted her huge eyes up to him, and they were liquid. They made a dismal and unwelcome connection with his heart, a connection he didn't want to acknowledge, and suddenly all this new-found compatibility was too much, with too much potential for pain. He seized the knife and chopped onions with gusto while Simon added ground beef to the bowl, raw eggs, a hefty squeeze of some red tomato stuff, salt and pepper. His euphoria of only moments before had evaporated, leaving a shallow grave of unwelcome guilt.

Without looking at his sister, Rob fetched two more beers from the fridge, and placed one of them significantly in front of Toby, then they rolled up their sleeves and delved into the mixture.

517

Granddad Robert had refused his blue tablets. He was fractious and unsettled. Todd, under the table, was playing with his little cars, making incessant driving noises and running the cars round and round his Granddad's feet. It felt like a mouse tickling his ankles.

'Mary! Mary!' he said, but Mary was at the other end of the table.

'What's the matter, Daddy?' Heather bent over him. He pointed mutely under the table. 'Yes, poppet, it's Todd. Isn't he playing nicely?'

Mitch sat at the table and drank his tea. Ellie's trip to the shops had not cheered her, it seemed; she was still pale and distressed, and cast frequent glances over to her brother where he kneaded something meaty in a bowl. His actions were frenzied and overdone and Mitch knew that he was all too aware of his sister's unhappiness. He could almost see the strands of emotional connective tissue stretched tautly across the room between them, and between Ruth and James, the boys under the table and their querulous grandfather, in a triangle comprising June, Muriel and Les. Like someone given a glimpse into the intimate centre of a sacred thing, Mitch was able to see right through them all, into the heart, and the heart was livid and bursting with things unsaid. It enraged him, their determination to ignore the elephants.

Suddenly, in spite of herself, Ellie began to cry. Tears quivered for a second on her dark lashes before rolling down the side of her nose. 'Oh poor Ellie. Poor Ellie,' Tansy murmured, under her breath. She put her arms around Ellie's shoulders and began to rock her gently to and fro. Mitch leapt from his seat as though jolted by an inner mechanism but found himself unable to leave the spot, restrained by an invisible brake. He folded his arms across his chest, trapping them. Conversation in the kitchen dried up. Outbursts of emotion were not something the McKays did. They all turned towards Ellie. Only Rob continued, feverishly, to mix something on a square of worktop by the back door. He was the only one to notice the figure who stepped into the last patch of grey daylight which filtered through the back door. Belinda had moved to Ellie's side. She perched on the bench and gently took hold of Ellie's hand.

'Oh darling. Do tell me what the matter is,' she said.

Tansy spoke into the silence. 'Unfortunately Ellie has been badly let down by someone who she thought she could trust. By someone she really ought to have been able to trust. It's made her very sad. Poor Ellie.'

'Who?' 'Who is it?' a few people enquired, but Tansy's wouldn't say more. Mitch's eyes bored holes into Rob's back. Mary, overwrought by the day's events, and against the family rule, also began to cry. Confusion gusted from the family; they didn't know how to cope.

In the doorway, Rachel stood aghast. She and Rob looked at each other, stranded from the rest by their mutual connivance in Ellie's unhappiness. Tansy's words cut them both like a knife, to their quick. They licked and burned at Rachel with the caustic flame of guilt and self-accusation. She welcomed the pain of it. She wished it could be more real, that they would see her flesh ablaze with it.

'It's one of life's hardest lessons,' Ruth said, coldly, from her seat by the Aga. 'People do let us down, and when it's the people that, over all others, we should be able to trust, the lesson is hardest of all. The ultimate betrayal.' A few people nodded.

James followed the direction of Ruth's steely gaze. It was aimed squarely at Belinda. He sighed. He would have to find a way to persuade Belinda to tell the truth. Hers was a secret he couldn't hold for her much longer. Ruth's muddle-headed misconceptions threatened to blow them all sky-high. He stood up and cast a significant glance at the back door, where empty air, grey as a ghost, made a curtain out into the night. Belinda followed his intention, and not many seconds after he had passed out into the evening, she, too slipped through the veil.

519

A thick and surprising mist surrounded Hunting Manor, rolling in from the sea and cloaking the house in impenetrable, unfathomable mystery. It quickly swallowed up even James' bulk as he walked away from the house and into the woods. He called Rachel's name a few times but it was like shouting into a pillow. Some yards into the woods he had to stop. It was impossible to see the path; the mist eddied through the trees and, in any case the night was so dark that, without a torch, even without the mist, it would have been impossible to find the way. He turned back with a sigh. Suddenly Belinda was in his arms, they collided before they had seen one another. Belinda pressed against him.

'Oh James,' she said, resting her head for a moment on his chest. Then she inhaled, as though gathering herself, and they stepped apart.

'I can't find Rachel in this mist,' James said, unnecessarily.

'No,' Belinda said. 'Ellie's lost in a mist too. I can't seem to get through to her. She won't speak to me.'

'Somebody has let her down,' James stated. 'Or she feels that they have. But of course,' he flung out with a cynical tone, 'she won't *talk* about it.'

They walked slowly back to the little gate. By unspoken consent, rather than returning to the house, they wandered along the line of the fence besides the trees.

Belinda nodded. 'It's a McKay thing. One of the many maxims we were brought up with; *'if you can't say anything nice, don't say anything at all.'*

James laughed grimly. 'So you can never express anger, sadness, dissatisfaction, fear...'

'No. Because they're not nice.'

'It might not be nice but it's *honest*. Surely we can be honest with one another? It shouldn't make any difference, in a family.'

Belinda shivered. James unzipped his fleece and put it round her shoulders. 'I hoped that this week would draw us back together but we only seem to be getting further and further away from each other. Ellie's done it right in front of my eyes.' Belinda shook her head, reviewing it all in her mind. 'I knew on Friday that there was something wrong, but I didn't ask her what it was. Heather told me that there was something going on between her and Rob, but I was too busy to get to the bottom of it. On Sunday they were at each other's throats – literally fighting......it isn't right that she doesn't feel she can confide in me,' she heaved a massive sigh, weighted with sadness.

'It's a maddening McKay trait,' James said, with unusual vehemence, 'and, you know, I'm not just thinking of Ellie, now. Things left in the dark only fester.' He gave her, though the gloom, a significant look. They had reached the end of the fence but lingered still, not ready to go back to the house, and in any case the mist boiled and eddied and disorientated their sense of direction. 'I mean,' James pressed his point, 'here's Ellie with some problem that she doesn't feel she can talk about but which is clearly making her very unhappy. Now which would you rather? That she preserved a few family taboos or that she was happy?'

'Of course I want her to be happy no matter what.'

'Of course, you want *her* to be happy!'

Belinda made a gesture of impatience. 'You're mixing up two different things.'

James said, 'No, Belinda, I'm not. They're the same. The only difference is the way you feel about the people involved. To you, Ellie matters so the rules don't apply. But in your eyes, *you* don't matter, you don't deserve to be happy; you're not important enough to be allowed

521

to upset the apple cart.' They turned and retraced their steps along the fence towards the gate. Belinda stared into the mist. It enveloped and protected them, blotting out every feature of the landscape, cocooning them in its moist silence. Not a sound or a glimmer penetrated it. They could be anywhere, anywhere at all, in time or space. She had only wanted to talk about Ellie but James wouldn't let her separate Ellie from the other issue. Suddenly she relented. She said, quietly: 'It's a case of the good of one against the good of the many.'

They ambled for a few moments more. Then James said, 'In a family, the good of the one *is* the good of the many. Wouldn't you like, at last, for them to see things as they really are?' They had arrived back at the gate. James put his hands on her shoulders and turned her to face him. Her hair was silvered by beads of moisture. It looked as though she was wearing a cap of jewels. Belinda looked into his eyes. When she spoke, her voice was barely more than a whisper.

'You make it sound as though I've been lying to them.'

'Hiding the truth *is* a kind of betrayal,' he said, looking past her into the mist, and thinking of Ruth.

There was silence between them. When he looked back at her he saw, in her eyes, only fear, and he knew he had failed.

A rustle in the undergrowth nearby broke the moment. She stepped a pace or two away from him.

'No,' she said, coldly. 'It isn't. I've been loyal. I've stuck to the script. I've done what was expected of me. *No-one* could accuse me of betraying the family. You know we talked the other day about kindred and kin, and I asked you which was stronger? Obviously it's kin. The integrity of the whole family is far more important than one individual member, or any friendship, no matter how close.' She turned to face him, her hands rubbed and twisted restlessly against one another, the ring on her finger turning and turning in a ceaseless spiral. She was beginning to cry. 'No-one could *ever* accuse me of betraying the family!' she repeated.

James took two steps towards her and gathered her into his arms.

'No, my poor darling,' he said, quietly, into her soft, damp hair, 'they could only accuse you of betraying yourself.'

Rachel lay in the undergrowth. Only four days ago she had romanticised this kind of existence; living rough, sleeping under the leaves, gleaning nuts and berries for food. But the reality was that the night was cold and the mist scared her. It had laid a coating of moisture on her jumper which was gradually seeping inward to her flesh with a clammy grip. The ground was hard and stony, and the pine needles, which felt so soft under foot, were sharp; they pricked and protruded through her layers of clothing. When she had heard someone coming she had dived into the small opening in the pile of branches and leaves she had spent the afternoon heaping up between and against the divided trunks of a tree some few yards off the main path and not far from the gate into the garden. The interior had been smaller than she had planned, and it was uncomfortable to be half squatting and half lying with her knees under her chin. At the sound of her father's voice calling her name she had wanted to cry out to him, but had steeled herself and clamped her mouth resolutely shut, in her den.

She had caught only snatches of their conversation. They had been discussing Ellie, and her betrayer. Then they had wandered away for a while, but when their voices once more became audible, Aunty Belinda had talked about loyalty, about doing the right thing by the family, and about family being more important than any other relationship. That meant that the family would unite against any outsider who threatened them. And for one family member to betray another was obviously the worst thing anyone could be accused of: 'Nobody,' she had said, with pointed inference, 'would *ever* be able to say that *she* had betrayed the family,' as though it was ultimate, the worst kind of treason which in the olden days would have been punishable by death.

Rachel remained in her hide after they had gone. The temptation to remain was very strong, but she knew what its inevitable outcome would be; eventually she would be found, and the truth would come out, and that was something she was determined to save them from if she could. The main thing was to ensure that Ellie's secret remained exactly that. Ellie *need* never, Tansy *would* never and Rob *should* never tell. The secret would bind them together in a circle of trust and by placing herself on the outside of its perimeter Rachel would seal them into it.

After tea people drifted away from the kitchen. Simon and the boys began to scoop the meat mixture out of the basin and make round patties with it on a floured board. The girls had disappeared upstairs with Heather and Mitch, to help put the baby to bed. Ruth remained fixed in the armchair, in a sort of reverie, staring at the back door which had now been closed against the night. Muriel was busy clearing away the tea things. Les had helped Robert to his feet and they had shuffled off in search of a television. Granny McKay sat at one end of the table rummaging in her handbag.

Mary arrived carrying two tubes, both red and white. She laid them on the table in front of Granny, who blinked up at her owlishly. Mary picked up the larger tube. 'Toothpaste,' she said, loudly, 'for cleaning dentures.' She picked up the smaller tube. 'Thrush cream, for.... well.... I think you've been getting them mixed up, Granny.'

The old woman swept both tubes into her handbag. Mary turned to Simon; 'you're being very industrious,' she said, 'what are you cooking?'

'Homemade beef burgers, jacket potatoes, coleslaw, and pancakes for afters.'

Mary stopped in her tracks. 'Pancakes?' She looked as though he had said they were to have sheep's eyes.

'Yes mother.'

'But it isn't Shrove Tuesday!' Eating pancakes on any other day was as inconceivable to her as eating Easter eggs at Christmas; it just wasn't the way they had always done things.

Simon laughed and put a floury arm around her shoulders. 'Oh Mum. You're such a slave to convention. You *are* allowed to eat pancakes at other times of the year, you know. They do it in America every day!'

Mary humped. 'Well,' she said, huffily, 'we always had them on Shrove Tuesday.'

'Don't worry, Grandma,' Toby said, nudging his cousin, 'it isn't against the law. We won't get arrested!'

'No!' Rob laughed. 'I think it's the pancake police's day off!'

'Now lads,' Simon said. 'That's enough.'

Mary said: 'Simon, after tea I'd like to speak to you and your sisters.'

Simon was grating carrots with gusto. 'Ok, fine,' he said.

'Did you catch that, Ruth?' Mary asked, folding the tea towel and draping it over the Aga rail.

Ruth drained her glass and reached for her bottle. 'I'll check my diary and see if I'm available,' she said, sourly.

'Somebody's nicked my Johnnies,' Grandma McKay announced, looking up from her handbag. Young Rob held his hands out. 'Not guilty!' he said.

Les got Robert settled in the games room. It was a struggle; the children had more or less appropriated the room. Their toys and disks and shoes and debris lay everywhere. There were cups and plates and glasses and discarded clothing. Les had to clear a space on the sofa before he could ease Robert into it, and the seat was really too low. Robert was querulous.

'Bloody mess everywhere. Noisy children. Can't tell what's going on half of the time.'

'I know, mate. Rum carry-on all round. But the youngsters seem to be enjoying themselves,' Les sympathised, tucking a cushion behind Robert. 'It'll be quiet in here for a bit, I think, and kick-offs at seven.'

'Where's that?'

'Right here, if I can get that thing to work.' Les approached the enormous television with some trepidation. There was no sign of the remote control and he began to search around the room for it; under cushions, behind the chairs. Finally he located it in the microwave of Starlight's toy kitchen. 'Alright. Now then. Let's see.' Les prodded at the control but couldn't get anything but a blizzard on the screen.

'Somebody needs to fiddle with the aerial,' said Robert. 'We've missed *Murder, she wrote* now, anyway. Where's Mary?'

'In the kitchen washing up. She'll be through in a minute. Maybe something's unplugged at the back.' Les stepped over the trailing wires and circuitry to examine the back of the set. At the same moment Ben and Todd came hurtling into the room, whooping and hollering, embroiled in some game. Robert tensed.

They skidded to a halt. 'What you doing?' Todd stepped out of the make-believe to observe Les on his hands and knees behind the set.

'Granddad wants to watch the football later. I'm trying to tune the telly in,' said Les, tentatively touching wires.

'Oh.' Todd picked up the remote control and mashed at the keys. The television leapt into life. 'You need to swap the in-put,' he said, as though it was obvious. He dropped the control and instantly he was back in his game, a super-sleuth on the trail of the ubiquitous Wriggly. Between them they kept up a continuous narrative of invention:

Wriggly hides behind the settee.'

'And the detective gets out his special detection glasses and scans the area.'

'And Wriggly puts up his special anti-detection shield.'

'There you are, Robert.' Les dusted his hands against one another. He wanted to check on Muriel, to make sure she was safe from June. 'I won't be a tick. I'll just fetch the paper,' he said, leaving the room. 'I can't remember who they've tipped to play up front.'

'Oh look, it's *Ready Steady Cook*. I like that,' Robert brightened at the sight of a familiar face on the screen. 'They cook things all in a rush and then the peppers and tomatoes say which they like best. It was better with Fern Brittain, though. Her hands always looked so clean.'

Wriggly crosses the deadly swamp. Snakes and crocodiles are near.'

'A crocodile spots him and crawls into the water.'

The ceaseless squeaking of the two boys was too much, setting off a whine in Robert's head which wouldn't go away and which interrupted the jocular repartee on the television. He cupped his hands behind his ears to try and filter out the boys' laughter but it was no good. 'Oh I can't hear it. Turn it up! Turn it up!' he raised his voice at them but the boys were too embroiled in their game.

The crocodile's jaws are enormous, and they clamp on Wriggly's leg.'

Wriggly struggles but the crocodile is too strong for him. Will our hero meet his end in the swamp?' The boys rolled and thrashed across the parquet floor, locked in combat.

529

The remote control had been left on another settee and Robert couldn't reach it. He couldn't get up, the seat was too low and he didn't have his stick.

'I can't hear! I can't hear!' he shouted, 'Mary! Mary!' but no-one took any notice of him, it was like being dumb, or being in a dream where no one will listen to you or do as you say, and the frustration of it all whipped up a fury in his head. Why wouldn't they listen to him? Why couldn't he make them? Why couldn't he move? The fury in his head got bigger and bigger, ballooning out of control, pressing on the backs of his eyeballs, making a rushing, pulsing sound in his ears. It was stopped up in his throat, strangling his voice, his breathing.

Todd and Ben scrambled to their feet, and raced round the settee, laughing and shouting in continuous circles.

'I'm coming to get you! I'm coming to get you!' Todd bellowed. Ben dodged and avoided him easily, behind the settee, lurching first one way and then the other. Todd, holding onto his Granddad's knees, lunged left and right, mirroring Ben.

Suddenly, in a rush, the balloon of Robert's fury burst. There was a seeping, melting ooze of escaping ire in his brain. A noise like an enraged animal burst from his throat. Todd was laughing, his eyes on Ben, loving the game, his hands to each side of his face, fingers wiggling, tongue waggling. The wrath was coursing through Robert's body, engorging, crackling with static. His arms flailed, out of control, and a bony-fingered hand caught Todd a glancing blow across his velvet cheek. Todd's laughter was reabsorbed in a sharp gasp of shock, and he raised his hand to his face, and his eyes widened in surprise and revelation. Ben, too, was shaken out of the game. He paled, and gaped like a fish. There was a moment of stunned silence in the room, with only Ainsley Harriot's sugary chocolate voice to fill up the void, before Todd's yelling drowned out every other noise.

Belinda and James re-entered the house through the front door, having blundered their way by a circuitous route through the garden and round the house. Reluctantly, she handed him back his fleece. Simon, running through the hall, stopped long enough to ask Belinda to finish frying off the burgers for him. 'Just seal them on each side and then finish them in the oven. Or watch over Rob while he does it – he's quite capable – but just hold the fort for me, will you, for a few minutes? There's something I have to sort out. I'm sorry, I'd ask Ruth but she's three sheets to the wind already.' He disappeared down the gallery towards the games room.

James took off his wet shoes. 'I'm going to search the house for Rachel,' he said. 'If she isn't inside we'll have to have a search party.' He strode off after Simon.

In the kitchen, Toby and Rob were clearing away the debris of their cooking. Simon had abandoned the first batch of burgers in a skillet on the warming plate and Belinda wearily tied her apron on before lifting the pan back onto the hotplate. Ruth remained in the armchair by the Aga. She raised her eyes to Belinda but they were bleary.

'You'll suffer for that, tomorrow,' Belinda cast a significant look at the almost empty wine bottle by the chair.

'I suffer every day,' Ruth said, indistinctly, with incongruous hauteur. 'How long have you been back inside?'

'Oh, a little while. We were looking for Rachel but there's no sign. James is looking inside the house for her, now.'

'Looking for Rachel,' Ruth repeated, 'I see.'

Belinda glanced round the kitchen. Ruth sounded the only gloomy note. The boys had made a huge bowl of coleslaw and set the table. The rest of the burgers were floured and ready for cooking, laid neatly on a board. The wonderful aroma of jacket potatoes rose from the baking oven. Rob was quite unrecognizable, laughing and being

531

useful, she watched him wipe down the work surfaces and then rinse his cloth. While he had his hands in the sink he flicked suds at Toby. They both laughed and dodged about. Then they had a game of tea-towel whipping which made them wince and shout. Watching him, she just couldn't believe that he was the cause of Ellie's unhappiness. It was as though he'd come out from under some cloud which had claimed him for the past eighteen months. She balanced between her children, the misery of one and the sudden release of the other, as she turned the burgers on the skillet. Then Rob suggested a game on the computer and he and Toby went off together, helping themselves to beers from the fridge on the way, leaving the kitchen quiet, except for the sizzle of the burgers.

The smash of a glass breaking on the stone floor broke the silence. Belinda gathered herself mentally before turning round to see Ruth rising unsteadily to her feet.

'I've broken a glass. It fell off my knee,' Ruth stated, through woollen lips. She stared down helplessly at the shards of glass on the floor.

Belinda sighed and slid the skillet across to the warming plate again. 'You'd better sit down or you'll stand on a piece. You haven't got any shoes on. We can't have poor Mitch clearing up any more McKay haemoglobin.'

'I don't want to sit down,' said Ruth, petulantly. 'I don't want to stay in this room with you.'

'Don't be silly. It won't take me a minute to sweep the glass up. I'll get the broom.' When she came back from the boiler room, Ruth hadn't moved, but her eyes glittered like the glass on the floor.

'When I said, the other day,' she enunciated carefully, 'that anyone was welcome to my husband, I didn't mean it.'

Belinda, squatting, using the dustpan and brush to gather the fragments of glass, looked up at her sharply. 'Of course you didn't.

You weren't talking literally anyway.' Belinda continued to sweep, efficiently, around Ruth's bare feet; they were white and vulnerable. 'You were making a point about June and Muriel, if I remember correctly. You said that you didn't think sisters should ever fall out, and you were right.' She swept the last of the glass into the dustpan and stood up. She looked Ruth square in the eye, or as squarely as Ruth's restless, unfocussed eyes and slightly askew spectacles would allow. Ruth blinked at her, trying to grasp hold of the words, but they were all slithering away from her and she couldn't be sure, any more, about anything. There was nothing, not a hint of guile, no shred of guilt, in Belinda's clear, steady gaze. 'Now go and try and pull yourself together, Ruth. At the very least you'll need to be there to hear Ben's song, and you might have to go out looking for Rachel if she doesn't turn up somewhere in the house. And Mum wants to talk to us all later, and you'll need to be clear-headed for that.' Belinda turned from her and went to the draining board. She wrapped the glass shards up in a piece of newspaper and buried them deep in the waste bin like the fragments of a shattered dream.

Simon held Todd on his knee and rocked him backwards and forwards. Todd had stopped crying but his breaths still came in heaving, shuddering gasps. No-one had ever hit him before. There was a nasty red weal on his cheek but his face was pale and his eyes were frightened. He was frightened of his Granddad, now, and frightened too of the anger which he could hear hammering away in his Daddy's chest, held back in his throat like a wild animal by the bars of his carefully controlled voice saying; 'Dad, we will be talking about this, in a minute, Dad, when Todd's calmer.'

Tansy was brought down and after a little while Todd was persuaded to go upstairs with her for a very deep bath. He began to cry again, at first, thinking he was being sent to bed, but Simon hugged him and said the he wasn't to be silly, *he* hadn't done anything wrong and anyway it was burgers and pancakes for tea and he'd made about twenty thousand because he knew they were Todd's very favourite.

Uncle James asked if Ben could share the bath, and Todd nodded, and while Tansy went ahead to turn on the taps, he scooped the two boys up onto his massive shoulders and they clung to each other while he mounted the stairs, beginning to laugh at the giddiness of it and at a funny story Uncle James was telling them about going out into the mist and getting lost in the garden. On the landing they met Rachel, cold and twiggy from a day spent in the woods, and Todd said that she could share the bath too if she wanted, but Uncle James said that Rachel was a big girl now and had to have baths on her own, but that in the morning, if they asked her nicely, she might show them her den. He put the boys down on the landing and stroked Todd's cheek and, very tenderly, Rachel's, and said that a facial injury was plainly this holiday's 'must-have accessory' and soon everyone would want one. Rachel smiled a little and went away, muttering about getting changed for tea.

Simon and his father remained in the lounge. Robert was stuck on the low settee. He wanted, with an instinctive, aching need, Mary to come. But she was nowhere to be seen. Simon stood and looked down on him, across the coffee table. His hands were shaking, and he clenched them in an effort to control it.

'You hit my son,' Simon said. 'You hit my son!'

Robert looked up at him. He wanted to explain about the game under the table, and the television, and the noise, and the green peppers and red tomatoes; it all made perfect sense, but the words wouldn't come. His own feebleness infuriated him. Then Mary was in the room and he turned to her and barked out her name. What emerged was an inarticulate grunt.

'Oh Simon, I'm sorry. Poor Todd. Is he alright?' To Robert's increased ire, Mary ignored him and went to stand next to Simon.

'No, Mother, he isn't alright. He's been hit. He's got a bruise and he's shocked and frightened. He's never been smacked, never, not once, and he doesn't understand.' Without meaning to, Simon was taking his anger out on Mary. He found he was shouting at her, and that wasn't fair. He struggled again to get himself under control. Robert made a small, faltering noise and they both turned to look at him, stranded on the settee.

'I'm sorry, love. I'm so sorry,' Mary went on, speaking to Simon but looking helplessly at Robert. 'I couldn't make him have his tablet and I left him alone too long. It's my fault,' Mary rummaged in her cardigan pocket for a tissue. 'He's been so difficult today and I just wanted a little break.'

Robert forced his tongue to form words; they tumbled and stumbled and jostled against one another, impeded by his uncooperative lips. It was quite useless. They stared at him, uncomprehending. The only words they could make out were 'fucking imbecile.' The effort of it exhausted him and he crumpled back against

535

the cushions Les had placed for him. The countdown music for *Ready Steady Cook* had started and the audience was counting backwards from ten to one while the chefs scurried round the kitchen finished off their cooking. The music and the counting filled his head and when Simon spoke again his words were double-dutch, like a language Robert had once spoken but which had become meaningless to him.

Simon took a pace towards him, a floodgate opening in some deeply suppressed part of him. 'Don't you *dare* speak to Mum like that!' he yelled. 'You're a bully, Dad. You always were.'

'Oh Simon, please,' Mary began, her voice in ribbons, but Simon could not hold back the ancient tide. 'But look at you! Just look at you. You're old and weak and we're not afraid anymore.' Robert stiffened; especially his weak leg and arm seemed to be in some kind of spasm beyond his control. He looked across at Mary, but speech was lost to him. His eyes were angry. Simon leaned over the table and spoke vehemently into his father's face. 'You have *no* power over me and *no* power over my children, and you will *never* lay a finger on *any* of us again.' He stared into the cold grey eyes. 'I am not afraid of you,' he enunciated, slowly, and realised at last that it was true. The freshness of the revelation made him step backwards, and the freedom of it flooded him like an in-rushing tide and made his eyes well. He raised his hand and pointed squarely at his father. 'I am *not* afraid of you,' he said again, louder, and his voice broke. Mary reached her arms around him and he allowed her to hold him.

Robert sat mute on the settee and observed them, his only response to his son's outburst a slight flicker in one eye and a grimace at one side of his mouth.

Ruth found herself on the tiny roof terrace looking out into the dense whiteness. Everything became more muddled in her mind the more she thought about it; swirling and bewildering, like the mist. She had always noticed, in the past, a general preference in James for Belinda above her other siblings. It was not surprising; they were alike in many ways, two of life's plodding, reliable types who liked to make themselves useful in practical if unspectacular ways leaving the centre stage available for more charismatic personalities. It hadn't bothered her in the slightest; indeed, often, it had been convenient to foist James onto Belinda so that she could spend time with April. But Elliot's words yesterday evening, and last night, the sight of them together on the terrace, and the look, the *look* on Belinda's face, had cast things in a completely new hue. An affair was unthinkable for a McKay, and in any case, Belinda didn't have the imagination or James the energy for such a thing. And yet….. And yet.

Ruth's old demons refused to be shaken off; Belinda was the only McKay even remotely associated with McKay's Haulage. Belinda was wealthy, with status – the high-profile, charity-working wonder McKay. Belinda was Mary's favourite daughter, whereas she, Ruth, had been nobody's favourite, not even, it had begun to seem to her, James'. She was an extraneous limb; entirely surplus to requirements. It had hurt and angered her, and engendered a crisis of confidence which had sent her scurrying to the wine bottle. But the deeper she sunk into her own despondency the less certain she was about anything. In her increasingly disorientated state the only strong impression she had was an uncomfortable self-doubt. The accusation she had levelled at Belinda had seemed, on the speaking of it, quite ridiculous.

As she stood now and gasped at the cold, laden air, out on the roof, feeling the clammy mist on her face and beading her glasses, she was forced to acknowledge that in all probability it was all in her skewed, unreliable mind. The bleakness of her impending depression

537

was casting its infectious pall on everything, and she could not trust it. The injudicious alcohol, too, meant that in the same way that she must not trust this substantial-looking vapour to hold her weight - she must not climb out upon the parapet and place her weight on the miasmic moisture roiling in the air before her - neither could she wholly trust any impressions or convictions which came to her mind.

Having spent the past hours trying desperately to dull and numb herself, she needed suddenly to be bright and sentient. It was too frightening to be out adrift on the mist, without an anchor. She needed something real to cling on to, amidst the doubts and uncertainties; something shocking and sharp and sobering. She looked longingly down at the shard of glass she had picked up off the kitchen floor. It glinted dully in the light from the landing. It would answer in so many ways; the pain of it would bring her round, like a slap to a woman in hysterics, it would shock her sober. A wound, a deep wound, would expiate the sense she increasingly had that it might all somehow be her own fault; it would feel like an atonement. It would be reassuring to see the McKay blood flow from her, unassailable DNA evidence of her kinship. Finally, when James found out, it would be the entry code to the quiet sequestered ward of a hospital, the cool hands of concerned nurses, the blessed oblivion of drug-induced sleep.

She settled the glass into her palm as though it were a precious jewel and closed her fist around it, but a step on the landing behind her made her jump. In one movement she swung around to face whoever it was, flinging her hand out wide so that the guilty crystal splinter spun out into the mist. It was Rachel. They regarded each other silently for a few moments.

'Come on inside, Mum,' Rachel said, at last. 'It's cold with the door open.'

Ruth took a deep breath. 'Yes, alright. I will.'

To Rachel's relief, Ellie and Tansy were not in the bedroom. The room was a bombsite, especially around Ellie's bed; clothes were strewn everywhere, the bed was unmade, makeup littered the crumpled coverlet and sheet along with screwed up sweet wrappers and ten pound notes. The floor was covered with discarded dirty underwear and cups and plates. Tansy's bed was tidier; her laundry was in the scented bag and her clothes were folded, but the girls had evidently been listening to CDs during the day and these were spread across her bed in a disorganised way, out of their cases, their surfaces scratching against each other. Rachel's Dad had a comprehensive collection of CDs, mainly jazz, and she had been taught at an early age how to handle and store the disks so that they wouldn't become damaged. Almost without thinking, Rachel began to restore the disks to their cases and to arrange them in the box in an organised, alphabetical way. Then she picked Ellie's dirty underwear up and found a carrier bag from their shopping trip to put it in. She folded up the clothes neatly and placed them on the little chest of drawers adjacent to Ellie's bed. She put the rubbish in the bin and straightened out the money and put it in the drawer. Then she made the bed. Finally she gathered up the cups and plates and stacked them near the door. She surveyed the room. It wasn't quite enough. She closed the curtains and switched on the little bedside lamps by each bed, and, recalling that Aunty Belinda had done something similar when she had come to look after them once, she turned down the quilts a little, to make an inviting opening, and laid their pyjamas out on the beds with their arms jauntily crooked at the elbow and one knee bent to the other ankle. They looked like people who had been surprised in the act of dancing an Irish jig by a steam-roller. It still wasn't enough but then, she knew, it never would be. She went into the bathroom and began to run herself a bath.

When she came out a little later, Ellie and Tansy were there, sitting on Tansy's bed, painting each other's toe nails. They looked close and companionable, and Rachel felt like an intruder. Little Todd, pink, like her, from his bath and, like her, with a blooming rose of bruise on his cheek, was playing quietly with Rachel's collection of furry animals which he had discovered behind the curtains.

'Hello Rachel,' Tansy said, brightly enough, 'where have you been all day?'

'Oh,' Rachel busied herself folding up her clothes, 'I decided to spend the day outside.' She wanted to add some self-deprecating remark about not being in their way, about understanding that she didn't belong with them and that they would be glad to be rid of her, but she couldn't quite bring herself to it; she hoped that her intention would be clear enough to them.

'She made a den; Uncle James said so,' Todd remarked.

'Oh.' Tansy said. 'That's nice. And you've been busy in here too, haven't you?'

'Well,' Rachel hesitated. 'I thought....'

'*We* thought that a house-elf had been in, didn't we, Ellie?' Ellie nodded.

'Like Dobbie!' Todd laughed. It suddenly occurred to Rachel that whereas she had intended to demonstrate a sort of self-conscious inferiority by tidying up their things, they might have considered it as meddling, or even as judgmental.

'I hope you didn't mind,' Rachel said, looking anxiously at the two girls.

Before they could answer Todd cocked his ear and said; 'oooh! Supper! I can hear Dad calling, come on!' He abandoned the toys and raced out of the room.

'I suppose we'd better,' Ellie said, listlessly. She and Tansy climbed off the bed, careful to avoid smudging the varnish, and made for the door.

Tansy said: 'Are you coming, Rachel?'

'Yes, in a minute,' Rachel made a great fuss about folding her towel. 'You go ahead.' When she came back in from the bathroom, she noticed that the girls had left their nail varnish things on the bed; small bottles and some remover pads blotched with red. They had been sitting on Tansy's pyjama person. It looked tortured and spoiled where they had squashed it and the red pads made it look as though it was bleeding.

The table was all set and the candles had been lit. The family took their places. It was like a stage, Mitch thought, and was suddenly, after his afternoon of brooding, glad to have no role to play. The complex web of relationship was a snare, too easy to trip up on; the script too full of ambiguity and nuance – words, once spoken, could not be taken back. The obscurity of the stalls gave him distance and detachment and a certain protection. But, on the stage, the lights were searing and cruel – no gesture would go unremarked - and the set was rocky and unreliable. Close-to, the masks of the actors were utterly unconvincing, and all-but slipping as they struggled to maintain the illusion of the charade. There were false notes in the lively hum of conversation, an enforced gusto in some to cover the broodingly subdued demeanour of others. Something had kicked off in the games room. Todd had been crying and had a bruise on his cheek now which wasn't there before. He was the centre of attention, now. His father and brother and sister were all making much of him, letting him sit in the big chair at the head of the table and giving him first pick of the food. Simon, in fact, was soaring, charged up by some new energy, he seemed to have taken control; directing the service of the food, getting people seated, flamboyantly juggling cooking utensils and looking deliberately ridiculous in Belinda's apron, he seemed to be trying to generate a festive atmosphere by the force of his own will. Toby and Rob were bobbing in his wake. In the intervals of meal preparation the two of them had been playing a computer game and drinking beer; plainly it was not their first of the day. Toby, only eleven years old, was getting decidedly giddy, and encouraged by Rob, he kept acting the goat. They hooted with laughter and engaged in mock scuffles and threatened food-fights which made Todd and Ben helpless with mirth. Scarcely less voluble was Granny McKay. Someone had been dispensing drinks, or perhaps Granny and June had had been helping themselves; they each carried glasses into the room with them. They were flushed; even June's usual high colour increased by several shades. Granny prattled on and on, not quite in control of her newly restored dentures; she was virtually incoherent, making up in volume what she lacked in clarity. Heather appeared with the baby in tow, rolling her eyes ruefully at Mitch; bedtime had been abandoned again. Starlight, slotted into her high chair, embarked on her own garbled tirade of gibberish. The noise eddied and flowed around the stony statues of Ellie and Ruth, and of Mary and Robert, who all sat in morose silence, and of Rachel, who arrived in the room last of all and slipped unobtrusively into a seat at the far end of the table, as far as possible from the other girls.

It was a smouldering volcano, volatile and fractured. The smallest shift could blow it sky high

When the food was served, Mitch took advantage of Tansy's preoccupation with her little brother to sit next to Ellie. She gave him a pallid smile, and picked listlessly at her food. Now he was next to her, he couldn't think of a thing to say to her. To ignore her distress by beginning a conversation about anything else would make him seem heartless, but to rake over, now, the coals of her unhappiness, would seem cruel. So he just smiled, and passed her the butter, and tried to exude manly sympathy and support.

'How was your golf yesterday?' she asked him, presently.

He made a moue. 'I don't think your Dad enjoyed it much.'

She gave a little laugh, then. 'He wouldn't have done if you beat him,' she said.

'I'm afraid I did. Clearly a bad move on my part.'

'*Very* bad,' she frowned, theatrically. 'He's a very poor loser.'

'Oh dear,' Mitch gave an exaggerated sigh. 'And I *so* wanted to ingratiate myself.'

'Did you? Why?' There was the merest twinkle in her eye, the slightest hint of flirtation, glimmering through her care-worn veil.

'Well,' he began, in spite of himself, moving closer to her on the bench, 'I was really hoping....'

'Yes?' she breathed, the beginnings of her dimple quivering in her cheek.

'I was wondering if he might consider...' recklessly, he lifted his hand and tucked a tress of her heavy, silky hair behind her ear. She could feel his breath. Her eyes opened in surprise, but she made no move to restrain him. She flicked her eyes swiftly round the table. No-one was paying any attention to them.

'Consider?' she prompted, mesmerized. He had dropped his hand to her shoulder. It slid, under her hair, round her narrow back and rested against her neck.

'Yes,' Mitch swallowed. He had gone too far now to retreat. He felt giddy, breathless, and a little sick, with the riskiness of it. 'to consider if I might make a suitable...'

'A suitable?' she prompted again, hoarsely. Her dimple, now, was fully realised. Humour, and, more deeply, a budding sexual response, was quivering under the surface.

He moved his mouth close to her ear. She thought, for a crazy moment, that he was going to kiss it. Her eyes, again, raked the relatives.

'Truck driver,' he whispered.

She gasped, and then the peal of her laughter rang out down the table. She flung her head back and hooted. It was as merry, as exuberant as water bursting from a spring. Rob, at the boisterous end of the table, looked up at the sound of it, and his heavy load of guilt lightened a little. Belinda found reassurance in it. Mitch drank it in. It was, he realised, the first time he had really seen her laugh. He sat back, to observe it, happy to have divined it. He poured her some wine, then, and nudged her plate towards her.

'Come on,' he said, blithely, 'eat up, or no pancakes.'

Granddad Robert sat in his customary chair at the bottom of the table. The old man seemed frailer and more disorientated than usual, a dribble of spit gleamed on his chin; he was having difficulty eating. On either side of him, Mary and Les were managing his cutlery and napkin with deft, discreet gestures, and chatting across him with determined brightness. James and Ruth made another moody pool in the central section of the table. After remarking 'Ah ha! Potato Jaquettes!' in that whimsical way he had, James had fallen silent. Ruth, at least, had eschewed the wine which had been offered to her and was drinking water. Presently she roused herself sufficiently to say: 'I found Rachel, you see.' Opposite them, Miriam and Muriel were making herculean efforts, Miriam paying fascinated attention to the unsuspected nobility of Roger's character. The top end of the table was ribald with hilarity, as Simon and the boys bantered amongst themselves, with only Tansy's occasionally reproving, 'Dad! Really!' sounding a restraining note. Rachel sat amongst them, and said nothing at all.

Ellie finished her food and gave a heavy, cathartic sigh. 'You've made me laugh,' she observed. 'I was beginning to think I never would again.'

'Things are never as bad as they seem.'

'It's hard to see it, though, from the inside. That's where you're lucky, being detached from it all.'

Mitch raised an ironical eyebrow. He had never felt so connected, so attached, helplessly pinioned by his irresistible attraction to the girl at his side and by the compelling lure of the interwoven mesh of personalities and relations around him.

'It makes me feel trapped. They,' she indicated her family, 'make me feel suffocated. Sometimes I think I *hate* them.' She drank some wine. Her hand shook, a little.

He had thought he had hated people, in the past, but it had only been a reaction built of fear and disappointment and bitterness and wounded love. He remembered, suddenly, a conversation he had had with a cell-mate about hate, words spoken into the darkness after lights-out. His voice, when he began to speak, was low, and she leaned her silky head closer to him. 'A bloke I knew called Billy thought he hated his son,' he said. 'By all accounts the lad was a complete loser; addict, dealer, thief, violent with it – off the rails....'

Ellie nodded, 'go on,' she said.

'He would smash the house up on a regular basis, kept his stash there, had people coming to the door at all hours to buy the stuff..... Billy had tried and tried to keep him in check but the lad was on a self-destruct mission. Eventually he'd just had enough. Anyway, they had a big row and Billy chucked him out and took his key off him. Then Billy went on a bender; he'd been sober for years but the stress of the thing was just too much for him so he went on a binge that lasted days. He woke up in a police cell to find that he'd driven home while he was off his head and knocked his son down.'

Ellie gasped and covered her mouth with her hand, her eyes wide with the horror of it; 'oh no!'

'It seems the son had been out looking for him, trying to make things right, spotted the car and stepped into the road trying to flag him down. Billy had been too drunk to see him and just mowed him over. Killed him outright.'

'Oh God!'

'Now Billy told me that the hate he thought he'd felt for his son had been love all along. He said hate and love run down opposite sides of the same street and sometimes the street's a very narrow one....Oh. I'm sorry....' He realised that Ellie had begun to cry; silent tears slid down her cheeks. He put his hand on hers. It was a tiny hand, almost child-like, and very soft. He was glad, now, that he hadn't intervened between her and her brother; that his attempt at it had foundered. He understood now, at last, the nature of it.

'What a sad story,' she whispered. She did not move her hand away.

'If you wanted a bolt-hole,' he ventured, 'there's always my room.' She raised her eyes slowly to his.

Ben had eaten too many pancakes. They sat in his tummy like stones, and the nervous fluttering felt like the wings of birds trapped underneath them. He and Bob sat together on the piano stool as the family gathered in the games room to hear their song. Granny McKay, Grandma and Granddad sat together on the sofa. Granddad was quiet again, he looked dazed, his eyes glassy and remote, as though focused on something a long way away. It was like the ugly scene only an hour or so ago had never happened. But Todd's bruise, and the way that he insisted on sitting on Uncle Simon's knee showed that it had happened and could never be undone. Some things were like that; once they had happened you could never un-happen them. This moment felt the same to Ben. Once he had sung this song with Bob it would be out, escaped from the captivity of their private, shared composing, released into the wild to fend for itself, something which no longer belonged exclusively to them. And he would never be the same either; he would have started on his path into the unknown. But he wasn't afraid; Uncle Bob would tread the path before him, making the footsteps, like Good King Wenceslas for the Page. Uncle Bob had told him that if the song got released there would be Ben's name there on the CD for all to see, and, less exciting but still pretty cool, that every time someone bought it there would be a bit of money going into a bank account with Ben's name on it.

He looked across at his parents; his Mum, perched on the arm of the settee, looked pale and distant, hardly present in the room at all, unnervingly like Granddad, and Ben knew that it would not be too long before she went away from them for a few weeks. His Dad stood behind her, but his size and strength could not save her.

The rest of the family had arranged itself around the room; nearest to them, at the end of the piano, Heather with Starlight on her hip, the two of them smiling at Bob. On the small settee, June and Muriel with Les between, looking uncomfortable. There wasn't really room for three of them but they were wedged in now. Simon, in the armchair, had Todd on his knee and Tansy perched on the arm of the chair, leaning against him. Miriam, away from them, and alone, leant on the snooker table, tapping one of the red balls restlessly from one hand to another. Ellie and Mitch slouched on adjacent beanbags, talking quietly, their heads close together; she seemed to have cheered up. Aunty Belinda hovered behind his Dad, and, away from them all, barely in the room at all, just in the doorway, Rachel, smiling at him, except that her swollen face could not quite manage a full smile. Rob and Toby came in last of all. There were no seats left so they perched ridiculously on two of Starlight's little sit and ride vehicles, their eyes unnaturally bright.

Bob gave him a nudge, and an encouraging wink, and for a second or two Ben looked into his grey, smoky eyes, and then they placed their hands on the keyboard, and began to play.

As soon as it was politely possible, after the applause had died down, Les switched the TV on to the football, and tried to interest Robert in the game. Mary took advantage of a few distracted moments to lead her four children into the small lounge and close the door. James suggested Ben and Todd play a game in their room for half an hour before bed. Surprisingly, they needed no second bidding. It had been a long day and they were tired. Muriel went off to tackle the ironing while June put Granny to bed. She was unusually compliant, allowing herself to be guided briskly through the bathroom and into her nightclothes and swallowing her two pills which took quick effect. Starlight was far more spirited in her efforts to avoid being put, for the second time, to bed; wriggling about on the changing mat, making a nappyless dash for the stairs and yelling remonstrance throughout. It took Bob ages to get her into her travel cot, where she stood defiantly and screamed at the top of her voice. Her piercing shrieks melded into the soundtrack of the boys' computer game; the roar of engines and screech of tyres issued from the study and permeated through the house. Finally Starlight made herself sick, a gush of half-digested grapes and vivid orange spaghetti. She observed it rather proudly, while Bob changed her sheets and pyjamas and the whole process had to be started again.

The match was a disappointment; it was well into the second half by the time they got the set switched on and City were being trounced by Spurs, 5 – 2 down and playing abysmally. Robert's blue pill was beginning to take effect. Les took advantage of a commercial break to switch off the set and help Robert to his feet. 'Come on, mate,' he said, mildly, 'time for bed, I think.'

In the kitchen, Rachel stacked the dishwasher and filled the bowl with soapy water. It looked as though the boys had used almost every pan and dish and bowl in the entire kitchen; what her father called 'man-cooking.' The skillets and trays they had used for the burgers were greasy and crusted, the floor was slick with food debris.

Roger has doing his best to clear it up; licking industriously at the floor. When they had left the kitchen, the table had been sticky with honey and syrup and sugar and orange juice from the pancakes, but it and all the crockery left on it were now suspiciously clean and Rachel suspected that Roger had been busy while everyone had been distracted.

Ellie, Rachel thought, had seemed much brighter at tea time and afterwards. Perhaps the more time that passed without Rob spilling the beans, the more convinced she would be that he would not in fact do so. Maybe seeing Rob in such high spirits had reassured her that in some way he now felt less need to betray her. Ellie's feelings for Rachel were blindingly obvious; she hadn't looked at her or spoken to her since the previous night, and it was clear to Rachel that she was to be cast out of the cousinly circle. Her betrayal would always be between them for as long as she lived, like a debilitating genetic defect; a birthmark, a harelip or prominent stammer; glaringly evident, politely unremarked.

Muriel pottered into the kitchen, her arms full of freshly ironed clothes.

'Hello, dear, are you all by yourself?' Muriel said, kindly. 'Let me give you a hand. I'll just put these...'

'Oh don't put them on the table, Auntie Muriel,' Rachel raised a soapy arm. 'I think...' she glanced at Roger, 'well, it might be sticky, I haven't wiped it yet.'

'Oh alright, dear. I'll put them on the chair then,' Muriel replied happily. 'There we are. Now then, let me get a tea towel. My! You *have* been busy! What a lot of washing up those boys made. You're like Cinderella here, all on your own, aren't you? You ought to be off having fun with the others. I could be like your fairy God-mother, and make a spell so you can go to the ball, would you like that? And dance with the prince. Gosh! Wouldn't *that* be lovely? Except I don't think there are any pumpkins....' Muriel wittered on in this vein for some

551

time as they washed and dried the mountain of dishes, and Rachel thought back to Saturday night, after the furore on the landing, when Rob had told them all the story of Muriel and June and Uncle Les, and how Muriel had not been able to bear the sight of Aunty June since then, and had cocked a snoot at the family. But the idea of this lady being so proud and bitter didn't seem to fit. She'd done virtually nothing but wash and iron since she'd arrived, between helping with Granny and making tea. And it came to Rachel in a sort of a flash that the reason Muriel had withdrawn from the family was nothing to do with saving her own dignity; on the contrary, it had been to save the family so that she would not be a constant reminder of that terrible, shameful thing which June had done and with which they had all, by their silence, been complicit. It accorded with the family creed; that one family member should be exiled for the sake of the rest of them. They were in the same boat; except that Muriel was really a McKay while Rachel wasn't, and Muriel hadn't done anything wrong while Rachel had. Perhaps she, like Muriel, would spend the rest of her life on the edge of the family, a tolerated, distant, poor relation who had sometimes to be included but never made much of, an embarrassing reminder of family indiscretion, long after Ellie's silly lie about the teacher had been forgotten. Impulsively, Rachel turned to Muriel and said: 'You're far more like Cinderella than I am, really. You're the one who deserves to go to the ball.'

Ellie followed Mitch up the stairs and along a narrow landing she had not explored before. From somewhere nearby, Starlight was crying, angrily.

'You don't have to go and help?' she enquired.

'He'll let me know if he needs me,' Mitch said.

He led her into a small, neat lounge. There was an old-fashioned, over-stuffed settee against one wall and a table with an ancient television set in front of the window. A dim lamp glowed over a desk. The curtains were open onto black, blank panes. A small collection of Starlight's books and toys were assembled neatly on the seat of an upright, ladder-backed chair. Through a far door she could see his bedroom; an impeccably made single bed, clothes folded tidily on a chair.

Now they were here, alone, together, Ellie felt shy. It was ridiculous, she told herself, she had only come to look at his room. He turned to her and held out his hands, palm up. 'Not much to it,' he said.

'You're very tidy,' she laughed.

'Yes,' he said. He did not tell her it was a habit imposed in the young offenders' institution. 'It's easy when you haven't got much stuff. I only brought a few clothes.'

'So did I,' Ellie said. 'But you should see *my* room. It's a bombsite! Although, actually,' she hesitated, 'Rachel tidied it up, earlier.' She had not said thank you, she realized.

'I haven't spent much time in here,' he said, looking round as though seeing it for the first time. They both looked at the toys.

'You're very good with the baby,' Ellie observed.

He shrugged. 'I just seem to know what she wants.'

'You seem to know what *everyone* wants.'

'I know how to make myself useful,' he acknowledged.

553

In this room, small as it was, Ellie looked even more insubstantial and fragile than before. Her baggy jeans rode low on her narrow hips, their hems frayed and grimy. Her feet were bare; tiny, they were, like a child's. She kept on sweeping her hair out of her eyes only for it to fall back. Her skin, clean of make-up, was pale, her eyes shadowed by tiredness.

He knew what *he* wanted. He could feel it; a reaching, yearning sensation; small, inexperienced tentacles groping towards her; need, want, a lonely soul searching for companionship from its hollow home. It was as innocent, as natural as milk. People belong with people, he thought. They belong in groups, in families.

He knew what *she* wanted, too.

He did not, when he took her into his arms, try to kiss her. He did not, as some boys would, press her urgently back onto the lumpy settee. He did not slide his hands under her shirt, nor did he press himself against her. He didn't get, as other boys had, that wild and fevered look in his eye. He didn't bombard her with words, he didn't say 'oh Ellie, oh Ellie,' between heavy, laboured breaths. He didn't say anything, at least not at first. He only held her, gently, in his arms, with her small bare feet between his, and her head nestled under his chin. They stood so for long minutes, feeling a million miles from anywhere or anyone, apart from each other.

It was, she realised, *just* what she had wanted.

Mary had taken the small armchair by the fire in the sitting room. Heather and Ruth sat on the settee, Belinda on one of the straight backed chairs behind them. Simon stood with his back to the fire although it was not lit. The big armchair remained empty; it was Robert's chair, the one he would have occupied if he had been with them, the best chair, left for him, the head of the family, the man of the house, in just the same way that the biggest portion, the choicest cut, the first pick was always his by unquestioned right. To meet and to discuss anything of importance without him made them all feel vulnerable and furtive; it was something they had never done in the past, as much because it had been practically impossible – he was always everywhere, liable to arrive home unexpectedly, burst in to any room, as though he had a sixth sense for subterfuge – as because it was unthinkable that anything critical *could* be discussed or decided in his absence. And as much as they might tell themselves that they were grown-up, now, independent, autonomous, yet still old habits were hard to break. They were indelibly stained with the colour of his control. They shifted uneasily in their seats; even Heather, who had never felt her father's control as a restriction, more as a form of security to be relied upon, felt uncomfortable to be engaged in a momentous family discussion without him, and she fiddled restlessly with the tassels of Ruth's shawl. It was as though they were all waiting for him to come in and get things started, and it wasn't until Simon eventually stepped across the room and sat down in the armchair that Mary felt that she could begin.

To their surprise and concern, she began with tears; they erupted without the preamble of words, and she could only shake her head, and hold her hands out in supplication before them as she tried to conquer her emotions. Eventually, she managed to choke out; 'you can see how he is. You can *see* how he is.' Belinda left her chair and perched on the arm of Mary's. 'Yes, Mum, we can. We can see how he is. He's too much for you.' Mary nodded, and dabbed at her eyes with her handkerchief. Belinda stroked her back.

555

'We all need to do more,' Heather said, breezily, as though it was a simple matter. 'You could come and stay with us for as long as you like. There's plenty of room at our place and we could bring in more help.'

'And you know you're welcome with us any time, too,' Belinda agreed.

Mary shook her head. 'I don't think it would really help.'

'No,' Ruth cut in, 'neither do I. I haven't got room for two extras even if you all have, and anyway I'm out at work all day.'

'I don't want to give up my home and I won't be a burden on any of you,' Mary said, quite forcefully. 'That isn't what I had in mind.'

'I should think not,' Ruth said. 'Dad isn't some sort of modern day King Lear to be shunted from one place to another.'

Simon said nothing. There was no way in hell, he thought to himself, that he would have his father to stay. Even before this afternoon's incident, it had been unthinkable. He leaned forward in his chair. 'What *have* you got in mind, Mother? A day centre? Respite care?'

But now she had made a start, Mary couldn't stop her roll-call of complaints. 'Some days he's alright and I can manage him, but other days, more and more, he's so difficult. He won't take his tablets, he won't let me get him dressed, he's lazy about the toilet....'

'You don't need to justify yourself to us, Mum,' Simon interrupted her. 'We've all seen just today how awkward he can be.' He hesitated a moment, before plunging on, 'and frankly, based on today's performance, I'm not convinced he's altogether to be trusted. Has he ever hit *you?*'

'Of course he hasn't!' Heather interjected, 'this is Daddy we're talking about!'

'Exactly!' Ruth laughed, coldly. Simon gave Heather a piercing, ironical look.

'He isn't himself, clearly,' Belinda tried to soothe the moment over.

'Well,' Simon muttered, 'I wouldn't say that.'

Abruptly Heather got up from the settee and went to sit on the step of the hearth, next to Mary. 'Poor Daddy,' she said, putting her head on Mary's knee and casting a glare at Simon, 'I'm sure it was just an accident today, hurting Todd.'

'You don't know the half of it, Heather.' The bitterness in Ruth's voice took them all aback.

'I'm afraid Ruth's right,' Simon nodded. 'You were the golden girl. *You* could do no wrong.'

Heather looked from one to the other. 'Was I?'

Their silence confirmed it.

'Poor Daddy,' Heather repeated, uncertainly, twining her fingers in the chain of her necklace.

'Poor *Mum*, I think,' Ruth ejaculated. 'It's time she had a break.'

'So do I,' Simon affirmed.

'No-one would think you were being disloyal, Mum, if you had a break from time to time,' Belinda remained on the arm of her mother's chair, stroking her back. 'We know you're not complaining.'

'Heaven forbid!' Simon got up. 'The McKays never *complain*. It isn't polite.' He brushed his hands together, as though the business was concluded. 'Whatever you decide will be fine. I'm right behind you.'

'But I don't *want* to decide, not on my own,' Mary was dissolving again. 'That's why I wanted to talk to you, and to see what you all thought. You see.... you see.....I don't think he's going to like it.'

557

Simon sat down again, next to Ruth. 'Tough,' he said, his voice flat and harsh.

Ruth leant against him, heavily. They both folded their arms.

'OK,' Belinda said, her voice like a tentative foot testing out new territory. 'So what are the options?'

James found Muriel and Rachel in the kitchen, trying to sort out the ironing into piles. 'Oh *there* you are!' he opened his arms and gathered Rachel into his embrace. 'It's *days* since I clapped eyes on you.' They stood for a moment or two wrapped in each other.

'I've missed you, too, Daddy,' Rachel mumbled, her face in his broad chest.

He kissed the top of her head. 'I came to find your den but I got lost in the mist.'

'Yes,' she nodded. 'I did too. I've been lost all day.'

'Poor baby. Are you alright?' She nodded again, not daring to say more. The warm, familiar scent of him was overwhelming, the sterile hospital smell overlaid by the sweet grease of canteen food and the salty tang of his skin, the way his chest rose and fell with each breath, like floating on the sea, and the whistle of the air in his nostrils; the smell and sound and sensation familiar since babyhood, evoked the deepest comfort imaginable. Muriel continued to sort the clothes, talking quietly to herself. Presently James loosed his arms.

'We're in the big lounge. Why don't you come and join us? We could play Monopoly if you like.'

'Yes, I might.' Rachel couldn't quite meet his eyes. 'I don't mind, if there are too many players...'

'Don't be silly. I'm making some drinks for us all.'

'I'll help you, then.'

'Alright. And Rachie?'

'Yes?'

James reached into his pocket. 'I bought this for you today. It's a present, from me to you. Open it later, if you like.'

'What's it for?' Rachel took the little package.

'Read the label!' James grinned.

Rachel squinted at it: 'A very happy un-birthday,' she smiled.

Rob steered the green Toyota Tundra at breakneck speed along the forested track. Last time he'd played this round he'd been wrong-footed by a sharp left hand hairpin which had thrown him down a ravine and into a swirling torrent. He eased up on the gas slightly to make the turn, the back of the car drifted fractionally but held the road and plummeted down the steep incline towards the narrow wooden bridge which spanned the gorge. Behind him, a blue Range Rover Sport was right on his tail. As long as he stayed on this route he'd be ok as there wasn't room to pass either here or on the bridge, but on the other side of the bridge the road opened out where the forest had been cut away and he knew that there would be enormous, slow, low-loaders piled high with logs to impede his path. He had to get rid of the Land Rover before that. Judging the moment as best he could, he stepped on the brakes hard. The tyres locked and he skidded down the loose shale path. The Land Rover, behind him, tried to adjust his speed, but as Robert skidded onto the bridge, the Land Rover, unable to stop, slid off the road, through the barrier and disappeared into the river. Dozens of points ratcheted up onto Rob's score. 'Fucking hell, that was good,' he breathed.

'Yeah. Fucking great!' Toby agreed, indistinctly. He was drunk. Rob smiled to himself.

'Your turn, Toby.'

'Cool,' Toby said.

There had been a dramatic shift of allegiances in the small sitting room. Heather and Ruth had found themselves unexpectedly in agreement on the matter of full time residential care for Robert, although for very different reasons. Heather had become tearful; 'He won't understand,' she cried. 'He'll think he's being punished, locked away. I don't know how you can even consider it.'

'The Oaks is hardly a prison, Heather. Five star luxury, his own room, four meals a day and the best nursing care money can buy.' Simon was phlegmatic. He stood once more, somewhat proprietarily, on the hearth.

'You can say that again,' Ruth was aghast at the cost of The Oaks. 'James is obviously in the wrong job. He'd nurse Dad for half that amount!' She remained seated on the sofa, but had shifted to one end of it.

'Daddy isn't mentally ill, Ruth,' Heather snapped, 'or criminally insane or whatever James' patients are. He's an old man who's had a stroke; he needs love and care.'

'I think they *are* very caring in The Oaks,' Belinda put in, 'and he's familiar with the place; he's been visiting Granny there for years.'

'I have no quarrel with the care at The Oaks. It's the money. I'm amazed you can afford it, Mum. Nine hundred pounds *a week*? Is that what you pay for Granny?'

'Yes. The money's there, Ruth, as long as the business thrives. It *is* still Dad's business, you know. We can increase our drawings.' Ruth was scandalised. She had had no idea that such funds were available from the business, while she had been allowed to struggle on week after week in virtual penury without a single offer of help. On the other hand, if the business was that lucrative, and ownership of it destined, as she had been led to believe, on Robert's death, to be divided between his four children, it seemed short-sighted to pour the contents of its coffers into the bottomless pit of The Oaks. However,

561

she voiced none of this, contenting herself with: 'I wonder what Elliot would say to that.' Silently, Belinda agreed.

'Elliot will do as he's told,' Simon cut in. 'He's employed to run the business, what happens to the profits is up to Mum. Of course there will be tax implications.'

'This isn't about money!' Heather shouted. She had taken up an uneasy position behind the settee.

'No. It's about what's best for Mum.'

'And Daddy.'

'Yes. But he has to allow us to be the best judge of that for him, Heather. You've seen what he's like. He isn't the man he was. Thank God.'

Heather put her hands to her head, an incredulous, impatient gesture; 'There you go again, Simon. What has he ever done to you that you should speak that way about him?'

There was an edgy silence in the room. Simon and Ruth exchanged significant glances. Belinda looked down at her hands. Mary, sitting still and very erect on her chair, clenched her handkerchief in her hand. Then Simon took a deep breath. 'Why do you think I went away, Heather?' He spoke quite softly but his voice was flat and cold. His face, too, was drawn. A muscle near his eye twitched.

Heather faltered a little; her words, in her head, before she even spoke them, sounded naive and lame. 'To.... to have adventures and..... see the world,' she said, eventually.

'Without saying goodbye?'

She shook her head, slowly. In contrast to Simon her colour was high, her cheeks, especially, were almost livid, and her neck was blotched with red. 'I.... I didn't think about it. You were like an explorer, out on the high seas, finding lost worlds.' She turned accusingly to Mary; 'That's what you told me,' she said, 'isn't it?' Mary avoided her eye. She stared at the ash in the empty grate.

'You were so young, Heather. We didn't know how to explain it to you,' Belinda's voice broke the silence.

'You don't know the half of what went on,' Ruth said.

Simon breathed heavily down his nose, his lips pursed in a hard line. With a sudden start he strode across the room to the cabinet and sloshed whisky into tumblers. 'I think we all need one of these,' he said, grimly. The room remained in silence while poured the drinks. Then, in a carefully controlled voice, like a witness called to give evidence, he recited his indictments. 'I was ignored, *for months*, because I wouldn't go into the business. It was like I was a ghost. He just refused to see me, even when I was in the same room. When he carved the roast, he didn't put any on my plate. If I was the last to get in the car he drove off without me. If I was out and everyone else was in, he would bolt the door. He didn't speak a *single word* to me all the time I was at college.'

'He was *so* disappointed,' Mary cried, suddenly, wondering, as she did so, at her need to justify what, even at the time, had seemed like inexcusable cruelty.

'Don't defend him, Mum,' Ruth snapped.

'No, no,' Mary sobbed. 'It wasn't right, what he did, even so.'

Simon stood again on the hearth rug. His proprietorial air of earlier had dissipated. He looked more, now, like a castaway, marooned on its dark plush. 'So I *ran* away, Heather, when I'd finished college, a day or so after I turned eighteen. I ran away with £32 in my pocket and my passport and a few clothes in a bag. *That's* the truth of it.'

Heather shook her head, incredulously. 'I can't believe I didn't see it,' she murmured.

'You were always in your own little world,' Simon waved his arm, indicating enchanted castles and make-believe. He drained his glass and put it on the mantelpiece. 'And anyway, he was *different* with you. It was almost as though you had some kind of *hold* over him.'

Ruth took a sip of her whisky and placed it with determination down onto the side table. 'It's ironic, really.'

'What is?'

She got up from the settee and joined Simon on the rug; he had looked so lonely there. Her eyes shone. She was pale, even in the muted lamplight of the room; her face was a mask of anger and pain. 'I wanted nothing more than to go into the business. I was *desperate* to, right from being little. But he just dismissed the idea. He was only ever interested in Simon, and you.'

In a tiny part of her, Heather acknowledged, she had always known that somewhere, deep in the heart of her family diamond, the brilliance was marred by a network of dark flaws. She did recall, on the periphery of her consciousness, raised voices; an oppressive atmosphere at home as one feels, in a headache, the pressure of a distant storm. But she had turned her little radio up louder, immersed herself more deeply into her make-believe world, closed the door more firmly on the unpleasantness she did not want to acknowledge. She turned now to Belinda. They were *all* looking at Belinda, that most stoical, most faithful McKay. Which side of this sudden-rearing family fence would she be on?

'We shouldn't be saying these things,' Belinda gasped out at last. 'It doesn't do to talk like this. It can't do any of us any good. It just isn't the way we do things.'

Mary looked resolutely at the floor over her sodden handkerchief. It was as though years and years of family laundry had been deposited on it, dirty laundry; vomit-encrusted sheets and faeces-marked pants and muddy, sweaty, stinking sports kit, blood-stained underwear and dribble-grimed bibs, snot-smeared sleeves, a thousand oily boiler-suits and a million urine-soaked nappies; the family effluent she had tried so hard to wash and scrub and bleach away, to make Persil-perfect and dazzlingly Daz white until her hands had cracked and bled: here it all was, back to confront her.

There was silence. Then Heather stepped round the settee and stood in the middle of the room. She held her hands out, one to Ruth and one to Simon. 'Perhaps we *should* have talked about them,' she suggested. The proposal hung in the air between them. At that moment the door burst open and Elliot stepped into the room. He looked from one to the other of them, taking it all in.

'What the *fuck*,' he spat, 'is going on here?'

Elliot had had a terrible day. Even setting off so early the traffic had been dreadful on the motorway, and he had forgotten until it was too late about the road works near the airport turn off and got himself snarled up in further delays there. No-one at the office had been expecting him; there was a dissolute, relaxed atmosphere about the place, people in casual clothing and a jocular gathering around the coffee machine when they should have been hard at work. They had literally scattered like panicking chickens as he strode into view. Carol looked pale and fearful as he entered the outer office, anticipating the sack.

'Good morning,' she had said, timidly.

'Coffee,' he had replied, closing the door of his office with a slam.

It had taken him all day to telephone the various recipients of the tenders and quotes, and sometimes he had had to wait many long minutes on hold or even hours for a call back from the MD or Purchasing Manager. By the end of the day he had his script almost word-perfect; 'Ted? Elliot McKay-Donne! How are you? Great! Wife and kids? Good, good. Now then I don't know if you've opened your post yet? I know, yes. No, me neither. Only the thing is, you won't believe it....' Sometimes the conversation concluded amicably enough: 'You'll put it in the shredder? Can't tell you how grateful I am, mate. Yes, yes, in the post as we speak......No really. I owe you big time.... In fact, I was wondering if you and your good lady might fancy a bit of a trip over to Amsterdam next month. My treat, of course....What's that? Oh no, of course not. We wouldn't *have* to include the ladies....' But far more often things had turned nasty: 'I think you'll find if you *read* the small print.... no, I know, no-one ever does, do they, but..... well, I'm sorry you feel that way about it..... of course, by all means consult your legal team although I'd be sorry to fall out over something like this. Yes, yes, I see. Of course. And the word of a McKay is *still* good, believe me....'

It had taken him until well after five o'clock to speak to everyone, amend the quotes and oversee Carol while she printed them off and bound them. They'd missed the post by then of course so he'd had to drive into town to the FedEx depot to get them all sent with a guaranteed delivery before nine the following day. The town centre had been choked with football traffic and it had taken him an age to crawl through it all and back onto the by-pass, which was itself thronged by then with people going to the shopping centres for late night bargains. He hadn't eaten, had had a gut-full of humble pie and was so riled that when a man cut him up on the motorway he could quite happily have got out of the car and beaten him senseless. The fog made the going through the country roads intensely difficult. The directions he had had at first were nowhere to be found in the car and he had spent a while driving aimlessly between high, grey, featureless hedges, cursing whoever had removed them. In an effort to calm himself he'd stopped at the village pub and downed two large whiskies. The portly, unattractive barmaid had tried to short-change him, insisting he'd given her a tenner when in fact it had been a twenty and he left the place, if anything, more irate than ever.

Entering the hall of Hunting Manor he was assaulted by the din of engines revving overlaid by the dreadful cacophony of some terrible heavy metal band. In the study, Rob and one of the other boys – he never could remember which was which – were hunched over the screen, their faces illuminated an unnatural blue. The noise was so deafeningly loud that he had to roar above it.

'I told you that computer had to go away today,' he shrieked, but the boys took no notice of him at all. 'Rob! Rob!' he yelled. Finally he strode across the room and yanked the plugs out of the wall. The hard-drive made an ominous bang and the screen fizzed with static.

Rob leapt to his feet. 'Dad! Dad!' he was inarticulate. The possible repercussions of such an action were incalculable.

'I told you that thing had to go away today,' Elliot shouted, pointing a bony finger. 'I told you. Now get it packed up and put it in the back of your mother's car. If I see it again I'll throw it out of the window. End of.' He didn't wait for a reply.

Back in the hall he encountered Ellie and Mitch descending the stairs; there was something, he thought, *smug* about them. James arrived from the kitchen, carrying a tray with glasses and a large jug. Behind him, Rachel held a bowl of snacks. Elliot managed with difficulty to plaster a genial smile across his features.

'Ah! Jim. Excellent. I see I'm just in time for cocktails. Will dinner be long?'

'We've had ours, Elliot, quite a while ago. But come and have a drink and see what the others are doing,' James smiled. 'This way, in the big room at the back.' He walked with unwonted briskness down the corridor and pushed open the door with his shoulder. 'Here we are, then,' he said, placing the tray down on a table. 'And look who I found in the hall?'

'Hello Uncle Elliot,' Tansy was busy setting out Monopoly on a low table. 'Would you like to play?' she asked. 'You can be the car...'

'Or the boot,' Miriam said, acerbically, picking up a small playing-piece.

Ellie and Mitch ensconced themselves on a small settee. Rachel handed round the nuts.

'I've had about enough high finance for one day,' Elliot grumbled, sourly.

Bob joined them. 'Child's asleep at last,' he said.

James poured generous measures into high ball-glasses and handed them round. 'Now then. Get your laughing gear round that. Cheers!'

'Gosh!' Miriam squeaked, 'That packs a punch James!'

Elliot took a long pull at his drink. Miriam was right; it was certainly a powerful brew.

'Ellie, take that game somewhere else, will you?' Elliot waved an imperious arm. 'I'm sure we said that this would be a child-free zone.' Ellie looked at him. The game wasn't anything to do with her! But Mitch gave her an almost imperceptible wink and she got up. Rachel helped Tansy sweep the board and pieces away and they all trooped out of the room.

'Now isn't that better,' crowed Elliot. Bob, Miriam and James exchanged looks.

'Give him another drink, James.' Miriam said. She helped herself to a nut.

'Don't mind if I do, Jim. Good stuff this.' Elliot held out his glass.

'Well,' Miriam declared, sitting back in her seat and tucking her slim legs underneath her, 'this doesn't happen very often, does it? Here we are, the McKay B team, alone at last. The never-will-be-quite-Real-McKays. What stories we could tell! "Living with the McKays – the Truth at Last!"' She gave a self-deprecating, artificial sigh, 'but don't worry,' she went on, 'I'm not going to interrogate you. I know you'll never talk. You're too well grafted in to the family tree for that.'

Bob chuckled. James said: 'Ah ha! The ubiquitous Family Tree. I wonder if Rachel found it, in the woods today.' None of them was prepared to take the bait Miriam had laid. A wary silence stretched in the room.

Then the door opened a crack and Les' head appeared in the gap.

'James?' he said. 'A word, if you please?'

'By all means.' He got up and stepped out of the room.

'Well there you are,' Miriam laughed. 'A rare moment, short lived.' She picked up a magazine and began to leaf through its pages. The three of them sat in silence for some little time. Bob drummed absent-mindedly with his fingers on the arm of his chair.

Miriam said, 'does anyone have a pen? I might tackle this Sudoku.'

Elliot drained his glass. Presently, he asked: 'Where *are* all the real McKays, anyway?'

'Oh? Didn't you know?' Miriam looked up from her puzzle. 'They're in the small sitting room having some kind of family powwow.'

Les took James upstairs. 'I might be wrong, but he hasn't seemed quite right all afternoon.'

'Alright. I'll have a look at him,' James put his hand on the door knob.

'I hope he's not asleep. He's all ready for bed but I left him in the chair.'

'Don't worry. Are you going to come in?'

Les shook his head. 'I have to find...... there's somebody I have to check on.' He was already backing down the corridor. With all the family otherwise occupied he couldn't trust June not to corner Muriel.

In the darkness and the unaccustomed silence of the study, Rob and Toby looked at each other. The sounds of the game and the music had been replaced by an unremitting fizzing, sizzling noise in Toby's ears. He felt weird; spaced out and sort of disconnected. 'That's a shame,' he said. He started to help Rob pack away the computer.

'Don't worry,' Rob said, quietly. 'We're not going to let *him* spoil things for us. You go and get the keys. There'll be in my Mum's handbag in the kitchen.'

'Oh. Alright,' Toby said.

He had some difficulty negotiating the passageway down to the kitchen. His feet wouldn't walk straight and he was sure that the walls were leaning. When he got there, the room was in darkness apart from the light over the cooker. In the gloom, the table seemed to be covered by small rounded heaps, like fresh graves, but on closer inspection they turned out to be piles of clothing. He looked around the room for Aunty Belinda's handbag, realising that he didn't really know what it looked like. There was nothing on the dresser or down on the floor under the table. He checked the back of the door to see if it was on a hook, but only Aunty Belinda's apron hung there, badly stained with the evening's cooking. He ran his fingers through his hair, a gesture he had seen his cousin Rob make a dozen times that day, and he said 'fuck' a few times, a word Rob also made frequent use of when there were no grown-ups present. In front of the cooker, the stinky dog had curled itself up on a worn, hairy, smelly blanket, and another dog, much smaller, nestled nearby, against the leg of the arm chair. Toby puzzled over the other dog for a few moments. Both dogs looked to be fast asleep but he knew that the stinky one was not to be trusted. He took a tentative step or two forwards, colliding with the big chair at the end of the table, which made an ugly scrawping noise against the flagged floor. The stinky dog raised its head and growled, but the other slept on. Toby tried to focus on the smaller dog, a puppy perhaps, round and barrel bodied. In spite of Stinky, he took another step towards it, and, as he was able to see more clearly, he realised that the second dog was a handbag. He reached for it. Stinky bared his teeth. Toby froze. Across the room, the enormous fridge shuddered into life, and Toby had an idea. He walked across to the fridge and opened the door. Inside, a plate of food kept back for Uncle Elliot rested on a shelf. He took hold of a beef burger and hurled it across the kitchen. The dog was after it with a bound, and before he had got his teeth around it, Toby was out of the room with the handbag.

In the hall, he met the girls coming from the direction of the lounge and heading for the games room. It occurred to him that he had better explain why he was carrying Aunty Belinda's handbag. He gestured in the direction of the kitchen.

'That Stinky handbag's eating Uncle Elliot's tea!' he said, indistinctly. They looked at him as though he had spoken gibberish.

Muriel and June were both on their feet, standing at opposite sides of the snooker table.

'Well here's Les, anyway,' Muriel was relieved to see him. 'I didn't know where anybody was!' she laughed. 'They all seem to have disappeared! But at least those boys have switched that awful music off now. Have you put Robert to bed?'

'He doesn't seem quite right.'

'Oh?'

'James is with him now.'

'Well that will be alright then, I expect. Do you mind if I wait in here with you?'

'Yes,' June snapped. 'I do mind. I mind about you being here at all and I mind very much about you being in the same room with me and *my* husband.' Les flinched at the deliberately emphasised possessive pronoun.

Muriel was nonplussed for a second or two. 'I thought we'd been managing very nicely up till now,' she said, quietly.

'I've been managing by avoiding you. When you've been unavoidable I've contented myself with thinking how ridiculous you are.'

'June!' Les barked, but June sat down on one of the sofas and pulled a newspaper towards her as though no-one had spoken.

'I'm sure I *am* very ridiculous.' Muriel lowered her eyes and examined her palms.

'Muriel!' Les' voice was softer, with a mild reproach.

'Well! You're hardly dressed for a country house party, are you, for a start?' June looked Muriel up and down with a nasty, narrow-eyed appraisal. In comparison to her own sharply cut tweed suit, Muriel's viscose trousers and nylon jumper were a bit dowdy. 'I've never seen such cheap, shabby, common clothes. Where do you buy them, anyway? Ethel Austin?'

'I'll go and find some of the others,' Muriel turned to leave.

'Oh they won't want you!' June shrilled, patting the back of her hair. 'They're in one of the back rooms hoping you won't find them.'

'That's a lie!' Les shouted.

'Can't *wait* to get rid of you on Thursday.'

'I'm leaving on Thursday?' Muriel turned back to them. Her eyes were full of hurt confusion.

'Of course you are! We're taking Mother back to The Oaks on Thursday and since you came to look after her, you'll be going back as well! You won't be required.'

'I didn't say that Muriel was going home on Thursday, only that we were,' Les corrected her.

'What?' It was June's turn to look confused. Her only comfort had been that if she had to quit the field on Thursday at least she would not be leaving Muriel in possession.

'I don't know how long Muriel's been invited for,' Les shrugged. 'I hope it's the full week.'

'Simon didn't really say, when he called me,' Muriel was hesitant. 'I just assumed...... but I certainly wouldn't want to outstay my welcome...'

'No,' June's mouth curled at the corners, a mirthless smile. 'Far better leave before you make a real social gaffe.'

Muriel looked at Les, miserably. 'Have I?'

Les shook his head. 'Of course not. You've been the perfect guest; helpful, accommodating....'

'Our Sandra would have been a much better help,' June snapped. 'If only you hadn't made her go home. And she had far more *right* to be here....'

Les couldn't contain himself any longer. He strode round the snooker table and bent over June, grasping the lapels of her jacket and hauling her halfway to her feet.

'Don't you,' his throat was so constricted with anger he could barely speak, 'don't you *dare* speak to anyone about *rights*,' he snarled.

'Leslie! Leslie!' June shrieked. Her feet pedalled at the polished wood floor, failing to get a grip. She flailed her arms behind her, trying to reach the back of the sofa, but she was held in mid-air, suspended from his hands, unable to rise, unable to sit. The sound of her voice drowned out the approach of footsteps down the gallery.

'Just shut up! And listen for once in your life!' Les roared into her face. June stopped struggling, but her face was beetroot. She dangled like a broken doll.

At the door, the three girls and Mitch were arrested, amazed.

'What's going on?' Ellie breathed. They had hung around, for a few minutes, in the corridor, trying to decide what to do. Eventually someone had suggested a film, and they'd trooped down to the games room only to stumble on a scene like something out of the worst kind of American soap opera.

'Oh, I think, well, Uncle Les and Aunty June are just having a little chat.' Muriel, from her position between June and Les and the doorway, tried to think of something, anything, which would distract them from the ugly spectacle in the room. 'There're lots of nice clean ironed clothes in the kitchen, waiting to be claimed. Maybe you'd better go and see.' She thought of it as a master stroke, but they didn't move.

Les hadn't even noticed them. 'For forty-five years I've listened to you whining on about your rights,' he shouted into June's face.

'Your *rights* to the business, your *rights* to a detached house, your *rights* to this holiday and that car, because you're a McKay, as if that gave you the *right* to everything.' As he spoke to her, to emphasise his words, he shook her, not hard, but firmly, renewing each time his grip on her suit as her weight drew it from his hands. June began to whimper. It was a struggle for her to keep her head forward. She reached up and grasped his pullover, as much to support herself as to exert some control over him. She dug her finger nails into his arms but he was unstoppable. It was going to slip away and there was nothing she could do about it. She looked desperately around the room. Muriel, just inside the door, was riveted to the spot, and, in the doorway, the children were open-mouthed.

'Leslie!' she pleaded.

He ignored her. 'Well I'll tell *you* something about right. *I'm* going to do right.' Shake. 'I'm going to do right by that lady over *there*.'

'Leslie! No!' June cried out.

'Oh yes! I'm going to take your mother back to The Oaks on Thursday.' Shake.

'No, Les, put me down!'

'No. Listen. And I'm going to take you home.' Shake. 'And then *I'm* going to go home, with *Muriel,* to her house. And I'm going to stay there.' Shake.

He stared into her eyes. Underneath the shadow and the liner and the mascara, they were McKay eyes, round and pale, steely grey. As he watched them, they swivelled up, and he thought that she might faint, but then he caught the movement, the slow creep of her hairline backwards, revealing a greater and greater expanse of forehead, an impossible area of temple.

Quite deliberately, then, he shook her once more. June's thick head of auburn curls slipped from her head and fell like a furry road-kill onto the sofa behind her. Her crown, startlingly white against the

577

unnaturally deepened hue of her face, was barely covered by a thin scraping of wiry, iron grey hair, much like her brother's. Abruptly, he dropped her onto the sofa, on top of the wig, his anger spent, and turned to Muriel.

'If that's alright with you,' he said.

In the study, Rob had the computer all packed up, its wires rolled into coils, the keyboard balanced on the tower, the monitor on the floor by the door.

'You've been a long time,' Rob said, rummaging in his mother's bag until he found the keys.

'Fucking dog!' Toby mumbled.

'Ah.' Rob smiled. 'Come on then. You get the door open and I'll start bringing the stuff out.'

The cold air hit Toby as soon as he got the front door open. The fog, drifting and grey, like smoke, obscured everything, and even the ground seemed to shift beneath him. Rob was stumbling too. One of the coils of cable unreeled itself and he fell over it and almost dropped the monitor as he tripped down the steps, and they both doubled up with laughter. It was almost impossible to see Aunty Belinda's car in the fog, dark grey in the greyness. Rob tried to balance the monitor with one hand while he stabbed at the key fob with the other. Eventually the lights flashed and the boot clicked open.

'There we are. Now you go and get the rest,' Rob said, 'and then I'll take you out for a drive.'

The girls and Mitch were back in the hallway. There was so much noise that Toby thought someone must have put another game on the computer but then he remembered that it was in pieces and they were putting it away in the boot. There was a dreadful, shrieking woman-crying noise coming from the games room. At the same time, from down the passageway towards the back of the house, there was raw, angry man-shouting. Toby went into the study and picked up the tower and keyboard. As he stepped back into the hall, the door to the lounge burst open and people began to spill out and into the sitting room.

'See you in a bit,' he said to Tansy. 'Off for a drive.'

579

The girls looked helplessly at one another. The sight they had just witnessed, down in the games room, had shaken them badly. To hear so many words from Uncle Les was unusual; he was not a man given to much verbiage, contenting himself to what the McKays called 'P's and Q's' and the odd general remark about football. His strength had surprised them; he was not an especially well-built man whereas June was stocky, a capacious size 18 or 20; it must have been the power of his anger alone which had allowed him to suspend her in mid-air like that, and it was the anger, probably, which had most stunned them. They had shrunk from it, all of them, and without thinking about it at all, Ellie had reached for Mitch's hand. Expressed anger was not something which Rachel and Tansy, anyway, had ever encountered. Ellie, of course, had witnessed anger; Elliot was always raving about something but somehow the frequency of it made it trifling and negligible. She and Rob would just shrug, and remark that their Dad was 'off on one' again. This anger, Les', had gushed with the force of a volcanic eruption from some deep and unsuspected place in his wiry frame; searing and dangerous. It had seemed, at first, to be literally slicing the top off Aunty June's head, and they had watched, first, with horror, and then, with a bubbling, inappropriate hysteria, the separation of her ghastly white head from her distinctive curls. Their preoccupation with this had distracted them, and they had not been ready for the sight of her as she hurled herself across the room and onto Aunty Muriel. The two women roiling on the floor in a dog-fight had galvanised them, and they had hurtled up the gallery in search of help, only to find another rumpus underway down in the sitting room and Toby, clearly as drunk as a skunk, heading out into the mist for 'a drive.'

Ellie and Mitch followed as far as the door. Her Mum's grey BMW was parked on the sweep, its lights blazing and its engine running. Its front passenger door and its boot gaped open. The fog of its exhaust mingled with the greyness of the mist, but its yellow lights barely penetrated the thick air. As they watched, Toby dropped the computer into the boot, slammed the lid shut and was making for the passenger door. Mitch, with a degree of objectivity and maturity unavailable to Ellie, dashed down the steps to try and put a stop to the ill-advised adventure. Toby was practically in the front seat when Mitch caught up with him. The car had already begun to creep forward. Mitch threw himself inside the car on top of Toby as the car spurted gravel from beneath its tyres and bound away. In seconds it had been swallowed up in the impenetrable denseness of the fog, and had disappeared entirely from view.

Tansy and Rachel remained in the hall. From down the gallery they could hear June shrieking like a banshee, the cries of Uncle Les ineffectual now against her. At the same time, the raised voices from the small sitting room were intensifying in volume and shrillness. The sounds of smashing ornaments and the thud of heavy objects crashing around reverberated from down the corridor. Upstairs, Starlight began to cry.

Ellie, in the doorway, looked over her shoulder miserably at her cousins, and out again, into the solid night. She knew for certain that her brother had been driving the car. Who else could it have been? He'd been having lessons and had been out in their Mum's car a few times. But he had been drinking, and the fog was so thick, and the local roads were so narrow and dangerous, and slowly she was flooded with a chilling sense of doom which had nothing to do with the mist which crept like insistent, icy fingers around her legs and into the house. Something connected itself up inside her, a previously unknown channel between her heart and her head, with fluid fibres which reached out and made her skin shrink into gooseflesh; it all pulsed with anxiety; she was afraid *for* him. Her anxiety about him overlaid every other emotion; her fear of his betrayal, her resentment of his interference, the way she hated his teasing, the sting of his frequent, unnecessary cruelty. It all seemed lined up in front of her; his pinching and hair pulling, his name calling and teasing, the times when

581

he had put spiders in her bed and salt in her tea, but, even as she reviewed it, it seemed to disintegrate, like the car, into the mist, and leave behind only solid but until now dimly recalled incidents of tenderness. Her first day at school, when he had sat next to her at lunch amongst the other tiny reception children while the bigger boys in his class laughed and jeered; the time he had gone with her to the staffroom when she had cut her hand on some glass in the playground, and let her use his shirt-tail to soak up the blood; the day he'd given her his bus fare when she'd spent hers on sweets, and walked the four miles home in the rain; his offer to beat up the creep on holiday. She knew suddenly, clearly, that he'd only told their parents about that holiday misadventure because he was genuinely incensed by the waiter's loutish behaviour towards her, in the same way that she knew absolutely that he would never have told them about Philip, about her stupid lie.

All at once she was running, down the steps and across the sweep, over the gravel and up the drive; running and running, and calling her brother's name.

Rachel and Tansy looked at each other for a few seconds, both white and shaking, while the house, the family, everything, seemed to crumble and dissolve around them. Then Tansy turned and walked swiftly down the corridor towards the sitting room, and Rachel ran, like Ellie, out of the house.

James walked slowly along the landing and stood at the top of the stairs. He couldn't be sure but he thought Robert had suffered another stroke. His blue pills made him drowsy and indistinct anyway but there was definitely a lack of mobility about the mouth and his speech was slurred. He had been uncertain as to what the day might be or where he was. He had been unwilling, or unable, to raise his hands above his head. Putting these things together had given James sufficient cause for concern, given Robert's medical history. He had used the extension in Belinda and Elliot's room to dial 999. Now he descended the stairs. The main door of the house was wide open, admitting gusts of cold, moist air. As he closed it, he became aware of the sounds of angry raised voices; females shouting, men yelling; they seemed to be coming from all over the house; the games room, the rooms at the back, the panelled walls, the vaulted ceilings. The tongues of Hunting, stilled for generations, seemed to be loosed in the dour portraits; ghosts yelled down the chimneys. Furniture crashed and slid around, restless from years of entrapment, crockery and glassware was shattering; it was as though the whole house was imploding. He ran down the corridor towards the sitting room.

'*There's no need* to speak like that, Elliot,' Simon said, sharply. 'I think we can have a family discussion if we want to, without your permission.'

'That depends what you're discussing.' Elliot took another pace into the room. Heather, in front of him, remained in possession of the main floor; she held her hands out, still, to her brother and sister. Simon took half a step towards her, bringing him to the edge of the hearth, and took her outstretched hand. Ruth, also, lifted her own hand up and clasped Heather's. Belinda had shot up from her seat on the arm of Mary's chair and retreated a pace or so behind it. She was obscured from Elliot's view by the open door. Mary remained on her chair, staring as though in a trance, at the hearth rug.

'What *is* this?' Elliot half laughed, although his face, puce only a moment before, was now bloodless. 'Some kind of weird family ritual I don't know about? A mystic McKay gathering? Are there to be incantations and a human sacrifice?'

'Don't be ridiculous, Elliot,' Heather said, in a low voice. 'We're just deciding things about Daddy.'

Elliot's face, anaemic before, now appeared to be virtually fleshless, the thinnest covering of skin over this sharp nose and prominent cheek-bones, his eyes sunken into bony sockets. His voice rasped, venomous and reptilian. 'About Robert? What about him?'

'Well we don't know yet, we haven't decided,' Ruth said, with studied reasonableness. 'We won't be too long, Elliot, if you'd like to give us a few moments...' She lifted her spare hand and held it out, palm tilted slightly, indicating the doorway behind him, inviting him to withdraw himself.

'Oh no,' Elliot shook his head and raised a hand in denial. 'Oh no. You can't decide anything without Belinda. I won't have you three ganging up on Mary without Belinda being here to speak up for her Mother.'

Simon shook his head incredulously. 'Of course we wouldn't decide anything without Belinda.'

The gaze of the three of them travelled past Elliot, to an area he couldn't see behind the door. Swiftly, and in defiance of Ruth's gesture, he stepped right into the room and closed the door.

Belinda's reaction, on being thus discovered by her husband, spoke volumes. It was as though a tract in an ancient, indecipherable cuneiform language had suddenly been translated and made accessible to them, clearly annotated, comprehensively illustrated and written in script ten miles high. She could not hide it, her secret, from them any longer. Belinda stepped backwards, an instinctive recoil, further into the corner of the room, behind the chair, and right against the standard lamp which occupied the far recess of the space. Her face, beneath its fine powder, was pale, and she lifted an automatic arm defensively across her face.

'Oh there you are,' he sneered, nastily, 'hiding, were we?'

A frisson of comprehension travelled between Simon, Heather and Ruth, still holding hands on the hearth rug. Then Simon let go and stepped carefully towards his mother. Without looking at her, he raised her gently to her feet and walked with her across the rug, away from Elliot and Belinda, pressing her with care back down into the larger arm chair.

For a moment, the McKays made an ineffectual attempt to revert to their default programming; to skim over, with polite, determination, the impending unpleasantness which they all felt mushrooming in the atmosphere around them. Heather spoke very brightly into the heavy silence which Elliot's question had spawned.

'I think that we ought to leave this discussion to another day. We're all very tired.'

'Mum certainly is,' Ruth said.

'And you won't have eaten, Elliot,' Belinda managed to say from between lips suddenly parched.

'We saved you some supper,' Simon reached out to take hold of Elliot's elbow, in an attempt to release Belinda from where she cowered in the corner. 'Come with me and I'll serve it up for you.'

Elliot shrank from Simon's hand and took another step towards his wife. 'Tell me,' he spat, 'what you have been talking about. Here. In this little secret room. Without me.'

'Heather told you, Elliot,' Belinda stammered. She could see it coming; she could hear it in his voice. The early start, the long drive, the problems at the office, the drive back, in the mist, finding everyone busy without him, no supper, and no wife to welcome him. 'We were just talking about Daddy...'

But Ruth found her reservoir of ugliness-avoidance had run dry. 'As a matter of fact,' she broke out, taking, also, a step towards Elliot, 'I don't think it's any of your damn business what we were discussing. This is family business.'

Elliot turned on her. 'And who do you think runs your precious family business?' he roared. 'Which one of us has been up since six and done seven hours driving and a full day's work and licked boots and arses all day for the benefit of your precious family business?'

'This wasn't really anything to do with the business,' Belinda tried to placate him. 'It was to do with the family proper.'

He turned back to her, further enraged, his voice increased by decibels. 'Aren't *I* family proper? Christ, I've changed my name and worked my balls off... what else do I have to do? Have a fucking blood transfusion? Jesus Christ! What kind of a wife are you, Belinda? You're *my* family, you're supposed to be loyal to *me*, not to them. You're supposed to have given them up for me! "Forsaking all others" you promised. But no! You're in here conniving and plotting behind my back....'

'Don't you talk to me about loyalty,' Belinda cried, but he was deaf to her, and to the remonstrance of her family as they spoke his name in increasingly louder tones. His shouting had brought Bob and Miriam into the room. They, too, tried to distract Elliot, but his anger was beyond control. Bob and Simon tried to restrain him as he rained imprecations down upon her, certain that his fury would soon erupt into violence, but he shook them off with such ferocity that Bob was thrown backwards into the china cabinet, smashing its glass frontage. Simon lunged at Elliot again; he was by far the bigger man and had every advantage of height and breadth, but Elliot's rage was uncontainable; he threw Simon away from him. He fell backwards over one of the small round tables; its collection of exquisite porcelain flower baskets went skidding across the floor. Simon landed on his back on the rug and cracked the back of his head on the hearth. Tansy, also, now, in the room, screamed.

As James entered, the family was in complete hysteria. Tansy was screaming. Simon lay on the floor, blood seeping from the back of his head. Mary, shaken from her reverie at last, was kneeling next to him, trying to dab at the blood with her handkerchief. Heather was helping Bob to his feet, as shards of glass fell from his shirt and skin and hair. Ruth was trying to interpose herself between Elliot and Belinda, who had wedged themselves into the corner of the room. He was shouting, haranguing Belinda, flecks of spittle spraying from his lips and landing, like cuckoo-spit, on her hair and on the lenses of Ruth's glasses. Then, almost in slow motion, he reached out his left arm and pushed Ruth away, into the back of the armchair. Then he raised his right hand, and, with a quick and practiced move, he opened his palm and slapped twice, forehand and backhand, across Belinda's face. The sound, like the clap of hands which the teacher uses to bring her class to attention, stopped time. Every face was turned towards him, all eyes aghast, each mouth agape. The blow seemed to have conjured his ire into some kind of tangible form which astounded even its creator and he stood appalled, they all did as, released, into the light at last, his fury flooded the confines of the room. It oppressed them like a swarm. The sense of menace was so real that when Belinda slowly raised her own right hand, James believed for a moment that she wanted to swat at it, ineffectual though that gesture would have been. A second later he wondered if she planned to return the blow, but the idea of it seemed to sit so uncomfortably with the gentle softness of the woman he knew. Then, in just a fragment of a second before she did it, he knew what her intention was, and although he stepped past Tansy and reached out his long arm past Elliot to try and prevent her, he was too slow, and her palm, with the cold blue glitter of the diamond cluster she wore on her third finger, flashed across her own face, leaving a whitened print on her cheek with a livid red weal at its centre. Slap. Slap. Slap. With cool, practised precision she expiated the punishment and pain which choked the air. Then she rested, and her eyes held Elliot's, until, with a sound like a maddened elephant, he stormed from the room.

He almost collided with June in the hall. She has manhandling a suitcase down the stairs. She had a black eye and her hair was askew.

'Leaving too?' Elliot barked as he strode past her. 'I don't blame you. This family is insane.'

'Oh yes. Are you? Take me with you,' June sobbed.

'I'm going right now,' he said, eyeing the suitcase. She let it fall, and the two of them hurried across the gravel, got into his car and roared away up the driveway into the mist.

The car kangarooed in second gear for a hundred yards or so up the drive. Mitch had bundled Toby between the front seats and into the back.

'Put your seatbelt on!' he yelled, struggling, as the car bucked and jolted, to secure his own. Rob had the lights on full beam and the window wipers going ten to the dozen. The sudden heat of three bodies in the cold car had caused the windows to mist up so he also had the demister going full blast. The noise of the revving engine and the fan heater and the thudding wipers made conversation almost impossible.

'It's a bad night.....' Mitch began.

'If you didn't want to come, why did you get in the car?' Rob shouted back. He stabbed his finger onto the CD controls and the curdled tones of Tammy Wynette filled the car. 'Oh fuck that!' he ejaculated, ejecting the CD. 'Look in the glove compartment. She must have *some* decent music in there, I think.' With a sense of acting out a dream, Mitch pulled at the latch and half a dozen CDs spilled out as the car made a lurch forwards. 'Shit! I'll get it in a minute, just a bit rusty. Are you alright Toby?' Rob screwed himself round in his seat to peer into the back of the car. 'Sit up, mate! You're going to miss all the fun.'

Mitch rifled through the CDs. 'Which do you want?'

'Thriller.'

The whooping tones of Michael Jackson reverberating full blast from the speakers of the car seemed to calm Rob somewhat. He managed to get a better control of the accelerator and the car made steadier progress. But the drive, deeply rutted and covered with a thick layer of damp and slippery leaves still made the car rock alarmingly from side to side and occasionally the wheels could be heard skidding on the vegetation and loose surface. Visibility was so poor – barely two or three feet beyond the bonnet – and the lights seemed to make the mist into a solid white curtain.

'Can you see where you're going?' Mitch ventured, over the din.

'Nope. Cool eh?'

'And where *are* you going?'

Suddenly, with a roar, the car pitched forwards, Rob crashed into third gear and they were hurtling blindly up the final third of the drive, between the trees, the suspension rocking and bouncing over the rutted surface. Rob gave a whoop, like a cowboy, clinging on to the steering wheel, jerking it left and right as the trees leered into view on one side and then on the other. Finally, they shot out between the stone gateposts and onto the tarmac road surface and Rob stepped hard on the brakes just before the low wall of a small house opposite the gates. There was a squeal of tyres and the ominous sound of grating on the front bumper.

'That was awesome!' Rob breathed. 'Much better than the game, wasn't it, Toby?' There was a groan from the back seat.

'I'm going to be sick,' Toby gasped.

Rob scrambled out of the car. Mitch leaned over to make a grab for the keys but Rob snatched them away from him before yanking Toby out of the car. Mitch clambered out too. They both watched Toby as he lay on his front in the road and heaved spume after spume of brown liquid.

'Look, Rob. Let me have the keys.' Mitch said, reasonably. 'I'll take responsibility for the bump if you like, only it's a bit dangerous you know, in the fog and everything.'

Rob looked at him. His eyes were glittering, his pupils unnaturally enlarged. 'You're not insured to drive this car,' he said, smugly, as though making an extremely clever point.

'Give me the keys, Rob. It's been great but it's time to go back now.' They faced each other over the retching body of Toby. Mitch held his hand out for the keys but Rob put his hand behind his back.

'Get lost. Fuck off,' he shouted, suddenly, backing a few steps away, 'who the fuck are you, anyway? This is nothing to do with you.' Mitch said nothing but continued to hold his hand out. Rob hesitated, and then withdrew a bottle from his deep jeans pocket and took a swig. The curtains at the window of the tiny cottage twitched. The sound of the tyres, or possibly of them hitting the wall, plus the continuing thud of the music, had evidently disturbed the residents.

'Time we weren't here.'

Toby felt himself being lifted back into the car, into the seat behind the driver, and somebody strapped on his seatbelt, before the two front doors were slammed shut and the engine restarted with a roar. There was some manoeuvring, backwards and forwards, with quick, jerky leaps and sudden harsh braking. Since he's been sick his head felt clearer, although the abrupt backwards-forwards motion of the car made his stomach contract and his mouth fill with spit. Music was playing; head-splittingly loud, from the speakers at the back of the car, the words fast and mainly indistinct, the voice shrill and knife-like; 'killer-thriller-killer-thriller,' was all he could make out. Then the car was off, with an enormous surge, the engine screeching, wheels spinning, the chassis bouncing off down the drive into the murk, the whiteness of it lit up like a curtain, like driving through a cloud, so that Toby wondered if they were flying instead of driving. Down they hurtled, pell-mell between the spectral trees, like falling, his stomach lifting into his throat. Then suddenly he was thrown violently forwards in his seatbelt, so that the edge of it grazed his neck, and the interior of the car was illuminated by savage yellow-white lights. Somebody shouted, 'shit, shit, shit.' There was a violent veering, off to the left, ('string, no string,' came inconsequentially into his head, his father's voice shouting across the water, from a very great distance away), the

591

left hand side of the car seemed to rear up, as though mounting a cliff, and Toby was thrown, in spite of his belt, against his door, his head smacking the window with a hollow thud. Then the car went dark again and very close, on the other side of the door, in the darkness, something enormous and solid ripped past them; he felt the drag of it as it passed alongside. There was an ugly, metallic tearing noise as the beast pressed them up against the cliff, and then a sigh as it released them. They crashed back on to the level, the savage forward motion of the car scarcely halted by the encounter. The boys in the front were twisting and shouting; somebody said; 'He's gone over.' Another voice screamed; 'Watch out! Watch out!' and Rob said, 'Ellie.' Then the car swerved sharply right, the back wheels drifted on the leaves and loose gravel. There was a soft thud, as though an angel had landed on the bonnet, and a lurch as the car plummeted down a steep bank, scraping past the hacked off branches of the trees and bushes and jolting over rocks. Toby was once more thrown viciously forwards against his belt, and then just as brutally backwards, and forwards again, as though he were being shaken. Then they were still, the car pointing downwards at a sharp angle, the engine cut out and there was the soft pop and hiss as the front airbags inflated. Then the only noise was the eerie laughter on the CD, shouting into the night.

The departure of Elliot sucked away with it the electric charge of anger and violence which had ignited the family. They reeled in its after-shock as it eddied and flowed, traumatised - as they might have been had an earth-quake or tsunami overwhelmed them - but alive. James was the first to recover, putting his arm round Belinda, lifting his big hand to touch, with infinite tenderness the whitened skin of her cheek and the raised red wheals. She did not cry; she seemed, for the moment, to have exorcised her distress, and simply leaned against him, spent and trembling. James was careful to look his wife squarely in the eye while he comforted Belinda. 'Now,' he said, in his penetrating gaze, 'now do you see?' In response Ruth stepped towards them, and took her sister's hand. The sudden revelation of Belinda's burden made her feel chastened, ashamed of her own self-indulgent introspection.

'You poor, poor thing,' she said. 'I didn't know. I didn't know.'

Heather held Bob tightly. He was bleeding, from cuts on his back from the shattered glass of the cabinet. Heather tried to pick the shards from his body, wincing at each one as though they were being plucked from her own skin. 'None of us knew,' she said, forcefully, shaking her head, and then, more quietly, wonderingly, 'I didn't know. I didn't know.'

'None of us did,' Bob said, under his breath, to comfort her.

'I think some of us did,' Ruth gave James a look, reproachful, but not challenging. 'How long has it been going on for, Lindy? For God's sake? How long have you been putting up with this?'

'I always thought you were a saint to put with him,' Miriam said, 'but it wasn't my place to say anything.' Practically, she had found a wad of napkins to stem the seep of blood from the back of Simon's head. He remained on the rug, Tansy and Mary kneeling beside him. Both were crying. 'You mustn't put up with it for another *day*,' Simon said, trying to get up. 'I'm alright. Really. I'm quite alright,' he assured them, probing the wound. 'I'm just winded, that's all.'

Belinda was unable, still, to see any alternative. 'It doesn't happen often. He must have had a very bad day.'

'I can't believe you're defending him!' Ruth cried.

The family was rallying, closing ranks, their differences rendered insignificant against this larger threat.

'It's the price I pay,' Belinda said, quietly, into James' comforting chest, 'for you all.'

'The price is too high,' Heather wept. She scraped her hair out of her eyes, smearing Bob's blood across her cheek.

'There are no circumstances at all,' Ruth said, stroking Belinda's shoulder, 'which would justify us permitting a person to harm a member of our family, no matter who he is. Why couldn't you *tell* us?'

Simon hauled himself to his feet and staggered across to the settee. His collar and the back of his sweater were soaked with blood. He pressed a wedge of tissue to the back of his head. 'Because she's a McKay, of course! It's in-bred; keeping up appearances, hiding the dirty laundry, keeping the skeletons in their cupboards.'

Belinda, at last, began to cry, feeling doubly attacked. 'You're very scathing, Simon,' she said, bitterly, 'and you make me feel guilty, Ruth, for trying so hard... for trying *so hard*.... to do the right thing....' James fished a large handkerchief from his pocket and Belinda cried into it for a few moments before blowing her nose and saying; '....but what choice did I have? Tell me that! There are the children, and the family, and the business. Too many consequences! And anyway,' she looked down at her hands helplessly, 'what would people *say?*'

Simon spread his hands, holding the blood-sodden napkins out in grisly evidence; 'I rest my case,' he said, bitterly smug. 'Nothing will change in this family until we start to tell each other the truth.'

'Be careful,' Mary spoke from the hearthrug where she had remained on her knees. 'There's only so much truth a family can stand.'

Muriel and Les arrived, carrying Starlight. She was hiccoughing from too much crying, blinking in the light, and when she saw Heather she held out her arms: 'Mummy,' she said, clearly. Her word provoked more tears from Heather.

We had something to tell you,' Les said. 'But it can wait. What can we do to help?'

'Daddy,' Tansy spoke up at last. 'Daddy,' she said, 'there's something *I* need to tell you, and it *can't* wait. It's about Toby.'

Toby pushed open the front door. Everyone was in the hall. All the Aunties were crying, and he wondered how they knew, already, what had happened. Aunty Muriel was pouring cups of tea out on the hall table. Her jumper was torn and she was limping. His Daddy was struggling into his big coat. It was difficult for him because he held a big white bandage pad thing onto the back of his head with one hand while he tried to get this coat on. Uncles Bob and James also had their coats on. They had big torches. Tansy saw him and shouted his name and they all turned round to look at him. Then his Daddy rushed across the hallway and picked him up, and even though he was much too big to cry, he did do, just for a little while. Aunty Belinda looked anxiously past him, towards the door.

'I was just coming to look for you boys,' Daddy said, squeezing him tightly. 'Had a little adventure, have you? Don't worry; nobody's cross. Where are the others? Are they coming?'

Toby shook his head. 'You need to come,' he said, his mouth quivering.

Simon and Bob and James went, and Belinda. The others waited, anxiously, behind. Toby was made to stay with them. He was shaking and white, and had a bump on his head. Les lifted him up to sit on the table next to the first aid kit, and Aunty Muriel gave him a mug of sweet tea and a large slice of cake, 'for the shock.' He wondered if they would pester him with questions, but nobody did. It was as though they did not really want to know. Which was fine. He couldn't really be sure what had happened and the little he did know, he didn't really want to tell them.

A little breeze had sprung up causing the mist to eddy and churn; it swirled and floated, like angel wings, across their eyes as they climbed the drive. Their torches probed the night, the thicketed undergrowth. It was a steep climb. About halfway up the driveway, then, muffled, through the fog, they heard voices. The first car they found was Belinda's; it was propped up almost on its front bumper, down a steep incline off to the left of the drive, its tail lights still glowing like demonic eyes through the gloom which clung between the trees in the hollow. It had smashed through half a dozen of the rhododendron bushes and wrapped its bonnet around the bole of a stout tree. Steam hissed from underneath the buckled hood, adding itself to the vaporous air. Belinda slid, without dignity, on her bottom, down the steep incline, through the leaves and tilth. Bob and Simon slithered down after her, James lighting their way from the elevated driveway with his torch. But the car was empty, its doors yawning wide, its interior weirdly illuminated by the lights of the dash.

They could still hear the voices, disembodied, from further up the drive and they scrambled back up the banking and hurried on up the drive.

Elliot's car was also down the banking to the left of the drive, but it was on its side. The underside of the car faced up the slope, the roof was caved in against a tree. It faced towards Hunting Manor, having somehow described a hundred and eighty degree arc to end up facing the way it had come. Its front windscreen was shattered into a mosaic of tiny fragments; the back window had been smashed, but its airbags had failed to inflate. Rob and Mitch were frantically trying to lever open the passenger door; it was badly buckled and misshapen; the car must, also, on its journey down the incline, have rolled. They were using a coppiced branch picked up from the ground, an inadequate tool for the job but the only one at their disposal. June hung from her seatbelt in the passenger seat across the central console and was shouting and thrashing around, inarticulate with hysteria.

597

Ellie's frenzied voice could also be heard from inside the car, calling her Dad's name; crying and shouting, and begging him to respond. As James and Bob and Simon arrived at the scene, Rob and Mitch got the door open. Mitch hoisted himself onto the side of the car, and reached in past the flailing arms and legs of the trapped woman, to release her belt. At first she flopped, with an anguished cry, onto the driver. Ellie, wedged between the two front seats was also, momentarily, crushed, and cried out. Bob went around to the roof of the far and leapt, like Mitch, so that he could lean into the car, and the two of them grasped June's clothing and pulled her, from behind, and with no regard at all for her dignity, out of the car, like a squalling baby in a breach birth. She was cut and bruised, and in a paroxysm of agitation, but seemed otherwise unhurt.

At the sight of the men, or, perhaps, because of the appearance of his mother, or because of June's successful release from the car, Rob folded suddenly into a heap on the forest floor. His limbs trembled uncontrollably; he wept, the sobs racking him, and his teeth chattered. Belinda, by him, could get no comprehensible word from him. His tongue and lips seemed only to be able to repeat the same syllable over and over again; 'li, li, li.' He shrank from her, and shook his head like an animal maddened by pain, in the soil.

Ellie seemed to have squirmed into the car via the shattered rear window. She could be still be heard inside shouting her Dad's name, her voice shrill. With June freed from the car, Mitch turned to the others with helpless hands; 'He won't reply. She can't get him to say anything.' Suddenly Belinda understood what Rob wanted.

'Ellie! Ellie!' she shouted, 'come out of the car; Rob needs you.' Ellie wriggled back out through the window and Bob took her place, squirming in the same way as she had got out. James hoisted himself up into the passenger door. They shone their torches and made a quick assessment of Elliot's condition. There was blood, a great deal of it, on his face, from his mouth, perhaps, or his ear. One eye was closed up and soft and spongy. His jaw was twisted out of shape so that his mouth gaped in a perpetual yawn. There was a lump, the size and shape of an avocado stone, on his forehead. James checked his airway, his breathing and his pulse.

'Call an ambulance,' he called, over his shoulder, to Simon. Simon dialled 999 on his mobile telephone but almost immediately the wailing siren of an ambulance could be heard permeating the thick night.

'That'll be the one I called for Robert,' James said. 'Tell them we'll need another.'

Ellie slithered through the leafy tilth of the floor and clung, briefly, onto her Mother.

'Yes, yes,' she assured her, 'I'm ok. Not hurt at all. You'd better see to June.'

Her Dad was in a mess. It had been dark and disorientating in the overturned car and she had had to use the tiny torch on her mobile to get her bearings. Aunty June hadn't helped, moaning and thrashing around. But now that the others were here, she didn't need to worry about him anymore, there was somebody else who needed her more. Being needed was a new sensation and one, she felt, she could rise to. She squirmed her way into the ball which Rob had made of himself, on the ground, his arms over his head, burrowing her head down so that she could whisper into his ear.

'We've got to find her, Rob.' Her voice was calm, amazingly level. She was surer of this than she had ever been of anything in her life. Rob felt it too. He lifted his head up. It was difficult, in the darkness, to see his face, and she lifted her hands to it and felt the filthy, dry soil and wet tears and waxy mucus. She used her thumbs to wipe his grimy face, and, in spite of everything, they laughed a little. Then they held one another for a long moment, while the men were

599

busy in the car and their mother tried to calm June, before they struggled to their feet.

'Yes,' he whispered to her, picking up Bob's discarded torch; 'come on, we have to find her.'

They gained the driveway once more, their feet heavy as they laboured up the slope. The last of the mist cleared, like a gauzy curtain being swept aside, and, above them a million stars pricked the inky sky and the palest of moons shed a milky light. They turned down the drive, back towards the place where they had last seen her.

When they did find her, she was some few yards from the driveway, nestled against the trunk of a coppiced bush, curled, almost as though in a nest, amongst the old leaves and the mulch, and she looked as though she was asleep, like a forest child, a woodland being, all covered with loam, with leaves in her hair. It was as though the forest had absorbed her into itself, or that she was transforming into it; they were entwined and connected by the splintered branch which sprouted out of her abdomen. Red flowers blossomed across her body, bright scarlet berries cascading onto the ground. Her face, in the pale moonlight, was winter-white. She curled around her precious bough, like a mother with her baby, as it protruded, not quite born, from her womb. They knelt down beside her, quiet, as though not to wake her, trembling. It was easier to believe that they had stumbled across a faerie nymph than that this was Rachel, their Rachel. Then Rob spoke her name very quietly, as you would to awaken a sleeping child, or your lover. She opened her eyes, and turned her head a little towards them.

'Rob,' she said, and her voice sounded dry and rasping, 'and Ellie.'

In the distance, the wailing siren of an ambulance, or a police car, or both, came nearer and nearer.

'We found you,' Ellie said. She was crying again. 'Help is coming.'

Rachel let go of her baby-bough. It hurt her to do it and she winced as she grasped their hands. Rob's tears were in spate; they would not let his words come. He shook his head, helpless. She turned her head to look at him. 'Promise me,' she said, hoarsely, 'promise me, and promise Ellie that you'll never *never* tell.'

Rob opened his mouth; a gum of thick saliva clogged his tongue. He shook his head again, not knowing what she meant.

'No,' she hissed, clutching his hand more tightly, 'you *must* promise. You *must.*'

He looked at her eyes, they were fevered with fierce intention, but he couldn't discern it. He nodded, dumbly, and managed to rasp out the words; 'I promise.'

'And promise Ellie.'

He looked at Ellie. He thought he could see in her face just a glimmer of comprehension. The noise of the sirens was loud now, and the strobe of the blue lights against the empty sky was like a meteor shower. 'I promise,' he mouthed. Both the girls nodded. Abruptly the noise ceased, and Ellie turned her head over her shoulder to yell 'Help! Over here! Help!' before turning back to Rachel. 'They're coming, Rachie. They're coming.'

'He never would have told, you know,' Rachel said.

'Yes, I know that now.' Rachel's grip on her hand, tight, only seconds before, almost crushing her fingers, relaxed now. Rachel herself seemed to sink back, down, into the ground. Her body, her flesh seemed to be ebbing away. But her eyes remained open, wide and lucid.

Ellie remembered running up the hill through the clammy fog with Rachel, behind her, trying to keep pace, breathless and panting, and wittering on and on between laboured breaths about her secret,

601

and how sorry she was, and trying to explain how it had all slipped out, and how sorry she was. It had been such an annoyance, in the midst of her concern over Rob, and eventually she had stopped in the road and grabbed Rachel's shoulders hard and shouted at her; 'what the hell are you talking about?' But then the lights of her father's car had come out of the mist, up the drive from the house, like crazed yellow eyes; she and Rachel, clutching each other, had leapt clear as one, and he had careered past them and the fog had closed around him. Then, from within its shroud, they had heard anguished screeching of metal on metal, like robots fighting in the fog. And at that moment, she remembered Rachel's voice wheezing into her ear; 'I'm trying to say that I'm sorry. For telling Rob your secret.' And she remembered distinctly how, at that moment, she had stepped away from Rachel, in disbelief, away from the author of her misery, so unsuspected, and yet so unimportant now, so that when, only seconds later, the lights of her mother's car had borne down on them, she and Rachel had been on opposite sides of the driveway, she on the right, Rachel on the left, caught like two rabbits in the beam. The narrowness of the drive, the sudden gulf which had opened up between them and the inexperience of the driver meant that the car could not avoid hitting one or other of them. And she remembered, before the car had swung away from her and down the slope, seeing Rob's face at the wheel before he, the car and Rachel had all disappeared.

'Help! Over here! Help!' Rob yelled, his voice broken.

Rachel was still looking at her. There was the sound of many feet pounding towards them.

'That's good,' Rachel said.

There was a crowd; uniformed paramedics, police constables, Mitch, Belinda, June, and James, roaring like a wounded lion, like his heart would break, and the sound of Rachel's little voice speaking into the melee; 'Oh Daddy,' she said, 'I knew you'd come and rescue me.'

Then they were all kindly moved away as the paramedics got to work. She was obscured by their broad backs and cumbersome bags, such a small body overwhelmed by the unaccustomed attention.

And the last thing Rachel remembered was her Daddy's face, and Rob's broken voice, saying her name over and over again.

More people arrived, from the house, unable to wait any longer for news. The crush of vehicles, the flashing lights, the crowd of busy, grim-faced officers served rather to increase than to allay their fears. The drive was like a traffic-jam. Elliot had been carried, at first, into the first ambulance, but its exit was blocked by those behind and so he had been transferred to the last vehicle. It reversed up the drive and sped off into the night. Belinda had refused to get into it to accompany Elliot, clinging instead to her children and James. In the end Miriam had consented to go. James, start-eyed, almost incoherent, managed to explain to one of the paramedics that there was an elderly stroke-victim at the house who needed attention. In the revolving emergency lights he looked bloodless and blue. A team set off down the driveway. A third ambulance waited. People were busy in the back with tubes and needles and blood-soaked pads and frantic, futile activity.

A police constable began to make enquiries. His colleagues were sealing off the area with yellow tape. He tried to establish a pattern of events, who owned the cars, who had been driving, but the family was too distressed to make any sense. A teenaged girl and her brother were inarticulate with grief; their father was seriously injured. A red-haired woman, who had been treated for cuts and bruises, a passenger in one of the cars, was quite hysterical. A large boned man, father of one of the victims, was clearly in shock, his wife, also, beyond a comprehensible sentence. The rest of the family gathered in a closed, clannish, huddle, and grasped each other as though physical contact could in some way reinforce the family relations.

Standing a little apart, Mitch surveyed the family; it was laid out before him; a corpse in its final throes. Its life hung in the balance, suffering from an assault so vicious, so pernicious, that it could never recover. James was white and overcome, eviscerated, his bulk melting into an insubstantial shadow, only Belinda, at his side, a silent buttress, infusing him with the warmth of her compassion. Ruth was hysterical, engorged with distress; one more ounce of it would destroy her; it took the combined efforts of Heather and Mary to hold her. She clung onto Rachel's jumper – the paramedics had cut it from the poor, limp, impaled body and Ruth had snatched it up. Its bloody fibres were smearing her hands and face. In fact blood was everywhere; oozing through the quickly applied bandage from the cut on the back of Simon's head, soaking into the back of Bob's t shirt. The blood on Ruth was larding Mary and Heather. Bob and Simon had Elliot's blood on them, and, as he looked down at himself, he too was marked with it, like a sign. Rob and Ellie and James were all smeared with Rachel's blood, and Belinda too, as she stood amongst them, with words which could never console. Mitch felt their agony; his detachment torn away. What else, *who* else, had he? He found that he could not separate himself from them. *His* precious family was bleeding to death and the truth would sever the last artery, spraying them all with the sanguineous consequences of the McKay way.

The truth would stretch loyalties beyond endurance; they would putrefy and stink. There would be a terminal taking of sides, fatal unforgiveness and shame like a cancer. It would rankle and fester, fed by bitter recrimination. Eye would not meet eye, flesh clasp flesh; there would be avoidance and excuse, distance, deceit. The truth, now, would pare flesh from bone, disconnect the living tissue, still the faltering pulse. It would mean the dividing of the ways, the end of the road.

At the crossroads, Mitch saw Ellie. She and Rob clung together, like conjoined twins, sharing, at last, the mutuality of sinew and marrow, each the others only hope. He knew at last what she needed from him – what they all needed, the thing which he and he alone could offer her that would be of any use; the value, suddenly, amongst them, of being the outsider.

He stepped forward, towards the police constable. 'I was driving,' he said.

The practical ramifications of the incident were as unwieldy as the emotional ones, but they gave the shattered family something to cling on to in the few hours which remained of the night. Discussing logistics over endless pots of tea – who would do what, how many each car could accommodate, who would drive whom and where to, how each member could most usefully be deployed – gave the family the bland comfort of the mundane. The details took up the hours, irrelevant, really, just hooks to hang words on, excuses to speak, to meet eyes, to nod and agree while the words which could not be said, especially the questions which could not be asked outright, remained too intimidating and thorny.

Mitch had been taken away in a police car, to answer questions, stalling Bob's shocked, confused attempts to intervene with a shake of his head. Why had Ellie clung to him before the guiding hand of the constable had ducked his head into the vehicle? What had Rob tried, and failed, to say? Events had piled up on one another in the darkness and the mist with all the chaotic, destructive power of a derailed train, leaving indecipherable carnage. The fog, the anger, hysteria and shock, the drink – they all clouded the facts. Unpicking it all would be like trying to unravel a piece of ancient lace. What purpose could it possibly serve? The truth was too terrible to pursue; Mary had been right; there was only so much truth a family could stand.

James slumbered fitfully in the easy chair by the Aga, Ben curled up on his knee. They had both cried themselves to sleep and been gently covered over with the crocheted throw. The lights of the kitchen were kept dim and people spoke in hushed voices. It had taken all their efforts to prevent James from accompanying Rachel's poor ravaged body to the hospital; he had needed physical restraint, bellowing like a wounded bull until Belinda's clear voice had arrested his maddened struggles and given him reason to stay: 'If you go, James, who will tell Ben?' Muriel had stepped into the hiatus while he had considered this; 'I'll go with her. May I? I'd like to. She and I were becoming such friends. I'd like to keep her company.' She had taken his agonised silence as assent and quickly stepped into the rear of the ambulance. Mary had had to go with Robert, of course, and Les had driven behind the cavalcade of ambulances and police vehicles with June, who had insisted on being taken to casualty to have her injuries assessed. 'Don't think for one minute,' she had been heard to say as the car door closed, 'that you're going to leave me here with *them*.'

Initially Ruth had been overcome; roaming in aimless, agonised distress from one room to another, clinging helplessly onto doors and furniture, her legs barely able to support her, throwing herself one moment onto James and the next onto Simon or one of her sisters, clasping Ben to her and then pushing him away again, wailing in paroxysms of inarticulate grief, tormented as though by a million demons. Presently Dr Gardner had arrived, his hair more dishevelled than ever, his clothes hastily put on over his pyjamas which peeped with inappropriate and mischievous cheerfulness from his cuffs and hems. He had administered an injection and advised bed but Ruth had cried like a child and begged not to be left alone. Now she sat at the table with the rest of the family, close to Simon, leaning heavily against him, withdrawn and silent as the others made gentle, carefully worded suggestions as to how things had best be arranged. She seemed to have arrived at a state of shocked detachment, her face a white, paralysed mask of traumatised bewilderment, her body overtaken from time to time by involuntary fits of trembling and shaking which it seemed that nothing, not even the powerful sedative, could still.

After a while Rob and Ellie withdrew to the games room. They sat together on the smaller sofa ('not the big one,' Rob had said, looking at it aghast, 'I sat on that with her....'), their arms around each other. If they communicated it was without words, the speech of instinctive, psychic communion. Only, at one point, did Rob turn his ashen face to his sister and begin; 'Ellie, I was...' but she shushed him with a frown and a shake of her head. 'We *promised* her,' Ellie said.

Later, Belinda found them there, overcome by sleep. She put the tray of tea and sandwiches down on the low table and lowered herself into the opposite chair, where she remained for a long time, just watching them, and wondering if it was too late.

Upstairs, in the boys' attic room, where Simon had, with difficulty, induced them to go to sleep, Tansy, Todd and Toby slept. Starlight slumbered in Ben's vacated bed, side by side with her new cousins. Below, Granny, oblivious, snored and muttered in her dreams.

Around 4am Les returned with Miriam and Muriel. Robert had had another stroke, and would be kept in hospital for a few days until its extent could be assessed. Mary had remained by his side. June, her minor cuts and bruises treated, had called Sandra from the hospital and was waiting to be collected. 'Nothing on earth,' she had proclaimed, 'could induce me to return to that house.'

Muriel sipped her tea and spoke Rachel's name. 'I left her lying very peacefully in the chapel,' she said. 'She looked lovely. All cleaned up and.....tidy.' The image made them all cry and they made no attempt to hide it. After a while Muriel withdrew from her pocket a clear plastic bag and laid it diffidently on the table in front of Ruth. 'The hospital gave me this,' she said, 'personal effects.' They all looked at it, the paltry, inadequate evidence of a life.

Then, into the quiet, because such things cannot be dwelt on for too long but must be handled in small amounts, Miriam told them about Elliot. The news was not good. He was being transferred to a bigger hospital in another county where the neurological facilities were better. However, the prognosis was serious.

'I'll drive you, Belinda,' Les offered, 'be happy to.'

Belinda smiled and thanked him, pouring tea - endlessly pouring tea, innumerable cups, countless gallons - but shook her head. 'Tomorrow,' she said, quietly, 'I'll go tomorrow, but my family needs me here now. There isn't much I can do,' she smiled wanly, and nodded towards the tea pot, 'but I can do this.'

Hearing the news from Miriam, and as Belinda spoke, something permeated the fug of Ruth's consciousness, a shred of possibility, a glimmer of future light. She had not given Elliot a second thought, her own loss was too pressing, but his absence created a practical vacancy which would need filling; the family would need someone to step into his shoes, or rather, into her father's shoes which Elliot had inadequately, for a time, occupied. She glanced across at James, in the chair, and Ben curled upon him, in his place of refuge. As Belinda has said, there wasn't much she could do, but she could do this. With an enormous inner effort she turned from the welcoming arms of the abyss she had been sinking gratefully into and roused herself, just a little, her eyes clearing, her colour warming slightly. She must make an effort, for James' and Ben's sake, and for the family, not to be overwhelmed.

With hesitant hands she drew the bag towards her and emptied out the contents; a pink Disney character watch, a single, woollen sock and a small, tissue-wrapped parcel with a neatly written label. 'A very happy un-birthday,' she read, in a wondering voice.

At last, the dawn broke, heartlessly bright and blue. Countless hundreds of birds, released from the blinding fog of the previous day, disturbed, perhaps, from their habitual nesting places by the disruptions of the night, careered and swooped around the roofs of the house like exuberant children released to play. The family roused itself and at last put in train the courses of action they had planned in the dark hours of the night. Ruth surprised them all by taking tender control, offering guidance and making suggestions, reminding them of the plan. With calm and orderly efficiency, like a regimental unit, a well-rehearsed team, the concerted organs and bones and sinew and flesh of one body, the family vacated Hunting Manor. Food was boxed and distributed between car boots, clothes claimed and packed away, books, games and CD's collected, wellies identified and sorted. James, working like an automaton, each tiny movement a mechanical step into an un-faceable day, swept out all the hearths and cleared away the broken glass and smashed ornaments from the small sitting room. Ben, his shadow, waxen-skinned, looked soberly on. His hands, holding the dustpan of fragments, trembled. 'Will we get into trouble?' he asked. His father smiled and shook his head. Bob and Les stripped all the beds and put the games room to rights, Heather and Ruth cleaned all the bathrooms, Muriel and Belinda scoured the kitchen. Simon arranged for Belinda and Elliot's wrecked cars to be towed away once the police had completed their investigations. Tansy played with Todd and Starlight while the grown-ups were busy, and kept an eye on Granny. Toby hunched over the toilet and retched and retched with nothing to bring up but acrid yellow bile. It took all of Ellie and Tansy's courage to go back into their room and pack their clothes. They wept over Rachel's new, unworn outfits, her collection of old toys. Bridget Jones, unfinished; her pack of sanitary towels, scarcely begun. Then James came into the room and packed them all silently away.

Gradually the men and women McKay withdrew from Hunting Manor. They lingered for a while on the gravel sweep, unwilling, at last, to depart, to separate. Then they took one last look at the silent house, climbed anyhow into cars – aunts and husbands, cousins and wives, brothers and sisters and uncles all randomly distributed amongst the available vehicles, - it didn't seem to matter, after all their endless talk of it, who sat where – and drove in solemn convoy up the drive, leaving the house to the birds, and the ghosts.

Epilogue – May 2005

The old parish church was packed with mourners and those who could not find a seat inside gathered under the laden blossom trees in the church yard. Neighbours, employees, representatives from the Masonic Lodge, beneficiaries from the various McKay charitable interests, local dignitaries, professional and commercial associates, alongside some who couldn't claim any direct connection at all with the family, other than the fact that they lived in the same town; they had all gathered to pay their respects, to bear witness, to observe or to be observed. They liked a good funeral; the familiar protocol, the pomp and ceremony, scrutinising the tightly reigned-in emotions of the bereaved, taking the opportunity to speak of the dead with effusive praise, or with thinly veiled criticism. A funeral meant a day, or, at the very least, a half-day off work, a good feed and free sherry at the local hotel. They could impress each other with claims of connection; 'of course I worked with him for years,', 'I knew him before he was anybody, you know,', 'our daughters attended the same Brownie pack. A quiet sort of man.' Someone else's death was comforting, ironically, and made them feel secure in their comparative permanence. Being there, included, at a big funeral like this one made them feel important and, importantly, alive. The McKays were a big family locally, influential, and everyone wanted to be a part of the occasion.

There were few, if any, friends. The McKays had never needed friends; they had each other.

The pink and white petals fluttered onto their shoulders as they stood beneath the trees, and gathered in drifts against the ancient mossy kerb stones; inappropriate confetti. A church warden was hastily paying out cabling to connect up to a portable speaker so that they would be able to hear the service. The vicar stood in the porch ready to shake hands with the chief mourners when the cortege arrived. His cassock flapped around his ankles in the May breeze with

611

the unfitting exuberance of a boisterous puppy. This was a big funeral; the McKays were a prominent family; he had high hopes for the collection plate. In the family plot, sequestered in a quiet corner of the churchyard, close to a particularly prolific damson tree – the Vicar's wife had famously made many a jar of jam from its fruit, much sought after at the annual bazaar, and, less well known, many a bottle of damson gin also – the grave was freshly dug and draped with green felt. It would be a peaceful enough place to rest. His sermon would contain the usual assurances of the Lord's love and comfort, His goodness and grace towards the faithful and the joys of heaven without stating with any absolute specificity that the deceased was an assured recipient of these good things. In these cases, it was best, he found, to be kindly vague. His business, to quote the Saviour, was more with the living than with the dead, who must, at this late stage in proceedings, be prepared to take their chances.

With an unpleasant squeal the PA screeched into life and the sonorous tones of the organ boomed into the air, making the mourners wince. A wave from another warden, stationed at the gate, indicated that the cortege was in sight. There was a collective in-breath, and the crowd readied itself.

The coffin was borne on a McKays Haulage low-loader, its paint and chrome polished to a high shine, its flat-bed draped in voluminous yards of black silk. A mass of floral tributes surrounded the casket, weighted down somehow against the brisk breeze. In their midst, and on the huge truck, the box looked small and pathetic. The on-lookers gasped at the splendour, or perhaps at the tawdriness, of it. The funeral director, in the first car following, was rather in the latter camp. He had spent the short journey giving the whole arrangement anxious glances; it seemed impossible that the coffin would not be dislodged, slide off the back of the lorry, or cannon into the back of the cab at any moment, or one of the wreaths fly off and get caught on the windscreen of a passing car, causing an accident. It would reflect very poorly on him professionally if anything were to go awry. He had tried hard to argue against the plan, offering various alternatives including a horse-drawn gun-carriage. He believed that some members of the family would themselves have infinitely preferred a traditional hearse, but it seemed that the staff at the yard had been so importunate and he had given way to them with the proviso that, in the event of inclement weather, the scheme be abandoned. It was important, with such high-profile clients, that everything went smoothly. Even now, as they approached the entrance, one or two disrespectful members of the press were aiming their cameras. He would have to instruct his staff to keep them well back while being sure to mention the name of the firm.

The first limousine drew up to the kerb and the funeral director skipped round to open the door for the mourners. The crowd outside the church stepped back in deference to them, keeping their eyes down but casting frequent furtive glances at the grieving family, curious to know how they were bearing up. The McKays were well known. Belinda, especially, was popular and active on various committees and charitable boards, even still, after the dreadful accident, managing to fit in a plethora of causes around the demands of full-time caring. Ruth they knew less well, although she was beginning to make her mark. Heather, of course, was quite famous. Simon was more of a mystery. He had eschewed the family firm and their town for the brighter lights of the capital. It was hard for them to forgive him, really. But he was handsome, suitably dressed, and, as they watched, took particular care to support his mother, which softened them towards him. He had been touched, they whispered to one another, by tragedy. Hadn't his poor wife died? Wasn't she buried in the family plot over in the corner? Yes, they sighed, but apparently he was a marvellous single Dad. Hadn't he a new partner? No, it hadn't lasted. He was on his own again, poor man. Yes, he had been touched by tragedy. But hadn't they all? Indeed this local family who, at one time, had seemed to float rather above the normal disappointments and grievances of life, had, in recent times, been all but deluged by them.

There was Mary, looking calm, but rather pale, commented the Chairwoman of the Townswomen's Guild. She'd been a stranger, recently, since Robert had gone into The Oaks. She'd been spending a lot of time at Simon's, looking after the poor motherless kiddies, remarked a neighbour, with a smug smile which would imply, she hoped, that she was privy to pretty much all of the McKays' private affairs.

The crowd of on-lookers wondered how the McKays would bear themselves in the face of this most recent loss. Almost in answer, the family collected itself on the pavement beyond the old stone wall, unwilling, it seemed, to join the waiting crowds, almost as though holding themselves aloof.

'Always were a proud lot,' someone mumbled. Mary hung on Simon's arm, Belinda and Heather stood close together; Heather clutched a handkerchief damp already. They were, the mourners had to admit, impeccably dressed; even Heather, the weird and wayward one, wore sober black. As they watched, Ruth stepped away from them all to take a call on her mobile with an apologetic look. The crowd shook their heads disapprovingly at one another, while furtively groping for their own 'phones to make sure they were switched off.

The children of the family stepped from the second car, uncomfortable in smart, formal clothes. They had all grown since November, especially the oldest, Belinda's boy, who had suddenly, about that time, left the school sixth form and gone to America to a military academy with a reputation for tough discipline. It had mystified the staff at St Hilary's, apparently. One woman, who knew the neighbour of a parent governor, hinted enigmatically about drugs. He looked very American, now; tanned, with closely cropped hair like a GI, or a convict. He had broadened out, his shoulders filling his well-cut charcoal suit. But he kept his eyes firmly on the floor. It was a shame, barked the Scout Commissioner, a boy like that should have been taught to look people square in the eye, not hang his head as though he was ashamed of something.

His sister, a burgeoning beauty, held his hand. It was rumoured that she had developed an unsuitable attachment. Oh yes! A man whose wife's sister was a regular prison visitor under a scheme organised by their church, sketched out the details. A ne'er-do-well taken in as a charity case by the family. He was back in prison (of course, these people were lost causes) and the girl visited him every week. His companion nodded conspiratorially; he had even more shocking news to impart. It seemed that the young man in question was none other than the feckless vandal who had caused the dreadful accident the previous autumn! There was a ripple amongst the mourners within earshot. Shocking! Wasn't there a death? Oh yes; not a genuine McKay. But still. The lone voice of a woman who served as a JP warned that in fact the cause of the accident had never been categorically established. The eye witnesses had been young, and unreliable, and their accounts had tended to be contradictory, she reminded them. There had been high levels of alcohol involved and the emergency vehicles had obscured tyre tracks and skid marks which might have established the exact sequence of events. But the crowd was not to be tempered. When they thought about the havoc wreaked on that poor family; it beggared belief. The hooligan would be out in a few years and free to go marauding round the countryside killing innocent men women and children again. No-one was safe!

The girl's father was livid about it but what could he do, poor man, now?

The other children, younger, hovered behind the older two, hesitant in their well-polished shoes. Poor mites. Too many funerals. This would be their third in as many years. A woman in a hat proving unmanageable in the gusty breeze lifted a handkerchief to her eye.

The last to emerge was the littlest one, the little African one they had all read about in the papers; it looked like the court case might drag on for months. She took the hand of one of her boy-cousins as soon as she got out of the car, a wispy-looking child, every bit a McKay. Ruth's boy – looked like her, didn't he? Oh yes. A real McKay. But fancy letting the little one come to a funeral! The crowd sucked its teeth disapprovingly again. They were all in favour of the couple being allowed to adopt the little thing but surely she was too young for this kind of occasion? Mightn't it prejudice their case? Not to mention the possible disruption to the service! They rolled their eyes at one another in their unspoken but shared vision of the irreverent interruption of the sombre service by a lively two year old dropping hymn books and running amok in the chancel, and began to be relieved, rather than annoyed, that they had arrived too late for a place on a pew.

The third car drew up at the kerb, a specially adapted black people-carrier. Two of the sons-in-law climbed out. One went round to the back of the vehicle and extricated a wheel chair. He was tall, dark haired; the father of the poor dead girl. At one time he had been very bulky but the weight had dropped off him, recently. Someone on the NHS Hospital Trust Board imparted the confidential information that after weeks of sick leave he had given up his job in the psychiatric unit. He stayed home full time now, apparently, and divided his time between looking after the son and helping Belinda with Elliot. He did a lot of things for the church. His companion made a sympathetic moue; an experienced nurse like that would be impossible to replace.

The crowd gave an involuntary thrill as the other son-in-law, with the distinctive grey ponytail, began to help Elliot into the waiting wheelchair. Such a lovely man, with the human touch; look how nice he had been with all those poor starving Africans, and raised ever such a lot of money.

They all knew Elliot of course; he had run McKays until his accident had rendered him so badly disabled. Not, frankly, a popular man; efficient, no doubt, but not a *real* McKay. Now he was a shadow of his former self; blind in one eye, his face disfigured by scar tissue, massive jaw reconstruction and dental work had failed to make his speech clearly intelligible and in any case the damage to his brain meant that he would probably never regain full mental capacity. They watched as he thrashed around angrily while the two others tried to secure him into his chair, making inarticulate attempts to speak which produced nothing more tangible than a dribble of saliva on his chin. The dark haired brother-in-law wiped it, efficiently, with a large white handkerchief. It was good of him, wasn't it, they murmured to one another, considering Elliot's blood-alcohol levels on the night of the accident? Hadn't the Coroner made specific mention of it as a significant contributing factor? Oh yes, the woman in the hat nodded, knowingly. And that was why the hooligan had got off so lightly. But still, wouldn't you have thought - she shook her head, sadly - every time that poor man looked at Elliot he must think of his little girl......

Seeing Elliot, with a cry of joy the little black child skipped over the pavement and clambered onto his knee. Elliot went suddenly rigid while his niece snuggled companionably on to his lap. His good eye widened and roved furiously over the crowd of McKays, but no-one met it.

Last from the people-carrier stepped the younger McKay sister and her daughter. June was classily dressed in appropriate black and wore dark glasses. No sooner was she out of the car than she had hurried along the pavement to where the chief mourners were gathering, keen to establish herself amongst them. Her daughter trailed awkwardly behind. There was no sign, yet of the older sister or the man who had been husband to one and was now husband to the other. What a scandal *that* had caused, the previous autumn! An ex-lady Golf Captain raised her eyebrows significantly at the treasurer's wife. The new wife was nothing like the old, had never so much as held a club, apparently. There they are, the treasurer nodded as Les and Muriel arrived on foot and joined the young people, who greeted them with hugs and smiles.

Then everyone's attention had been drawn to the arrival of the final cortege vehicle. The mini-bus from The Oaks disgorged a number of staff come to pay their respects to the recent patient, and an extremely elderly woman, bright eyed, walking unaided, smartly dressed and closely supervised by two uniformed nurses whom she regaled with a detailed account of Sir Winston Churchill's funeral, which she claimed to have attended as a guest of honour.

Complete at last, the family came through the gate and walked slowly up the gravelled pathway. Behind them, the pall bearers struggled manfully to remove the coffin from the low-loader with a modicum of dignity. Along the path, Ruth stopped to shake hands here and there with a supplier, a customer, an employee. 'Thank you so much for coming,' she said, again and again, 'it means so much to us, and Daddy would have been so proud.' Since she had replaced Elliot as MD of McKays, or, perhaps, since the loss of her step-daughter, she had bloomed, her hard edges softened, her angst had melted away. The employees all liked her; she didn't pretend to know everything, but asked for their advice and opinion. But she was no push-over: suppliers who tried it on were swiftly dealt with and years of surprising wayward delinquents up to no good meant that any malingering staff members had to be on their guard. Customers were charmed by her. And, of course, she was the real deal, a true McKay. She was her father's daughter, alright.

The Vicar stepped from the shelter of the porch and shook hands with the widow and the children of the deceased. He murmured words of comfort to the children, squeezed Elliot's shoulder and stroked the cheek of the little girl on his knee. Presently, the pall-bearers began the journey up the pathway. The crowd fell silent. Men removed their hats. The family divided briefly as Robert passed between them for the last time, then united seamlessly behind him as the Vicar led them slowly through the doors and down the aisle.

'I am the way and the truth and the life,' he said, and the mourners in the pews rose to their feet.

AC 28.03.11

If you have enjoyed this book please visit amazon.co.uk to leave a review.

Reviews provide great feedback to the writer and are very useful for other readers.

Visit the author's website at allie-cresswell.com to find out more about her novels, see her recommendations for great reads, leave comments and to source materials for reading groups

Coming soon, by the same author

Lost Boys

A small boy falls into a river in spate. And so begins a sequence of events which will affect and connect the lives of four unrelated people.

Iris Fairlie, proud and prickly, who has been sent against her will to live at Bridge House, a home for the elderly. The enthusiastic efforts of a piano-playing spinster, well-meaning visits from the congregation of a 'happy-clappy' church and a constant supply of confectionery all fail to compensate for the shameful lapses of old age; the home is pervaded by the pungent aroma of biscuits and wee.

Sulking in her room, Iris is forced to question everything: life is over, what has she achieved? What is it that separates her from her daughter? Where on earth is her son?

Witnessing by chance the boy's tumble into a racing river, Mrs Fairlie is galvanised at last into action; if she cannot rescue her own boy she will try to rescue this one.

Matt, a teenage boy whose parents' separation has meant a move from The Fairways, an affluent executive estate on one side of the valley, to The Mere, a run-down estate of social housing on the other.

At first the victim of their cruel and thoughtless bullying, and later in rebellious fascination, Matt becomes embroiled with the wild and ungoverned estate boys while he struggles to come to terms with his beloved father's defection. Matt's bitter envy of his father's new step-son forces him to desperate measures – he will make his father choose between them.

But then the other boy is lost in the raging river and Matt discovers that it is he, and not his Dad, who has to choose.

621

Megan works at a motorway service station café situated on a bridge which spans the carriageways between one artificial no-place and another; an en route stop-off on the journey to somewhere else. It is perfect for Megan, in hiding from a violent ex and ever fearful of discovery. But the legacy of the past prevents her from embracing the future; she finds herself trapped between the two and desperately missing the son she left behind.

The glimpse of a young boy caught in a flood changes the course of both their lives.

When the local paper prints her story, it is inevitable that Megan's past will catch up with her; not only the son she abandoned, but the husband she is so desperate to evade.

On the day her nephew is lost in the river, **Jade** and Ryan, a boy she has only just met, are inadvertently caught up in a clash between rival gangs of football supporters and take refuge in a semi-derelict church. While out on the streets all is violence and anger, inside Jade is overcome by a tangible flood of love and peace, different to anything she has ever experienced before. So far her joyless life on a run-down estate has resulted in a world-view literally jaded by pessimism and despair, but the kindness of strangers makes Jade's world a more hopeful place, where it is never too late to change and where even she might be truly loved, if only Ryan, absent since that night, would call.

Log on to allie-cresswell.com to find out more about the background of Lost Boys, read excerpts and be the first to get your hands on a copy.

2206340R00312

Printed in Great Britain
by Amazon.co.uk, Ltd.,
Marston Gate.